Prophet

FRANK E.
PERETTI

PROPHET

Living Books®

TYNDALE HOUSE PUBLISHERS, INC., WHEATON, ILLINOIS

IN CASE YOU WERE WONDERING

This novel is a creative work of fiction imparting spiritual truth in a symbolic manner, and not an emphatic statement of religious doctrine.

As usual, while I *am* dealing with real ideas, I'm not writing about any real persons, places or institutions.

—the author

Designed by Jacqueline L. Noe

ISBN 0-8423-7111-7

Printed in the United States of America.

06 05 04
5 4

To Jan and Lane
true prophets in their own right

ACKNOWLEDGMENTS

I owe a debt of thanks to many precious people
whose invaluable experience, assistance,
and advice helped bring this project together:

Susan the anchorlady, who let me tag along with her
throughout her workday and get a feel for her job.

Nick the jack-of-all-news-gathering-trades, who showed me
around and checked hundreds of pages for accuracy.

Kevin the reporter and John the cameraman,
who took me with them into the field and
shared their perspective with such honesty.

Good ol' Roger the attorney, who has helped me with more than
one book, always explaining things so I understand them.

Bob the physician, who advised me on the medical aspects of the
story and who also checked hundreds of pages for accuracy.

Frank the "Skank," one terrific cop who was always available.

Dana and Joe, two dedicated men in the emergency profession
who took me through their procedures.

Carol, the "Lady in Scarlet," who knows the
abortion industry firsthand.

Randy and friends who shared their intimate sorrows with me
and helped me understand the abortion experience.

Hey, all of you get the credit for the things I've captured
accurately—I'll take the blame for the mistakes.

Thanks.

one

John Barrett heard God speak when he was ten years old. Years later all he would clearly remember about that Sunday night meeting at the Rainier Gospel Tabernacle was that it was close and sweaty, in the dead center of summer's heat. Noisy, too. It was altar time at the front of the church, the saints were praying and praising, and it was not the quiet, introspective kind of worship but the hollering kind, the throw-back-your-head-and-cry-to-Heaven kind as the women wept, the men shouted, and the piano kept playing over and over the strains of "I surrender all, I surrender all . . ."

Pastor Thompson, young and fiery, had preached a sermon that caught John by the heart. And when the altar call came and Pastor Thompson said, "If this word is for you, if God is speaking to your heart, I want you to come forward, lay your all on the altar . . ." John knew God was speaking to him, and he went forward, almost running, to kneel at that long mahogany prayer rail, his face flushed and his eyes streaming tears.

"'Behold the Lamb of God, who taketh away the sin of the world!'" Pastor Thompson quoted the Scripture. "Will you receive that Lamb tonight? Will you find Jesus?"

John was ready to receive the Lamb, he was ready to find Jesus, and as he called on the name of the Lord, he could even see a lamb, small, gentle, spotless and white, right there in front of him, right on the other side of the prayer rail, so close he could have reached out and touched its nose. He was later told he'd had a vision, but at that moment he thought there really was a lamb in the church, as real as anything. The Lamb of God, like Pastor Thompson said. It was so real then, so long ago. It was a moment that truly stirred his soul.

But that moment, with all its feelings, its meanings, its transcendent, eternal words, even its little vision, would fade with time, and John would eventually tuck it away in a lost and forgotten corner of his memory.

He would not remember that he had done business with

God, that he had made a covenant with the Creator when only a young boy—"Jesus, come into my heart and take away my sins. God, I give You my life. Use me, Lord. I'm Yours."

The memory of his father's hand on his shoulder would fade with time and adult ambitions, as would his father's words, spoken loudly and prophetically in the child's ear, as if from God Himself: "Ye are called, My son, ye are called. Before I formed thee in the womb, I knew thee, and before thou wert born I consecrated thee to My service. Walk in My Word, listen for My voice, for I will speak to thee and guide thee in all the paths you may take. Behold, I am with thee always . . ."

He would choose not to remember. ". . . in all thy ways acknowledge Me, and I shall direct thy paths . . ." Good words, useful words. Forgotten words. "And lo, I am with thee always, even unto the end of the age . . ." He would not remember.

But God remembered.

two

GOVERNOR, I plead with you, search your heart and change your course, for if you do not, God will change it for you. Though you have said to yourself, 'No one sees, and no one hears,' surely, the Lord sees, and He hears all that you think in your heart, all that you whisper, all that you speak in your private chambers. There is nothing hidden from the eyes of Him with whom we have to do!"

It was the Friday after Labor Day, still sunny, still summer, the early-evening shadows just beginning to stretch. Crowds of giddy party supporters were coming from their homes, jobs, early dinners, and schools to converge on The City's Flag Plaza for Governor Hiram Slater's big campaign kickoff rally. The Hi-Yo, Hiram! straw hats were already blooming in profusion and floating along on hundreds of heads like leaves on a river. Before the backdrop of the plaza's fifty state flags, a platform had been set up, draped in blue, festooned with red, white, and blue balloons and American flags, neatly arranged with rows of folding chairs and garnished with a full nursery's worth of potted chrysanthemums. Soon the rally would begin, and Governor Slater would make his campaign kickoff speech.

But as people entered the plaza, a stocky, gray-haired man in blue warehouse coveralls was already making a speech, standing on the edge of a concrete planter box, primroses at his feet, his head well above the crowd. The governor may or may not have been within earshot, but this man was going to shout to the governor anyway, his voice tinged with pain, with desperation.

"Like Nebuchadnezzar of old, you have set up an image of yourself for all men to follow, a towering image, a mighty image, an image far greater than yourself. But please take heed: the Lord would remind you, you are not that image. Though you may say, 'I am strong and invincible, I tower over the masses, I cannot be touched or harmed,' yet in truth you are as weak as any man, about to be harmed, about to be toppled!"

"Why don't you just shut up, big mouth!" yelled a beer-bellied contractor passing by.

"The Truth must be heard though the lie be a tumult," the man replied.

"Not him again," griped a mother with four children in tow.

"Get off that planter!" ordered a realtor in a business suit. "You don't belong up there."

A radical feminist publisher responded with the slogan "Hi-yo, Hiram!"

Those nearby picked up the slogan, louder and louder, and threw it at the man for pure spite. "Ho-yo, Hiram! Hi-yo, Hiram! Hi-yo, Hiram!"

They had stung him. He looked into their faces as pain filled his eyes, then pleaded, "The Lord is in His holy temple; let all the earth be silent before Him!"

Through the chanting a few voices could be heard responding in mock horror, "Oooooooooooo!"

"Our God is there, ever present, and touched with our infirmities. He is speaking. We must be silent and listen!"

"Hi-yo, Hiram! Hi-yo, Hiram!"

Behind the platform, screened from visibility by blue curtains, Governor Slater, small, balding, with an unimpressively high-pitched voice, went over final details with the rally's organizers.

"Thirty minutes," he said. "I want thirty minutes even if you have to cut something."

Wilma Benthoff, the governor's campaign manager—and presently his harried rally organizer—pushed her wildly curled blonde hair away from her face so she could see her clipboard. "Okay, we'll do the 'National Anthem,' then Marv will introduce the dignitaries. Marv!" Marv didn't hear her; he was busy directing photographer traffic while tying balloons to the platform stairs. "MARV!"

He looked up. "The governor wants more time, so keep the introductions brief!"

He nodded and said something they couldn't hear. Benthoff went on, "Then the band will play . . . uh . . . Joyce, how many songs is the band going to play?" Joyce didn't hear her; she was standing too close to the trombone player practicing his scales. "Oh, forget it. We'll cut a tune out. I'll tell her."

The governor felt a hand on his shoulder. It was Martin Devin, one of the governor's staff members and would-be chief of staff. The tall, former college linebacker had an amused sneer on his face. "Our old friend the prophet is here."

The governor chuckled and shook his head. "As sure as the sun rises." He sneaked a peek through the curtain and could just see the old man's head above the crowd. "I wonder what his son must be thinking right now?"

"Especially when he sees the ruckus on his own newscast! I called a friend at Channel 6 and they're moving their camera. They want it."

The governor's face brightened. "Always thinking, Martin, always thinking!"

Devin nodded, acknowledging the compliment. "So we just might have an opportunity coming up here . . ."

Leslie Albright, Channel 6 news reporter, carefully placed a molded earpiece in her ear and then found one square foot of ground to call her own as Mel the long-haired cameraman brought her face into clear focus. There were better places to shoot this story, better views of the plaza, better backgrounds, but orders were orders. Someday she was going to shoot Tina Lewis.

"John, this is where is all begins for Governor Hiram Slater . . ." she rehearsed in her professional news voice. "Undaunted by challenger Bob Wilson's showing in the polls . . ."

With one hand she held her NewsSix microphone and with the other her quickly jotted notes, which were trying to elude the grasp of the three fingers holding them. She tried to straighten her breeze-tousled blonde hair as she examined her reflection in the camera's lens. Gawkers were already waving to Mom behind Leslie's back.

"Undaunted by how well his challenger is doing in the polls . . . Even though Bob Wilson . . . Even though the polls show Bob Wilson coming on strong . . . uh . . . show Bob Wilson gaining support . . ."

"We've got about ten minutes," her earpiece crackled.

"Okay," she replied, and went back to rehearsing. "The governor has proven he has supporters too, as you can see by the vast crowd behind me . . ." And then she waxed sarcastic just to vent herself. "—which you could have seen better if we'd stayed up on the stairs instead of moving down here."

She adjusted her red suit jacket and tried to think her report through again. That guy standing on the planter behind her wasn't helping much.

"The Word of God says, 'Before you were formed in the womb, I knew you!'" he cried.

Oh brother. Now he's going to bring up that subject!

"I like it," said Tina Lewis, executive news producer. She was in the Channel 6 control room for this one; she knew it was going to be interesting.

Above the console where the show producer, director, and video switcher sat, the monitors on the wall flickered a visual three-ring circus with different things happening everywhere all at once so fast youcouldhardlykeepupwithit. Monitors One, Two, and Three showed the views from the three studio cameras on the news set below; the Preview Monitor framed whatever view would be next; the On Air Monitor showed what people at home were seeing; the news anchors were still in the middle of NewsSix at Five Thirty, pushing news stories through like cars on a speeding train.

"Camera Three, head-on to John," said Susan the director.

Camera Three moved in. Monitor Three and the Preview Monitor showed a tight head-and-shoulders shot of handsome, fortyish anchorman John Barrett looking into the camera.

"Pan for box." The camera moved to the right. "Box." The

video switcher hit a button, and a nicely drawn beer can in a frame appeared in the upper-right corner of the screen.

"More trouble brewing for Bayley's Beer," said John Barrett. "Ever since the Bayley Brewery in Tobias contracted its aluminum can recycling to Northwest Materials . . ."

"Stand by Cassette Two." Cassette Two appeared freeze-framed on the Preview Monitor.

". . . environmentalists have been hopping mad and foaming up a real storm . . ."

"Roll Cassette Two." Button pressed. Cassette Two began to roll.

". . . that could be coming to a head . . ."

Cassette Two counted down—Three, two, one . .

". . . Ken Davenport has the story."

On Air, Cassette Two: a shot of the brewery. Bayley Brewery title across bottom of screen. Ken Davenport's voice over the picture.

"Board Members of the Bayley Brewery met today in a closed meeting to determine what action, if any, they will take . . ."

"Stand by Camera Two, head-on to Ali."

In Monitor Two, Ali Downs, co-anchor, a former model with jet black hair and almond eyes, sat ready to begin the next story.

In a black-and-white monitor near the ceiling, Leslie Albright stood before the remote camera, microphone, earpiece, and hair in place, waiting her turn to report. Behind her a fracas was growing.

"Look at that!" said Tina Lewis, almost awestruck. "Will you look at that!"

"You have turned your eyes from the slaughter you have championed! You have robbed the innocent of their lives!" said the man on the planter. "The Lord formed our inward parts. He wove us in our mother's womb, and we are fearfully and wonderfully made!"

That was all some of the crowd needed to hear. Hiram Slater

was a pro-choice governor, and this was a pro-choice crowd. Things started getting quite vocal.

"You're at the wrong rally, bub!"

"Keep your bigoted views away from my body!"

"Would somebody pull him down from there?"

And through all the shouts and threats "Hi-yo, Hiram!" never missed a beat.

Leslie thought she heard a question through her earpiece. She held her hand over her other ear. "Say again please."

It was Rush Torrance, producer of the 5:30 newscast. "John still needs a scripted question to close your package."

"Um . . ." Leslie looked behind her at the crowd coming to a rapid boil. "Things are changing kind of fast around here. He might want to ask me about the abortion issue . . . you know, how that might be affecting the climate of the rally."

"So . . . how do you want it phrased? You want him to—" The man on the planter was shouting something, the crowd was hollering louder than he was, and all of them were louder than Rush's voice in the earpiece.

"I'm sorry, I can't hear you!"

"I'll have him ask you about the hot issues, all right? He'll ask you how it looks from where you stand. What's your outcue?"

"Um . . . I'll end with, 'This campaign could be an exciting roller coaster ride for both candidates, and the whole thing begins in just a few minutes.'

"All right. Got it."

Leslie was getting nervous, anticipating an elbow in her ribs or a projectile on her head any moment. She asked Mel the cameraman, "You think we ought to move back a bit?"

"No," said Tina Lewis. In the studio they could hear everything Leslie was saying. "Stay right there. We're seeing everything. It looks great."

Rush Torrance passed the message along through his headset.

In the monitor Leslie cringed a little but stayed where she

was while the crowd behind her became more dense and noisy. Fists were waving in the air.

The man on the planter was clearly visible above the crowd, gesturing and shouting, "Hear me! Volume and chanting and numbers and repetition and television coverage will not make a lie true!"

Then some coat hangers appeared, waving in the air above the crowd.

Tina chuckled. "They know they're on-camera."

Rush informed Leslie, "You're on after the break. Stand by."

On television screens all over the city and beyond, Ali Downs finished up a story. "Legislators hope the move will help displaced timber workers in time, but the timber workers say they'll believe it when they see it."

Two-shot: John Barrett and Ali Downs seated at the expansive, black-and-chrome news desk. In the upper background NewsSix in large blue letters. Center background: false TV monitor screens with faces, places, titles frozen in photographs. In the left background, through a false window, a false city skyline.

John Barrett started the tease: "Coming up next, Governor Hiram Slater's campaign for re-election starts with a citywide rally tonight. We'll go to the Flag Plaza live for an update."

Ali finished the tease. "And iguana lizards running for your health? See it for yourself!"

The screen cut to the teaser video: lizards pawing and licking at the camera lens.

Commercials.

"All right, Leslie," said Rush. "We're coming to you in two minutes."

The governor scanned his notes. If things kept going the way they were, he might have to change his text a little. "Sounds like things are heating up out there," he hinted to Martin Devin.

Devin had just returned from a reconnaissance peek. "Mr.

Governor, you've got the crowd, you've got the camera. I think we ought to take advantage."

"You have something in mind?"

Devin lowered his voice. "I think we can get things a little rowdier. It could stir up some emotions, really get the crowd on your side, and it'll get the attention of the TV viewers."

The governor looked at his watch. "It's close to 6. When is Channel 6 going to carry us?"

Devin looked at his own watch. "Any minute. I think they want to close the 5:30 show with a live teaser and then come back at 7 to pick us up again."

The governor mulled it over, then smiled. "Okay. I'll be ready."

Devin smiled and hurried away.

In a tight little area behind some trees, out of sight, he dialed a number on his cellular phone. "Yeah, Willy, he went for it." He looked at his watch. "Keep your eye on that blonde reporter down there. Go when she goes."

"Fifteen seconds," said Mardell, the attractive, black floor director standing behind the cameras. "Leslie will be to your right."

John Barrett looked to the right unconsciously. At home viewers would see the anchors looking at a large screen with Leslie Albright on it. In the studio John and Ali would be looking at blank space, pretending a screen was there.

Mardell counted down with her fingers silently. Five, four, three, two, one . . .

In the control room Leslie had jumped from the black-and-white monitor to the large, color Preview Monitor, and the picture was impressive. There she was, her tension showing and her hair tousled despite her best efforts, holding her ground as a sea of enraged humanity boiled and bubbled behind her and one lone man continued his struggle to be heard above the tumult.

On Air, John Barrett intro'd the story, looking into Camera Three and reading the teleprompter script mirrored on the glass over the camera's lens. "Well, today is Day One of Governor Hiram Slater's campaign for re-election, and Leslie Albright is at the Flag Plaza right now for the big kickoff rally." Both he and Ali Downs turned and looked toward the wall. "Leslie?"

On televisions at home, there she was on what looked like a three by four foot screen propped on the end of the news desk.

Leslie looked right into the camera and started her report as rehearsed. "John, this is where is all begins for Governor Hiram Slater. Even though the polls show Bob Wilson gaining support, the governor has proven he has supporters too, as you can see by the vast crowd behind me."

As viewers at home saw the shot of Leslie jump from the screen that wasn't there to the full television screen, it wasn't clear just what that vast crowd was indicating, other than an impending riot.

But as John glanced sideways at his own monitor hidden in the top of the news desk, his attention was drawn to that one lone character sticking up above the crowd, his mouth moving, his hands gesturing. It seemed he was leading this mob.

"Roll Cassette One," said Susan the director, and Leslie's prepared video report began to play on the screen with Leslie's prerecorded voice narrating.

Video: the governor meeting folks, shaking hands, waving to the crowds.

Leslie's voice: "Governor Slater admits it will be a tough campaign, but insists he is ready for the battle and will pull no punches."

Video of the governor being interviewed. Sound up. The governor: "I think we have a head start, really. The past four years are a clear record of our accomplishments, and I stand on that record. We've moved ahead on education, employment opportunities, and women's rights, and we're going to keep after those issues."

John's face was getting redder, and it showed, even through the makeup. As he watched the live camera monitor showing what Mel's camera was seeing at that very moment, he could still see that rabble-rouser standing above the crowd. The monitor had no sound, but he could easily imagine what the old man was shouting. He dared not curse—he might be on the air. At least Leslie's video was still running on the air and people weren't seeing what he was seeing right now.

Leslie was ducking her head and looking behind her, at least while the video report was running. She kept trying to hear her next cue through her earpiece.

The crowd was starting to chant, "Pro-life, that's a lie—you don't care if women die!"

John grabbed his desk phone to talk to Rush Torrance. "Can't we get that kook off the screen? Rush? You there?"

No answer. Leslie was coming back on.

Mel the cameraman nodded furiously. "Yes! You're on, you're on!"

Leslie straightened, held the mike in a trembling hand, and almost shouted her cue line. "So, John and Ali, this campaign could be an exciting roller coaster ride for both candidates, and the whole thing—" Someone screamed. "—the whole thing begins in just a few minutes!"

The old man on the planter couldn't believe it. Suddenly two characters he'd never seen before, one with stringy hair and a bald spot on the back of his head, the other black-haired, hulking and tattooed, came from nowhere and started throwing punches at his audience, hitting men, women, anybody—on his behalf!

"Dirty baby killers!" shouted one.

"Hallelujah!" shouted the other.

"No . . . no! Don't do that!"

Too late. Some of the audience were switching from shouting to slugging.

"No! This won't solve anything!" *Oof!* Something—it sounded like a can—bounced off the man's head. Hands were grabbing at his legs. He started pulling away, dancing on the planter.

John could see it all on his news desk monitor, as could every viewer watching the news at that moment. He'd been given his cue, but his mind went blank. He searched his script and found the question he was supposed to ask, scribbled in at the last minute. "Uh . . . Leslie . . . this . . . uh . . . campaign seems to be loaded with a lot of hot issues . . . how does it look from where you stand?"

Leslie just about said, "How do you think it looks?" but simply replied, "I guess you can see for yourself, John and Ali. And if you don't mind, I think we'll move a little further away so we can keep covering it from a safe distance."

"No!" shouted Tina Lewis. "Don't lose it!"

"Stay on it," Rush instructed through his headset.

Leslie ducked sideways out of the picture. If she heard the instruction she wasn't indicating so. The picture wiggled, tilted, jostled. Mel was moving the camera.

"Stay on it!" Tina ordered. "Mel, stay there!"

The camera came down solid again. Mel had planted the tripod.

No Leslie on-camera—only the crowd, the scuffle.

Producer Rush Torrance barked the order into his headset as he yanked pages from the show's script and dropped them on the floor. "We're bumping 480, Boy Pilot, and 490, the Running Lizards. We'll stay with this!"

"Oh terrific!" John moaned.

From beside the planter a big black man, his eyes full of fire, leaped into the crowd. "You wanna fight, I'll teach you to fight!"

He was after those two intruders who'd started the fight in the first place. He found the first one, the weasel with the stringy hair and bald spot, and put him out of commission with one well-placed haymaker to the jaw. The big guy with the tattooed arms was a little more of a match, and they both went down to the pavement, taking several other bodies with them.

Three big college jocks finally got their paws on the old man and wrestled him from the planter, locking him in a painful hold with his arms behind his back. "Come on, old man! Party's over!"

His face was etched with pain and fear as they began forcing him along, almost carrying him from the plaza, two holding him from behind, one pulling him by his hair, the prophet's body bent forward, off balance, tripping, stumbling. He cried out.

Suddenly—it looked like a violent, tumbling play from a football game—the black man burst through the crowd, pushing bodies aside until he could reach the old man. With his tremendous weight and powerful arms he grabbed the first two men by their necks and smacked their heads together like melons. They went limp, falling backward, releasing their hold. The third let go of the old man's hair right away and only wanted to defend himself, holding his arms in front of him.

"No, Max, don't—" cried the old man.

But Max did, grabbing the young man by his hair. "See how it feels, sucker!" He flung him into the crowd, where several people fell like bowling pins.

Mel kept his camera on the whole scene, capturing the grappling bodies, the flying KEEP ABORTION LEGAL signs, and the whipping American flags. There was no telling who was on which side or who was winning, but it was exciting footage, no question about that.

John couldn't say a word, so Ali jumped in. "Leslie? Leslie, are you still with us?"

Leslie's voice came from off-camera somewhere as the camera captured the first police arriving on the scene. "Yes, Ali and John, we're a safe distance away now and as you can see, the police are intervening, so this should clear up quite soon."

"Do you have any idea what started this?" Ali asked.

John knew; he never would have asked that question.

Leslie answered, "Well, uh . . . you may have seen that man in the background, the one yelling at the crowd . . ."

"Yes, and I think our viewers did."

"Well, he was obviously anti-abortion, and as we all know, that's one of the hot issues in this campaign, and I think there was a pretty strong disagreement back there."

"Thirty seconds. Close it," came Rush's voice in their earpieces.

Ali closed with, "Well, hang in there, Leslie, and we'll get more from you tonight at 7. Be careful."

"Oh, I'll be here, on the scene."

John was happy enough to tell Camera Two, "And that's NewsSix at Five Thirty. Stay tuned for the 'CBS Evening News,' and we'll see you again at 7 o'clock."

"Good night," said Ali.

Theme music. Wide shot of studio. Credits. The anchors engage in unheard small talk with the weather and sports announcers, gathering and shuffling their scripts. Commercials.

"Mel," said Tina Lewis, "you hear me?"

"Yeah, you're coming in," Mel's voice came back. It sounded a little high with excitement.

"Keep the picture steady now. Keep rolling. We'll use some of this at 7."

"Okay."

Tina and Rush watched the live camera monitor as Mel zoomed in on the police grabbing the old man and his black friend and muscling them out of the crowd. The old man's feet weren't even touching the ground.

The old man was scolding his friend even as the police dragged them along. "Max, you shouldn't have done that!"

Max was fuming, sweating, too angry to speak. He could

only curse the old man, curse the crowd, struggle against the four cops it took to contain him.

"All right, take it easy," said a cop, brandishing his nightstick.

The old man chided his friend. "Max, now you cooperate! You can't afford to make things worse!"

Max came to his senses and calmed down with unnatural quickness. "Sorry, officer. Didn't mean no trouble."

"You're gonna clear out of here now or we'll haul you in, got it?"

"Oh, we'll leave, right away," said the old man.

"Yeah, we outa here."

On the outskirts of the plaza the police let them go, and they hurried away, thankful for freedom.

As for the two strangers who'd thrown those first punches, they were nowhere to be seen.

Martin Devin was all smiles when he reported back to the governor. "You should have seen it!"

"Did it get on the air?"

"We'll know in a minute. But that cameraman was really scrambling to cover it."

"Okay, we'll play on that."

The studio cameras were off, the show was over. Ali and John removed their earpieces and lapel mikes. The news set was cut off from the outside now, a small, empty, plywood box of a place.

"Poor Leslie," said Ali. "That was supposed to be an easy assignment."

John didn't even hear her as he grabbed the desk phone. "Rush? Rush? Could you get me Rush please?" He slammed the phone down. Apparently Rush wasn't available.

Ali looked him over for just a moment. "What's the matter?"

John glared at her, not meaning to. But right now glaring was all he could do. "Aw . . . that . . . stupid story . . ." He grabbed his script and left the desk, muttering to himself more than answering her question. "Of all the things we could've put on the air we had to put that on . . . and now we're gonna see it over and over 'til they wear it out . . ."

John circled behind the stud-and-plywood backdrop of the news set and immediately into the newsroom, a large, gray-carpeted, open floor partitioned into small cubicles, each with a desk, a telephone, and a computer monitor, where reporters, producers, editors, and anchors worked at gathering, sifting, condensing, cutting, and pasting together each day's news.

So where was Rush? Where was anybody responsible for this?

The room was relatively quiet at just a little after 6 o'clock. The Five Thirty was finished, and half the personnel had gone home. The Seven O'clock producer, Pete Woodman, had already chosen the material that would run, and now his five people, sitting here and there around the room, were putting the finishing touches on the show, updating the script, tailoring the videos, reslotting and prioritizing the stories.

Oh, there was Rush, at his desk in the corner, having a hurried, impromptu script conference with Pete Woodman. It had to be about this latest development. Brother. This thing had so much momentum it was going to be unstoppable.

"Leslie's there right now," Rush was saying, "and Mel got footage of the scuffle if you want it. It's great stuff . . . looks really good."

Pete was perusing his script for the Seven O'clock, scanning it with the point of his pen. "Now I take it she's getting the governor's speech. I've got that slotted near the top."

Rush checked his watch. "He was scheduled to start about a quarter after. He wanted to get on the Seven O'clock, I know that." He looked up. "Hi, John. Good show."

"Hello . . ."

Rush went right back to his discussion with Pete. "So Leslie ought to be feeding that in any minute."

"Good. Bill's expecting it." So the Seven O'clock would feature highlights from the governor's speech. No doubt

Leslie and Mel were feeding it back via microwave to Bill in the editing room. Bill, the fastest editor around, was recording it on tape this very moment and would then work with one of the newswriters to find the most poignant eye- and ear-catching clips to paste together for a feature on the Seven O'clock. And if he really wanted to catch the eyes and ears of the viewers, what better footage than—

"So let Bill have that scuffle footage," Pete said. "That would really give a sense of the . . ."

"Yeah," Rush completed the thought, "the heat of the issues, the feistiness of the campaign. That'll fit right in with the governor's kickoff."

"And that's what I'd like to talk to you about," John cut in.

"Yeah?"

"That footage, Rush. I . . . I just don't know about that."

Rush, not much more than a kid with a floppy blond forelock, had great strengths as a producer. He could put together a tight, gripping newscast, he could draw a story out of a vacuum, he could inventively defy time in making deadlines. But one thing he could not do was fathom, much less endure, the petty misgivings and foot-draggings of the station's "talent."

"What's the problem with it?" Rush was being polite, not interested.

John stumbled trying to come up with an answer. "Well . . . it's violent, it's . . . well, I think it's tasteless."

"I think it happened," Rush answered curtly. "It happened, and we were there, and that makes it news. You tell me any other station in this market that had an opportunity like that fall right into its lap."

Okay, John thought. *My spine's as stiff as the next guy's.* "I would say the brawl was an opportunity, yes. But that religious nut in the background, you went after him, didn't you? You wanted him in the background."

Rush threw up his barrier right then and there, his hands raised. "Okay, okay . . . Discussion ended . . . No comment. If you have a problem with it, talk to Tina. I took my orders from her. I liked the whole idea. I still do, and I'd do it again, but for this one, talk to Tina. Your problem's with her."

And with that, Rush went back to consulting with Pete as if John weren't even standing there.

Tina Lewis, a sharply dressed professional, removed her designer glasses as her gold bracelets jingled, then gawked at John with incredulous eyes. "John, come on, we've got forty minutes until the Seven O'clock and you're telling me you want the lead story changed?"

"Well . . ." John was frustrated and angry. Time, only a few minutes, had degraded his original concerns from possibly legitimate to silly and outlandish. "I had no idea what Leslie was going to be shooting. Had I known I would have said something earlier, and now . . . of course, it's too late and my concerns no longer have merit and . . ." He threw up his hands in surrender and turned to leave her office. "I've got a promo to do."

"John . . ." She sank into her chair and leaned her elbows on her desk. "I'm sorry if the situation is awkward for you. But when news happens, it's our job to report it. You know that."

John turned toward her and took a purposeful breath to control himself. He spoke slowly and carefully. "Tina, I have worked in the news business for twenty-four years. Please don't use that line with me. I've used it all too often myself. I know that line."

Now came the contest to see which of them could remain a collected and controlled professional the longest.

Lewis spoke slowly, in carefully measured tones. "I wouldn't think of using a line with you, Mr. Barrett. And I'm a little disappointed that someone with twenty-four years experience still can't separate his profession from his personal concerns."

"You chose to put him in the background," John said flatly. "You could have shot the platform, the banners, the flags on the plaza, any number of backgrounds, but you chose to show him. Isn't that right?"

She grimaced and wagged her head as if she'd never before

encountered such idiocy. "John, I wasn't there, and as far as I'm aware, he never called us and said, 'Hey, I'm going to be preaching to the crowds over by the 4th Street entrance, come and get me on television!'"

John pointed his finger at her, a sign he was losing his temper. "You were in the control room. You were calling the shots. You made the decision."

She let out a disgusted sigh and said, "Okay. You're embarrassed. Is that my problem? Is that even any concern of the business we're in?"

John saw the clock on the wall. Time, the boss of all bosses, was ordering him out of the room. "I've got to do that promo."

The last word was hers. "I'm sorry we can't resolve this for you. But really, it's your problem, you're the only one in a position to do something about it, and if I were you I would."

He just turned his back on her and walked out.

He went into the makeup room to check his face in the big, illuminated mirror. The makeup was still good from the Five Thirty. It was the expression on his face that needed some work. *Come on, guy, loosen up. Nobody wants to look at that.*

Back in the newsroom he took off his suit jacket and hung it on a hook just as Pete Woodman handed him the script for the promo. He glanced over it as he sat in the stool in front of the flashcam, a small television camera set up just behind the rear wall of the news set. This was where all the live-from-the-newsroom shots were done. It was a handy arrangement, almost a one-man television studio: a remote-controlled camera, some lights, a remote-controlled teleprompter.

John checked the monitor and tilted the camera up slightly with the remote control. Now he was centered in the screen. The teleprompter in front of the camera was cued and ready. He planted the flashcam earpiece in his ear so he could hear his cue from the control room.

Okay. An on-the-air monitor showed the "CBS Evening News" just ending. Then two CBS news promos.

"Five seconds," came Pete Woodman's voice.

Network identification: "This is CBS."

"Two, one . . ." Theme music.

John appeared on The City's television screens in shirt sleeves and loosened tie, looking like he'd been hard at work in the newsroom visible behind him. Title across the bottom of the screen: John Barrett, NewsSix.

John went right into it, his eyes smoothly scanning the teleprompter script. "This is John Barrett. Coming up in a half hour on NewsSix at Seven, Governor Slater's campaign kick-off rally . . ."

Video rolled. A jerky, groping camera scene of grappling bodies. The old man fighting off his assailants and then being yanked off the planter and into the crowd.

"The governor came out fighting . . . and some fights broke out. We'll have a live update at 7."

John on the screen again. "We'll also have more on those two high schoolers lost in the mountains. They've been missing for twenty-four hours now, they were not dressed for weather, and in the mountains there is *weather*. Those stories and an update on the rest of the day's news ahead on NewsSix at Seven tonight."

Commercial.

Well, that was that. Twenty-five seconds. Now to proofread the script for the Seven O'clock and hope the governor had something interesting to say, something that would draw attention back to him and his campaign.

" 'The governor came out fighting, and some fights broke out,' " John repeated mockingly, settling at his desk and calling up the script on the computer. "I'm gonna kill him!"

three

The rally was over. The plaza was now empty except for small clusters of party boosters who still wanted to talk politics with their fellow diehards. Clean-up crews worked around them, sweeping up the paper cups, candy wrappers, and fallen placards. The big blue platform was coming down piece by piece, and the chrysanthemums had been adopted by whoever grabbed them first.

The governor had left the moment the rally ended, rushing away in his limousine and heading back to his mansion. He'd left everything in good hands.

Martin Devin's hands. Chief of staff Martin Devin. Yes, the governor had finally made up his mind which man would get that distinguished job description, and Devin was floating, buoyant with joy, satisfaction, and in a way vindication. So the gov finally saw the light! Yeah, results, the kind Devin could provide, were effective persuaders.

The rally could have gone well, but it went *great.* The news coverage could have been matter-of-fact and routine, but now it was sensational; it got noticed. The governor could have just spoken on the issues from his prepared speech, but instead, spurred on by . . . certain unexpected conditions, he verbally fought, clawed, and snapped for his views on the issues to a crowd fired, inspired, and ready. Devin had to laugh in delight. By the time that crowd went home, they would have thought it was the end of the world if Hiram Slater failed to be reelected.

Devin made the rounds quickly, slapping backs, congratulating the hardworking volunteers and the once harried, now relieved Wilma Benthoff, still carrying that clipboard. Special thanks from the governor went through him to all of them.

There was one item left on his list, and then he'd be out of there as well: Ed Lake. Now where was he?

Ah, there he was, walking across the almost-empty plaza, carrying four helium-filled Hi-Yo, Hiram! balloons and looking like a convalescent celebrating his ninetieth birthday. Well, looking at his rival, Devin had to admit to himself that the governor's choice had been all too easy to make.

"Ed!"

The old man looked his way and smiled broadly, quickening his step.

How old was he really? Sixty-something at least. *Old enough,* Devin thought.

"Quite a rally, eh?" said Lake.

Devin smiled and laughed. He was laughing at how stupid Lake looked carrying those balloons, but he didn't say so. "Great rally, Ed. The governor was quite pleased."

Lake shook his white head. "Well, I'm glad we managed to survive despite the disturbances."

Devin put his arm around Lake's shoulders and gave him a brotherly, wrestling squeeze.

Lake hated that kind of thing. That's why Devin did it.

"Oh, we did more than survive, Ed. We capitalized on the disturbances. We were prepared."

"It's getting to be a dirty world."

"Well, one man's dirt is another man's capital. If it's there, you find a way to use it. That's how you survive."

Lake looked toward the concrete planter where the old man in the blue coveralls had stood. "That old prophet fellow gives me the willies."

"He gives us free publicity, that's what. Our side gets noticed, the other side looks . . . like him: stupid, backward . . ."

"Oh, don't be too sure about that. I understand he's a respected businessman, and isn't his son—"

"He's nothing but a blue-collar kook," Devin said with a smirk. "He belongs on First Avenue carrying a sign and passing a hat."

Lake scowled in harsh disagreement. "But he was here, wasn't he? And at the opening of the hospital, and then at the state teacher's convention. And each time the message was the same." He paused to reflect on it. "To hear what he had to say—and then know how the governor—and his staff—have been conducting themselves, I would not be shocked to someday find out he was right all along."

"That's the problem with you, Ed. Guys like that can get to you."

Lake scowled at him. "So what's wrong with having a conscience?"

Devin laughed heartily and deliberately at the question. "He did get to you!"

Lake was annoyed. "Oh, come on . . ."

"Well, hopefully he got some sense knocked into him. I don't think he'll be back."

Lake only looked glumly at Devin. "It was a disgusting show, Martin. Deplorable behavior on everyone's part. Even the governor. I hope I never see it again."

Devin nodded knowingly. "Well, Ed, maybe you won't." Dramatic pause. "I was going to wait until tomorrow, but tonight's as good a time as any, I suppose. The governor's appointing me chief of staff."

Lake froze. He stared blankly at Devin as if hearing of his own death.

Devin just kept cutting into him. "The gov will tell you all this tomorrow, of course. I imagine he'll tell you how valuable you've been to his administration and how your knowledge and experience will always be appreciated, but . . . I think you and I both know that when it comes down to job descriptions, what the governor needs right now is fresh blood, people with the guts to go after and get whatever the governor needs, no holds barred. You're a good man, Ed, maybe a little too good. You're too timid at the wrong times."

Lake answered in a mutter that was barely audible, "I thought we had a good combination, Martin . . . your aggressiveness and my experience . . ."

Devin shook his head. "We just don't have room for two heads at this level, Ed. The gov says we have to cut back, so that's where it stands."

"So you're in . . ."

Devin looked straight at Lake. He wanted the blow to be direct, not glancing. "And you're out."

Lake was resisting believing all this. "Out?"

"You're retiring, if that's what you'd like to call it."

Lake struggled. "But . . . by whose order? Whose decision? The governor didn't say—"

"My decision. I'm chief of staff now. The gov says to trim back, and quite frankly I can't think of any job description on the staff that would fit your qualifications."

Lake had to take time to let it all sink in.

Devin continued, "You can come in and clean out your desk tomorrow. Hey, look at it this way—you can start a new life now, get out of the rat race—"

"As if I don't know exactly what you're doing!" Lake snapped. "You've wanted this job all along, and you've never missed an opportunity to try to muscle me out!"

Devin didn't deny it. He just nodded and replied, "You prepare, you make your move, you survive."

Lake waited to reply. He'd gathered some new thoughts. "But you're not prepared, Martin."

"I'm in."

"But I'm not out. Not yet."

"It'll sink in. Just give it time."

"You think I didn't see you working on this ever since you came on staff? You think I didn't do some preparing myself?"

Devin thought for a moment, then chuckled derisively. "Hey, take it easy, Ed. You're scaring me."

"Remember last April? I was in on that, you know. Sure, you thought the governor was trusting you with everything, but perhaps you didn't notice me standing in the doorway of your office when he gave you that material to destroy."

Devin grew sober. No more chuckling or smirking. "What about it? I tossed it, threw it out."

Lake's eyebrows went up in challenge. "Oh, did you now? Maybe not. Maybe you kept it in your desk instead of destroying it. What were you thinking, Devin? Were you thinking of writing a book someday, a terrific exposé by someone who was really there in the halls of power?" He laughed at the thought. "Eh . . . that material would have been a nice addition to a book like that."

Devin tilted his head as his face grew tight. "So *you* took it?"

Lake smiled in happy surprise. "Oh, so you did miss it. I was beginning to wonder."

Devin just about grabbed Lake by the collar. "Why you—"

Lake held up a hand. "Careful!"

Devin backed off. "You took it?"

"First chance I got. I couldn't let you have something so destructive all to yourself."

"But that was months ago!"

"I'm a patient man. I knew the day would come when I might need some leverage, when I'd have to make you squirm. Looks like that day has come all right."

Devin was holding back his anger. He talked quietly. "So this is where the bargaining starts, is that it?"

"What was it you said? 'One man's dirt is another man's capital'? Well, I do have capital, and it is dirt all right. Dirty enough to cost you your job."

Devin thought for a long moment and then said grimly, "You're walking on very dangerous ground, old man."

"I assure you, sir, I am up to the challenge."

They had a short stare-down. The old man was still bold and strong.

"Okay," Devin finally agreed. "We'll talk."

Lake nodded slowly, grimly. "Yes, I would give it some thought if I were you. You don't want to be too hasty in your decisions, eh?"

Devin forced himself to keep looking confident and in control; there were still people around. "Okay, tell you what. It's getting late. Let's take the night to think about it. I'll think about it. You think about it. We'll talk again Monday morning. All decisions can wait until then."

Devin put on an overly nice, hopefully pacifying smile and waited for Lake to agree.

Lake did not return the smile, but only replied grimly,

"Monday morning then" and walked away, angrily releasing the balloons to float into oblivion.

"You have seen . . ." Pause for effect. ". . . with your own eyes . . ." Another pause. ". . . the kind of people we are up against in this election!" The governor was shouting into the microphone, his hand pointing toward the concrete planter. The crowd began to stir, voicing its acknowledgment. "What better way to illustrate the gravity, the mission of the campaign that begins here today!"

The crowd went absolutely nuts, banners and flags waving, KEEP ABORTION LEGAL signs rocking and bouncing like bluebells in the wind.

It looked great on television. The governor seemed to know exactly where the cameras were. He played to that crowd, and he especially played to those cameras. Mel's camera, over by the planter, didn't miss a drop of his venom.

Nine o'clock. In his apartment overlooking the city, John Barrett sat and watched it all, some of it several times, his VCR remote control in his hand.

"Bob Wilson, listen up!" said the governor. "We believe in freedom! We believe in choice! We believe in the fundamental right of every American to chart his own course and choose his own path!" Applause, cheers. "So rest easy, Bob Wilson. We will not send mad prophets to break up your rallies and infringe on your rights." The crowd began to stir, anticipating a real zinger. "We will not send worthless ruffians and hoods to batter your supporters!" The emotion, the fire in that crowd came across even on television. "We will not infringe on your God-given freedoms, Bob Wilson!" Just the right pause to let the crowd cook up its impending storm, then the zinger. "But God help you if you think you can infringe upon ours!" The crowd began to roar its agreement, and the governor yelled his final line over the tumult. "Mr. Wilson, *this governor and the people of this state will not allow that!*"

Spontaneous demonstration, the crowd going wild. Cut back to Leslie Albright, live, closing the package.

"And as you can see behind me, the rally is still going strong, with a lot of enthusiasm, a lot of support. If this rally is any indication of the tone Governor Slater intends for the rest of his campaign, we're in for a fiery campaign indeed. John?"

John Barrett, news anchor, faced the screen that wasn't there with Leslie on it and asked, "Well, Leslie, has the challenger Bob Wilson had anything to say in response to the governor's words tonight?"

John grimaced and hit the Pause button. His image froze on the screen. He looked at John the news anchor's hands. Did he always wiggle his thumbs like that? He rewound the tape. He hit the Play button.

John Barrett, news anchor, faced the screen that wasn't there with Leslie on it and asked, "Well, Leslie, has the challenger Bob Wilson—"

Pause button. John cursed. Those thumbs! They looked awful. Distracting. He made a note of it on a yellow pad: "Watch those thumbs!" He must have been nervous. He could remember wondering how long this report was going to be. The excerpt of the governor's speech seemed long enough.

Play button. "—nything to say in response to the governor's words tonight?"

Pause. *Did I sound natural?* Rewind. Play. "Well, Leslie, has the challenger Bob Wilson had anything to say in response to the governor's words tonight?"

Pause. *Yeah. Okay. Need to relax more, but . . . okay. It's a good thing I got that question in time to tailor it a bit,* he thought.

Play. Leslie on full screen. "John, we understand that candidate Bob Wilson will be making a brief statement in an hour or so."

John at the news desk, seeming to look at the screen with Leslie on it. "Yes, at about 8 o'clock we understand, and we'll be covering that on NewsSix at Eleven tonight. Thanks, Leslie, you've had quite a day."

"Thanks, Joh—" Pause. *Great, John, brilliant. You knew the answer to the question and you let everybody know it.* He made another note: *Remember: You don't know the answer to a scripted question.*

John dropped the yellow pad on the coffee table, hit the off button on the remote control, and leaned back in his soft couch, letting his eyes drift toward the ceiling. He put his hands behind his head and let out a deep sigh.

Yeah, really, I'm better than that. I've had better days. Today was tough. Too many distractions. Well, only one big one actually. I mean, give me a break. Do the riot, do the rally, get the great shots . . . just don't stick him *in the middle of it all and then give me this professional, objective news gathering malarkey.*

He sat forward and stared at the blank television screen. What a business. For a moment John tried being honest with himself and admitting that had he been Rush or Pete, responsible for the content, or Tina Lewis, responsible for all the shows together . . . well, yeah, he would've run that stuff. The viewers would have loved it. Even if they didn't like it, even if they wrote and complained, they still would have stayed glued to their sets, and that would have made the Advertising Department happy. *Yeah, to be honest and downright practical, material like that you don't pass up.*

And the material from that rally was spicy stuff, no doubt about it: wild gestures from everybody, yelling, grappling, arms and legs flying everywhere, cops pulling people off each other, dragging others away, including the old man.

The old man. Yep, he had to be famous now. He'd be recognized on the street. John didn't know what that would do for business at the old man's warehouse. His customers had to have recognized him. What a way to advertise.

John heard something outside, some kid crying or something. Kind of late for a child to be out on the street. *Go on, kid, go home. I've got things to think about here.*

John was wearing his sweatpants and NFL T-shirt. He'd had his dinner, then a nice glass of wine, and he'd planned to relax, review the day's work, take it easy. But tonight was not relaxing. Reviewing the day's work on the VCR wasn't the usual enjoyment either. Seeing it all again was miserable, frustrating, and maddening and stuck in him like a sliver he couldn't pull out.

He slapped the couch resolutely. "Dad . . . we're gonna have to talk. Yeah. You and me. We're gonna . . . I mean, we are really gonna have it out!"

He rose from the couch and went toward the telephone, then hesitated. This may not be the best way to do it. *Maybe I should call him tomorrow. Maybe we should just have lunch. I need time to cool off, get over this.*

The phone was on the kitchen counter, near the sliding glass door to the balcony. He could hear that kid again. No . . . Now it sounded like two kids. Maybe three.

But it sounded like an adult crying as well. Or was it two adults? Or three? What in the world—He slid the door open and stepped out onto the iron-railed balcony.

It was a pleasant evening with a warm land breeze wafting down the hill, weaving through the iron-and-glass forest of The City's downtown, now a festival of amber, yellow, and silver lights below. To the west, cut into short pieces by the skyscrapers, a bright layer of pink sky showcased the jagged silhouette of the distant mountains.

John listened raptly. Traffic noise was pretty steady around here. Though the apartment building faced a small residential street, there was a major arterial at either end of the block and the interstate only a few blocks down the hill. *Strange,* he thought, *that I would hear those kids crying in the first place with all this noise out here.* Maybe it was some sirens or a loud radio. Maybe it was mating season for cats . . .

No, wait a minute. There it was again. Someone crying. Heartbroken wails. One voice. Now two. Anguished wailing. Three?

Maybe someone was having a domestic struggle of some kind. Brother. Why didn't they close their window if they were going to carry on like that?

Yes, there were several voices out there, he was sure. But where were they coming from? He cocked his head this way, then that. For some strange reason he couldn't tell the direction. It just seemed to be everywhere.

More voices—some quietly weeping, some wailing, some speaking words. Women's voices, men's voices, high, low, soft, loud . . .

Oh brother. It must be a TV show . . . TV sets all over the neighborhood, all tuned in to the same show, some weird movie or something. Sure, that's it.

But it sounded so real. He listened some more, fascinated, perplexed. He'd never heard anything like it.

One of the voices was saying something, just weeping out the words over and over. He couldn't make out the words; there were too many other voices crying at the same time, too much traffic noise, too much breeze.

Curiosity started setting in. Then he checked it with the question of whether this was any of his business. He overcame that with a reminder that he was a newsman—or at least he used to be before he became an anchor—and there could be a breaking story happening out there. *So what do I do?* he wondered for just a moment.

Well, I'm in my sweats, I've got my running shoes on, it's a nice evening for a walk . . .

He went inside and grabbed a sweater. Then, on impulse, he grabbed his cellular phone. If there was a breaking story out there, he'd want to be in touch with the assignment desk right away, or even Owen Wessel, the Eleven O'clock producer. After all, here he was, on the spot, right where it was happening.

He ran out the door, down the hall, and down the stairs to the street, figuring times and schedules in his head all the way down. *Let's see, it's about 9:30 . . . that's an hour and a half before news time. If we got a crew here within half an hour we could get the tape back to the station by 10:30, but that would be tight. We may need to send a remote truck out here, use a microwave to do it live. Yeah, yeah, go for it—that'll work, if it's a story. But who do we have available at this hour?*

He ran out onto the sidewalk. No need to strain to hear it

now. It was clear as a bell, all around, on every side, up and down the street. Wailing, weeping, crying, sobbing . . .

". . . help me . . ." he thought he heard. Then again the words, barely discernible through all the other sounds, all the other voices, ". . . help me . . ."

That was no television. Good grief, someone was in trouble!

"Hello!" John shouted. "Can you hear me?"

". . . dying . . ." He could hear that word, he thought. It came from another voice, a deeper voice.

"Where are you?" John called. Then he thought, *Good question.* It sounded like they were everywhere. And who were they? And what was happening to so many people at the same time? Something about this whole thing just wasn't right. *Careful, John, careful.*

He stood silently, cautiously, and listened some more.

Now, beyond those immediate voices, he could hear throngs of other anguished cries, and beyond those . . . far beyond those, still more, blending together in a long, ceaseless moan like a mournful wind, like a distant, whispering ocean.

His heart began to race. His muscles tensed, ready to run. This was getting to him. He was afraid. Fear, real fear, was creeping up on him. Up to this moment he had no idea there was anything to be afraid of, but now it hit him: *I'm right in the middle of something. There's something dreadful happening out here, and I don't know what it is, and it's harming a lot of people, which means it can harm me too.*

He looked all around, up the street and down, up into the utility wires and tree limbs, the windows of the apartments, the lights of the city. He saw nothing strange, nothing sinister or threatening. That only made the whole experience more sinister, more dreadful.

The sound continued. He felt he could talk out loud and not be heard over it.

Enough. He was sold. He believed it. He ducked behind a utility pole for safety from whatever was going on out there and banged out the newsroom number on the cellular phone.

"Hi. This is John Barrett. Got a story breaking here. Let me talk to Owen."

He sold Owen on the idea. NewsSix had a cameraman on call. They would send him over. John would do the stand-up, reporting the story himself.

Then, having called the station, John called the police and reported a strange disturbance.

Then he looked himself over. Brother. He couldn't do a stand-up in a T-shirt! He ran back into the building, up the stairs, back into his apartment, breathing hard and starting to sweat. He stripped off the T-shirt, wiped his sweating body down with a damp washcloth, then groped through his closet, finally settling on a casual shirt he would wear open at the collar, and a red windbreaker.

As he pulled the shirt on, he rehearsed. "The evening quiet was broken tonight as a major disturbance erupted in this Baker Hill neighborhood . . . uh . . . the peace of this Baker Hill neighborhood was disturbed tonight . . . abruptly disturbed . . ."

Looking in the mirror, he wiped the sweat from his face, ran a comb through his hair, even checked his teeth for left-over salad. *Yeah, good, good.* This would look like a remote, on-the-scene, spur-of-the-moment stand-up.

He grabbed the ringing cellular phone off the bed. It bleeped and he dropped it, startled, then picked it up again.

"Yeah?"

"John, this is Benny. I'm pulling out of my garage. I need to verify where you are."

Benny was the on-call cameraman for this week. He drove home after work in one of the NewsSix camera cars so he'd be ready to cover any fast-breaking story on a moment's notice. Now he was rolling and calling John on his car phone.

John gave him the address and directions as he scurried out the door, down the hall, down the stairs—he almost lost contact with Benny while in the stairwell—and back outside onto the sidewalk.

A squad car had just gone by and was moving slowly down the block, apparently looking for the trouble. Sure. They had to be as perplexed as John was. With all these voices wailing on every side, where do you even start to check it out? They'll be calling in backups for sure.

John had to make sure he got these guys on camera, got reactions from them, information on what was happening. He stepped into the street and waved his arms, shouting. "Hey! Hey, back here! John Barrett . . . NewsSix!"

The car's brake lights came on. It came to a stop, then reversed, backing up the street toward him. John shot a quick glance up the street. Nuts! Benny wasn't too far away, but it was all happening too fast. They weren't going to get it on camera.

The squad car backed to a stop just opposite John, and an officer rolled his window down. "Hello. Did you call the police?"

John looked both ways and then dashed across the street. "Yeah. Hi . . . John Barrett, NewsSix. This all started about . . ." He checked his watch. ". . . fifteen minutes ago. I haven't been able to pinpoint the source of the problem . . . Maybe you can get a better handle on it."

The officer looked at his partner, then back at John. Then both got out of the car.

"You're with the press?"

"Right. I anchor the news on Channel 6. I've got a cameraman on the way, and we're going to be covering this."

"So what's the problem?"

John could still hear the weeping and wailing up and down the block and beyond. He threw up his hands. "Beats me. I haven't the slightest idea what this is all about. I've never encountered anything like it."

The officer was getting just a little impatient. "Like what?"

John was puzzled by the officer's inaction. "Well . . . there's got to be a reason for all this noise."

The other officer had come around the car and now both were facing him.

"Do you have some ID?"

John took only a moment to realize he didn't. "Oh, well,

no, I'm just wearing my sweatpants . . . I don't have my wallet on me."

Just then Benny pulled up in the NewsSix camera car, a little white fastback with NewsSix and the station's call letters emblazoned in big red letters on the side.

"Oh," John said, relieved. "Here's Benny Hake, our cameraman. Maybe we can get some reaction from you after you've gotten to the bottom of all this."

Benny's arrival seemed to authenticate John's claims about himself. The officers let the ID question go for the moment, but the officer pressed him. "Mr. Barrett, we need to know the nature of this disturbance. What's the problem? Where is it?"

Benny flipped open the back of the car and started pulling out the camera equipment.

John was unsure of what the officer wanted to know. What more did he need to know, for crying out loud? "Um . . . well, all this started up about fifteen minutes ago—"

"What started up?" the officer demanded.

"Well . . . all these voices . . ." Right about then, a suspicion crept into John's mind that he didn't want to entertain.

"What voices, Mr. Barrett?"

The suspicion became stronger.

Benny had the camera, the tripod, and a rack of camera lights ready to go, carrying them braced against his shoulder as he approached. "Hey, John, where's the best place to set up?"

John looked around, aware of the police officers. *Better not block the street,* he thought. "Oh, how about there on the sidewalk? We can get a good shot of the street behind me and the squad car."

Benny started setting up the camera. The officers were looking all around and exchanging glances with each other. They were also exchanging low mutters.

One officer asked, "Are you hearing voices, Mr. Barrett?"

John hesitated. The question was sensible, but he suddenly had the feeling he was being asked if he were crazy. Now that suspicion he'd been trying to resist came flooding in: *They don't hear the voices.*

Impossible. Of course they do.

"You're kidding . . ."

"We haven't done any kidding so far," said the officer.

"You don't . . ." John looked up and down the street. He noticed the voices were beginning to fade now. "You don't . . . hear any voices?"

The two officers looked at each other, their arms crossed, then looked back at him with poker faces. "No, sir. We don't hear anything."

"You don't hear . . . people crying for help, anything like that?"

'No, sir."

John couldn't believe it. It just wouldn't sink in. He turned to Benny. "Benny, you hear all the crying people, right?"

Benny looked out from behind his camera's eyepiece. "What's that?"

"You hear all the people crying?"

Benny repeated the question to make sure he'd heard it right. "Do I hear all the people crying?"

John was desperate. "Yes."

"What people?"

"You don't hear anything?"

The officer asked, "Have you been using any drugs tonight, Mr. Barrett?"

Oh no. This couldn't be happening. "Well . . . no. I don't use drugs at all."

"Do you live around here?"

"Well, yes, that's my apartment right up there."

The officers turned to Benny. "Sir? Could you come here please?"

Benny left the camera and walked over to the squad car.

"Now . . . you know this guy, right?" the officer asked.

"Sure," said Benny.

"He's hearing voices."

Benny thought that over and then asked John, "You hearing voices, John?"

John listened, just to be sure. The voices were gone. The street was quiet. He was afraid to answer.

"Are you hearing voices, Mr. Barrett?" the officer asked.

John shook his head. He was too troubled to speak.

"You're not hearing voices?"

"Not now," he muttered.

"Beg your pardon?"

"I . . . I heard them. I could hear them even after you got here, but now I don't hear them anymore."

"And you haven't used any drugs lately?"

John was horrified at the only explanation that came to his mind. "I . . . I used drugs in college. I was into LSD back then. But that was years ago." He was starting to shake.

"Well," said the officer, "it sounds like you're hallucinating."

John was troubled, mortified. He felt absolutely naked standing there.

"You okay, John?" Benny asked.

John couldn't answer. He didn't want to admit anything.

Finally he said, "I guess there isn't anything happening then. Sorry."

The officer asked, "That's your apartment up there?"

"Yes."

"Then if I were you, I'd get off the street and back inside. Go to bed. Sleep it off."

"I haven't used any drugs!" John protested, resenting the insinuation.

"Could be an LSD flashback," said Benny. "I've heard that people get those sometimes."

"I've never had anything like this happen to me before . . ."

"Let's call it a night, guys," said the officer. "Benny, can you take care of him, make sure he gets inside?"

"Yeah, sure."

"All right." The officer nodded to his partner, and they got back in the car.

While John and Benny stood there, Benny feeling bewildered and John feeling stupid, the police drove off.

John looked up and down the street, at all the windows in all the homes and apartments. Everything was quiet. Wherever those voices came from, they were gone now. Just gone. Simple as that.

"It was weird, Benny," he said. "I mean, it was absolutely real. I was convinced something was going on here. I wouldn't have called the station if I wasn't convinced."

Benny gathered up the camera and headed back for his car. "Yeah, well . . . it's pretty weird all right."

"Sorry to bother you."

"Well, I'm getting paid for this, so I guess I don't mind."

"Okay. Okay. Uh, say, Benny, could you give me some time to work this thing out? I mean, let *me* tell Ben about this. I'll get to a doctor, find out what's going on . . ."

"Hey, don't worry. You can tell the boss about it if you want—it's none of my business."

"Thanks."

Benny finished loading the car, said good night, and drove off, leaving John standing there, a lone figure under a streetlamp. The street was quiet again. John paused to take one more look up and down the street and then stood very still, not breathing, just listening.

There was no sound but the sound of the city. The fear had not left him. He hurried inside, up the stairs, down the hall, and back into his apartment, not resting, not pausing until he had locked and bolted the door and checked every room.

Then he found a spot on the couch, his back against the wall, the whole living room visible, and tried to calm down. It would end up taking half the night.

four

Ed Lake and Martin Devin had their meeting, first thing in the morning in Devin's big office—it used to be Lake's—with the big oak door closed. It didn't last long, perhaps fifteen minutes. Then, without a word of good-bye, and with most of the governor's staff oblivious to what had happened, Lake hurried down the long, paneled hall, past all the well-lit, touched-up portraits of past governors hanging on the walls, and out into the daylight, never to return. No one took much notice of it. It was typical for Devin or Lake to be out of the office on business for whole days at a time. It was also typical for them to have heated discussions and for one of them—usually Lake—to walk out.

The governor dropped in on Devin not long after that. "So how did it go?"

Devin smiled and gave a little shrug, sitting behind his big new desk. "Oh, not altogether pleasant, but I would say we reached a very clear understanding."

Barrett Plumbing and Fixtures was a wholesale business in an old warehouse in The City's south end, a semi-sagging building with peeling blue paint and windmill vents along the roof ridge that whirled and squeaked the same tune all day long. Every once in a while a jet would tiptoe right over the roof on final approach to the airport, and a salesman on the phone would have to ask the caller to say something again. John Barrett, Sr. had run this business for the past thirty years, knew everybody who was anybody in plumbing, and could talk sinks, faucets, showers, toilets, rubber washers, and compression fittings with the best of them.

The warehouse looked like it had to contain close to anything and everything in the world having to do with plumbing. If Dad Barrett or his four employees couldn't find it somewhere in all those rows of carefully labeled racks, shelves, bins, and boxes, they could sure find something else that would work just as well if not better. Cast iron? No problem. Copper? PVC? ABS? CPVC? They had racks of the stuff both in the warehouse and in the yard out back.

Yeah, thought John as he eased his Mercedes into the gravel parking area, *Dad knows how to run a warehouse and turn a profit.* But that's the part that didn't make sense. How could a man who worked so hard and did so well as a businessman be so irresponsible with his public image? Hey, marching in a pro-life march and holding a sign was no big deal; even respectable people did that. But this "mad prophet" stuff, this highly visible, public preaching, was getting to be an embarrassment, especially Dad's vendetta against Governor Slater. It seemed everywhere Slater appeared publicly, Dad was there as well. Slater was even starting to recognize him, and this last time Dad even made it into the governor's speech.

John turned off the engine and sat there for a moment, trying to keep cool. It was difficult. All he had to do was think of Dad's embarrassing behavior and how the resulting stress triggered that ridiculous hallucination last night, and his anger returned. The cops and Benny had to think he was a lunatic. *Thanks a lot, Dad.*

Well, now they had an appointment. John had called Dad that morning to say nothing more than "I'll be there to see you at noon," and Dad said okay, and now it was noon. John got out of the car and went around to the front entrance.

The front door had a window so covered with product posters and ads you couldn't see inside. John swung the door open and triggered the electric eye so that the old buzzer buzzed to let someone know he was there. Not that anyone paid that much notice. The front counter always had plenty of plumbing contractors leaning against it like cowboys in a saloon, asking for obscure parts, placing and picking up orders, swapping stories. Buddy Clemens, the skinny little salesman with the glasses and suspenders, was manning the counter as usual, and right now Jimmie Lopez, the beefy warehouse worker, was helping out. The walls and counter were plastered with more product posters, everything from septic system distribution boxes to fine, gold-plated bathtub faucets. No girls though. Dad never allowed any girlie ads.

Buddy spotted John and smiled a hello, which John returned. Jimmie had his nose in a thick catalog and didn't even look up.

John went around the end of the counter, right at home in this place. "Where's Dad?"

Buddy jerked his thumb over his shoulder. "Back in the office, I think." He went back to his customer.

John ducked down Aisle 7, the shelves of brass fittings towering on either side of him.

Buddy stole a glance at Jimmie and wiggled his eyebrows. "Here come the fireworks."

Jimmie looked back to see John walking briskly down Aisle 7. He said to his customer, "Just a second" and ducked down Aisle 7 himself.

"Johnny," he called not too loudly. John was trying to build some momentum, working up to the task. He didn't like having to stop and turn.

Jimmie caught up with him and spoke softly. "I know it's none of my business, but if it'll help . . . your old man's really broke up about what happened. He only talked to one salesman early this morning, and he hasn't come out of the office since. I mean, he's hurting. And I don't know why I'm saying this . . . I mean, it's none of my business, but . . . I guess I just want to ask you to go easy on him."

This was typical. As nutty as Dad could be, people who knew him liked him. Maybe Jimmie's plea helped John ease up . . . A little. He answered politely, "Okay, Jimmie. Thanks."

"Thanks, man." Jimmie hurried back to his customer.

John went back to building up momentum. He emerged at the other end of the aisle and paused for Chuck Keitzman to go lumbering by on the forklift, hauling a huge bundle of galvanized pipe to the loading dock. That machine had to be as old as John by now, still working, still smelling up the place with exhaust.

And there, back in the corner of the huge room, was the

office, a structure within a structure, several rooms framed in, drywalled, and painted a nondescript off-white. John went to the main door, marked "Office—KEEP DOOR CLOSED," and went in, closing the door behind him.

Jill the bookkeeper, a sweet and bubbly, heavy-set gal, greeted him with "Hi, Johnny. He's back in his office" and then watched with inordinate curiosity as he walked back to the door marked, "THE BOSS."

It was ajar. He knocked gently.

"Yeah, come on in, son."

John looked toward the front of the office, and Jill jerked her head back toward her work. He went inside.

Dad was behind his desk, wearing the same blue coveralls with his name stitched on the left breast. The desk was cluttered with invoices, orders, and a few catalogs, but on top of all that was a portable cassette player with headphones. As John came in, Dad picked up the cassette player and stowed it in a drawer. His eyes were red from crying.

John noted Dad's emotional state, but he was armed for bear nevertheless. "Well . . . I was going to take you to lunch, but perhaps . . ."

"Son, if you don't mind, I've had Jill order us some sandwiches. I figured we'd better just talk in here . . ."

John was quick to agree. "Yeah, I think so."

Dad didn't raise his voice when he said, "Jill, those sandwiches ought to be ready by now."

"Okay, John," she said.

"And then we'd like two coffees, all right? One black, one with sugar. Please."

"Okay."

Dad got up to close the door. "She's a very attentive lady."

He returned to his desk and eased into his chair, rubbing his eyes, then his face, exhaling a slow, mournful sigh. "It's been quite a morning." He forced a smile as he looked at John and gave him his full attention. "But my time is yours now, son."

John had a decision to make. Should he end it here, forgive

Dad, let it go? Or should he deliver what he had come to deliver?

It had to be done. He would deliver it. All of it. "Well, Dad, I have something to say, and I want you to listen because you need to hear it."

Dad rested his elbows on the desk, rested his chin on his clasped hands, and looked at his son. He was ready to listen.

John could have backed down. His father already seemed broken, not needing any more lashes, but John had anger he needed to vent, anger he'd been saving for a long time. The anger gave him strength; it drove him forward.

"I saw you on television last night. Several times. The coverage was quite thorough."

Dad nodded.

"Even during my own newscast I saw you standing above the crowd, shouting and railing against the governor like some kind of rabble-rouser. Then I saw you get involved in a fight, a near riot that jeopardized our reporter, until the cops came and dragged you and your pro-life friends out of there. And during all that, being a professional with a duty to report the news, I had to sit there in front of thousands of people and report . . . report what an absolute fool my father was making of himself. My own father!"

Dad nodded again, his gaze dropping.

"I'm . . . I'm more than embarrassed. I'm hurt, I'm mortified, I'm slandered. I'm a public figure in this town with a reputation to preserve, and my worst enemy, my greatest liability, is my own father who just can't seem to control his behavior in public.

"I'm not sure how many people at the station know you're my father. My executive news producer knows, and she rubbed my nose in it. I wouldn't be surprised if she had that camera aimed at you just to get at me. And then, when I saw you on the screen, I was so upset I couldn't read the script right, I asked stupid questions, I looked tense on camera . . ."

John stopped to take a breath. He still had more. "The producers put you right out front, did you notice? Right at the top of the hour. They slapped me in the face with you. I can imagine the undercurrents going through the newsroom right now. If anyone didn't know you were my father before this, they probably know now. I don't know what I'm going to have to face this afternoon at work."

John had enough anger to go on all afternoon, but not the time. He jumped to the bottom line. "So I don't know what you've decided, if anything, but my input on this is simple: This kind of behavior has got to stop. *Now.* It has absolutely got to stop!"

Dad nodded a third time, then sensed the pause and asked, "May I respond?"

"You have the floor."

Just then Jill knocked on the door.

"Come on in, Jill."

Jill slipped in, tiptoeing for no apparent reason. She set the sandwiches and coffee on the desk ever so quietly and slipped back out, closing the door behind her.

At the moment neither man made a move for the sandwiches. Neither felt like eating.

"May I tell you what really happened out there?" Dad asked.

"I saw what happened."

Dad hesitated at that statement, thought for a moment, then said, "Well . . . let me tell you what really happened."

"All right, tell me. I'm listening."

Dad leaned back in his chair and dabbed his eyes with his handkerchief. "Son . . . I didn't go to that rally because I've got something personal against Hiram Slater. I'm not his enemy. I was only giving him the warnings God laid on my heart. I just had to tell him." He gave it just a little more thought and then admitted, "If I did anything wrong, it was talking in generalities. Maybe I should have been more specific."

John couldn't believe this. "Dad, you shouldn't have been up there talking at all! Can't I get that through to you?"

"But how else can I warn him?"

"Did you ever think of writing him a letter?"

"I did that. I never got anything back but a form letter that tells me he hasn't read a word I've said. I'm hurting for him, son. That is one tortured man. He's so far into the dark he's tripping over his own lies, and now he's deceiving others. There's a lot of pain out there right now, and there'll be more, and he's going to be held accountable for a good portion of it."

John knew arguing with that would be pointless. "Okay. Fine. But what about that fight?"

"The fight . . . I don't know what that was all about. I don't get into fights, and you know that. I was standing there trying to be heard . . . I guess that crowd didn't care much to listen . . . And then two guys, two strangers, jumped into that crowd and started beating on people, just stirring things up, cussing people out, calling them baby killers, things like that. But, son, I don't know who they were. I've never seen them at any pro-life events, and they were never at the Women's Medical Center when we'd go there to sidewalk counsel. But anyway, that crowd was already hot enough, and when those two guys started hitting people, boy, a lot of anger broke loose."

"And you don't think you're to blame for that?"

"Not for the fight." A look of resignation came across his face. "But I guess I did rile those folks a bit. I didn't mean to, but I did." John remained quiet, so Dad continued, "Things went wrong, son. I just wanted to say what needed to be said and hopefully be heard by someone out there, but all of a sudden here I was in the middle of a big fight, and I never asked for that. And I remember being up on that planter, trying to calm people down, and I was shaking I was so scared, and then—I don't know where they came from, but these three big guys grabbed me and pulled me down and started muscling me out of there, and then . . ." He smiled sheepishly. "You see, I've got this friend named Max. He's a big guy, a shipyard worker. We met outside the Women's Medical Center one Friday back in July, and we've been close ever since. Max'll do anything for me. The problem is, he still thinks brute force is the answer to everything, and I keep telling him he has to get over that."

"I did see him brawling."

Dad nodded sadly. "He was trying to protect me. But that just got us in more trouble when the police came. They dragged us out of there like common thugs, and it's a good thing Max finally controlled himself or we both would have ended up in the pokey."

John grimaced and took a moment to respond. He had to hold back his anger at the sheer idiocy of it all. "Dad, I hope you can see the foolishness of all this. At least admit that your actions were not cost effective, okay? For all the trouble you caused yourself and everyone else, the returns were very poor."

"Well . . . I said what I had to say."

John pounded the chair arm in anger and cursed. "They used you, Dad! Don't you see that? That whole Hiram Slater bunch used you, and you helped him by what you did. You made it look like the only people who would oppose him are narrow-minded, fanatical, loud-mouthed kooks! Kooks and brawlers, and . . . and . . ." He stopped. He hadn't come here to insult anyone. "Now I'm not saying you're any of those things. But you don't understand the game, Dad. You're up against the big leaguers out there, and I don't think you realize the power of television."

Dad shook his head. "I didn't mean to be on television. My words were for the people who were there, for the governor . . ."

John leaned forward and gestured in Dad's face. "Dad, you were there, you were happening, you were visually interesting. Television viewers want something to look at, something to watch. Producers are looking for what the viewers want, and, well, you were it. You asked for it, you got it. You drew those cameras, Dad. And Slater took advantage of the whole thing—you hollering, the fight, everything. That's because he knows television. You don't."

Dad thought it over and then nodded. He understood. "Yeah, you're right."

"Well, I'm going to need more satisfaction than that, Dad. I want to know for sure—I want to hear it from your lips that you're going to stop this public preaching-and-prophesying stuff. It isn't working. It's making a fool of you, a fool of me, and it's only helping your enemies. Do you see that?"

Dad rested back in his chair and looked at the wall, pondering the whole thing, his eyes full of pain. "It's hard, son, to have God show you things and tell you things and then not know what to do with what you've been given."

John sighed. This was one of those little quirks of Dad's—subjective experience. How do you reason with someone who's been hearing from God? "Well, Dad, there are proper avenues . . ."

Dad didn't seem to hear him, but continued speaking in quiet tones, his eyes full of sorrow. " 'Eat the scroll, John.' That's what the Lord said. 'In your mouth it will taste sweet, but it will make your stomach bitter.' And He was right. Up front when you hear thing and see things and God entrusts you with knowing things, you think of how privileged you are, how wonderful it is to see Truth parading right in front of you. And then . . . when you try to speak it and nobody listens . . . and you see people heading for a cliff and you just can't turn them back . . . and when you find out things you would have been happier not knowing . . . and when you hear the cries of lost souls . . ."

Dad's eyes filled with tears. He dabbed his eyes again and looked at his son. "I could hear them last night, son. I could hear them as plain and clear as I can hear you now. All over the city. Souls without God, lost and dying and crying for help." His voice broke and he struggled to continue. "Oh, on the outside they laugh and they mock and they sneer and they try to look good to all their friends and keep right on having a good time, keep right on accumulating things and being entertained because it's the only way to get away from the pain. But I can hear them crying. I can see them drifting further and further from the light, just like they're walking into shadows, into darkness, never to come back." He drew a breath and then spoke out of anger and frustration. "But who can I tell? Who's going to listen to me?"

John heard what his father was saying, and yet, with a willful stubbornness, with a determined denial, he would not accept it. No way. *I'm not going to be a part of this,* he told himself. *If Dad's got a screw loose, it's not going to happen to me.*

"You won't listen," Dad said—not accusingly, just sadly. Truthfully. "And you know something? One of those crying voices was the voice of Governor Hiram Slater."

Well, it makes sense, John thought. *We're genetically similar, we've both been under stress. I get the same allergies he does too.*

"Funny that we could be so much the same and so different, isn't it?" Dad said, allowing himself to chuckle, even through his tears. "You know, son, you and I were having this same conversation some twenty years ago, except you were sitting in my place and I was sitting in yours. What was it you were doing at the university? Taking over the Administration Building for three days until the cops finally broke in and hauled you and all your fellow saviors of the world out of there?"

John smiled ruefully. "Yeah, I remember that."

Dad shook his head. "I was so frustrated with you . . . and embarrassed."

That's one for you, Dad. "Guess the shoe's on the other foot now, huh?"

"Yeah, son, I guess it is."

"So there you go. You've been through it with me. You know how it feels."

Dad nodded a strong nod. "I know." Then he smiled. "And I guess it gives me a ray of hope, knowing we're so much alike."

No, Dad, we're not alike, John thought.

"It's just so sad that you and I can't be devoted to the same things, that we can't see eye to eye. It would be so wonderful to be able to tell you things and talk about things, I mean, just open up and lay it all on the table and both look at it and come to the same conclusion. Son . . . I can remember when it used to be that way, and I think it can be that way again."

No, Dad, that's not likely. John stole a glance at the clock on the wall. He had to be at the station by 1.

Suddenly, with a new resolve, Dad turned to face his son head-on, leaned over the desk, and spoke so directly that

John cringed. "Well, son, all right, you've had your say. So now I'll have mine, and don't worry. I'll be finished in time for you to get to work.

"You know what? I've got plenty of things I'd love to share with you right now. Right now. I've got things I've learned today, just this morning, that I'm busting to share with you . . ." His hand went to the desk drawer where he'd stowed the cassette player, but then he drew it back, having second thoughts. "But I can't. I can't because so far, son, you and the Truth have a real problem with each other."

"Now, Dad . . ."

The elder Barrett waved him off. "No, no, now you listen. It's my turn. So you just listen. One of these days, son, I'm going to give you what I have, every bit of it, but not until you're ready to receive it. Right now I'm over a barrel. I'm not politically correct, I don't have anyone to appear on camera, and I can't squeeze it into a minute and a half."

Maybe he does know television, John thought.

"No, but I know you, and you mark my words, son, or at least file them somewhere in your brain until you're ready to hear them." Dad stopped so he could slow down. "Son, the days ahead are going to be difficult for you. I want you to know that ahead of time. The Truth is coming after you, son, and it's going to sink its claws into you and not let go until you start paying attention. There's something you need to keep in mind about the Truth, John. Depending on where you stand, the Truth can be your best friend or your worst enemy. So let me tell you something. I mean, if I never get the chance to say anything else to you, at least let me say this: Make friends with the Truth, John, as quickly as you can." Dad looked at the clock. "All right, I did that in just a minute and a half."

Dad sat back in his chair, finished.

John assumed he had the floor again. "Okay, Dad. Message received and filed. But now, how did I do? Did my message get through?"

Dad answered quietly and firmly, "Son, I heard you. And

I'll give the matter serious thought. Just you do the same with what I gave you."

Well, John thought. *What did I expect?* "All right. So long as we understand each other."

Dad sighed and looked out the window. "I guess I've said all I need to say."

John rose from the chair. "Yeah, I've got to get going."

"Take your sandwich."

"Yeah, sure."

"You bring a coat?" Dad was looking out the window, and it was raining hard.

"Oh, brother. Well, I'll make a dash for it." Dad went to the coatrack and grabbed his old overcoat.

"Here. The weather's changing. You're going to need this."

"No, come on, I don't need—"

Dad shoved the coat at him. "Go on, take it. Humor your religious old man."

John resigned himself to wearing the coat and slipped it on over his suit. "Don't know if it'll fit me."

'You'll grow into it."

"Well, thanks. I'll get it back to you."

"No, it's yours now. You keep it."

John was about to protest again, but there just wasn't time for more discussion. "I love you, Dad."

"I love you too, son."

It was close to 1 o'clock. John rushed out of there.

Audio: Low, rumbling music, rising in intensity. Video: The sun just on the horizon, burning a window of fire through the dusty red haze of dawn.

Low voice, heavy on the glottal flutter: "A new day, a new dawning, broke upon our state four years ago. Now that rising sun is approaching its zenith, and we, the people, have the power to keep it there."

Cut to head and shoulders of Governor Hiram Slater just turning his face toward the camera. Coat off, tie loosened, his face earnest, full of business.

Voice: "Governor Hiram Slater, a pioneer who will not be turned back, is working for you!"

Quick-cutting, rapid-fire shots of Hiram Slater, shirt sleeves rolled up, brow furrowed, shuffling papers, consulting with VIPs, talking on the phone.

Voice: "A growing economy and new jobs. A bold new approach to education for the twentieth century. Environmental awareness. These are the Slater legacy."

Shot of the state capitol dome silhouetted against a massive rising sun, the whole picture rippling with heat waves.

Voice: "The new dawn lives on." Hiram Slater's face appears to the left of the capitol dome in stark relief against the sun.

Voice: "Governor Hiram Slater—for Governor!"

Small title across bottom of screen: "Paid for by the Committee to Reelect Governor Slater, Wilma Benthoff, Chairperson."

The governor, Martin Devin, and Wilma Benthoff were seated at one end of a massive conference table, watching the towering, powerful images assaulting their senses from a deluxe, 50-inch television screen in the corner of the room. Wilma Benthoff, the harried organizer from the rally, was looking much better today, decked out in a tailored black suit, her spine straight, her billowing, blonde curls perfectly behaved. All three sat in calm, objective, critical-eyed judgment on the presentation as Rowen and Hartly, their hired media consultants, unveiled the television spots that would persuade the populace to keep Slater in office.

Waves playfully lapping against the round stones and mussel shells. The cry of sea gulls. Seals on a rock, barking, sleeping, clapping. Killer whales sporting and spouting. A blue heron skimming just above the water in slow motion. Windswept, outdoorsy music.

Voice: "The Bay, for millennia a showcase of nature, a playground for sea life. A precious treasure."

Shots of black oil swirling around the rocks, dying birds, limping otters. The music becomes dark and ominous.

"Governor Hiram Slater has determined that what has happened elsewhere will not happen here."

Shot of The Bay. Blue water, blue sky. Hiram Slater's face appears superimposed over the scene, the guardian of these placid waters.

"Two years ago Governor Slater presented—and saw passed—a law requiring double hulls and backup containment systems on tankers operating in The Bay . . ."

A tanker appears on The Bay as Hiram Slater's superimposed image keeps a watchful eye on it.

". . . the first law of its kind to protect our precious environment."

Shot of Hiram Slater, in shirt sleeves again, standing on a wharf with The Bay in the background, addressing a group of people, all with their backs to the camera.

Slater: "This is not only *our* world, but our children's world. What we have here is a precious legacy, and what I inherited I intend to pass on in even better condition than when I found it."

Several people nod in agreement. Shot of mountain streams, jumping salmon, soaring eagles.

Voice: "Your world. Your children's world. Your governor, Hiram Slater!"

Title: "Paid for by the Committee to Reelect Governor Slater, Wilma Benthoff, Chairperson."

More ads followed, with more images moving quickly, jump-cutting from one to another.

Scene: The governor in close-up on grainy film stock, in jerky stop-motion. Hardworking. Gritty. Determined.

Governor's voice over the pictures: "Fiscal responsibility is still one of my goals for the state. I'm happy to say that last year we realized our first budget surplus, and if I can help it we're going to see another one this year, and the next, and the next."

Scene: Women cheering, waving KEEP ABORTION LEGAL

signs. In the center, Governor Hiram Slater, greeting them, shaking their hands. Cut to:

Governor addresses a gathering of women: "I once dreamed of a state where reproductive freedom was a fundamental right of every woman. We have seen that dream come true, and as long as I am governor that dream will live on!"

Cheers. Some tears.

Scene: The classroom. Teachers dashing ABCs and famous names onto blackboards. Kids listening attentively, hard at work. Hiram Slater in the middle of it, talking to the children, addressing the class, taking questions, laughing.

Slater addressing a group of teachers: "History has carried our world forward, but our schools have lagged behind. I say it's time not to catch up with history but to outrun it. We must live, and we must educate, as if the future were today."

The teachers nod, exchange positive looks.

The ads tumbled colorfully out of the television screen, the music rising, the sun continuing to shine. From every angle, at every film speed, in backlight, sidelight, stark light, faces, faces, faces, happy, hopeful, adoring, prospering, a moving montage of political satisfaction.

Title: "Paid for by the Committee to Reelect Governor Slater, Wilma Benthoff, Chairperson."

The screen went black. Slater, Devin, and Benthoff exchanged pleased expressions and applauded.

"Bravo!" said the governor.

"Good enough, good enough," said Benthoff.

"Boy," said Devin, "they're going to think they're electing God."

"Well," said Rowen, the smaller of the duo, the one with the horn-rimmed glasses and crooked tie, "the ultimate benefactor at least. We're showing the people that Governor Slater is good for the state and good for them."

"Image is everything," said Slater.

"Image is everything," echoed Hartly, the taller of the two, and the better dressed. "Uh . . . you may have noticed we emphasized the bass on your voice a bit. In those . . . uh . . . outdoor scenes, you know, the higher tones tend to carry."

"Good move," said Devin.

"Yeah, fine," said Slater. "Well? Questions? Comments for these gentlemen?"

Benthoff referred to her notes. "Now . . . you just showed us six commercial spots. How many do you have planned overall?"

Hartly replied, "These six will open up the campaign starting next week if you're all agreeable. Then, after they've reached saturation, we'll start rotating our celebs through to recapture the public's attention."

"That's a great lineup, too," said Devin.

"I think it's outstanding," said Rowen. "We have Rosalind Kline, the star of 'Who's Got Problems?' "

"Ever seen the show?" Devin asked the governor.

"I don't watch that slop," he said under his breath.

Rowen continued, "She'll be doing a spot emphasizing the women's rights issues. And then there's Eddie Kingsland, who's really into environmental issues, so he'll do a plug from the environmental angle."

"Help me out," said the governor.

Benthoff rolled her eyes. "Oh brother, you guys! Haven't you ever watched 'Love Thy Neighbor'? He plays the hunk next door."

"These are household names," said Rowen, "faces the public will instantly recognize and identify with."

"Uh," Devin prompted, "you do have Theodore Packard doing an ad, right?"

"Oh?" said the governor, his eyebrows going up.

"Got him," said Hartly. "He'll be doing an ad on pluralism, freedom of artistic expression, cultural diversity. We picked him for the classy folks."

"Thank you," said Slater, and they all laughed. "Well, that's what we want. Whatever will get their attention where they are."

"And what about the posters, the billboards?" Devin asked.

"Those should be ready for posting next week," said Rowen.

"I think . . . uh, Mason, do we have photocopies of the revisions?"

Hartly dug into his valise. "Right. I think you'll like these." He gave a small pile of papers a shove and let them slide across the conference table to the three. "You'll notice we took the same style from the TV spots and translated it into provocative stills that evoke the same image. The public will see the TV ads, so they'll immediately recognize the billboards. Their eyes will be drawn to the familiar."

Slater, Devin, and Benthoff perused the sketches and nodded approvingly.

"And did we ever get any mention of the Hillary Slater Memorial Fund?" the governor asked.

"Oh!" said Rowen. "I believe we had Anita Diamond lined up to do a TV spot. You'll recall she's very active in animal rights—"

"Animal rights!" The governor cursed. "I want people to see how I care about young women needing an education and you give me someone identified with animal rights?"

Rowen and Hartly looked at each other for a suitable reply. Hartly took the question. "Oh, beg your pardon, Governor, I'm afraid we may have misunderstood—"

"If image is everything I don't like the image!"

Devin tried to intercede. "Guys, the Hillary Slater Memorial Fund provides grants for girls going to college. It doesn't have anything to do with animals."

Rowen and Hartly stopped cold, then chuckled, then laughed a very socially soothing laugh. Hartly addressed the problem. "Hey, I think we're still okay. Eugene said we had Anita Diamond lined up. Uh . . . that means we've talked to her, but it's nothing firm. But using her might work anyway. She's a successful young black singer who overcame poverty and hardship and racial prejudice, that sort of thing . . ."

The governor was not appeased. "We've got enough black footage in the TV ads. We've established that I like blacks. What I need now is a young woman with some brains."

The two media consultants looked blankly at each other. "Who do we have who's known?" Hartly wondered.

"How about a lesbian?" Devin suggested.
The governor cursed again.
"Hey, they vote!" said Devin.
"I know that!"
Devin turned to Rowen and Hartly. "What about Packard? Isn't he gay?"
Hartly shrugged. "He isn't telling, sir."
Slater mulled it over. "Well, Martin's got a point. Get me a gay. Somebody famous, with some credibility. And I don't want any lisping limpwrist. Have him say something nice about me. I've been nice enough to them."
"Yes, sir."
"And then maybe we can get an actress to plug how I've formed the Hillary Slater Fund. I don't know who."
Rowen brightened. "Why not a local girl, someone right from the area, who benefited from the Fund?"
The governor was silent. Devin quickly answered, "We've only funded one girl so far, and . . ." He wiggled his hand, palm down.
"How about a woman athlete?" suggested Benthoff.
"Yeah, right," said Slater. "What's wrong with that? A tennis champ or something, talking about me helping girls reach their full potential and all that crap."
"Better get on it," Devin goaded.
Rowen was taking notes. "Yes, sir. You've got it, sir."
"Now have we covered everybody?" the governor asked.
"What about the homeless?" Benthoff asked.
"Not this election."
"They don't vote," Devin quipped.
"Well, next election."
They had to laugh at that. It broke the tension.
Benthoff perused the list in front of her. "So we're talking about TV ads, with adaptations for radio . . . billboards, bus posters . . ."
"We've purchased space on twenty Metro buses."
"Okay. Bumper stickers, yard signs, balloons . . ." Devin flipped to the next page. "Not to mention public appearances. You're going to be busy, Mr. Governor."

"How public?" the governor asked.

Rowen read down his list. "Oh, many different venues. The University, the Kiwanis, the Teachers' Union . . ."

The governor asked Devin, "Any places where that prophet might show up?"

Rowan's eyes went blank. "Sir?"

Devin glossed over it. "Oh, an old friend. One of the governor's most faithful followers."

five

John slammed the receiver down. He was fully awake and out of bed without a thought, scrambling for his clothes. It was 8:32 A.M., Wednesday. There'd been an accident at the warehouse. Dad was hurt. Buddy wouldn't say how badly, but he emphasized, "You'd better get down here right away."

Rush hour. The northbound interstate was jammed and sluggish, but southbound was moving. John made it to the Industrial Street Exit without delay and worked his way through the industrial grid, through alleys and over railroad tracks, to the warehouse. He could see the flashing lights blocks before he got there.

He pulled around the back, drove through the big yard gate, and jerked to a stop beside two police squad cars. Near the loading dock, a large fire truck and an aid car stood ready. A fireman was just going up the stairs to the loading dock with some cable in his hand.

John spotted Buddy Clemens on the dock waiting for him, waving frantically. John was there in an instant.

"What happened?"

Buddy stood in his way. "Johnny, let's go in the office."

John pushed Buddy aside and ran into the building, past the office, past Aisles 8, 9, and 10, then into the open area where the galvanized stock was kept.

The images that confronted him would haunt him for days afterward, every time he closed his eyes.

Firefighters scrambling, lifting, shoving heavy pipe aside. Chains, hooks, pulleys. Shouting.

A toppled pipe rack now lying on the concrete floor, twisted and bent.

Heavy, twenty-foot lengths of galvanized pipe strewn on the floor like jackstraws.

Paramedics working, moving . . . but not hurrying. No urgency in their manner.

Police officers watching, muttering into their portable radios, looking grim.

Some guy with a camera snapping pictures.

A white cloth on the concrete floor, covering . . .

Jimmie Lopez saw John and walked toward him, heading him off, blocking his way. "Johnny, hang on, man. Just hang on."

John tried to get around him, but Jimmie outweighed and outsized him. "Jimmie, what's happened?"

Jimmie held him back, then somehow turned him around. He spoke gently. "Johnny, your father's dead. He's gone."

It didn't sink in. John kept trying to look. "What happened?"

"Your father's been killed in an accident. Just work on that."

The realization, like a spear, reached John's heart. He grabbed hold of a shelf. Jimmie held him, braced him from falling.

"Let's get into the office where you can sit down," said Jimmie, guiding him with a strong arm.

John's vision went blurry. He felt like he would smother. His breaths were short, shuddering. He was trembling all over.

Jimmie got him through the office door and into a chair. Jill was at her desk, completely beside herself, whimpering into her clenched fists, stealing horrified glances through the office window and then turning away with anguished cries.

"Is your husband on the way?" Jimmie asked her. She couldn't answer. He asked her again, gently, "Did you get ahold of Kevin?"

She nodded.

"Is he coming to get you?"

She nodded again.

"Okay. Just sit tight."

In came Buddy Clemens, helping Chuck Keitzman along. Chuck, shaggy-haired, mustached, and built like a tank, was cradling his right arm and cursing over and over. His right hand was wrapped in paper towels; blood was soaking through them. Chuck flopped into a chair, threw back his head, and cursed in violent anger. Then he wilted in the chair and wept. Buddy raced into the washroom and returned with more paper towels.

"The medics will be here," said Buddy, his voice high and rushed. "Just sit and be quiet. Just take it easy."

"I couldn't get the pipes off him," Chuck wept. "I couldn't get 'em to move."

"It's okay. You gotta calm down."

"What happened?" John demanded.

"Johnny," Chuck cried, "Johnny, I'm sorry. I couldn't get the pipes off him."

John cursed and shouted, "Chuck, *what happened?*"

"The rack of pipes fell over on him."

Nothing would sink in. John just couldn't fathom anything. "What do you mean, it fell over?"

Chuck let his head fall backward against the wall and cried some more.

"Chuck, what rack of pipes?"

Chuck controlled himself. "The big galvanized. Two-inch, one-inch, one and a half. I just don't get it. I don't know how it happened. The thing weighed a ton. We've never had anything fall over like that."

"Did you see it fall?"

"No. I got here at 8 and saw it dumped over and the pipe lying all over the floor, and then . . ." He choked back his emotion, drew a deep breath. "And then I saw John underneath. I tried to get the pipes off him, but there were just too many, so I tried using the forklift, but I couldn't get under 'em, they were all crooked. I tried to get 'em off by hand and they kept rolling back and then I busted my fingers and I cut myself up. I couldn't do it."

John was disoriented. He could only sit there, let things happen around him, and try to take it all in.

The police and a medical investigator had questions for everyone, and John sat in numb shock, listening to all the answers. "No, no one saw the rack fall. John was here before anyone else; he always got to work an hour early. John was the boss . . . Chuck got here first, a little after 8, and then the rest of us, at 8:30 . . . No, we've never had a rack fall like that before. Maybe the pipe wasn't stacked evenly, maybe Dad was climbing on the rack and that could have tipped it over, but we can't say for sure . . . No, his wife doesn't know yet. His oldest son is sitting right here . . . The company is privately insured, not state insured . . . "

"Did he have enemies?" asked a cop.

"No."

"Maybe he did," John answered.

"Who?"

John shook his head, sorry he'd said anything. "I don't know."

Two paramedics worked on Chuck's arm while the police asked their questions. He'd broken two fingers and lacerated his knuckles. They bound the wounds, applied a temporary splint, and arranged for Jimmie to drive him to the hospital. Jimmie and Chuck left immediately.

Kevin, Jill's husband, came and picked her up. He stayed just long enough to find out from Buddy what had happened, then away they went. Jill had to get home. Kevin would get the details later.

The police and medical investigator completed their work. Don't disturb the site, they said—they might have to come back after the autopsy.

Then, quickly, quietly, and unobtrusively, they conveyed the shrouded form into a transport and drove away.

Only Buddy and John remained in the warehouse, sitting alone in the office, the clamor suddenly chopped off as with a knife, the shock ebbing, giving way to grief.

"Guess I'd better close up the place," Buddy murmured just to break the silence. "We won't be doing business today."

"I've got to tell Mom," John said.

"How're you doing?"

John was staring at Dad's office door, still ajar, the one marked "THE BOSS." "That's the last time I ever saw him alive, Buddy . . . Right in there."

The last time. And perhaps the worst time. Just one more

conversation, John thought. Just one and things could have been better. He and Dad could have ironed things out. They could have had time to make changes, adjustments, meet on some kind of middle ground.

But they never did, and now they never would. "We never finished the boat either," John muttered.

"Hm?" said Buddy.

"Oh . . . Funny . . . I just thought of the boat Dad and I worked on and couldn't finish before I left for college, and after that we never did finish it, never got back to it. Good grief, that was years ago. It's funny the things you remember."

The boat. The little rowboat. They were going to build it in Dad's shop and then take it out fishing. "I think it was the last thing we really did together."

The last thing . . .

"Steady now, not too fast. Light pressure. That's it." They were in Dad's shop, pushing a plane along the edge of a board, Dad's hand on his, his body wrapped around John's like a cloak, guiding John's every movement.

"You start at one end, pick up the chip . . . Yeah, just pick it up, no deeper than that, and away you go, on down to the end . . . Keep her flat, keep her flat. You're Mr. Level, the board's counting on you . . ."

The chip curled like a blonde tress out of the planer, one clean strip, and Dad chuckled with delight. "That's it, that's it, all the way down. Hmm, boy, ain't it lovely!"

John was eighteen. He knew how to use a plane, he didn't need Dad showing him for the umpteenth time . . . but Dad sure had the touch, and he was having so much fun showing John how to do it—again—that John didn't want to complain about it. *Okay. I'll humor him,* he thought.

It was summer. John would be leaving for college in the fall. He had other things to do, and yet . . . when would he get the chance to do this again? It was right to be with Dad, working on something together. If only this silly project didn't take so long!

"Well, just think, son. Jesus used a plane and a saw and a

hammer, and they didn't have power tools back then, so it was even slower than this. Guess that's one way He learned such patience. Good thing, too, 'cause He's working on us every day, just like we're working on this boat, and *we* take a long time too . . ."

That boat took so long . . . so long. And they never finished it.

Saturday afternoon. Brother Moore, deacon, with tears in his eyes, stood amidst the congregation to give a brief tribute. "I will always remember John as a lover of life. For him, every good thing really was a gift from God, and he never neglected to give God the glory . . ."

When Brother Moore had finished, Sister Larson, now in her eighties, rose to her feet and spoke. "I guess I knew John longer than anybody, and I can remember when he was a little fellow in my Sunday school class. He was a cutup, like kids are, but you know, there was never any doubt about his commitment to the Lord . . ."

Betty Pierson, a young single mother, rose to her feet and spoke through great emotion. "He was Jesus to me. The kids and I were living in that old place on 32nd, behind the apple orchard . . ." There were some hmmm's and nods from some who were familiar with the place. ". . . and the plumbing was just shot, and John found out about it, and I think it was that very week, he was there with a sink and a toilet and all new things, and he put it all in for nothing, and it wasn't even my house . . ."

The Rainier Gospel Tabernacle was a different place now. It had a new sanctuary with a high, arched ceiling and large windows to let in light and fresh air, and it had a new name, the Rainier Christian Center. For Dad's memorial service, every pew, every folding chair, every seat in the choir loft was filled, and John recognized many faces, some a lot older, some pretty much the same. They'd sung some of Dad's favorite hymns—"It Is Well with My Soul," "And Can It Be That I Should Gain?" and "Amazing Grace." Young, bearded Pastor Phillips—this was his fourth year at the church—gave a well-worded eulogy, full of hope and assurance, just the way Dad would have wanted it.

And then the floor was opened for fond memories, meaningful recollections, and there were plenty.

"An honorable man, who wanted to leave his children an honorable world."

"He had such patience. He could listen to your problems for hours . . ."

"I think he was a modern-day prophet. He spoke in love, but he always spoke the Truth."

John was sitting in the front pew with his mother. Sitting near him, as well as interspersed throughout the room, was the rest of the Barrett family. Uncle Roger, Dad's younger brother, was there with his wife Marie and their four children, all grown, with their own families taking up several pews. Dad's sister Alice was there with her husband Robert and their three children and their families. Mom's siblings, Doris, Elizabeth, and Forrester, occupied some more pews with their spouses and families. The whole church sanctuary seemed interlaced with Barretts, Barretts-in-law, and shirt-tail Barretts.

Seated right next to John was Mom Barrett, Lillian Eve, Dad Barrett's sweetheart for forty-six years, John's ever-present, ever-patient friend and counselor throughout his childhood and, to be honest, ever since as well. She was grieving, of course, but John knew she'd done her weeping at home over the past few days so she could be strong today, for her family. Now, in a pastel blue dress—not black—her face angelic under hair of spun glass, she silently journeyed through years and years of her own precious memories, her visage hauntingly serene.

The tears kept recurring in John's eyes until finally, in a delayed decision, he let them come, let them spill over and run down his face. He pulled out his handkerchief to dab them away. *Dad, I'm sorry. God, I'm sorry.*

He felt—he couldn't think it clearly yet—that for the past twenty-plus years he had missed something. These friends, this precious family, knew his father better than he had. Their memories were a rich, enduring treasure of joy, admiration, and love. They really knew the man.

His own recollections? The rowboat project was his most recent fond memory. His most vivid memory? His "lunch" with Dad, where pleasant words were few and lunch stayed in the paper bags uneaten—that and his bitter words, "My worst enemy, my greatest liability, is my own father . . . If anyone didn't know you were my father before this, they probably know now . . . They slapped me in the face with you."

It was like being impoverished in the midst of great wealth. The lives and circumstances of these relatives, friends, and strangers were not ideal. None of them were rich in a material sense. None of them "had it all" or ever would, but wealth was here: families, children, love, faith, an enduring spiritual heritage, and because of these, the ability to express deep joy and steadfast hope, even through tears of sorrow.

In the center of them all, John sat alone. Separate. Disconnected.

He glanced across the room and a few pews back. Yes, he had a family too . . . once. A wife and a son. They were sitting over there right now, on the other side of the church, apart from him, from the family, far away, a sort of monument to the missing side of his life, to the great failure the vast viewing public never saw, never knew about. Ruth was as gorgeous as ever, once a fashion model and now a fashion designer in Los Angeles. That beautiful face still had the same radiance, but like the radiance from a distant star, it had no warmth.

And then there was Carl, John's nineteen-year-old son, a stranger who'd grown up with his mother and hardly known his father. John had to use some imagination to even recognize him. He'd changed, and that was an understatement. His face was ghostly pale, and his hair, jet black, was shaggy atop his head with an unruly lock falling across his forehead and sometimes over one eye, then cut in sharp stair steps down the sides and back. A gold chain linked a ring in his ear with a ring in his nostril. Everything he wore was black.

Even as John looked, he didn't want to look. The sight hurt

him. Their even being here hurt him. Why had they come? Just so they could sit far across the room from him? And how could he proudly introduce them to his family—"Hi, I'd like you to meet my pride and joy, my son, whom I haven't seen in years, don't know, and whose appearance I have no explanation for"?

But Carl was *weeping*. John had to look almost to the point of staring at the contradictory image. Here was what appeared to be a bizarre, defiant rebel, an almost gruesome, morally lost character with a heart of stone, and yet Carl was weeping openly, unabashedly. The kid was heartbroken, and John had to wonder why. Carl hardly knew his own father; why would he be so grieved over his grandfather?

So here was something else John was missing. *Carl, why are you crying? What's that grief you're feeling? Hey, I'm your old man—you can tell me.*

John looked forward, down toward the floor, toward the red-and-gold carpet, not wanting to look at faces or anything else. For so many years John had resigned himself to wondering about Carl and never knowing the answers. Carl, like Ruth, had become distant, faraway, a stranger. Ask him about the weather, about school, about LA, but don't ask the big questions.

So Dad was gone. In a way Carl was gone too. So much for belonging. So much for family. So much for wealth. *O God, I can't let this go on. Help me.*

Uncle Roger and Aunt Marie's house on 28th was one of those big, gabled, dormered structures built in the 1940s, when full-width, pillared front porches and bedroom dormers were popular and concrete was cheap. This was the big house John always remembered as the fun house, the hide-and-seek house, with all the cherry wood doors with the glass doorknobs that opened into rooms, halls, stairways, closets, and nooks in a teasing, maze-like sort of way. It was a perfect house for childhood chases in vast, meandering circles, through Aunt and Uncle's bedroom, into the hall, into Cousin Tim's room, through the bathroom, and back into

Aunt and Uncle's room again, then down the big stairway with the banister you could slide down but weren't supposed to, down the hall, and through the kitchen and dining room where the moms and dads would finally tell you not to run in the house.

Today some of the third generation, the youngest children of the children of Roger, Alice, Doris, Elizabeth, and Forrester, were running through the big house and being told not to by John's cousins. The squeals and laughter of the children made the gathering sound like Christmas or a wedding or a birthday, but today, of course, the adults were more subdued, keeping the conversation quiet and reserved, the laughter confined to gentle, social chuckles.

Mom was the center of attention, but it was a delicate kind of attention. No big, heavy questions, nothing disturbing or burdensome. Just love, gentle embraces, and, for as much as Mom wanted to remember and reminisce, listening ears.

"He was ready to go," John heard her saying to her sisters Doris and Elizabeth and Dad's brother Roger. "I don't know how I know—but we've paid off all the debts. He made sure of that. And he was talking with our attorney just the other day. I think he wanted to set everything in order. I just know that somehow he knew."

In the dining room Lindsey and Mandy, Dad's sister Alice's daughters, shared the table with Chuck, Trish, Mark, and Ben, Mom's sister Elizabeth's children, and talked about something—who could tell what—while Mom's brother Forrester's son Clay stood between the dining room and living room with Alice's other daughter Candice and her daughter Susan, while Debbie the daughter of Burt and Linda who was the daughter of Dad's brother Roger rounded up Bobby and Jason the twins to feed them and put them down for a nap, while Lindy and Dori, daughters of Mom's sister Doris and her husband Marv sat in the living room visiting with Brent and Michelle, children of Mom's brother Forrester, as well as Mary and Jeff who was the son of Roger, Dad's brother, and Jeff's younger brother Tom and his wife Stephanie, who was trying to get their young son Tyler to eat some turkey off a paper plate, sitting next to Eddie and Jerry, the sons of Mandy the daughter of Alice, and James, Roger and Marie's youngest son who was still single, and all the cousins were talking with each other while they and some of the second cousins were trying to get caught up while keeping up with their children who were still running through the house and slamming doors. And in the corner of the living room, with a faint, social smile on his face but no one to talk to, sat Carl.

John had his turkey dinner on a paper plate and a cup of coffee and knew that if he moved quickly enough he could grab that one folding chair next to Carl and say something to the boy. Everybody else in the house had a family, kids, stories about the kids, messes to clean up or behavior to correct, pride to show off, grandchildren to introduce, sons and daughters to encourage in pursuing their dreams, and doggone it, John had a family too . . . of sorts. It was sitting in that corner looking repulsive and, apart from answering polite social questions—"Whose boy are you? Where are you living now? Haven't seen you lately; you get up this way often?" —was not really conversing with anyone.

John stepped from the dining room into the living room, carefully slipping between Clay, Candice, and Susan who were still in the doorway. He caught Carl's eye and said, "Hey!"

Carl smiled at him.

"Hey, John." It was Roger, Dad's brother. He looked a lot like Dad across the eyes, and the graying hairline was sure the same. "Can we talk for a minute?"

"Sure . . ." They were still close to the huddle in the doorway. They moved into the center of the living room, surrounded on all sides by cousins and kids, and even had to step over a few of the smaller ones.

Roger moved close and spoke in a quiet voice that would be lost anywhere else in the room. "It looks like your dad and mom were ready for this. That's a real comfort."

"Mm-hm. Dad was thorough. He always liked everything in its place."

"I understand you'll be overseeing the estate, making sure Lil's taken care of."

John smiled. "Oh yeah. Mom and I already met with the attorney, and the papers all look good, and Mom's got a real handle on it. She'll need to get some accounts switched over, but that won't be hard, and the way Dad budgeted everything out, she should be taken care of the rest of her life. Besides that, she'll always have me around, if I can help it."

"That's great, John. But listen, if there's anything I can do, please let me know."

"I've got something for you right now."

"Shoot."

"The plumbing warehouse is all Mom's now, but we'll have to get someone to run the business, do all the managing Dad used to do."

Roger nodded. "Right. I'll get some feelers out."

"Buddy and Jimmie are manning the counter and keeping the place open, but the back office is dead in the water and falling behind."

"Mm. I've got a good man, semi-retired, who could fill in for a short time until we get someone permanent. I'll call him on Monday."

"Great. Let me know." John looked. Carl was still sitting there.

"Oh, one more thing," said Roger.

"Yeah?"

"Do you have any feelings about the autopsy? Do you think . . . uh . . ."

John shook his head in bewilderment. "I don't know, Roger. There could be any number of explanations."

"But . . . if some of John's injuries didn't come from the accident, then . . ."

"Well, all the medical examiner said was that some of Dad's injuries weren't consistent with what the accident would have caused. But that isn't a sure thing, and he hasn't drawn any conclusions. So far the police haven't said a thing."

"Mmmm . . . Just makes me wonder, that's all."

John nodded. "I know what you mean. I just hope I'm seeing straight. The whole thing, Dad's death, is just so unacceptable, so . . . pointless. I'm afraid maybe we're trying to come up with a reason just so we can have one."

Roger gave a quiet, sad chuckle. "Yeah. I think that could be it." He turned to the huddle in the doorway. "Clay, what's this I hear about you moving up in the world?"

John was free. Carl was still there. John let some youngsters scramble after a rubber ball while two mothers corrected, "Not in the house!" and then hurried over to that folding chair.

"This seat taken?"

"No."

John sat down, carefully placing his paper plate in his lap and his coffee on the windowsill. "So how're you doing?"

"Okay, I guess."

"Did your mother leave already?"

"No. She never came."

"Oh."

"She had to catch a plane back to LA, so she dropped me off. I've got all my stuff out on the porch."

John didn't mean to make a puzzled face, but this did seem rather odd. "Hmm . . . Well, I'm sorry I missed her. We didn't say more than two words to each other at the memorial service."

Carl didn't respond, but just looked into the center of the room. Now there was silence. Dead air. It made the broadcaster in John nervous.

Say something, John. Anything.

"I'll be—" Carl and John said at the same time. Pause. John prompted, "Go ahead."

"I'll be in town for a while."

John felt happy about that. It was good news. "Oh . . . No kidding. You . . . uh . . . you have friends here? Business? What?"

Carl seemed a bit hesitant to answer. "Oh, both I guess. Got some painting I want to do . . . just . . . stuff."

It was beginning to sound like a television interview, John asking, Carl answering, the clock ticking.

"So how is your mother?"

"Fine."

"Still working at Wembley and Myerson?"

"Promoted. Head of the department now. She's doing all right."

"Well, that's great. How about yourself? You heading back to school pretty soon?"

"Not for a while. I need to get out and explore a bit."

"Mm . . . Sure." They both looked toward the center of the room for a moment, and John took the time to munch on some turkey and drink some coffee.

"Well," John said finally, "it's good to see you again."

"It's good to see you again," Carl returned.

It sounded like the conversation could end there, but John didn't want it to. He got an idea. "Um . . . well, listen, if you're going to be around for a while . . . why don't you come by the station sometime? I can show you around, you can see where your old man works, and then we can go somewhere and grab some dinner."

Carl's face brightened noticeably. "Yeah . . . All right."

"You going to be busy Monday?"

"No, I'm open Monday."

"All right. Why don't you come by the station about . . . oh, say, 5? I'll show you around a bit and then you can watch me do the news. You have a way to get there?"

"I think I can borrow a car."

"Okay. Well, I'll clear it with the front desk and then give you a call with the details. Where are you staying?"

"Oh . . . a friend's house."

"Got a number there so I can call you?"

Carl hesitated. "Uh . . . no, not yet."

"Well, okay." John pulled out his wallet and produced a business card. "Here's my number at home and at work. Give me a call Monday morning and I can let you know what to do, where to park, all that stuff."

"Okay."

More dead air. The noise in the room was noise enough. Plenty of conversation, distraction, action. But what a lousy place to try to get some kind of conversation going with your son. Maybe Monday, at dinner. Then they'd be alone. They could work at it.

"Well, okay then," said John, getting up. "See you Monday."

"Monday," said Carl, giving John a thumbs-up.

John found that simple gesture encouraging. Perhaps some ice had melted.

six

CLICK. Two bare light bulbs on the ceiling came to life, and Carl Barrett remained in the doorway of the building for a moment spellbound, almost afraid to go inside.

"This was your grandfather's workshop," said Mom Barrett, still wearing the pale blue dress. It was Saturday night. The memorial service and afternoon get-together were over. Now, at the Barrett home, it was just Mom and Carl. "When he wasn't working at the warehouse it seemed he was always out here, he and your father."

Carl, still in black, still wearing the chain across his cheek, went inside, walking slowly among the power tools that stood neatly arranged about the floor like a gray steel platoon: the band saw, the table saw, the power planer, the drill press, the radial arm saw, the power sander. The room smelled of sawdust and machine oil, wood and iron, paint and lacquer, but it was remarkably clean. The floors had been thoroughly swept, and though faint traces of sawdust were visible in the rafters, on the windowsills, and along the top edges of the tool racks, this place was no typical messy woodshop.

"It wasn't always this clean," Mom said. "Close to it maybe, but Dad took a lot of time out here just getting the place spick-and-span, just like everything else he did in the last few days. Everything taken care of, everything in its place."

Carl looked down and watched his own feet taking steps across the worn boards. *This was where Grandpa walked,* he thought. This was where he worked. He placed his hand on the knob of the drill press, the finish worn off long ago by repeated use. *This is your hand, Grandpa.* He gave the crank a little turn and watched the drill's chuck drop toward the table. He could imagine the rumble of the machine, the chips flying out of the drilled wood. *My father used this machine too,* he thought. This was part of his world.

Along the entire far wall was a heavy-built, nicked, gouged, spilled-upon but kept clean workbench with heavy drawers beneath it and tools, tools, tools hanging on the wall above it, each one carefully traced on the wall with a black marker so the eye would immediately know if a tool was missing, not in its place. Right now no tool was missing. All had come home to stay.

Mom's eyes were filling with tears. "I'd better not stay out here long. I can see Dad everywhere I look."

Carl knew what she meant. This room was just full of Grandpa. His touch and his personality were everywhere. Carl could feel it.

"But see?" Mom pointed, wiping her eyes clear with her other hand. "Down there at the end, right by the windows. Couldn't you use that area?"

They walked down to the south end of the room where a row of large windows would welcome the daylight. Carl looked the area over thoughtfully. In the corner was a large pile of lumber, some kind of project under a tarp, but apart from that there was plenty of open space here. Near the windows was a perfect spot for an easel, and on the next wall plenty of room to hang his paintings. This end of the workbench had space for his paints, palettes, and brushes, and in the center of the area was a fine worktable. During the day the light would be ideal.

He wanted to be here. "It'll be a beautiful place to work."

"Then that's that."

"But I don't want to cause any problems, you know?"

"You belong here."

"Well, I mean, with my father. He doesn't know I'm staying here, and I was afraid to tell him."

"Oh, I'm sure he'll find something to fuss about. But that's because he doesn't know you and you don't know him, and he'll be concerned for me."

"What kind of a person is he?"

She raised an eyebrow. "Ask him yourself. That's why you're here."

Carl looked around the room again, fascinated, captivated by this world—his world—he'd never known. "I still feel like I'm intruding."

"No, now remember, this was my idea." She touched him, got him to look at her. "Carl Barrett, my name is Lillian Eve Barrett. I'm your grandmother, the mother of your father. And you, young man, are my only grandchild." She put her arms around him and gave him a squeeze. He didn't know how to respond to that and just stood there stiffly, his hands awkwardly at his sides. "This is called a hug, Carl. It's one of the things I do to people I love. You'll get used to it."

He absorbed the hug and the words that came with it and then shyly agreed, "Okay."

She let him go and stepped back to smile at him and to even point a motherly finger in his face. "If you get to be a nuisance, I'll let you know, so don't be. I expect you to keep this place clean, like your grandfather kept it and your father never did. You can have your father's old room. The bed's still there and his dresser. Right now I've got my sewing in there and a bunch of boxes from the Women's Missionary rummage sale, but we'll cart all that stuff upstairs and out of your way. If you start feeling guilty for mooching off a little old widow, I've got plenty of work for you to do around here to earn your keep. I'll give you a list."

He smiled, nodded, feeling a bit nervous, on the spot. "Yeah, okay. Fair enough."

"Any questions?"

"Oh. Well . . ." His eyes drifted toward the pile of lumber and whatever else under the tarp. "Would it be okay if I moved that stuff there? Then I'd have this area all clear. It'd be perfect."

She stepped over to the pile and lifted the corner of the tarp, folding it back over the top. Underneath were several planks cut to precise, curved shapes, mingled with finely cut wood ribs.

"Looks like a boat," said Carl.

Mom didn't answer right away. She seemed drawn by those unassembled parts into another world. Her eyes filled with tears again. "I'd better get inside now. I see Dad everywhere I look . . ." Her hands went to her face and she turned away, heading for the door. "Come in when you're ready, and we'll get you moved in."

"I'm sorry. I didn't mean to—"

"It's all right." She stopped and turned toward him one more time, wiping her eyes, speaking with quaking breath. "I want you here. Dad wants you here too. I know."

She went out the door. Carl stood there, unsure of what to do next. He finally heard the back door to the house open and close again. She was safe inside now. She was home.

Who is she anyway? he found himself wondering. *Who was Grandpa?* Then he chuckled. *Who's my old man?*

He reached out and touched one of the boat ribs. And for the longest time, he just couldn't take his hand away.

Monday afternoon, at ten to 1, John parked in his designated stall under the building, punched in the security access code at the stairway door, and entered the bowels of Channel 6, The City's Premiere News and Information Station. Up one flight of stairs, through the steel fire door, and straight ahead was the newsroom.

"Hey, George."

George Hayami, assignment editor, waved from the assignment desk, an elevated station everyone passed on their way into the newsroom. From the newsroom floor it resembled a sort of lunch counter, built at chest height, from which George, Ruth Sutton, and Diane Bouvier served up a constantly changing menu of fast information. The Desk, as the staff called it, was in many ways the only window in this windowless room, the station's electronic, telephone, fax, and print eyes and ears that were open to the outside world. On the left end a bank of radios tuned to police and fire frequencies carried the chatter of dispatchers, fire trucks en route, and cops on capers. In the left back corner a radio and telephone switchboard kept the Desk in touch with reporters in the field via radio, cellular phone, and, when all else failed, public telephone. Just under the back counter all the latest City newspapers, plus the *Wall Street Journal,* the *New York Times,* the *Los Angeles Times,* and the *Washington Post,* were stacked in wire bins, already divided up, folded over, highlighted, and clipped. On the back wall were large maps of The City proper, The Greater City, the county, and the state for quick reference by the assignment editors so they could tell reporters where a story was happening and how best to get there. On the desk below the maps were the computerized feeds from the news services—United Press International, Associated Press, and Reuters. At the other end, sifting and selecting, George Hayami and Ruth Sutton sat at computer consoles updating the "24-Hour Outlook," a multi-paged, computer printout, the day's menu of what news was happening and where, what stories were being covered and by whom, who was working, who was sick, who was on vacation.

John picked up a copy, updated at noon, and at a glance could see what was happening and what might be news:

> M! (M! stood for murder) BROCKVILLE—33-year-old Cora Ann Bayley found dead in home. Friend who found her thinks she was strangled. Cops won't say how she died.
>
> MURDER PLOT—Three teenagers arrested in Greenport for plotting to kill parents.
>
> B! (B! stood for a body found) DILLON PARK—Woman's body found in Dillon Park Sunday (not reported Sunday). Reported missing on Friday. Apparent suicide.
>
> C! (C! stood for a plane crash) MANILA—We *really need* to put Southcott on this today. Benson Dynamics is, of course, issuing the usual meaningless doubletalk. Southcott last year reported on similar engine problems.
>
> F! (F! stood for fire) VARIOUS—Couple of good fires with good flame pictures from Sunday. Yacht in Lake

Swayze. Cause? Grandstands at Summerville Raceway burned up in an arson fire.

And so it went. Three pages of it. They wouldn't all make it on the air, but John always found the wide selection fascinating, especially when compared to the final script for the evening news.

He sat at his desk in the back of the newsroom and clicked on his computer monitor. A small, blinking mailbox in the upper-right corner of the screen meant he had a message in his mailbox. Of course, this didn't mean a physical mailbox, but a message left for him in the computer. He called up his mailbox to retrieve the message.

Well, messages, plural. A lot of them. "We're thinking of you, John." "Much sympathy in your time of loss." "Chin up, sport, and remember, you're the greatest." "God bless you, John." "Condolences to you and yours."

Oh. And here was a message from Leslie Albright. "John, my sincerest condolences. Please come around to talk. I owe you an explanation and apology for last Friday. Leslie."

Well, what do you know. He pushed the tears back down, smiled warmly, and typed in a return message for general distribution through the system. "Many thanks to all of you for your good wishes and support at this time. We've got a great team. God bless."

He hit the enter key, and the message went into the system just that quickly. He looked around the newsroom. Leslie wasn't at her desk. She was probably out covering a story, as usual for this time of day.

He entered the code for her computer mailbox and left her a message—"Thank you for your kind thoughts. Sure, let's talk"—and hit the enter key.

Now back to work. Back to business. It was time to look forward, time to lose himself in the rush and hubbub of the daily news. He loved it.

He hit a series of keys, and the script for the Five Thirty came up on the screen, still under construction. Now he'd find out which stories from the "Outlook" survived the sifting process and would actually be on the air.

He was betting the fires with the "good flame pictures" would make it. Good video was always a strong seller.

As for the plane crash in Manila, the plane's manufacturer was a major employer in The City, so that story was of great local interest and would get into the lineup somehow, whether there was any fresh information or not.

Two pervading questions that guided news reporting in a local market were, How can we localize this? and What's hot? If a Benson Dynamics plane crashes overseas, you definitely have local interest because people in the area probably built that plane. As for "hot," well, if enough planes were crashing and enough people wondering why, that topic would be hot; there would be plenty of cause for related spinoff stories and sidebars. Even if there were no new news, you could still get reactions from people on the old news, you could take a poll, find a relative, look for another angle.

John could recall other "hot" topics over the past few months. AIDS was hot since two more celebrities had tested positive for HIV; NewsSix localized the story by running a piece on the local gay community and what they were doing to curb the epidemic. The Middle East hostages were hot because they were finally being released after years of captivity, and since the sister of one of them lived in the area, NewsSix had a perfect opportunity to "localize" the story. Sexual harassment on the job was hot since a major politician was accused of it. Gun control was hot after another mass shooting. Crooked televangelists were hot after another TV preacher got caught with a prostitute. News fed news, and hot news fed a lot of news.

But this was all part of the gauntlet, the gathering and sifting process every news story had to run through before it got on the air. The broadcast news business involved a day-long chain of human, journalistic, and business elements that tugged on the news, often from opposing directions, here promoting it, there opposing it, other times shaping, discarding, or rebuilding it.

Even though the people who gathered the news made every effort to be professional—meaning *objective*—news gathering was still a human business. Reporters, producers, and even viewers perceived things differently and held different facets of the news to be important, and that alone was enough to reshape reality, however unintentionally.

But even after that, the news gathering process still involved a balancing of journalism and business: What are the people out there interested in, what are we as journalists interested in and concerned about, and—this one nobody talked about openly—what material is in the best interests of our News Department as far as ratings and advertising accounts are concerned? It was a complex world.

Bingo. John saw the Summerville fire in the script for the Five Thirty. The good video of the flames must have sold it to Erica Johnson, the managing editor. And here was the plane crash story. No new information on the crash itself, but to keep the story alive—right now it was hot—Wendell Southcott had filed a piece on how thrust reversers work and how they might have had something to do with the crash.

These were stories passed down from the assignment desk and then approved and assigned at the 9 A.M. meeting around Erica's desk, where Ben Oliver, the news director, Tina Lewis, the executive news producer, and the producers for the Noon, Five Thirty, and Seven O'clock shows met with reporters and writers to decide what would be news that day. From there, with their marching orders from Erica, the reporters went out in company cars with their assigned cameramen and got the video footage and pertinent information so they could put together their video packages, their perception of what was happening. The writers would remain in the newsroom and get their information over the phone, from the papers and wire services, from the public information officers of the police departments, or any other reliable source, and then write a story to accompany some separately shot video—or perhaps no video at all, the anchor would simply read it.

Then the stories were all sifted again, this time by the show producer, who placed each one where he or she wanted it within the half-hour time slot, which really meant twenty-two minutes of actual news time plus eight minutes of commercials.

Finally, whichever portions of the stories were to be read by the anchors were proofread by the anchors, and that was where John was right now.

Okay, here was a story about gubernatorial challenger Bob Wilson speaking at his kickoff rally. After last week's story—the one John hoped everyone would forget—the public was no doubt curious about how he would respond.

And here was a hate crime story about a cross burned on a lawn out in Woodard. Racism was always hot; people were interested in that.

Oh-oh. A gay/AIDS story. These were hot but also tough to do because they were so politically and morally loaded and stirred up a lot of cross fire. This story was a follow-up on a Sunday demonstration by gays during a Catholic mass. Ah, this was where Leslie Albright was today, gathering this story. She'd be on-camera, reporting live from the newsroom during the Five Thirty broadcast, sandwiched around her video package. John perused the script for the question he would have to ask her. Hmm. "Leslie, can we expect more demonstrations of this kind?" John chuckled. He already knew the answer to that one, but he made a mental note. *John, remember, you don't know the answer to a scripted question.*

Here was a story about one of the ferries that carried commuters across The Bay breaking down, and that would be of interest to the commuters who rode that ferry. The volcano still erupting in the Philippines was a big story that all the other stations and papers were covering, so naturally NewsSix would be covering that. But this story about a lady finding a tarantula in a bunch of bananas and suing the grocery chain probably qualified as filler or maybe human interest. There was certainly no plague of tarantulas threatening the area as of yet.

Speaking of filler, here were some more stories of that nature: the new uniforms for the Irish Girls' Drum and Bugle Corps (and whether or not you could join if you were not

Irish or not a girl or didn't care to wear a skirt) and an oyster eating contest! These were bound to end up on the floor if time got tight.

John continued to scroll through the script just to give it an overview, tapping away on the PgDn key. He'd be spending most of the afternoon proofreading and polishing, as would his co-anchor, Ali Downs. Most of the stories had already been assigned to either Ali or John and marked with an A or a J, but both anchors read and edited all of the script in case either one missed something—and to make sure the stories made sense and were understandable and readable. Sometimes the script could tie your tongue up and had to be changed.

Anyway, this was great. This was life as usual, and John was happy to let himself become lost in it, absorbed by it. Now he could just work on getting normal again.

Normal. Something about that word made him think of Carl. Oh brother . . . Carl . . . He'd gotten a call from him that morning and set the whole thing up, but he still hadn't cleared it with the front desk. He picked up the phone—

He spun his head around as he held the receiver. The scream came from across the room. A woman. An accident. Something terrible.

He bounded from his desk and weaved through the maze of desks toward the sound.

Now he could hear words. "I didn't do anything . . . I didn't do anything! Leave me alone!"

The reporters, writers, producers stayed on their phones, kept at their computers, even conversed with each other. Good grief, what was wrong with these people? They didn't care! They didn't even turn their heads!

"What's happened?" John asked Hal Rosen, the weatherman.

Hal, a lanky, good-natured guy, was at the weather desk, shuffling through weather wire copy and watching the computer-enhanced satellite photos on the monitor. At the look on John's face he jumped up, alarmed. "What?"

John heard the woman's voice again. "Get away from me! *Please!* I haven't done anything!"

It was coming from Tina Lewis's office.

"Tina!" John dashed into her office with Hal on his heels.

Tina was facing the wall, a script in her hand. At the sound of their entrance—and it was not a quiet entrance—she spun around, started and irritated. "What in the world—"

"Are you all right?" John asked, his words rushing with urgency.

She slowly, deliberately dropped the script on her desk and demanded, "Don't you ever knock? I don't recall inviting you in here."

"She's okay," said Hal, ready to look elsewhere.

"I heard you screaming," said John.

She glared at him, even let her mouth drop open with incredulity. "Screaming?"

John saw her glaring at him the way she always did.

But then, in a weird dissolve, the glare melted into an anguished expression, the head thrown back, the eyes running with tears, the mouth contorted in a scream of agony. This face cried out, "You leave me alone! I had the right! It was my right!"

John froze. He stared at her. "Are you . . . are you sure you're all right?"

"Barrett," another voice demanded, "is there something you need?"

It was Tina Lewis's voice. It came right through that anguished face.

No. Now it was that angry face. That impatient, condescending face.

John blinked. He looked at the floor. He looked at Tina Lewis again.

She was wringing her hands, wagging her head in torment. "Barrett?" The voice didn't match the face again. It sounded alarmed, curious.

Now he saw her rise, not weeping or screaming, but a little concerned, bewildered, looking at him as if he were . . . as if he were . . .

"Are you all there?" Now she was weeping again, moaning in pain.

John mentally broke in on himself. He purposely aborted the program going on in his head, forcing himself to muster all the acting ability he had, look straight at the weeping, desk-pounding image, and say, "Boy, that computer printer! We've got to oil that thing or something. It sounded just like a woman screaming. I thought it was you!"

"Get out of my life!" she cried, cowering, her arms covering her head. "I don't want your pain! Just leave me alone!"

"You need to get your ears checked," said the other Tina. The real Tina? One of the Tinas? "Go on, get out of here." She picked up the script again and sat down with her back to them.

"Come on," said Hal. "The lady's got work to do."

They went back to the weather desk, Hal leading John by the arm, steadying him a little. John wiggled his finger in his ear. He could still hear the terrible cries coming from Tina's office.

"Man oh man."

"Here, sit down," Hal said, pulling a wheeled chair closer.

John sat.

"You still hear something?"

John listened. "Not now." He forced a little laugh, tried to gloss it over. "I'm too close to the printer, I guess. Or maybe it's my telephone."

Hal set his elbow on the desk and studied John for a moment. "You're sure you heard Tina screaming?"

John shrugged. He tried as best he could to look like a normal, sane, responsible human being. "Isn't that the wildest thing you ever saw? Boy, I sure thought . . . Boy, what a deal."

"You okay?"

"Yeah . . . Sure."

Hal didn't seem satisfied. "You know . . . you just went through a real tragedy, John. Maybe you're not ready to be back here yet, back under the pressure and everything."

John was ready to get away from this discussion. He rose,

looking at his watch. "Well, you know, my son's coming to visit the station today, and if you think I'm hearing things, just wait 'til he gets here—you'll think you're seeing things. Gotta call the front desk."

"Well, take care."

John got back to his desk and rescued the telephone receiver which he'd left dangling by its cord.

Rush Torrance was standing at his desk, only a few feet away, gawking at him. "What happened?"

"Oh, nothing. I thought I heard someone hollering for me. False alarm."

Rush accepted that and went back to work at his console. John tried to look as normal as possible, realizing that others in the room were also gawking at him. He put the receiver to his ear and punched in the number of the front desk. As he talked to the receptionist and made sure Carl was expected, he could feel their curious gazes gradually turning away.

Then he slumped in his chair and stared at the computer screen. The computer kept prompting him, *Make a correction, escape, do something.* But it would have to wait for a moment. John was scared.

It had happened again, but this time more directly, more personally. Instead of vague, faraway, unidentifiable voices, he'd heard Tina Lewis. He knew he'd heard her, and he'd seen her so clearly, so vividly that he mistook it for . . . reality? But was it?

He cursed under his breath. LSD flashbacks. That had to be it. The sixties pseudo-intellectual, acid-dropping, college radical was now paying the price. Back then Dad always warned him there'd be a price to pay someday. He used to think of Dad every time he popped that little sugar cube into his mouth: "This one's for you, Dad." Now all the recent strain, first with Dad's behavior, then with his death, must have jarred something loose somewhere in his head, and he was back there, back in the old rebellion. How poetic. Every time he took a drug trip he thought of Dad; now thinking of Dad too much brought on drug trips without the drugs.

And, oh yes, wasn't it Dad who helped aggravate this thing

with his mutterings about the "cries of lost souls"? That had to be a part of it too. Dad's last words, the tragedy that followed, John's own deep regrets coupled with the emotional upheaval . . .

He just had to be careful; he had to take it easy. This kind of thing probably passed with time and rest. He was an otherwise healthy man who took good care of himself, jogged five miles a day, watched his diet, got plenty of rest . . . it should fade, it should go away . . .

Aw, so forget it, John. Let it go. It'll pass. You're forty-two, all that stuff's behind you, and you have a career to think about.

He leaned forward and got back to work on the Five Thirty script. What was that he was saying earlier? Something about getting back to normal?

seven

AT close to 5, Carl drove Dad and Mom Barrett's gray Chevrolet down under the Channel 6 building and found one visitor's slot still available. Following his father's directions, he found his way around to the front entrance.

The reception area was big enough to . . . well, to hold a reception. It was a vast, high-ceilinged room with lots of glass, a deep, sound-deadening carpet, and a wide-screen television in the center of an inviting sitting area. The television was carrying Channel 6, of course, and at the moment a syndicated, prerecorded, controversial talk show host was interviewing what appeared to be prostitutes.

In the center of the room was the reception desk with an attractive young lady wearing a headset and taking calls.

"Oh," she said, "you must be Carl Barrett."

He smiled. The meaning was clear. With his weird hair, clothes, and jewelry he was easy to identify, hard to miss. "That's right."

"I'll let your dad know you're here." She made a quick call, then had Carl sign in, identifying himself and the car he had parked down below.

Then he was free to wait, to stroll about the reception area and take it all in. All around the room Channel 6 was putting its best foot forward. There was, of course, the huge television providing a nonstop sampling of the station's wares, but there were also several glass display cases filled with impressive memorabilia: a football jersey and an autographed football from The City's football team; a baseball bat and autographed baseball from the baseball team; several trophies awarded to Channel 6 for excellence in broadcasting, broadcast journalism, and sportscasting; photographs of Channel 6 bosses meeting with dignitaries and celebrities.

But it was that wall behind the receptionist's desk that really caught the eye. Here, in brightly lit, full-color, three-foot-high photographs, were the talent, the stars, of Channel

6: Hal Rosen, weatherman; Bing Dingham, purveyor of a stick-it-to-'em sportscast; Ali Downs, news anchor; Valerie Hunter, special assignments; Dave Nicholson, consumer specialist; Barry Gauge, editorial commentary.

And, of course, John Barrett, news anchor. Carl paused. So this was his father. He'd never seen his father stand still like this. There he was, clean and polished, in a dark blue suit, color-balanced burgundy tie, and a white shirt. His left hand rested on the news desk in front of him; the right rested on the left and held a fountain pen. The pose looked like he'd just finished doing the news, giving vital information to the public, and had now turned aside to pay special attention to just Carl. He sat tall and straight, though relaxed. His face was without blemish, his eyes keen and insightful. Hmm . . . The eyes were brown. Carl had never noticed their color before. He stood before that picture for the longest time, just gazing into those eyes, trying to read them. The only problem was, those eyes were not looking at him, but at a camera.

A door opened at the end of the room. "Hey, Carl!"

It was him. The guy in the picture. No suit jacket at the moment, but he was wearing a white shirt and a tie. A dark blue tie. The smile looked the same. He looked smaller than in the picture. And . . . whoa! He had makeup all over his face! Carl looked at the picture again, at that perfect, unblemished face. Well, maybe it was the makeup that made it seem so perfect. He couldn't tell.

John extended his hand. "Any trouble finding the place?"

Carl shook the man's hand. "Uh, no . . . Came right to it."

"Did you sign in?"

"Yeah. I think I'm okay."

"Great. Well, come on." With that, TV anchorman John Barrett headed back toward the door he'd just come through, and Carl followed. The receptionist was watching, and when she got a glance from John, she released the lock on the door. They went down a few hallways, turned a few corners, and went into the newsroom.

"George, this is my son Carl." They shook hands.

"Erica, this is my son Carl. I'm showing him where his old man works." They shook hands.

"Hi, Rush. I'd like you to meet my son Carl. He'll be watching us do the show today." They shook hands.

Rush said, "John, the cassette on the curfew story's no good. We're going to have you read it instead."

As Carl watched, they conferred—reading, pointing, nodding their heads.

"Right . . . got it," said John. Then to Carl, "Okay, come on and I'll get you situated."

They went past all the desks, past the young Asian gal talking on the phone and the grim-faced guy with the horn-rimmed glasses typing at his computer and the black man tapping his pen on his writing pad, waiting for inspiration. They reached a crude-looking plywood wall braced with two-by-fours, painted to match the rest of the room but looking very much like plywood and two-by-fours anyway. A long computer-printed streamer proclaiming "WE'RE NUMBER ONE" covered up some of it, and various tack-ups decorated the rest, at least as far off the floor as human arms could reach—complete game schedules for football, basketball, and baseball, and adjacent to that, a sign-up sheet for the football pool, almost filled. Some news clippings about the station had been there a while, and the tape was getting yellow, but some of the news-related gag cartoons were new, such as the picture of the two men in an office setting, one with his hindquarters chewed off and the other asking, "Well, what did ("the boss" was scratched out, and "Mr. Oliver" was penciled above it) have to say?"

They turned right and went down to the end of the plywood wall, where a small camera perched on a stand looked down at them like a curious, one-eyed crow.

"This is the flashcam," said John. "You'll see how we go to reporters in the newsroom for their stories and how they use this camera."

John kept going, around the plywood wall, and Carl followed.

Now they entered another world, and Carl felt he'd just

plunged into a big, brightly lit aquarium, full of human fish but no water. Lights bore down on them from above and from the walls, washing out the shadows, putting every detail of their clothing, their faces, their movements, on display. The back wall, the one made of the plywood and two-by-fours, looked impressive, even intimidating, from this side. On the left was the city skyline, painted on a mural behind a false window. In the center was an array of false TV screens showing photographs of events, news frozen in time. On the left was a waving, blue-green-gray-purple pattern.

In the center of the room, decked out in mahogany, chrome-edge trim, and black formica, was the news desk, a podium for four, with swiveling leather upholstered chairs at four stations, the one on the left for the sportscaster, the one on the right for the weatherman, and the two in the middle for the anchors, each with its own television monitor tucked into the surface of the desk, hidden from the cameras' view.

The cameras. Yes, if this was an aquarium, the three cameras were the fish watchers. They stood there looking like just-landed alien probes, all staring one-eyed at the news desk, each bearing its own name like some kind of livestock ear tag: One, Two, and Three.

Across the top of the backdrop were television monitors, even now flashing forth images. The one on the left showed the controversial talk show still in progress, the sound off, the mouths flapping without meaning. Then came three monitors showing the world as seen through the eyes of Cameras One, Two, and Three. Camera One was looking at a black leather chair with no one in it, Camera Two was looking at a crisscross test pattern on a stand right in front of it, and Camera Three was looking . . . well, at them, just behind the news desk, looking up at the monitor.

John showed Carl to a chair situated to the right of the news desk, back behind Camera One. "Have a seat right here. You can watch part of the show from here, and when we have a commercial break somebody will take you upstairs so you can see the control room."

With that, John ducked out of the room for a moment.

Carl, fascinated and bewildered by it all, took his seat in the chair and just watched without a word.

The floor director, a pretty black woman, came onto the set, headset in place, script in hand. Two men and one woman took their places behind the cameras. It was almost 5:30.

In came an attractive, dark-complexioned lady in a gray suit jacket and black skirt, a black scarf perfectly arranged over a white blouse, her hair a complex, ebony sculpture. This was, of course, Ali Downs, his father's co-anchor, looking just like her big picture out in the lobby. She took her place in the second of the center chairs, picked up an earpiece from the news desk, and carefully installed it in her ear, then clipped a tiny microphone to her jacket. It virtually disappeared against the black scarf. Then she reached into a slot in the news desk and picked up a round mirror, checking her appearance, arranging her hair just so.

Anchorman John Barrett returned, a little rushed. His face looked different; perhaps he'd touched it up a bit. His hair was perfect though. He probably used hair spray. He took the first of the center chairs and then went through the same quick preparations, installing his earpiece and lapel mike and taking a quick look in a mirror of his own.

"Thirty seconds," said the floor director. The news team of Barrett and Downs was ready. In the monitor atop the backdrop the controversial talk show was over, and now commercials were racing one after the other across the screen.

"Ten seconds." Then the floor director's hand went up with five fingers extended. Four . . . three . . . two . . . one . . .

Point.

John Barrett looked at Camera Two and spoke in a resonant voice. "Tonight on NewsSix at Five Thirty, Candidate-for-governor Bob Wilson has his say at his own campaign kickoff rally."

Ali picked up where John left off. "And Governor Slater says he's ready for Wilson's challenge anytime, anywhere."

"There's a lot of fingerpointing going on over what caused

the crash of that airliner in Manila. Is the airline to blame, or is Benson Dynamics covering up?"

"And this weekend's tragic fire at the Summerville Speedway has raised some hot questions on who will eventually pay to have the grandstand rebuilt."

"Next, on NewsSix at Five Thirty."

Music.

Carl watched the monitor right next to him. The pictures galloped out of the screen and right into his lap.

Moving aerial shot of The City. Traffic rushing back and forth, ferries pulling out from the dock.

Voice: "This is Channel 6, The City's Premiere News and Information Station, your number one source for up-to-the-minute news."

Pictures, fast pictures: a cameraman aims his camera toward the screen, a female reporter runs up some stairs, a chopper with a big 6 on the side lands with a bump, a team of reporters set up an interview, some guy in a white shirt hands papers off screen . . .

Voice still going: "And now, from the NewsSix newsroom, NewsSix at Five Thirty, with John Barrett . . ."

John Barrett, in a portrait that moves, flashes a knowing smile at the camera.

". . . and Ali Downs . . ." She grins pleasantly as if meeting a friend.

"Bing Dingham with sports . . ." He looks at the camera and cracks up.

"And Hal Rosen, weather . . ." He looks at the camera and winks.

"The NewsSix News team. NewsSix at Five Thirty!"

Music resolves.

Carl saw a wide shot of his father and Ali Downs seated behind the news desk. He watched his father's lips move but heard his father's voice from within the room.

"Candidate-for-governor Bob Wilson began his campaign today and wasted no time in addressing the assault launched against him by Governor Hiram Slater last week."

Close-up of Ali Downs. "Wilson was ready with an assault

of his own as he addressed his own kickoff rally at the Memorial Stadium this afternoon."

Video: The Memorial Stadium. Crowds, balloons, WE BACK BOB posters. Ali's voice over the pictures: "Wilson says he's ready and willing to take on the issues and considers Hiram Slater's opening salvo nothing more than a cheap shot."

Video and sound: Bob Wilson, a nice-looking guy, dark hair, Kirk Douglas chin, stern expression, addressing the crowd. "The governor has set the tone for his campaign, and it looks muddy brown. (Cheers) But this campaign is going to be built on the issues, and I'm not afraid to say the words: Abortion. Back-to-basics education. Balanced budget. Family. Tax cuts." Cheers start.

Cut. Close-up of Ali Downs. "More rallies are planned for the coming month."

Close-up of John Barrett. "There are allegations tonight . . ."

The camera panned a little to the right and a small picture appeared over Barrett's left shoulder: an airliner broken in two and burning.

". . . that the Philippine government is interfering with the investigation of the crash that killed more than two hundred people. Meanwhile, the owner of the airline thinks *he* knows what caused it all: faulty thrust reversers. Wendell Southcott, our aviation specialist, has more on that."

Shots of planes landing at the airport. Wendell Southcott's voice starts explaining how thrust reversers work.

In the studio John Barrett grabbed a sip of water, and Ali Downs primped, looking into the little round mirror.

More stories, one after the other.

Carl had trouble remembering what he'd just seen before he was seeing something else. A fire at a grandstand, a woman's body found in Dillon Park, three kids trying to kill their parents.

Cut to commercials.

While a lady on the screen tried to get the last precious drops of dish soap out of the bottle, John took another sip of water and looked at Carl, sitting in the dark behind Camera One. "Holding up okay?"

Carl shrugged, then nodded. The monitors in the news desk were suddenly filled with a blood-red sunrise as the audio carried a deep, rumbling voice. "A new day, a new dawning, broke upon our state four years ago . . ." Oh, so this was Governor Hiram Slater!

The ad was captivating from the very start, and Carl found himself mesmerized by the colors and the quick-cutting, rapid-fire shots of Hiram Slater, his shirt sleeves rolled up, his brow furrowed as he shuffled papers, consulted with VIPs, talked on the phone.

Voice: "A growing economy and new jobs. A bold new approach to education for the twentieth century. Environmental awareness. These are the Slater legacy."

Then came the shot of the state capitol dome silhouetted against a massive rising sun, the whole picture rippling with heat waves.

Voice: "The new dawn lives on." And there was Hiram Slater, his huge face appearing to the left of the capitol dome in stark relief against the sun.

Voice: "Governor Hiram Slater—for Governor!"

Wow!

"Okay," came Rush's voice through John's earpiece. "Gay protest, Leslie Albright on DVE Box, to your right."

John checked his script. This would be the follow-up story on Sunday's gay protest at the Catholic cathedral.

Countdown from Mardell the floor director. Four . . . three . . . two . . . one . . .

She pointed, and John read from the teleprompter. "The Catholic Archdiocese has not yet responded to demands made by The City's gay community in a demonstration at St. Andrew's Cathedral yesterday, and a gay spokesman says they are still waiting. Leslie Albright is live in our newsroom with an update."

Mardell held her hand out to the left, and John and Ali followed it with their eyes, looking to their right.

"Leslie, has there been any response from the Archdiocese?" John asked.

Carl followed his father's and Ali Downs' gaze and looked at the wall, but nothing was there. Then he heard Leslie Albright's voice some distance away. "John," she was saying, "so far the Archdiocese has released only one brief statement maintaining the Church's position on birth control . . ."

Carl looked from the wall to his father, but his father was still paying rapt attention to the wall. Where in the world . . . ?

Oh . . . Carl could see Leslie Albright just out of the camera's view around the end of the plywood backdrop, sitting in front of that little camera perched on the stand, the flashcam.

". . . Harley Cudzue, spokesman for the Gay Rights Action League, is not satisfied."

Carl looked at the monitor. Oh . . . Here was some guy carrying a sign and looking upset, hollering. "We are here to call attention to the callousness and indifference of organized religion to the plight of gays and straights alike. AIDS is everyone's problem, and everyone needs to be involved in stopping it."

John perused his script once again for the scripted question and Leslie's outcue. He found the outcue: ". . . free condoms available."

And the scripted question. Hmm . . . Leslie came up with a different question. Funny she didn't mention it. But John liked it. It was more probing, more interesting, and definitely more risky.

Leslie, you've got guts, I'll hand you that.

Carl watched the monitor.

Leslie's voice: "Yesterday was the first of many planned demonstrations, with several confrontations between gays and parishioners."

Video: Homosexuals handing free condoms to parishioners just leaving the church.

Cut to video: A parishioner and a gay having it out. The gay: "The Church needs to own up to its responsibility! You are to blame for thousands of deaths!" The parishioner: "You people need to turn back to God and turn away from this sin!"

Cut to video of the guy with the sign again. Title at bottom of screen: "Harley Cudzue, Gay Rights Action League."

"Condoms are the answer to stemming this plague, and we will not surrender until the Catholic Church amends its murderous policies!"

Cut to Leslie, live from the newsroom, with desks and people working behind her.

Carl looked. His father and Ali Downs were looking at the wall again, while Leslie, only a few feet behind them, talked to the flashcam.

"So that's where it stands, John. Regardless of what the Church eventually decides, Cudzue and his fellow gays say they will continue to make free condoms available."

As Carl watched the monitor, Leslie suddenly appeared on a screen perched on the end of the news desk. Carl looked at Leslie in the newsroom, then the monitor, then his father.

My father's talking to the wall, he thought.

John was ready with his scripted question and addressed it to the wall. "Well, Leslie, how does he reconcile his position with the fact that he's had over three hundred sexual encounters in the past year and never uses a condom himself?"

Dead air.

"Well . . ."

Carl looked at the lady sitting behind the backdrop. He was waiting to hear the answer.

"Well," she said, her script falling limp in her lap, "that's a good question, John."

Carl detected a note of sarcasm, and now she sat there with a very testy expression on her face.

An expression John could not see, but could certainly feel in her tone. He'd better let her go, and quick. "All right, thank you, Leslie."

On the monitors, the screen that wasn't there vanished.

John and Ali looked toward the front again as Camera One zoomed in for a close-up of Ali.

Ali started the next story. "The tax initiative for the Public Swimming Pool is in deep water again . . ."

Carl watched as Leslie Albright rolled limply out of the flashcam chair, her mouth open and her eyes looking toward Heaven. The first person she encountered back there, she grabbed, gesturing, waving her script.

John paged through his script, getting ready for the break coming up. There was tension in the air; he could feel it.

Camera Three's red light flashed on, and the monitor showed the camera capturing the two anchors plus Bing Dingham, newly arrived, ready at his post at the right end of the news desk.

John looked into the script mirrored on the glass over Camera Three's lens and started the close-out for this section. "Coming up next, a two-dollar rubber washer is blamed for a million-dollar flood."

Ali added, looking to her left, "And Bing Dingham brings us Sunday's Sorry Saga."

Bing Dingham looked into the eye of Camera One for the close-up shot. "Hey, you've heard of the instant replay. Well, how about a perfect repeat of last year's game against Kansas City? Stop me if you've heard this one."

Camera Three came on again, showing all three. John intro'd the break. "We'll be right back." Music. Cut to commercials.

John's earpiece crackled with Rush Torrance's voice—"What the @$#!!*& was that?"

Ali heard the question through her earpiece as well and looked toward John for the answer. Mardell the floor director was just now flipping through her script, ready to ask the question if no one else did.

The show was over. They'd made it through with no further train wrecks. Rush, Ali, Mardell, and Leslie were huddled in the studio around the news desk—around John—every one of them spring-loaded and ready to strike.

"Where's Carl?" John asked.

"Show it to me!" Rush demanded, his finger tapping the show's script.

"Carl's upstairs in the control room," said Mardell, "but he's probably on his way back down."

"Then we'll settle this before he gets here," said John, flipping through his script.

"What's to settle?" asked Leslie. "We agreed on the question, we put it in the script, it was there all afternoon. You could have checked with me, given me just a little warning, but no, you had to wait until we were smack dab on the air to make up your own question and make me look like a jerk!"

John insisted angrily, "I asked you the question I was given in the script!"

She shook her head in wide sweeps, her blonde hair waving like pennants. "No, no, *no,* just look at it, will you look at it?"

John found it. "Okay. Right here." He didn't read it out loud because it said, "Leslie, can we expect more demonstrations of this kind?"

His silence was rewarding for all of them. They had a glance-exchanging party right then and there.

"Well?" asked Rush.

John was nonplussed. "It said that thing about the sexual encounters and him not using a condom . . . It was right here."

Mardell suggested, "Well, did you see it on the teleprompter?"

"Well, I think I read it here, but . . ." Rush was already back to the teleprompter table, scrolling through the long paper strip, the script that was projected on the front of the cameras. "Nope. It's the same here."

It was too perfect. Too flawless. Too much without any explanation. John smiled wryly and suggested, "Okay, it's a gag, right? Who did it? What's the occasion?"

No one cracked a smile. Least of all Rush. "Do you want the gay rights activists storming this place?"

"Rush . . ."

"You ought to see what they did to that church! You want them doing that to this place? I'm not going to have that on my head!"

Ali tried to intercede. "Rush, all right, it was a mistake, okay? Maybe it was a gag. It was a bad gag, but—"

Rush was too riled to turn back. He counted the items off on his fingers as he listed them. "They broke the windows out, they spray-painted" (Rush didn't mind repeating the graffiti verbatim) "all over the walls, they broke a bunch of glassware in the church, and urinated" (Rush's language was not so gracious) "all over the altar! You want those people coming in here next?"

John was shocked, disgusted. "They did what?" He looked at Leslie.

Leslie nodded.

John looked puzzled. "I didn't know that."

"Well, now you know. You know what kind of garbage we're up against every time we have to do a gay story. So use some common sense, will you, just a little common sense?"

John was not satisfied. Something was gnawing at him. "But . . . we haven't shown any of this. We haven't told anyone about it."

"You better believe we haven't!"

John could feel some anger building. "Now wait a minute. The gays virtually ransacked a church and defaced property? . . . Was anyone arrested?"

Leslie answered, "Not that we know of."

"Not that we know of? Did anybody ask? Did we get any pictures of the damage?"

Rush was incredulous. "Yeah, right, John, like we're going to show everybody spray-painted profanity during the dinner hour! You want to take the phone calls?"

Leslie piped in, "John, not all gays are like that!"

Now he knew he was getting angry. He locked eyes with Rush again. "Rush . . . everything you told me, everything they did—it was happening, wasn't it? And we were there, weren't we?"

Rush threw up his hands and started walking away. "Oh boy. I'm outa here."

John went after him. "No, now, Rush, don't walk away. It was happening, and we were there, and now you're telling me it wasn't news?"

Rush turned and stood his ground. "Listen, we're not here to discuss that! We're here to discuss you fouling up, that's what we're here to discuss!"

John threw a question at Leslie. "Was it true?"

Leslie wasn't ready. "Was what true?"

"Three hundred sexual encounters, never uses a condom. True?"

She thought it over, then nodded and admitted, "Well, one of his friends says he's proud of it." But she was puzzled. "But how did you know about that?"

Rush cut in. "John, c'mon, that has nothing to do with this story anyway."

John didn't buy that. "Oh? Maybe it just depends on who we're covering, which way the political winds are blowing, who we want to protect . . ."

Rush tried to control his voice but didn't do very well. "John, wake up and smell the coffee. We are in this business to inform, not inflame."

John could see inflaming videos playing in his head this very moment. "Yeah. Yeah, right, Rush." He was reaching full temper and purposely lowered his voice. "Where was all this journalistic idealism last week?"

Rush rolled his eyes, shook his head. "John, we're not trying to hurt anybody!"

"Well, you can tell that to my father!" He started out of the room.

"John . . . !" Leslie called after him. He was just about to dismiss her with an oath and a gesture, but bumped into Carl first.

Dead air. No script. No one could think of what to say. Carl was staring at them, each one of them in turn.

As one, they relaxed. They became pleasant and smiled. They looked a bit stiff, but they smiled and chuckled anyway.

Ali came up with a quick ad lib. "Well, Carl . . . now you've seen how we do it!"

eight

The warm-toned, low-lit, heavy-beamed restaurant known as Hudson's offered a much needed escape, a pleasant place to get away from the station and everything that had happened that day. John often came here after work. He was known and recognized by the lady at the reservation desk, and tonight, happily, she gave him and Carl his favorite table near the gas-fired stone fireplace.

After that big mess on the Five Thirty, the Seven O'clock was an uphill morale and concentration battle all the way, and now John was tired. Spent. This had been a dreadful day after a devastating week. His mind, and maybe his life, seemed to be on the edge of something disastrous, and his career was currently careening through a mine field of bad breaks, foul-ups, and embarrassments. What a time to be sitting across the table from his son, a stranger, wondering what in the world they would talk about.

Looking at Carl, he was almost afraid to ask what was on the kid's mind. Carl had been silent up to this point, not open to much conversation, just perusing the menu. His complexion looked a little warmer in the glow of the table candle, but he did not look happy. He seemed troubled, constantly and unrelentingly troubled; his eyes, though directed at the menu, didn't seem to be reading it. He seemed to be thinking, thinking, thinking.

John piped up, "The prime rib is good. I've had that a few times."

"Mm," was all Carl said, nodding slowly. Up came the waitress, a pretty black girl not too long out of high school. "Hi, I'm Rachel. I'll be your waitress tonight." She seemed a little tired too. *Well,* John thought, *I know the feeling.* "Are you ready to order or should I give you a few more minutes?"

John was ready and was surprised to find that Carl was too. John ordered the prime rib. Carl ordered the chef's salad.

Rachel took the menus and left. Now there was nothing to look at but each other.

"So what did you think of the station?" John asked.

"It was . . ." Carl took time to choose the right word. ". . . interesting."

John figured he'd better deal with that little scene after the Five Thirty. "Oh, it can be interesting all right, some days more than others. Like that conversation you came in on the middle of . . . That was another one of those things that make the news business . . . well, like you say, 'interesting.'" Carl was looking at him and listening. *Okay, John, just maintain a flow here.* "When you're in this business there's a constant challenge, a question out in front of you, What is news? What's important and what isn't? What do the people really want to know about? It all revolves around how you define 'the people's right to know.'"

"It ended up on the floor," said Carl.

John didn't understand, obviously. "Hm?"

Carl became stronger, his voice more firm, his eyes reaching directly for John's. "The people's right to know. The news. I stood in the control room and watched the producer toss page after page on the floor."

John smiled and nodded. "Sure. When all you have is a half hour, you often find you can't fit everything in. That's why we'll often do some last-minute cutting."

"So what happens to the news that gets tossed?"

"Oh, we might run it again at a later time if it's still current."

"What do you mean, 'still current'?"

"Well, still happening, still . . . still news. Fresh news stories are breaking all the time, and if a story misses the train the first time, well . . . unless we can use it for a follow-up or something . . ."

"So if it gets tossed on the floor, it probably won't make it on the air."

John thought for a moment, then admitted, "Well, chances are it won't. Events happen too fast, and if the train's left . . .

I guess it's like a contest, with winners and losers. But most of the time the stuff that gets tossed is dispensable."

"So it isn't really news?"

"Oh, it's news, sure, but it's dispensable news. I mean, to be honest, it's news that people would enjoy, would find interesting, but they can do without it."

Carl nodded thoughtfully, digesting that.

"But like I was saying, it's a human business, and we all see things through different eyes. But if we're going to do our job and gather the news in any kind of thorough, objective manner, we have to let others tell us when they see things we may have overlooked. Sometimes that leads to some fierce differences of opinion, but that's what the information business is all about."

"I take it they didn't like the question you asked."

John chuckled. "Well, right, see, that's what I'm saying. You have a lot of cooks in the kitchen, and sometimes they butt heads."

"Why do you do that?"

"Do what? Butt heads?" A little joke. A dumb joke.

"Ask a question."

John had to think a little on that one. "Well . . . I guess it helps to blend things a bit, sort of bring the anchor into the story . . . uh, it helps make the anchor look more involved in the gathering of the news, more a part of the process. And I guess it adds a human touch to the show."

Carl seemed perplexed. "But don't you get that question off the script?"

"Yeah, it's a scripted question."

"So who writes it?"

"Usually the reporter who filed the story. The reporter gives us a question, we ask it, and then they have an answer prepared, and we end the package with that."

Carl thought about that some more. "So you're not really asking them a question, you're acting like you're asking them a question."

John was getting uncomfortable. Was the whole evening going to be like this? "Well, sometimes the anchor can ask a question of his own, but it's wise to let the reporter and the producer know in advance. The problem tonight was that we got the wrong question into the script somehow and the reporter wasn't ready for it. We try to avoid surprises like that. It doesn't look good on TV, let me tell you."

Carl actually smiled. John guessed he was amused. "I liked your question," Carl said. "It was yours."

"Well, I appreciate that." He really did. Then he reflected for a moment, just a short moment. *Hm . . . The content of that question was true. How did I know that?*

But now back to Carl. Eye contact. Look into the camera. Maintain the flow. "But anyway, it's all part of the TV news game. The technology is complex, so the policies, the whole presentation of the news can get complex. There are just so many different tools at our disposal for informing the public, and doing it in an interesting, entertaining way . . ."

"Is that why you were talking to the wall?"

This conversation wasn't flowing, not the way John wanted it to. Too many rocks in the stream. He paused to gather himself. Very small pause, not much dead air. *All right. Now we'll work on this one.*

"Well, did you see the monitors, and how we were making it look like we were talking to Leslie?"

"But she was sitting right there behind the background. Why didn't you just bring her in and talk to her?"

"Well, we do that sometimes."

Carl just made a face. "I don't get it."

John just rested his face against his hand and stared at the table trying to think of his next line. "Well, we were—" He had to laugh. He was stuck, and it felt kind of funny. "Carl, I don't know why we do it that way. I guess we want people to see the newsroom, or get a view of somebody working back there, somebody still digging out the story."

"So you end up talking to the wall and pretending you're talking to somebody who's actually sitting behind the plywood?"

John's voice was getting a little tense, but he couldn't help it. "Well, what's wrong with that? I mean, you're an artist, you deal in a form of expression, you embody truth through how you create a painting . . . We do the same thing using technology. TV news is an art form, I think. We use technology to paint reality."

Carl looked away and said abruptly, "I'm sure going to miss Grandpa."

Hey, come back here, kid, we haven't settled this yet. John adjusted. New subject. And now this.

"Yeah," said John, "I'm going to miss him too."

"I wish I could've known him better. It was like he knew what he believed. He knew where he was going."

'Yeah, he did have a strong belief system, no question about that."

"What kind of belief system do you have?"

Suddenly John knew how Leslie Albright must have felt after his "scripted" question. "Well . . . I respected Dad's beliefs. I always knew where he stood, and that's good. We all have to stand by our convictions, and I think Dad was a good example of that."

Carl was still waiting for an answer.

"Excuse me," said a lady passing by the table. "Are you John Barrett?"

Oh, good. An interruption. "Yes, hello."

"I watch you on the news every night. Love the show."

"Well, thank you very much."

The lady fumbled in her purse for a small scratch pad and then sheepishly held it toward him. "Could I . . . trouble you for your autograph?"

"Sure you can." John took his pen, scratched out his autograph, and pleased another fan.

Carl watched the whole thing, just like he watched everything. He was absorbing it all, John could tell.

"What's it like, being a celebrity?" Carl asked.

Good, a comfortable question. "Well, it's . . . it's fun, sure. It's part of the job, of course. Television makes you a public figure, and then, looking at it the other way, you have to be a celebrity, a well-known face that people want to tune in and watch every evening. So the news program feeds the celebrity, but the celebrity also feeds the news program."

"So there's a lot of show biz involved."

"Oh, sure. It's part of the business, part of the machine."

Oh, here came dinner, carried in the steady hands of Rachel the waitress. She placed a plate in front of John—"Careful, the plate's hot"—and the big glass bowl of salad in front of Carl.

She's hurt, John thought.

"Okay, now can I get you anything else?"

"Umm . . ." John couldn't think of anything. He looked at Carl, but Carl was leaving it up to him. "I don't think so . . ." *She's hurting.* "How about you? You doing okay?"

"No. I'm bummed out. I want to cry." *Watch it, John, watch it. Did she really say that?* He looked at her carefully. She was smiling and sociable. No, she didn't really say it.

But John could see a deep sadness in her eyes. "I'm doing all right," she said. "Now, the salad bar is included with your meal, so you can help yourself anytime."

"Great. Thank you." She hurried away. John felt clearly that she was escaping. He stole as long a look at her as he could without staring. But enough of that. "Well, dig in," he said to Carl, picking up his fork.

They started eating. "So, uh . . . tell me about yourself. Tell me about your painting."

Carl furrowed his brow and formulated a reply. "Just finished a magazine layout before I came up here. It paid pretty well. Maybe I'll be able to survive until I get the next thing done."

"Which is?"

"Oh . . . a friend of mine runs an underground theater. He wants me to do the set design."

"Mm . . . Sounds interesting."

"Don't know if I'll take him up on it. I'm . . . I'm searching for style right now, I think. The last couple of years I've been themeless, painting in circles. The same old stuff keeps coming out and I can't seem to find direction."

"Think you'll go back to school?"

"What for?"

"Well, if you've lost direction, that might help."

Carl considered that a moment, then shook his head. "No. School won't help."

John got fatherly even as he felt he shouldn't. "Well, you know, it would be a smart idea to hone your craft, get a good skill developed."

"Why?"

John leaned back, raised his hands, and gave the answer that to him seemed very obvious. "So you can make a living."

Carl stayed serious and implored, "Why?"

So you won't be a bum, John thought. He didn't want to get into some big exchange, so he tried, "Well, I guess I still have that old-fashioned idea that the way to make it in this world is to set a goal, work hard, and make something of yourself."

Carl just looked at his salad. "But . . . I can't paint that. It just keeps coming out wrong, it isn't . . . it isn't about anything. It isn't enough."

"Well, it's enough to start. Think about that first and then you'll survive to think about the rest." It was getting tense. Time for a break. "Hey. I forgot about my salad. Be right back."

He got up and headed for the salad bar. Nuts. This just wasn't going very well. Carl didn't seem capable of plain, simple, comfortable conversation, which would have made for a more pleasant evening. The kid was troubled, mixed-up, unsettled, insecure . . . a natural product of a lousy, blown-apart marriage. John literally patted himself on the back. *Way to go, John, you should be proud.* Well, maybe he'd go ahead and let Carl ask some ridiculously hard question. Maybe they could pick a tough topic and go for it, just really chew it up—just so long as they didn't chew on each other.

Okay, John, so talk about your belief system. Oh please . . . He got to the salad bar, grabbed a cold plate, and started stirring around in the lettuce.

I wonder if Dad ever felt this way about me? Then he laughed to himself. *Brother. Am I kidding? Move over, Dad.*

"Annie . . ."

John knew, even as he heard that voice, heard that name, that he wasn't really hearing it with his physical ears. After a few times through this ridiculous hallucination stuff he was finally getting wise. He put some lettuce on his plate and stole a glance toward the kitchen.

There was Rachel, standing alone near the serving window, absentmindedly sorting through some checks. He could hear her crying, though outwardly she was not crying.

He picked out some broccoli and cucumbers in a very normal fashion.

"Annie . . ." He stole a quick glance. Maybe this time he did see some sorrow in her face. She wiped her eye. Perhaps there was a real tear involved.

He picked out some sprouts and onion slices. Hm . . . Three hundred sexual encounters and never uses a condom . . . and I was right. Somehow I knew it was true.

He looked at Rachel again. She was putting the checks back in her pocket and picking up another dinner for someone. If he wasn't imagining it, she did seem like she was taking a deep breath, trying to control herself. Behind her an unnatural darkness filled the room—deep shadows that gave John an eerie, gloomy feeling.

But . . . no. This just wasn't what it seemed. He plopped several cherry tomatoes on his plate, then added some croutons, some bacon bits, and a good ladle's worth of low-calorie Italian dressing, and headed back toward his table.

Again he saw Rachel, now serving a table across the room.

Sorrow. Uninvited. Unexpected. He stopped to look her way, and as if they were of one heart, he could feel her pain. She was hurting. He just knew it, and now he was hurting too.

All right, now hold on here, enough is enough. I don't feel a thing. I didn't really hear anything. It's over, it's done, I'm through with it.

He looked away, setting his eyes straight toward his own table where Carl was still working on his chef's salad and looking dismal.

I'm going to whip this thing. I'm going to ignore it and keep right on being a sober, level-headed professional.

But the sorrow lingered in his heart, heavy and troubling, and by the time he reached the table and sat down, he thought he would burst into tears.

Come on, Barrett, snap out of it. Control, man, control. Pretend you're on-camera.

Carl must have noticed the troubled look on his father's face. He was paying close attention.

John wiped his eyes but made an excuse. "Too much pepper."

"Are you crying?" Carl was being so true to form John couldn't believe it.

"No, I'm not crying." He forced a laugh. "Hey, look out for those hot peppers."

Enough of this. John got out his handkerchief, cleared his nose, wiped his eyes, and regained control. He stuffed the handkerchief back in his pocket and stabbed after the first piece of lettuce. A cherry tomato popped out sideways and went bouncing across the floor. Carl was watching the whole thing. John could feel him watching the whole thing. John was winding up as tight as a spring.

Finally he hit the table with his fist. "What are you looking at?"

Carl's eyes were a little red now. "What were you crying about?"

"I was not crying! I ate a hot pepper and it made my nose run and my eyes run and . . ." John rested his elbow on the table and his chin in his hand and just looked at his son. Then he rubbed his neck and stared at his salad. Then he looked across the floor trying to locate the cherry tomato. Then he sighed and faced his son again.

"Just what is it you want from me? What do you want to know?"

"I'd sure like to know what would make you cry."

"You're making me cry," John said in frustration, shaking his finger at his son. Then he got a bad case of motor mouth, and he realized it but too late. "Carl, since you're so intent on asking questions . . . blunt, difficult questions, I might add . . . Perhaps you'd like to ask one more blunt, difficult, tactless question so we could find out what I'm crying about—if I'm crying at all!"

Carl's eyes locked on his. "Yeah. Yeah, I'll do it."

John just shook his head. His attempt at cutting sarcasm didn't work, and he'd said too much. "Oh, forget it, forget it."

Suddenly Carl grabbed his hand. "Dad, you haven't said a word to me all night. Now talk to me!"

John really felt that hand gripping his. He couldn't ignore it. He could hardly think of anything else. He looked at his son for a long, awkward moment, and Carl just looked right back at him. No escape. The director couldn't switch to another camera. John couldn't even break for a commercial.

"Let me think," he said finally, letting his eyes drop. He played with his fork a moment, then looked across the room. Rachel was gone now. He asked himself, *What if? . . . What if Carl did ask her?*

"You know the waitress . . . Rachel?"

"Yeah."

John turned it over in his mind one more time before speaking. "Why don't you go find her and take her aside . . . casually . . . and ask her if the name Annie means anything to her?"

Carl didn't make a face or seem perplexed. Rather, he seemed fascinated. "Annie?"

"Yeah . . . Annie."

"Just ask her if the name Annie . . ."

". . . if the name Annie means anything to her."

Carl rose from the table and walked casually across the room, looking for Rachel. He got back near the salad bar, still looking, and then disappeared around a corner.

John stared at his prime rib, getting cold by now. He found it hard to have interest in his salad. He picked up his fork and forced down a few bites of dinner, feeling like he'd just made a colossal mistake, a fitting topper for a terrible week. Now Carl would come back embarrassed, with nothing but a negative report, and John would have to settle for the fact that he was really, undeniably losing a screw. Ah well. At least he'd know.

He felt someone approaching and turned. Carl and Rachel. Carl was excited, the most excited John had ever seen him, and Rachel was wide-eyed and just staring at John in awe.

"You're . . . you're John Barrett, the guy on the news?" she asked.

"Yeah, that's right."

"How do you know about Annie Brewer?"

John wasn't sure he'd heard her—really heard her. He looked at Carl.

"She had a friend named Annie Brewer who died," Carl said.

"You have to hear about it," said Rachel. "This ought to be on the news!"

John looked at Carl, then at Rachel, then at his watch, and fumbled, "Uh, well, when do you . . . how do you—"

"I get off at 9. We could talk then. That's only in twenty-five minutes."

Yeah. Follow it, John. Follow it through. "Well, okay . . . Sure."

Rachel went back to work with new strength in her step. Carl slipped back into his seat, somewhat more animated.

"What do you know about her anyway?" Carl asked.

"Who? Rachel?"

"Yeah."

John probed his mind just to be sure. "Nothing."

"So what do you know about this Annie Brewer?"

There was no other answer available except, "Nothing."

A few minutes after 9, it was a simple matter to pay for their meal, find a booth near the back of the restaurant, and order some decaffeinated coffee.

Rachel Franklin, eighteen, a recent graduate from Jefferson High School, was tense and troubled but glad to be talking to someone, especially someone connected with the news media.

"I went to school with Annie last year," she said, nervously crinkling a napkin on the table in front of her. "We were good friends."

John had an appointment calendar from his pocket open in front of him. He'd found some empty dates already past and was using their space for notes. "You were both seniors?"

"Yeah."

"And when did she die?"

"It was about two weeks before school was out. It was in May."

"Late May."

"Uh-huh. She got sick on a Friday and died on Sunday, and we never saw her alive again. We all thought she died from some weird infection, 'toxic shock' or something. That's what we were told. We never did understand it, how it could happen so suddenly."

"Who told you?"

She thought about it, then shrugged. "I don't know. It was just the word that got around."

"So none of you ever heard this from Annie's parents themselves?"

She shook her head widely. "Uh-uh, no way. You don't go near Annie's father. He's mean."

"I see. So . . ." John figured it out. "Annie died a little over three months ago."

"Uh-huh." Rachel gathered strength and then just said it. "I think she was killed." She stopped to choke back some tears and wiped her eyes with the crinkled napkin. "I'm sorry. I got over this once, I really did."

John tried to clarify the term, and he tried to do it gently. "Killed? Do you mean, by someone else? Somebody killed her?"

"Yeah. The Women's Medical Center killed her. You know, that abortion clinic down on Kingsley?"

NewsSix had covered a few protests down at that place before they became "same old, same old" and just weren't news anymore. "I'm somewhat familiar with it. Go ahead."

"I just figured it out. I went to that clinic myself the Friday before last . . ." She stopped. "Let me start over. I was going with this guy during the summer, right? And . . . you know how it is, I thought maybe I got pregnant. So . . . I knew about the Center. All the kids knew about that place. We knew girls who'd been there. So I went in to have a test, you know? To see if I was pregnant. And while I was sitting in the waiting room waiting to hear how the test came out, four, maybe five girls came in, and I knew some of them were from Jefferson. I think I even recognized one girl. And I knew why they were there—I mean, that's obvious, right?

"So we were all sitting there in the waiting room, and nobody was talking, and then the nurse came in and got the first two girls, and they went into the back to do the abortion. Then this lady that did my test called me over to the window and said, 'Honey, you're pregnant. If you get in line we can have you done today and get you taken care of.' But I asked her how much it would cost and she said $350 in cash, up front, and I didn't have $350, and she said, 'Well, do you have VISA?' and I didn't have VISA, and I had another week until payday, and then she asked me how much I had in savings and could I go get it and come back, and then she started asking what my income was in case we could show the state that I qualified for the state to pay for it, and it just got ridiculous.

"And then . . . there was this door open to the back, back behind the lady I was talking to, and somebody was screaming back there, and the doctor was yelling at her to shut up—I think it was the doctor. I hope it was the doctor—I don't know what other man would be back there yelling at her like that. And the lady I was talking to jumped up and closed that door so I wouldn't hear it anymore, and then she tried to get me to stay and get an abortion, and it was too much. I had to get out of there.

"So . . . I didn't get my abortion, and I thought I was pregnant, and I went home and tried to figure out what to do, and . . . I looked in the Yellow Pages and found another place that gave pregnancy tests. They were the first thing in the phone book. So I called them and went in on Saturday and got tested again, and the test was negative. I wasn't pregnant. So that lady at the clinic lied to me."

"What was this other place? Another clinic?"

"Human Life Services. It's down on Morris Avenue. It's an abortion alternative place. You know, pro-life."

"Of course. Now . . . I'm just asking this because I'm a reporter and I have to, okay?" Reporter. John liked that title. "Uh . . . how do you know that the second pregnancy test wasn't faulty? How do you know which person was lying?"

She thought for a moment, cocked her head to one side, and replied, "Well, those people at the second place weren't gonna get $350 if I was pregnant."

"No, I suppose not."

"And besides, my period started last Wednesday. It was late, but it started."

John smiled apologetically. "I guess that settles that. Pardon me, I didn't mean to infringe on personal areas . . ."

She shrugged. "Well, just so you know. But here's what got me thinking. While I was there I read a pamphlet they had sitting out on the table—you know, anti-abortion stuff, and the pamphlet talked about some of the dangers, some of the bad things that can happen, and it talked about an infection you can get if the abortion isn't done right.

"And then I remembered seeing a van parked outside the clinic, and I figured out, hey, that's the van that brought all the girls to the clinic, and I recognized it. It's that same brown van that we used to see around Jefferson High every once in a while, usually on a Friday, and we all knew where it was going, but we didn't talk about it much because . . . you know, a lot of us had been on it.

"But . . . now it made sense. You see? Annie got sick on Friday, went home, died on Sunday. That fast. And nothing else was ever said about it. She went in that van to have an abortion, and they botched it, and she got some kind of infection and it killed her, and nobody's said anything, and nobody's done anything, and . . . well, who knows how safe that clinic really is? Who knows if anyone else has been hurt or killed by those people? How would we know?"

John looked at Carl. Carl was spellbound.

"This ought to be on the news!" said Rachel.

"Well," John asked, "I take it Annie's parents don't know about this?"

She made a puzzled face. "They might. That's that part I haven't told you yet. Last summer Mr. Brewer was going around asking questions and scaring everybody, looking for all of Annie's friends, trying to find out if anybody knew anything about Annie getting an abortion. He came in here once, trying to find me, but I hid in the ladies' room 'til he left. I'm not gonna talk to him. He's a bad man."

"So what does he know—or do I have to ask him?"

She wagged her head and even chuckled a bit. "Oh, you'll have to ask him. I don't know anything about that, and I'm not gonna ask. But I don't think he knows much. Nobody's gonna say anything, because once you say you know something, the question's gonna come up, How do you know?, and like I said, a lot of us have been on that van, and our parents don't know. Nobody talks about it and nobody asks about it because nobody wants people finding out about them. And you don't go near Mr. Brewer. He's mean, and he's dangerous. Everybody's afraid of him. So I wasn't gonna stick my neck out. But that was before I went to that clinic myself. Now it's all hitting me at once. Whatever Mr. Brewer's after, he's probably right."

"But . . . there are no witnesses at all, no one who actually saw Annie on that van or saw her go into the clinic?"

"Somebody had to see it, but they aren't gonna tell. They were on that van too, remember."

"Mm-hm." John looked at his notes, mostly to stall for time. This wasn't going to be an easy thing to say. "Well, Rachel . . . I have to be honest with you . . . All of this may be true, I'm not doubting your word or anything, but . . . we can't put anything on the news unless we have some real facts. Now you heard—not directly, but from others—that Annie's father was asking people about her having an abortion, but . . . apart from that, do you have any way of knowing for sure that she was even pregnant?"

Rachel had to admit, "No."

"She never told you herself?"

"No, and I don't blame her. Hey, if you're pregnant and you're planning on getting an abortion, you don't talk about either one. And she was dead afterward, so she never had a chance to tell anybody."

"And so far no one has come forward who actually saw Annie go into the clinic? You don't know of anyone willing to confirm, as an eyewitness, that Annie went into that clinic to have an abortion?"

She was getting discouraged. "I don't know."

John tried to let her down easy. "Well . . . if you could get us anything else. A witness. Someone who knew for sure that Annie was pregnant, or someone who rode on the van with her that day, anything like that, it would really help your case, because listen . . ." Hoo boy. She wasn't going to like this. "Rachel, there isn't a day that goes by that someone doesn't call the station or write to us—I get a lot of letters—and they have some horrible story about how they've been unjustly accused of something, or someone's cheated them, or the system has failed them somehow, and . . . you know, it's the kind of thing you hear every day. I don't mean to sound insensitive to your problem, but . . . I've got producers, I've got editors, I've got a boss, and I can't go to them with what you've given me so far because . . . so far, number one, we can't prove any of it, and number two, even if we could prove it, it wouldn't be news. It isn't . . . big enough, important enough for us to spend time and money on."

Her mouth dropped open a little. He knew she wouldn't like his answer.

Carl was more direct. "Are you kidding me?"

John lifted his palms just a little and said, "Hey, I'm sorry to say, it's the nature of the business. If Annie was the daughter of the governor, or she'd been raped by a movie star, or she was somebody famous . . . anything different, unique . . ."

"Juicy," said Carl.

John couldn't argue with that, though he hated the sound of it. "Well, yeah, something the public would be interested in, something that would catch their attention, then maybe it would be news, it'd be something worth pursuing. But even then we'd have to have something really clear-cut, something we could prove."

Rachel's eyes were becoming clear and strong with anger. "So if Annie was a movie star or somebody important, then you'd care that she was killed?"

"Well, it's not a matter of me caring—"

"But if she's nothing but a poor black girl living in the city who dies because some abortion doctor was sloppy or in a hurry or drunk—who knows?—you don't care?"

John tried to say it more clearly, "It's not that I don't care—"

"You said it isn't news!"

John sighed. "I know it's hard to understand."

"Yeah, and maybe poor black girls die all the time, but who cares? If they were somebody, and if they didn't do it so much, maybe then it would be news!"

She got to her feet.

"Wait, don't go."

"That'll be a buck for the coffee. Don't worry about a tip." She hurried away.

Carl shoved against John. "Let me out."

John slid out of the booth so Carl could get out, and then stood there in silent frustration as Carl hurried after the girl.

Good. Now the day's perfect. Totally consistent from start to finish.

He dropped a dollar bill on the table and got out of there.

He walked slowly out to his car, hoping Carl would catch up. He'd reached his car by the time the door to the restaurant opened and Carl came out, looking for him.

"Hey!" Carl yelled.

John just acknowledged him with a wave and leaned on his car.

"So did you make peace?" he asked as Carl hurried over.

"Well . . . I think she still trusts *me.*"

"Oh, terrific. That's encouraging."

Carl wasn't so cool-headed himself right now. "Man, I

don't believe this. I've been watching this stuff all day and I just don't believe it."

Okay, John had had enough. A full day of it. "Hey, I've had enough dumped on me for one day, all right?"

But Carl was ready. He'd stored, analyzed, and sorted it out, and now he was ready. "I saw you! I saw you have a big, stinking fight with your producer about picking and choosing the news, and I thought it was because you were concerned about honesty! But then you turn right around and tell this girl—"

"Carl, you don't know anything about—"

"You tell her that her girlfriend getting killed isn't news! It isn't important. People don't care about it. Well, maybe Annie Brewer's dispensable news, huh? Maybe she can end up on the floor with the Irish Girls' Drum and Bugle Corps and the oyster eating contest—"

John went nose to nose with him. "Listen, buddy, you were at the station two and a half hours, just two and a half lousy hours, and now you're telling me about the news business? You're telling me how to do my job?"

"When Grandpa got killed I didn't see that on the news, but when he's up there making a fool of himself it's all over the TV! Why? Who's doing this stuff?"

John was all set to yell right back, but he couldn't. Carl was on his side. He stopped cold, threw up his hands, and fell back against his car to simmer. Carl joined him, and they both leaned against the fender, silent.

John finally said, "So what happened with Rachel?"

Carl answered in a low monotone, his eyes on the pavement. "She's gonna try and find a witness. She wants to make it news. Now that's what *she* said—I didn't say it."

"Okay. Okay."

"And she gave me the Brewers' number in case you want to call them."

Carl took a slip of paper out of his shirt pocket and handed it to John. John took it and just fiddled with it.

"You gonna call?" Carl asked.

"I don't know."

"If you don't, I will."

John looked at Carl, opened his mouth about to say something, then abandoned the idea and just looked down at the pavement, shaking his head. "It's a dead end. Trust me."

"Hey, I'm not the one who started this whole thing. You're the one who told me to ask Rachel about Annie and all that."

"I don't need to be reminded!"

"So if it isn't news, what was that all about?"

"I don't know."

Carl turned toward him. "And how did you know about Annie in the first place? How did you know Rachel was thinking about that?"

John answered impatiently, "I don't know."

"But you nailed it right on the head—"

"I said I don't know, all right?"

Carl absorbed the verbal punch and then answered quietly, "All right."

John looked at the slip of paper and read the number. "Max Brewer. Okay. I'll call him tomorrow. And then I'll call you."

"I don't have a phone number."

"Sure you do. You're staying at Grandma's."

Before Carl could ask, John spoke up. "She told me, all right? I do keep in touch with my mother from time to time."

Carl's demeanor softened a bit. "You don't mind?"

"No. If she doesn't mind, I don't mind. You need to get to know her. We all need to get to know each other."

And we're off to a great start, John thought bitterly.

nine

TUESDAY, his mind full of images, his heart pounding with feelings, sentiments, angers, and perhaps some pleasures—but not many—Carl set to work in his grandfather's shop, clearing the area near the south windows, setting up his easel and brushes, and starting to paint again.

He'd brought some of his previous work with him, and he hung the paintings here and there just to get his creative juices flowing. Over by the window he placed a cold, predominantly blue landscape, a picture shattered by broken lines and incongruity, and on the workbench a surrealistic face full of tension and agony, the hands clapped over the ears, surrounded and overwhelmed by loud, clashing colors. On the wall he hung what looked like a temper tantrum, a violent explosion of chaotic colors that drew the eye to the center where there was nothing.

It was time to begin anew. The light through the windows was perfect, just as he expected. He took brush in hand and stared at the blank canvas. If he could just capture the lostness, the drifting. Yes, the aimless, rootless drifting . . . like a lonely planet without a sun, or a balloon let go, or a sailing ship on an infinite plane of featureless water. Yeah, maybe so.

The brush moved over the canvas. Smallness. The smallness of one tiny dot, one tiny soul in the middle of . . . what? Confusion? Then confusion of an exquisite kind. Not chaos so much as voices, colors on all sides, all in conflict, pulling and flinging, rending, drawing the eyes this way and that, a battle for the mind, for attention, for belief. The viewer should not rest, so his brush did not rest.

Before long he paused. *It's coming out the same way again,* he thought. *I'm painting the same old stuff. I'm a little speck being swept along in endless, meaningless circles.*

But what about his old man? Where did he fit into all this? Was he attached to anything solid, or was he drifting too? Were they both tumbling in this whirlpool together?

Carl stared at the canvas, waiting for something to awaken in his mind, for some image to leap into his consciousness, through his hand, and onto that blank sheet. Where would John Barrett fit into the scheme of this . . . this reality he was trying to capture? Not in this corner. That would be somewhere. No, not near the center either. Not yet anyway. Right now a void would capture him better, a vacuum somewhere behind the immediate face of the painting. But no. To capture his father, there would have to be some kind of presence, but it would be subtly hidden. So hidden it made him angry. Like life. Like meaning. Like destiny.

All hidden. Teasing him. He was hide-and-seeking with Truth.

He set the brush down. He was getting nowhere. Then his gaze was drawn to the small portable television sitting on the workbench. Grandpa had never had a television out here. Carl had borrowed it from his father's room. This was his father's television.

My father. My father's television. My father is television.

He approached that little machine and stared back at the unblinking screen. It was like a shark's eye, totally neutral, unfeeling, without a soul.

John was sitting at his desk, tapping away at the computer console, editing the script for the Five Thirty, when he felt a gentle tap on his shoulder. It was Leslie Albright.

"Got a minute?"

"Sure."

Leslie pulled a chair slower and sat down. She really was a good sort—a little brusque at times, but those deep brown eyes were kind eyes, always caring, never cold. "After yesterday I don't know where to start, but, John, we've got to talk this out." She saw the script on his computer screen. "I won't take long."

"I'm sorry about yesterday. I had a terrible day. A terrible week."

"Yeah, you did. You really did, and we should have remembered. We should have cut you some slack instead of ganging up on you. I'm sorry. Sorry for the pain we caused you."

John didn't mean to stare at her, and he didn't mean to go so long without replying, but it just seemed so different, so rare to have anyone in this newsroom taking this tone, apologizing like this. "I . . . I appreciate that, Leslie. Thank you."

"And, John, for whatever it's worth, I didn't know that was your father at the rally. It wasn't even my idea to have him in the background."

He smiled to reassure her. "I know. Tina and Rush put you there. I've been able to piece that together."

"I'm sorry anyway. Maybe I should have just gone with my own better judgment. I should have just stayed up on the stairs. The view was better, I could've been heard better, I could have heard the director better . . ." She stopped and looked across the newsroom full of people doing the news. "But I couldn't. I had to do what I was told."

"I understand."

"Yeah, I guess you've been there."

"Sure. You're out in the field, right in the middle of what's going on, being told what's happening by a producer sitting in a windowless room with his own ideas about reality, saying 'paint it my way, this is the way it really is, show me this, not that.'"

She had to laugh. "Yeah, you've been there." Then she asked, "So what would you have done?"

"The right thing."

It was a joke. She knew it was a joke, but not the kind you laugh at.

"Well, that's what I thought I was doing at the time."

He tried to let it rest. "Well, don't worry about it. It happens."

She was still troubled, "But it's more than just that . . . I don't know. I don't mind being the grunt, the soldier out in the field . . . But it seems like something's controlling all of us, even the generals." She was struggling with thoughts and searching for words to embody them. Finally she wagged her head and said, "It's hard to put my finger on it, but . . . it's kind of like we've all walked into the belly of a big monster without knowing it, and now that we're deep inside, we think we're in control, but it's swimming away with us, anywhere it wants."

John just shrugged. "Mm . . . I suppose all of life is like that to a certain extent."

"I suppose. Well, I won't keep you any longer. Thanks for your time."

"Thank you."

She went back to her desk, back to work.

John's phone rang. "John Barrett."

"John, this is Ben. Come into my office for a minute."

Well . . . John was kind of expecting this. Ben Oliver, news director, John's boss, was calling him in for a meeting. On his way to Ben's office, John passed that little cartoon taped to the back of the news set, the one with the employee minus his gluteus maximus. He began to ponder what it would be like to anchor the news standing up.

Ben's office was at the far end of the newsroom, just past the weather desk, adjacent to Tina Lewis's office. It was not a big office, but Ben usually had it so cluttered with books, papers, videos, and memorabilia—the big, full-color photo of Chopper 6, the NewsSix helicopter, was a treasured prize—that it seemed quite small, more like a cave or a . . . a lion's den? . . . than an office.

Ben was waiting for him. "Close the door and have a seat." His voice sounded like an old, tired, radio commentator, low and resonant, somber, with just a little bit of gravel.

John closed the door. That meant this would not be any casual, shoot-the-breeze meeting.

Ben was a level-headed, roll-with-the-punches sort of guy, but his crusty demeanor gave him a reputation as a hothead. Hence the cartoon taped to the wall. He was thin, his face etched with worry, and he chewed gum a lot to replace the pipe he was trying to give up.

As soon as the latch clicked into place, Ben started the meeting, sitting back in his chair, holding a pencil in his mouth as if it were that longed-for pipe, and not looking at

John at all, but the opposite wall. "I got a call from this Cudzue, Harley Cudzue, president of the Gay Rights Action League. He wanted to talk to you, but I told him he'd come to the right place, the top, and that his concerns would carry a lot more weight with me, that I'd pass his concerns along in no uncertain terms to the parties responsible, that I would take care of the whole thing, that I would straighten you out and chew your everlovin' butt off."

John was not one to cower. "What can I say, Ben? We made a mistake, and that's all there is to it. Sorry."

Now Ben swiveled in his chair and looked at him. "I also got a call from the Catholics. They invited us to come out and get some pictures of the damage to their church before they clean it all up, since we didn't seem to notice it the first time. They were rather pushy about the invitation."

John had no comment. He just nodded his head a little, so Ben would know he was listening.

Ben kept going. "I asked Cudzue, if he didn't have three hundred sexual encounters in the last year, then how many did he have, and he hung up on me." He saw the questioning look on John's face and responded, "Well, we said something about him; I was getting his response for the record." Ben swiveled back toward his desk and chuckled quietly. "He's had plenty, we know that much. One of his lovers works upstairs in Accounting right now. But let's get to the agenda here. I talked to Rush about this . . ."

"Oh boy . . ."

Ben looked directly at him. "Hey, he doesn't blame you. Yeah, he gets hot when you foul up on his show, and even if he thinks you're right he won't tell you to your face. But he knows what happened, what we didn't say, and I told him what I'm going to tell you right now: that you were right in being upset. Your question was a dumb move. I took the flak this time, so you owe me one, but you were right. We didn't handle the story well. We weren't fair to either side.

"But now that I've patted you on the back I'm going to whip you on the butt. We'll keep it balanced that way. I'm going to tell you to watch yourself and be careful. 'News' is a term we all play with, and we all know it. We do have room, Barrett, slack. We can make choices about what we see and what we say about it, and none of us wants more trouble than our pockets can afford. Private sex lives we don't talk about. That's Cudzue's business, that's his sex partners' business. Lawbreaking, vandalism, violence, destruction of property we do talk about, but with our eyes open to cover our behinds."

John asked, "So you're not going to send a cameraman out there to video the damage to the church?"

Ben shook his head. "That's what we should have done, but now we'll just have to let it cool off. Maybe next time. The train's left—it isn't news anymore. But I told Erica to be on the lookout for something nice to say about Catholics, and I think she's already found something nice to cover about gays, something about the Gay Men's Chorus doing an AIDS benefit. So we'll do some good after we've done some bad and hopefully come out objective on this thing."

"Sounds good to me."

"All right then."

John stood to leave.

"Oh, one more thing," said Ben. "I don't like talking to people like Harley Cudzue. So you foul up again and don't clear a question first, *you're* gonna talk to 'em!"

John smiled. This was Ben's idea of a slap on the wrist. "It's a deal."

"Otherwise you're doing fine."

"Thanks."

Carl had his easel ready. He figured he'd start with pencil, just get the portrait sketched out. He knew the subject would be moving, changing rapidly, so a lot of the interpretation, the capturing of the face and the soul behind it, would be up to him.

The clock hanging from the hook above the workbench indicated 5:30. He clicked on the television, and the cold, gray eye awoke, beginning to flicker and flash colors into the room.

Then Carl heard music—quick, compelling rhythms. There was the aerial shot of The City: traffic rushing back and forth, ferries pulling out from the dock.

And there was the voice: "This is Channel 6, The City's Premiere News and Information Station, your number one source for up-to-the-minute news."

Pictures, fast pictures. It was all the same as yesterday.

The voice said, "And now, from the NewsSix newsroom, NewsSix at Five Thirty, with John Barrett . . ."

Carl was ready. John Barrett appeared on the screen for one second.

And then he was gone, chased away by images of Ali Downs, Bing Dingham, and Hal Rosen.

Well, wait. He'll be back.

Voice: "The NewsSix News Team. NewsSix at Five Thirty!" And there was his father, sitting next to Ali Downs.

Carl held his pencil to the canvas. This was that opening two-shot again. John Barrett's face was pretty small on the screen right now.

"A train derailment near Mendleston . . ." John Barrett was saying.

Carl sketched a few lines. "Metro bus drivers are growing concerned over muggings and robberies on Metro buses . . ." said Ali Downs.

Video: Metro buses pulling out of the garage.

Carl sketched some more, at least from memory, from initial impression. He would capture John Barrett somehow, even if it was in tiny, fleeting pieces, moments, glimpses, hints. Somehow the puzzle would fall together.

C'mon, John Barrett! Just stay on the screen a little longer. Just a little longer.

Okay, the Five Thirty went fine. No foul-ups, no glitches, just a smooth, professional, neat newscast, the way it ought to be, the way it used to be. No, maybe even better. John didn't wiggle his thumbs this time, he made sure of that.

Back to normal at last? Maybe, maybe not. He went across the newsroom to his desk and plopped into his chair. It was ten after 6. The "CBS Evening News" was on. Maybe Max Brewer was home by now. Maybe he was sitting down to dinner and wouldn't want to be called.

Maybe John didn't want to call him anyway. But maybe Carl would ask John if he called, and then John would have to make up some excuse for why he hadn't called which Carl probably would not believe.

Okay, John, dive off the deep end just one more time, and then life can get back to normal.

He dug the slip of paper out of his wallet, set it on his computer keyboard, and dialed the number.

"Hello?" Not a kind hello, and this guy didn't sound very small either.

"Hello . . . Max Brewer?"

"Yeah. Who's this?"

"This is John Barrett, from NewsSix—"

The guy swore a blue streak at him!

"Excuse me?"

"You think you pretty funny, huh, like nobody gonna touch you, nobody gonna find you . . ."

"Mr. Brewer, this is John Barrett from—"

"No, you ain't John Barrett! Listen, you kill him, that's one for you, but I'm dead too, you got that? I'm dead, and you forget about me 'cause I forgot about you!"

"Mr. Brewer, I don't think you understand—"

"You show up 'round here, you just try it, I'll rip your head off! I'll cut you into pieces so small the dogs won't find 'em!"

Clatter, fumble, *click.* Dial tone.

John slowly hung up the phone. "Well, good evening to you too." Rachel did say this guy was mean.

No. This guy isn't mean. He's scared. And what did he say? Something about killing John Barrett?

Dad. John Barrett, Sr. A tape replayed through John's mind. The black man at the governor's rally, the big guy on the videotape, throwing bodies around, fighting, scrapping, right up there next to Dad.

Max. Dad called him Max! He picked up the phone and

dialed again. He had to explain the mix-up, explain who he was.

But Max Brewer was not answering the phone now. John dialed Mom's number. *Okay, Carl, you want to pursue this, now's your chance. I'm not going to this guy's house alone.*

ten

John used a crisscross directory to find Max Brewer's address, and Carl was able to contact Rachel at Hudson's Restaurant to verify the location. Everything matched.

The Brewers lived toward the south end of The City in a predominantly black neighborhood, a low-income area where the houses and yards were small and clusters of kids played on concrete and asphalt more often than on grass; where both sides of the street were lined with aging, parallel-parked automobiles, and vandals cursed their enemies with spray paint. It was a rough neighborhood too, known for its unemployment, gangs, crack houses, and shootings.

It was an especially uncomfortable area to be driving through in a nice car and white skin. John and Carl moved slowly up the block in the ebbing daylight, trying to find the right address.

"There," said Carl, peering out the window. "Is that it?"

John looked out Carl's window and could barely make out the house number, little black numerals tacked to the lap siding of a small, gable-roofed house. There was one large maple tree in the front yard with a tire swing hanging from it. No fence. The porch light was on, and the lights inside the house were on, so somebody had to be home.

They found a place to park halfway up the block, got out, and locked the car. They stayed close together.

"What did he say again?" Carl asked.

John recited it in a near whisper. "He said if we ever showed up he'd tear our heads off and cut us up into pieces so small the dogs wouldn't find them."

"Thanks. I'd almost forgotten."

"Be bold. We're not here to hurt anyone, we're not sneaking around. We'll just walk right up to the door and knock."

"Okay."

"Incidentally, what happened to your earring and your chain?"

Carl had left off all his facial jewelry. "Less for him to grab."

They turned up the front walk to the house. As they mounted the porch, they thought they saw some movement inside, some shadows against the drapes. *No sneaking now. Stand up straight. We're here on legitimate business.*

John couldn't find the doorbell, so he knocked. The porch light went out. "Oh-oh," said Carl.

"Uh . . . hello?" John called through the door. "Mr. Brewer? It's John Barrett and his son Carl. Uh . . . I talked to you on the phone today. We'd just like to talk to you—"

They heard the heavy footsteps pounding up behind them, but not in time to do anything about it. John had no sooner turned to look when a ham-sized fist grabbed his tie and made a lasso out of it, yanking him off the porch and sending him sprawling into the yard, rolling in the autumn leaves and just about hanging himself on the tire swing.

Carl tried to leap from the porch and get away, but the shadow in the white T-shirt grabbed him by the scruff of the neck and yanked him backward, pulling him off balance. He fell but didn't make it to the porch floor. The huge hand was still gripping him by his coat and he was hanging there, limp with fear. He looked up and saw the shiny surface of a knife blade in the dim light.

"Okay, sucker, you wanna live?" huffed a big voice above him.

John shouted, "No! Don't—"

"Yes!" Carl insisted. "Yes, I do want to live!" Now Carl could see the man's scowling eyes looking him over.

"Kid, I don' like the way you look." The porch light came on, and the front door cracked open.

A woman's voice pleaded, "Max, don't do anything!"

"Get inside! Get in there!" the man shouted. In the light they could see Mr. Max Brewer, as big as a football lineman, raging and wild-eyed.

John was on his feet but trying not to make any sudden moves. "That's my son. That's Carl Barrett. He's . . . he's a pacifist, you know? He's never hurt anybody."

Max agreed. "He couldn't if he tried."

The woman said through a crack in the door, "Max, don't hurt him! You don't know—"

Max yelled at John, "Stay there, man, or I cut him!"

"No!" Carl whimpered.

"Max!" the woman cried. "Don't! Please!"

"Now who are you?" Max demanded of John.

John tried to answer clearly, without yelling. "I'm John Barrett—"

"Yeah, and I'm Ray Charles!" He waved the knife in small circles near Carl's face. "And maybe this kid needs a better haircut."

"I'm John Barrett, *Junior*. John Barrett, Senior was my father! You're holding John Barrett, Senior's grandson there."

Carl stammered, "You . . . I saw you at Grandpa's memorial service! You were sitting on the right-hand side, toward the back, you and your wife, right?"

That seemed to register. Max held the knife still, but didn't let go of Carl as he took another look at John. "John Barrett, Junior?"

"My Dad must have told you about me."

"You on TV?"

"Yes. Channel 6. The news guy."

The front door of the house across the street burst open, and a neighbor hollered, "Max, what you doin' over there?"

The knife dropped out of sight. Max lifted Carl gently to a standing position. "Ain't doin' nothing, Henny! These are friends."

"Well, keep it down, man. I was gonna call the cops." The door slammed.

Max released Carl. "Hey, I'm sorry, man. I didn't have no idea who you were. Deanne!"

The door came open, and an attractive, fortyish woman cautiously poked her head out.

"We got company here." He beckoned to John. "C'mon, c'mon, get inside before somebody sees you. Deanne, c'mon, open the door. Let's go."

She opened the door, and John and Carl went inside. Max was right behind them, closing the door again.

"Have a seat," he said, still brandishing the knife.

John looked at the knife. A man could dress out a deer with that thing. "Are you . . . through with that . . . uh . . ."

Max noticed he was still holding it. "Oh . . . Yeah." He dropped it into the drawer of a small end table. "I don't guess you guys want trouble."

Deanne Brewer, visibly shaken, was concerned with proper hospitality nevertheless. "Max, why don't you introduce your two friends?"

Max eyed them a moment to make sure, then gave it a try. "Deanne, this here's John Barrett, Junior. He's John's boy. And this here is . . . uh . . ."

"Carl."

"Yeah, Carl . . . John's grandson."

Deanne extended her hand, still trembling a little, and they greeted each other. "May I bring you something to drink?" she asked.

John and Carl looked at each other. "Uh . . . coffee?"

"All right. Please sit down." She looked at Max and he said, "Yeah. Sit down. Sit down."

There was one couch in the small living room, so they took that. Max sat on the edge of a worn-looking stuffed chair. Deanne went into the kitchen, a small area divided from the living room by a dining table and six unmatched chairs.

"Daddy . . ." came a timid voice from down the hall.

"'s okay, honey. Come on in here, say hi."

Two bedroom doors toward the back of the house opened. From one room came a boy about ten. From the other room—the one with the Michael Jackson poster on the door—came two girls, one about twelve and the other in her midteens. They moved gingerly down the hall toward the living room.

Max waved them in with his hand. "C'mon, c'mon, it's all right. Nothing wrong here . . . These are friends."

They came into the living room and stood side by side, like notes in a musical scale, ten-twelve-midteen.

Max introduced them. "This is George." "Hi" was all George would say. He was being shy. "He likes fast cars. And this is Victoria." The twelve-year-old just gave a little wave and stared at them, rubbing the back of one foot with the other toe. "She's the dancer."

"Daddy, I'm a fashion model," she protested.

He laughed. "Okay, honey. Seems like the same thing to me. And this is Rebecca. She's the artist."

"Hello. I'm pleased to meet you."

They were beautiful children, though clearly frightened.

"You go on now. We're talkin' in here. Get your homework done."

They scurried down the hallway, obviously relieved. Max continued to gaze down the hallway even after the kids were back in their rooms. Then he nodded toward the end table where he'd put the knife. "I'd kill for them. Yeah, you know I would."

John swallowed and ventured his first full sentence since they'd become guests. "We're terribly sorry for any alarm we may have caused you."

Max smiled a devilish smile. "How'd you like my ambush?"

"It was great," said Carl.

"Gotcha good, didn't I? Turned out the light, snuck 'round the back, nailed you. Pow!"

Carl held up his hands in surrender. "I wouldn't want to be on your bad side."

"Yeah, well, some people are, and I thought you were them." He looked straight at John and added, "I thought you were the ones that killed your father."

John had to look at Carl. Carl's expression must have matched his own—dumbfounded disbelief.

"Uh . . . Say again?"

Max explained, "You know, callin' me up and sayin' you were John Barrett. Well, ever'body knows John Barrett's dead, so I thought you were them, just tryin' to scare me."

"Them? Who?"

"The people that killed him. I thought they were comin'

after me now. They killed my Annie, then they killed John, so I figured now they're after me."

"Oh . . ." John was lost and groped for a starting point. "We got your phone number from a girl named Rachel Franklin. She's a waitress at Hudson's. Fine young lady."

"I know who she is. Ain't seen her since Annie died though. I think I ran 'em all off, all of Annie's friends. I wasn't handlin' it too well."

"Uh-huh. Rachel said you were asking around, trying to find out if Annie'd had . . . an abortion. Is that right?" Max didn't answer, but just glared at him. "Well, listen, we don't know anything about this. I never knew you and Dad were friends . . ."

"And I never seen you before. I guess you 'n' your ol' man didn't hang around together much."

John admitted, "No, I guess we didn't. So . . . I just didn't know about you, and I never knew anything about Annie."

Max went over to the bookcase in the corner and picked up a framed photograph. He handed it to John, who shared it with Carl.

"That's Annie," said Max. "That's her senior picture."

She looked a lot like her mother, smooth-featured, lovely, with a captivating smile.

"She was seventeen," said Max. "Senior at Jefferson. Sweetest thing you ever saw." He hesitated as tears came to his eyes. He looked toward the kitchen. "Coffee ready, babe?"

"Just about," she replied.

He looked back at them and wiped his eyes. "I gotta be careful what I talk about."

"I'm very sorry, Mr. Brewer."

"Just call me Max."

"Max."

"Annie died in May . . . May 26th, Sunday. I'll never forget that. We didn't know nothin' 'bout what happened to her. She came home sick from school on Friday and went to bed. We thought it was the flu or somethin', and she never told us different. We put her in George's room and had to move George outa his room, put him on the couch here so Annie'd have a room of her own. We didn't want the other kids gettin' it. She kept gettin' worse all night long, getting a bad fever and complainin' 'bout her stomach, so we took her to the doctor on Saturday and he gave her somethin' for flu, for the fever, but it didn't help. Finally took her back to the doctor on Sunday and he says, 'Get her to a hospital,' so we did, but—" He couldn't finish.

Deanne came in with coffee in mugs. "We were too late. Annie died in the hospital from a severe infection. We just never knew that's what it was. We thought it was the flu, and the gynecologist who examined her told us it was toxic shock syndrome." Now she was trying to control her emotion as she asked, "Would you like any cream or sugar?"

John figured she could use the diversion. "Uh, both please." He held his coffee for a moment. The room was silent. Finally he ventured to ask, "So . . . Annie died from toxic shock syndrome? Rachel Franklin was thinking it may have been an abortion, at least that the impression she got, and . . ."

Max began to answer but broke into tears and buried his face in his hands, his huge body quaking.

John felt foolish. "I'm sorry . . . I've overstepped . . . I'm sorry."

"No, you're right," said Deanne as she brought the cream and sugar. She sat in a chair next to her husband and said in a quivering voice, "Annie died from a septic abortion. We never knew she was pregnant. She never told us. But we found out that she'd had an abortion, and . . ." She blinked away some tears. ". . . and somehow it wasn't done right, and she became infected, and the infection spread through her body until it killed her."

John was stunned. So Rachel was right. He leaned forward just to think, to digest this, his fingers over his mouth. He could feel Carl looking at him and looked back. Carl sat there motionless, his eyes intense.

John ventured another question. "So is that what the hospital told you?"

Max wiped his eyes on the sleeve of his T-shirt. "No. There was this other doctor, this woman's doctor . . ."

"An ob-gyn," said Deanne. "Our doctor said he couldn't handle it, and he told us to get Annie to the hospital, and this other doctor, his name was . . . Lawrence, Dr. Lawrence, he took care of Annie 'til she died, and then he's the one who said it was toxic shock. That's all he ever told us, and that's what he wrote on the death certificate."

"Then how did you find out it was from an abortion?"

Deanne gave a smile and said, "Your father."

"My father?"

Max explained, "Annie was gone and buried for . . . what? Close to two months, and we just accepted it, you know, didn't know any better. Then, it was one Friday, I was drivin' home from work and goin' by that Women's Medical Center, and that's when I saw your dad, John Barrett, Senior, jus' walkin' back and forth outside the clinic, him and about ten other folks, all carryin' signs and protestin'. And then it hit me. Don' know why it never hit me before. Friday. Annie got sick on a Friday. And these people, seemed like they was always protestin' on a Friday. I don' know, I just pulled over, thought I'd have a talk with 'em."

Max wiped his eyes again and took a moment to take some coffee from Deanne. "Thanks, babe." He took a good gulp. "I picked out your dad 'cause he was the oldest. I don't know. Just looked like he'd know what was goin' on. And he did."

"Yeah, he did," Deanne agreed.

"I walked over to him, and he took one look at me and said, 'Brother, you're hurtin'. Tell me what's wrong.' I mean, he knew I was hurtin', and so I told him. I told him all about Annie and what happened to her, and you know, he told me things I never knew before. Did you know that clinic sends a van down to Jefferson High like every Friday to bring girls back to get abortions and their parents never know nothin' 'bout it?"

John and Carl let their eyes meet. Well, they knew since Rachel had told them. "We weren't aware of that . . . not until recently."

"Well, your dad told me what mighta happened to Annie,

tol' me about abortions gettin' too fast, and doctors makin' mistakes and nobody knowin' when they do, and what he said was too close, man, too close to what really happened. So I knew what killed her. I knew. And I was gonna go in that clinic and just ask 'em about it, but your dad said, 'No, let's go back to the hospital first and ask 'em again,' so we did."

He drank some more coffee, exchanged a look with Deanne, and then continued, "We went back and cornered that Dr. Lawrence and asked him again what killed Annie, and he told us the same thing, but then John said we wanted to see the autopsy report." Max enjoyed the memory and laughed a little. "Your dad was a fighter, man, he didn't give up easy, didn't let those doctors bluff him. Ol' Dr. Lawrence, he wasn't ready for us pushin' him like that, I could tell. But he said we'd have to go down to the Records Department, so we did.

"And then when we get down there, here they go again. They gave us a buncha trouble and said they didn't have no autopsy report or nothin' . . . said they lost it, couldn't find it. But John seemed like he'd done this before. You couldn't turn him around, you know? He says, 'Then let's see the pathologist, the guy that did Annie,' and . . ." Max cursed. "They weren't gonna let us see him neither! Started makin' excuses, but we got to him. Seems like we ran all over that hospital, but we found the Pathology Department, and then we still had to wait all afternoon, but we got in there and we saw him. Mark Denning, that was his name."

John took out his writing pad. "Denning. Okay if I write that down?"

"Yeah, write it down. Denning was cool. Wouldn't tell us a thing out in the open, and when we got into his office he talked real quiet." Max leaned forward and lowered his voice, as if mimicking Denning's manner. "He was afraid of somethin', you know? He talked quiet and said he really couldn't discuss the case, but then he got out a folder and left it on the desk and said, 'I gotta step out for twenty minutes, guys. You didn't hear anything from me, and if you want to sneak a look at this, I won't see you do it,' and then he went out of the room."

Deanne got up and went into their bedroom as Max continued. "So, hey, what do you think ol' John and me are gonna do? We got that thing open, and we started lookin' through it tryin' to find out what really killed Annie, and we did. We could see it. Mosta that stuff you couldn't understand what Denning was talkin' about, but the last paragraph he wrote it out pretty clear, so we copied that paragraph and anything else we could find that we figured said somethin'."

Deanne returned and handed several sheets from a yellow legal pad to John, along with a document. He quickly perused them.

"This is Annie's death certificate," Deanne pointed out, "and you can see what Dr. Lawrence wrote."

"Mm-hm. 'Primary cause of death: septic shock . . . due to septicemia . . . due to toxic shock syndrome.'"

"And then . . . well, here's what your father and Max managed to copy from the autopsy report."

Max's handwriting was done in a hurry, that was certain. John easily recognized Dad's handwriting, had the usual trouble reading it, and found himself dwelling there, just looking at the words because Dad had written them.

John read the first paragraph they'd copied, this one in Dad's handwriting. "'Septic shock due to septicemia due to . . . septic abortion.'"

Deanne commented, "That's where we found the first contradiction to the death certificate."

Max pointed. "Check out that paragraph on the second page there, the one I copied."

John read as Carl watched, "'The most attractive hypothesis that would explain the mechanism of death in this case would be that initially this person had an abortion complicated by staphylococcal infection resulting in peritonitis and septicemia leading to septic shock and inadequate oxygenation of the vital organs, leading to death.'"

John shared the report with Carl, and they continued looking it over as Max continued. "All those big words, we didn't know what we were copying mosta the time, but I think we got enough. We know what killed Annie. Your father even took it to another doctor to have him check it over, and he said that's what it was, if we copied it right."

"But Denning wouldn't tell you himself? That seems so bizarre."

Max shook his head. "He wasn't supposed to tell me, and he said I didn't have no legal right to see the report 'cause of the privacy laws, but . . . he took a chance, didn't he? He walked out so he wouldn't see us lookin' at it."

John shook his head. "Strange."

Max gave a knowing sneer. "Tell me all about it."

"But . . . my dad was there too, involved in your situation."

"He was in it all the way. He was a good man."

"Who was the doctor?"

"What's that?"

"Do you know the name of the doctor Dad took the report to?"

Max and Deanne looked at each other and drew a blank. John made a note to check into that. Mom might know. "And do you have any positive link to the Women's Medical Center? Is there any way you can prove Annie was there?"

"Hey, sure she was! She went to Jefferson, she got sick on a Friday, the clinic sends the van over to Jefferson every Friday, the clinic does abortions, Annie died from a bad abortion. That's it. They did it."

John admitted, "Well, that sounds convincing, but . . ."

"But nothin'!"

"Have you asked the—" John stopped and reversed gears. "Mm . . . I don't suppose the Women's Medical Center has told you anything?"

That was a laugh. "No, not quite. But don't think I didn't ask. Your father tried to stop me, but I went into that place and told 'em what I knew and I asked 'em, 'Did you do an abortion on my daughter, Annie Brewer?' And they wouldn't tell me. Said it was confidential. And I said, 'We talkin' about my daughter. Now if you did it I wanna know,' and they wouldn't tell me nothing . . . just told me to get outa there.

"And I got mad. Ain't nobody gonna do that to my little girl and tell me it ain't none of my business! Well, I didn't touch nobody and I didn't break nothin', but they called the cops and told 'em I did, and I spent the night in jail. Good thing I didn't really bust anything or I woulda been in jail a long time. The judge said I have to stay away from there and if I'm good he'll let it go." Then his eyes burned with fury. It was frightening to see. "But that place is still there, and that van's still runnin' every Friday."

He drank some more coffee, taking time to calm down.

John held up the pathologist's report. "Is this the only copy?"

"We got some more copies made. Your father has one, we've got a few."

"May I have one?" John stole a glance at Carl. "If we . . . pursue this, we'll need all the information we can get."

"What do you mean 'pursue' it?" asked Deanne.

"Well . . . I can't promise anything, please understand that, but we're talking about a young woman, a minor, dying due to a botched medical procedure and how nothing was ever done about it, nothing was ever reported, no one was ever held accountable. That bothers me, I know it bothers you, it bothered Dad, and it should bother the people who watch our newscasts."

"You gonna put this on the news?"

John could feel Carl waiting for the answer. When he did answer, he felt he was answering Carl as well as the Brewers. "I can't promise that."

Carl mumbled derisively, "I can't promise that . . ."

John spoke more firmly; he may have even raised his voice a bit. "I'm sure we'll need more information first."

Max sneered a bit. "Well, good luck. We were thinking 'bout contactin' a lawyer, but your dad said the same thing: we don't know enough. I told you what happened at the hospital. The clinic wouldn't tell me nothin', the school counselor wouldn't tell me nothin', and the law says they don't have to. Who else you got to ask?"

"Well . . . give me some time to think about it, do a little homework. I might be able to find out something. In the meantime, Max, try to rest easy until you hear from me. Don't . . . uh . . ."

"I gotta stay outa trouble, I know. I've caused a lot of trouble for a lot of people. After we got that stuff from Denning I climbed all over those people at the hospital for holding out on me. Got the people at the high school mad at me. Scared away most of Annie's friends." Max added in a somber tone, "I made trouble for your father too. Got him pulled into my troubles, got into that fight at the rally. Good thing I didn't get arrested again. Him and me, we got a lot of people mad at us. I been layin' low. Whoever got him, they gotta be after me."

"But . . . I don't follow you yet. Why would anyone want to kill my father?"

"'Cause we was coming after 'em. They killed Annie, and they didn't want us findin' out about it."

Okay. Was this guy just paranoid? Had he been in too many street brawls, lived by jungle rules too long? "But you've no idea who?"

"No. But your dad and me was seen together lots of times. We was seen together at the governor's rally. We got thrown out of there together. I even saw us on television on Channel 6!"

John grimaced inwardly. "Uh, yes . . ."

"So they knew I was after 'em, and they knew John was helpin' me, so they wasted him, and if I stick my nose out again they'll waste me too—if I don't waste them first."

John held his hand up. "But . . . now hold it there. You don't know for sure that anyone *killed* my father. It was an accident."

Max just cursed at that. "Hey, these people kill young girls every day and it looks like they never killed nobody. You think they're gonna kill your old man and let it look like somebody killed him?"

"You don't know these people kill young girls every day—"

Max didn't stop. "You think somebody wouldn't figure out how to make it look like an accident?"

John stopped short. "All right . . . All right . . . Walk me through it. How did they do it?"

Max didn't shy away from the question. He was quite sure of himself. "First they killed him, probably beat him to death, and then they dumped the pipe rack on him to make it look like the pipes smashed him."

John shook his head. "Max, those racks weigh tons. You don't just dump them over."

Max got loud. "What you mean, you don't just dump 'em over? The pipe rack dumped over, didn't it? Or didn't you notice that little detail?"

Deanne put her hand on him to calm him down.

John tried to answer quietly. "They figure it could have been metal fatigue."

Max shook his head. "Man, you talkin' to a welder. I know steel—I know good welds and bad welds. That rack was fine."

"How do you know?"

"I been in your dad's warehouse. I've seen it."

"Well . . . the rack could have been out of balance too. A killer couldn't just dump the rack over."

Max looked insulted. "John, ain't you never heard of a forklift?"

The next morning John was at the warehouse. The stand-in manager was doing well and was considering accepting a permanent full-time position. The customers were still coming through at a steady rate. Jill the bookkeeper was back on the job and was almost her bubbly self again. Buddy and Jimmie were optimistic.

Okay, good enough. Now to talk to Chuck Keitzman, the warehouseman—and forklift operator—who found Dad under the pipes that fatal morning. He was hard at work in the warehouse, rearranging wooden boxes of ABS fittings.

"Hey, Chuck!"

"Hey, Johnny! How's it going?" Chuck looked better. One hand was still in a cast, but he was doing well enough with the other hand just tossing parts from one box to another. They engaged in shop talk for a little while. Yeah, Chuck was doing all right, but was anxious to heal up so he could do the heavy loading again. He and Jimmie had switched jobs much more often, which Jimmie didn't mind, but Chuck didn't like working at the counter—he couldn't put up with pushy customers.

John approached the key subject casually. "Say, do you know Max Brewer?"

"Sure. He was a friend of your dad's. Didn't know him real well, but he's been around a few times. He came over a few days after John died, just to look around. A lot of John's friends have done that."

"Well . . . Max has come up with a theory about how Dad may have died, how the pipe rack may have fallen. Remember when you used the forklift to try to get the pipes off Dad?"

Chuck grew quiet and somber at the memory of it. "Yeah."

"Was the forklift already warm when you started it up?"

Chuck thought for a moment and then recalled, "Yeah. Yeah, it was. I choked it, but then I didn't need to because it was ready, it wanted to start. I figured John had been using it."

"How about exhaust in the air? You know how that thing stinks the air up in here."

"Well . . ." On that, Chuck couldn't be sure. "You just don't notice that after a while."

"Yeah, right. Well, say, whatever happened to that pipe rack?"

"We tore it apart."

Oh-oh. "You tore it apart?"

"Yeah, the cops were through with it, and it wasn't any good anymore, and we sure didn't need the thing in here to remind us."

"What did you do with the pieces?"

"I think they're still out in the yard, out by the ADS coils."

They went out to the loading dock, hopped down to the ground, and crossed the gravel yard to the ADS pipe—large, plastic, corrugated pipe stored in coils that resembled stacks of monstrous black earthworms. Next to one stack of ADS, in several mangled lengths, lay the remains of the fallen pipe rack.

John looked carefully through the pile. "Okay, Chuck, can you tell me which of these long pieces were on the bottom?"

"Brother, I don't know."

"Well, give it a shot."

They picked through the pile, sorting them a bit. The short girders were crosspieces, the log rods with the turnbuckles were diagonal braces. The smaller L-shaped pieces were built to hold shelving. All these were put aside. That left four main rails that spanned the length of the rack. They were heavy, L-shaped, and very much alike.

"Okay, Chuck, here's what I'm looking for: I want to see if any of these rails got bent or marred or scratched in a way that would show the forklift was used to dump the rack over."

Chuck stared at him a moment. "Are you kidding?"

"Is what I said possible?"

Chuck gave it serious thought. "Yeah. Yeah, that's possible."

"The forklift could've gotten in on the other side of the rack, gotten the tines under it, and tipped it over?"

Chuck was getting disturbed at the prospect. "You really think somebody *killed* John?"

"I don't now. But let's check these rails."

The first rail was twisted on the ends, but the fall did that. The second rail was obviously a top rail the way the bolts were anchored, and it matched the first, so they were top rails. The third rail . . .

"Hang on," said John. "What about the fourth one? Does it have a bend in the middle like this one?"

They checked the fourth rail. It was straight. They looked carefully at the bottom surface of the third rail. It had a definite upward bend in the middle, with paint scratched away in two key places.

"Let's get this over on the dock." Each man took one end of the rail, and they hurried back to the loading dock. They set the rail on the dock and hopped on up. Then Chuck ran into the warehouse. In just moments the old forklift came chugging out into the daylight, and John knelt low by the paint scratches to have a good look as Chuck eased the forklift closer.

The tines of the forklift eased up to the bend and the scratches. The left tine touched one scratch; the right tine came close.

Chuck leaped from the machine for a look. "What do you think?" John asked.

Chuck took hold of the right tine and gave it a light yank.

The tine lined up with the scratch. It was a perfect match.

Chuck let out a quiet, long, salty phrase of amazement.

"I'll call the police," said John.

eLeven

BOb Henderson was good-looking, a little heavy but trying to lose weight, had a wife and three boys he loved, coached Little League baseball, and went to church every Sunday. He dressed neatly, didn't smoke, didn't mutter or talk fast. In other words, he wasn't what one would expect a homicide detective to be. One attribute did fit the stereotype: he'd grown so used to the job that nothing seemed to excite him.

"Yeah," he said, looking down at the long, bent steel rail. "Could be."

Henderson, John, and Chuck Keitzman the warehouseman were standing on the loading dock at the warehouse, looking over John and Chuck's discovery.

Henderson took another close look at the bends in the rail the forklift made—or could have made. "How many people have operated the forklift since the morning of the accident? We'll call it an accident for now, if that's okay."

Chuck knew where this was leading and had already had the realization. "Myself, Jimmie, maybe Buddy."

Henderson stood up. "So in other words it's been used regularly ever since the accident."

Chuck was sad to report, "Yep."

"And I suppose you drove it out here to match it to the bends in the rail?"

That was the most painful to admit, for both John and Chuck. Chuck answered, "Yep."

"Well, we'll fingerprint it anyway, but I doubt we'll find anything. Eh, that's tough. If we knew then what we know now . . ."

John asked, "What about the autopsy report? Weren't there injuries that didn't quite fit what the accident would have caused?"

"We'll check it again. But I recall the findings being inconclusive. Your dad was . . . well, pardon me, but it would have been hard to tell. Was anything missing from the warehouse after the accident? I'm looking for a motive here."

Chuck shook his head. "Nothing disturbed that we could find, and we usually keep a tight control on the inventory."

"No cash taken?"

"The cash box was safe and sound."

"So, how about enemies? Help me out. Who'd want to kill a nice old plumbing wholesaler, and why?"

"Well . . ." said John. "He wasn't just a plumbing wholesaler. He was also an outspoken . . . uh . . . religious person."

"What kind of religion?"

"Uh . . . Christian . . . Fundamentalist. He was active in the pro-life movement, and I think he may have made some enemies in the pro-choice camp."

Hoo boy. That did sound dumb, and Henderson's expression reflected that. "Is that so unusual?"

"Well . . ." John finally shook his head. "I admit it's pretty flimsy."

"Yeah, it's flimsy." Henderson looked at his watch. "Well, okay . . . I'll reopen the case. But do some homework for me, okay? Do some thinking, some remembering, ask around, find out if anybody might know something that would shed some more light on this. Right now we don't have a suspect, we don't have a clue about who the suspect might be, we don't have a motive, we don't have much of anything. Show me the way. Give me something to hang my hat on, I don't care what it is. I gotta go."

"Well, thanks."

"You're welcome. Don't touch the forklift. I'll get somebody out here."

With that he was gone, and somehow John felt ignored, passed by . . .

. . . neglected . . . abandoned. Even as he sat at his computer that afternoon, editing for the Five Thirty, he couldn't help brooding about it all, turning it over and over in his mind. Was this how Rachel Franklin the waitress must have felt?

"John?"

It was Tina Lewis, of all people. "Yeah, Tina. What's up?"

Tina grabbed a chair and settled into a fashionable pose. "John, the subject of your father came up at the 9 o'clock meeting, and I felt I should talk to you about it."

You, of all people? John thought. He could feel himself bristling. "What about my father?"

Tina was displaying a rather gentle demeanor at the moment. It was jarringly uncharacteristic. "Well, we all know it's been difficult for you, and of course the choices we made in covering the governor's rally were . . . Well, they were not good choices. I admit that. I'm sorry."

John remained cordial, but he didn't believe a word she was saying, and he had no trouble with that at all. "Okay."

"Well anyway, the subject did come up about your father's death and whether we should do anything on that. It is an old story by now. We'd be a little late if we covered it, and there really isn't much to show. We have no video of the accident, no shots of the police or aid unit or fire department, nothing to put the viewer on the scene."

"No, you don't."

"But the bottom line is, we really agreed that we had to consider your feelings. We didn't want you to feel your father's death was unimportant to us, that we were just ignoring it. But at the same time we were concerned about dredging up matters that were best left alone and could cause you embarrassment."

"I appreciate that," he lied.

"But let me ask you something . . ." Oh-oh. John had a feeling she was getting around to the real reason for this conversation.

"Have there been any more developments in your father's death? Any investigations by the police, anything that might make it newsworthy? Because if it's important to you, we want to air it."

Don't tell her. The thought shouted clearly and emphatically in John's head. *Don't tell her.*

"Well, uh . . . Tina . . ." John looked at his computer screen and away from her just to get his mind clear, then faced her again. "I can't think of anything newsworthy, that's for sure. Dad's dead and gone, and I think most of the excitement is over."

"Mm-hm." She nodded, and her expression dripped compassion and understanding. "Well, if anything arises and you want to tell me about it, please don't hesitate."

Pain. Cunning. Both together in the same person at the same time. She was like a cornered, wounded animal.

"Well, thank you," was all John could say, and he tried not to stare.

She rose, put the chair back in its place, and floated toward her office. John just looked at the floor, trying to process what had happened, what he suddenly knew about Tina Lewis. What do you do with a cornered, wounded animal? Try to help, or run from the danger?

John looked back at the Five Thirty script on his computer screen, but it was all he could do to pay attention to it, to get the editing done.

Anything newsworthy, she said. My dad is killed outright, suddenly, tragically, and she wants to know if there was anything newsworthy. He tried to put the subject out of his mind. This script wasn't going to edit itself.

Newsworthy. Speaking of newsworthy, sure, there were plenty of important and legitimate news stories in the script for tonight—the ongoing campaign of the gubernatorial candidates for one, as well as a major traffic rerouting on the I-40 bridge. But what in the world was this item all about? And this item?

He looked over his shoulder. Rush was at his desk, working on the script as well.

"Rush . . ."

"Mm?" he said, not looking up. Hoo boy. John tried to soften his approach as much as he could. He didn't want another fight. "Could I ask you about a few stories here?"

Rush finally looked up. "Sure."

John looked at his computer screen and called up the first story in question. "Uh, this one here, Number 230, the lady dying at the zoo?"

Rush didn't look at it himself; he was too busy with something else. "What about it?"

"The way I read this story, the zoo had nothing to do with her dying. I mean, it wasn't an accident, it wasn't due to anyone's negligence, she wasn't mauled by a lion or stepped on by an elephant or anything."

"No, they figure it was a heart attack."

"Heart attack." John thought it over for a moment. "So . . . she just died." Rush didn't respond, so John dared to press the question. "Why is this news?"

"Channel 8 got some good video on it," said Rush, going back to his computer screen. "Somebody was there and got a home video of it, and it was good stuff, and Channel 8's going to run it, so we're picking up the story."

"So we're running the story because Channel 8's running the story because they happened to get some home video of it?"

"Right."

"So what are we doing for video?"

"We sent Ken down there today to get some shots of the zoo."

"Of what? Gorillas playing with their toes?"

Rush was getting red in the face. "Hey, just look at your script. We're slotting thirty seconds for the story. It's a voice-over. You read the copy, we roll the video. It's that simple."

"Yeah, but I still don't see the news in this. I'm going to be telling people that a lady died an unremarkable death that was not due to any accident or negligence while we roll video of . . . of animals lying around and pacing back and forth and kids throwing food to the pigeons, which really has nothing to do with it."

Rush was eager to get back to his work. "Well, sometimes that's just the way it turns out."

"Hang on. I've got one more."

It was only professionalism that made Rush pay attention. "Okay . . . quickly."

"This story from England about the protester shooting several bystanders and police. Who was he?"

"We got it from the network feed, and they didn't say."

"It says he was protesting the rezoning of a public park. Which public park?"

"The feed didn't say."

"So . . . we don't know what was happening to the park or what he was disgruntled about in particular?"

"Nope."

"Whom did he shoot?"

"Some press and some cops. It's on the video. Somebody had a camera right there."

"Any charges filed against him?"

Rush slapped his desk. "Look, does it matter?"

"That's exactly what I'm asking. I admit it makes for some great television, but really, what does this have to do with anything?"

Now Rush had reached his limit. "Listen, if you're bummed out because we didn't run anything on your father I can understand that. But, John, life has to go on. Now, I have slotted that story into the program, and I want you to read the copy. I also want to carry the story on the 5 o'clock promo. CBS is running it, we're running it. It's hot. It's what people want to see. End of discussion."

Rush went back to work in a huff.

John turned back to his computer and scrolled through the script. News. Newsworthy. John was starting to feel sour about this, as unprofessional as that was.

If only we could've gotten some shots of the pipe rack falling, or Chuck's bleeding hands, or the blood stains on the floor . . . If only there'd been a camera right there in the clinic when Annie—

John stopped himself. *Come on, John. Ease up. Let it go.*

Carl worked that afternoon on his portrait of John Barrett, but found the task agonizing, unreachable. The face lacked expression. It seemed cadaverous.

He checked the clock. Almost 5. There would be a promo coming up, a whole twenty-five seconds worth. He didn't know why he even bothered, but he clicked on the television set and waited, pencil in hand. Maybe something would come across that would reach his soul, a glint of warmth, of humanity, of . . . whatever.

As he waited, his eyes drifted to that pile of unassembled parts, Grandpa's and his father's boat, still resting and waiting under the cloth. He went over to take another look, to fold back the cloth and touch the wood. He felt sorrow for Grandpa.

A voice came from the television. "Hello, this is John Barrett in the NewsSix newsroom. Coming up in one half hour on NewsSix at Five Thirty . . ."

Carl dashed to his easel, compared the television eyes with the penciled eyes. They were—

What was this? Some old geezer shooting people?

". . . we'll have a shocking report of a protester opening fire on several bystanders and police . . ."

Carl stood there, watching the gun go off, watching people scurry for cover.

". . . and a woman dies at the zoo, apparently of a heart attack."

There was John Barrett again, in shirt sleeves, the newsroom behind him. "All this and other top news of the day, one half hour from now, on NewsSix at Five Thirty."

Commercial.

Carl turned the television off, stared at that blank screen, and cursed.

John set down the camera remote control, got off the flashcam stool, and cursed.

Tina Lewis, in her office with the door closed, spoke quietly into her telephone. "I have talked with John Barrett. He says there are no developments in his father's death at this time. No . . . he said nothing about any police investigation. Yes, I'll let you know."

She hung up and went back to work.

Martin Devin hung up the phone and went down the hall to

the governor's office. Miss Rhodes, the governor's secretary, announced him and waved him in.

Wilma Benthoff, the hard-working campaign manager, was already there for the meeting and had laid out some new billboard designs on the governor's desk.

"So how goes the battle?" Devin asked.

The governor was pleased. "We are whipping Wilson's butt, that's how it's going! Take a look at these!"

Devin came around to the governor's side of the desk to view the new artwork. The photographs and graphics were lofty, eye-catching, even transcendent, and made Hiram Slater bigger than life, no question.

Wilma Benthoff reported, "The early analysis finds more people identify Hiram Slater with the issues that concern them than they do Bob Wilson, especially in the areas of civil rights and environment."

Devin laughed. "Well, what else did we expect? When you control the images, you control the high ground. Too bad we can't carve the governor's face in the side of Mount Blanchard."

Benthoff was delighted to report, "Well, maybe we have. Look at this poster."

Hmm. There was Mount Blanchard, and if you looked a second time, you could see the governor's face cleverly hidden in the rocks, glaciers, and crevasses. The lettering below the scene read, "Slater = Environment."

Devin moaned in mock disappointment. "Aww, and I thought I had a brand-new idea!"

Wilma pulled out some photo proofs. "So now, to get stronger on the family values side of things . . ."

Devin received the proofs from Wilma's hand. Family portraits. The governor with his silver-haired wife Ashley and their two remaining children, Hayley and Hyatt. "Well, if that doesn't look like the typical All-American family!"

Slater's smile was a little crooked. "Beaver Cleaver's family, if you ask me! Hayley never dresses that way—and look at Hyatt! His hair's combed! You can't even recognize him!"

Wilma gave the governor's hand a mock slap. "Now, now! You all look charming! It'll sell, believe me!"

"Well, at least we look happy for once . . ." He shook his head. "Sometimes it's like pulling teeth, but they do it for me."

"Image is everything, Mr. Governor," Devin reminded him.

"Image is everything," the governor admitted, leaning back in his chair and switching to thoughts about success. "The polls are favorable. We've gone up fifteen percentage points since we started our ad campaign, so don't tell me people don't learn by watching TV!"

Devin chuckled. "Don't worry, sir, I won't."

The governor looked at Benthoff. "So, let's hear the latest on the rally over in Sperry."

Benthoff handed some copied reports to the governor and Devin. "They're ready for you, sir, in two weeks. I think you'll have a full house, and of course the press will be there. We have a press conference set up afterward, and I've gotten confirmations from a local station in Sperry, plus the four big news stations from over here. I'm flying to Sperry tomorrow to do some advance work among the businessmen. The local organizers aren't pulling enough support from them."

The governor nodded, scowling. "Yeah, kick their butts, will you? The eastern half of this state isn't a different world, no matter what they say, and I'm still their governor and they need to be rowing this boat with the rest of us." The governor quickly scanned the letter from Sperry, his flight schedule, and the attendance projections. "Well, at least there won't be any mad prophets over there."

Hiram Slater shuffled through the papers on his desk. "Well, it's after 5. I'm about to call it a day." Then he stopped and considered, "But isn't it interesting how we never knew about the prophet's death until now, even with the media connection in the family . . ."

"No one else did either. I imagine most people in this state don't . . . and never will."

"Well, that's nice. We want the people to be thinking about me and only me, right?"

"That's my concern," said Benthoff.

"So I'm glad my little messenger from God hasn't gotten any more attention than he has."

Devin looked away for a moment. "So am I, sir. So am I."

Carl had dinner with Mom Barrett right after the Five Thirty News and was back out in Dad Barrett's shop in time to catch the Seven O'clock. Now he attacked that canvas, that portrait, with a growing anger. Where was that man anyway? Who was he?

The face on the canvas was lifeless. It was perfect, it was impressive, it was strong . . . but it was lifeless, as lifeless as that gray screen when the television was turned off.

So what did I expect? Carl thought. *I'm not looking at my father—I'm looking at a machine. Well, my father isn't looking at me either. There's a machine between us, always there. Even when we sit in the same room, at the same table together, it's there. He talks to me just like he talks to that camera. His words come from a teleprompter in his head. My father is television. Yeah, a machine who expresses love on cue cards, caring in TV scripts, compassion—or lack of it—in policies and excuses.*

Carl had a ticket to a rock concert that night, and by now he was ready for it. He was ready to go out and rock himself silly. Maybe by tomorrow, when he came in for a landing, things would look different. Perhaps something would finally connect.

He cleaned up his brushes, turned out the lights, and got out of there.

On not much more than a whim, John drove to a large shopping mall on the north end of town and started walking aimlessly past the storefronts, looking at clothes, gifts, clocks, toys, cameras, anything to get his mind off . . . well, things. Dad. Annie Brewer. The job. News and newsworthiness. What was it Leslie Albright called it? A shark or a whale, or something like that, a big beast, that swallowed everybody without their really knowing it and then just swam away with them inside, wherever it wanted.

Well, he figured, *before I get swept away with all this, a change of scenery might help to get everything back in perspective. You brood on stuff like this too long, everything starts looking bad.*

He passed a computer store. Yeah, he was into computers. Maybe he could find an interesting innovation, some new software, a new toy. He went inside, past the displays of desktop and laptop models with their VGA screens flashing colorful demos, all seeming to call to him, "Buy me! Buy me!" He loved this stuff. Say, here were some new notebook-size computers.

"Hello," said a salesman, "can I help you?"

"Well, sure. I'd like to check out these notebook computers here."

Something about this salesman looked so familiar. He stood there rather still, wearing a dress shirt and tie, with computer monitors flickering and people going about their business in the background, and it just looked like he was—

"Hi, this is Tim Miller in the Tyde Brothers Computer Showroom. Coming up this week in Tyde Brothers' Incoming Tyde Sale, a startling development in notebook computing as the Martin-Androve 486 weighs in at only 4.4 pounds. Also this week, the controversial Bookkeeper II system is trying for a comeback, but will it make it? We'll see what the customers have to say." A telephone warbled. "More after this." Reporting live from the newsroom . . .

The salesman picked up the phone and engaged in a brisk, copy-perfect conversation. "Well, in this age of rapidly changing computer technology it's no surprise to find that some people are having trouble keeping up with it. Our software specialist Hank Baxter has been looking into a new program that promises to help those of us who can't tell a bit from a byte." He handed the phone to another man. "Hank?"

Hank took the phone and spoke in a resonant voice. "Tim, its makers claim it's the software of the decade, and though critics said it wouldn't succeed, Dumbyte, the DOS Tutorial for Idiots, has virtually sold itself . . ."

John expected a cassette to roll at this cue, but thankfully nothing happened. He slipped quickly and quietly out of the store. *What have we done to these people?* he wondered.

Carl had grown up in LA. He was used to crowds. But for some reason, as he was swept along by the river of people flowing into the large arena, he was bothered, almost frightened. *I couldn't turn around if I wanted to,* he thought. *I couldn't get out of here.*

John was having trouble staying in one place for very long. He tried to look at some jackets in a leather store, but couldn't stay long enough to try them on. He thought he might check out some pens in a stationery store, but there were too many; he'd never be able to see them all. He had to keep moving.

He came to a camera store. Sure . . . He enjoyed photography and had a pretty good camera himself. He stepped inside, not knowing what he'd find. Even as he went in, he had a feeling he'd better find it fast.

Here was a nice, lightweight video camera standing on a tripod. The prices on these things were coming down slowly but surely. Pretty soon every home would have one of these.

"Hi," said the salesman. "Pretty nice camera, huh?"

"Sure," said John. "What can you tell me about it?"

The salesman suddenly pointed in John's face. "Hey! John Barrett? NewsSix?"

John smiled kindly. "Yeah, that's right."

The salesman turned to the older guy behind the counter. "Hey, look who's here!"

The older guy looked and asked, "Who?"

The salesman just waved him off. "Never mind. Hey, John, a lot of your news footage comes from little jewels like this one, huh? Home video. It's a whole new wave, right?"

The salesman started showing John the features on the camera: the zoom lens, the automatic white balance, the high-speed shutter, the backlight feature, the calendar and clock, the battery pack, the AC adapter socket, the remote cable attachment, the . . . He was taking too long. . . . One-button review, the leather carrying case, the ninety-day warranty, the . . .

John thought he saw a woman behind the camera counting down with her fingers. Five . . . four . . . three . . . two . . .

John interrupted the salesman. "Well, in the few seconds we have left . . ."

"Hey," said the salesman, "I've got 'til 9, no problem."

John caught himself. "Oh . . . Sorry."

Carl had a ticket with a number on it, so he knew he was entitled to that one seat with the same number, but he also knew he would probably never sit in it.

He was right. When the lights in the arena went down, everybody in the place stood up and stayed that way, bellowing and shrieking as one huge hysterical organism, blasting out a sound shock so loud it made your cheeks buzz.

Carl was on his feet too, hollering and breaking loose, waving his arms, cheering, just venting everything. He was among friends, thousands of them.

The band came onstage in the dark, groping through thick stage fog. The anticipation of the crowd was like an electric charge.

Lights. A flurry of brilliant shafts waved and groped through the fog—red, blue, pink, purple, gold. Five musicians, like ragged wraiths from the sixties, seemed suspended in boiling clouds.

Then came the *sound.* The *sound.* The crowd gave itself to the sound. It pounded through their chests, grabbed them by their guts, clutched their hearts, cut into their minds. It led, they followed; it soared, they flew; it crashed, they cried; it thundered, they roared; it leaped, they danced.

It took them it took them it grabbed them and took them it ripped them and it tore and it pounded and took them the drums and the lights and the cry of the strings and the smoke and the sweat and the volley of screams took them on. And on. And on. And on.

And Carl was dancing—but suddenly found himself asking a question he never had asked before, a question he never had even thought of before. *Where are we going? Where are you taking us?*

He stopped dancing. He looked all around—at the sea of arms, faces, and rumbling, quaking bodies. He clapped his hands to the beat, but soon that stopped too. He couldn't shake the question from his mind.

Where are we going? Where are you taking us?

John tried not to hurry through the mall. There was no need to hurry. Good grief, he'd been hurrying all day long; all he really wanted to do was slow down, take it easy. Finally he stopped and got an orange drink, then sat on a bench just to hold still, sip the drink, and watch the people.

Shopping malls are great for people watching. Here you can see all kinds: ladies shopping in twos and threes, taking their time; a few husbands tagging along and wishing they weren't; moms with kids in strollers; kids with treats; kids fighting over treats; and always—always—a kid screaming bloody murder because he sees something his parents won't let him have.

Then there were the older kids, the teenagers, both junior and senior high schoolers, walking fast and talking fast, sipping, chewing, munching, teasing, flitting from one store to another like hummingbirds after pollen.

Hm. And they all looked the same, as if they all lived in the same big family, sharing and handing down all the clothes, as if they all lived . . . well, in this mall, and every store in the place was their closet. The same styles kept going by him—styles in pants, dresses, jewelry, hair. And then John noticed something else. Had he started counting the rock, television, and movie stars, not to mention cartoon characters, radio station call letters, and movie titles, that passed by on a T-shirt or on a jacket or on shoes or purses or folders or shoelaces or in the form of a toy or painted on a toy just to sell the toy, he could have counted steadily until the place closed. It was an odd feeling, like having hundreds of billboards driving past him instead of the other way around. Somebody was making a lot of money from all this stuff.

Or fluff. Yeah, fluff. At the station they had their own version of it, and that's what they called it. This was, of course, the light feature material, the human interest stuff, the "dispensable news," the show biz. It wasn't necessary, nobody's life would be measurably changed by it, it rarely had anything significant to do with anything else, it wasn't harmful as far as anyone knew—it was just . . . fluff.

In a sense he was watching fluff walk by. It all took time to watch on television, it all took money to consume, it all demanded a significant niche in the culture, but none of it really mattered. As a matter of fact, very little of it was even real.

But they were buying it, wearing it, eating it, screaming for it, identifying with it; it was so important to them. The place was saturated with it.

I could tell them anything, John mused. *Hey, I know the media. Give me graphics, music, tight editing, maybe a TV star, and I could tell them . . .* He laughed. He was getting silly. *I could tell them the color brown gets moldy when it rains—I could ruin the sellers of brown!*

"Aaaw!" came a shriek behind him. He looked over his shoulder to see a young girl dressed like a rock star confronting a friend who happened to be wearing brown.

"You didn't buy brown!" she cried, incredulous. "Brown gets moldy when it rains—everybody knows that!"

Just then three high school jocks came marching by, harassing a smaller kid in front of them, pointing at his brown shoes and chanting, "Mold-ee! Mold-ee! Mold-ee!"

John wasn't shocked or even alarmed. It was happening again! He surrendered to it. He leaned back on the bench and just had a good laugh. It was a great show. He was going to enjoy it.

The *sound* carried the crowd onward as one tribe, one voice, one spirit. The young men rocked with the rhythm and pounded the air with defiant fists. The young women swayed as if in a trance, their arms reaching heavenward. The priests on the stage cavorted and blasphemed.

But Carl sank into the seat he'd paid twenty dollars for, dying in a way, falling like a single tree in a thick forest. The question still pounded in his head and not even the *sound* could drown it out: *Where are we going? Where are you taking us?*

But there was no answer. There was only this moment. There was only the *sound.*

John felt a cold draft moving through the mall as if a huge door or window was open somewhere. Well, he'd just had a cold orange drink, and he'd been sitting still. He got up and got moving. That would warm him up again.

Now he was part of the throng, just moving along with it, being careful to watch for cross traffic buzzing from window to window, store to store.

It seemed so noisy in here. What was everyone talking about anyway, and did they all have to shout like this?

Oops! He lost his balance and staggered sideways, almost bumping into some junior highers, their startled faces as close as his nose. He made it to a wall and stood still for a moment. Did the ground really move or was it his imagination?

There! Again! An earthquake! He could feel the ground stirring to life under his feet. He stayed right there, close to the wall, looking about. Some hanging light fixtures were rock steady. Maybe this was hallucination as well.

What about the people? Had they felt anything? They were walking faster, exchanging concerned looks, talking more loudly. Maybe they'd noticed the shaking, maybe not.

More cold. That draft had become a breeze blowing toward the far end of the mall. There had to be a huge door open.

What in the world—? He pressed against the wall, trying to find a handhold of any kind. The floor was shaking again, and now, like a sinking ship, the whole mall was tilting, settling at one end!

Steady, John, steady. It's happening again. Get over to that bench and just sit down. Wait for it to pass.

He set out across the floor, heading for the bench, working

his way through the people passing by, trying to look normal, trying to walk a straight line.

But now . . . was it really just him? The people were acting strange. They were noticing it, looking at each other, looking excitedly around, up, and down the mall, talking faster, more loudly.

A rumble. He was sure he was really hearing it—a low rumble—building, growing louder, like an underground train approaching. He looked toward the far end of the mall. The people, the storefronts, the displays had disappeared in darkness as if the lights had gone out.

He made it to the bench and sat down to watch, to listen, to wait. The mall continued to sink, to tilt. The far end grew darker.

Then he heard screams, cries for help, wailings, shrieks of pain. The voices! The voices were crying again, just like the other night! He gripped the edge of the bench tightly and strained to see.

This was no show. This was no amusement, no silly hallucination. This was the worst of nightmares.

Now the darkness at the far end of the mall was growing, rising, beginning to spin like a deep, black whirlpool, a bottomless vortex. It was drawing, pulling, yanking people toward it. The whole mall was sliding in!

At this end, where John sat, no one seemed to notice. They kept walking, talking, laughing, teasing, buying. Well, of course this had to be an illusion. Surely these people would see the same thing he was seeing if it was really there.

John gripped the bench. The floor lurched again, tilted some more. The monstrous throat was coming closer, consuming the mall, sucking in the people.

Wow, he thought. *I remember having bad trips, but this one's a doozie! Just hang on,* he told himself. *Take it all in. It'll be over soon enough.*

Oh-oh. The people around him were starting to notice. That was not encouraging. John would have preferred to be crazy just by himself. But the shoppers were starting to hurry, to talk more loudly and more quickly, to tug and pull at each other in all directions. A weird panic was setting in, and the people were getting frantic.

But they were not frantic to escape, to get out of this place, to flee the other way. They were frantic to buy things, see things, hear things, handle things. They ran into the stores, began grabbing the first items they could get their hands on and shoving money and credit cards at the merchants. They talked more loudly, they laughed, they mocked, they teased in desperation. In the home entertainment store they turned up the volume on all the stereos and televisions, and hundreds of voices and little talking faces shouted and sang deafening bedlam. The shoppers laughed with relief, cowering amongst the shelves and rows, looking toward the screens and listening to the booming speakers, looking away from the darkness approaching.

John kept telling himself he was having a delayed drug trip, a hallucination. That vortex, that monstrous swallowing tunnel, wasn't really there.

But it was so big, so terrifying, and so very close now that he was getting unnerved. He could hear it swirling and sucking, roaring like a tornado. He could see unwary people disappearing into its depths, tumbling headlong down its throat, screaming, clawing to get away, their bags and packages flying from their hands.

And as far as John could tell, the mall was still sliding into the vortex, just like a ship going under or, worse yet, like a log being fed into a gigantic grinder.

Now the people who would not look began to fall and tumble down the sharply inclining floor, grabbing onto benches, posts, planters, doorways, each other.

John couldn't hold on to the bench any longer. He slipped off the end, slid along the crazily slanted floor, and grabbed hold of a post where he hung on for dear life.

Shoppers, still clinging to their packages, went sliding by him. Two girls were comparing prices and colors of their new clothes as they slid by, and here came those three high school toughs, still tormenting the little guy: "Mold–ee! Mold–ee! Mold–ee!" One woman came rolling by and grabbed hold of a quaint jewelry stand in the middle of the mall. She frantically waved money at the young salesgirl, who let go of the stand to grab the money and went tumbling toward the vortex.

Half the mall was gone now, and the vortex kept sucking, swallowing, destroying. The cavernous throat was getting closer, closer, wider than the whole mall, higher than the ceilings, unrelenting, insatiable.

Tables, chairs, dressers went sliding by, then cameras, computers, Tim and Hank the computer salesmen still on the phone, whole racks of clothing, jewelry, knickknacks, clocks, televisions. Here came a huge portable tape player, tumbling in time to the rock music it was playing.

John wrapped himself around that post in stark terror. *Please, God, please make it stop!*

Carl burst from the doors of the arena and grabbed a light pole, trying to steady himself. He'd come here to enjoy this concert, to rock out, to be a part of it.

But he'd been scared to death.

"Hey, mister, are you okay?"

John awoke with a start. "Huh?" He was clinging to a post in the mall. A security guard was nudging his shoulder.

The mall was still there. People were still passing by, though now the crowds were starting to thin down. There was no tilting floor, no cold wind, no black, gobbling vortex.

Well, of course not.

"Are you okay?" the guard asked again.

John let go of the pole and looked himself over. "Uh . . . sure, sure . . . I'm fine."

The guard was looking at him suspiciously. "Well, it's getting close to 9, closing time. If you've got any more business here, you'd better get done with it and then head for home, okay?"

"Sure . . . Right . . . I was just on my way out."

"Good." That sounded rather emphatic.

John looked up and down the mall. It was back to its

usual, peaceful bustle, and yet . . . if he stood still, if he listened not just with his physical ears but with his soul, he could hear that rumble. It was faint, distant, behind the scenes, but it was there.

Enough. He got out of that place and out to his car. But he wouldn't be going home tonight. Not yet. He wondered if Mom was still awake. Probably. He had to see her.

twelve

John sat at the big, round, oak table that had been in the family since he was a child. He could still see the scratches he put there with his tricycle, then his model spaceship, and then the tape deck from his car. The silverware Mom placed in front of him, and the cup from which he drank the freshly brewed coffee, were as old as his memory.

"Can I get you anything else?"

He couldn't think of anything. He wasn't thinking too well anyway.

"How about some toast?"

"Yeah. Okay."

"Peanut butter and jam sandwich?" That sounded better.

"Yeah. Yes, please."

She went into the kitchen—it was divided from the dining room by a counter and some stools—and started making the sandwich. It was a special picture, her standing there at the counter, slicing the homemade bread with that same bread knife and dropping it into that same old toaster. How many times in his life had she done that for him?

And this old, faithful kitchen! There'd been some changes over the years—new wallpaper five years ago, a microwave about that same time, and a light fixture to replace the old white globe that Dad broke with a ladder he was carrying through. But overall it hadn't changed much. The dark walnut cabinets that Dad put up years ago still gave the kitchen its warm atmosphere. And the smell of the place, that smell John associated with home, with love, with growing up, was still there.

Mom seemed the same too. Her hair was silver now, and her shape a little rounder, but her glow, her spirit, the depth of her love and convictions were always the same. And just as always, she was there when her son needed her.

She finished the sandwich, sliced it in half on a plate, and set it in front of him. Then she sat quietly across the table from him just to be there. She knew he'd speak when he was ready.

He took one bite of the sandwich and realized he wasn't hungry. With a sigh he set the sandwich down and attempted conversation. "I've been having some real problems, Mom." *All right . . . Now how in the world do I describe what's been happening to me?* "I think . . . well, you remember how when I was in college, the things I was doing . . . the drugs and all that . . . well, I think—"

The front door opened and in came Carl. John stopped abruptly, resenting the intrusion.

Carl was visibly surprised to see his father there and didn't seem entirely comfortable about it. "Oh . . . Hi."

John said curtly, "I thought you were at a concert?"

Carl crossed the living room and plopped into a chair at the table looking tired, worn, even shaken. "I walked out."

"Who was playing?"

"Bloodie Mary."

John felt his stomach turn. Bloodie Mary. He'd seen them walk by on a T-shirt more than once tonight. His disfavor showed plainly on his face. "You've got nothing better to do than put your money in *their* pockets?"

Carl was immediately defensive. "I left early . . . I got out of there."

That calmed John a little. "Well, that was a wise move." Then another thought, brewing in his mind, broke to the surface, and he spoke it. "Boy, if I ever catch you using drugs . . . !"

Carl got mad. "I don't do drugs."

"Well, you better not or there'll be hell to pay."

Mom asked quickly, "What happened tonight, John?"

Suddenly he wasn't as willing to talk about it. "I . . ." He looked at Carl again. "I think I had a flashback. I heard once how, if you took LSD years ago, the effects could still pop up again years later. I don't know, but maybe that's what's happening. I started seeing things, having hallucinations."

Mom seemed intensely interested. She leaned forward and asked, "What did you see?"

John wasn't ready. "I don't think I can describe it. But it scared me spitless." He paused to gather some thoughts, any thoughts. "Maybe what triggered it was seeing all those kids virtually living in that mall, buying up all that . . . that junk as if their lives depended on it!"

Carl asked flatly, "What else is there?"

John gave Carl a quick warning glare and kept going while he still had the thought. "I saw . . . it seemed like a huge . . . well, there was this black hole or something, and the whole mall was sliding into it, and people were being sucked in. But it was like they didn't want to know it, they didn't want to see the . . . the black hole. All they wanted to do was keep buying things and keep watching the televisions and listening to the music, and they didn't want to see what was happening, and so . . . they never got away, they just got sucked in." John looked at them and shook his head. "I can't describe it. It was weird, that's all."

He couldn't say any more. He took a bite from his sandwich just to fill the gap in the conversation.

Carl thought about it for a short moment and then spoke quietly. "They're all running. They know the black hole's there, but what can they do about it?"

John glared at Carl again. "What are you talking about?"

"It's death . . . annihilation . . . the whole universe going down the tube, and people know they can't do anything about it, so they try not to think about it. They buy stuff—they try to have fun any way they can before they get sucked in. That's what I meant when I said, what else is there?"

John wasn't in the mood for this. "Carl, I don't want any big . . . message here . . ."

"I just think that's what you saw."

"What I saw was a hallucination."

"Yeah? Well, I saw something tonight."

John said, "Yeah, I'll bet you did," and took a sip of coffee.

Carl looked away in anger. "You don't even give a rip, do you?"

John was ready to grapple. "Hey, I know what you saw, Carl. You're looking at an old Hendrix fan, a Doors fan. My money helped get all that crap started. I know what you saw." Then he added, "And yeah, maybe you're right . . . maybe I don't give a rip. Why should I care if you devote your time and money to . . . to cheap exhibitionism . . . contrived thrills . . . outrageous conduct and antisocial behavior?"

"Hey, now hold on, man . . ."

"Why should I be upset when I sit in the mall and see a nonstop parade of kids all wearing that stuff and wandering around with ten-second attention spans and then find out my son's part of the same great tradition?"

Carl slammed the table and cursed. "Are you going to listen to me or not?"

"Boys!" Mom tried to caution them both.

Carl held back on the volume but still held his finger in John's face. "Don't you talk to me about exhibitionism and . . . and contrived thrills and outrageous conduct! Not when you're the one showing us the kook in England shooting everybody and the lady keeling over in the zoo and cops beating up blacks night after night and dead, burnt bodies from the war—"

John was riled and ready to fight. "Carl, that's news!"

"Oh yeah? Then Bloodie Mary is art!" Carl dropped back into his chair in a huff.

John devoted his attention to his cup of coffee.

In that one moment of brooding silence, Mom tried hard to find something to say to build a bridge between her son and grandson. "Well, I'm glad you two are in such strong agreement."

Carl calmed himself and started over. "I saw something at the concert tonight and that's why I left. Well . . . I didn't *see* something . . . I just . . . thought of something."

John had put a check on his temper as well. "So what did you think of?"

"You really want to know?"

"Yeah. Yeah, tell me. I'll listen."

Carl stared at the table and kept control of his voice. "Bloodie Mary . . . They were taking us somewhere. We were all going with them, we were following them, but nobody knew where." He was playing back the memory in his mind. "Everything they told us to do, we did. Everything they did, we did. We did it all together. We were like one big . . . one big organism, one big machine. And I kept asking myself, Where's this machine going? Where is it taking us? And I didn't know. I kind of felt trapped. I just had to get out of there."

John mused quietly, "Use enough wattage, lights, volume, show biz . . . and brown gets moldy when it rains."

"Huh?"

"They follow you."

Carl thought about it, then nodded. "Maybe we're all following something and don't even know it."

"And we don't know where either."

A sad despair filled Carl's eyes. "Maybe down that big black tube you saw."

John looked at Mom. "So you weren't just being sarcastic, were you?"

Mom shook her head. "I think you're both upset about the same thing." Then she added, "But you know what I really think? I think God's talking to you."

John loved his mother. He wasn't about to hurt her feelings. "Yeah, well, maybe so."

She wasn't bluffed. She repeated, just as sure of herself, "I think God is talking to you. He's trying to get through."

John smiled at her. "Okay, Mom." He wouldn't let himself consider what Dad had said about the cries of lost souls.

Carl was more interested. "Grandpa was into that, wasn't he?"

Mom only replied, "He was very close to the Lord, yes."

John was quick to respond, "Well, I'm not Grandpa. I'm his son and I'm proud of it. I believe in God, but I don't think God does things like this."

Mom smiled, actually amused. "Well . . . Daniel saw four great beasts coming up out of the sea, and Ezekiel saw dry bones come together to form a nation, and Peter saw unclean animals lowered from Heaven in a big sheet, and the Apostle John saw the glorified Christ and the whole book of Revelation on the Island of Patmos. Why wouldn't the Lord want to show my son a shopping mall being gobbled up by a big vacuum cleaner?"

That sounded so silly John couldn't help laughing. Mom was a good sport. She laughed along, but still gave her head that little tilt that meant she was serious and said, "You just wait, John. One of these days . . ."

"Okay, Mom, okay. Message received and filed. You too, Carl. Thanks for your input. And I'm sorry I climbed on you like I did."

"Yeah, I'm sorry too."

John rested his elbows on the table and relaxed a bit. "I've had a lot on my mind lately, that's obvious."

"Yeah," Carl agreed. "We all have."

They talked a while longer, not about anything vitally important; they just needed to depressurize. John got a little more into his sandwich and Mom made one for Carl.

Finally John returned to a pressing matter. "Carl . . . what do you think about the Brewer situation?"

Carl brightened a little. "You've been thinking about that?"

"Oh yeah."

"What about the Brewers?" Mom asked.

Oh-oh. John had to be careful. Mom knew about Annie, of course, but what Max had said about Dad's death . . . well, that was nothing more than a very thin lead, and nothing to concern her about. "Oh, it's just Annie, and how she died. I'm bothered about it."

"So am I," said Carl.

Mom nodded. "And so was your father."

"So let's do something about it," said Carl. "We've got to be able to find out something."

John looked at Carl, that weird, young man who seemed so lost, so far away. And yet . . . their vastly different worlds seemed to have common ground in this one situation. "You . . . uh . . . you want to go after this?"

"You bet I do," Carl answered.

"Well . . . so do I. I still don't know if this is going to be a news story or not, but what the heck, so what if it is or isn't?

It was important to Dad, and if it was important to him, it's important to me."

"And me."

"Well . . . okay. Let's do it."

Carl brightened. "All right! Where do we start?"

John had been thinking about it. He was ready even now with some first steps. "Mom, would you happen to know which doctor Dad and Max Brewer took that handwritten autopsy report to?"

Mom thought the answer was obvious enough. "Dr. Meredith."

"Of course." Dr. Meredith had been the Barrett family doctor for years.

"Max and Dad went to him, and he explained it. I wasn't there, so you'll have to go ask him about it and get it straight from him."

"Okay, we'll do that. Now, Carl, I thought of one other thing. I don't know what good it will do, but since we're scraping for anything and everything, we should get Annie's attendance records from Jefferson High School and see if she was absent the Friday before she died. I think Deanne Brewer can go to the school and get those."

"Okay. I'll call her and get that started."

"But listen now, this is important: Before Deanne goes to the school herself and asks for the attendance records, see if you can find out from her just which classes Annie was taking in the spring trimester of last year. Then have her contact those teachers and get their attendance records first. I'm just guessing and hoping that, even if the school office tries to cover up her absence, maybe some of her teachers won't be in on the secret."

"Okay."

"So . . . you call Deanne Brewer and get started on that, and I'll check with Dr. Meredith about that autopsy report. I want to hear what he has to say before I try to track down the pathologist . . . uh . . ."

"Denning, I think."

"Yeah, Denning. Oh . . . one more thing. Rachel Franklin,

the waitress. If she can find anyone who was riding on that van with Annie . . ."

"I'll call her tomorrow, just say hello, kind of remind her."

John took one last bite of his sandwich—it was a little dry by now. "Well . . . let's do it."

Carl was excited. He even gave his father's shoulder a light punch, a rare show of enthusiasm. "Let's do it."

The next morning, John drove to the office of Dr. Irving Meredith, the senior Barretts' general practitioner.

Dr. Meredith was a kindly sort, an older fellow who looked a bit like Mark Twain, though his smooth voice and mellow personality broke that image right away. He'd known John and Lillian Barrett for years and was glad enough to see John Barrett, Jr. the next morning between appointments. They went into his office, and John showed him a photocopy of the hand-copied report. Dr. Meredith pulled his glasses from his pocket.

"Ah yes!" he said with recollection. "You got this from the Brewers?"

"Right. I need to have you explain it to me."

"Well . . . you understand, of course, this isn't much of a document. It's only some excerpts copied by hand from a document that should exist, certainly, but I understand can't be found."

"That's right."

"So, as I told your father—may he rest in peace—I'm only telling you my conclusions from what I read right here on this paper, and I can't be held to them. The best thing, the only thing really, is for you to contact this Dr. Denning and get the actual information directly from him."

"Understood. But what can you glean from what we do have?"

Dr. Meredith perused the pages in his hand. "Well, it appears they got some of this from the first page of the autopsy report, and maybe some of the last paragraphs. Most of it is summarizing without a lot of the detail you find in an autopsy report—gross examination of all the organs, then microscopic examination. It can go on for pages; they're very thorough."

"What does that term 'gross examination' mean?"

"Simple, visual examination, how the organs look upon examination by the prosector, the pathologist who does the examination. Weight, appearance, any signs of trauma, infection, whatever."

"Okay."

"But what's clear to see here are the primary and secondary causes of death, probably a summary your father and Max Brewer found on the first page of the report.

"'Primary causes of death: Generalized septicemia.' That's bacterial infection in the bloodstream. It was generalized; that means it had spread everywhere.

"'Pneumonitis.' That's infection of the lungs. 'Peritonitis.' That's infection of the lining of the abdomen.

"Then you have the secondary cause—the problem that caused the primary causes that killed her, and that's 'septic abortion.' That means an infection introduced in the process of a termination of pregnancy. Of course, in medical language, 'abortion' could mean a natural termination of pregnancy such as by miscarriage as well as a termination induced from the outside. But be that as it may . . ." He scanned the pages, flipping through them. "And they say my handwriting's bad . . ." He found what he was after. "Ah! Your father's handwriting. He must have been looking for this; it's the gross examination of the uterus. Look here:

"'The uterus was examined . . . surface smooth and glistening, gravid, or appears to have been gravid'—that's pregnant—'. . . on its posterior surface there is evidence of a recent perforation . . .' Mm . . . and look here: '. . . these findings show there has been a recent pregnancy . . . products of conception still attached to the endometrial lining of the uterus . . .'"

John asked, "You mean parts of the baby left inside?"

"Oh, maybe, maybe not. Could be some of the placenta. Even in a normal birth you have some product that may remain for a short time before being expelled naturally.

But . . . yeah, could be baby parts too. You'd have to ask Denning. If it was baby parts, I'm sure he'd remember. Come to think of it, if it was baby parts, that might explain why no one can find the actual autopsy report. Don't quote me on that.

"But this perforation . . . that would do it. That would be enough to kill her. Some of the contents of the uterus could have been introduced through that perforation into the peritoneal cavity—the abdomen, okay?—and if those contents were not sterile, they would carry the infection in there. Or even if product were left inside the uterus, and the uterus couldn't clamp down and expel it, the infection would fester in there, and because the uterus has such an abundant blood supply, the infection would be introduced into Annie's bloodstream. It would be carried all over her body, into her vital organs, and the toxins would kill her. And yes, it would take as long as it took—what? from Friday to Sunday?"

"Aborted Friday, died Sunday."

"Mm-hm. That makes perfect sense." Dr. Meredith set the pages down on his desk. "So . . . any way you read the findings, the conclusion's the same: Somebody did a lousy job of abortion. But listen, John, you've got to get the real documents, you've got to talk to the pathologist. For one thing, I'm not a pathologist, and obviously I can't commit myself to anything scribbled on pieces of paper. I can share my knowledge with you, but this is strictly on an unprofessional basis, off the record, understand?"

"Certainly. Thanks."

Dr. Meredith was showing some anger now. "But then again, if the autopsy report does indicate death from abortion, as these notes indicate . . . then the parents are legally barred from seeing it." His face was grim as he said, "If you're to go any further, I think you'll need a lawyer."

As John left Dr. Meredith's office, his eyes were drawn to the poster on the side of a passing bus. Marvelous graphics, wondrous image, eye-catching colors. A red sun rising over the capitol and the words emblazoned across the sky, "The

New Dawn Lives On." Governor Hiram Slater's face, grim with determination, faced the capitol dome, and under his chin were the words, "Governor Hiram Slater—for Governor!"

Wow. His opponent Bob Wilson should look so good.

"You wanted to see me, Ben?"

News Director Ben Oliver was rummaging through the papers on his desk and rapidly filling his wastebasket. "Yeah, John, come in and close the door."

John closed the door and was about to take a seat, but the only other chair in the room was occupied by a stack of magazines. "Um . . . should I move these?"

Ben didn't look up from his desk. "Put 'em on the floor. They're going into the recycling bin, along with this other stuff." He gathered a stack of letters, phone messages, notes, daily news outlooks, and junk mail and dumped them all in—or rather, on—the wastebasket. It was full by now, and half of the pile slid onto the floor. He didn't seem to notice.

"I don't like trouble, John. I'm trying to rid my life of trouble. I'm getting rid of the old trouble so I'll have room for the new trouble, you follow me?"

John didn't and felt apprehensive. "Uh . . . no, sir, I don't."

"You realize, of course, that we have the number one newscast in this market?"

"Yes, sir." That fact was touted time after time on the air, around the newsroom, and in the station's advertising. Of course John realized it.

"Do you realize that the other stations are currently working at a fever pitch trying to bump us out of that spot?"

"Yes, sir."

"Do you realize what this station's been able to charge for advertising because of where we are?"

"Yes, sir."

"We are making money for the station, John, and when the station makes money, we make money. We're not cleaning up, we won't retire rich, but we are doing a good business. We are presenting the news to people in a way they seem to like, and they are tuning in. Now . . ." He threw one more pile of old files, papers, magazines, and mail on the floor.

"Two things, neither of which you are to discuss with anyone outside this room. Number One: I just got out of a meeting with the general manager and the Board of Directors, and they are bound and determined to stay on top. That's why they've put together a new plan of attack and the budget to launch it. We're expanding the Five Thirty to a full hour, starting at 5, which means more news coverage, which means more work for you, which means more exposure, and of course more money."

John was impressed and pleased, of course. "Well, that's very interesting . . ."

"Don't get too happy yet. They're planning on doing some big image campaigns with you and Ali Downs. Billboards, bus posters, TV promos. They were talking about building a new set for the show too, a new look."

"Wow."

"So just hang on now and listen to what I'm about to say." He looked at the shelves behind his desk, considered an old calendar from a videotape company, and chucked it on the floor. "John, we do a good job around here, and I think we have one of the best news teams in the business. But you and Ali, you're the ones who are right up front. You're the ones the people associate with the station. You're the ones the people tune in to see." Ben rested his elbows on his desk—he'd found enough bare area to do that now—and looked at John probingly. "So, John, I need to know something. Are you losing your marbles?"

"What?"

Ben waved his own question aside. "No, no, strike that—I withdraw the question. Let me tell you this and we'll let it go: we're betting a lot of money on you, a lot of reputation and viewership and revenue, and that's because you're good. Now I have no doubts whatsoever that you'll carry the ball for us—all the way into the end zone, and we'll all come out winners. When people see you out in public, they'll see a sharp, in-control kind of guy, the same guy they see every evening on the tube, the same guy they've trusted, a guy who's going to make Channel 6 look good."

"That's who they see now, Ben." John was quite firm on that.

"Well, sure they do. Sure. But just tell me, John . . . Tell me I can be sure that's how it's going to be in the future."

"Of course! I'm troubled that you would even ask the question."

Ben leaned forward and eyed John carefully, one eyebrow strangely cocked. "So people . . . those people out there, those viewers, are going to see a man they can trust to bring them the news with sobriety, integrity, and grit, right?"

"Of course!"

"And they're not going to see a man who reads things in the script that aren't there . . . or hears voices calling to him in the night . . . or goes running to rescue people who don't need rescuing?"

Tina Lewis, John thought. Rush Torrance. Maybe even Benny the cameraman who came to John's apartment that one night. They'd been talking about him. "So you've been talking to Tina. Ben, that was nothing. And that mistake with the scripted question, it was just a mix-up."

"And the voices calling in the night?"

John was thinking fast. He shrugged it off. "Kids, I suppose, pulling a prank. I guess I was wired that night, just too anxious for a breaking story. Hey, you win some, you lose some, but you keep trying. You stay as far ahead as you can."

Ben nodded approvingly. "Yeah, yeah, that's right." He leaned back in his chair and picked up a pen to put in the corner of his mouth. "I guess I just want you to be . . . predictable, know what I mean? I'd like to be able to tell myself, Yeah, I know what John's going to do now. I know how he's going to handle this. I don't have to worry about it."

John had trouble keeping his voice down. "Listen, Ben, I don't know what you've been told, but I'm not too happy that someone would try to upset you or try to smear me."

Ben held his hand up. "John, John . . . The real problem, as I see it, is that you and Tina need to cease fire. Listen, I don't find snitches all that impressive either, and I don't need to hear this kind of crap; but when I do, I have to look into it." Ben tried to look like he was relaxed, but his face was still tense. "Power goes down the ladder, but responsibility for screw-ups goes back up, so we in management are always looking out below. It's the nature of the beast, you know that."

Ben got up and crammed some more paper into the wastebasket. "And now, thanks to those guys upstairs and their big ideas, I've got a whole new batch of trouble coming and I don't need any of the old stuff still hanging around, you know what I mean? So okay . . . we've talked about it, the matter's settled, it's finished. Just do a good job. Make me glad for every decision we made today, all right? That's all I'm saying."

Back at his desk, John hammered away at his computer, whacking out excess words, tightening the rhetoric, rephrasing, clarifying, editing with a vengeance. And it was *vengeance.* He was angry. He was a pro. He was going to write like a pro and report like a pro, and Tina and whoever else had it in for him was going to like it, and that was all there was to it.

And if any more of this hallucination stuff tried to force itself on him, he would ignore it, overcome it, do whatever he had to do to stay in control of his life. *His* life! He banged his desk in anger and even mouthed the words, "It's my life!"

The phone rang. "Hello!" Oops. He really sounded angry.

"Dad, this is Carl. I've got something."

John held the receiver against his ear with his shoulder so he could keep working. "Yeah?"

"Deanne Brewer got the names of Annie's teachers from last year. She'll call them tonight at their homes to ask for those attendance records, and then I suppose they'll have to check and get back to her."

"Okay. Good."

"And I think Rachel Franklin found somebody."

John forgot about working. He held the receiver with his hand. "She found somebody?"

"Yeah. It's real touchy. The girl won't give her name or anything, and she won't talk to us. She says she might talk to Deanne."

John had to be sure. "Now . . . this is a girl who rode on the van with Annie Brewer?"

"That's what Rachel says."

"Who is she?"

"Rachel doesn't know anything about her."

"Well . . . she must know something. Did they go to school together or what? How did Rachel find her?"

"Hey, like I said, it's touchy. Remember Rachel telling us how she went to that other place to have another pregnancy test?"

"Yeah."

"Well, she went back there and talked to a counselor about all this, and the counselor called her back today. It turns out that one of the girls who's been coming to her for counseling says she was on that van with Annie."

John's pulse was quickening. "So . . . all right, what's this girl willing to do?"

"The counselor said—now I'm getting this from Rachel, I haven't talked to the counselor yet—the counselor said that this girl might talk to Annie's mom, but she doesn't want anyone to know who she is or even to see her, and the counselor has to be there."

"What about a reporter? I wonder if she'd mind a woman reporter being there?"

"I don't know."

"Find out. Get on it."

"Okay. I'll get right back to Rachel and then call Deanne. But I don't know how this thing's going to turn out."

"Thanks, Carl. Good work."

"I love it."

They hung up, and John looked around the room for Leslie Albright. She'd be perfect for this, if it ever developed.

What was it Carl said? I love it or I love you?

thirteen

That Saturday Leslie Albright picked up Deanne Brewer, and they drove together to a small, storefront location between a laundromat and a used bookstore just off Morris Avenue, an obviously low-budget operation in a low-rent building in a rundown district. If Leslie had not called first and gotten clear directions, they may have had trouble even finding the place. It was Deanne who first spotted the posterboard sign in the window: "Human Life Services. Free Pregnancy Tests, Counseling, Referrals, Support Services. Abortion Alternatives."

Leslie parked just across the street, turned off the engine, and then looked at Deanne. "Well, are you ready for this?"

Deanne was uneasy but gave a firm nod. "Oh, I'm ready. I know I'm not going to like it, but I'm ready."

They got out.

"Better be sure you lock it," Deanne said.

They locked the doors and crossed the street. Leslie was here as a friend, not a reporter. She was on her own time, with no plans as yet to make a news story out of this. She was here just to listen, to get the facts for John since he couldn't participate. Since she felt she owed him some favors, she'd let him talk her into it. Besides, at the very worst it would be a chance to see a side of the issue she'd never really seen before.

And she'd never taken a close look at anything like this place before either, this humble little enterprise with the pretty curtains in the weathered windows, and the simple painted sign to identify the place. While doctors could make over a thousand dollars per day in large, abortion-providing clinics with paid staffs, here was an organization mostly run by volunteers and operating on donations. She was impressed by how unimpressive it was.

Marilyn Westfall, the director, was waiting for them and met them at the door, introducing herself. She was a lady somewhere in her forties or fifties, professional in her demeanor, and soft-spoken, especially now. "Please come in and have a seat. We'll talk for a bit."

They stepped inside without speaking, careful not to make any noise, as if a baby were sleeping somewhere. The reception area provided a small table with coffee and cups, four padded chairs, and a coffee table with literature—obviously pro-life—arranged on it. Deanne and Leslie sat down on one side of the table, and Marilyn sat across from them.

Mrs. Westfall explained in a quiet voice, "The young lady you'll be talking to is waiting in a counseling room. For our purposes today we'll give her a pseudonym; we'll call her Mary. I told her I would speak with you first so we could all understand and agree on the conditions for this visit.

"Just to give you some background, I'm a licensed counselor, married, with two grown children, and I donate my time here twice a week. Mary came to us about a month and a half ago, post-abortive—psychologically distressed from the abortion experience—and I've been working with her on a regular basis.

"Now you can call it coincidence—I think God had something to do with it—but just a few weeks ago she told me about a particular struggle she was having." Mrs. Westfall spoke carefully, slowly. "She'd been living with the knowledge that your daughter, Mrs. Brewer, was there at the clinic at the same time she was and possibly could have died from the abortion she received."

Deanne only nodded, expecting this.

Mrs. Westfall continued, "Well, she told me about this in confidence, so I couldn't take any further steps until Mary was ready to do so herself. But then, right about the same time, Rachel Franklin came to us—and I understand Rachel's already told you about that."

Leslie nodded. "That's right."

"So you recall that while she was here she read some of our literature and pieced together her theory that Annie died from a septic abortion. She later shared that with me. Well, that put me in a bind. Two girls coming to the same conclusion at practically the same time, and here I was in the middle, unable to tell either about the other . . . until this week. I understand Rachel had told your friend . . . uh . . . Carl?"

"Yes, Carl Barrett, and his father, John Barrett."

"Mm-hm. She told Carl and his father about her theory, and then Rachel came back to me and said they wanted to talk to someone who'd actually been there and seen Annie getting the abortion . . ." Mrs. Westfall allowed herself a muffled laugh. "Isn't it amazing how God works? I shared all this with Mary, and she said she'd like to tell what happened, but only to you, Mrs. Brewer, and I agreed that she should. So here we are.

"Now, this might seem a little strange to you, but here is how she wants the interview done: she's going to be inside the counseling room, and I've moved a screen in there for her to sit behind because she doesn't want anyone to see her; she doesn't want anyone to know who she is. I told her you were going to bring a friend along, Mrs. Brewer, someone to give you support, and that's fine with her, because I'll be there giving Mary support, so she'll have someone and you'll have someone.

"Now as we discussed over the phone, Mary does not want to be tape recorded, but if you'd like to jot down any notes about times and places, that's fine. She wants you to know what happened; she's just very concerned about protecting her privacy."

"We understand," said Leslie.

"So what we'll do is go down the hall to the counseling room, and I've arranged two chairs in there for you, on this side of the screen. We'll go in, get you seated, and then I'll go behind the screen to be with Mary. All right?"

They rose, and Mrs. Westfall led the way to the counseling room, passing a tight little office with a telephone, desk, copy machine, and literature, and then a large room filled with maternity clothes, baby clothes, toys, and folded cribs.

The last door on the right was the counseling room. Mrs. Westfall knocked lightly, said "Hello, we're here," and opened the door. Quietly, as if approaching a timid deer, Leslie and Deanne went into the room and sat in the two chairs on the near side of a collapsible screen. Then Mrs. Westfall went behind the screen, out of sight.

"Mary," she said, "I'd like you to meet Deanne Brewer, Annie's mother."

There was no response from behind the screen, so Deanne ventured a gentle "Hello, Mary."

"Hello," came a young woman's voice.

"And Mrs. Brewer has a friend with her, Leslie Albright."

"Hello," Mary said first.

"Hello, Mary."

Mrs. Westfall said, "Mary, why don't you just tell Mrs. Brewer what happened, what you know, and then, if it's all right with you, perhaps Mrs. Brewer or her friend Leslie would like to ask you some questions. You don't have to answer any question you're uncomfortable with, all right?"

"All right." Then there was an awkward pause. They could hear the girl fidgeting, now knowing what to say.

Mrs. Westfall helped with, "You were a classmate of Annie's, isn't that right?"

"Yes."

"And . . . well, why don't you tell them how you found out you were pregnant?"

"Mrs. Hannah told me."

"And Mrs. Hannah is . . . ?"

"The nurse at school, at Jefferson."

Leslie got out her notepad and started jotting down the details.

"And when was this?"

"Last year."

"In May?"

"Yeah, it was on a Tuesday." It sounded like Mrs. Westfall was looking at a calendar somewhere. "That would be . . . May 21st, right?"

"Right."

"Tell us about that."

"I thought I was pregnant, and so I went to see Mrs. Hannah, and she gave me a pregnancy test, and the test came out positive, and she asked me when my last period was and figured out I was about seven weeks pregnant."

"And how did you feel about that?"

"I was scared. I didn't know what to do. But the first thing Mrs. Hannah said was, I didn't have to tell my parents. She said nobody had to know and we could get me an abortion right away and nobody would have to find out about it."

"And what about the father? Did he know?"

"No. I never told him. I don't even talk to him anymore. I don't know where he is or what he's doing."

"So . . . Mrs. Hannah told you you could get an abortion right away and that your parents wouldn't have to know . . ."

"Yeah. And then she asked me if I had some money to pay for it, and I said no, but she said that was okay because she could file for state assistance and the state would pay for it, no questions asked. Mrs. Hannah had the forms right there in the office. So I never had to pay any money, and I think the clinic got paid a few months later, but they're set up for that. Anyway, she set up an appointment for Friday and told me there'd be some other girls going."

Deanne's eyes began filling with tears.

"So," Mrs. Westfall prompted, "did you go to school on Friday?"

"For the morning. And then, instead of having lunch, I went to Mrs. Hannah's office, and then me and two other girls got on this van that came from the clinic and they took us over there and we got our abortions."

Leslie asked, "And that was the Women's Medical Center?"

"Uh-huh."

Mrs. Westfall prompted, "And you knew the other two girls?"

"Yeah. One of them was Annie."

Deanne tried not to make a sound, but she couldn't keep from crying.

Mrs. Westfall asked, "Are you all right, Mrs. Brewer?"

Deanne could hardly answer. "I'm all right. I want to hear it."

"We can stop for a moment."

"No . . . No, I want to hear it. I *have* to hear it."

Leslie took Deanne's hand, and Deanne received her comfort.

"Go ahead . . . Please," Deanne said.

Mrs. Westfall asked Mary, "This is one of the big, important questions, Mary. Did you see Annie receive an abortion at the Women's Medical Center?"

"Not the whole thing."

"Well, tell us what happened."

"Well, the van took us there, and we went in and they had us fill out some forms—stuff about diseases we've had or drugs we were taking or allergies . . ."

"Well," said Mrs. Westfall, "medical history, I suppose."

"Yeah. And then there was a consent form that said we agreed to have the abortion and we were aware of the risks."

"Did you read the form before you signed it?"

"I didn't understand it, and I didn't have time. Everybody was in a hurry. A bunch of other women and girls were there, and it just seemed like everybody was in a hurry. But there were some girls in the waiting room before us. They were already there when we got there, and they went first, and then . . . um . . . the other girl . . ."

"The one who wasn't Annie?"

"Yeah. A counselor came and got her, and she went first . . ."

"What do you mean when you say a 'counselor'?"

"Well, they had some women there who kind of took you through the whole thing. They answered your questions and tried to make you feel relaxed, things like that."

"All right."

"So then my counselor took me into one room, and when I was in there sitting on the table I could see Annie through the doorway, out in the hall with another counselor. They were going to put her in the room across the hall, and I remember her saying . . . well, I don't want to say the other girl's name, but see, the other girl was done, she was on her way to the recovery room, and Annie was talking to her, asking her how she was, and I remember Annie sounded scared."

Mrs. Westfall said, "Could you hear the other girl's voice at all?"

"No, not from where I was. My counselor and some other lady . . . maybe it was a nurse, but she didn't look like one . . . were talking and I couldn't hear. But I heard Annie say to the other girl, 'Are you all right?' and then somebody out in the hall with her, one of the counselors, told her, 'She's all right, just come in here,' and then the doctor came into my room, and they closed the door, and he started doing the abortion on me and . . ."

They could tell Mary was crying.

"And . . ." Mary struggled to speak. "And it just hurt so much . . . and I told the counselor, 'What's he doing, you said it wouldn't hurt,' and she just held me down, and I started screaming, I couldn't help it, and the doctor yelled at me to hold still and he said, 'You want your parents to find out?' So I tried to keep quiet, but then I heard Annie screaming . . ."

Mary broke down completely.

Deanne also broke into bitter weeping, and Leslie embraced her.

That evening, troubled and torn with emotion, Leslie reported her findings to John, Carl, and Mom Barrett around the Barrett dining table, referring to her notes.

"From the way Mary described it, the doctors were in a hurry, rushing it, not gentle but cold and insensitive. Apparently Mary got through it without serious physical injury, but . . ."

"But Annie wasn't so lucky," said John.

"No," Leslie agreed. "She wasn't so lucky. I guess Friday is a busy day for them. According to Mrs. Westfall, the clinic runs a van to three different schools—Jefferson High, Monroe Junior High, and Gronfield Junior High—to handle the girls who can't supply their own transportation. They do all their school referrals on Fridays and Saturdays so the girls can recover over the weekend and not miss school and hopefully get around their parents finding out."

Mom asked, "You mean the schools send the girls over there?"

Leslie nodded. "The clinic gives a discount if any girl is referred by a school counselor. This is a business we're talking about, involving a lot of money. We're talking about fifty abortions per day for a price of $350 each, many of them paid for by state funds and the others paid for with cash or credit card only, in advance, with virtually no paper trail, no regulation, no accountability. There is room for corruption. But be that as it may . . ." Leslie eyed her notes again. "This particular day must have been hectic—like I said, on a good day the clinic will do up to fifty abortions—and Mary says the abortion was very painful and, she thought, rushed, and she was in a lot of pain afterward. The girls spent about a half hour in the recovery room, and since there didn't seem to be any major problems they were given a sheet of follow-up instructions and a month's worth of birth control pills and taken out to the van. Mary says she was in a lot of pain, with a lot of bleeding which eventually stopped. As for Annie, she had to be helped, practically carried, back to the van. They were taken out the back door of the clinic—so they wouldn't be seen, according to Mary—and then taken back to the school where they spent the rest of the school day, which would have been an hour or so, in the nurse's office, lying on beds and recovering."

Carl added, "And the school records just marked them as being in school, not absent for that day."

John responded, "So it was a good thing we checked with the teachers first."

"Sly move." Carl looked at his notes. "Mr. Pomeroy marked her absent from U.S. Government, fifth period, and . . . Mrs. Chase marked her absent from Art, sixth period. Deanne heard from three of Annie's other teachers who taught morning classes, and they marked her present. So it matches what Mary said."

John looked at Carl's notes. "Gone for half the day, and

her parents none the wiser. How's that for a new interpretation of *in loco parentis?"*

"Well," said Leslie, "it all has to do with privacy."

"Yeah," said Carl, "so Annie died privately when she could have lived publicly."

Leslie didn't argue with that. "Granted."

"All that aside," John interjected, "this whole thing raises some serious questions. How many women go through that place every week? How many minors? And what do we even know about the doctors, the staff, the hygienic standards?"

"Virtually nothing, and that's my concern," said Leslie. "As far as we know, over four thousand abortions are safely performed in this country every day, and we're simply dealing with an anomaly—one very bad apple. But how do we know that for sure? How many other bad apples are out there? How can we find out? Besides, one is one too many. Listen, whatever Marilyn Westfall knows, she's pieced together by talking to people who've either had abortions at that clinic or who have worked there. But it is in little pieces, none of it is provable, and just try finding something out directly. The clinic can hide behind the reproductive privacy laws and never have to come out."

Mom shook her head. "Well, don't blame me. I didn't vote for those laws—and I didn't vote for Hiram Slater."

Leslie admitted, "I voted for both."

John ventured, "You sound like you regret it."

Leslie gave a wry smile. "I'm watching and listening—let's just put it that way."

"So how's Deanne Brewer taking all this?"

Leslie breathed a deep sigh. "She's holding up. It's hard for her, hard for both of them, but they want to know."

"We'll have to be sure we don't let Max get too riled."

Carl asked, "But who are these doctors? We must be able to find that out."

"Sure, we can find out," said Leslie. "But it's interesting how Mary has no idea who they were. Those doctors go through the whole thing so fast the girls hardly even see their faces. There are no doctor/patient relationships, no introductions, nothing. And along those lines, the clinic tries to minimize the paper trail by paying the doctors in cash, no 1099s, no W-2s.

"But if you're looking for some way to link the clinic with Annie Brewer, I've thought of four things: Number One, every patient has a chart—a record of the procedure, what was done, what the results were, and so forth—and every chart has a little tear-off coupon at the bottom. After the doctor does the abortion, he signs the chart and the coupon, tears off that coupon and puts it in his pocket. At the end of the day he then turns in a whole stack of coupons so he can get paid. Now that would be one way to tie a doctor to a patient."

"So if Annie's chart still exists, that would be evidence," John said, "if she used her real name."

"She didn't," said Leslie. "But Mary knew what her code name was: Judy Medford."

"Judy Medford," John rehearsed as he wrote it down.

"A lot of the girls use code names. The clinic doesn't mind as long as the same name is always used by the same patient. Incidentally, Mary's code name was Madonna."

"So there's still hope," said Carl.

"Hm?" asked Leslie.

John nodded. He and Carl had talked about this.

Carl explained, "Well, think of it: Here comes Max Brewer into the clinic, asking if they did an abortion on his daughter Annie Brewer and making so much trouble they have to call the cops to get him out of there. If you were running that clinic and found out one of your patients died and her old man was after you, what would you do?"

Mom had no trouble with the answer. "I'd get rid of all the records. I'd get rid of anything that had anything to do with Annie Brewer."

Leslie and John didn't dive in to agree. Leslie countered, somewhat reservedly, "That would be . . . pretty dishonest."

But John just looked at her, prodding further thought with raised eyebrows.

Leslie asked him, "Do you think they'd do that, John?"

John pursed his lips, scanned the table for the answer, then replied, "If they thought they could get away with it."

Carl finished his point. "But if they didn't know Annie Brewer's phony name was phony . . ."

"They wouldn't know which records to purge," said John. "So we may still have a chance here."

Leslie went back to her notes. "Okay then, here's Number Two: Every woman, every girl, has to sign a consent form. Whether they understand it or not, whether the form really informs them of the dangers or not, they have to sign it to get an abortion. Number Three, the clinic probably has a daily schedule sheet for each day's abortions. If they've kept that record, then Annie, alias Judy Medford, would be on it. Number Four, there might be a bookkeeping entry or a receipt for Annie's $350. She did pay in cash, isn't that right?"

John nodded. "I called Max about that, and he said Annie's savings account shows a $350 withdrawal the Thursday before the abortion."

"Okay . . . so there we have four possible documents that could establish Annie being at the clinic."

"Now if we could only get those records . . ."

Leslie shook her head. "It's going to take a lawyer, John."

John searched the card file in his head for a name. "I know a lawyer we can talk to: Aaron Hart. Maybe he can get us a subpoena or something." Then he scanned his notes, saying to no one in particular, "But what do we have to show him? We're sure now that Annie was at the Women's Medical Center for an abortion on the 24th of May and that she died two days later on the 26th . . ."

"Depends on what you mean by 'sure.' Our witness Mary has vanished back into the woodwork."

"Hoo boy. We've got to hope we can draw her back out somehow. But besides Mary, we have hand-copied excerpts from an autopsy report that suggests Annie died from a botched abortion. Dr. Meredith says we really need the original, along with the pathologist himself."

"And there's Rachel Franklin who can assert that she was

given a phony pregnancy test result, as if that has anything to do with it."

Carl added, "And we've just heard about the $350 taken from Annie's bank account."

"And we have the circumstantial stuff," said Leslie. "The van running from the three schools, and Jefferson High being one of them."

"And the Friday factor, the . . . well, the coincidence of the day the school-referred abortions are performed and the day of Annie's illness."

"Well," said Leslie, "I know one thing I'm going to do, and that's get together with Deanne and try once again to track down Denning, the hospital pathologist. If he's still on the planet anywhere, we've got to find him and get him to attest to the fact that Annie died from a botched abortion. But by all means let's get an appointment with that lawyer before the trail gets any colder."

"So . . ." John ventured, "you're in?"

"I have my views on all this," said Leslie, "and I'm no witch-hunter. Choice is still choice, and privacy is still privacy. But an innocent girl is dead. I've seen and heard enough. I'm in."

John trudged up the stairs to his apartment at about 8 that night, fumbled with the key in the lock, and finally got inside where he flopped on the couch, his forearm over his eyes, tired, troubled, not wanting to move, wanting only to lie there and process, process, process. He had to get away from the emotion and the momentum of this thing before he got carried away. Regardless of what the others thought, felt, were doing, or were going to do, what was *he* going to do? Where did he stand on all this? He had to sort it out before going one step further.

All right. First of all, was he convinced Annie Brewer had died at the hands of a sloppy abortionist? Yes, he was. But that wouldn't mean much if he couldn't prove it, and proving it would be troublesome and, if he wasn't careful, hazardous. Here he'd be, the supposedly impartial, reliable newsman, caught in an activity that would brand him a pro-lifer or, worse yet, an anti-choicer. That might be bad for ratings, and Ben Oliver wouldn't like that.

But what about the wrongness of it? he wondered. Was what happened to Annie Brewer wrong? He thought so. Okay, how wrong? Certainly a skilled lawyer could demonstrate that the physician—indeed, the whole clinic—had acted within the law, according to their good faith judgment; and if so, the Brewers, and by association John Barrett and Company, would be left high and dry without a *bona fide* complaint.

So okay, it might be legal, but did that make it right? *Oh please, let's not get into that,* he thought. These days it was all too frequently demonstrated that the law could not settle that argument one way or the other.

So why should he even bother himself with this? The answer came to his mind: Because what happened to Annie Brewer was evil, and evil prevails when good men do nothing.

Okay, so what is Evil? He could be like Dad was—thump a Bible and say what's right and what's wrong—but how well would that fit in a society that looked to majority opinion, legislation, and court precedents for its rules—rules that were constantly changing? Just who had the final say? Maybe the whole notion of Evil was a catch-all created for anything the majority didn't like.

Well, if he couldn't nail down what Evil was, why fight it? Whatever was evil today could be voted, legislated, or judged good tomorrow. *Maybe if we just wait long enough,* he thought, *we'll get comfortable with the way things are. Maybe next year what happened to Annie Brewer won't be such a bad thing, and we'll be looking back, glad we didn't bust our guts for nothing. Or our careers.*

What if they did pursue this? John tried to imagine the best thing that could happen.

Perhaps the Brewers would receive some kind of compensation. But a jury would have to award it to them, and what wrongdoing could anyone prove in court with the laws the way they were?

Well then, could this incident be used to stir up a public outcry for tougher laws regulating the abortion industry? Well, it would fuel the debate, of course, but did the debate really need more fuel? Right now it was roaring along just fine on the fuel it had.

And what about Dad? John went limp as hope left him. As much as they knew about the Annie caper, nothing pointed in the tiniest way to Dad's death.

Such uncertainty! If only he could find just one little guarantee somewhere!

So John turned to the worst thing that could happen. They wouldn't find out anything, nobody would get caught or held accountable, and his name would become associated with unfounded pro-life vendettas, thus ruining his image as a—how did Ben Oliver put it?—a "sharp, in-control kind of guy . . . a man the public can trust to bring them the news with sobriety, integrity, and grit . . ."

Well, one answer, one course of action, was becoming obvious. *John,* he mused, *you've got to stay clear of this. No matter how it turns out, you cannot let yourself be associated with it. A news story is one thing—political meddling is another—and it isn't a news story yet anyway, not without something more solid.*

So now he had decided. He'd made up his mind. No, he hadn't. His heart was almost physically pounding with it: What happened to Annie Brewer was wrong.

Yes, wrong. But what about . . . ? It was *wrong.* He knew it was wrong, felt it was wrong, would go to his grave convinced it was wrong.

But the other factors kept plaguing him—his career, his image, the vagueness of the law, of society's present moral code, the elusiveness of the whole concept of Evil.

It was wrong, he said in his heart—undeniably, emphatically, unequivocally, categorically wrong.

But what can anyone do about it? Why even try? He jumped up from the couch ready to do battle with his doubts, angry at the whole situation, at himself, at that cursed clinic, at the whole red-handed world. Hey, a man had to have some remnant of a conscience, for crying out loud!

"It's wrong!" he told himself, and then went on to tell the world, "No, sorry, your arguments don't wash! I know wrong when I see it, I know when someone's been taken advantage of, I know when someone's made a tragic mistake and tried to get away with it, and it's *wrong*, and you won't take my conscience from me!"

He looked out the glass balcony door toward the city, now aglow with its myriad of lights, glimmering, roaring, hurrying about its business, with things to do, deals to make, places to go, appointments to keep. For a moment he felt a strange sensation, a kinship in sin with all those people out there.

"How'd we ever get ourselves into this mess anyway?" he asked.

And then, as he stood there quietly before the city, the voices reached him once again. He could hear them clearly but not "audibly," not seemingly with his ears as before. His heart heard them. His humanity heard them. Every fiber within him that could mourn—but also hope—heard them. And it was no big shock. He was not surprised or dismayed. He welcomed the knowledge, the awareness of their cries.

Perhaps it was because to a certain degree he now understood what they were feeling. They were hurting, yes, and dying, pulled steadily downward by despair, but they were crying out because they knew they would be heard; they were reaching desperately for hope because they knew it was there. They knew. As much as they would argue against it and deny it in the light of day and in the clatter and diversion of their social circles, in their souls they still knew.

And John knew. He'd always known. For years he hadn't given it much attention, hardly any conscious thought, but he always knew hope was there, like a life preserver hanging on the wall which he passed every day but never used.

And sometimes, just sometimes, he too had cried out just as these voices were doing, and only because he knew he would be heard.

"You know," he said to the city, "there really is an answer.

I mean, here I am talking about Evil and right and wrong, and here we all are wailing about how tough life is and what a joke it is and how much it hurts, and you know what? If there weren't anybody to hear us, we wouldn't be whining like this. If . . . if I didn't truly believe in some ultimate Good, I sure wouldn't be having trouble with Evil. I wouldn't try to fight it. No, I'd just let it go, I'd accept it. I wouldn't be looking for answers because there wouldn't be any."

He leaned against the wall and peered intently into the night scene below him. Could they hear him? No matter. "But listen to me . . . There is an ultimate Good. There's a God, and He cares about us; He cares about all this mess we're into. If you're hurting, well, He's hurting too, because He's fed up with the evil, He's fed up with the pain, and I think He wants to fix it, if we're willing to let Him."

Behind him, so quietly he didn't hear it, the door to the apartment opened. He was so troubled and distracted when he got home that he'd failed to latch or lock it.

"God's patient, sure, but He's righteous too. He's laid down the law, and He did it for our good, and what we need to do is quit playing games by our rules and get our acts together and do things His way again. It's our fault we're in this mess!"

John felt he would weep over the city. He didn't know where these thoughts and feelings were coming from, and he didn't really care. He just had to express them. He had to spill his guts.

"He's . . . He's God, you know? But listen, He's compassionate, and He's gracious, and He's slow to anger and full of love and . . . and faithfulness too! He'll stick by us. He loves us, and He'll forgive us if we just turn to Him and trust Him. Sure, we've rebelled against Him, we've gone our own way, and we've . . . well, yeah, we've sinned. I'll say it. We've sinned, and we're all feeling it tonight, right? Well, let me tell you, God is holy, and He won't leave the guilty unpunished. Just look at us! Our fathers got lazy about God, and now we're away from God altogether, and our kids . . . they don't know where they are! You don't think we're paying for our sin?"

He was starting to weep. Though he'd been able to contain himself when he felt sorrow for Rachel the waitress, he felt no need to contain himself now.

"Listen, we need to wise up, because God won't help us if we're going to keep pretending with Him, throwing His name around and acting like we're praying, because He won't take it. He'll just hide His eyes from us, and we can pray all we want, but He won't hear us because . . ." He could see it so clearly now. "Our hands are full of blood! Annie's blood! Dad's blood! How can we claim to be good when there's blood on our hands? We need to do some real cleanup."

Someone came in and silently closed the door behind him.

John didn't notice. He had to get something off his chest. "In the Bible God says, 'Come now, let us reason together. . . . Though your sins are like scarlet, they shall be white as snow. Though they are red as crimson, they shall be like wool.' We've sinned against God, but His Son paid the penalty for us. Jesus is the Lamb of God who takes away the sins of the world. He can be our peace and our comfort, and He can wash us clean—"

Then he noticed. He spun around expecting a demon. It was Carl, standing in the middle of the living room, frozen in place, looking like he'd just seen the burning bush.

John just stood there himself, looking at his son's awestruck expression and unable to come up with the first word of a coherent explanation.

Carl spoke first, his voice quiet and quaking. "You . . . uh . . . forgot your coat. I was going over to . . . well anyway, I came by here and . . . here's your coat . . ."

Carl held it out to him. It was Dad's old overcoat, the coat Dad gave to John the last time they were together.

John reached out and took it, and then he held it with tears in his eyes, looking out at the city. Carl came and stood beside him, looking the same direction, not saying a word.

John knew he'd have to say it. He'd have to admit it. "I'm just like Dad," he said.

fourteen

CARL kept looking at his father, and though for an instant he thought he shouldn't be staring, he rebuffed that notion with the weightier thought that he was entitled to all the staring he wanted. "What did you say?"

John had had enough trouble saying it the first time. "I said . . . I said that . . ." John's gaze dropped to the floor. He didn't want to say it again. "I gotta sit down."

Carl moved toward the living room. John passed him and sank into the couch, still holding Dad's old overcoat. Carl sat in a chair opposite him and tried to relax a bit. He was staring so much he had to be making his father nervous.

"Carl," John said in a near whisper, not looking at his son but at the coffee table, almost forcing the words out one at a time. "I . . . have heard voices . . . Lots of voices, all crying and wailing in pain and despair and pleading for help. I've heard them all over the city." He paused just long enough to denote a new paragraph. Carl didn't insert a comment or question. "I heard a gal at work screaming for help when she wasn't really screaming for help. I saw . . . you were there for this one . . . I saw a question in the TV script that exposed something politically damaging to certain parties, but I asked it anyway, and it turned out that what I said was true. I knew . . ." He had to take a breath and calm himself. "I knew that Rachel Franklin, the waitress, was hurting and grieving over someone named Annie. I felt her pain, and it was all I could do to keep from crying right there in front of you. For some reason I was right about that too, and you know the rest of that story. I saw people, hundreds of them, being sucked down into a black pit at the mall. I already told you and Mom about that one. And tonight . . ." John had to think about how to express it. "Tonight . . . I didn't hear the voices again, but I knew they were crying anyway, and I knew those voices belonged to real people out there in that city who are hurting and without hope, and somehow I just had to tell them there really is hope because there's a God. God! Can you believe that? I haven't been to church—of my own free choice anyway—since I was nineteen, and here I am, telling them about God, and . . . it was like every sermon I ever heard from my church-going days came back to me, because it all came rushing out as fast as I could think of it, sometimes faster, and I don't know that I've ever carried on like that before."

John looked at the overcoat he still held in his lap. "And so I said, 'I'm just like Dad,' because . . . what I was doing when you came in . . . that's what your grandfather used to do, all the time, so much that it drove me bananas." He looked at Carl. "And now . . . I'm wondering if I'm going to end up like him—a prophet who can't help but speak, and . . . I don't want to, and I'm scared of what's happening to me."

"What if it's God?" Carl asked.

John gave that some thought, then looked at the coffee table again, tired, beaten, despondent. "Well . . . I would almost prefer that to . . . uh . . ."

"But didn't Grandma say God was talking to you?"

John recalled it. "It would be nice if He was. Maybe we could discuss this whole thing; maybe I could negotiate to get my brain back."

Carl pressed it. "But . . . all the things you've seen, and what you were saying tonight . . . Dad, it's all true."

John gave Carl a testy look. "Son . . . an entire shopping mall being devoured by a black . . . vacuum cleaner?"

"But maybe it meant something."

John nodded with recollection. "I believe you were the one who gave the interpretation. People running from annihilation and death or something . . ."

"And what you said tonight . . . You believed it, didn't you? You were crying, Dad. You had to believe it. You had to mean it."

Now John found himself staring at Carl. "You . . . uh . . . you want it to be God, don't you?"

Carl considered the question, but could only look away, unable to answer.

"Hey, come on," John prodded. "There's nothing wrong with that. I don't blame you."

Carl turned back toward his father and cried, "Don't you believe anything?"

"Well . . . sure I do. I believe in God."

"So tell me about Him. Where is He? Does He care about us? Does He even give a rip?"

"I don't know, Carl."

Carl pointed toward the city. "That's not what you told them."

"Oh, come on. What I told them was just . . . Well, I don't know what it was."

Carl's eyes were filling with tears. "Well, do you believe what you told them or don't you?"

Forced to think about it, John knew the answer. Of course he believed. Every word he'd spoken to the city that night was his own. The pain was from his own heart, the thoughts from his own mind, the conviction from his own soul. But all these things had been buried and neglected, so far from his mind, for so long that their sudden resurrection caught him unawares. His answer surprised him even as he spoke it. "Yeah, Carl, okay, I believe it. Every word of it." Then he added, "I just don't know what stirred it all up."

Carl's eyes softened at the answer. "Maybe God is talking to you!"

"Hey, easy now, easy! Listen, everything I said tonight is out of the Bible. I learned all that stuff in church, it's in my head, it's buried in there somewhere. So I wouldn't say God sent it straight to me tonight on a lightening bolt."

Carl nodded toward the city. "So why were you telling it all to them? What was that all about? And what was Grandpa doing?"

John dug hard and deep for an answer. "Carl . . . I need time to think about it. It's not like a guy can go through something like this and just—wham!—have it all figured out." With great hesitance, he continued, "What if it really is God? I mean . . . I can't even fathom that. Can you imagine what it would be like to come around a corner one day and boom—there's God, right there. I mean, let's consider what we're saying."

At any other time the notion of actually bumping into the living God would have brought a chuckle and a not-so-serious discussion. But right now, in this place, in this time, it brought a stunned silence. What if . . . ? What if . . . ?

Carl ventured, "But haven't you known God before? You went to church with Grandma and Grandpa all those years."

John only shook his head. "I don't know, Carl. Hey, blame it on me—maybe I didn't pay enough attention—but right now it doesn't seem like the same thing. In church we talked about Him, we sang about Him, we read about Him, we gave testimonies about Him, we had emotional fits and shouted hallelujah . . . But what would we have done if God came right into the room and we all met Him face to face? It's one thing to feel the sunshine, but it's another thing to fall into the sun."

Carl asked in all seriousness, "Are you afraid of Him?"

"Wouldn't you be?"

Carl thought it over. "I don't know Him, and right now I'm feeling pretty small. Yeah, I guess so."

John looked down at the overcoat again. "But I do believe in Him, Carl, and if you really pressed me on it, I'd have to say I believe everything I ever learned in Sunday school and church. It's just that I've had it all tucked away for a long time and I'm not clear on it . . . except for one thing, and for now it's all I can say to you: Because I believe in God, I believe that Good, what's right, is worth fighting for. Sometimes, at least for me, what's right is a little hard to nail down, but I do believe it's worth fighting for, and I think God is pleased when we do."

Carl's eyes teared up again. "All right. That'll do for now. Thanks."

The next day Carl stood before a fresh canvas and found himself actually painting something. Trees. A forest scene. A stream. Mom Barrett's big maple was visible through the windows, just now building to a finale of red, gold, and yellow, and today it struck him: *This is beauty.* Yesterday he would not have seen it. Beauty had been an elusive concept, a vague, unknowable ideal, a myth conceived out of vain wishes. But today there was beauty. It was really there, in and of itself. Before it slipped away or his eyes closed to it again, he hurried to bring it inside with his brush.

Sunday afternoon John called Mom Barrett to arrange a time alone with her, a time they could talk without outside interruptions.

"Well, how about right now?" she asked.

"Is Carl there?"

"No, he's gone for the day. He's got some artist friends he wants to meet with, so I don't expect him back until tonight. You ought to come over now."

"But what about evening service at the church?"

"Son, you're more important. Come on over."

He got right over there, and he and Mom sat down at the same round table in the dining room where many a family conference had been held.

"How're you feeling?" Mom asked, and John knew it wasn't a mere formality.

Considering that they were alone, and that neither one of them would live forever, and that one of the family had already passed on without a chance like this one, John figured it was time to be as open as he could be, to take some risks and get some things said and heard.

"Well, Mom . . ." John pulled out a crinkled sheet of paper on which he'd scribbled some notes. He wanted to make sure he covered everything before the opportunity was lost—or before he chickened out. "I'm feeling like . . . Well, Mom, I need to talk things out."

She nodded. "Okay."

John looked at his notes. "Uh . . . first thing you ought to know is that the brass at the station are expanding the show. Tomorrow the Five Thirty goes to one hour, from 5 to 6, with some big TV and print promotion, more exposure for me and Ali Downs, and a raise."

Mom was genuinely pleased. "Oh, that's very exciting."

"Yeah . . . exciting is right."

Mom took a careful look at him. "You don't seem too excited."

"Well . . . you remember the last time I came in here by myself . . . after I had that flashback or whatever it was at the mall?"

She chuckled. "Oh, I sure do."

"You said that maybe God was talking to me."

"I still think that."

"Okay. Well then, two things: How do you know it's God, and secondly . . . did Dad ever have experiences like I've had?"

Her eyebrows raised just a little. "You mean there's more?"

He nodded. "A lot more." He looked at his notes. It was confession time. "I was alone in my apartment one night . . . the night before I had lunch with Dad, the last time I ever saw him alive, and . . . I heard all these voices outside . . ." He then recounted everything: the voices in the night, the time he heard Tina Lewis "screaming," the weird scripted question that wasn't in the script, the vision in the shopping mall (which she already knew about), and then the strange experience of just the other night. "I was preaching, Mom. I mean, I just about sounded like Pastor Thompson used to sound . . ."

"Pastor Thompson?" Mom almost laughed. "Ohhh, yes. Yes, I remember his preaching."

"I do too. Yeah, I listened once in a while—and that's what I sounded like. It was unreal. But it hit me, and I told Carl—Carl was standing there, wondering what in the world I was doing—I told him . . . I remember I said, 'I'm just like Dad.'"

Mom went "Mmmmm . . ." and gave a slow, thoughtful nod.

"Mom . . . I'm getting a raise, I'm getting more exposure, more responsibility, and do you know, Ben Oliver—that's my boss, he's the news director for Channel 6—Ben Oliver called me into his office this week and actually wanted to know if I was losing my marbles. He'd heard about some of this stuff, and Mom . . . the pressure's on, and I've got to know . . ."

"John, you're not losing your marbles."

"Well, that's nice to hear, but how do you know?"

Mom was already on her feet. "Let me get something to show you."

While John sat there worrying and wondering what to say next, she went to the back hall closet, rummaged through the photo albums and scrapbooks, and returned with an old spiral notebook. "Remember this?"

He began to recall it as she slid it across the table to him. He recognized his own handwriting—the juvenile version—on the cover: *The Private Journal of John Barrett, Junior.* He hadn't seen this in years, but Mom, of course, saved all this stuff.

"You used to guard this thing with your life," she said with a twinkle in her eye. "But—I forget when it was, maybe when you turned thirteen or so—you quit guarding it and left it lying around until I put it away in the closet."

John began to page through it. It was like a time capsule. Here were the thoughts, feelings, and scrawlings of John Barrett, Jr. during the ages of nine through ten, along with some doodles, some drawings, and even a few stories, including "The Lazy Dinosaur Who Wouldn't Work," "Who Ate My Apple?" (complete with illustrations), and "Sam's Big Feet."

John felt he was holding a real treasure, of course. "Incredible."

"Find July 19th, 1959," Mom said.

Even as John turned the yellowing pages to the journal entry he'd made on that date, the memory, some thirty years old, came back to him.

It read, "Tonight I heard God speak and I saw a vision of the Lamb of God who takes away our sins. Tonight I gave my life to Jesus. I am a new creation in Christ, and whatever God wants me to do, I will do it, because I told Him He could have my life and He could use me. Haleluyah! I can't wait to see what wunderful things God will do in my life."

Mom was ready to make her case. "I remember that night, and Dad always remembered it. I remember how you went forward at the Sunday night meeting and prayed at the altar, and Dad prophesied over you."

John nodded as the memory slowly reassembled, pieces at a time.

"You see, son, we can forget our promises, but God doesn't forget. A thousand years is as a day with Him, so what's a mere thirty-two years?"

How comfortable it would be, John thought, how nice, to retreat into his usual skepticism, give Mom an indulging smile, and walk away from her theory. Had there been no rude intrusions into his soul and mind by . . . whatever it was . . . he could have done that. He was well practiced at it. But now, with the journal entry before his eyes, he remembered that night in the summer of 1959. He remembered his prayer and the intensity of that moment—the little church, the close, sweaty smells, the smooth, lacquered surface of that prayer rail, the praying saints, Sister Ames playing at the piano. He could recall his vision, hallucination, whatever, of that little lamb standing right in front of him, so real he thought he could touch it, its eyes so gentle and lucid. He could hear once again Dad's prophetic words, the cadence of Dad's speech and the timbre of his voice.

And it struck him how last night felt so much like that night thirty-two years ago.

"I remember I said, 'Use me, Lord.'"

"Well," Mom said, her hands folded on the table, her expression gentle, "you asked me how I know it's God, and this is one reason. You've been fighting it, I know, but I think God is holding you to your promise."

John figured he should at least explore Mom's theory. "So . . . if you're right . . . am I going to end up like Dad?"

Mom was wondering if she should be offended. "Oh? And how is that?"

"Well . . . that last time we had lunch, he told me he'd heard the cries of lost souls. Has he ever had experiences like mine?"

"For years."

John's mouth dropped open. "For years?"

Mom nodded.

"Well, how come I never knew about it?"

She gave a little shrug. "You were never around. You were away at college, and then you took that radio job in Wichita . . . and then the TV job in Los Angeles . . ."

"But he never told me. He never said a thing about it."

"What if he had?"

The answer was clear, and it was only under Mom's unrelenting gaze that John admitted, "I would have said he was crazy."

She nodded. "You have been known to say that."

John had to know for sure. "Was he, Mom?"

"What you really want to know is, are *you* crazy?"

"I have no doubt that I got it from him. I just want to know what it is."

She shook her head. "John, you didn't 'get it' from him. You don't inherit it like . . . like your noses being the same or something. It's more like a legacy. Dad wanted you to have a ministry like he had. Remember when he gave you his coat?"

John almost did a double take. "His coat? That old overcoat?"

"That was the prophet's mantle."

"The what?"

"The prophet's mantle. That's what Dad called it. He got the idea from the story of Elijah. You know, when Elijah's time to leave the earth approached, he took his mantle and put it on the shoulders of Elisha, his successor."

John remembered. "Come on," Dad had said, "humor your religious old man." John considered the Barrett estate and how everything—the bank accounts, the stocks, the house, the business—had been cleared of debt and put in Mom's name before Dad was killed. "Do you think Dad knew he was going to die?"

She thought for a moment. "That's one thing he never shared with me, which I can understand. All I know is, when it did happen his house was in order and he was ready." Then she added, "And you had his coat."

John had heard enough. He wanted to close the subject. "Okay. All right."

"I'm not finished, John."

By the look in her eye John knew he was going to get an old-fashioned talking-to. "If we're going to 'talk things out' like you want, I've got a few things to say too. Son, if all you want to believe is that you're crazy like your old man, then . . . are you listening now? . . . you could be missing your very last chance to get right with God. Now I agree that what's happening to you is extreme, but if I'm right, and if your father's prayers and my prayers are really being answered right now—if God is speaking to you, you would be the greatest of all fools if you harden your heart against Him. You hear me?"

She was going to get an answer out of him if she had to sit there all day.

He obliged her. "Yeah."

"Okay, now here's another thing: I'll grant that you're fooling your public. They see you on that TV and they think, Well, here's a man who knows what's happening, who's in control of his life. But, John, you aren't fooling me, and I guarantee you, you aren't fooling God.

"You've cut yourself off from life, John. You're like a branch cut from a tree, and you're going to wither up and die if you don't get reconnected. You know all those voices you heard? How do you know one of them wasn't your own? Are you listening to me?"

One thing about Mom's lectures, John could never get too old for them. This was Mom at her best, as only she could be. He wouldn't have taken it from anyone else. "Oh, I'm listening, Mom. You're . . . uh . . . you're doing just fine."

Mom paused to let it sink in, then began again. "John, I'm sorry I have to be so blunt with you, but . . . well, maybe that's part of being a prophet, or a prophet's widow. You get used to being direct and saying what needs to be said because no one else will do it." She leaned forward and spoke gently, urgently. "And, John, that means you can make enemies. There are people out there who will not appreciate honesty, who will not want to hear the Truth. They're the ones Jesus said would flee from the light lest their deeds be exposed. They don't want you exposing what they're doing. But that's what a prophet has to do sometimes. He has to lay bare the secrets of men's hearts so they'll know they're sinners and get right with God, and that can be a miserable job. You can make enemies."

John received the warning. But the warning also made him think of Dad and another question John had on his list. "Was that true in Dad's case? Did he have enemies?"

She didn't take her answer lightly. "I believe he did. Prophets are never without enemies."

"Any idea who they might be?"

She almost laughed. "Well, where would you like me to start? I have over thirty years to cover."

He smiled back. "Then how recently? Anyone who may have meant him harm recently?"

"You mean, who may have killed him?"

John wasn't sure he heard that. Then again, he knew he did. "Well . . . yes."

She shook her head. John didn't want to disturb Mom with his theories.

"Well . . . of course, I'm not saying he was killed . . ."

"No, John. But that's what you're thinking, and that's what I'm thinking."

John had to doublecheck. "You think Dad was killed?"

She nodded.

"You mean murdered?"

"Yes."

"What makes you think that?"

"What makes *you* think that?"

John felt they'd skipped a question in here somewhere. "I . . . uh . . . well, I do think he was killed. At least I lean heavily in that direction."

"Which is something those pipe racks never do."

Another surprise. "You know about the pipe rack?"

"I know about all of them. I helped your father buy them and set them up when we moved into that warehouse sixteen years ago. I know what they'll do—stand there for years—and what they won't do—dump over for no reason when no one but Dad is there. And I went down there and had Chuck show me what was left of that pipe rack, and he told me about the forklift theory."

"He told you about the—"

"Now, now, I asked him directly, and he knew he'd have to tell me. I'm his boss now, remember? But I do appreciate you wanting to spare me some pain."

John was stuck for a moment. He still had some things to learn about his mother. "So, okay . . . any theories, Mom? Why would someone want to kill Dad?"

"I don't know. But I have faith that someday we will."

"But what about . . ." John hesitated. "Mom, I hate to ask a question like this, but . . ."

She shook her head. "John, all your father ever did was sell pipe. He never sold drugs or laundered money or did anything else that would make him a criminal." Then she chuckled and said, "Except for blocking abortion clinics. He has done that."

"What about his friendship with Max Brewer?"

"They spent a lot of time together. Dad was hoping he could find out who killed Annie. You know about that."

"What about Max Brewer's circle of acquaintances or enemies? I wonder if Dad crossed any of them?"

She shrugged. "Son, I think you and I know basically the same things, and God knows the rest."

John gave a wry smile. "And I'm supposed to be a prophet. Do you think God will tell me?"

She could only answer, "Son, God will do as He pleases." And then her eyes twinkled as she reveled in the thought. "You can count on that."

Monday John reported to the station at 9 in the morning, quite early for him. His regular shift began at 1 in the afternoon, but this was the week of the Big Push, as Ben Oliver called it, and he and Ali Downs were scheduled for some photo and video promotional shoots.

The news set was already undergoing some changes. A crew of carpenters, tool belts jingling and saws screaming, were tearing out a whole wall to make room for the camera boom, a giant, mechanical arm supporting a robotic camera that would provide an extreme high-angle shot of the news set and then swoop down on the cast of performers for a dramatic entry into the show. One of the conceptualizers for the project was even pondering how to combine that moving shot with another taken from Chopper 6 as it swooped down on the Channel 6 building, creating the effect of one continuous swoop from the sky, through the roof, and into the news set.

"The viewer must have no doubts," Ben said, "that this is NewsSix! No other station can top this one!"

In front of a bank of monitors with still pictures pasted over their screens, Ali Downs was ready for the camera, looking stunning as usual. John looked good, all made up and suited up and ready to sell the news. Marvin the photographer, a chubby, bearded, fretting little man in a purple T-shirt and blue jeans, had several strobes, umbrella reflectors, and floods set up, and now he was peering through the viewfinder of his big camera on a tripod.

"I want news, I want action, I want . . . I want intensity," he chattered. He would have made a good acting coach. "Okay, now read that copy."

Ali and John had some dummy scripts and looked at them.

"Ali," Marvin said, waving his hand at them, "you're checking a story with John. You're concerned about its accuracy, okay?"

Ali held her script for John to see it. "John, what do you think of this? I don't trust the source. And look at that spelling!"

Flash.

"Hmmm," said John, furrowing his brow at the script. "Does this reporter work for us?"

They both cracked up. *Flash.*

"Hey, come on, come on, let's get serious!" said Marvin.

John read from the script, "A retarded chicken hatches a billiard ball, that story coming up next!"

"Yeah, that's good, that's good." Marvin kept peering down through the viewfinder. All they could see was the top of his head. "Now look at me. Make me trust you."

"I wouldn't lie to you," said Ali in mock seriousness. *Flash.*

They smiled. *Flash.*

They looked at the script again. *Flash.*

They posed with a TV camera. *Flash.*

John in shirt sleeves. *Flash.*

Ali close-up, jotting notes. *Flash. Flash.*

"Wet your lips and smile." *Flash.*

"Lean forward, John. Ali, move in." *Flash.*

"Okay, turn this way a little. Closer together." *Flash. Flash. Flash.*

Then the video shoot. Mounted cameras, hand-held cameras, high angles, floor angles, close-ups, traveling shots. News in the making. Faces full of business—the world's going to end if we don't get this story out, working, editing, rushing about, hand-held shots racing through the newsroom, quick conversations, zoom-in shots of John, then a blurry pan, then Ali brought into focus and zoomed in some more. Intensity, intensity, more intensity. John with sleeves rolled up, banging away at the computer, not just taking but tearing news copy from the printer, nodding in agreement with no one in particular. Ali busy at work, then consulting with a reporter (over the shoulder shot), then a wry, you're-not-fooling-me smile at someone off-camera.

Ben dropped in from time to time to get a taste of what was brewing. His orders were clear and crusty at the start of the day: "*Sell* it." So the strobes kept flashing, and the video cameras kept grinding, and John and Ali kept looking busy, intense, and outstandingly honest. Ben didn't say much, but his narrowed eyes and tight smile indicated he was pleased.

That same morning, before Leslie had to report to the station for her shift, she and Deanne Brewer met at the Westland Memorial Hospital, walked down long halls past numbered doorways, work stations, patients in wheelchairs, a green plant or two, and much inscrutable art, turned corners, took elevators, read floor directories, asked directions, and finally found themselves in Medical Records, a pleasant, glassed-in office with six desks neatly arranged and quiet people seated behind them shuffling papers, marking files, answering phones.

At the nearest desk a lady named Rose with neon-red hair asked if she could help them, and they asked her for Annie Delores Brewer's autopsy report.

"Do you have a release form?" Rose asked.

Deanne had it ready. She'd gotten it the day before, and she and Max had filled it out meticulously, answering a volley of questions: who they were, where and when they were born, where they now lived, where they worked, their income, their Social Security numbers, any run-ins they may have had with the law (Max had had a few).

"And I'll need some picture ID," Rose instructed. Deanne produced her driver's license. Rose then typed Max and Deanne's names and numbers into a computer and waited for the results.

The results were immediate but not good. "That file is not accessible."

Leslie wasn't surprised. She had to hold her tongue.

"What do you mean?" Deanne asked, her temperature rising.

"It's protected under the privacy laws."

"But I'm Annie's mother!"

Rose only shook her head. "I'm sorry. The document is not accessible."

Deanne was visibly angry. "Now wait a minute! You are talking to Annie's mother! Her blood parent!"

Rose only raised her hands and shrugged. "By law the autopsy report is not accessible to the parents if it contains certain information protected by the privacy laws."

Now that was interesting. Leslie asked, "Certain information?"

"Yes."

"And just what kind of information would that be?"

Rose played dumb, and very poorly. "Oh, I would have no idea. It could be anything."

Deanne knew she was addressing one tiny wheel in a very big machine, but she had to lecture somebody. "Well listen, my husband and I have been through the wringer with this hospital before, and we've been put off and shuffled around and given excuses and told all kinds of things that we can't do and can't know and can't ask and can't find out, and I am getting sick of it, you hear?"

Rose didn't like being lectured. "Mrs. Brewer, if you wish to see the autopsy report, you'll have to come back here with a court order. Otherwise . . ." and her long fingernail tapped the counter with each word, "the file is not accessible."

Deanne's face sank as she began to lose hope.

"Wait a minute," said Leslie. "What about the pathologist who performed the autopsy? We'd like to speak with him."

Rose shook her head. "He's legally barred from saying anything."

Leslie lost no momentum. "His name is Denning. We'd like to speak to him please."

Rose sighed. "You're not going to like this either—he's not here anymore."

"Then can you tell us where he went? We'd like to contact him."

"Well, all we have is his office number here at the hospital, but like I said, he doesn't work here anymore."

"What . . ." asked Deanne, "did they fire him?"

Rose was getting impatient. "I don't know, Mrs. Brewer!"

"What about a home phone number?" asked Leslie.

Rose smiled apologetically. "I'm sure we wouldn't have it, and even if we did, I couldn't give it out."

Deanne waxed sarcastic. "Woooooo, you have been a world of help today, sugar!"

Leslie checked her watch. She had to go. "Come on, Deanne, let's get out of here."

Deanne was not ready to leave. "But I . . . there has to be something we can do."

"Yeah, there is. We're going to get a lawyer." Leslie glared not so much at Rose as at the bureaucracy she represented. "We'll just have to take the gloves off."

fifteen

TUESDAY morning, John met Max and Deanne Brewer at the law offices of Hart, McLoughlin, Peters, and Sanborn, attorneys-at-law, located in a remodeled, turn-of-the-century mansion of brick, rough beams, and stucco.

"We're here to see Aaron Hart," John told the receptionist.

"And then I'm outa here," Max muttered, his eyes exploring the deep carpets, ornate woodwork, heavy oak doors, and fancy fixtures. "How much this gonna cost?"

"We can't afford an attorney," Deanne said flatly. She was having second thoughts as well.

John urged, "Well, just talk to him first and see what he says."

A young man with thinning, neatly parted red hair and a dark blue suit walked briskly into the room and extended his hand toward John. "Hey, John!"

John shook hands with him. "How you doin', Aaron?"

Deanne tried not to gawk at Aaron Hart. Max gawked and didn't care who knew it. Who was this wimpy white kid, and what was he doing in a place like this? He was so short his tie hung below his belt.

John turned to Max and Deanne and introduced the attorney. "Max and Deanne Brewer, I'd like you to meet Aaron Hart. He's a good attorney, and he's pushed some important papers for me on more than one occasion."

The wimpy white kid extended his hand. "Hi—glad to meet you."

Deanne rose and shook his hand, feeling timid despite herself. Max stood boldly and towered over the attorney, giving him a firm handshake and staring him down a bit.

"Why don't we step into my office?"

"You're a lawyer?" Max asked.

"Yes, sir."

"How much you gonna charge us?" Max demanded.

Aaron didn't mind answering. "That depends on what I do.

Why don't we talk first—that won't cost you anything—and then we'll know what I can do and whether you want me to do it. Fair enough?"

Max stole a glance at John, whose face and little shrug answered, Fair enough—sure, what the heck.

"Okay."

John said, "Okay, I've done my part." He touched Max's shoulder. "Hear him out. He'll deal squarely with you."

Max nodded.

"Keep in touch." And with that, John made his exit.

"Right this way," said Aaron Hart.

Max and Deanne followed him down the wainscoted hallway to a bedroom-become-office where he offered them two comfortable chairs in front of his desk.

"Can I get you anything?"

They decided on coffee. Aaron called someone named Linda on his intercom and made the request.

Then he relaxed in his chair, picked up an NFL paperweight to play with, and said gently, "John told me about your daughter. I'm very sorry."

"Thank you," Deanne answered. Max just nodded.

"John's told me a little bit about your case. Why don't you tell me what happened and how I can help."

It took time to establish trust, to find the words, to feel right about this appointment, but as Max and Deanne got into their story and Aaron Hart showed a genuine interest and concern, the images, feelings, and frustrations they'd experienced since May 24th gave them plenty to talk about until they were almost crowding each other to share everything replaying in their minds. With tears of sorrow and sometimes a raised voice of anger, they worked through it until finally arriving at the bottom line, the reason for this meeting: their daughter was wrongfully dead. What could they do?

Sometime during their story, Linda had brought the coffee. Now Aaron moved his cup aside and began to scribble on a legal pad, thinking a little out loud, a little on paper. "Hm. So . . . the first thing you want to do is make sure Annie died due to negligence on the part of the Women's Medical Center, and in order to do that you need to find a legal way to get Annie's records from the clinic."

Max and Deanne exchanged a consulting look, and then Max answered, "Yeah, that's one thing," and Deanne added, "I just want to stop that clinic so they don't hurt somebody else."

"Mm-hm." Aaron stopped scribbling and thought for a moment. "Well, initially you have two courses of action. The first is to file a lawsuit against the clinic, but . . ." He smiled whimsically. "Kind of a Catch-22 in that. You can't sue the clinic unless you have a case against them, and you can't build a case against them unless you have Annie's medical records to prove she got her abortion there, and you can't get those records without filing a lawsuit so you can subpoena the medical records as part of the discovery, which you can't do unless you have a case, which you don't have without the medical records . . ." With a waving of his hand he concluded, "Let's forget that idea."

He leaned forward and wiggled his pen in his hand as he spoke. "There's a simpler way to do it which would not involve a lawsuit, and that's only because—and please pardon me for saying this—it's only because Annie is now dead. If she were still alive, then her abortion would have been a fundamental right, and any records or chart the clinic might have on her would be protected and confidential, even from her parents. Only Annie herself could request them. But now, since she's dead, you can take steps to stand in her place legally and request her medical records."

Aaron got lively and animated, as if telling a story, talking with his hands. "Now, anytime somebody dies they usually leave something behind, something they owned. That's called their estate. If you own a big house and three cars and you have a couple million in the bank, that's your estate—that's what's left when you die. If you own the clothes on your back, one ballpoint pen, and two nickels, that's your estate. So Annie had an estate too, and that's what we'll be working with."

Max and Deanne did a quick mental inventory.

"She didn't own much," Deanne said.

Aaron only smiled, undaunted. "Well, that's what I'm getting to. She did own one thing that's important to us now, and that's a claim for damages she may have suffered at the Women's Medical Center. But I'm getting ahead of myself.

"Here's what we can do: we can file a probate of your daughter's estate. Now probate is the process of transferring assets that your daughter owned at her death, which is no big deal since she was a minor, your daughter, and didn't own much anyway, but it would still provide a legal way for you to get those records. You could have yourself appointed as the personal representative of Annie's estate, meaning you'd be standing in her place to . . . we call it 'marshalling' . . . it would be your duty to marshall the assets of the estate, which means to figure out what the deceased person owned, what monies, property, and claims she owned or had a right to at the instant of her death.

"And it's the claims part of Annie's estate we're going after here. One of her assets left behind for you to marshall is a potential claim for damages from the doctor, the nurse, the abortion clinic, whoever's responsible, and you, as the personal representative of your daughter's estate, would not only have a right but a duty to determine whether or not Annie had a valid claim. Are you with me so far?"

"I'd be standing in for my dead daughter," Max said.

"Right."

"And that means her right to an abortion and privacy, that'd be *mine*. Those records would be mine."

"Once you're appointed as personal representative of her estate, yes. You've received enough information to cause you to believe that she has a claim against the clinic as an asset, and in order to marshall that asset, you'd have to have those records, and the clinic would have to produce them."

Max liked the sound of this. "Gotcha."

"How do we do that?" Deanne asked, a glint of hope in her eyes.

Aaron went back to his legal pad and started a list. "Okay,

first thing would be to get one of you appointed as the personal representative of the estate. We could get those papers prepared and then have you in to sign them and then file them with the court to get you appointed.

"In the meantime we would draft a letter for you to sign, a Request for Medical Records. The letter would state . . ." Aaron scribbled it down as he said it. ". . . that Annie was in the medical clinic for medical treatment . . . that you've been appointed as the personal representative of her estate . . . and . . . in order to settle her estate, you need to obtain her medical records. We would enclose a check for, say, twenty-five dollars, to cover copying costs. So you would send them the letter, and . . . well, usually a clerk in a hospital or clinic handles that routinely and releases the records, but I'm not sure how routine such a request would be for an abortion clinic." Aaron hesitated just a little, then mused, "With a little luck, the clinic's records custodian would just fill the request and none of the clinic's bigwigs would ever see it. But if things don't go our way the people in charge are going to know about it real quick and then you'll have to deal with them."

"Well, I'll tell you one thing," said Max. "I ain't mailin' them nothin'. I'm takin' that letter in there and puttin' it right in their face."

"Well . . . these things are routinely handled through the mail, but . . . I can understand your going there personally. I don't recommend it, but . . . sure, I understand."

But Deanne had a problem with that. "Babe, you can't go in there."

Max deflated with a recollection and cursed. "Excuse me. I've given that clinic trouble, Mr. Hart. The judge said he would jail me if I didn't stay away from there. I can't go."

"How about Deanne?" Aaron asked. "Is she under any judge's order?"

Max laughed at that. "No . . . no way, she's too good a woman for that." He grabbed her hand when he said it.

"So we could make Deanne the personal representative. Is that all right with both of you?"

"So *she* takes the letter and puts it right in their face?" asked Max.

"Well . . . I imagine she would be courteous about it, but . . . yes, she could go."

Max and Deanne consulted each other with their eyes, and it was all right.

"Good enough. Now, Linda's our paralegal, so if you decide you want to go with this, she'll prepare the documents in the next day or so to get you appointed, and then she'll call you. You'll have to sign several papers to have you appointed by the court as the personal representative of your daughter's estate. Now while all that's going on, I'll prepare a letter for you to sign, a Request for Medical Records. Once your appointment goes through and the letter's drafted and signed, you'll be all set to go to the clinic and get the records.

"Now, do you think that's enough?" Max and Deanne started thinking about it, and Aaron further clarified, "If there's anything I've left out, or anything you need to have explained, or any other action you want to take . . ."

Deanne asked, "What if they really did kill Annie? I mean, what if we can prove it? How can we stop them?"

"How can we *get* 'em?" asked Max.

Aaron scribbled some more. "We have another lawyer in our office, Bill McLoughlin, and all Bill does is personal injury claims such as this one. Tell you what—let's get those records first, and then, having proof from which to build a case, I'd like to turn this claim over to Bill for further action. For now I'll run this by him and see if he thinks of anything else we could be doing at this time to get those records."

Max held up his hand to call a halt. "Well, this all sounds fine, but . . . we gotta talk money here."

Aaron smiled. "Yes, there is that final detail. Well, we're willing at this point to proceed on this as a contingent fee case. That means that our fee is based on a percentage of the recovery. No recovery, no fee. Our usual percentage is thirty-three and a third percent. You'll have to pay for our out-of-pocket expenses, but we can defer those in most cases until the case is over. Once our investigation is complete and we see what's there, we'll sit down with you and map out the case. Or, if there isn't enough, we'll advise you not to proceed. If you're willing to go ahead on this basis, I'll have Linda prepare an agreement along those lines."

Max and Deanne exchanged another consulting look, and then Max answered, "Let's do it."

Thursday afternoon, close to 4 o'clock, Tina Lewis gave Leslie's notes a quick, cursory scan and then tried to hand them back. "Hm . . . Yeah, Erica's right, you don't have a story here."

Leslie wouldn't take the notes back, but left Tina holding them in midair. "Now wait a minute, Tina. You hardly even looked at it."

They were in Tina's office. Tina was seated behind her desk, busy, now interrupted, and about to become irritated.

She dropped the notes on Leslie's side of the desk just to be rid of them. Now she was getting angry. "You don't have a story. Who's going to believe a bunch of allegations made by an unknown, anonymous, alleged witness who won't even appear on-camera, who can't prove a word of it? This isn't news, it's abortion baiting, it's inflammatory. You don't have a story!"

"I have a family who lost their daughter!" Leslie tapped on the notes with her finger as she spoke.

"So what do you have that's solid? We can't go on the air with severe allegations like this and nothing to back them up, no one to appear on camera, no proof. We'll have the pro-choicers all over us—not to mention our peers, anyone out there who still has some respect for fair journalism!"

Leslie was ready to fight for this one. She picked up her notes and flipped the pages to the last item, holding it toward Tina to show her. "Tina, had you given my notes a fair reading, you would have seen that the Brewers have taken legal steps. The mother, Deanne, has been appointed as personal representative of Annie's estate, and she'll be hand-delivering a Request for Medical Records to the Women's Medical Center tomorrow morning. Now if some records do turn up and the Brewers can prove Annie was really there, we'll have some strong pieces to fit together, to build into something. All I'm asking is to be there at the clinic with a camera to get some footage we can use if this thing develops into a story. Hey, how often do we get to be there right when a story is breaking?"

Tina probed, "And of course you're not after an anti-choice piece?"

Leslie took that like a slap in the face. She recovered, leaned on the desk, and spoke in a controlled voice. "Last week we did a story on new home construction rip-offs, and before that we reported on that dental clinic using poisonous amalgam in its fillings. Now, when there could be a case of malpractice so severe that a young woman is dead . . ."

"We don't know that."

Leslie pressed on. "But we're close to finding out, and I think it's worth looking into, regardless of our political positions. I'm not talking about a woman's right to an abortion. I'm talking about current abortion industry standards and safeguards, or the lack of them, a subject that would be of great interest to our viewers. Hey, why did we wave all those coat hangers at all those rallies if we can't be sure women are really getting safe abortions?"

Tina's expression remained hard, but Leslie had prevailed enough to make her pause. She looked at Leslie, then at the notes still lying on the desk, and finally, with a sigh of resignation, picked up the notes and looked them over carefully. "Who's this . . . Judy Medford?"

"Annie Brewer. 'Judy Medford' was her alias. A lot of the girls use false names to protect their privacy."

"What about the autopsy report? Where's the real one?"

"Deanne Brewer and I went to the hospital on Monday, but they'd misplaced it, couldn't find it. We still haven't heard anything."

Tina gave a concessive sigh and rested against the back of her chair. "So . . . Annie Brewer's mother is now the legal personal representative of her daughter's estate." Tina sat and stared. It seemed this was something new to her.

Leslie was glad to know something Tina didn't. "As such, she now stands in the place of her daughter and has a legal right to her daughter's medical records. The clinic has to release them. They can't hide behind their usual confidentiality."

Tina smiled wryly—it was almost a smirk. "Well, you'd better hope the Brewers get something for all their trouble or you won't have a story." And then for emphasis, "Right?"

Leslie conceded, "Right. But it's worth a little time in the morning. Let me have it, and then I'll cover another story the rest of the day."

Tina studied Leslie for a moment, thinking it over. "Okay, I'll authorize that much. You haven't sold me yet, but . . . let's call this a test drive, and that's all it is."

"That's all I'm asking."

Tina turned to her computer console and called up the Next Day Story Outlook. She typed in Leslie's photographer request, followed by the letters, HP—NFAT, which stood for High Priority, Not For Air Today. The entry would clue in the assignment desk the next morning, and a cameraman would be reserved for Leslie's use for this story as well as her regular assignment.

All set. Leslie felt giddy as she left Tina's office. Now where was John? He'd want to know.

It was 4:30. The Five O'clock was coming up fast, and people were scrambling around the newsroom to assemble twice the amount of material as before and have it ready half an hour earlier. Hal Rosen sat at the weather desk putting his graphics together in the computer, watching the clouds moving off the blue ocean and over the green continent, swirling in time-lapse animation. Another monitor showed a weather map with temperatures all around the state, wind velocities, and precipitation. The five-day forecast wasn't on the screen yet. No sneak previews this time.

"Hal."

"Nnyehh." He wasn't entirely verbal when he was working on his maps.

"Have you seen John?"

"Yeah, lots of times."

"Any idea where he is now?"

Hal turned and smiled mischievously. "Try the set. They're tinkering with the lights or something."

Leslie hurried around the big plywood backdrop and into what was beginning to look like a Disneyland ride or a scene out of "Star Trek." The set was wide, expansive, awesome. The backdrop had been extended upward as high as the ceiling, but the lighting gave the illusion that it stretched upward forever, far beyond the eye's reach. The news desk was roughly the same shape as the old one, but this one seemed to hover there like a spacecraft, carefully planned shadows and angles hiding the supports underneath. To top it all off, high above the set, poised like a steel tyrannosaurus, was the camera boom, a new state-of-the-art robotic camera perched precariously upon it, ready for that big swoop-down shot to open the show.

John, Ali Downs, and Bing Dingham the sportscaster were all sitting at their places, along with Walt Bruechner, the late-night news anchor, sitting in Hal Rosen the weatherman's usual spot. Mardell the floor director was pointing and directing the camera operators as they experimented with different angles, dollying this way, then that, back and forth. Up above, on a narrow catwalk, a lighting technician adjusted some floodlights.

"Heads up, John," said Mardell, and John looked up at Camera Two. "Give me more wash from the right."

"From the right," echoed the lighting tech.

Leslie gestured to Mardell and mouthed the words, "Is it okay if I talk to John?"

"Sure, come in and sit in the weatherman's chair for a minute. Walt, you can take a nap now if you want."

Walt jumped from his chair. "Ah, thank you so much! I need my beauty sleep."

Mardell cracked, "Better make that a long nap."

Walt waved at Leslie with the same motion one would use washing a windshield. "Hi there, bye there."

She ducked under his waving arm, scampered across the

floor, stepping over cables and gaffer's tape, and took Hal Rosen's chair on the right end of the news desk.

"Okay," said Mardell, "pretend you're Hal."

Leslie sat up straight and smiled at Camera Three. She muttered to John, "I talked to Tina and she gave me the okay to shoot the request for records tomorrow."

John sighed a worried sigh. "I don't know if you should have done that. The story isn't ready yet, and you know the policy. We don't have to pitch it to anyone until we have everything."

Leslie felt defensive. "John, I couldn't wait for a free camera. Deanne's serving the request tomorrow morning, and I've got to have a camera there when she does it."

"It's your telling Tina that bothers me."

"Well, that was Erica's doing. She didn't have a camera to spare during the day shift, so the only thing I could do was ask for one extra stop in my schedule, and Erica wouldn't approve that unless Tina approved it."

"Ohhh."

"So I tried, okay?"

Mardell paced back and forth, eyeing the set's colors, textures, balance. "Looks good. Bing's heinie's in the dark, though."

"I beg your pardon!" said Bing, and they all laughed.

"Yeah," said Nate the light man, "let's shine some light on that subject. Be thankful, Bing, it's your best side."

Leslie leaned toward John and spoke quietly. "Well, Tina isn't sold on the idea yet, but she said I can get the footage, so I've got the assignment for tomorrow morning."

John nodded, still looking toward Camera Three. "Well, we're gambling. Something really solid would be nice."

"Or we don't have a story. Tina was clear on that."

"She doesn't like abortion stories."

Mardell called, "Okay, everybody straight ahead—let's try the boom."

The intercom from the control room squawked, "Hurry it up—we've got fifteen minutes."

"Fifteen minutes, everybody," Mardell echoed. "Okay,

straight ahead. Look busy." They looked straight ahead; they looked busy.

Leslie whispered, "Well, this story's different, and I think I can convince her of that."

John touched her hand to caution her. "But don't say anything to anyone, okay?"

"Let's roll it," said Mardell. "Music: Tumm . . . didi didi didi dahh . . . Bring it down!"

In the monitors they could see the aerial shot of themselves, taken through the camera high above them on the boom as it began to descend. It was a marvelous sight, like a lunar landing.

"That's good, that's good!" Mardell shouted in glee.

John whispered to Leslie, "I think this is going to be an ambush story, if you know what I mean. We don't want the clinic to know."

Leslie's eyebrows went up. "Right."

Mardell ordered, "Look this way, you two!"

They both smiled at Camera Two, along with Ali Downs and Bing Dingham.

"Okay," said Mardell, "one more time, with the theme music!"

The camera boom lifted toward the ceiling for another swoop. Then came the music, busy, *big,* sounding like *news:* Didi didi didi daahhh, Boom Boom, Didi didi didi daahh . . .

"And now," came a voice over the music, "The City's most up-to-the-minute, most accurate newscast from the City's Premiere News Team, NewsSix at Five, with John Barrett and Ali Downs!"

You couldn't help but be impressed.

sixteen

The Women's Medical Center was housed in a two-story brick structure in the midst of a quiet neighborhood of older houses and new apartments. The shrubbery lining the front walkway was neatly trimmed, there was an attractive lawn between the building and the sidewalk, and in the center of the lawn the clinic's sign was mounted in a matching, understated brick pedestal. To someone driving by, the clinic could have been a dentist's office, a counseling center, even a law firm—a Mercedes and two BMWs were parked in reserved stalls in the black-topped parking area.

But as Leslie, Deanne Brewer, and Mel the cameraman stood across the street in the cold, gray morning, knowing what they knew, the building had an imposing, ominous feeling about it.

This was Friday, and, as was their custom, two women and a clergyman, pro-lifers, were on the sidewalk ready to counsel and, they hoped, dissuade any women or girls who might be approaching the clinic. Right now there were no patients approaching, and the three appeared to be praying.

Leslie was dressed properly to appear on-camera—if not for this story, for the next one. Deanne was dressed to show she couldn't be intimidated. And Mel wore his usual jeans and army jacket. Leslie and Mel had come in one of the NewsSix cars, a little white fastback with the show's logo emblazoned on its sides. Deanne had come in her own car.

Mel knew the gist of the story and set to work, the camera perched on his shoulder, walking up and down the street to get some establishing shots of the building and the pro-lifers.

"Oh, and be sure to get some shots of those cars," said Leslie, pointing at the BMWs.

She brought out her reporter's pad and jotted some thoughts for possible voice-over. "The Women's Medical Center, contrary to appearances, is not a peaceful place. This is where two oceans of sentiment and conviction clash with opposing tides. Anywhere else, the issue of abortion is debated, even fought over, in abstract terms, but here it is felt, it is seen. Here is where words become actions and sentiments become deeds."

Too wordy perhaps, but it was how Leslie felt right now. The whole area was tight with tension.

She gave her watch a nervous glance. It was 8:25. The clinic had been open since 8.

"Deanne . . ."

"Mm-hm." Deanne was visibly nervous, trying not to crinkle the envelope that held the Request for Medical Records.

"I think it would be a good idea to get a shot of you going up the front steps of the clinic while no one else is around."

"By myself?" She didn't like that idea.

"It's an establishing shot, something to give the viewer the idea of you going into the clinic with your letter."

"But aren't you going in there with me?"

"Sure, I'll go with you, but I'm the news reporter, so I can't be in the picture."

Deanne crinkled her face with puzzlement. "Huh?"

Leslie tried to explain. "Well, you see, it's not you and I who are requesting those records, it's you. I'm the reporter covering the story, I'm not part of the story. So when we shoot this and then show it on TV, we'll probably have me saying something like, 'Deanne Brewer, legally appointed as personal representative for her daughter Annie's estate, hand-delivered a request for her daughter's medical records,' and while the viewer hears me reading that off-camera, they see you going up the front steps and through the door."

Deanne looked across the street at the clinic and the front walkway. "I have to walk through the door all by myself?"

"No. You can stop before you open the door. We just need a shot of you walking down the sidewalk and up the front steps with that letter in your hand."

She shook her head. "Man, this is like Hollywood."

Leslie admitted, "Well, it's . . . it's television. We have to give the viewers something to look at. We have to have pictures of what we're talking about."

Deanne shook her head, shrugged, and said, "Okay . . ."

"Oops. Hold on." A car pulled into the clinic's parking lot. Mel was a short distance up the sidewalk. Leslie waved to get his attention and then pointed to the two young women getting out of the car. One was dressed in sweatpants and a jacket. She was probably the patient; clinics often advised their patients to wear loose, comfortable clothing to their abortions. The other young woman was probably the friend who would drive the patient home.

The women immediately encountered the three pro-lifers, and Mel caught the scene as a short conversation ensued on the sidewalk in front of the clinic. *Good grief,* Leslie thought, *those people stand out there and do that all day long!* She jotted another note in her notepad. ". . . where women still come to exercise their right, but not without confrontation . . ."

The patient and her friend ended the conversation abruptly and brushed by the pro-lifers. Mel followed them with his camera until they went in the front door.

"Well, okay," said Leslie, "let's shoot it and then let's do it."

She advised the pro-lifers of what was coming, and they were happy enough to serve as extras on the sidewalk, subtly holding their signs toward the camera and being peaceful.

Deanne walked down the block until Leslie said she was far enough, then turned around and walked back toward the clinic, the letter visible in her hand, not knowing where in the world to look as Mel backpedaled in front of her, the camera on his shoulder, capturing her "performance." When she got to the front walk, she turned and approached the clinic's front door, hoping Leslie would say, "Cut" before she had to open it. Mel stayed on the sidewalk, now shooting her walking away from the camera, toward the clinic, while Leslie looked over Mel's shoulder, directing. Deanne felt better with her back to the camera.

She went up the steps and almost got to the door when Leslie called, "Good. Great. Come on back."

Relief! She hurried away from the door, glad it was over.

But it wasn't. Suddenly the drama became real. She heard

the clinic door open and a curt voice behind her demand, "Can I help you?"

Mel kept the camera on the scene as Deanne turned to face a stern-looking woman now peering out the clinic door at her. Deanne froze, clutching the letter in both hands, holding it close.

The lady gave Mel and Leslie a wary eye and said to all of them, "Unless you have business here, you'll have to leave."

Deanne thought of Annie and forgot about being nervous. She didn't like this lady's tone. "Are you open for business?"

"Yes, we are."

"Then we do have business here."

Now the lady was looking at the pro-lifers too. "What business?"

Deanne held the letter high. "A Request for Medical Records."

Mel kept grinding away. Leslie stayed behind the camera. This was great stuff.

The lady was still staring icily at the pro-lifers. Deanne demanded her attention again. "I'm not with them! I represent myself and my daughter's estate, and I'm here on my own business!"

This lady wasn't quick to believe her. "So what about the camera there?"

"If you don't want your picture taken, why don't you invite me in and close the door?"

The lady considered that for about one second and then said with a jerk of her head, "Come on."

Deanne looked over her shoulder at Leslie. "Come on, Leslie, let's go."

"Uh-uh, no way!" said the lady.

Deanne objected, "She's a friend. We go way back."

"She's press! Don't try to fool me!"

Leslie had come alongside Deanne by this time. "I would think by now that you were used to the press dropping by from time to time. Besides, have we ever hurt you before?"

The lady studied both of them. "Why are you here really?"

Deanne answered, "I told you. I have a Request for Medical

Records, and I'd like to have it taken care of." She looked at Leslie. "And if I have a friend along, well, that's my choice, isn't it?"

The word "choice" seemed to work. The lady hesitated, then swung the door open. "All right, you can come in, but the camera stays outside."

Leslie and Deanne went up the steps. Then the lady blocked their path. "You don't have any hidden microphones on you, do you?"

Leslie only laughed. "You watch too much television."

The lady let them in. Mel switched off the camera and waited.

The waiting room was large, with enough chairs to handle at least a dozen patients, if not more. The young woman who was driving for her friend was the only one in the room at the moment. She stole a quick glance at them, then returned to focusing on nothing in particular. Here and there stood a large potted plant, and on the walls were posters of pleasant countrysides, fuzzy animals quoting witticisms, and happy, independent people who'd made the right decisions in planning their families.

The lady—her name badge said "Laurel"—walked across the room and stepped behind a white, formica-topped counter where a young receptionist busied herself with some patient charts and stayed out of the discussion.

"Now," she said coldly, "how can I help you?"

As Leslie stood at her side, watching and listening, Deanne opened the envelope and ceremoniously unfolded the letter. "I have here a Request for Medical Records for my daughter, Annie Brewer, also known as . . ."

"Annie Brewer's the name," Leslie cut in, catching Deanne's eye.

Deanne said no more.

Laurel smiled a meaningless business smile and replied, "I'm sorry. That information is confidential. We can't release it."

"Can we speak to the person in charge?" asked Leslie.

"I can make an appointment for you."

Deanne unfolded the letter just enough for the Hart, McLoughlin, Peters, and Sanford letterhead to show, and let Laurel see it. "Laurel, you aren't talking to the Weeping Mothers Sewing Circle. We're talking about legal action here. We want to see the person in charge."

Laurel seemed confused. "I'll have to talk to her. Would you like to have a seat please?"

"Thank you."

Laurel left the room, going through a big blond door that latched with a metallic clunk.

They took two chairs near the counter, not saying a word, and not hearing one from the young woman sitting across the room all by herself. She never looked at them, and they only stole quick glances at her. Without being told, they knew the unspoken rule: You don't know me, and I don't know you, and hopefully we'll never see each other again.

Deanne whispered, "They're not going to find anything under Annie's real name."

Leslie whispered back, "I know. I just don't want to let any cats out of the bag until we're eye to eye with the director."

The front door opened, and some cool air wafted in. They stole a glance to see three teenage girls enter. Two were hesitant and uncertain, their eyes on the walls, on the floor, on anything but other people. The third seemed more sure of herself. As her two friends found chairs and sank into them, she remained standing, looking for a familiar face. One of her friends began to whimper, and she bent down to whisper comfort to her. "It's okay—you'll be okay."

Laurel returned through the big blond door, stepping quietly but quickly into the waiting room. She came just close enough to Leslie and Deanne to say softly, "She'll be right with you," and then went straight to the three girls who had just come in. They had a hushed conversation, and then Laurel brought the two uncertain girls some forms on clipboards for them to fill out. One girl took time to read the sheet in front of her. The other girl just signed it.

Leslie and Deanne tried to be careful about staring, but

they were both thinking the same thing: Forms. Paperwork. Records. Clues.

The big blond door opened again, and a woman entered the room, her appearance immediately catching their attention. Beautiful? Yes, but in a perverse sort of way, with black hair oddly pin-striped with gray, cascading in waved locks over a snow-white silk blouse. Mascara and eye shadow made her dark eyes even darker, and her polished fingernails were long and curved.

"Yes," said the woman, "can I help you?"

"Come into my parlor," said the spider to the fly, thought Leslie.

Leslie stood to meet the woman, but stood alone. She looked back at Deanne, who remained in her chair.

Deanne had lost her strength. She was trembling.

"Hello," Leslie said to the woman. "I'm Leslie Albright, and this is my friend"—she reached and touched Deanne just to get her moving—"Deanne Brewer."

Deanne forced herself to her feet, took a few steps, and faced the woman with Leslie at her side. "Hello."

"Hello," said the woman, offering her hand. "I'm Alena Spurr, director of the Women's Medical Center. How can I help you?"

Deanne's hands were still trembling as she tried to get the letter out of its envelope. "I'm Deanne Brewer, and I'm here to get my daughter's medical records. I believe you gave her an abortion back in May . . ."

Ms. Spurr looked at Deanne with nothing but disdain in her eyes. "Brewer . . ." she said, now recalling the name. "Mrs. Brewer, I already told your husband that we had nothing to do with your daughter's death. I'm sorry it happened, but we were in no way involved. I just don't know how I'm going to get that through to you."

"You could take us through your records."

Ms. Spurr smiled the same business smile. "I'm sorry, but that information is strictly confidential and protected by law. We can't release it."

Deanne hesitated. Leslie was just about to speak for her,

but Deanne found some new strength and pressed ahead. "You need to look at this letter." She held it up for Ms. Spurr to see. "You see, since my daughter is dead . . ." Her voice cracked with emotion. She kept going, her voice clearing. ". . . I've been appointed as personal representative of her estate. So . . ." She took a breath and spoke firmly. "So you're not talking to Annie Brewer's mother. You're talking to Annie Brewer. And Annie Brewer wants her records!" Deanne read from the letter: ". . . 'any and all medical and other records in your possession, custody, or control which relate directly or indirectly to medical services or any other services provided or performed for the deceased, Ann Delores Brewer . . ."

Ms. Spurr's eyes were icy as she looked at Deanne, then the letter in her hand, and then asked, "Will that satisfy you?"

"It's the only reason we're here today. All we want are Annie's medical records."

"Very well. I'll tell you what. Just to satisfy you once and for all, I'm going to violate the rules and maybe even the law and let you come back into our office to see for yourself."

She went to the big blond door and swung it open, her posture inviting them to step through it.

They found themselves in a large hallway lined with shelves, supplies, some small work stations, more posters, and a weight scale. There were several rooms off this hall, but at the moment every door was closed. There was no sign of a nurse, or a doctor, or a counselor, or a patient, but behind one of the doors were muffled voices, and a machine was running with a low hum.

"Come this way please," said Ms. Spurr, hurrying them along. They followed her lead through a door into an office with voluminous file shelves against one wall. She entered after them and closed the door. "Now, you want the charts for Annie Brewer, correct?"

Deanne looked at Leslie, and Leslie nodded. "And for Judy Medford. That was the false name Annie used when she came here."

Ms. Spurr froze on the spot. "Excuse me?"

Deanne held up the letter again. "It's the last item, right

here on the second page. You might have Annie's records filed under her false name, Judy Medford. We'd like you to look under both names."

Ms. Spurr stood perfectly still, digesting this new development. Then with a slow, deliberate turn she called to a young woman, apparently a secretary, "Claire, we need to pull schedule sheets, patient charts, and consent forms for Annie Brewer and Judy Medford."

Claire hesitated, looking at Leslie and Deanne with a perplexed expression.

"This is Annie Brewer's mother," Ms. Spurr explained. "She has a lawyer's letter requesting her daughter's records."

Claire rose from her desk and went to the file shelves to look.

Ms. Spurr went to help her. "Let's just pull out the sections . . ." There had to be hundreds, if not thousands of color-coded folders, and with Claire's help Ms. Spurr pulled out an armload of them and brought them to a table in the center of the room.

Deanne stepped forward, anxious to find her daughter's name, but Ms. Spurr stopped her politely. "Excuse me . . . these files are private. If you'll give me just a moment, I need to cover the names—at least the last names—to protect our patients' privacy, you understand."

Deanne looked at Leslie, who nodded and said, "It's okay." Deanne stepped back while the two women spread the first group of documents across the table in a neat, overlapping row with just the patients' names showing. Then Ms. Adams covered the last names with some sheets of paper, leaving only the first names exposed. At her signal, Deanne and Leslie approached the table.

"You are seeing something no one else will ever see—I hope you realize that. These are the patient charts—all the information pertaining to each patient and the service they received, filed alphabetically. You'll notice the signed consent forms are included. We pulled everything from Ba- to Bu-, so Brewer would be in this group. You'll notice I've concealed the last names. I hope you'll scan them now and look only for the name of your daughter."

There were at least fifty charts. They scanned down the names. They did not find an Annie, nor a Delores. Deanne's face sank a little.

"How about Medford?" Leslie asked, hoping.

"All right, step back please," said Ms. Spurr, and then she and Claire repeated the process, laying out the other set of files in the same way as the first, again covering the last names. "All right."

Leslie and Deanne approached the table and scanned the names. Deanne's heart leaped. "There she is!" She pointed at a Judy about a third of the way through the stack.

Ms. Spurr carefully pulled that file from the others, looked it over, and then risked showing it to Leslie and Deanne. "Are you sure about your daughter's code name? This Judy's last name is not Medford. She's white, twenty-five, has two children already and a husband named Jack, and she was here a year and a half ago."

Leslie grabbed at a possibility. "Perhaps the first name was wrong. Are there any Medfords in here?"

Ms. Spurr's voice and expression were especially grim. "What I'm about to do is unlawful. But just to show you how serious I am about settling this matter . . ." She lifted the paper away from the files just enough for them to scan the last names. "I never let people see these records, and Claire is my witness, but here—let me pull these . . ." She pulled out about a dozen files to show them. "Here, see the names? Mavis, Meacham, Mead, McKling, Medina, Meaker, Melanetti, Melvin, Mendelson, Michaels, Mitchell, Montgomery. No Medford."

"But she's got to be in here somewhere," said Deanne.

Now Ms. Spurr actually used a comforting tone. "Mrs. Brewer, there are eight different abortion-providing facilities like ours in this town. Your daughter could have gone to any one of them."

Leslie had one more card to play, "What about the schedule sheet from May 24th?"

Ms. Spurr only sighed impatiently and pulled open a file drawer and thumbed through the tabs. She found the folder for May and withdrew it, then went through the schedule sheets arranged inside. "May 24th. This year, right?"

"Right," said Deanne.

She found the schedule. It was several pages long. She scanned it, saying, "I could simply tell you that we show no Annie Brewer or Judy Medford here, but I suppose you'll want to violate all policy and privacy laws and see it yourselves?"

"I want to see it," said Deanne.

Ms. Spurr held the pages so they could see them. "Please, quickly scan the names for your daughter's names, and try to forget the rest."

They scanned one page, and then the next. The schedule reflected about twenty to twenty-five patient names per doctor for that day.

Madonna. Leslie saw it but said nothing. The girl Mary, who told her story from behind a screen, had been here on the 24th of May, just like she said.

But there was no record of Annie Brewer or Judy Medford receiving any kind of treatment that day.

They prevailed upon Ms. Spurr to show them the schedules from the two days previous and the two days afterward, but found nothing.

"That's it," said Ms. Spurr. "That's all I have. I hope I've satisfied you."

Deanne didn't raise her voice, but did firmly inquire, "Did you destroy Annie's records?"

Ms. Spurr took the question as an insult. "Mrs. Brewer . . . this is a medical clinic. We do not destroy patient records!"

Deanne pressed ahead. "My husband Max was in here, and he gave you so much trouble he got arrested. You knew who he was, and you knew the name of his daughter. You could've cleaned Annie's records out of your files to protect yourselves."

Ms. Spurr's face turned to stone, and her eyes burned at Deanne. "Mrs. Brewer, first of all I deeply resent what you're suggesting. But if I must argue with you, let me tell you this, and I'll tell you only once: I could have cleaned out Annie Brewer's files only if her files bore her real name, which they didn't—you said so yourself. And you can ask your husband—he didn't say anything to us about anyone named Judy Medford. I imagine neither he nor you knew anything about that false name at the time. If you didn't know Annie used a false name, how would *I* have known it?"

Deanne was speechless—incredulous. It wasn't supposed to happen this way.

Leslie knew it was over. "C'mon, Deanne. Thank you for your time, Ms. Spurr. Sorry for the trouble."

"I'll see you to the door," Ms. Spurr replied.

As they walked out of the clinic, Mel got them on videotape.

"How'd it go?" he asked when they reached the sidewalk.

"You can put the camera away," Leslie answered. "We came up dry. Nothing. All bets are off."

Mel stowed the camera gear in the back of the NewsSix car and then watched from behind the steering wheel while Leslie saw Mrs. Brewer back to her car. It would have made a good shot if this were a news story: the clinic in the background, the pro-lifers still out there with their signs, and Mrs. Brewer weeping with her hands to her face, walking slowly up the sidewalk with the reporter holding her arm, trying to cheer her up.

What a mess, he thought. *Leslie got into this one too deep, getting that lady's hopes up like that, and now we have all this footage we'll never use and a lot of the day gone. Oh well. You win some, you lose some. This wasn't the first story to ever come up dry, no sir.*

When Leslie got back in the car, she was not too conversational.

"Well . . ." was all Mel said, not sure what he'd say after that.

Leslie cussed the whole thing off and grabbed the cellular phone. "Hey, George, we've just finished at the Women's Medical Center. Scratch it. The whole thing came up dry.

Yeah. We're heading for the next stop, Avalon Elementary, the self-esteem program. Are they ready for us? Okay. We'll grab that one and see you this afternoon. Car Twelve is clear." She slapped the phone back in its rack and went limp with pain and frustration. "Let's go."

Mel hit the pedal, and they sped away from the Women's Medical Center, passing a brown van carrying some high school girls. Leslie had immersed herself in her notes for the next story and didn't even see it.

seventeen

LESLIE got back to the station at just about noon, ready to sum up the day in one fabulously fluffy soft feature about Carol James, the second grade teacher at Avalon Elementary School who dressed up as Mr. Gullywump to teach kids that even though we sometimes feel we're nothing but a Gully-wump, there's a Beautiful Prince or Princess hiding inside every one of us if we're only willing to see him or her. Charming. Heartwarming. Great video. Mr. Gullywump put his big nose right up to the camera lens for a terrific comic shot.

Quite a switch from the story that could have been. She dropped her carrying case and purse on the floor under her desk and slumped into her chair. *Please,* she thought, *nobody talk to me, nobody ask me how my day went.*

She flicked on her computer terminal, trying to formulate a clever opening for the Gullywump story.

Halfheartedly tapping the keys, she came up with: "For children who feel rotten about themselves . . ." No. How about: "A second grade teacher has come up with a novel approach to teaching self-esteem . . ." Maybe, but she couldn't get excited about it. Then: "Of all the stories we could have covered today, we chose this one . . ." Followed by ". . . d;gl;a;oiwejt;lkahsd;gh . . ."

Leslie sighed and rested her brow on her fingers, her eyes closed, shutting out the world for a moment. All she could think about, the only thing she could see in her mind's eye, was Deanne Brewer, crushed and disappointed, walking that long, tearful walk back to her car, wondering what she would ever tell Max. In retrospect, Leslie knew she should have stayed with Deanne longer. They should have taken time to talk it out, depressurize, regroup. She never should have left Deanne in such a state.

But they didn't talk it out, they didn't regroup, and Leslie did not stay. She had the Gullywump story to do, the ever-so-important Gullywump assignment. Time was tight, deadlines were approaching, she had her assignment to do.

She had to call Deanne. That was all there was to it. They had to talk it out. It wasn't over yet. What about Mary, that anonymous girl hiding behind the screen? She'd been there at the clinic that day. Her false name, Madonna, was still in the records. Her story checked out. Everything else checked out.

Annie'd been in the clinic that day. Leslie was sure of it.

So why was there no record of it?

And why was Alena Spurr willing to go out on such a long, shaky limb to show them the records against all established ethics and procedure, unless . . .

The conclusion was as easy as it was disturbing. The clinic destroyed the records. Cleaned them out completely. They could have done it after Max first caused them trouble.

Okay, so how did they know to clean out Judy Medford's records?

"Leslie!"

Leslie looked up and saw . . . Tina Lewis, beckoning from her office door.

Leslie stared, then glared as her mind began to race. She felt she'd been hit with a brick. *Careful, Leslie. Don't jump to conclusions. You don't know for sure.*

Oh, don't I now! Didn't Tina see the name Judy Medford in my notes yesterday? Why that—

Careful! Leslie wanted to curse silently, but Tina was familiar with the language and would read her lips. She took a deep breath, composed herself, got up from her desk, weaved through the rows of desks and computer terminals, and followed Tina into her office.

"How'd it go this morning?" Tina asked, circling behind her desk.

As if you didn't know! "It didn't. We shot footage of the clinic and Mrs. Brewer approaching the clinic, some pro-lifers, some cars parked outside—the whole nine yards. But when we got inside, the Request for Medical Records came up dry. We didn't find a thing. It's a non-story."

Tina sat down. "Well, things have changed. It's a story now, and we have to run it."

That was like a punch in the stomach Leslie wasn't braced for. "Excuse me?"

"Abortion's a big issue in the gubernatorial campaign, and the candidates were talking about it today. On top of that, Channel 12 and Channel 8 got wind of what happened at the Women's Medical Center and sent crews down there. I hear they've interviewed the Brewers and the director of the clinic, and I suspect they're both going to be running a piece on it tonight."

Leslie could not help the accusing tone of her question. "I would be fascinated to know how they found out about it."

Tina shrugged innocently. "I guess the clinic called them."

Leslie repeated the words, having a very hard time swallowing them. "The clinic called them . . ." Would Tina actually spill a story to the competition just to make sure the story would run? Could she do such a thing?

Tina was still talking. "But, hey, who came up with the idea in the first place? We were right down there, right when it was happening. Mel tells me he got video of Mrs. Brewer walking up to the front door of the place. You've had a relationship with the Brewers for quite some time now. We could outshine the competition on this one."

"And I'm very curious to know the angle . . ."

"The abortion issue. Use the material you've gathered and put something together along the lines of, 'The abortion battle is still with us, and here's another example of it, another skirmish.' We'll tie it in with the campaign story."

Leslie tried to keep her voice down, but the content of her words imparted her rising fury. "Don't you mean something more like, 'another failed attempt by anti-abortionists to skirt the privacy laws'?"

"Well, if that's what happened, we should report it."

Leslie was just now beginning to believe she was really hearing this, and her acting ability was giving out. She could not hide her anger. "Tina . . . I told you what the story was about . . . malpractice . . . an innocent girl killed . . . parents at a loss, unable to do anything about it. That's the story I went after, and that story, as far as I'm concerned, is dead. It's over."

Tina gave a little shrug and a tilt of her head. "You got something else instead, and we can use it. So your work paid off."

Leslie was trying to find a thought she could actually speak. "I can't . . . Tina, the Brewers trusted me. They confided in me. I can't turn this story around and make it say something it wasn't meant to say."

Tina took on the expression of a perturbed schoolteacher and asked, "Leslie, I think the crusader in you is showing. We're talking about news here, not causes."

A slap in the face. Leslie had had too many of those lately, especially from this . . . this . . . executive news producer. She tried to control herself, but knew her hands were shaking. Now her voice quivered as very quietly, very carefully she warned, "Please don't try that one on me. I've been with this station for six years now, and you know me better than that."

Tina let the warning go right past her, as if expecting it. "Leslie, I gave you the story. It's still yours. All you have to do is finish it for the Five O'clock. There's still time to get an interview with Mrs. Brewer, and we've rushed a crew to the Women's Medical Center to get their comments. It's nearly in the can. All you have to do is write it, voice it, do the package."

Leslie knew, she just knew, that Tina already had another reporter lined up as she said, "Tina, I can't do it. I can't turn this story around like that. I couldn't do that to the Brewers."

Tina cocked her head in a carefree way and said, "Well, Marian Gibbons is ready to take the story if you don't want it. Just give her your material and the video from this morning and let her do it. That puts you in the clear, okay?"

"Tina . . . that was my story!"

"It's still yours—unless . . ."

"You know what Marian will do to it."

Tina demanded, "I don't have all day. Now do you want the story or don't you?"

Leslie rose from her chair and backed toward the door, afraid she might get sick. "I can't do it. I can't have my name on it."

"Then bring me the video so Marian can get going on it. We've got deadlines here." Tina picked up her telephone. Leslie hadn't moved yet. Tina glared at her. "Well? Let's get moving. You've got Gullywump to do, and I need to see that video!"

Leslie got out of Tina's office and hurried across the newsroom, weaving between the desks, bracing herself against a partition or a desk several times, afraid her legs would buckle under her. Then she dropped into her chair, sickened to the point of nausea. She had to think. What could she do? Did Ben Oliver know about this? Whose decision was it? She had to calm down before she talked to anyone else.

The little mailbox icon was blinking in the corner of her computer screen. She hit the keys that called up her messages. Deanne Brewer had called and wanted her to call back.

Leslie picked up the telephone and punched in the number. She had a pretty good idea what this would be about.

"Hello?" came Deanne's voice.

"Deanne, this is Leslie. How are you doing?"

Deanne sounded hesitant and troubled. "Well, I don't know. I thought we weren't going to have anything on the news, and now it looks like we will, and so I guess I just wanted to talk to you and find out what's going on."

"I'm . . ." Leslie didn't know how to sound or what to say. "Have you talked to any reporters yet?"

"I had people from Channel 8 and Channel 12 come by as soon as I got home, and now I just got through talking to somebody from your station."

"Marian Gibbons?"

"Yes. She said she was a friend of yours—"

Leslie's voice rose in volume despite her best efforts. "She's already been there?"

"Yes. She left about an hour ago."

Leslie needed a moment to let that sink in. "So you . . . you did an interview with her?"

"Yes, I did. She worked for Channel 6, so I was glad enough to talk to her, but I was wondering why she came here instead of you. Is this going to be on the news tonight?"

What else could Leslie say? "Well . . . I guess it is, Deanne. I guess . . . I guess things have changed."

"Well, I was surprised, but I guess it's okay. Marian was very nice. I was glad to meet her."

"So what did she ask you? What did you talk about?"

"Oh, just about everything. I told her about the Request for Medical Records and how we didn't find anything, and she asked me how I knew Annie died at the Women's Medical Center, and I told her about the autopsy report and what Mary said."

No, no, NO, Deanne! "You told her about Mary?"

Deanne got defensive. "I didn't tell her anything about Mary herself. I just said that we had a witness but I couldn't say who, and that the witness saw Annie at the clinic."

"And how . . . I mean, did Marian seem . . . sympathetic? Did she believe you?"

"Oh, I thought she was very nice."

As if that means diddly-squat, thought Leslie. "What about the other stations? Did they ask about the same things?"

"Well . . . they said they'd heard we had some concerns about the Women's Medical Center and they were doing a story on it, and they wanted to know what we'd been doing and what we knew."

"And you talked to them on-camera?"

"Just standing on the porch. I didn't let anybody inside—my house is such a mess right now, and I didn't have a chance to clean."

"What about Max? Was he there?"

"He's still at work. I called him, but you know, he's out in the shipyard and can't come to the phone right away. He'll call me when he gets the chance."

"What did they ask you? Can you remember?"

Deanne got flustered. "Aw, Leslie, this day's just been so

crazy, I don't know which end is up . . . I don't know what I said."

Leslie tried to calm her own voice for Deanne's sake. "It's okay, Deanne. It's all right."

"So when's this gonna be on TV?"

Please, don't watch it, Leslie thought as she answered, "Five o'clock—Channel 6. I don't know about the other stations."

"Well, guess I'll turn it on and see how I did."

"Deanne . . ." Leslie stopped.

"Hello?"

"I'm still here. I was just going to say . . ." *Go ahead, Leslie. Tell her not to trust newspeople. Tell her not to trust Channel 6.* "Well, we'll see how it turns out. But don't expect too much. I'm working on another story, so I couldn't do anything on this one. I don't know how it's going to turn out."

"Well, at least people are going to hear about it."

"Yeah. Yeah, they'll . . . they'll hear about it." Leslie hung up. So the story was well on its way, out of her hands before she even surrendered it, taking whatever form Marian Gibbons determined it should have. Tina Lewis was never one to waste any time with foot-dragging reporters. This shop seemed to be full of people like her.

Tina would be coming after Leslie's video any moment if Leslie didn't get it to her. Leslie reached into her carrying case and withdrew the cassette Mel had shot that morning, the story that could have been. Shots of the clinic, of Deanne walking up the sidewalk and up to the front door, of the pro-lifers holding their signs. Now Deanne Brewer would see pictures of herself on the Five O'clock, but Marian Gibbons would be voicing a different story.

Leslie held the cassette on her lap, feeling a strong sense of ownership. This was *her* work, *her* time, *her* effort. This was also a token of trust. It carried images of a dear lady only because that lady trusted Leslie.

Leslie hesitated. Oh, if only she could—But . . . no. She was a professional, and this job demanded painful decisions at times.

Tina wanted this cassette, and right away. Leslie could envision her patronizing expression and her outstretched hand.

And that image persuaded Leslie to at least explore the notion pressing itself upon her heart and mind. She took a pen and poked it into a tiny slot on the side of the cassette, pressing a release button so that the cover flipped open. Now the playing surface of the tape was exposed. Yes, she thought, it would be easy for something bad to happen to this tape.

Like what? Well, somebody could put their fingers right on it . . . and they could even pull it out of the cassette . . . and there could be an unfortunate accident . . . and they could pull the tape out . . . like this . . . and like this . . . and like this . . . and like this!

The process started slowly, and she felt like a bad little girl who shouldn't, but after the first ten feet or so she yanked and pulled with a vengeance, with a blind leap into angry, reckless irresponsibility. This one's for Deanne, and this one's for Max—oh, this was exhilarating! —and this one's for me, and this one's for John, and . . . and this one Tina can shove right up her nose!

"This story will not have my name on it!" she said to herself. "Right is right, and wrong is wrong, and . . ." She lapsed into words of fiery judgment.

"What are you doing?" came an alarmed voice behind her. She jumped, startled, caught in the act. But it was John Barrett, staring at her, his face full of questions.

She didn't wait for him to ask. She just started reporting as she gathered the strewn tape into a brown tangle at her feet. "The story's been hijacked!"

"What—"

"We were there at the clinic this morning and gave them the Request for Medical Records, and the files were clean, absolutely clean—no Annie, no Judy, nothing, and I'll tell you why. It's because that woman in that office over there, that Tina Lewis, tipped them off! She heard the whole story from me yesterday. I told her all about Annie Brewer, and I told her about Annie's code name Judy Medford, and by the time we got to the clinic this morning they knew we were coming and they had the files picked clean and made us look like dumb pro-life idiots—just that easy, cut and dry, neat and clean, and . . . and guess what? Now we're newsworthy!"

John pulled a chair over and sat close to listen. Leslie was too upset to slow down. "And you know what else I think? I think Tina leaked this story to the other stations, because now they're on it, which is Tina's way of making sure NewsSix is on it. But it's not my story, no way! It's not going to have anything to do with malpractice or what happened to Annie. It's going to be about the . . . the vicious witch-hunt by anti-abortionists that failed, and it's going to rub their noses in it, that's what it's about. And Marian Gibbons is going to write it and voice it and do the package because I won't, and that means the Brewers and Annie get used. Used, that's all, and then dumped."

"Marian's doing the story? How did she get it?"

"Tina wants it run, but I won't have my name on it! I didn't go after this story to have this done to it."

She could see John looking at the pile of tape on the floor and explained, "This is the footage from this morning. *My* footage. This is the story that never was, and it's going to stay that way!" She got to her feet, her arms draped with loop upon loop of tape. "Excuse me. Tina wants this video right away."

John stood just to keep from being run over. "Leslie! You . . . you can't take her a ruined pile of tape!"

"Bump into me, will you please?" She didn't wait. She bumped into him. "*Oof!* There, I've had an accident. She'll understand."

And with that, she was off for Tina's office, dragging several feet of tape behind her, parading through the newsroom, drawing stares, questions, even a few laughs, heading for disaster, maybe the loss of her job.

"Leslie!" He had to stop her. He took three steps . . . And then he stopped. By now the whole newsroom was watching. He looked back at them.

"What's going on, John?" asked Dave Nicholson, the consumer specialist.

John looked toward Leslie, still heading for Tina's office, then back at his colleagues, still waiting for an answer. The roof was falling in on the Annie Brewer story, and if Leslie made it to Tina's office with that pile of videotape, everything and anything was sure to hit the fan. His first instinct was to run, as if fleeing from a leaking gasoline truck before it blew. *Back off, get away, stay clean.*

He went with his first instinct. He was still clean. He faced his colleagues . . . and shrugged, his arms upraised in befuddlement. He shook his head. He didn't know. He went—fled, actually—to his desk to await the storm.

Meanwhile, Leslie stepped briskly into Tina's office and without introduction, explanation, or invitation let the tape tumble and pour onto Tina's desk. Tina jumped from her chair as if someone had spilled coffee in her lap, her arms upraised, her mouth and eyes at full width.

John could hear Tina's expletives from his desk clear across the newsroom. His hand was shaking as he turned on his computer and tried to get to work. A futile notion, of course. There was no way he could concentrate on his tasks, not with this going on. He had to get involved; he had to stand by Leslie and hopefully diffuse this explosion.

But he still sat there, strangely paralyzed, unable to move. If he went in there now and sided with Leslie . . . He could just see Ben Oliver bursting in and seeing the lines drawn, hearing the accusations, seeing that pile of ruined videotape. He and Ben had reached an understanding, and if John were to be associated with Leslie's behavior . . .

What to do, what to do? Perhaps the best thing, the professional thing, would be to wait, to let the storm subside a bit, and then carefully and calmly step in—if invited—and help all the parties sort it out objectively, professionally. That's what John Barrett, news anchor, would do, and John was sure Ben Oliver, news director, expected no less.

So he waited, working on nothing except justifying remaining in his chair, until a wise and rational endeavor occurred to him; he needed information. Yes, information. He couldn't jump into this thing without all the facts, right? Remaining safely in his seat, he scrolled through the story lineup for the Five O'clock: the gubernatorial campaign, a body found up on Highway 16, an apartment fire on Magnolia Hill . . .

Oh-oh. "Abortion battle." The story was slotted in the computer already. John looked around the newsroom but didn't see Marian anywhere. She might still be on the assignment. She had called in the lead-in: "As if to underline the debate over parental consent, one family confronted that issue head-on today in an unsuccessful attempt to pierce the veil of privacy at a local clinic. Marian Gibbons is live in front of the Women's Medical Center . . ."

You gotta be kidding. No. Please, no. So Marian would be live at the clinic, doing a stand-up before and after a videotaped package. But it got worse. John was the anchor assigned the lead-in and the scripted question at the end. It would be his face, his voice, his name framing the story. He was in this mess, like it or not.

Max Brewer wouldn't like it, that was for sure. Deanne Brewer wouldn't like it. Rachel Franklin wouldn't like it. Carl wouldn't like it. And Mom wouldn't like it.

And no, John Barrett wouldn't like it either. Not one bit.

The door to Tina's office was closed, but he could still hear some shouting going on in there.

He had to get involved; he had to enter the battle. Hopefully he could bring peace, perhaps a little reason. But he had to contain this mess. He had to stop it.

He took a deep breath and rose from his chair. Then he marched with the utmost sobriety and self-control across the newsroom toward Tina's office. The shouting became more discernible the closer he got, and by now no one in the newsroom was working.

Hal Rosen the weatherman was fascinated and not at all timid about staring toward Tina's door.

"I wouldn't go in there if I were you," he said, and then clawed the air like a scrapping cat, making the appropriate sound.

John approached the door anyway, but didn't get there

before the door burst open and Tina Lewis came strutting out, her jaw well ahead of her.

"Move, John, if you don't want to get run over!" she ordered with a wave of her hand.

Leslie was right behind her and caught John's eye. "John, you talk to her!"

John tried to head Tina off, blocking her path as politely as he could. "What seems to be the trouble here?"

Tina stopped but resented having to. "Don't you patronize me, you son of a—"

Another voice. Like subtitles. John could hear it—he could feel the pain in it.

The Tina in front of him was saying, "I know you and Leslie are in this together, so don't act so innocent. I'm taking you both to Ben. I've had enough of this—"

But as Tina unloaded on him from her storehouse of epithets and outrage, another voice cried in agony and fury, "Leave me alone! It's my life! How dare you call me guilty! How dare you remind me!"

John listened intently. The last time this happened, he was disoriented and confused. This time he was fascinated.

Leslie worked her way around Tina so she could face both her and John. She was trying to use a controlled, professional voice, but it still quaked with emotion. "I have confronted our executive news producer with several accusations, and she is understandably upset."

Tina spit angry words at Leslie along with an expletive.

But the accusations were true. John knew it. He could hear it, even see it. He could see Tina sitting at her desk, talking on the telephone, saying Leslie's name, consulting a slip of paper and pronouncing the name Judy Medford—M-E-D-F-O-R-D.

But what could he say? He didn't get the chance anyway.

"What the @$#!!*& is going on here?" Ben Oliver, news director, hater of waves and wavemakers, ultimate decider between life and death, had come out of his office, down the aisle, and right into the discussion, pouring out salty language where no further salt was needed. "My job isn't hard enough, now I've got to break up fights in my own newsroom?"

Tina immediately gathered herself together and got in the first word. "Sorry for the intrusion, Ben, but we have something here that needs to be settled."

Ben was unsympathetic. "What are we paying *you* to do?"

She countered skillfully, "Ben, I'm too upset, too wrapped up in this problem to be objective and professional. I need your balance in this."

Ben grimaced at that line, but listened anyway. "All right, what . . . what?"

"We have a story here that's—"

Leslie cut in, "I'd like to start please, so it can be told from the beginning."

Tina was indignant. "I believe I was talking—"

Ben pointed his finger right in Leslie's face. "You start." He pointed in Tina's face. "You finish. And I'll ask questions." He glared at John. "Are you in this too?"

John shrugged and looked bewildered. "I don't think I've heard it all yet myself."

"Then what are you doing here?"

"I might be involved."

Ben locked eyes with Leslie. "All right, talk, and talk fast."

Leslie rose to the challenge. "We were pursuing a story on possible malpractice at an abortion clinic. We had good reasons to believe that the clinic was responsible for the death of a seventeen-year-old girl."

"What clinic?"

"The Women's Medical Center."

"What girl?"

"Um . . . her name was Annie Brewer . . . an African-American."

"What reasons?"

"An autopsy report, for one thing . . ."

Tina broke in. "Hand-copied excerpts from an alleged autopsy report, incomplete, with the pathologist unavailable to corroborate."

Leslie pressed on, fighting for her life. "The pathologist's name is Mark Denning, and he was at the Westland Memorial Hospital where Annie Brewer died on May 26th. He performed the autopsy and filed the report—"

"Which can't be found," Tina added, "and neither can Denning."

"We also had a witness who was in the clinic at the same time and saw Annie get an abortion there—"

"Unwilling to go on the record or appear on-camera. And, Ben, ask her who the parents are."

Ben looked at Leslie for the answer.

"Max and Deanne Brewer."

That meant nothing to Ben. "So who are they?"

Tina provided an answer. "You might recall the governor's rally and the riot that broke out. Max Brewer was right in the middle of it and we got him on-camera, brawling and assaulting people. Prior to that he was jailed for assaulting people at the Women's Medical Center. The man is a pro-life fanatic."

John had to clarify that. "Now just a minute!"

Ben's eyebrows went up. "Oh, so you *are* part of this?"

John explained, "Max Brewer and my father were friends, and I don't appreciate—"

Ben put it together. "You're part of it. Hang on . . . we'll get to you." He looked back at Leslie. "Keep going."

Leslie was losing steam, knowing she was losing her case. "We thought we might have a story of malpractice. All the facts seemed to indicate it. So when the Brewers filed to become legal personal representatives of their daughter's estate and then took a Request for Medical Records to the clinic, we wanted to cover it in case something turned up and the Brewers could prove that the clinic was indeed at fault."

Tina countered, "And their legal tactic produced nothing. The Request for Medical Records came up dry."

Leslie stared daggers at Tina and said, "And we both know why, don't we?"

Tina looked at Ben and said, "The Request came up dry because the Brewers are unreliable, impulsive, and vindictive over the death of their daughter, and they're simply looking for a scapegoat, which happens to be, in this case, the

Women's Medical Center. I tried to tell Leslie that when she first came to me with the idea."

Leslie's face opened up as if she'd just heard a horrendous lie. "Ben! Mr. Oliver, I have good reason to believe that Tina Lewis—" Leslie stopped. Tina was looking toward her office, toward that pile of ruined videotape. Now she was looking back at Leslie.

Ben demanded, "What about Tina?"

Leslie withdrew visibly. "Nothing."

Ben studied both of them for a moment, then asked Leslie, "Are you finished?"

Leslie gathered up any remaining momentum and finished with, "I started pursuing the story because I was convinced there might be a problem at the Women's Medical Center. I knew the evidence was sketchy, and I was hoping the Request would turn up something. When it didn't, I figured the story was dead and I wanted to leave it that way and just let the Brewers be. Now Tina wants to turn it around—"

"I do not want to turn it around! I only want to report what happened—just what happened. We're already running the story on Slater and Wilson and their differences on parental consent, and I thought this would make a good sidebar. The other stations are running it, they've already interviewed the Brewers and the people at the clinic, they're all set to go, and I figured since we were there, right there, and had footage and good contact with the Brewers, it was our story—it was our idea in the first place. The problem here, as I see it, is that Leslie is interested in running the story only if it's to the advantage of the pro-life position, and I for one can't abide that kind of bias."

"Bias!" Leslie squeaked. "You're talking about bias?"

Tina butted right in. "And as for Max Brewer, he's already been in the news because of his behavior at the governor's kickoff rally. Leslie ought to know that; his brawling almost endangered her. He's newsworthy. We have video of him already."

John jumped in. "Now wait a minute! We've been through this before, remember? My father's on that tape!"

Tina jumped right back at him, "News is news, John! It happened!"

Leslie spouted behind them, "Tina, you're the one who made me shoot the story that way!"

And now all three of them were talking at once.

Ben heated up quickly and brought the meeting back to order with a nerve-quaking string of cusswords. "If you people don't shut up I'm gonna fire all three of you!" They ceased immediately. "Now I want to know what happened and that's all I want to know, and I don't give a rip what your political persuasions are, is that clear?" He pointed at Leslie. "You were there, weren't you?"

"Yes, sir," she answered, her voice greatly subdued.

"So tell me what happened."

Tina started, "They—"

Ben's hand went right in front of her face and she stopped.

"Tell me what happened," he told Leslie.

Leslie recounted the events of that morning as clearly as she could recall them, trying not to be biased but factual.

"So you didn't find anything?" Ben asked when she was through.

"That's right. We were hoping something would turn up—"

"See?" asked Tina. "They were hoping. She's clearly on the Brewers' side!"

Leslie tried to remain calm as she countered, "Deanne Brewer was hoping to confirm the cause of her daughter's death and the people responsible, and I was hoping to have a story. Neither occurred."

Ben digested Leslie's account for a moment, then asked Tina, "So what do you have on this?"

"Marian Gibbons went back today to get interviews from the clinic personnel and from Mrs. Brewer. She's doing the package for the Five and Seven O'clock, and we've slated her to do the story live from in front of the clinic."

"So did she get reacts from both sides?"

"Both viewpoints will be represented. I emphasized that with her."

Ben shifted his weight backward and looked them all over. "Then why don't you people just do your job like the reporters I thought I hired and leave your politics out of it?"

John raised a finger to be recognized and suggested, "Uh, Ben . . . why don't we just not run the story, or at least wait until we know more?"

Tina was right on top of that. "Ben, Marian is at the clinic right now, she's on location, and we've got a microwave truck out there. Besides, John is involved with this story personally, we know that. His father was a friend of Max Brewer, and it's obvious that he's been pursuing this with Leslie. The right thing, the professional thing, is to run the story despite personal conflicts. Besides, the other stations are going to run it, and the candidates are talking on the abortion issue. If we don't run the story, the question's going to come up why we didn't. Not running it will be more politically biased than running it."

Ben closed his eyes, shook his head, and put his hand to his forehead, muttering something about the sacredness of manure. Recovering—slightly—he asked Tina, "The other stations are running it?"

"Yes sir, both 8 and 12."

Leslie demanded, "And just how do you know that?"

Tina actually got cocky then. "Hey, that's part of what I get paid for."

John tried once more. "Ben, it really isn't that big a story . . ."

Ben snapped back, "Then act like it. All of you. Run the story . . . Tell it like it happened . . . Cover both sides . . . Let the chips fall where they may. Isn't that the job we all signed up for?" He saw John about to say something and cut him off. "And you, Mr. Anchorman, you're on the spot, you follow me? You've cost us a lot of money this week and you'd better be worth it. Got it?"

John got the message loud and clear. He nodded resignedly. "Got it."

"Now get back to work, all of you." Ben turned and went back into his office.

Tina made sure John and Leslie could see her triumphant smile before she went back into hers.

Leslie wanted to say something to John and he wanted to say something to her, but neither could think of a word. They returned to their desks in silence.

eighteen

FOUR forty-five. John checked his face in the huge, illuminated dressing room mirror, brushing on his makeup, straightening his tie, making sure he would look good for the cameras. *Keep smiling, John, whether you feel like it or not. Smile for all those people out there who trust you. You're the professional, you know, the man people trust to bring them the news, to show them what's really happening out in that big old world.*

In the newsroom Leslie sat at her desk, tapping out a tighter version of the Gullywump story for the Seven O'clock. It wouldn't take long, and then her shift would be over at 5, and she could go home . . . although she was planning on sticking around for a while.

Four fifty. John went onto the news set, its floodlights now coming to life and the camera operators rolling silently into place as they got their orders from Susan the director up in the control room. Mardell the floor director was there, headset in place, ready to take charge, and high atop the boom one technician readied the robotic camera for the big swoop-down shot.

Four fifty-two. Ali Downs took her place in the chair to John's left, looking over her script, making circles, underlines, and arrows to clarify late changes.

John had gone over the script, first in the computer and in the printout before him. He was ready. The candidates were going to be the top story tonight, followed by the sidebar story about the ongoing abortion battle. After he'd read Marian Gibbons' package he'd tried to swap stories with Ali Downs so he could do the candidates story and she could do the abortion sidebar, but she didn't like last-minute changes, and, not surprisingly, Rush Torrance wasn't tolerant of the idea either.

So now it was up to him to do the lead-in and the scripted question, professionally and objectively. He had no doubts that Ben Oliver would be watching to make sure he did. He even wondered if Ben had already ordered that John Barrett, the costly news anchor, would do the story and no one else.

But the Brewers would be watching as well, not to mention Carl. He would have some explaining to do, and it was not going to be easy.

If they'd only been here, he thought. *If they'd only seen all the factors involved, all the forces and interests and circumstances . . .*

Four fifty-four. Weatherman Hal Rosen joined them at the right end of the news desk, while sportscaster Bing Dingham took his place at the left end.

Four fifty-six. Time for the teaser that played right after the syndicated controversial talk show.

Mardell counted down, then pointed.

Busy music. Camera Two, four-shot of John, Ali, Hal, and Bing sitting at the news desk, ready to go. They were on the air.

John started. "Good evening. Coming up on NewsSix at Five . . ."

A videocassette began to roll. Governor Hiram Slater in a rather animated speech, followed by challenger Bob Wilson, even more animated.

John's voice over the video: "The race for governor is heating up over the abortion issue."

Video: The Women's Medical Center, followed by a close-up of Deanne Brewer talking on her front porch.

Ali read the copy over the pictures: "And the abortion battle rages on as parents try to break through the privacy barrier at a local clinic."

John intro'd Hal Rosen. "And Hal will have our weather, what there is of it."

Camera Three on Hal, close up.

He laughed apologetically. "Hey, what can I say? More of the same cool gray stuff, typical for this time of year, but the weekend does look better, so there is hope!"

Ali intro'd Bing Dingham. "And Bing Dingham will tell us what in the world happened to Billy Graylark."

Camera One, head-on to Bing.

"Billy's nursing his wounds, and so are his promoters.

We'll have highlights of the bout, and reactions from Graylark and Bengal. It sounds like they're still fighting!"

"In and out of the ring," John quipped. Bing answered, "Most definitely," and John chuckled at Camera Two as the camera got all four of them in a wide shot. "All those stories and more coming up on NewsSix at Five."

The monitors in the news desk cut to a commercial, and they knew they were off the air.

Up in the control room Rush Torrance stood at his post, headset in place, nervously paging through his script. "Brother, we're still too tight. Marian's package on the abortion parents is . . . what? Two minutes! That leaves . . ."

Susan the director leafed through her script. "We're full up to the first break. We can move 199, the Lanford trial, ahead and open up another thirty, but that crams the second section."

Rush found a solution. "Okay, go to section three and we'll pull 399, the Gullywump story. Then move the dead body from section two to section three."

Susan found the Gullywump story and pulled the pages. "Okay, 399 is out." She pressed her intercom button and advised the anchors. "John and Ali, pull 399, Gullywump, and move 299, the dead body, up to the first place in section three, right ahead of 301, car dealer protest."

Susan dropped 399, Gullywump on the floor.

Rush pulled out 399, Gullywump and tossed the pages in a trash can.

On the news set, John pulled the pages. "There goes your story, Leslie." He dropped them to the floor.

"Ready . . ." said Mardell.

Show time. They struck a busy pose, checking their scripts, looking serious. In just a few seconds viewers everywhere would be able to soar out of the sky, crash right through the roof of the NewsSix broadcast house, and land in front of John Barrett and Ali Downs, ready to hear the day's news.

Carl Barrett was one of the viewing public this night, sitting beside his easel in his grandfather's shop, watching the little portable television on the workbench. He'd set up a new canvas on his easel for his next project, an expression of order in the universe even in the midst of chaos. Sure, it was a lofty goal, but he was excited about it and excited about being excited. Excitement about anything had been far from him for years, but this work he could actually see finished from the beginning, before he'd even started. He knew what he wanted, in a way he'd never known it before, and though he still needed to find which direction, which approach would best get him there, he knew where he was going.

But now he paused, set down his brushes, and turned on the television, feeling uneasy. He hadn't heard from his father all day, and that bothered him. When he finally called Deanne Brewer that afternoon, he got bad news and perhaps good news. The Request for Medical Records had turned up nothing, and yet it seemed the story—or a story of some kind—was going to run anyway. Somehow John and Leslie were going to have something on the air. He'd called Rachel Franklin to make sure she knew about it.

But something didn't feel right.

Deanne Brewer was too nervous to sit still, which made Max edgy too. "Babe, now sit down, you gonna wear out the carpet."

Deanne had called Max at the shipyard and told him about her day, so he hurried home to be there, and now he, Deanne, and the three kids, Rebecca, Victoria, and George, were all gathered in front of the tube, waiting to see Mom on television.

After Rachel Franklin heard from Carl that the story might run on NewsSix at Five, she tried to keep an ear tuned to the wide-screen TV in the restaurant's lounge, now tuned to Channel 6. Her boss said she could take her break early if that would help, and she was ready to take him up on it.

Marilyn Westfall had no idea the story would be running until she'd closed up the Human Life Services Center and gone home. The phone was ringing just as she came in the door.

"Marilyn! Turn on Channel 6 . . . they're going to say something about the Women's Medical Center!"

Oh, goodness! Had the Brewers actually found out something?

She clicked on her set before taking her coat off.

Music. Big music that sounded like news, rushing along, charging along, sounding the call, *News is happening, happening, happening.*

Video: moving, aerial shot of the city, the Adams Tower, downtown. Traffic rushing back and forth, ferries pulling out from the dock.

Deep, sandy, booming voice: "This is Channel 6, The City's Premiere News and Information Station, your number one source for up-to-the-minute news."

Pictures, fast pictures: a cameraman runs toward a fast-breaking story, zooming in, focusing; a female reporter stands in front of more news, hair blowing, microphone ready; a male reporter scrambles from a NewsSix car, his eyes locked on an off-screen event; Chopper Six lands with a bump as technicians bang switches in the control room . . .

New video: The city skyline from high above, the picture rocking, dipping a bit with the helicopter as it banks over the skyscrapers, catching the glint of the evening sun off the vast panes of glass . . .

Voice still going: "And now, from the NewsSix newsroom, this is NewsSix at Five, with John Barrett . . ."

As the camera flies through the air, circling over the I-5 freeway where the traffic flows like blood through an artery, a box appears at the upper left: John Barrett, new, fresh, improved, flashes a knowing smile at the camera.

". . . and Ali Downs . . ."

Box at lower right. She has a new hairdo and a new look and delivers a shining smile.

The boxes disappear as the camera drops toward an imposing tower of glass adorned with a big red 6.

"Bing Dingham with sports . . ."

A box containing Dingham's face leaps out from the tower and slams into the upper-right position. Bing Dingham looks at the camera and cracks up as always.

"And Hal Rosen, weather . . ."

His box flies out of the tower and comes to rest at the lower left as he looks at the camera and winks.

The boxes disappear. Here comes that tower, closer, closer, we're coming in for a landing, the big red 6 filling the screen, closer, faster, closer, faster . . .

"The NewsSix News team. NewsSix at Five!"

Crash! We're inside the building, sailing past rafters, cables, floodlights, and then, like a roller coaster going over the top, we nose over, dropping down past rigging, wires, lights, monitors, into the open expanse of the NewsSix set, heading for the floor and the news desk where John Barrett and Ali Downs are ready and waiting to inform us, accepting with ease that we have fallen from the sky and through their ceiling to get there.

Two-shot: John and Ali at the desk, looking into Camera Two.

"Good evening," said John, "and welcome to NewsSix at Five."

Camera One, head-on to Ali. A graphic of Slater and Wilson nose to nose appears over her left shoulder.

"The gloves came off again in the race for governor as Hiram Slater and challenger Bob Wilson exchanged verbal punches over the issue of parental consent and this state's reproductive privacy laws. Todd Baker has that story."

Todd Baker's prerecorded package begins to roll.

Video: Governor Hiram Slater addressing a huge luncheon crowd.

Todd Baker's voice over the pictures: "Addressing the National Freedom League, Governor Hiram Slater minced no words in defending the pro-choice legislation he has championed during his administration."

Sound comes up as the governor speaks: "Bob Wilson claims he wants to protect families, but what he really wants is to tear away a woman's right to control her own body. I'd like to remind Mr. Wilson that you, the people, spoke when you approved the Reproductive Privacy Act and guaranteed every woman's fundamental right to abortion, free from interference by the state, the church, the family, anyone. And I think you should remind him as well and tell him where you stand when you go to the polls in November!"

Cheers, cheers, cheers.

Video: Bob Wilson addressing another crowd, a huge BOB WILSON FOR GOVERNOR banner behind him, framed by red, white, and blue balloons.

Todd Baker's voice: "But at a rally today at the Pendergras Hotel, Bob Wilson called for a moratorium on the privacy law, insisting that the law comes between parents and their children."

Sound comes up for a Bob Wilson soundbite: "A child needs her parents' permission just to receive an aspirin from the school nurse, and yet she can be driven to a clinic by that same nurse to undergo a risky medical procedure without her parents' knowledge or consent. And what if there's a complication? The abortionist can hide behind Hiram Slater's favorite law while the parents are left to bear the pain and expense of repairing the damage. If this is the law of the state, then we need to have another law; if this is what our governor stands for, then we need to have another governor."

Cheers, cheers, cheers.

Todd Baker, standing in the lobby of the hotel, microphone in hand: "And it isn't over yet. With less than two months before the election, the candidates are going to get all the mileage they can out of this issue as if emotion meant votes, and right now there is plenty of emotion. At the Pendergras Hotel, this is Todd Baker for NewsSix."

Camera Two, head-on to John, close up.

With a deep, quaking pain in his stomach, John pushed himself objectively onward and read the copy from the teleprompter in front of the camera lens. This was it.

"Well, as if to underline the debate over parental consent, one family confronted that issue head-on today in an unsuccessful attempt to pierce the veil of privacy at a local clinic. Marian Gibbons is live in front of the Women's Medical Center . . ."

Mardell held her hand out to the anchors' right, and they turned their eyes in that direction. On television screens all over The City they appeared to be looking at a large, rectangular screen perched on the end of the news desk. Marian Gibbons was on that screen looking back at them, microphone in hand, the Women's Medical Center behind her.

". . . and has the latest on that. Marian?"

Marian went to full screen and began her package. "John and Ali, this was another case of anti-abortion sentiment still at work even in the face of strict laws protecting reproductive privacy."

A cassette began to roll.

Video: head-and-shoulders shot of Deanne Brewer standing on her front porch, the front door just behind her.

The Brewer kids knew better than to talk over the TV when Mom was on the screen, but they still jumped, pointed, and squeaked in excitement.

Marian's voice over Deanne's talking head: "Max and Deanne Brewer lost their daughter to toxic shock syndrome in May of this year, but they are convinced the Women's Medical Center is to blame."

Deanne's voice comes up to volume: ". . . we saw part of the autopsy report, and it said Annie died from a septic abortion, and we didn't even know she was pregnant . . ."

Video: The Women's Medical Center.

Marian: "The Brewers had themselves appointed as personal representatives of their daughter's estate in order to gain access to confidential records at the Women's Medical Center."

Video and sound of Alena Spurr, director, Women's Medical Center, her office walls in the background: "Mrs. Brewer presented us a legal request for her daughter's records, so of course we cooperated, and of course we didn't find anything . . ."

Video: Alena Spurr going through the files in the back office of the clinic, thumbing through hundreds of folders. A reenactment.

Alena's voice over the video: "We do keep thorough records, and there is simply no record of Annie Brewer ever being here, ever receiving our services."

Video and sound of Deanne Brewer on her front porch: "I went and talked with a young lady who was there at the clinic, who saw Annie get an abortion there, and that's how we found out who was responsible."

Video and sound of Alena Spurr in her office: "We have offered our services to hundreds of patients over the years, and not one of them has ever complained of mistreatment."

Video: The pro-lifers out on the sidewalk holding their signs and stopping patients to talk with them.

Alena's voice over the video: "What's really tragic is how these people are being used by the enemies of choice. The anti-abortionists are grabbing at anything they can find now."

Video: Shots of the clinic, of patients (their faces turned away from the camera) approaching the door.

Marian: "So who is the eyewitness the Brewers claim saw their daughter receive an abortion at the clinic?"

Video and sound of Deanne Brewer: "I can't say who it was. She wanted to remain anonymous."

Marian: "And what about that autopsy report indicating Annie Brewer died from a septic abortion?"

Video: Pages of the hand-copied autopsy report being slowly turned for the camera.

Marian over the video: "All Deanne Brewer could show us were five pages supposedly hand-copied from the original autopsy report. But where is the original?"

Video and sound of Deanne: "Well, the hospital can't find it. They've lost it or something."

Marian's voice, interviewing Deanne from off-camera: "Well, what about the pathologist who performed the autopsy? Couldn't he explain the cause of death?"

Deanne gets flustered and looks down. "Well, we couldn't find him either. He doesn't work at the hospital anymore."

Cut to Alena Spurr in her office: "It's harassment, pure and simple. They can't prove one charge they're making and yet they come in here and harass us, intimidate us, and scare our patients. You know, we have had trouble with the Brewers before."

Video: Old footage from the governor's kickoff rally. Max Brewer scuffling, slugging it out in a near-riot as an older man stands above the crowd on a planter and hollers. A circle highlights Max so he can be picked out visually.

Marian over the video: "Indeed Max Brewer was arrested and jailed for trespassing on clinic property and later was ejected from Governor Hiram Slater's campaign kickoff rally for assaulting the participants."

Back to Marian live, in front of the Women's Medical Center: "So, John and Ali, if nothing else, today's incident serves to remind us that the abortion battle is far from over, despite the recent public approval of laws protecting the rights of women."

John was ready with the scripted question, written for him by Marian Gibbons. "So, Marian, are the Brewers now satisfied that the Women's Medical Center was not at fault in the death of their daughter?"

Marian answered from the screen, "Well, John, when I asked Mrs. Brewer that question she said they were not yet satisfied and would keep fighting to find out what happened. So unfortunately the Women's Medical Center is bound to see some more trouble before this is over."

"Okay, Marian. Thanks."

Camera One head-on to Ali. "A semi truck carrying two thousand live chickens caused a real flap when it overturned on Interstate 40 . . ."

John flipped the page of his script. That was that. Funny how so much struggle, pain, emotion, and information could be hyper-simplified, skimmed, and spit out in under two minutes. It went by so fast he had no time to think about it. He had no time even now. The next story was up, and it would be his turn in front of the camera. He'd have to ponder all this later.

Max and Deanne just sat there as Ali talked about the body found near Interstate 40, and John introduced a story about an Army Surplus store's fiftieth anniversary, and then Ali talked about a house fire. They couldn't think of a word to say; each was afraid of what the other might be thinking.

Twelve-year-old Victoria spoke up first. "Mom . . . did you do a bad thing?"

"No, honey . . ."

Max slammed the arm of his chair and then leaped to his feet. "Son of a—"

"Okay, kids." Deanne roused the children. "Go on to your rooms and work on your homework. Supper will be ready soon."

They went. Daddy was angry, and Mommy was crying. It was best to get away from them for a while.

Carl turned away from the television and stared at his canvas, just stared into the white, featureless expanse. He was trying to see his vision again, his goal, his project as he'd imagined it.

It was gone. He couldn't recall it.

Rachel Franklin went back to work, cursing under her breath. John Barrett had not surprised her, not really.

Marilyn Westfall sank back in her chair and shook her head. *People just don't know,* she thought, *and maybe they never will.*

The story ran again on the Seven O'clock, cut down slightly, but essentially the same. And then the Seven O'clock, like the Five O'clock, ended in a rush, with hurried good-nights over push-you-along music, with closing credits against shots of The City, and then commercials one upon another. The News of the Day went by like a speeding train and then disappeared to return at 11 that night and the same time tomorrow to speed by again to return at 11 and the same time the next day with a few chuckles thrown in along the way.

"Max, the news business is a very complicated process, there are a lot of factors involved—" John winced and held the receiver away from his ear, so very thankful that Max Brewer was on the phone and not in the same room. "Max, Max, now listen . . ." Anyone nearby could have heard Max's oaths and threats squawking out of the receiver. "Max, I can understand why you're angry, believe me, but I don't pick the news around here." More hollering. "Well, yes, I read it. That's my job." Max began to tell John what his job ought to be. "Max, you ought to let my boss know how you feel about this. Talk to him, tell him what you're telling me right now. Well, he's not here, he's gone home. But you can call him tomorrow." Max didn't seem ready to receive any more suggestions about anything from John Barrett, news anchor. "Max, why don't we talk some more about this tomorrow, okay?" No way. *Click.* "Max?" Dial tone.

"Aw, for crying out loud . . ." John slammed the phone down.

The day shift had all gone home, and the newsroom was fairly quiet—no one there but the late-nighters, getting ready for the Eleven O'clock. John pushed and pulled—no, he did more than that; he threatened to kill Owen Wessel, the Eleven O'clock producer, if Owen so much as thought of putting the abortion story on that night. Owen got the message. *Yeah, okay, John, sure thing. You can trust me.*

John clicked off his computer, his way of clicking off the whole cussed day, the whole miserable mess, the whole circus that made him the clown. He just wanted to get out of there.

Leslie pulled up a chair and sank into it, looking very tired. She'd stuck around almost three hours longer than she had to, watching the entire outcome.

"Was that Max?" she asked.

"Hoo boy, was it ever. Forget the dark alley—I wouldn't want to meet him in broad daylight right now."

She nodded. "I would guess we've exhausted our friendship with the Brewers. We've blown the whole wad." She added a thought she wasn't too excited about. "I could probably call Deanne tomorrow and try to explain this to her." Then she just sighed through her nose and shook her head despondently. "But how good an explanation am I going to have? Right now I don't like the explanation myself." She glanced across the newsroom. "I had it out with Marian and I talked to Rush too and . . . I knew what they were going to say."

John supplied the answer. "It was news. It was happening . . ."

Leslie prompted, "And . . ."

"And . . . everything in the story was true, factual."

"And . . ."

"And they got reacts from both sides."

Leslie threw up her hands, rested back in her chair, and said, "And I am quitting."

John stopped short upon hearing that. He shouldn't have been surprised, but he was. "You sure?"

She wanted to answer right away, but then hesitated. "I'm not sure about anything anymore. No, I take that back. I know one thing for sure: I've let down my friends, I've compromised my ideals, I've gone with the flow, but . . . at least I saved my precious little rear. Leslie Albright the reporter is safe." She stopped to brood about that.

John suggested, "Well, really, did you have any choice?"

She leaned forward and spoke intensely. "You better believe I did! Surprised? Well, it dawned on me today—no, actually I've known it all along, but it's been so easy, so handy to forget—I have a choice. I can choose right from wrong—we all can. The problem is, it's this beast, John. We're in the fish's belly and it's swimming away with us, remember? Once you get inside this workplace and you get so used to going with the flow and protecting your rear, you don't even think you have a choice, and you don't even consider choosing the right thing over the wrong thing, you just do what the machine tells you to do. Sure, you gripe about it in the news car or at the lunch table; you talk about the blind producers sitting in the windowless room forcing their reality on you, telling you what they want to see whether it's really there or not—but you do it. Even for the dumbest reasons, you do it. I let Tina walk all over me because I was afraid for my job, and you let Ben Oliver crack the whip over you and make you do your tricks because you're afraid for your job, and when it comes to keeping our jobs, our important, hard-to-get, major-market jobs, we have to be professionals, so right and wrong don't even enter the formula because we think we don't have a choice!"

John was getting uncomfortable with this. "Leslie, come on, you're not being fair—not to the business, not to yourself. You . . . you can't bring morals into it when there's news to report—"

She didn't raise her voice, but just whispered so hard she hissed. "John, don't we get to be people? Who are we anyway? I don't now who I am—or who I'm supposed to be. I don't know who you are!" She stole a glance around the room, hoping no one was overhearing them. "John, what were we when we talked to the Brewers? Who was I, what was I when I spent all that time with Deanne? Was I just a news gathering machine or did I really care, did I really feel for Annie Brewer? What do you do, John? Hang up your humanity when you come into the newsroom? Does John Barrett ever feel anything?" She swallowed her emotion and ventured, "You intro'd a story that betrayed people who trusted us, and you did it so well! You were so . . . so professional!

"Well, I can't do that. John, the Brewers have been through the machine, they've had their two-minute spot on television and now they're gone; they'll probably never come across that assignment desk again, but you know what, the Brewers, the real-live, breathing, feeling Brewers, are still out there, still living in that little house with one less daughter, and I can't just crumple them up, toss them, and go on to the next story."

"Leslie . . ." John had to make sure she knew. "I felt something."

Leslie was pained as she grappled with that. "Then . . . John, in God's name, why did we let this happen?"

John couldn't fight it anymore. His head, his professionalism, told him one thing, but his heart kept listening to Leslie and to what he knew deep inside. He had to give in. He leaned his elbows on his desk and rested his forehead in his hands. For a moment he said nothing, but then, as if confessing, he spoke in a weak, barely audible voice, forcing himself to say it. "Tina Lewis called the Women's Medical Center right after you talked to her on Thursday. She told them all about the request for Medical Records, and she told them about Annie's code name, Judy Medford. She even spelled it for them. She told Alena Spurr that you and Deanne were going to be there the next morning, and Alena Spurr told Tina about Max Brewer being arrested and his jail time, the whole thing. That's how Tina knew about it this afternoon.

"Last night Alena Spurr went through all the records and purged Judy Medford's name out. She even rewrote the daily schedule by hand so she could omit Annie's code name."

Leslie was speechless. Sure, it's what she'd thought, and yet . . . this sounded so direct, as if John really knew, as if he'd been there.

John continued in the same quiet voice, as if he were spilling his guts, confessing secrets he'd been hiding. "Tina is a deeply wounded woman . . . She's scared, and she's running, and when she fights and pushes like she does, it's because she's trapped, she's trying to defend herself."

Leslie leaned close to hear him better, his voice was getting so quiet.

John stopped to gather strength and then continued. "Three years ago . . . September 16th . . . Tina had an abortion. It was a boy. The only child she ever had. The anniversary was just two weeks ago, and I heard her screaming."

"Screaming?" Leslie whispered.

John held his hand up. "*I* heard her screaming . . . Screaming inside. She's still thinking of him, and every time an abortion story comes along, it reminds her, and so she has to fight it off. She has to show herself, show the world, that what she did was all right, that she had the right to do it, that she isn't guilty of anything. Leslie . . . when you pitched the story idea to her, you came too close to the wounds."

For the first time John looked at her. "It's not you or me she hates. She's not fighting against us. It's the Truth she hates. The Truth won't let her alone, and she hates it." He stopped as another thought came to his mind. "And . . . I don't know who they are, but . . . Annie isn't the only one. Some other girls have died there."

Leslie believed him. "John . . . how do you know all this?"

He looked as if he would break into tears and shook his head. "I don't know."

"You mean . . . What do you mean? I don't follow you."

He started gathering things together, preparing to leave. "Leslie, all I know is . . . well, please don't quit. Please stick around and . . . there's more to this, that's all. The beast doesn't have to win. We don't have to let this fish swim away with us. Something will happen, something will break."

She had her doubts. "Well, I don't . . ."

"Well, think about it, will you? Give it some time. I'm giving it time. Do the same. If you don't you might miss something." He got up from his chair. "I've got to get out of here. I've got to get to Carl."

He seemed so urgent she became concerned. "Is he all right?"

John shook his head as he put on his jacket. "No. He saw the newscast tonight and . . . well, I'd better get over there."

nineteen

Paint was everywhere. The canvas was all but invisible under splatterings, smears, globs, and dashes of paint of all colors. The walls were speckled and splattered too, as were the floor, the windows, and several of Carl's other works.

And he was still digging it out of jar after jar, clenching it out of tube after tube, throwing the stuff blindly, crazily, his vision blurred with tears. He whimpered, sometimes he growled, lashing at the canvas with his brushes, beating and whipping the paint in merciless, exploding patterns.

His universe had exploded into meaningless, detached particles.

"Carl!" John burst into the room and right into the middle of Carl's painted *scream*. "Carl! Stop it. Please."

"I don't hear you!" Carl cried. "I don't hear anything anymore! I don't see anything! I don't know anything!"

John tried to grab him, to contain him. "Carl, c'mon now, you're making a mess . . ."

Carl thrust him away. "What's a mess? What's art? What's love, what's hate, what's Truth? I don't know, and neither do you!"

"Carl . . ."

Carl spun around, his face splattered with paint, his hands covered with it, his eyes the eyes of a savage. His words were rehearsed; he'd been brooding on them with every splash of paint. "I needed answers, and the whole world ignored me! I sought for God, and He gave me you! So I looked to you for Truth and . . . and you blew up my universe and cut to a commercial!"

"Okay, Carl . . . okay. I know it's hard to understand. It's a complicated business." John looked at the splattered canvas. "And if this is what you think of me . . . well, I don't blame you—"

"I've already painted you. I've painted the only father I could find."

"I'd like to see it, Carl."

"I can't find it. Nobody can."

"What do you mean?"

"I cried at Grandpa's memorial service. Did you know that?"

John was surprised to hear Carl bring it up. "Yes. I wondered about it . . . I really wanted to know why . . ."

Carl looked all around the shop, at all the machinery and tools set in their places, hanging on their hooks, tucked into their slots. "Because he knew something. He knew where he was, who he was. If he'd been alive just a little longer, I could have gotten to know him, we could have touched, you know?" He took one more look around the room and then cried, "I don't belong here!" and ran for the door.

"Carl! Carl, don't go! We can talk it out!"

Carl slammed the door behind him, leaving green, blue, red, and black paint smeared on the knob.

And John was alone, standing in the middle of the most intense work Carl had ever created. All around, on every side, could be seen chaos, anger, despair. The little shop that Dad Barrett had built and organized with such purpose, such care and love, was now disrupted, desecrated, by an explosion of placeless, meaningless colors.

And in the middle of it all the little television on the workbench was still chattering its nonstop, clamorous message: buy, buy, buy, have, use, indulge, forget; laugh, laugh, laugh at everything, care for nothing; look at this, look at that, now look at this, it's new, it's now, it's different, it's wild, it's naughty, you've never seen anything like it, don't miss it!

Then another nauseating, overdone ad: "In these times a man of integrity is needed to keep you informed, a man you can trust!"

John cursed. *As if this stupid tube's chatter isn't bad enough, now I've got to hear another Slater-for-governor ad!* He reached for the on-off knob, that precious escape route back to sanity.

"John Barrett!" the tube trumpeted. "The voice of integrity, bringing you the world as it is!"

And there was John Barrett's face. Big, bold, honest. The real thing. You couldn't help but be impressed.

John stood transfixed for the few seconds his face remained on the screen. He could sense it so clearly: that little box was laughing at him, mocking him! He could hear it cackling! It was slapping him in the face with . . . himself. First he listened and watched; he received the whole message; he let it hit him full force. Then, stunned and heartsick, he silenced that little machine. He switched off its life.

It went blank and stared at him without expression. He backed away from it, staring back at it, hating it, hating himself.

A sight in the rafters made him jump—an apparition, a face lurking overhead!

It was cold. Lifeless. Mechanical. It was perfect. Honest. Impeccable. Professional. His face. Ready to bring you the news reliably and accurately, up-to-the-minute. Number one. Premiere.

Carl's painting. An image without blemish. It was everything John Barrett, anchorman, was.

And it was up high. Lofty, out of reach, untouchable. *I can't find it,* Carl had said. *Nobody can.*

The little box had mocked him. Now this painting, this image, shamed him.

That's me? he wondered. "O God," he whispered, "who am I? Who am I really?"

God heard his question.

And John knew it. *No, no, I shouldn't have asked that. I don't want to know. At least let me figure it out myself . . . Don't tell me . . . Please don't tell me.*

But God heard the question.

John knew he'd gotten God's attention; he'd disturbed God. He didn't mean to, but he could sense what he'd done. Somewhere in the big wide universe, maybe everywhere, God had heard John's voice. He'd heard the question, stopped, and turned.

God. . . . don't look at me. It isn't that important, really. I didn't mean—

An answer was on the way. From God? From Almighty God? The little building was dead quiet. Not a sound. The little box sat lifeless on the workbench. John could hear the wind outside, the barking of a dog, a tiny creak in the rafters . . . the beating of his own heart.

He could hear any sound that might come. Any voice. An answer was on the way. God was going to answer. John looked up into the rafters again. What were they, two-by-fours? He could imagine them snapping like toothpicks. They could never hide him from God. He looked around at the old, single-paned windows. Some were cracked even now. He'd broken one when he was a boy. They could never shield him from God.

This whole building was only a tiny shell made of sticks. A hurricane could blow it away, a mighty earthquake could topple it, lightning could consume it. It could never hide him from God.

God was on His way. God would be here soon. Oh brother. What if God sees that painting? What if He sees this awful mess? What if He talks to Carl?

John looked up at his image in the rafters. The news anchor just gazed back at him, same as usual, cool, collected, in charge . . . paper-thin.

A lie? O God, don't let that be me. I'm not that guy up there . . . I'm not.

But please . . . don't tell me who I really am. Not yet. I couldn't stand it.

John took some deep breaths and tried to clear his head. He had to calm down.

He decided to pray. Sure. Why not? He'd grown up in church. He believed in God, and he'd always said so. He was a good man . . . At least he tried to be.

"God . . ." *Oh man, don't pray, you'll give away your position! He'll home in on you! You want Him to see you like this?*

This is nuts, he thought. *I've got to get out of here.* He went to the door. Carl's paint was still on the knob when he grabbed it. When he got outside he noticed the slickness of his fingers against his palm. He dropped to one knee and frantically rubbed his hand in the grass. He had to get rid of this paint. *No, God, it wasn't me, it wasn't my fault. I didn't know Carl was going to do this. I don't know why he did. His mess isn't on my hands!*

He got to his feet and walked briskly out to the sidewalk. A change of scene, that's what he needed. Fresh air. A different environment. He hurried through the quiet neighborhood, past all the quaint old homes that had been here for at least half a century. He kept waiting for the fear, the holy dread, to ebb away, but nothing changed. As a matter of fact, being outside under the open sky felt even worse. He felt naked out here, a sitting duck with a big target on the top of his head.

O Lord, where can I flee from Thy presence? The Scripture echoed in John's mind.

He started running. *Nowhere,* he thought. *God's everywhere. No matter which way you turn, you're looking Him in the face.*

If I flee down this alley, You're there. If I get in my car and get out of town, You'll be right in the car with me. If I duck into the subway, You'll be right there in the tunnel. I could turn on the television and maybe drown You out, but that won't make You go away. I could buy things to push You from my mind, but You'd still be there when I tired of them.

He kept running, trying to shake the terror. Either he was crazy or God was really after him, but either reason was reason enough to run wildly down the sidewalk, duck around a massive maple tree, and flee down another street past warmly lit windows and friendly porchlights, then up a narrow alley where two dogs barked and chased him along a Cyclone fence until he was past them. What was the matter with them—couldn't they see he was in trouble, that God was after him? He could see the strangeness of this. God was chasing a man down the street while the poor guy ran for his life, but no one in the neighborhood even noticed. Perhaps they had nothing to fear.

God was getting closer, and He wasn't a bit tired. John knew God would run him down eventually, but he kept running. He couldn't stop.

He came to Snyder Park, the local play area for generations

of kids. It was night, so the place was empty; the swings were motionless, the baseball diamond vacant. He stumbled across the expanse of grass, found a picnic table, and collapsed on the bench, unable to run any further and seeing no use in it anyway.

He couldn't get away from God, couldn't outrun or outfox Him. There was nothing left to do but surrender.

"All right," he gasped. "All right. You've got me. I can't run anymore. I can't run. Here I am. Do what You want with me."

That sounded strangely familiar, like words he'd prayed thirty-two years ago.

Who are you really, John Barrett?

"Aw!" He couldn't hold that cry inside. He looked around, his eyes darting here and there. He saw nothing but the park.

I have laid bare the secrets of men's hearts and you have seen it.

No, no, John thought. *He's going to rip my heart out, I know He is!*

Now I will show you the secrets of your heart.

John began to realize what he was. He could not turn away from it. The Truth poured over his spirit, mind, and soul like a wave and he had to face it, confess it, know it.

He could not deny it any longer. His soul was naked before God.

"Son," Dad had said, "the Truth is coming after you, and it's going to sink its claws into you and not let go until you start paying attention."

The claws of the Truth were painful. The lies tore away like scabs, and John bled there for hours, stifling his cries of pain in the sleeve of his overcoat—the overcoat he'd received from his father.

Carl finally returned to Mom Barrett's at just a little before midnight, carefully opening the screen door to the back porch, painstakingly dragging his feet several times over the doormat, turning the back-door knob delicately and slowly until the latch finally released, easing the door open in hope of minimizing its characteristic squeak—and finding himself face to face with Mom, sitting at the kitchen table reading her Bible and waiting up for him.

He looked pathetic, cold, shivering, his eyes red from weeping, his face smeared with paint and tears.

"So how are you?" she asked.

He knew no more appropriate answer than, "I feel like Hell."

"Have you seen your father?"

The question irked him. "I have never seen my father."

She raised an eyebrow and directed a finger at his nose. "Oh, you've come close, now be honest."

"I have never seen him, and I don't care if I ever do. There's nothing there to see."

She rose from the table and beckoned with her finger.

He resisted. "Naw, c'mon . . ."

"You come on."

"Grandma, I am not going to talk to him!"

"I don't care if you do or don't, but I do care about the mess you made. Now come on."

He followed her. He had anything but a right attitude about it, but he followed her out the back door and down the path to his grandfather's shop, getting a quick update on how she felt about this whole thing.

"The Word of God says not to let the sun go down on your wrath. Well, the sun's down, but I'm still up, I'm getting tired and cranky, and I'd really like to sleep tonight knowing you two are working this thing out instead of wandering around the neighborhood like a couple of nutty vagrants in war paint."

"Grandma, he's just going to give me the same old routine!"

She stopped right outside the shop door and turned to fire her reply straight into his eyes. "Not tonight he won't."

She opened the door, swinging it quietly aside as if unveiling something.

Carl stopped in the doorway. He had no response. He could only stare.

There was his father, John Barrett, on his hands and knees

in the corner of the shop, hand-scrubbing paint off the floor, working slowly, deliberately, rubbing the floor with a rag, wetting the rag from a can of turpentine, then rubbing some more. He had to have heard them open the door—he had to know they were now watching him—and yet he didn't turn, he didn't look up.

Mom said softly, "It took both of you to make this mess, so it's going to take both of you to clean it up." Carl was about to offer a reason why it could never work, but she held up her hand and wagged her head. "No, no, now I've got you where I want you. You've defaced my property, so I'm calling the shots. Get started."

Carl surveyed the extent of his artistic expression. "It'll take all night!"

"Oh, longer than that. But tonight you start." And then she stood there, her feet firmly planted, her face providing no option.

Carl turned toward the room, took a moment to accept the idea, and then worked his way past the table saw and drill press, along the workbench and past the hanging tools, until he was just behind his father. He looked one more time at Mom Barrett, but all she did was point to the workbench. "You'll find more rags in that third drawer."

"What about . . . paint thinner or something?"

"You father has a can of turpentine. I'm sure he'll be happy to share it with you."

And then she closed the door on them.

Carl looked down at his father's back. John Barrett had changed into some old clothes, probably Grandpa's ragged jeans, an old blue shirt already stained with housepaint, and a scuffed pair of work boots. He didn't look one bit like a news anchor. And he still kept working, not saying a word.

Carl found another rag and got to his knees on the floor, not too close to his father. He started scrubbing out a long streak of yellow paint he'd thrown across the floor, but finally realized he'd need some solvent.

He looked toward his father. John Barrett's eyes were

watery, and his face was pink. He'd been crying. Maybe he still was.

"Can I have some of your turpentine?"

His father handed him the can, and their eyes met for a moment.

John Barrett's eyes were looking at him, really looking at him. There was no machine, no camera, between those eyes and Carl; no script, no cue cards, no teleprompter. Carl's eyes were locked on his father's, and he couldn't break his gaze until his father looked back at the floor.

Then Carl realized he was staring and tried to break his stare into quick glances as he poured some turpentine on his rag. There was something different about his father's face. It was hard to pin down what it was, but . . . it looked softer. Vulnerable. Warm. Human. It was even sweating a bit. Maybe he'd seen this face before, that night in his father's apartment, that time when he heard his father say, "I'm just like Dad." *I wonder what the voice would sound like?*

"You know," Carl ventured, "you don't have to help me. I'm the one who made the mess."

"I owe it to you, Carl." The voice was soft, broken. John Barrett borrowed back the can of turpentine, wetted his rag, and continued scrubbing. "I made the mess too. This is our mess. We've been working up to this for years."

Carl couldn't argue with that, so he just kept scrubbing. The yellow paint came up easily enough. Maybe this wouldn't be an insurmountable task after all.

He saw a small circle of water on the floor directly under his father's face. Then another.

"Hey . . . you okay?"

His father set down his rag, sat on the floor, and pulled out another rag, this one for his eyes and nose. "Oh . . . I guess I'm okay."

"You been hearing from God again?"

That brought a new flood of tears to John's eyes. He couldn't speak; he could only nod yes.

Carl digested that for a moment, then said, "Then pass the turpentine." John passed it to him and he set to work again, this time on a streak of blue. "We'll get the oil-based stuff up first. The watercolors will come off with soap and water, so they can wait 'til morning."

John put his nose rag back in his pocket and returned to work. "Is this one oil-based?"

"Yeah. All the yellows are oil, all the blues, and all the blacks. Don't worry about the reds—we can mop those up."

They scrubbed for a while without saying a word, and then John said, "Like eating an elephant, right?"

"Yeah," said Carl, familiar with that little saying, "one bite at a time."

They finished the job at about 1 in the morning and then tiptoed into the house to take showers and turn in for the night. Carl went to bed in John's old room, while John got some blankets and slept on the couch. He'd be going back to his apartment soon enough, but for now, maybe for a few days, he wanted to be right here, in this house, close to his family.

Saturday morning Leslie Albright woke up almost unemployed. Ben wouldn't accept her resignation yesterday, but told her to take the weekend to think about it. He must have noticed that she was angry, indignant, beside herself, ready to spit, and probably unable to make a cool and rational decision she would not later regret.

Well, as Leslie sat in her little studio apartment sipping her morning coffee and facing a brand-new day, she was able to conclude that Ben had done the wise thing. A good night's sleep and a new day could bring a fresh perspective on things. Maybe this job was worth another chance, another try. This was, after all, her chosen profession, the field she'd schooled and prepared for, and it was a worthy profession, all things considered. Besides that, if she quit now, she would never be able to find Dr. Denning, get a *bona fide* copy of that autopsy report, and shove it up Tina Lewis's nose. That alone was going to make staying at NewsSix worth any amount of pain.

So, having settled at least that much, she pressed on to the next item on the day's agenda: sliding her half-eaten toast aside, pushing her coffee cup forward, and making space for the phone book. Okay, the Request for Medical Records idea didn't work, thanks to good ol' Tina, and if the hospital wasn't going to give out Denning's number, fine. But if Dr. Denning still lived anywhere in the area she was going to find him. Her first course of action was the most obvious: find his home number and just call him. She flipped through the phone book until she found some Dennings: Albert Denning, David Denning . . . all right, here he was, Mark Denning, M.D.

She set the phone right next to the table and dialed the number.

The phone rang a few times, and then an answering machine cut in: "Hello, you've reached the Denning residence. We're unable to come to the phone right now, but if you'll leave your name and number and your message, we'll get back to you as soon as we can . . ."

After the beep she left a message: "Hello, this is Leslie Albright. I'm a friend of Max and Deanne Brewer and also of John Barrett, Jr. At any rate, this is regarding the autopsy you performed on Annie Brewer back in May of this year . . ."

She left her number, at home and at work. Okay. Done. Now, what else? Well, if she could check a crisscross directory she might find his address and perhaps leave a note on his front door. She began to seriously consider that. She was playing hardball now.

John carefully lifted the canvas cover aside, exposing a pile of planks, ribs, and parts he could no longer identify for certain. "Hoo boy, it has been a while."

As they stood in Dad's shop, eyeing that forgotten project, Carl found himself just watching, detached, not saying a word, not diving into the idea with any premature enthusiasm. Before yesterday he would have been thrilled at the thought of finishing this rowboat with his father, but that was before yesterday's tumble from hope. The fall had been long and hard—and the crash at the bottom more than painful. He could still feel the bruises deep in his soul and healing was going to take time if it happened at all. Sure, he'd seen tears last night, and he even thought he saw his father, his real father, working alongside him. But what was this now? His father's idea of "quality time"? A kiss to make it better? Carl couldn't help feeling a bit testy. His father was doing the right thing years too late.

"Grandma says you and Grandpa quit working on it when you left for college."

"That's right." John began picking through the pile, trying to sort it out and remember what was what. "This was our project, the one we were going to do together. I guess that's why Dad never finished it by himself. He was waiting for me to come back."

"Guess you came back too late."

Carl was right—John knew that. But the kid was being a little blunt and John didn't exactly welcome the pain. "Yeah. Yeah, that's right, Carl. That's how it is. But I'm here now, and so are you, and we've got some choices to make."

Carl just looked at the wood pieces. That's what they were—confused, scattered pieces.

"Right?" John prompted.

Carl was ready to walk out again, but he knew that would be cowardly. No, he was going to test this thing. Then he'd know for sure. "I know I don't want to build any stupid boat."

"I was thinking we could finish what Dad and I started." Then John was careful to add, "And I thought we could talk."

"Talk about what?"

"Anything you want."

Carl tried to lock onto John's eyes, and John let him. This guy was really leaving himself wide open—if he meant it. "Anything, huh?"

"Hey, it isn't going to be fun, but what are the alternatives? The way I see it, we can either deal with things the way they are and start putting the pieces together from here, or just walk away from each other, get out of each other's lives, and keep the mistakes the way they are."

Test him, Carl. Throw him a punch and see what he does.

"Why did you and Mom split up?"

John grimaced. "Oh boy . . ."

Carl threw up his hands. "Yeah, right, we could talk about anything!" He started to walk out.

"Well, give me a second to think, will you?"

Carl stopped as his father got riled.

"You start right out tearing into the big wounds, the really big ones, and you expect me to have some news and commentary all prepared for you or something? You think the reasons are simple?"

Carl thought for only a moment and then nodded, "Yeah, I think so."

"Oh, give me a break!"

"She was selfish and you were selfish; all you could think about was your career, and all she could think about was not letting you—or any man—walk on her."

John stopped short and stared at his son. "Then why'd you even ask?"

"Are those the reasons?"

"Yeah, those are the reasons."

"Okay."

"I take it you've had some long talks with your mother."

"Her name's Ruth."

"Okay . . . Ruth."

"You must not feel too friendly toward her."

Now John was mad. He let a curse slip out.

"What did you say?"

"I said . . ." John wilted a bit. "I'm sorry . . ." But then he just got angry again. "And why am I apologizing to you? Have you heard your own mouth lately?"

"Hey, I'm still a sinner! I haven't been talking to God like you have!"

John was about to throw a counter-remark, but got as far as drawing the breath when he held it, let it out as an amused sigh, and then just smiled, shaking his head, looking down, thinking for a moment. Then he looked up. "Okay, Carl. You want to communicate? You want to be honest? Tell me something: When you were throwing all that paint around last night, who were you thinking of?"

Carl smiled. Touché. "Me."

"So you weren't thinking of Grandma or Grandpa and their nice little shop here and the sanctity of their property and how a guest in someone's home should conduct himself?"

"No . . . I was mad." Before John could comment, he added, "But like I said, I'm a sinner. I do things like that."

John looked around the room, sharing an incredulous expression with the shop tools. "So . . . hey, give another sinner a little slack, huh?" Carl didn't have a comeback ready, so John kept going. "I'm a sinner. Sure . . . I'm a sinner, and I do sinful things. When you meet God, that's the first thing you have to face up to or you aren't being honest." John looked toward the rafters. "You can't be like that painting up there. Good job, by the way."

Carl looked up at the anchorman in the rafters, still cool, collected, immaculate, professional. "I hate that painting."

"Well, sure, and we both know why. So just try to get God to believe that image up there. Forget it! God sees right through it. He knows who you really are, so you may as well come out and be honest about yourself."

Carl looked at the painting and then at his father and then returned to unfinished business. "So . . . how do you feel about Ruth?"

"I feel . . . Initially I feel like I don't want to talk about her."

"Well . . . she doesn't talk about you much either. But do you hate her?"

"No, not at all."

"Do you still love her?"

John had to probe his thoughts, his feelings. "Back then I had no question that I loved her. But looking back from here I can say I loved myself more. And now . . . now I'm not sure how I should feel about her. If love is only a matter of feeling, that's gone completely. If love means commitment, we never had that in the first place."

"Do you love me?"

John worked on his answer for a moment before he shared

it. "You may not like the answer, but I don't think it'll surprise you."

"Okay."

"I've always loved you, Carl. In the wide sense, in the big picture, I love you, and always have. It's in the smaller, narrower sense that things start breaking apart. As far as love being a feeling, I've always loved you, no question. But as far as love being commitment . . . Hey, you know the answer. I loved myself more." He wanted to make sure he was coming across. "Is that . . . Does that make sense to you?"

Carl blinked away some tears. "Yeah."

John looked down at the wooden parts in disarray. "I don't know. I guess—no, I don't guess, I know—I've always regretted what Dad and I left undone, unsaid, unlived. We both lost something that would have been . . . just the most wonderful thing, you know? And now—" His emotions—his love—overcame him. "I just don't want to lose it with you." He wiped his eyes and took some deep breaths, trying to stabilize. He couldn't. He kept going anyway. "Carl, you've just got to forgive me . . . please . . . forgive me, and let's go on from here. Let's . . ." Words failed him.

Carl turned to the wooden parts for his answer. "Let's build a boat."

twenty

Let's see . . . 19202 N.E. Barlow. Ah yes. Leslie remembered this neighborhood with the high-priced homes and clean, paved streets. She'd been up here perhaps a year ago, right after a windstorm had toppled some of the trees and they'd fallen on power lines, cars, and homes. One of the big fir trees had almost cut an English Tudor in half when it fell—it did manage to flatten the Mercedes parked in the circular driveway. It was big dollar damage—great stuff for the evening news.

Okay, Dr. Denning, if you won't call me back, then I'll track you down.

Actually she'd only waited half a day for Dr. Mark Denning to return her call, but she was too primed and pumped to wait any longer without taking some action on her own. She had to talk to this guy, she had to learn something, anything substantial, and hopefully before Monday. One more smirk from Tina Lewis without something really devastating to throw back at her—like a *bona fide* autopsy report—and her decision to quit would be firm. On the other hand, if she could get something that would truly vindicate the Brewers and herself, then, oh boy, electronic news gathering just might be fun again.

Now that she'd driven around the neighborhood a few times looking for 19202 N.E. Barlow, she began to recall how hard it was to find an address in this place. All the houses were built on rolling, forested hills, so the streets tended to weave and wind around like a plate of spaghetti instead of a neat, predictable grid, and the number sequences had an aggravating way of changing, skipping, even reversing unexpectedly.

Whoa! She stopped the car. There was 192nd, and this time it looked like it really might go somewhere. She backed up and turned left, driving slowly up the hill.

She craned her neck this way and that to read the numbers.

19190 . . . 19192 . . . Still one more block to go, if there was a block—but it looked promising. She crossed an intersection and wound down a quaint street with big houses on either side, all tucked back among towering evergreens. *Yep. Next windstorm we'll be up here taking pictures again,* she thought.

There it was! 19202 N.E. Barlow. Nice place. Two stories, a steep, shaked roof, a few dormers, a two-car garage, a big yard with lots of beauty bark and rhododendrons. There was a Jeep Cherokee parked in the driveway, and lights were on inside. She parked out front, checked her appearance in the rearview mirror, and went up the front walk, passing a brightly colored playhouse and a child's dirt bike.

An attractive young woman with long, brown hair answered her knock. "Hello."

Leslie felt a little hesitant and acted like it. "Hi . . . uh, I'm Leslie Albright. I'm with . . . well, ordinarily I work for Channel 6 News, uh, NewsSix? But . . . um . . . that's not really why I'm here—well, not directly anyway." *Great start, Leslie.* "I'm not making much sense, am I?'

The lady seemed tolerant enough. "I suppose you'd like to talk to my husband?"

"Um . . . you are . . . Mrs. Denning? Dr. Mark Denning's wife?"

She nodded. "My husband isn't here right now. He's in Sacramento on a job interview."

Leslie hoped her disappointment didn't show. "Oh . . ."

"Would you like to come in?"

Leslie relaxed. "Oh, yes . . . certainly. Thank you." She stepped into the entryway, a nice, well-lit space with a high ceiling. "Beautiful home."

"Thank you. My name is Barbara."

"Nice to meet you." They went into the living room, a pleasant, thick-carpeted place with soft furniture and dark-stained cabinetry. The large windows gave a perfect view of the backyard where a little girl and boy were chasing a Frisbee.

Barbara Denning took a seat on one end of the couch and offered Leslie the other end. "I got your message on our answering machine. Are you the one who did that story on the Brewers yesterday?"

Leslie wagged her head emphatically. "No, no, I sure didn't. That was Marian Gibbons. I was working with Deanne and Max Brewer on a story about what happened to their daughter, and . . . well, to put it simply, the bosses at the station yanked it out of my hands and turned it around to say something I never intended it to say. So . . . I take it you're familiar with the Brewers' situation?"

"It's why my husband is out looking for a job."

Leslie's eyes widened as bells went off in her head. *You're onto something here. Pay attention.*

The little rowboat was seeing the light of day again for the first time in over twenty years. John and Carl had cleared the area near the windows and then used some sawhorses and planks to extend the worktable. Now all the pieces of the boat were laid out flat on the table, and Carl began to arrange them, piece by piece, one over here, one over there, moving this one, reversing that one, to somehow figure out how they all went together.

And there was hope. As nearly as Carl could tell, all the pieces were there. Right now he was trying to make sense of the ribs. One was placed backward, so he turned it around, and then two had to be interposed because they were in the wrong order. The keel was easy to spot and was already marked for where the ribs were to go. The whole process was encouraging. To look at that pile as it was originally, one would have thought the project was a lost cause. But now, having a better view of it, having a better picture of what needed to be done, the task was not so overwhelming. It wouldn't come together in a day, but given time, they just might have a boat.

The door to the shop opened, and John came in, moving briskly, his face full of news. Carl could tell something was up; his father's mind was grinding away so hard he could almost smell the smoke.

"Whooo!" was the first thing John said.

"What's up?"

"That was Leslie Albright on the phone. She found Denning."

They could read each other's face and knew they both felt the same reaction—mixed feelings: joy with doubts, excitement with misgivings.

Carl verified, "Denning? *The* Denning?"

"Denning's wife actually. Leslie says they had a really nice visit. Denning himself is away, down in Sacramento, interviewing for a new job. Get this: He was fired from his job at Westland Memorial Hospital over the Brewer affair."

Carl nodded. "Yeah, that's kind of what we figured."

"The hospital let him go right after he let Dad and Max see Annie's autopsy report. They've got some strong politics going on at that hospital, some unwritten rules."

"Like, 'Don't snitch'?"

"'—or you die.'"

"So what's the verdict? Were we right?"

John felt vindicated. He couldn't help smiling as he nodded yes. "Annie Brewer died from a septic abortion. But that's from Mrs. Denning. When Denning gets back, we'll get it straight from him."

Carl took a moment to lean against the workbench and process all this. John was too agitated to sit. Carl asked, "So . . . what about the autopsy report?"

Now John shook his head. This was where the mixed feelings came in. "Denning's wife says he has a copy of it in his own files, but—and this makes sense—she can't release it. Only Denning can do that." And then John added, "And only to the Brewers."

At that, Carl fell silent. He'd let John address that problem.

John finally did. "So . . . hey, if we want to stay in this battle we're just going to have to regroup, that's all. I think it's worth fighting, and I know Dad did. We'll just have to get the hurts patched up and keep going."

"You remember what it was like meeting Max the first time."

"Yeah, and now he's mad. But I've got to try calling him

again. Maybe he's cooled down by now, I don't know . . . he's got to be interested in this. Leslie's going to call Deanne anyway."

Carl tried to sort it out, and it wasn't easy. "If we had the autopsy report—if we had the Brewers working with us again so we could get it—we could prove Annie died from a bad abortion at the Women's Medical Center. And if that girl—'Mary'—was willing to come forward, if she hasn't been turned off by what happened on the news . . . which brings up that woman who runs that . . . uh . . . Human Life Center, whatever it's called . . ."

"Marilyn Westfall," John reminded him. "Human Life Services Center. Another person who trusted us and got stung."

"And then there's Rachel Franklin."

John could only shake his head. "Hoo boy. She was mad at me in the first place."

"She's probably mad at *me* now." Thinking about Rachel brought a distasteful question to Carl's mind. "So . . . even if we found out everything . . . do you suppose it would be news? After what's happened, I can't help feeling that nobody will ever hear about it anyway, that something will happen to . . . to the story, to the . . ."

"To the Truth."

"Yeah. Things happen to the Truth. I mean, even if we could prove everything, how do we know somebody isn't going to cut it all up and mash it and paste stuff on it and turn it around and ignore parts of it . . ."

John chuckled. "Everybody does that with the Truth, Carl, not just the news media. It's what we do as human beings with . . . well, with things we don't want to face."

"Yeah . . ." Carl became glum. "But then, even if we did get the Truth out, who'd even give a rip? Who'd even want to know about it?"

John held his hand up. "I don't think that's even the question here. Let's go back to where we started: What happened to Annie Brewer was wrong, and that mattered to Dad, and we decided it mattered to us as well, and . . ." John took another look at the boat parts all laid out on the table. "It's . . . I can't explain it exactly, but it's like another unfinished project, another goal that meant a lot to Dad but never got finished, you follow me?"

"Oh yeah."

"So even if nothing ever comes of this, nothing big and open and public . . . at least we'll know that we did what we were supposed to do—we didn't sit on our rears and just mope about it. Dad never moped about anything he could do something about."

Carl felt it and was sure his father felt it too. "Do you think that's why he was killed?"

John had no trouble answering. "Absolutely." Then he looked around the shop as he tried to understand the man who built it. "That's what really bothers me. All of this must tie together somehow. Max may not be as paranoid as we think." John just about laughed at a sudden recollection. "Remember what we said about Denning getting fired? That unwritten rule?"

" 'Don't snitch or you die'?"

John gave Carl a look that said, What do you think?

And Carl nodded in a way that said, I think you're right.

John summed it up. "Dad knew something." And then, as if waiting for just the right trigger, just the right time, John's mind fired off another thought. "And he said so! He told me he knew something and that he wanted to share it with me, but . . ." John recalled and understood. "He said I wasn't ready for it. I wasn't ready to receive it because . . . oh brother . . . because I wasn't on good terms with the Truth."

Carl was thinking, *Yeah, he was right,* but he didn't say anything. He just looked around the shop so he wouldn't have to look at his father.

"And he was right," John said. "He was right."

"So . . ." Carl stopped. Maybe he shouldn't ask.

"I'm trying to be," John answered. "I'm trying to be on good terms with the Truth. It's going to take time, I've got a ways to go, but . . . I'm willing. God's patient—I've discovered that. It's like Jesus said to that one woman that . . . what was she? A tax collector or . . . no, a prostitute, I think. He forgave her and then said, 'Go and sin no more.' God has time and patience for us if we have time for Him."

Carl could accept that. He liked the sound of it. "Okay."

"We've got to go down to the warehouse," John said abruptly.

Oh-oh, thought Carl. "What for?"

"I don't know specifically. But I need to go back to where Dad and I left off. I need to go back to his office."

"Governor, I plead with you, search your heart and change your course, for if you do not, God will change it for you. Though you have said to yourself, 'No one sees, and no one hears,' surely, the Lord sees, and He hears all that you think in your heart, all that you whisper, all that you speak in your private chambers. There is nothing hidden from the eyes of Him with whom we have to do!"

The prophet was so distant and appeared so small as he stood on the far side of the Flag Pavilion shouting and gesturing, and yet his powerful voice carried over the heads of the crowds, clear and distinct above the clamor and cheers.

The governor had acted as if he did not hear the man's words, and yet, try as he might, he could not help but hear them. Now, as he sat in first-class on his flight to the TriCities for some more campaigning, he was haunted by how clearly he could replay the whole event in his mind, almost every word the prophet spoke, even the old man's inflections and cadence. He could also remember how it felt—it felt that way right now—to hear the prophet's words. It felt the same as being caught cheating by your elementary schoolteacher, or hitting a ball through the neighbor's window, or being lectured by the high school vice principal.

"Like Nebuchadnezzar of old, you have set up an image of yourself for all men to follow, a towering image, a mighty image, an image far greater than yourself," the prophet had said.

How did that old geezer know about my ad campaign? The

governor laughed to himself. *C'mon, it's TV; everybody knows it's glitz, it's show biz. Nobody really believes that stuff.*

"But please take heed: The Lord would remind you, you are not that image."

Well, people don't believe everything they see on the tube . . . or on the posters . . . or the billboards. They know it's a campaign, it's selling. It's just . . . image.

"Though you may say, 'I am strong and invincible, I tower over the masses, I cannot be touched or harmed,' yet in truth you are as weak as any man, about to be harmed, about to be toppled!"

Slater had a hunch then, but he was almost certain now: The old prophet knew. The governor could hear it indirectly through the prophet's words. That old man knew.

But he's dead now. He's dead. Now he can't tell anyone.

"Hiram?"

The governor looked at Ashley, his wife, seated next to him. "Mm?"

"Are you all right?"

That winning smile came to his face automatically. "Sure. How are you doing?"

"Oh, just fine."

She went back to her magazine, and he went back to staring out the window.

That's the way it was between them and had been for . . . how many years? She never asked another question after the first one; she never pressed it. He said only as much as he chose to and showed nothing beyond that, and she bought the image, or at least acted like it.

When they'd first met, they talked about politics, about their classes at the university, about cars, sports, architecture, almost anything. But he would not talk about true feelings, wishes, concerns, hurts, love, needs, sentiment. These were not comfortable subjects, but rather comprised a realm in which he felt lost and without words, like a perpetual novice always stumbling along. During their first years he ventured into that realm just long enough and often enough to win

Ashley's heart, become a family man, and achieve what he considered domestic success.

But soon thereafter he was naturally drawn to a mistress that would not demand intimacy or vulnerability, but let him stay where he felt safe, self-assured, and powerful: the cold machinery of politics and power. This was a world in which he could truly be the molder of his own fate and, through the System, the fates of others. His god was The Task, his religion The Goal, his creed . . . Well, the rules were derived from the game, and the game's object was the Goal, and he was very good at writing new rules for new games. In any event, his protective shield could always be in place—the man everyone thought he was.

Ashley hadn't understood this shift at first, this change from the courting, calculating aspirant to the slightly warmer and vulnerable charmer who married her and then back to an even colder, more distant, more calculating man of ambition and drive. She had her needs, but he had his work, so they had their exchanges, their scraps, their discussions—and in the end nothing changed. She remained empty and needful, and he remained comfortable. He became what he had set out to become from the very beginning.

He couldn't remember a precise date when she changed her approach to their relationship. He'd been too busy to notice. But it did occur to him after a time that she no longer pressed him for his thoughts, his feelings. She no longer distracted him with a touch from her hand or an arm on his shoulder. She shared no more secrets. She remained at his side as his loyal wife, but the old sense of closeness was gone. Somehow they'd arrived at an unspoken covenant that they would not speak, not in any real sense. That way things remained comfortable. He had his ambitions, she had the goodies that came with them, and beyond those matters that directly affected the smooth acquiring of those goals, they did not talk.

Were they happy? They did not talk about it. He was The Governor, and she The Governor's Wife, and for the sake of the call, for the sake of The Image, their marriage was one of external peace, cooperation, and mutual support. Their roles were established, and they played them well.

So Governor Hiram Slater was alone with his thoughts and his fears as he sat and looked down at the clouds. The prophet was dead. But somehow he found no comfort in that. The prophet's words were still alive, and his knowledge could have been passed along to someone else.

Hiram Slater was considering how to expose, quantify, and then contain this threat—at least until the election was over. What the voters didn't know would not hurt them; and after all, what was good for Hiram Slater was good for the state.

Barrett Plumbing and Fixtures was open for half a day on Saturdays, but the back office was usually closed up and Jill the bookkeeper was not there, which would make it easier for John and Carl to let themselves in with John's key and do all the snooping they wanted without raising questions. Chuck Keitzman was working today, moving things around with the old forklift, even with a cast on his hand. He was busy at the moment and didn't ask any questions; he just said hi.

John and Carl hurried to the back office, and John opened the main office door with one key, then the door to Dad's office in the back with another. They stepped inside, and John flicked on the light.

Dad's office was still the same, as if he'd only left it a moment ago. The smells were the same: paper, old lumber, a hint of pipe cement, maybe even a lingering hint of the old man himself. The calendar on the wall had not been turned since September 11th, the morning Dad was killed.

"Now . . ." John said, moving slowly toward the desk, "what we're looking for is anything unusual, anything that might tell us what Dad was getting his nose into. Carl, why don't you go through those files, and I'll see what's in his desk."

Carl went to the file cabinet in the corner. The drawers were locked.

"Oh, right," said John, sliding open the center drawer of Dad's desk. He found a little key right away. "He always hid the key in this drawer." He tossed it to Carl, who opened the file drawers and began thumbing through the files. "Dad always had little hiding places for things. If I could remember what they were, it would help."

Carl was intimidated by all the files confronting him—hundreds of them. "Man, this is going to take all day."

John was going through the desk drawers. "Well, do a cursory scan first, just look for anything unusual, and then if we don't find anything, we'll look a little deeper."

Carl started at the front of the top drawer and began thumbing through all the accounts, receipts, suppliers. If he'd been intensely interested in plumbing, it would have been exciting. Carl was not intensely interested in plumbing.

John sorted through the contents of the center drawer, moving things aside, pawing through it a bit. This was the junk drawer, the little-things drawer, the catch-all for pencils, paper clips, stick-'em pads, a jackknife, a few rulers, several small pipe fittings, and several pads of personalized stationery, to name just a few things.

Top drawer on the right: envelopes, invoices, a flashlight, and some extra D batteries.

Second drawer on the right: Plumbing catalogs and some trade magazines, plus a few boxes of computer disks.

Third drawer: Junk. Lots of it. Some gadgets for wall-mounted heaters, a bag of shop cloths, a small radio, and . . . a portable cassette player with headphones but no cassette. John pulled that from the drawer, carefully untangling the headphone cord from the other items.

A cassette player, a walkman. Now he remembered it. When he'd first come into this office to have that talk with Dad, Dad had this sitting on his desk. John even recalled how he put it away as they began talking.

And . . . hmm, was he recalling this correctly? When Dad was saying something about knowing something, having something he really wanted to share with John but couldn't, he almost opened the third drawer. "I've got things I've learned today, just this morning," Dad had said.

A walkman in Dad's desk was a little strange. It didn't seem like Dad to have one of these on the job. Dad was always thinking, always counting things; his mind was always hard at work. What would he want with this?

"Carl . . ." Carl turned. "I might have something."

They flagged down Chuck Keitzman as he came by on the forklift. He recognized the walkman immediately. "Hey, so there it is! I've been missing that!"

"Oh, so it's yours?" John asked.

"Sure," said Chuck, taking it back. "Your dad wanted to borrow it and . . ." Chuck hesitated. He'd talked himself into a corner. "Well, he never got a chance to return it, obviously."

"When did he borrow it?"

Chuck thought a moment, then recalled, "Oh . . . it was that Monday right after the . . . well, you know, when he was at the governor's rally and got on television, the Monday after that."

"The Monday I came to see him."

"Yeah. Right."

"Did he ever ask to borrow it before?"

"No. I'm the only one who uses this thing around here, and only when I'm loading with the forklift or doing something where I don't have to think too much."

"Well . . . would you have any idea . . . did he say what he wanted to listen to?"

Chuck shook his head. "He just asked to borrow it for a little while, that's all."

John thought out loud, "Jimmie was here that day . . . he said Dad had a visitor . . ."

"He's out in the yard." They went out to the loading dock. "Hey, Jimmie!"

Jimmie recalled the visitor. "Yeah, I remember telling you about that. There was one guy who came to see John about 10 in the morning, and after that John just stayed in his office and wouldn't come out."

Chuck put it together. "Sure. After that guy left, that's when he borrowed my walkman, and I guess he was sitting in there listening to something. I don't know."

"Do you know who the guy was?"

Chuck and Jimmie drew a blank.

"Never saw him before," said Jimmie.

"What did he look like?"

Jimmie shrugged. "Young dude, wearing a suit, carrying a briefcase. He looked like a salesman to me."

"Color of hair?"

"Dark brown, maybe black."

"Height?"

"A little shorter than me." Jimmie was a big man, over six feet.

"Race?"

"Anglo."

John was getting frustrated. "He didn't have a card or anything?"

Chuck suggested, "Maybe we could ask Buddy. He was working up at the counter. He must have talked to the guy."

"About how long did he stay?"

Jimmie and Chuck looked at each other again as they agreed on an answer. Jimmie tried, "Man, I don't think it was long at all. Just a few minutes."

Chuck nodded. "For all I knew, the guy was just asking directions. He was in and out, that quick."

"Well . . . here's your assignment, guys. Find out who it was. If you see him again, if you know anybody else who might know anything . . ."

They exchanged a look that said, *That's a tall order.* "Okay, Johnny, we'll do what we can."

John turned to Carl. "Let's take another look in Dad's office."

A thorough search turned up no cassette tapes of any kind. Now John was all the more intrigued. "Let's go back to Mom's. We'll check the car, the shop, the tape player in the living room, we'll ask Mom . . ."

Sunday morning they went to church with Mom, something Carl had been doing regularly as part of his lodging agreement with her, and something John was ready to try again, for better or for worse. It wasn't all that bad.

The Pentecostal culture and worship style—pull out all the stops and get on with it—were distinctive, of course, and something you either liked or didn't, but God was there, and John could sense His presence.

And once again he heard God speak. He could hear God's voice in the singing, in the testimonies, in the love and sharing, and especially in the written Word of God. John knew that voice when he was ten, and he knew it now. Jesus is the Good Shepherd, he recalled, and His sheep know His voice; they recognize the same old ring of Truth, that same durable, virtuous tone, and, of course the same, unfading love and mercy. Perhaps John wasn't home yet, but he felt close.

As for Carl . . . "Let's work on the boat," he said. Sunday dinner was over, they'd all cleaned up and loaded the dishwasher, and Mom now was reclining in Dad's easy chair, a quilt up to her chin, resting her eyelids. John thought that activity—or nonactivity—looked terribly inviting, but Carl's idea prevailed easily, and they went out to the shop.

"I'm checking it out," Carl admitted as they began to fit the boat ribs for gluing. "Hey, I want God to be there—I want Him to exist. And if He's there, I want Him to speak to me. But right now . . . well, it's kind of wait and see."

John was marking the keel for drilling screw holes.

"Okay, I can understand that." What John really understood was that Carl was testing everything, examining everything, especially his father, to see if any solid ground was beginning to take hold under all that shifting sand. Wait and see? John had the same feeling about himself even now. God he was sure about. John Barrett was another matter.

Not to change the subject entirely, but slightly, John said, "Well, let's hear these tapes."

Dad owned a small radio/cassette player and used to listen to preacher/teacher tapes and music while working out in the shop. It wasn't hard to find; Dad had it in its rightful place on a shelf above the workbench, a shelf labeled "radio." Now they had it perched on the workbench near where they were working, and beside it was a stack of cassette tapes gleaned from Dad's car, his bedroom, the shop, the living room stereo, the closet, and anywhere else Mom could think of where Dad might stash tapes. Most of the tapes were preacher/teacher tapes and were so labeled. Some were copies of old phonograph recordings Dad put on tape so he could listen to them out here or in the car. But some were suspiciously unlabeled, and John wanted to review them carefully.

So began an afternoon of old-time religious culture as John and Carl began gluing and fastening the boat together. They heard southern gospel quartets, one after the other, with thundering bass singers, soaring tenors, and tinkling pianos. Then there was Brother So-and-So bringing life to you from the Such-and-Such Church somewhere in California. And last Easter's cantata by the church choir, recorded from the back of the sanctuary and sounding ten miles away—Sister Schmidt still came through above all the others—followed by a very distant, fuzzy voice squeaking to a pro-life rally from behind a thick curtain of tape hiss. The clock kept turning, and the tapes kept rolling, and John tried to work on the boat while keeping one finger available for the Fast Forward button. It didn't take long to determine that a particular cassette was not going to bring any significant revelations about Dad's death or whatever he may have discovered, and yet . . . John sometimes delayed ejecting the cassette because the contents did something for him: it brought back vivid memories of his father.

They worked, they listened, and occasionally John would remember.

"Sixteens," he said with a chuckle. "Dad was really into sixteen penny nails. That and Atco tar."

"Huh?" Carl asked. It was a fair question.

"Well, sixteens . . . I mean, they were the binding element that held every major project together, like this shop we're standing in. It wouldn't be here without good old sixteen penny nails. But you could use 'em for all kinds of things: you drive 'em into the wall and hang stuff on 'em, use 'em for stakes and markers when you pour concrete, pick your teeth with 'em . . . I mean, they're just a very straightforward, no-nonsense, functional nail. Dad loved 'em."

Carl nodded without comment.

"And Atco tar . . . Boy, there was always plenty of that."

"What is it?"

John only had to look under the workbench to find a can of the black, gooey stuff. "You use it for patching leaks in the roof. You know, gluing roll roofing or three-tab together, sealing up flashing, covering over nailheads. Great stuff."

"Uh-huh."

"But Dad used it to seal up the wounds in the fruit trees too, and it worked great and it was cheap. I mean, we're talking function here, good down-to-earth function." And then John laughed. "Like Vicks."

Now Carl laughed. Vicks he knew about—that all-purpose, gelatinous goo with the strong, camphoraceous smell.

John kept laughing. "Man, Vicks was good for everything. Dad used to smear it on his chest and put it on his chapped lips and smear it up his nose . . . You always knew when he wasn't feeling well—the whole house smelled like Vicks."

John got a whim, dashed over to a small cabinet in the corner, flung open the door, and . . . "Voila!" He produced a large jar of the stuff with a flourish. And then he just held it a moment with a distant look in his eyes and a warm smile.

Carl was enjoying this. "Grandpa was quite a guy, huh?"

John put the Vicks back. "Yeah, quite a guy."

During another taped collection of old recordings, Carl finally asked, "Man, he really listened to this stuff?"

"Yeah," said John. "We both did. We'd be working out here and we'd listen to it."

The Smokin' Gap Boys came on with their humorous rendition of "A Woman Ain't an Idol, But She's an Idle Thing," and John knew all the words. He could even sing the tenor part. Carl didn't try.

As Pastor Reynold J. Brimley of the Church of the Full Gospel in Dallas, Texas, came on with his view of the seven bowls of judgment from the book of Revelation, John showed Carl how to plane the edge of one of the boat ribs. "Yeah, right, just hold it steady . . . What we're after is a nice chamfer, about a quarter inch . . . Yeah, right, steady, steady, don't let it get away from you. Beautiful!"

As evening approached, the boat began to take shape. It had no skin yet, but the keel and ribs were impressive, to say the least. This was a marvelous consolation, a reward for a full day of enduring Dad's favorite obscure tapes from years gone by. Now that was beginning to be a real test. Carl didn't say anything, but his face was weary as John slapped in another tape and the vociferous "Give God Glory" songs of the Blue Mountain Quartet filled the room, followed by one more scratchy recording of Momma Tanner and the Gospel Belles singing about going home to Heaven where Momma's teaching angels how to sing.

"I'm goin' hoooome over yonder, beyond the crystal sea . . . across the River Jordan, where Momma's waitin' for me . . ." John knew all the words to this one too.

All it took was a look from Carl, and John ejected that one and slapped in another.

"Wouldn't you love to hear some good old Led Zeppelin right now?" Carl asked.

John was startled. "I used to listen to Led Zeppelin! How old are you anyway?"

Carl stole a look at the cassette player. "I'm getting old, Dad. I'm getting real old real fast."

In another hour the tapes were exhausted, and so were John and Carl. The boat's framework was assembled, and now the glue needed time to dry. John took the last cassette out of the player and tossed it into the box with all the others that had had their say or their song. The tapes had provided some great memories, some great music if you liked that kind of music, and some new perspectives on the Scriptures, but not the kind of breakthrough John and Carl were looking for.

"It was a good time anyway," said Carl.

John had to agree, still feeling a special warmth deep inside. "Sorry if I prolonged the experience with some of these tapes, but . . . It was just like I was spending the day with Dad again."

"Well, I got a better glimpse of him today too." Carl

stepped forward to check one joint on the boat. It was mostly just an excuse to touch it, admiring the work they'd done. "And I got a better glimpse of you."

John knew what Carl meant. "So did I. It's been twenty years since Dad and I were that close. Well . . ." John had to be careful lest his emotions rise again. "We had those days back then at least. And that kid who worked with his dad . . . he's still in me. He's still there."

Now John did break into tears and just gave himself time to feel it through.

Carl was enjoying the mystique of this old shop. The whole day had been a fascinating chain of little discoveries, and even the silly ones—the Vicks and the Atco tar, for example—were special in their own way. This building was full of Grandpa's personality, his heritage.

"You must have built a lot of stuff out here, huh?"

John was wiping his eyes, just coming back together. "Yeah, we did, especially around Christmas. We tried to build something special every year."

"Yeah. I saw the rocking horse and the bookshelf."

"Did you notice that chandelier in my room?"

"Yeah."

"I made that when I was fourteen."

"No kidding!"

"Yeah, and Dad made surprises too, things I never knew about. One Christmas he made a whole wooden chess set. Have you seen that?"

Carl was amazed. "The one in the living room?"

"Yep."

"He did that?"

"It must have taken him months. He turned all those little pieces on the lathe over there."

Carl just shook his head in wonderment.

"I knew he was up to something, but you know, when Christmas is coming you're not supposed to ask questions. I'd find out on Christmas." John chuckled with the memory. "And he always hid my present in the same place, and I always knew where to go find it—"

John stopped so abruptly that Carl thought he'd been shot or had had a heart attack or a stroke or . . . he didn't know what.

"Dad?"

John was frozen there, his eyes first gaping and then darting across the room, locking on the lower wall near the workbench. Almost with a leap, he dashed across the room to that corner and began moving some tools aside.

Carl raced up behind him. *Oh brother, now what?*

John had uncovered a hinged panel in the wall, the kind that usually concealed plumbing or a furnace or ductwork. It was held shut by a small brass bolt that slid aside easily. In seconds John had the door open.

There, in a small alcove where firewood had once been stored, lay a fat manila envelope. Scrawled across the face of the envelope in black marker pen were the words, "For John."

It was all Carl could do to keep from grabbing the envelope and ripping it open himself, so great was his curiosity.

As for John, his movement was arrested by awe. He reached out slowly, timidly, as if approaching a sacred object. He picked it up with both hands, not wanting to upset it, rip it, bend it. There was no telling what it was.

But it had been placed here recently. It was still clean; there were no spiderwebs on it, no dust or mildew.

Carl couldn't help himself. "C'mon, open it up!"

John got to his feet and went to the workbench. A utility knife was in its place in the second drawer, ready for use. John carefully slit the envelope open and pulled out the contents, laying it all on the workbench. Carl was right there to see everything.

Some photocopies of legal documents . . . another copy of the excerpts hand-copied from Annie Brewer's autopsy report . . . some names and addresses . . . pages of notes in Dad's handwriting . . . copies of some letters . . .

The last thing John pulled out of the envelope was a plain, unlabeled tape cassette.

twenty-one

John laid the papers out flat on the workbench while Carl moved a few cans and tools to make more room.

John was shaking. "He knew . . ." He stared at the papers in front of them. "Do you see all this, Carl? You see what he wrote on the envelope? He knew I'd find it. He hid it there, knowing I'd find it."

Carl couldn't think of a thing to say. He could only take it all in, gawking at the contents of the envelope, leafing through it, arranging it.

Then he spotted something and pointed at it so hard he almost stabbed the paper, immediately drawing John's attention to that spot.

The name jumped out at them from a filled-in blank near the top of a State Death Certificate: Hillary Nicole Slater.

"The governor's daughter," said John. "His oldest." He found the date of death. "April 19th, 1991. Yeah, that's her, no question."

"I didn't know the governor's daughter died."

"It was a big news story. She died from taking some mislabeled medicine . . ." John scanned down to the cause of death. "Hypovolemic shock . . ."

"What's that?"

"Uh . . . I'm not sure. But . . . let's see, that was due to 'exsanguination.' She bled to death. And that was due to . . . Hang on . . ."

Carl saw the long word and couldn't pronounce it either. John gave it a try. "'Hypo . . . pro . . . throm . . . binemia.' Hypoprothrombinemia."

Carl was waiting for an explanation.

"Um . . . as I understand it, she took some pills by mistake . . . they were mislabeled or something . . ." John scanned further down the page. "Sure. 'Accidental overdose of Warfarin.' That's a blood thinner. The governor was having trouble with blood clots in his leg . . . Remember Nixon having blood clots?" John considered his son's age. "Oh, well, I don't suppose you do. Anyway, the word was that Hillary thought she was taking medication for menstrual cramps, but took the governor's blood thinning medication instead, and suffered a fatal hemorrhage. Yeah, we covered the death, the funeral, and we did some consumer spin-off stories on drug labeling and safe medicine cabinets at home, that sort of thing. It was a real hot topic for a week or so."

Carl scanned the materials. "Grandpa had everything he could collect on Annie Brewer. Some of the autopsy report . . ."

"Yeah, and what's this? Hey, Annie Brewer's death certificate."

"All right. Yeah, look here. It's just like the Brewers told us: 'Primary cause of death: septic shock, due to . . . septicemia, due to . . . toxic shock syndrome.'"

John brought another page alongside. "But here's the hand-copied excerpt from the autopsy report. Let's see . . . Yeah, right here: 'The most attractive hypothesis that would explain the mechanism of death in this case would be that initially this person had an abortion complicated by staphylococcal infection resulting in peritonitis and septicemia leading to septic shock and inadequate oxygenation of the vital organs, leading to death.' "

"Well . . . it wasn't toxic shock syndrome anyway," Carl said sarcastically.

"Yeah, there's a direct contradiction. But look at this—another copy of Hillary Slater's death certificate." John looked at the receipt paper-clipped to the certificate's upper-right corner. "Eleven bucks, paid by check to the Bureau of Vital Statistics, May 2nd, 1991. So Dad went down to the Public Safety Building and got a copy."

"Why'd he buy two?"

John shook his head. "I don't think he did. The first one we looked at is different. It's newer . . . printed at a different time, different paper stock. And the receipt's for eleven bucks. That would be the price for one."

Carl was getting the picture. "Two girls, two death certificates . . . Annie's death certificate is definitely phony . . ."

John picked up the thought. "And it could be Dad thought

Hillary Slater's was phony too. That seems to be the direction he's leading."

"Man, let's hear that tape."

"I'm with you." John took the cassette over to the cassette player, dropped it in, and paused just long enough to look at Carl before he hit the Play button.

A period of silence seemed to go on forever. John and Carl were both leaning on the workbench, their weight on their elbows, their heads near the speakers.

A sudden sound cut in, a male voice on the telephone: "District Twelve Fire Emergency."

A female voice. Young, frantic. "Hello, my girlfriend's in trouble—she's bleeding and it won't stop!"

"Your location please?"

"Um . . . it's in the governor's house. You need the address?"

"Yes, please."

"Um . . . 1527 Roanoke West."

"And what is the phone number you're calling from?"

"Um . . . it's . . . I can't—"

"Is the number written on the telephone you're using?"

"Oh. 555-9875."

"And your name?"

"I'm . . . my name . . . it's . . . uh . . . Hillary Slater."

"Is the patient conscious?"

"She's . . . I can't see her from here."

"Is she breathing normally?"

"She's gasping real hard."

"You say she's gasping?"

"Yeah, like she can't breathe."

"Is she choking?"

"No, she's . . . she's breathing real hard."

"And did you say she's bleeding?"

"Yes, and it won't stop!"

"Where is the blood coming from?"

The girl said something unintelligible.

"Where is the blood coming from? Where is the wound?"

"She had an abortion."

"Has she soaked more than two pads in the last hour?"

"She's . . . we've run out. We've used . . . about seven."

"Okay, stay on the line. I'll send help."

A clunking sound. A receiver set down.

The dispatcher's voice: "Hello, are you with me?" No response. "Are you there? Hello?" Tones. One high, one low, two more in between.

Dispatcher's voice: "District Twelve, Rescue 231, Medic 231, vaginal bleed, the governor's residence, 1527 Roanoke West." Then, back on the phone: "Hello, are you there?" No reply.

Dispatcher on radio: "Rescue 231, Medic 231, be advised, unknown age female experiencing breathing difficulty, unknown if conscious at this time, possible induced abortion. I have an open line into the residence at this time."

A radio voice with a siren in the background: "Medic 231, we copy."

Long pause. Some radio chatter.

And then, background sounds. A woman screaming frantically, hurried footsteps.

Then the clunking sound of the receiver being picked up again.

The dispatcher's voice: "Hello? Are you there?"

A man's voice, desperate, urgent: "Who is this? I need the phone—"

"Sir, this is District Twelve Fire Emergency. We have dispatched Medic One and an aid unit to the governor's residence. Who are you, sir?"

"I'm Governor Slater! It's my daughter!"

"Is she conscious, sir?"

"No, no, I don't believe so."

"Is she breathing normally?"

The governor called off the phone, "Is she breathing? Ashley! Is she breathing?" A woman screamed something in the background. The governor came back on the phone. "She's breathing, but we don't think she's conscious."

"Does it sound like she's breathing normally?"

"No . . . No, she's gasping . . . It's very labored breathing."

"Would you like to do CPR? I can help you."

"Yes! I just need to—"

The woman shouted something. There were thumping sounds, doors opening, footsteps, voices.

"Oh, they're here! Thank God!"

"The aid crew is there, sir?"

"Yes!"

"Very good, sir, they'll take it from here, all right?"

"Yes, thank you."

"Good-bye."

Click.

The tape went silent.

John had to sit down and sank right to the floor. "O Lord . . . O Lord God . . . O Jesus . . ." he prayed, his eyes shut, his voice trembling.

Carl hit the Rewind button. He had to hear it again. They listened to it three more times, straining to hear every word, to know it thoroughly. Then they went back to the papers Dad had gathered and hidden . . . for John.

"Yeah," said John, his hands shaking, his throat tight, "look at this letter here. Dad told me he'd written to Governor Slater, though he never did get a direct answer."

The photocopied letter read:

> *Dear Mr. Governor:*
>
> *First of all, let me join with all the citizens of this state in conveying my condolences to you upon the untimely death of your daughter Hillary. My wife Lillian and I are remembering you and your family daily in our prayers.*
>
> *With sorrow and humility, I now come to the main purpose of this letter. I realize I'm in no place to judge any man, but nevertheless I must say what God has laid upon my heart and call attention to facts you are already aware of but have not dealt with, which could be much to your harm, as well as the serious harm of many others.*
>
> *Knowing the true cause of your daughter's death, I am deeply dismayed that rather than bringing to light that true cause and dealing with those persons, practices, and policies that allowed it to happen, you have let politics choose your*

course for you, meaning nothing will change, all things will continue as they were, and a great danger will remain unaddressed.

We are reminded by Scripture that "all things are open and laid bare to the eyes of Him with whom we have to do," and that "nothing is hidden, except to be revealed; nor has anything been secret, but that it should come to light." You have presented an image of yourself to the public, but it cannot endure. It must soon fall, and when it does, what then? Will an honorable man be found standing in its absence? What more can I say than to admonish you, even plead with you, to turn from deception and to walk truthfully? No political success is worth the eternal cost you will incur upon yourself and the unprevented pain that will be inflicted on others if you do not turn from your present course and choose to do right.

To provide hope, let me remind you that "if we confess our sins, He is faithful and just to forgive us our sins and to cleanse us from all unrighteousness." The God who requires righteousness has also provided a way to attain it. May you turn to Him now.

I remain sincerely yours,
John W. Barrett, Sr.

"Hm. Yeah, that's Dad all right," John said. "I can see why he got on the governor's nerves." He noted the date at the top of the letter. "May 6, 1991. That was before Annie died." He looked at Carl and saw the same incredulous expression that had to be on his own face. "He knew, Carl. He knew. Can you imagine . . . When Max Brewer met him in front of the Women's Medical Center and told him about Annie, Dad already knew about Hillary Slater. So what he feared, the . . . the 'great danger' he talked about in this letter . . . really happened. Another girl died, just like Hillary."

And then a thought, a fact, a bit of knowledge, hit John as clearly as if he'd always known it. "Carl, I'll bet they both died in the same clinic. Dad knew that all along." Another thought hit him. "And . . . I think God told me too, just the other day . . . All of a sudden I knew Annie wasn't the only one. But that's what Dad was hoping to prove."

"And somebody killed him."

"And somebody killed him."

Now both of them sat down, John on a stool, Carl on the floor. This sort of thing you didn't just learn and then go on to the next thing. They had to think it through and process it, and before that they had to believe it.

John reached over to the workbench and leafed through some more of the papers. "Yeah, look here: 'Glen Murphy . . . Al Connors, paramedic,' and here are the phone numbers. Dad may have contacted the paramedic who was on that Hillary Slater case. Here's Max and Deanne Brewer's number, and . . . good grief, here's Dr. Mark Denning's address and phone number. Wonder if Dad ever got through to him?"

"Well, Leslie has anyway."

"And you can be sure we'll talk to the others." John set the papers back on the workbench. "We've got to think, Carl. We've got to brainstorm this thing. What do we know? Where's all this going?"

Carl started with the easiest conclusion. "Hillary Slater died from a botched abortion . . . and it sounds like it was really botched."

"And covered up—the whole Warfarin overdose story released to the media, including NewsSix—and now it looks like even the death certificate was falsified. We'll have to check into who filled it out. Something went a little strange at that point."

"So how did Grandpa find out? When did he find out?"

"Maybe the Lord told him, I don't know. But he got the death certificate on May 2nd, which is about two weeks after Hillary died—so he was checking it out, we know that. Then, only four days later, he wrote to the governor about it. From what he told me, he never got through, as if that's any surprise."

Then John shook his head. "Hm . . . No wonder he was at the governor's rally saying all those things. He was going to get the governor's attention one way or another." John smiled slightly at a recollection. "He'd been following the governor for quite a while, from May through September, just trying to get the governor's attention. I think he really started getting under Slater's skin."

"He got somebody's attention—whoever gave him that tape."

"The visitor . . ." John mused. "It was the same day I went to have lunch with Dad. Jimmie and Chuck say a man came to see him around 10 o'clock. He didn't stay long, so it doesn't sound like he did much business. I think he was there just to drop off the tape . . . and probably that other copy of Hillary Slater's death certificate." John nodded as the pieces came together. "Sure . . . When I got there Dad had Chuck Keitzman's walkman on his desk, and he'd been crying, and he said he'd learned something he really wanted to share with me but couldn't because . . ."

Carl filled in, "Because you weren't on good terms with the Truth yet."

Good old Carl, as blunt as ever. But John saw no sense in objecting. "Yeah . . . yeah, that's right. But now at least I'm trying."

Carl accommodated that. "Okay. But I've got a question—Why Grandpa?"

John could only entertain theories. "It could be that after Dad was at the rally . . . you know, he got himself on television that night . . . somebody must have thought this was a perfect enemy of the governor to leak the tape to."

"Do you suppose the leaker knew Grandpa's son was a TV news anchor?"

John's face said, *Good thought.* "That could be. But that tape . . . The way I understand it, you don't just drive down to your local fire station and pick up a copy. Those tapes are privileged, they're confidential."

Carl was intrigued. "Oh . . . so now we're talking about an insider."

"Yeah, probably someone close to the governor. It could have been someone who read Dad's letters and maybe saw him at the rally . . . and maybe even knew about the Brewers and how Dad was helping them find out what happened . . ."

"Right. Right."

". . . and may have known that I was his son, somebody in the media."

"Well . . . we're guessing, and that's all."

"But here's something that spooks me: If . . . and that's if . . . Dad was killed because he had the tape, then what about that girl on the tape who called 911? She's a witness. She could confirm that Hillary had an abortion; she said it was an abortion, right on the tape. And from the way it sounded, Hillary was in bad shape, so I wouldn't be surprised if this girl . . . Well, yeah, she said Hillary was her girlfriend, right?"

"Yeah. So they were friends. So . . ."

"So I wouldn't be surprised if it was Hillary's girlfriend, probably a close friend, who drove her home from the clinic after the abortion. So she'd know which clinic it was."

"And it sounded to me like she ran, she got out of there, when she heard the governor and his wife coming."

"Sure. It was a secret abortion—the parents aren't supposed to know. The girlfriend drives Hillary to and from the clinic, but something goes wrong; the friend calls 911, but then the parents come home right in the middle of it; the friend drops the phone and gets out of there."

Carl blurted out another thought. "Yeah! And remember? She didn't want to give the dispatcher her name! She fumbled around and said her name was Hillary Slater."

"She was scared. She didn't want to be discovered."

The next thought was grim. "So . . . would the governor know who it was?"

"I . . . I think he'd want to. We're looking at a cover-up here. That Warfarin overdose story was a smoke screen. If I were the governor, I'd want to know who that girlfriend was. She'd know a lot, and she'd certainly know that the Warfarin story was a lie."

"But would he even know she was there at all?"

John thought for a moment. "He had to. Hillary was in no condition to make that phone call. She was semiconscious at best when the call was made—and in a different room from where the phone was by the sound of it. The phone was already off the hook and the emergency call made when the governor got there. If I were the governor, I'd think Hillary had a friend along."

"If he heard this tape, he might recognize the voice."

"But first he'd have to get a copy of the tape." John looked at the cassette player. "Which he did. And now we have it."

Carl stared at the cassette player. "We're holding on to dynamite, you know?"

John was staring as well. "Yeah, we are. The governor's up for re-election, abortion's a hot issue in the campaign, his daughter died from a botched abortion, and he covered it up . . ." Then John's head sank. "And . . . if it was the same clinic . . . that means Annie Brewer's death could have been prevented."

Carl added, "It also means this girlfriend of Hillary's could be in big trouble."

John went to the workbench. "Let's gather this stuff up and get it put away. I'm going to call Leslie. We've got to get going on this."

On Monday the faces of John Barrett and Ali Downs began to appear in bold, splashy billboards all over town, holding their scripts, peering down at the passing traffic like ever-vigilant observers of the times, like godlike guardians of Truth, their expression kind, their gaze incisive.

Against a field of video-grid blue, the fiery letters proclaimed, "BARRETT AND DOWNS, YOUR PREMIERE NEWS TEAM," and then the next line read, "NEWSSIX AT FIVE, A FULL HOUR OF NEWS!"

The Big Push was on, and the whole city was hearing about it.

Video: The interior of a large church packed with people. The camera pans slowly over the crowd, catching the mournful faces, some people weeping. A sad occasion.

Cut to a minister in a black robe speaking from the pulpit.

Audio: "All our children grow as flowers in a garden, and sometimes God decides to pick one for His own bouquet. In Hillary, God found the fairest flower of all. We will miss her. We will miss her smile, her laughter, her love of life . . ." Fast forward. The minister's mouth chatters rapidly, his head twitching from side to side and down at his notes.

Another angle: The governor and his family seated in front.

"Hold it there," said John, and Leslie released the fast forward and put the tape on pause. As the minister continued speaking, Governor Hiram Slater sat beside his wife and two remaining children.

"Okay, what are the names again? Who's who?"

It was Monday night after the Seven O'clock newscast. John, Leslie, and Carl were seated in John's living room, watching videotapes Leslie had checked out from the station archives—raw footage of Hillary Slater's funeral.

"That's Ashley Slater, of course, Hiram Slater's wife."

"She's taking it pretty hard," Carl commented.

"She did. The night they found Hillary, she had to be hospitalized and sedated." She looked at John to check. "We didn't say anything about that on the air, did we?"

John shook his head. "We kept this whole thing pretty low-key, which was only right."

Leslie hit the Pause button. "The girl is Hayley Slater. She's fifteen, the second oldest, currently a sophomore at the Holy Names Academy. Both she and her brother are attending there now."

John noted that with interest. "Uhh . . . is this something new? I don't remember them going to a Catholic school."

"They didn't. Last year all three kids were going to the Adam Bryant School, a private K through 12. A lot of the state senators and representatives send their children there while the legislature's in session. It's a good school, not real posh, good academics. All that to say . . . the governor took Hayley and Hyatt out of the Bryant school right after Hillary died and put them in Holy Names, just that quick."

"We'll keep that in mind."

"Anyway, that's Hyatt. He's twelve, I think. He's a sharp

kid. I interviewed him once." Leslie hit the Pause button again, and the video continued. They noted the people in attendance—many VIPs, of course, and a sizable throng of unidentified friends and family members.

"And," said Leslie, "that's about it for that one."

John prompted, "You said you had some video of reacts from Hillary's friends?"

"Coming up." Leslie ejected the funeral cassette and reached into her carrying case for the next one. She pushed it into the machine and hit the Play button.

Video: Exterior of the Adam Bryant School.

Leslie explained, "I remember this one. Joyce Petrocelli did the package, and this is footage of the school. You can imagine the copy while this ran. Joyce read something like, 'Students at the Adam Bryant School mourned the loss of a friend, and counselors were available to those who needed to talk about it . . .'"

"Right, I remember this," said John. "What we're looking for now is that friend who's on the 911 tape, so watch and listen carefully."

"Oh-oh."

A pretty blonde girl appeared on-camera, looking forlorn, talking to the interviewer whose microphone was visible under the girl's chin.

"She was . . . she was really nice. I'm going to miss her."

Joyce Petrocelli asked off-camera, "Did you do a lot of things together?"

"Well, kind of . . ."

"That's not her," said Carl.

"Nope," said John.

Leslie held the Fast Forward button until another face appeared, a young man. She went past him to the next face. A young black girl. "It's just so sad . . . we were looking forward to graduation . . . I mean, she had her whole life ahead of her . . ." She began to weep.

"I don't think so," said Leslie.

John looked at Carl. Carl shook his head.

Fast forward. A round-faced girl with curly brown hair.

"She was always the cheerful one. I mean, she wasn't stuck up or anything even though she was the governor's daughter—she just acted like the rest of us. She was great."

Nope. Fast forward.

Two more boys.

Then another girl with short blonde hair, fidgeting and jiggling nervously. "Well . . . we sang in choir together, and she was a great singer . . ."

Carl leaned closer, and so did John. Leslie looked doubtful.

"It's just scary, you know? One day she's there, and the next day she's gone. You just don't know what to think, what to say . . ."

"No," said Leslie.

"No," John agreed.

But those were all the reacts on the tape. They hadn't found Friend 911.

"What else?" John asked.

"Three more," said Leslie. "I've got that story we did on the Hillary Slater Memorial Fund, and a few of the spin-offs we did. Um . . . this one on product tampering and mislabeling, and this consumer story by Dave Nicholson on how to safeguard your medicine cabinet."

John waved the last two off. "No, not those spin-offs, unless they've got information about Hillary on them."

"No. But lastly, I have . . ." She asked for approval with her eyes. ". . . the footage at the governor's rally, the shots of your father."

John braced himself and said, "Okay, run it. Maybe we'll be able to make out what he said, you never know."

It was familiar stuff—painfully familiar. There was Leslie in front of the camera, and there was Dad, visible above the crowd behind her. She was apparently waiting for her cue to start her stand-up.

"Weird, huh?" said Leslie. "I'm not even saying anything but they taped the whole feed back at the station. I think Tina Lewis wanted the footage—that's all there is to it."

John felt like cursing right then and there, except that now he was trying to quit. Dad was talking, but they couldn't quite hear what he was saying. "Uh . . . turn it up a little, could you?"

Leslie cranked up the volume until John Barrett, Sr.'s words became intelligible. ". . . Governor, I plead with you, search your heart and change your course, for if you do not, God will change it for you . . ."

Carl was spellbound by the image and sound of the old man prophesying from the concrete planter and leaned toward the television, watching intensely.

John watched with a whole new set of eyes. Suddenly he realized how much he identified with that one pitiful soul up on that planter, that one lone voice against a contrary multitude.

"Like Nebuchadnezzar of old," Dad said with tears in his eyes, "you have set up an image of yourself for all men to follow, a towering image, a mighty image, an image far greater than yourself. But please take heed: the Lord would remind you, you are not that image."

John could see the reaction of the crowd—the animosity, the hatred. But Dad kept going; he just kept preaching with a desperate fervor.

And no wonder, John thought. During this moment, while the crowd mocked and jeered and his own son was ashamed of him, he knew about Hillary and he knew about Annie. He was crying out for them, and for how many others? And how much more did he know that John, Carl, and Leslie hadn't discovered yet? How many times had he wished for someone, *anyone,* to listen to him, and no one would listen? The governor probably never saw his letter. His own son gave no credence to his message. No wonder Dad stood there alone, shouting to that crowd.

This was not a kook or a religious fanatic. This was a heartbroken man pushed to desperate measures, just trying to do right, trying to be heard.

"Why don't you just shut up, big mouth!" came a voice from the crowd. John strained to see who'd yelled that, but couldn't tell.

"The Truth must be heard, though the lie be a tumult," Dad replied.

"Not him again," came a woman's voice.

"Get off that planter!" yelled someone else. "You don't belong up there."

Then the crowd started chanting into Dad's face, "Hi-yo, Hiram! Hi-yo, Hiram!" and Dad's words were buried under the clamor.

John watched as Dad tried to reach them, tried to be heard, pain filling his face. But his voice had vanished under the noise. A forest of shaking fists sprouted up at his feet.

"Hold it," John said. "Stop."

Leslie hit the Pause button. The picture froze into a silent tableau. There was Dad, his arms outstretched toward the crowd—and there was the crowd, so much like an angry mob, shaking their fists, their faces twisted in anger and loathing. The caption could have read, "Let him be crucified!"

John's head sank, and he covered his face. He needed a moment to gather himself.

Leslie considered whether to continue the tape. "I don't know . . . Maybe that's all there is of your father . . . Well, later on he gets grabbed and hauled off. I don't know if you want to see that . . ."

John took some deep breaths to pull himself together and then wiped the tears from his eyes. "Leslie . . . Carl . . . that was no kook . . ." When he raised his head, they were not looking at him.

They may have been listening, but their attention was fixed on the still screen.

"No," said Leslie, her face troubled. "It wasn't."

"No way," said Carl.

John looked again at the screen, at the lone prophet becoming the object of a mob's hate. "He was right. Everything he said was true."

Carl gazed at the screen, at John Barrett, Sr. standing his ground. "That was my Grandpa. That was him! That was the man . . . the man with a creed!"

John too gazed at that hurt old man, his heart filled with

yearning. "The man with a creed," he repeated, and then a phrase came to mind from his religious tradition. "His feet planted on the Rock."

Leslie fell silent, her eyes on the screen, her fingers over her mouth. John Barrett, Sr. was speaking to her. John could see it in her face.

"Leslie?"

She jumped a little, startled out of her contemplation.

She looked at John and Carl and then back at the screen. "He . . . he couldn't be moved, could he? Look at that—a whole river of humanity moving all around him, and there he is, holding still, just standing firm."

"Mm." John nodded, fully realizing her point. "Yeah, we've talked about that, haven't we?"

"We've talked about it." Leslie pondered it just a moment longer, and then, tucking it all away somewhere in her heart, she left it there and got back to business. "Well . . . I guess we've gotten the message from that tape."

John agreed with the shift back into gear. "Sure. At least we have a rough idea of what he was talking about, and knowing what we know now, it all makes a lot more sense."

Carl suggested, "Well, how about the last one?"

"Sure," John said. "Let's get on to that."

Leslie explained as she changed the tapes, "Well, this is whatever NewsSix did on the governor announcing the Hillary Slater Memorial Fund. I think Joyce Petrocelli was on this one too. I don't really remember it." She hit the Play button and they waited, starting to feel a bit weary.

Video: An auditorium filled with students.

"Oh, right!" said John. "The student assembly at the Adam Bryant School. Any date on the tape?"

Leslie ejected the tape momentarily and checked the label. "May 3rd, 1991. What's that? Just about two weeks after Hillary's death."

"Yeah, two weeks."

Leslie put the tape back in and let it play.

The governor was starting his speech, speaking informally from note cards. "I know many of you were close friends of

Hillary's, and her passing is a tragic loss to all of us. Her years here at Bryant made up a substantial part of her brief seventeen years, and you, her friends, were the center of her life. She spoke of you often, and . . . well, you know how it is with high schoolers, how they get so wrapped up in activities and school functions with their friends, you hardly ever see them. That's how it was with Hillary. Her friends were important to her, they were her joy, and I know she was your joy . . ."

John put a quick note on his mental bulletin board: Then why did he yank Hyatt and Hayley out of Bryant? What about *their* friends?

The governor went on to praise the school, its principal, and its teachers, all longtime acquaintances whom the governor admired. Then he came to the focus of his talk, holding up a special envelope. "Education is a top priority for me as governor, and had Hillary lived, I would have done all I could to be sure she got the best education possible. But I want you to know that the dreams I had for her are still alive, and I want them to live on—if not through her life, then through the life of other students who exemplify the joy, the character, the virtue and tenacity which so characterized Hillary Nicole Slater."

The governor looked toward the side of the stage and smiled. "Well, when it came time to decide who would be the first recipient of the Hillary Slater Memorial Scholarship, we didn't have to look very far. I think it's only fitting that the first recipient is not only an honor student from Bryant, but also one of Hillary's closest friends. Shannon?"

The auditorium erupted into thunderous applause and cheers. The camera zoomed back, quickly focused, and caught a young lady, smartly dressed, dignified, and lovely, striding across the stage to join the governor at the podium.

As one, Leslie, John, and Carl leaned forward a little and peered at the screen.

She was beautiful, but she seemed ill at ease and her smile weak. As she came and stood beside the governor, her hands clasped nervously in front of her and her eyes on the podium, not on him, he finished his comments. "I know that if Hillary could see us now, she'd be cheering and saying, "Go, Shannon! Go after your dreams!" He looked toward the audience again. "The very first Hillary Slater Memorial Scholarship is hereby awarded—with pride—to Shannon DuPliese!"

Applause, applause. Now the kids all rose to their feet, applauding and cheering as the camera panned the auditorium.

"Speech, speech!" said Carl spontaneously.

"Does she say anything?" John asked Leslie.

Leslie gave a shrug. She couldn't remember.

The governor handed Shannon the envelope, shook her hand, and then . . . Shannon turned away and went back to her chair on the stage, sitting between her teachers and what must have been her parents. Her mother gave her a hug and a kiss on the cheek. Shannon took it all with a sorrowful, troubled expression.

They kept watching. Perhaps there would be an interview.

The tape ended in snow. No speech. No interview.

"Don't you just hate it?" Leslie moaned.

"Where's Shannon now?"

"Probably off to college somewhere, spending her scholarship."

"Yeah . . . her scholarship," John mused. "Only two weeks after his daughter dies, the governor has a memorial fund set up and a recipient picked out—Hillary's best friend."

"Well . . ." Leslie was dubious.

"Oh, I know I'm being suspicious, but . . . right now we're scratching for anything."

Carl understood John's drift. "So you're saying he bought her off?"

"We've got to hear her voice, I know that."

"Okay," said Leslie, "I'll check the library for news clippings. There might be some info on what college she planned to attend. Then I'll call the college and see if I can find her."

"And then what?" Carl asked. "What are you going to ask her?"

Leslie shrugged. "I haven't thought of that yet."

John sat up straight and started scanning the list in his head. "We've all got plenty of work cut out for us, and I think we need to move fast, before we get found out and the governor can bury everything."

"We have seen that happen," said Leslie.

"You got that right," said Carl.

"Well, that's why we have to keep this all under wraps. I don't even want the police to know, not until we have something they can really run with in a hurry. I don't think we'll be interfering with any investigation because right now there isn't one. And besides, NewsSix has a reporter on the police beat, and if he gets wind of it, Tina Lewis and various other elements at the station will get wind of it too."

"So what are the assignments?" Carl asked. He was raring to go.

"Carl, let's you and I call these numbers here in Dad's notes and try to find out who this paramedic is and what he knows. Then, based on whatever we find out, Leslie can track down this . . . uh . . . the MD who filled out Hillary's death certificate."

Leslie found the death certificate and the name. "Dr. Leland Gray."

"So, Leslie, if you would, track him down and see if he'll release any information at all. Did he do the autopsy, and if not, then who did, and . . . what we're finally after is the real cause of death. Something got altered or covered up somewhere along the line."

"What about Dr. Denning?" Carl asked.

"I'm still waiting for him to get back from Sacramento," said Leslie. "But I feel good about that contact. I think it's in the bag."

"What did Deanne Brewer say?" John asked.

"I'm respecting her more as I get to know her. We talked this afternoon by phone, and I think she understands what happened, and she trusts us. Max still doesn't, which makes it hard for her. She's hesitant to associate with us again until he simmers down."

"That autopsy report would help, wouldn't it?"

Leslie smiled. "If we can come through with that—and it's

still going to take Deanne's help—it would make a nice peace offering. We have to convince Max he isn't being used again."

John made a grim face. "That's why we have to keep this quiet until we can play the game on our terms. I've still got my theory—maybe more than a theory—that both Hillary and Annie died in the same clinic. But if we're going to prove that, we're going to need on-the-record testimony from both Shannon DuPliese and that other girl, the one called 'Mary'—if Shannon DuPliese is the girl on that 911 tape and if 'Mary' will come forward again and go on the record. And if we're going to do that, we can't have any more confidence crashes or foul-ups."

"Good luck," moaned Carl.

John replied directly, "That's the goal, folks. That's what we're after."

"That's what we're after," Leslie agreed. "Plus any revelations about your father's death?"

"I've got a sneaking suspicion that we'll stumble over those in the process. So . . ." John scribbled as he spoke. "I've got a friend at the capitol—Charley Manning. He used to feed me tips all the time, years ago when I was still a reporter . . ."

"Exciting days, huh?" asked Leslie.

John smiled. "Oh, they're getting exciting again. But anyway, I'll ask him if there have been any upheavals in the governor's office. I'm just wondering if someone close to the governor has any reason to want to get back at him."

"By leaking a sensitive tape to a plumbing wholesaler?" Carl asked not needing an answer.

John stopped short. "Hm . . . Whatever Dad was finding out, it could have been enough reason for somebody to kill him. Now that they've killed him, the heat's got to be turned up for whoever it is." He took a moment to be sure he had their eyes and then said, "Whatever, whoever this ultimately leads to, they're not going to like what we're doing."

twenty-two

AS it turned out, Glen Murphy, the first name on one of Dad's little note sheets, was one of Barrett Plumbing and Fixtures' longtime customers, a partner with his brother in Beacon Hill Plumbing, a nice little retail supply and repair service on the south end. The guy sounded jolly enough over the phone, one of those loud-laughing characters who lived to hunt, fish, and watch football on wide-screen TV. In person he was big, wide-waisted, and a real back-slapper.

"Well, no kidding," he bellowed, standing behind the counter in Beacon Hill Plumbing with his burly arms crossed. "I am really talking to John's boy face to face?"

"You sure are," said John, accepting Glen's firm handshake. "And this is my son, John's grandson, Carl."

Glen grabbed Carl's hand and pumped it with his big fist. "Well, good to meet you, Carl." He told John, "Nice looking boy you got there."

Carl smiled. This guy was making him feel a little shy, but at least Glen Murphy would not be put off by his appearance, which certainly had changed. Carl had let his grandma cut his hair into something conventional, trimmed evenly on the sides, parted on the left, quite mute as far as any statement was concerned. As for the jewelry, it had remained in his drawer at home. Carl gave no reason for the change other than he just felt it was time for one.

"Well," Glen said in a somewhat more sober tone, "Al's here, so let's go on into the office. Jack, cover the counter." Jack, a young man in a blue apron, nodded and took his post, while Glen led John and Carl down an aisle past shower heads and flexible tubing to an office in the back of the store.

Glen made the introductions. "Al Connors, this is John Barrett, Junior . . . John Barrett's son. And this is John Barrett's grandson, Carl. John and Carl, Al Connors; he's a paramedic."

Al Connors was a young, blond, mustached man about

thirty years of age with a somber expression, dressed informally in jeans and plaid shirt. "Well . . . pleased to meet you. I've seen you on TV. Your father told me about you."

Glen cleared off a portion of desk to sit on, and the others found chairs. "Al, just to get you caught up, this is almost a repeat of last time. Remember, I called you about the elder John Barrett wanting to pick your brain a little."

Al nodded. It seemed he was feeling things out before saying too much.

Glen continued, "I already told John here about that—how his dad and I got talking about the governor's daughter and . . . When was that?"

"May, I think," said Al. "Early May."

"Yeah. I know the governor's daughter had just died, and they'd buried her . . ."

"And that's when you and I talked about it," said Al.

"Yeah, right . . . since you were there and saw the whole thing." Glen said to John and Carl, "We're fishing buddies. When you're out in a boat you talk about all kinds of things."

"Sure," said John. "So you came to Dad's warehouse the week after that . . ."

"Yeah, and your dad saw me and right away, like it was the first thing on his mind, he took me aside and asked me, 'Glen, you've heard something about Hillary Slater. Can you tell me what you know?' and I was kind of . . . you know, surprised that he'd just ask me that, like he knew I'd been talking to Al or something. But I told him what I'd heard from Al and how I thought it was a real sad situation—"

Al interjected, "But he already knew about the abortion thing."

"Yeah, right. That's why we got him and Al together." Glen could tell from John's face that some parts of the narrative had gotten lost somewhere. "Well, you see . . . Al and his buddy on the medic crew had a feeling about the Slater case . . ."

Al interjected again, "You know what the final story was on it, right? That Hillary Slater died from an overdose of Warfarin?"

John and Carl nodded.

"Well, that's what it turned out to be in the end, that's

what the doctor at the hospital said it was, but up to that time . . . Well, we were never sure, but we had it in the back of our minds that we could be working with a fouled-up abortion. I mean, it looked bad, and we both remember the dispatcher saying there may have been an abortion. That didn't pan out, but . . . boy, the whole time, from what we saw, it sure could have been. I remember Joel, my partner, whispered to me so nobody could hear him, 'Maybe this is what a coat hanger does,' but we thought that out and knew it didn't make sense, not with the abortion laws making it so easy for anybody to get one. But anyway, we were thinking about it."

Glen spread his hands and asked John, "So how did your dad know about that? He wasn't there."

John was about to venture an answer, but Glen kept going, not needing one. "So anyway, I told your dad what Al and I talked about, and your dad said he wanted to talk to Al himself, so we set it up, just like we set this up."

"So Dad met with you . . . when?"

"Oh, first or second week in May. It wasn't long after the Slater girl had been buried and things were beginning to settle down." Al paused a moment to reflect on the memory. "I liked your dad. I'm real sorry he died. I'm sorry for your loss."

"Thank you."

Al looked at John and Carl with inquisitive eyes. "Talking to you, I almost feel like I'm talking to him again. You know how it is. You don't like to make waves or ask too many questions. But your dad seemed to be the kind of guy who did, and I liked that about him. I can't speak for him; I don't know exactly why he was going after this, but . . . I don't think it was just to get some spicy stuff on the governor. I think he had something more in mind. He was feeling pain for somebody." Al turned to Glen. "Don't you think so?"

Glen shrugged a little and said, "I think he was grieving for Hillary—maybe for a lot of Hillarys."

"Well, anyway," said Al, "maybe you'll be able to finish where he left off."

"We hope to," said Carl.

John added, "Right now we're trying to find out where he left off. So . . . why don't you tell us what you told him? Tell us what happened."

"Sure . . . Okay." Al pulled a piece of paper from his pocket, some brief notes to aid his memory. "I'm with District Twelve. Been a paramedic there for the past five years. I was on the evening shift on Friday, April 19th, when we got the dispatch at 18:02, a 'vaginal bleed' at 1527 Roanoke West, which is the governor's residence, his mansion."

Glen jumped in with, "Hey, Al, tell him about that . . . how much you hear about vaginal bleeds."

"Well, they're not uncommon. I've noticed it, and the people I work with have talked about it—not out in the open, but, you know, just here and there, just a little bit. But when you come right down to it, we get 'vaginal bleed' calls on a pretty regular basis. It makes you wonder."

"How many are from abortions gone wrong?" John ventured.

Al shook his head. "We just don't talk about it. And you know, the manual we use doesn't say a thing about it either. It mentions spontaneous abortion, which is miscarriage, but not botched, intentional abortions."

"Hm."

"But anyway, we don't always go out on vaginal bleeds. A lot of times they aren't real serious, and the aid units and EMTs handle those by themselves. But this was a bad one. They had an aid unit and us together. Anyway, we responded, and while en route we got our short report from the dispatcher: 'unknown age female experiencing difficulty breathing, unknown if conscious, possible induced abortion.'"

John wanted clarification. "So the dispatcher actually said 'abortion'?"

"'Possible induced abortion.' Until you get there, you don't really know. But the reporting party must have said something to that effect or the dispatcher wouldn't have relayed it to us."

John and Carl exchanged another glance. So far Al's account was lining up with the 911 recording.

Al continued, "So we got to the governor's mansion, and that's a nice big place. I don't know if you've ever seen it . . ."

"Never been inside."

"Oh, it's nice. Big entryway and a long, curving staircase and fancy paneling, all that stuff. Governor Slater's wife met us right at the door. It was kind of strange, seeing her upset, frantic, just like real people. You forget they're people like anybody else. But she took us upstairs and down the big long hallway to their daughter's bedroom, and there Hillary was, laid out on her bed, and we knew we had ourselves a real problem. Mrs. Slater had been trying to sop up the blood with towels, and we almost had to grab her and wrestle her to get her out of the way so we could do our job. The patient was gasping for breath, cyanotic—"

"What's 'cyanotic'?"

"Uh . . . turning blue. Her lips and her fingernails were turning a bluish purple, from loss of blood and oxygen."

"Mm."

"So we got an oxygen mask right on her and worked on her vital signs. Her pulse was weak and rapid, and the blood pressure . . . Well, we couldn't hear well enough to get a reading with a stethoscope, Mrs. Slater was hollering so much and the governor was hollering trying to keep her from hollering and . . ." Al had to pause for a moment. The memory was obviously still disturbing to him. "Well, it was just a real mess, I want to tell you. We finally got a blood pressure reading by palpitating . . ."

"Mm, you mean, by touch?"

"Right—holding her wrist and feeling for a pulse. And we counted respiration, which was rapid. She was in trouble all around, to put it simply. She was bleeding to death, just bleeding out. The EMTs were there then, and they shared the load. We gave her an IV, got a tube into her airway, got the bag valve hooked up to the tube to assist her breathing—you know, pump air into her lungs because she wasn't getting enough. Then we radioed the police to do a blood run for us."

"What's that?"

"Well, we draw blood samples from the patient, fill three

vials, and then send the cop after blood. He meets us at the hospital and then we're ready to transfuse."

"Got it."

"So . . . we got the stretcher in, got her on it, and got ready to transport her to the hospital. Oh . . . while we were doing that, I asked the parents some real quick questions. I asked them if Hillary was pregnant or if she'd ever given birth before or if she was under a doctor's care for any special medical problems or if she was taking any medication. It didn't really matter what I asked—they didn't know anything."

"So they had no idea she was pregnant?"

"They weren't aware of it."

"And so I imagine they knew nothing about any abortion?"

"They . . . well, all of this was new to them. They had no idea what was going on. I had my suspicions, but it wasn't my place to tell them that. Once we got her to the hospital and the doctor had a look at her, then he could determine what the cause was and handle the parents. So anyway we transported her to the hospital."

"Bayview Memorial?"

"Right. We got her into the Emergency Room, and that was when the governor's family physician, Leland Gray, got into the loop. He was waiting there at the hospital, and he basically took over, calling the shots. We told him everything we knew, including our suspicions that it might be an abortion, and he took it from there. But obviously it was too late. She died on the table. Dr. Gray called it at 7:14 P.M. The governor and his wife were both there at the hospital, along with their other two kids, and I remember Dr. Gray going out to the waiting area to tell them, and I remember Mrs. Slater really going hysterical. She had to be sedated and admitted to the hospital for the night."

John wanted to double-check. "You did tell Dr. Gray about the abortion factor?"

Al nodded with a resigned look on his face. "Yeah, we did, and it surprised us a little when we checked back and heard it was an overdose of Warfarin. But what the doctor says, that's what it is. You just don't know everything when you're on the scene, and you don't have the whole picture 'til you bring the patient in. So when the whole picture finally comes out, well, that's that. You had your own theories, but the doc says what it really is."

John asked, "Dr. Gray in this case?"

"Well, him and the pathologist who did the autopsy. We didn't find out the true cause of death until a few days later. I think they did the autopsy the next day, Saturday, and we found out on Monday."

"We saw it was Dr. Gray who filled out the death certificate."

"Yeah. He certified the cause of death."

"And after all this, what do you think of Dad's idea?"

"That it was a botched abortion? Well . . . I'm still wondering how he knew about it. But the big problem with that whole theory is that you'd have to have Dr. Gray and then the hospital pathologist both be liars or in cahoots or something. When the governor's physician and the pathologist agree it was an accidental overdose of Warfarin, and the doctor signs the death certificate to that effect, what else are you supposed to think?"

"I might take into consideration the influence the governor and his personal physician might have."

Al smiled. "Yeah, you might."

John's brow wrinkled a little. "And . . . how do you know the pathologist even agreed with Dr. Gray's finding?"

Al's face went a little blank. "Well . . . the pathologist did the autopsy . . ."

"But how do you know the autopsy found the same cause of death that Dr. Gray states on the death certificate?"

"Well, it's a pretty safe assumption to make, isn't it?"

John said, mostly to himself, "It would be nice to see the autopsy report."

Al shook his head. "Not without a court order, you won't. It's confidential. But you know the official version."

"Tell us again so we can compare notes."

Al drew a deep breath, gathered an outline in his mind, and laid it out succinctly. "The way I understand it, the governor was taking Warfarin for a blood clot in his leg. Dr. Gray prescribed it. It was no secret or anything. When Hillary took those pills by mistake, well, Dr. Gray said it was just one of those freak accidents—bad timing and bad labeling at the same time. Hillary Slater was having her period and probably thought she was taking pills for menstrual cramps when she took her father's pills by mistake, which makes sense, I suppose. The doc said the dosage of pain medication she would have taken would have been about right, but the same dosage of her father's medication would have been enough to bring on a hemorrhage from her uterus and . . . well, that's what we found—an obvious hemorrhage from the uterus—and that's the explanation we got."

"Let's go back to the governor's house for a minute. Now you say you found the governor there and his wife."

"Right."

"Did you see anyone else in the house?"

"Well, the other two kids."

"Hayley, the daughter, about fifteen?"

"Right. And the boy. They were pretty shook, of course."

"Anyone else?"

"Well, besides our crew, the aid crew, and then the police who came for the blood run, no."

"No other friends or relatives?"

"I didn't see anyone else."

"Uhh . . . I'm curious. Any idea who called 911?"

Al thought about that a moment. "Mm, well . . . I always thought it was the governor. Nobody said who made the call."

"What about the dispatcher? Would he know more about that?"

Al shook his head. "That's out of bounds. 911 calls are confidential, and the dispatcher sure isn't going to give you any details if he values his job."

"What about the recording of the call itself? How would someone get a copy of that?"

"I don't think you could, to be honest. First you'd have to be a family member or a close relative, and even then you'd have to file a Request for Information form and have the station captain okay it, and then you could get a copy taken from the master tape, but . . . there's no way some reporter with no connections at all is going to get a copy of that conversation. It just isn't done, not without a court order, which you won't get without a really good reason."

John and Carl exchanged a glance.

Now Al spoke more out of fantasy than hard possibility. "It would be great if you could get the hospital pathologist, the guy who did the autopsy, to tell you what really happened. That would settle everything, wouldn't it?"

"Dr. Matthews? Harlan Matthews?"

Dr. Harlan Matthews, pathologist at Bayview Hospital, looked up from his desk to see an attractive blonde woman poking her head through the open door.

"Yes?"

Leslie stepped in and came up to his desk, offering her hand. "I'm Leslie Albright. May we talk for just a minute?"

Dr. Matthews was young-looking, although his tired expression was giving his age away, which was forty-five. "We'll have to make it quick. I have an autopsy coming up in just a few minutes."

"Oh, I'll be brief. This is regarding an autopsy you performed on Hillary Slater, the governor's daughter, back in April."

He smiled courteously. "I'm not going to be able to say much about it. The information is confidential."

"Oh, I'll be careful. I was just wondering—"

"Now wait a minute . . . What business brings you here anyway? Just who am I talking to?"

She smiled, feeling awkward. "Well . . . this is going to sound funny, but . . . I'm Leslie Albright, and though I work for Channel 6, I'm not here as a reporter for them. I'm here on my own."

The light dawned. "Oh, yes! I've seen you on NewsSix. I thought you looked familiar." He chuckled. "Now I know I'm not going to have anything to say."

Leslie chuckled only to keep things loose and friendly, if

that was at all possible. "Doctor, I assure you there are no cameras . . ." She opened her suit jacket. "No hidden microphones either. I'm not after a scoop."

Dr. Matthews looked at his watch, making sure she saw that he was looking at his watch. "You have one minute to clearly state your business."

Leslie spotted a chair near the door. "Um . . . may I sit down?"

He extended his hand toward the chair, offering it to her. She sat.

"Of course," she began, "everyone has been told that Hillary Slater died from an overdose of Warfarin, resulting in a hemorrhage from her uterus." She could see the immediate tension in the doctor's face. Her time with this man was going to be quite limited, she could feel it. "Um . . . that's what the death certificate indicates."

"That's correct," he replied, and his tone indicated he hoped that would be the last word on the subject.

"Well . . . I did a little checking with the Records Department—I was trying to find out who did the autopsy, and that's how I found you—and I happened to find the transcriptionist who transcribed your remarks. She remembered it right away. It was a big deal, you know, the governor's daughter and all. It was easy to remember."

He looked at his watch again and began to clear his desk. "I have to be going."

Leslie started talking faster. "Well, before you go, sir, could you help me out with one thing?"

"I doubt it," he quipped, his eyes on his papers and paper clips, not on her.

"The transcriptionist thought the autopsy report was quite remarkable, especially since it contradicted the death certificate. According to her, your finding was that Hillary Slater died from . . . uh . . . 'exsanguination' . . ."

"That's correct," he said crisply, rising from his desk and stashing some reports in a file drawer.

"Uh . . . due to hemorrhaging from the uterus . . ."

He kept filing as if not hearing her.

"Due to . . . incomplete removal of the placenta and the products of conception. An incomplete abortion, in other words."

Suddenly he turned and just locked eyes with her. She couldn't tell if he was going to admit it or throw her out or both.

"I'm sorry," he said firmly, deliberately. "The autopsy report and everything connected with it is confidential, and I cannot discuss it."

"Well, without discussing the report itself . . ." Leslie stood up, planning to block the doorway if necessary, for as long as she could get away with it. ". . . I noticed that the governor's doctor, Dr. Leland Gray, signed the death certificate as the certifying physician. Apparently he was content with the Warfarin story, but . . . could you explain the discrepancy between the autopsy findings—which we won't discuss—and the cause of death indicated on the death certificate?"

He stopped on his way to the door. He was apparently a gentleman—he didn't trample her. He seemed to be thinking about what she'd said, reviewing his options. "I really can't explain that."

"Well . . . without discussing the report itself . . . were you aware, sir, that Hillary Slater had received an abortion the day she died?"

He shook his head and took one step toward the door. "I can't discuss that."

She held her hand up in one last hope of detaining him. "Off the record, sir, off the record . . . if . . . if I were to believe that Hillary Slater had an abortion the day she died . . . would you have trouble with that?"

"I can't discuss it! Now if you'll please step aside—"

"Don't tell me she did or didn't! Just . . . just for my own peace of mind in this, okay? If I . . . okay, if I thought Hillary had an abortion that day, would you have trouble with that? Would I be all wet?"

He smiled at her tenacity. She was thankful he was smiling at all.

"Ms. Albright, you can think whatever you want. It's a free

country. Now . . ." He motioned with his hand for her to step aside.

She held both hands out pleadingly. "Just one more question . . . Just one more . . . Please."

"It doesn't mean you'll get an answer."

"Off the record . . ."

"Off the record."

"If . . . if I were to say to you that Hillary Slater didn't die from a Warfarin overdose but from a botched abortion, would you . . . and you don't have to say if she did or didn't . . . would you have any trouble with that?"

He pointed his finger right at her nose, so close she almost crossed her eyes to see it. "Ms. Albright, you learned nothing new from me today, isn't that correct?"

She took a quick inventory and then replied, "Yes, that's correct."

"I've told you nothing you didn't already know?"

"Correct."

He looked directly into her eyes with a gaze that seemed it would push her backward. "The answer to your question is no. I wouldn't have any trouble with that. All right?"

She maintained a meek and courteous stance, and she truly was grateful. "Thank you, sir. Thank you for your time."

He stepped past her, took just a few steps down the hall, and then turned and pointed at her with that same forceful gaze. "Now don't bring this matter into my presence again, understand?"

"Yes, sir."

He turned his back on her and hurried down the hall.

She turned away, used the doorpost to keep her balance, and mimed a wide-eyed, silent whistle.

The nurse/receptionist sitting in the little glass window at Dr. Leland Gray's private practice took the call, made a note of it, and then informed Dr. Gray the moment he'd finished with a patient. "Dr. Gray, you received a call from Dr. Matthews at Bayview. He'd like you to return his call ASAP."

Dr. Gray was an older man with thinning gray hair combed

straight back, a firmly set jaw, and cold blue eyes that could stare down an army. Upon hearing this message, he maintained an even, general-like demeanor, but did take a peek through the window to see who was out in the waiting room. Mm. Nothing urgent.

"Mrs. Demetri is next?" he asked.

The nurse consulted her chart. "Yes. She's complaining of a sore throat."

"Mm . . . Okay . . . I'll be just a few minutes."

"All right."

He walked, almost marched, into his office and closed the door behind him. He quickly banged out a staccato tune on his touchtone phone and waited while the other end whirred a few times.

"Dr. Matthews," a voice answered.

"Harlan, this is Lee."

"Lee . . ." There was an uncomfortable pause.

"Well, come on, man, I have patients waiting."

"Bad news, Lee. I had a reporter from Channel 6 drop by my office. She's been sniffing around and knows about the Hillary Slater thing."

Dr. Gray's eyes narrowed, but his spine stayed straight.

"What reporter?"

"Leslie Albright."

"Never heard of her."

"She's no big name or anything, but she does news reporting for Channel 6."

"So what does she know, what did she ask, and what did you tell her?"

Matthews fumbled a bit at the rapid-fire questions.

"Well . . . first of all . . ."

"What did you tell her?"

"I told her nothing, Lee. I told her I could not discuss the case."

"So what does she know?"

"She knows . . . or at least she's in the process of finding out . . . the cause of Hillary's death."

Gray was getting angry. "Well, can't she read? The death certificate is quite clear!"

"She knows it doesn't line up with the autopsy report."

"How does she know that?"

"Well, I didn't tell her—I want to make that clear."

"Then who did?"

Matthews was getting flustered. "Lee . . ."

"Who did?" Then Gray spiced his question with some cursing which underlined his impatience.

"I've got an autopsy to do, so I haven't had time to ask around. Albright said it was the transcriptionist who typed up the autopsy report."

Now Gray just cursed without saying anything else.

Matthews kept going while he had the chance. "I do not know what got this Albright woman started on this, especially after all this time, but . . . obviously, there's been a leak somewhere, and I'll be direct about this—it didn't start with me. She already had her information before she came in here."

"Well, who's the transcriptionist?"

"I'm going to find that out."

"When you find out, tell me."

"I'll do that. Any other suggestions?"

"None at this time except keep your &$#@! yap shut!" Gray slammed down the receiver, thought a moment, and then picked it up again.

Miss Rhodes, Governor Slater's secretary, answered the phone at her desk. "Governor Slater's office." Upon hearing who the caller was, she put the call right through.

Governor Slater picked up the phone and then swiveled his big chair toward the window, the high back hiding him from the rest of the office. "Yes, Lee." He listened intently for a few minutes, his face turning grim, his hands making and unmaking fists on the arms of the chair. Looking out his window toward the capitol dome, he suddenly felt naked before the world and swiveled toward his desk again. "Thanks, Lee."

Less than three minutes later Devin rushed to the governor's office, strode in fast enough to kick up a breeze across Miss Rhodes' desk, and closed the door behind him.

"Sit down, Martin," said Slater.

Devin knew from the governor's face that there was trouble. The governor couldn't even come around to speaking for a moment, but brooded and steamed and then slammed the desk with his fist as he barked out a curse.

"Sir, what is it?"

Slater flopped back in his chair, his hand over his mouth, his eyes scanning the desktop as if it were covered with tiny pests he wanted to squash. "Martin . . . I'm afraid our wall has been breached."

Devin felt a spear go through his stomach. He knew what was coming. "What is it, sir?"

"I just got a call from our family doctor, Dr. Gray. As you know, he was there when Hillary died. He determined the cause of death and filled out the death certificate. He did what he could to protect my family's privacy."

Devin nodded. He'd been a party to all this.

The governor was seething and trying very hard to control his voice. "All it takes is an election year!" He cursed, and not too quietly. "Of all the years for her to die, and die this way, it had to be an election year!" Then he winced at his own words and backed down a little. "Aw, Hillary, I'm sorry." He seemed to be praying, addressing his daughter through the ceiling. "It wasn't your fault, I know." He looked at Devin. "But sometimes I can't believe my bad luck." He leaned over the desk and delivered the news. "Dr. Gray just got a call from the pathologist who did the autopsy—what was his name . . . ?"

"Uh . . . Matthews, I think. I have the records in my office—"

"Matthews, that's right. Matthews says a reporter from Channel 6 came by to see him. She was asking questions about Hillary's death and seemed to know what the real cause was!"

Now the spear in Devin's stomach twisted painfully. "Oh no . . ."

The governor just kept leaning over the desk with fiery eyes, so Devin had to ask the question. "You did say Channel 6?"

"Channel 6."

"Which reporter?"

"Albright. Do we know anyone named Albright?"

Devin nodded. "Why . . . yes . . . She was the one at the rally. It was her report that we . . . spiced up a little."

Slater reared up on his haunches and gestured widely. "Martin, how in the world did she find out? No one was supposed to know! Not even my wife knows!"

"I . . . I don't know, sir!"

"Well, I want you to find out, and I want you to kill whatever they're working on at that station. This is my business, my family's own personal business, and it is not for public consumption! You make them understand that!"

"Well, sir, I can't just—"

"You have friends there, Martin! Don't tell me you can't!"

"Tina Lewis has some influence, but she isn't the top power there. What about Loren Harris, the station's general manager? I thought you were friends with him."

Slater shook his head. "No, no, that's a last resort. Loren's too big, too visible, too . . . Well, don't you see the problem? If I lean on him, it will look like I'm trying to kill a story, like I'm trying to use my influence to cover up something, and if that gets out . . . !" He rolled his eyes at the very thought of it and took some time to pronounce fiery judgment on the whole situation. "I don't want to look like I'm doing anything about any of this. I want this handled quietly, under wraps, nothing visible, you understand?"

"Yes, sir."

The governor brooded some more, glared some more at the pests on his desk, and then appeared to spot one pest in particular. "Lake!"

Devin looked horrified because he was. "Lake? But . . ." His voice stuck in his throat, and he had to clear it. "We didn't . . . we didn't share any of this with him. How would he even know about it?"

The governor sneered at the memory of Lake's old, conniving face. "He could have found out if he really wanted to. He's not above anything if it'll give him power over his enemies. Well, we're his enemies now, Martin. I should have seen that coming."

Devin admitted, "Lake did leave here quite angry, that's true, sir."

The governor held up one finger to count. "I want you to find out what's going on, and then . . ." He held up two fingers. "I want you to stop it, if at all possible." And then the next thought. "And I think you ought to track down Mr. Lake and have a talk with him. Come to an understanding if you can."

Devin rose from his chair, not expecting his legs to be so wobbly. "Consider it done, sir. And don't worry."

"I'm worried, Martin," said the governor quite sternly.

"I'm worried too," Devin mouthed to himself as he went out the door.

Devin settled just a few other matters—made a few phone calls, implemented some office policy changes, and forwarded some speaking invitations to Wilma Benthoff, the governor's campaign manager. Then he buried himself in his office, the door closed, without a word to anyone. He was careful to make it look official—serious business, confidential, urgent, big stuff, only he could do it, don't ask, I won't tell you, it's only for us special people to know these things, especially me, the governor's most trusted confidant.

Once he was in his chair, behind his desk, behind his closed door, he had a chance to grope, curse, fume, worry, fret, and try to sort out what was happening. There had to be a way out of this. He'd taken too long, worked too hard, stepped on too many people to get where he was. There had to be a way out, an answer, a solution to the puzzle.

And he would find it. That was part of his job, wasn't it, to keep the governor on a smooth, even road, to keep his boss clean above all else? Well, he hadn't failed yet, and he had no plans to start failing now.

Okay, let's get it down, he mused, *let's get it organized.*

He scribbled some names on a piece of paper and then flipped open his desk directory for the phone numbers. Information was the first step. He was going to know what was going on, and once he knew, the next step would be control—lots of control, as much as he could muster.

First on the list: Dr. Harlan Matthews, the pathologist. He

would have to hear directly from the governor's office; it would remind him of the gravity of his duty . . . and the consequences should he fail in his duty.

"Dr. Matthews," came the voice on the line. Devin had a pen poised over a yellow legal pad, ready to scribble notes. "Dr. Matthews, this is Martin Devin, chief of staff and special assistant to Governor Slater."

"And what do you want?" He didn't sound too impressed by Devin's title.

Devin dove in, undaunted and ready to put the leash on this guy. He spoke rather curtly. "It's come to our attention that you've been speaking to a reporter from Channel 6. I've called to verify that."

Matthews was even less impressed. "Yes . . . Yes, I have been talking to a reporter. I even sent her home with a kidney and a gall bladder."

Devin did not take kindly to being toyed with. "Excuse me, doctor, I believe I asked you a question."

"Not yet you haven't."

"Have you been talking to a reporter?"

"Turn it around, Devin. A reporter came to see me, uninvited, unexpected. I turned her away and went about my business."

"Did she ask you questions about the Situation?"

"She did, and she received no answers."

"How can we be sure of that?"

Now Matthews was mad. "Because I'm a professional, Mr. Devin. I operate according to certain ethics."

Devin hadn't written anything yet. He drew back a little and tried a gentler approach. "Well . . . of course you understand that the governor and his family will appreciate your continued cooperation in keeping the whole matter in strictest confidence."

"The governor's wishes are none of my concern, and his worries are ill-informed. Listen, I do between ten and twenty autopsies a week, all of them according to the same procedures and protocol. The results are confidential, the information is not released to the public or the press, and it never has been. The governor's daughter was one case among many; I view it no differently, nor have I treated it any differently. Now either the governor is overestimating his own importance or he's underestimating me, and either way I'm more than perturbed."

Now Devin eased way down. He still needed information, and he was beginning to fear Matthews would hang up before he got it. "I understand, sir. But for my own information, could you tell me who the reporter was?"

"Leslie Albright, from Channel 6. She claimed to be here on her own and not as a reporter, but of course I couldn't trust that."

"Of course. But what questions was she asking?"

"What do you think? She wanted to know about the Situation. She already had all the basics."

That felt like death to Martin Devin. "Uh . . . did she say how she found it out?"

"Oh . . . she talked to one of our transcriptionists, but I'm sure she knew before that. She knew just what to look for and whom to ask."

"Did she mention John Barrett at all?"

"The anchorman?"

"Yes."

"No mention of John Barrett."

"And you told her nothing?"

Matthews was getting short of temper. "Hey, don't worry. I protected you, I protected Gray, I protected all of us. I know how the game is played, Devin. A thing like this could give the medical profession a bad image, and I don't want my neck on the block. I did my job, I filed an accurate and truthful report, I followed professional ethics, and I've kept my mouth shut. Whatever happens beyond my control . . . hey, it's your problem, and none of my doing."

"Well, I'm sure the governor will appreciate—"

Matthews cursed the governor and then said, "Just leave me alone, all right?"

Click.

twenty-three

Martin Devin slammed down the phone and took a moment to recover his resolve—and his ego. *Okay, Dr. Bigstuff Matthews, be a jerk.* There were other sources, the prime one being Tina Lewis herself, executive news producer at Channel 6. If there was anything going on of any consequence, she would know, and she would be willing to tell him about it. He'd helped her out in the past; he had no qualms about calling in a favor.

He tapped out the number, and Tina answered.

"This is Tina Lewis."

"Tina . . ." Devin felt like busting a few heads over at that station, but he knew he had to maintain a good relationship, especially in an election year. He used his old-buddies-from-way-back tone of voice. "Martin Devin here."

She was glad to hear from him. "Well, Martin, how are you?"

"Well, I'm quite all right."

Tina stepped over to her office door and closed it.

"So what are we going to do for each other today?"

"Well . . ."

Tina sat down and spoke in a lowered voice. "Sounds like we might have a problem."

"Yeah, we just might, and I knew you'd be the one to ask about it. The governor and I spoke this morning, and Tina . . . he's concerned about his personal privacy, his family's privacy." That was a cue, a hint about the problem.

But Tina didn't pick up on it. "Mm-hm. Hello?"

Come on, Tina, don't act so innocent! "Well, listen, I think we've had a good relationship with you and with other members of the press. You and I have always been open and straightforward with each other . . ."

Well, she didn't think he was being straightforward right now. "Martin, I'm not clear on what the problem is."

He couldn't help the cutting edge on his voice. "Then of course you're not aware of your reporters snooping around for private information on Hillary Slater, the governor's daughter?"

This was news to her. "What?"

"Hey, if you're after a story, just tell me what you need, Tina. Just come to me and let's talk about it. I gave you that camera opportunity at the governor's rally. I've tried to be a reliable source for you—"

She wasn't following him. "Martin—"

But he was rolling and didn't hear her. "—and as always, if you people want to know something or if you're planning a story, don't be afraid to let me know, or contact Wilma Benthoff. We'll give you what we have."

"Martin!"

"Do you follow me?" He was not asking but demanding.

Now Tina felt free to be angry herself. "No, Martin, I don't. Now suppose you back up a bit and tell me what's going on."

"Well, correct me if I'm wrong, but we happen to know that one of your reporters has been prying into some of the governor's private concerns."

"And did I hear you say something about Hillary Slater?"

Devin gave an exasperated sigh. "Yes. I'm talking about the governor's daughter Hillary and the details surrounding her death. I think we covered that sufficiently when it happened, and there's nothing more to be said about it."

"All right. You've finally made yourself clear."

"So let's hear about it."

"Well, hang on . . ." Tina reached for the latest Outlook Sheet, the computer printout that kept the newsroom up to date on who was doing what where and when. "How about a few details, or do I have to guess those too?"

Devin drew back to think. He had to decide what he could tell her. He knew a lot, but that didn't mean it was available. Sure, they had a good professional relationship, but the emphasis was on the word *professional.* Professionally speaking, Hillary Slater died from a Warfarin overdose, and that's how the media had covered it. Professionally speaking, Devin wanted it to stay that way.

"I can give you a name. Leslie Albright."

That was the right button to push. It got Tina on Devin's side immediately. "Leslie Albright! What's she been up to?"

"We understand she was snooping around Bayview Memorial Hospital today trying to dredge something up on Hillary Slater's death. It was all very tasteless. I thought maybe you would know about it."

"I wouldn't know about that, Martin. If I knew about it, it wouldn't be happening." Tina quickly perused the Outlook Sheet, muttering, "Of course, with Leslie there's no guarantee." Then she found Leslie's name. "I see here she was assigned to a story on automotive emissions."

"Now, Tina—"

"Hey, I've given you some good information in the past, and I'm not about to lie to you now. That's what the printout says, and to the best of my knowledge that's what she was covering today. So whatever she's up to, we didn't assign it. I'll just have to ask her. She might be researching a possible story on her own and we haven't heard about it yet. Reporters do that all the time. The station encourages it."

Devin took a moment to decide whether he believed that or not. "What about John Barrett? Is he involved in this?"

Tina looked out through the glass partition and surveyed the newsroom. Well, what do you know! There were John and Leslie right now, at Leslie's desk, having their own little private conference. "He . . . might be. I can ask both of them. But first I need to know what you know."

Devin hesitated a little. How much should he tell her? "I think . . . well, I think Albright, and maybe Barrett, are after something they hope will damage the governor. Albright was bothering a pathologist at Bayview Memorial Hospital this morning, trying to get him to reveal the contents of Hillary Slater's autopsy report, which, as you know, is confidential. It was a tasteless thing to do. I might even say it was vicious. It's the kind of thing you'd expect in an election year, I suppose."

Tina knew he was trying to rile her, to get her defensive and wanting to prove him wrong. She knew what he was up to, but it was working nevertheless. She could feel her anger rising as she spoke. "I don't think that kind of thing would be condoned by the management of this station, Martin. I know *I* would not condone it."

"Well, I certainly hope not."

"So what else? Anything more?"

Devin hesitated to answer. He didn't want to tell her.

And she knew it, which made her all the more curious. "Come on—I can't hang them without charges. Just what deep, dark secret are they trying to pull into the open?"

Devin took a moment to decide he could trust her to handle the information correctly and then settled on a half-truth. "Well, Tina, for some reason Albright seems to want to blame Hillary's death on a legal abortion."

"What!"

Ah, good, Devin thought. *She's mad but in the right direction.* "It's a preposterous notion, really, but this is an election year, and you know how the muck gets dredged up, whether it's there or not."

It's the Brewer thing, Tina thought. *Albright and Barrett are eating sour grapes because they couldn't get around the law. These people never rest!* "All right, Martin, I think I see what might be happening here. I'll check into it."

"I would appreciate hearing back from you right away."

"You will."

Devin hung up on Tina Lewis and went to the next person on his list, the principal at the Adam Bryant School where the Slater children were once enrolled.

"Erica Tyler."

"Ms. Tyler, this is Martin Devin, chief of staff and special assistant to Governor Slater."

She knew who he was. "Oh, yes . . ."

"We have a rather discreet matter to discuss. I won't take long."

"Yes, Mr. Devin."

"As I recall the conversation we had back in early May, you really had no answers to give to any questions, and that was fine with us—we were happy enough not to ask any questions. Do you recall that?"

She sounded just a little leery as she answered, "Yes, that's how I recall it."

"And we were happy to let things remain as they were, correct?"

"Yes, that was our understanding."

"Fine. Very good. Now the reason I'm calling and going over this once again is because we've just recently learned that some people in the press are beginning to ask questions, and though we don't know this for sure, they may very well come to you with those questions."

"Oh really?"

"As you can well understand, it would be the governor's desire that the same policy apply in every case, to all persons—namely, that you simply have no answers, that everything must remain confidential. Do we understand each other?"

"Oh, we certainly do, Mr. Devin. As I said to you before, this school desires no connection, no involvement whatsoever, with . . . uh . . . the Situation."

"Yes, and we agree with that. We both know, don't we, that any revelations that leak out would be very harmful to us and to you."

"Yes, we're aware of that. There will be no information available here, not for anyone."

"Excellent. We're more than happy to have it that way. But you should be advised, and also advise others on your staff, whoever needs to be forewarned, that some people from Channel 6 might come around asking questions, and maybe even some other members of the press, who knows? You might want to remind your staff of the understandings now in place."

"I'll do that."

"And I should ask at this point, have there been any questions? Any visits by the press? I'm thinking of Channel 6 in particular."

"No, Mr. Devin, not yet, not that I'm aware of."

"Good enough. Then so far we've contained everything. We'll have to be sure it stays that way."

"You have our fullest cooperation, Mr. Devin."
"Thank you. Good day to you."
"And you, sir."

Leslie and John had had a productive day—with assigned work and with their own research. As soon as Leslie returned from the field—with her auto emission story—they met at her desk, discussed some of the material being slotted for the Five O'clock, and then lowered their voices to discuss their investigation.

John gave a quick report, leaning on the partition, the day's Outlook in his hand. "I spoke with Charley Manning, my friend down at the capitol. I asked him if there'd been any recent firings or resignations or gripes in the governor's office, and he said he'd heard there'd been some kind of stink, but he didn't have any details. He's checking into it."

Leslie opened a manila file and produced some photocopied news clippings and some notes. "Here's a story from the *News Journal* on the governor's presentation of the Hillary Slater scholarship. Shannon DuPliese was planning on going to Western, right here in this state, but since she received the scholarship, she's enrolled at Midwestern University. It's an upper-crust school, no question; quite an opportunity."

John scanned the article and took another look at Shannon DuPliese. This time she was smiling for the camera as she stood by the governor holding her award, but John could still remember how troubled she seemed when she'd actually received it. "The governor's taking really good care of her, isn't he?"

"And . . . if I may take such a leap . . . he's also making sure she's far, far away."

John's expression said, Good point.

"Anyway," Leslie continued, "I'll give the university a call as soon as I can and see if Shannon's really there and try to get her phone number, her address, whatever." She lowered her voice even more. "I don't want to use a line here at the station."

John nodded in agreement. The phone records would be a perfect trail for someone like Tina Lewis to follow.

"I'm just not sure yet what I'll say. I don't think I want to identify myself with NewsSix. I just about lost Dr. Matthews because of that."

"Whatever you do, record the conversation. We've got to hear her voice."

"If I can get her talking about anything, we'll have at least half a success."

"Right."

Then Leslie quickly and nonchalantly stowed her materials, her eyes following someone's approach. John knew right away it had to be Tina.

It was. She wore a pleasant expression as befitted a professional, but they could tell a brooding storm cloud lay just under the surface.

"May I have a word with you two?"

Well, there was nowhere to run and no place to hide.

"What's up?" asked Leslie, standing to meet Tina.

Tina joined them by Leslie's desk, and now all three of them were standing in the aisle, almost blocking any traffic that should happen along.

"How's that auto emission story?" Tina asked, and they could tell she was hoping it wasn't finished.

"I gave it to Rush," said Leslie. "It's slotted and ready."

Tina turned to John, "And how's the editing going?"

John was honest. "Just fine. Same as usual, I suppose."

Tina looked at them just as a first grade teacher would look at two class cut-ups who weren't getting their work done.

"Well, great. Leslie, might I have a word with you?"

"Sure."

John took his cue and started for his desk.

"John," said Tina, "I may want to speak with you in a moment."

"Sure thing," he said over his shoulder. Silently he was praying for Leslie.

Tina pulled a chair over and sat down next to Leslie's desk as she said, "Go ahead, sit down."

Leslie sat.

Then Tina just sat there for a moment, eyeing Leslie in a way that used to make her nervous and timid, but now just made her angry.

Leslie pretended to be busy, tapping away at the computer console but doing nothing in particular. "You can look all you want, but I hope you won't mind if I try to get some work done."

"I'd like to know what you and John are working on."

Leslie looked directly at Tina, her anger and resentment fueling her courage. "Tina, first of all, we both understand that things are not too good between us."

Tina cut her off with, "And you do understand, don't you, what my position is and what my responsibilities are and who you answer to?"

Leslie considered herself interrupted and said no more.

But she was determined to stand her ground, and if it had to get nasty, then so be it. "I understand, Tina."

"Then I'd like to know what you and John are working on. It's my responsibility to know and your responsibility to tell me. I just paid a visit to the archives, and I noticed that you'd checked out the video of Hillary Slater's funeral. What do you have going?"

"We are pursuing a story, but so far we don't have anything solid, just some ideas, and we're not prepared to pitch it to you. It'll need some more time."

"Were you at Bayview Hospital this morning?"

The question was direct, and Leslie knew she couldn't lie. "Tina, I was there during my lunchtime, representing only myself and not this station, and I said so."

"Said so to whom?"

Leslie stopped, carefully rechecked her knowledge of newsroom policy, and then took a tough position. "Tina, I could sit here and evade your questions, but I don't like it when somebody does that to me, so I won't do it to you. To be perfectly honest, I just plain don't want to talk about it. The story hasn't been sold to any editors or producers, and neither has it been officially assigned, and therefore the station has no direct interest and you have no direct authority. Hey, if you don't like the idea once I pitch it to you, then the story's dead right there anyway. But until we're ready to pitch it and it's time for you to approve it, I don't want to talk about it."

Tina's spine straightened. It was her way of bracing for a fight. "Would you like to talk to Ben about this?"

"Sure. Let's go." Leslie stood up, got into the aisle, and even got several steps toward Ben's office before Tina finally broke and said, "Hold on." Leslie turned slowly, noticing Tina's icy glare, and returned to her desk. She sat down again, enjoying her first tinge of hope; she'd called Tina's bluff and actually come out on top. Newsroom policy had saved her bacon.

Most everyone in the newsroom understood how Ben encouraged the reporters to sniff around for scoops and exclusives, even on company time as long as their assignments were done and done well. And until the stories were actually bought by the producers or managing editor and officially assigned to the reporter, they were a reporter's privilege and domain. It was an effective incentive, and one way to protect a scoop from being stolen by other media. Tina must have been hoping Leslie would not invoke that rule, but unfortunately for her, Leslie did.

"So . . ." said Tina, visibly stewing, "the story's still yours."

"What there is of it, yes."

"How about John Barrett? Is he working on it too?"

Leslie was cornered on that one. She could lie and say he wasn't, but Tina would see right through that; if she refused to answer, that would be as good as answering. "We both are. But like I said, there isn't much there right now. We might have something to show you after a while."

Tina slowly wagged her head and pronounced sentence. "I'll never approve it. Better quit wasting your time."

Leslie objected, "Tina, you haven't even seen the story yet. You don't even know what it's about."

"I know enough," Tina replied, "and I promise, you'll never get it past me."

Leslie studied Tina's face, now hard, cold, and scowling about the eyes but showing the slightest hint of a devilish smile about the lips, and she recalled what John had said about Tina's secret wounds. It all fit. She could almost sense it herself as Tina sat there as hard as stone but at the same time as brittle as glass. For the first time, she understood what forces drove this woman.

Leslie spoke gently, her final word. "We'll see."

Tina rose and took a moment to glare down at Leslie from a higher eye level before she turned and walked jaw first back to her office.

Leslie looked across the newsroom. John was watching the whole thing. She hurried over to his desk to quickly fill him in.

"It looks like Tina's onto us and not at all happy about it," she said.

"So I observed," John answered. "But how much does she know?"

"We weren't very open with each other." John laughed, and Leslie continued, "She knows we checked out the video on Hillary Slater's death and funeral, and somehow she heard I was at Bayview Memorial today. Maybe Matthews complained, I don't know, but I think she picked up on the abortion angle. She promised me the story would never get past her."

"Well, it's safe to say she knows a lot. And judging from past performance, we might just have a race on our hands—we're trying to get the story and Tina's trying to blow it open and bury it before we do."

"She's good at that."

"We've got to call Shannon DuPliese *tonight.*"

"We've got to do anything and everything yesterday."

"Carl's working on rigging up a phone. I'll call and see how he's doing."

Only a little later, when other business, other subjects, and other people had put some time and distraction between herself and her frustrated conference with Leslie Albright, Tina called Martin Devin's office.

Devin was rather brusque. It was getting toward the end of the day. "What've you got?"

"Leslie Albright and John Barrett are working on something."

"So John Barrett is involved?"

"I'm quite sure he is."

"What do you mean you're quite sure? Is he involved or isn't he?"

Tina held the receiver away from her ear, offended, then warned, "Martin, please watch your tone of voice."

Devin tried to tone down. "I'm sorry. This whole thing has me upset, in case you hadn't noticed."

"Well, are you going to let me in on what's going on?"

"Just tell me what they're working on."

"I don't know exactly."

Devin cursed. "They work for you, don't they? Don't you know what your own people are doing?"

"Martin, the story isn't assigned, and they haven't pitched it to the managing editor or to me or to anyone, so at this point it isn't really the newsroom's business. It's their scoop until they sell it to us."

"What the *^!@$# are you talking about?"

"I'm talking about Channel 6 policy, that's what."

"Tina, now come on, give me a break. I need the story stopped. You've got to kill it before it gets out of hand."

This sounded big. Tina had to ask. "Martin, what's the story about?"

"I told you! It's a slanderous piece of trash just to smear the governor, dredging up slime about his daughter. I can't believe the audacity of some people!"

"Did Hillary Slater have an abortion?"

Devin seemed to drop out of existence for a moment. The silence on the other end spoke volumes. Finally he said, "Don't be ridiculous!"

Now it was Tina's turn to curse, and she made sure Devin knew her opinion of his character. "Don't you play your little games with me! You know where I stand on that issue, and I won't be lied to! I've done plenty for you. I've checked around for you. I've confided in you. Now if you want friends in the media you can start with me. Otherwise, we'll say good-bye right here and now!"

Devin thought it over for a long time and then gave in. "Then I guess we'd better have lunch tomorrow."

"Dinner tonight."

"All right . . . Dinner. How about Keaton's, at 7?"

"That'll be fine."

Devin fumed for another moment, then asked, "So . . . what do you think about the story they're working on? I mean, can you stop it?"

"It's already dead, Martin. I told Leslie I'd never approve it. They can do what they want, but they won't get anything on the air."

"Thank God."

"No, thank me. But, Martin . . ."

"Yes?"

"That doesn't mean this won't get out. Whatever it is, people are going to find out about it—other media are going to pick it up. You'd better be ready for it."

Devin sighed, cursed, and moaned, all at the same time.

That evening, immediately after the 7 o'clock newscast, Leslie and John rushed over to Mom Barrett's. Mom and Carl were there waiting, Mom with some snacks and coffee, Carl with a tampered-with-and-taped-together telephone, a vast tangle of wires, two pairs of headphones, and a reel-to-reel tape recorder.

"Does it work?" John asked before he'd even taken off his coat.

Carl gave him a thumbs-up. "We were picking up the radio station for a while, but hey, I'm a genius, what can I say?"

John gave him an excited and grateful pat on the back.

Leslie removed her coat as Mom went around the table to collect it and John's. "I'm just glad the office at Midwestern University was still open. Thanks, Mom. There's a two hour difference as it is."

"Where'd you make the call?"

"The pay phone across the street from the station." She

produced a notebook from her handbag. "But I got the number of Shannon's dorm room. If she's there tonight . . ."

John looked at his watch. "It's 8:10 . . ."

"So it's 10:10 over there. She might still be up."

"We'll just have to be rude," said Carl.

"Well, we can always pray," said Mom.

Leslie sat in front of the telephone sitting on the table, a pair of wires protruding from the receiver. "So how does this work?"

Carl explained, "No different from a regular phone. I tapped into the wires to the earpiece and ran them through the tape recorder here, so we'll be able to record the call, everything you hear, and then we'll be able to listen with the headphones."

Leslie was impressed. "Good work."

"How about a quick test run?" John suggested.

"And I think we'd better pray," said Mom again.

"Fine," said Leslie. "Who do we call?"

"How about . . . your sister?" John suggested.

"Sure . . . okay."

Carl sat in his chair, the tape recorder in front of him. John sat between Carl and Leslie and picked up one pair of headphones. Mom sat on the other side of Carl, and Carl turned one earpiece around on his headphones so Mom could press up against it and listen.

"Ready?" Leslie asked, her hand on the receiver.

"Go," said Carl, starting the recorder.

Leslie picked up the receiver as the reels started slowly winding and dialed her sister's number. John, Carl, and Mom listened raptly. John was delighted; the sounds were coming through loud and clear.

"Hello?" came a voice.

"Hello . . . Angie?"

"Oh, hi, Leslie. What's up?"

"Well, we're running a little experiment here . . ." Leslie went on to explain Carl's make-do invention without saying a whole lot about what it was really for. Angie wanted to go on talking, but Leslie asked to cut the conversation short, and Angie understood.

"Okay," said John, "good enough."

Carl wound the tape back to check the recording, and Angie's voice came through fine. Mom handed Leslie a piece of paper she'd worked on that afternoon—a complete transcript of the 911 call.

"Mom, you're beautiful!" said John.

"Carl made copies, so everybody gets one," Mom said, passing them out.

Leslie perused the transcript, underlining key words. "I suppose one goal would be to get her to say some of these key words, anything that she pronounces in a distinct way."

"It'll be tough," said John. "If she had a lisp or something it would be easier."

"Well, hopefully the same inflections will come through."

John looked at his watch again. "8:34. It's getting later and later over there."

"We'd better pray," said Mom.

"Go ahead," said John.

They all bowed their heads in customary fashion as Mom led in a short prayer. "Dear Heavenly Father, we ask for Your divine hand upon this undertaking. May we find the Truth, dear Lord, and may the Truth set free all those concerned. And we ask this in Jesus' precious name, Amen."

"Amen," they agreed.

"God help us," said Leslie as she picked up the receiver, consulted her notepad for the number, and dialed it.

Carl turned on the tape recorder, and he and John put on their headphones. Mom leaned close to Carl to listen.

The phone rang. No answer. Leslie scanned her scribbled notes, not sure how to start.

The phone rang again.

Clunk. "Hello?"

Leslie had been looking at John and Carl. Now all her concentration went on that young lady two time zones away.

"Hello, this is Leslie Albright calling Shannon DuPliese."

"Who's calling?"

"Uh, Leslie Albright. I'm with Channel 6 News. Is this Shannon?"

"Yes." She sounded hesitant, wary.

"Well, hi."

"Hi."

"I apologize for calling so late. I didn't wake you up, did I?" Leslie rolled her eyes at having to use such a line.

"No, I'm not in bed yet."

"Well, listen . . . uh, we were thinking of doing a follow-up story on the first recipient of the Hillary Slater Memorial Scholarship, you know, just see how you were doing and what reflections you might have . . ."

"Uh . . . excuse me?" Shannon didn't seem to be following Leslie's line of thought.

Leslie saw a word on the transcript. "Uh . . . you know, we tried to write to you to see if we could set it up, but we couldn't get your address. It's at Midwestern, but after that we're not sure how to write you."

"You need the address?"

Leslie knew she'd triggered a key phrase but didn't have time to think about it. John underlined it on his copy of the transcript.

Leslie kept going. *Keep her talking, keep her talking.* "Uh, sure, could you give it to me?"

"It's Box 9921, Midwestern University . . ."

Leslie wrote it down. "Great. Now anyway, what I was calling about, we'd like to ask if you'd be interested in letting us do a follow-up story on you—where you are now, how you're doing. We're kind of keeping track of the Hillary Slater thing and the scholarship program the governor set up."

"Uh-huh." That was all she said.

Leslie had to ask another question; this girl just didn't roll easily into a conversation. "Okay, well, first of all, we understand that you and Hillary were best friends, right?"

Hesitation. "Yeah, well . . . yeah, that's right. We wen—" The last phrase was unintelligible.

"Pardon me? I think we have a bad connection."

Shannon spoke louder. "Oh, I said we went to school together."

"Okay, great. Well, what would you say is your fondest memory of her?"

Hesitation. "Uhh . . ."

"Well, what do you remember about her the most?"

"Well . . ." Long pause.

"Hello?"

Suddenly, "I don't . . . I—I can't talk about Hillary."

Oh boy. Now what? "Oh . . . I am sorry. That must still be a very painful area for you . . ."

"I probably shouldn't be talking to you at all."

John and Leslie caught each other's eye immediately.

"Oh," Leslie continued delicately, "is this not a good time? It's late, I can understand that. There's a two hour difference, right?"

"I can't talk to you."

"You can't talk to me?"

"No. I . . . I really shouldn't. I don't want to get into any of this, okay?"

Leslie could feel it—she was losing the contact.

"Well, we don't want you to talk about anything you're not comfortable talking about—"

"I don't . . . Well, it's not you, okay? I just can't talk about it."

"So . . . you're not interested in any follow-up story, any—"

Click. Shannon DuPliese hung up.

Leslie became angry with herself as she hung up the phone, but John countered her reaction right away. "Hey, you did fine. I think we got enough."

But Leslie was still upset. "There is something wrong with that girl!"

Carl rewound the tape. "She's scared, did you hear it?"

John scanned his transcript. "Well, we got one complete phrase—'You need the address,' plus an opening 'hello,' one 'Hillary,' and three 'can'ts.' There might be more when we listen again."

"It's her," said Carl. "No question about it."

"It's her," said Leslie.

"Let's hear it again," said John.

They played the tape until Shannon said, "You need the address?" and then John signaled Carl to stop there. John had Dad's cassette player with the 911 tape cued. He let the tape roll until the 911 girl said the same phrase, "You need the address?"

"A little more hysterical, I would say," said Mom.

"Let's play them close together," said John, winding the cassette back just a touch. Carl used his hands to manually cue the tape reels. With a nod from John, Carl played the phrase again, "You need the address?" and then John played the cassette, "You need the address?" John looked at the group for their reaction.

Leslie heaved a sigh and reiterated with all the more certainty, "We've got her."

Carl shook his head. "No doubt. It's her."

Mom nodded. "She wasn't frantic this time, but . . . it was her. It was the same voice."

John withheld his vote just yet. "One more test. Let's find where she says 'Hillary.'"

John found the one mention of the name on the 911 tape, while Carl sought out the one occurrence in his recording. They played them close together.

"Same vote," said Leslie.

"It's her," said Carl. "Now I'm even more sure."

Mom raised her hand and said, "Praise the Lord, it's her."

John looked at them one by one and finally cast his vote. "We've got her!"

Leslie was troubled. "But how in the world are we going to get through to her? How do we get her to talk to us?"

"We pray!" said Mom.

"Well . . . besides that."

John was new at this matter of faith and prayer, but he was learning. "No, you mean *after* that. If God's on our side at all, we need to include Him in our deliberations. Mom's absolutely right—let's pray."

Leslie smiled. "Well, it's been a while, but I guess even a backslidden Baptist can do that. It can't hurt."

Carl was watching John intently. "You really think it will help?"

John tried to be honest. "Son, I'll admit I'm still befuddled about a lot of things, but there's one thing I know for sure: God is there, and He can speak, and He can listen, and if we're doing the right thing, what He wants us to do, then I think He'll help us out." Then John turned it right back to his son. "How about you? What do you think?"

Carl thought about it. "If you pray, I'll pray."

"Well, then we're all in agreement," said Mom.

So with a slightly fumbling but willing faith, they gave it a try, and though they couldn't prove it in a test tube, they all knew they'd connected with the Creator by the time Mom said the final "Amen."

twenty-four

shannon DuPliese, nineteen, honor student, sat on the edge of her bed in her dorm room and ran a brush through her long, brown locks, pulling hard, almost tearing through any tangles, her expression grim, her mind and heart fiercely debating. On her desk were her studies, almost completed for the night, but abandoned ever since that call from the Channel 6 lady, that call that brought a buried ghost back to life so it could return and haunt her.

Back to life? Really? As Shannon continued to brush her hair and think it through, she realized the ghost was never dead or buried in the first place, but alive and well. It had followed her to the university and was sure to follow her everywhere through her life. Yes, during the few weeks of classes she'd tried to turn her back on it, but now this phone call had jarred her and spun her around to see it still there, its fingers of pain and regret still entangling her as relentlessly as ever.

And then there was the matter of the invisible, subtle string attached to her education. No one mentioned this string, or rather this leash, when she was awarded the scholarship, but she hadn't asked about it either. The agreement was made without a word spoken, and now it was there, attached to the money and to her, a choke collar that tightened every once in a while and had just about gagged her to death when Channel 6 called.

She was imprisoned in a cage with a horrible secret—gagged and unable to scream.

The phone rang again. It was 10:45. Who would be calling at this hour?

"Hello?"

"Hello, Shannon. This is Martin Devin. How are you?"

The leash! The choke collar! She always felt it whenever Martin Devin called to extend his best wishes and see how she was doing—to pry, in other words. Tonight, especially since that call from Channel 6, she could feel his loop around her neck as she'd never felt it before—teasing her, yanking her, continually keeping her in line. This was going to be another little session with her keeper and trainer, Martin Devin. He would crack the whip and toss her treats, and she would do her tricks.

Or would she?

"Shannon? Hello?"

She fumbled, her mind disoriented, distracted by a new defiance that surprised her. Tonight, this time, she didn't feel the usual intimidation. Instead she felt anger.

Finally she repeated, "Hello."

"Sorry to be calling so late. I've been trying to get through to you, but the phone's been busy." He was asking what she'd been doing on the phone; he was hinting to know whom she'd been talking to.

"Uh-huh," was all she said.

"I suppose you were having a nice visit with someone, right?" That was no hint; that was a nosy question.

None of your business, creep! "A friend."

"Mm-hm." Then an abrupt leap into easy, friendly territory. This guy could switch into social gear so easily it was disgusting. "So how are the studies going?"

"Just fine."

"Well, that's good. We're all rooting for you."

"So I'd like to hear from the governor sometime." It was her way of saying, I'm sick of hearing from you. She'd not heard from Governor Slater since his grand media performance in awarding her the scholarship, but she had heard from Martin Devin more than she'd heard from her own parents.

"Well," said Devin, "the governor's been really busy with his campaign. But I'll pass the word along that you'd like to have a call from him."

"I'd appreciate that."

"So, Shannon, I won't keep you long, but I do have some very important matters to discuss."

She didn't acknowledge the statement but remained silent.

Let him do the talking, she thought. *He made the call—let him carry the conversation.*

He carried it. "Shannon, have you gotten any calls from the media? Anyone calling to ask questions?"

"Yes, as a matter of fact." She wasn't ashamed of it. *Put that in your pipe and smoke it, Marty!*

Devin sounded alarmed. "You have talked to the media?"

"Not really. But I got a call just now, right before you called."

He got confrontive. "Was that the . . . uh . . . friend you told me you were talking to?"

"Yeah."

"Who was it?"

"Somebody from Channel 6." She couldn't hear it clearly, but she knew he was swearing to himself. "They called because they wanted to do a follow-up story on me, something about the first recipient of the Hillary Slater scholarship."

His voice was strained. "Do you remember the name of the reporter?"

"Uh . . . Leslie something."

"Leslie Albright?"

"Yeah, that was it."

This time she could hear his swearing distinctly.

"What about John Barrett? Did you talk to him?"

"No. Just Leslie."

"So what did you say to her?"

"I told her I couldn't talk about it."

"You did? Really?"

"Yes, really."

"So . . . you didn't answer any of her questions?"

"Hey . . ." She actually laughed a little. "You sound really paranoid, you know that?"

Devin didn't laugh. He sounded nervous, upset. "Well . . . Shannon, I'm sorry to have to put this kind of a burden on you, but you have to realize this is the governor's family, his own private matter, and now it's an election year, he's out campaigning, and there are people in the media who would really jump at the chance to destroy him, to dig something up that would hurt him. You understand that, don't you?"

Shannon was understanding it more and more, even as she heard Devin fuss and squirm. "I think I understand."

"So . . . I'm very glad you didn't say anything to them, and I know the governor will greatly appreciate that. But I should warn you, they may call you again, and if they do, please don't talk to them. I really need to have your word on this, that you won't discuss Hillary's death with anyone."

Shannon could feel that leash; she could feel this guy trying to control her life. She was amazed at her courage even as she asked, "Mr. Devin, what if I do talk to them? What will happen?"

Devin didn't answer right away. Apparently he was taken aback by the directness of her question. "Shannon . . . really, you have to believe me, that would not be a wise thing to do. It would hurt some people. It would be a betrayal of a sacred trust."

So now he was trying the old guilt trip! The governor had used that one on her in the very beginning! "Mr. Devin . . ." Oh no, now her emotions were choking her. The last thing she wanted to do was cry! "I don't think you care how *I* feel. I don't think it even occurs to you."

He switched into a sympathy mode. "Oh, Shannon, of course I do. You've been through a terrible ordeal. We're trying to protect you as well. We don't want the media prying into your life either."

"Mr. Devin . . ." She'd never thought about this before, but right now, at this moment, it seemed like a marvelous idea. "Mr. Devin, I'm considering withdrawing from classes and coming home. I could just give you back the money. I'll work for a while and just go to school there."

That alarmed him. "Shannon, now wait. You're just upset."

"You'd better believe I'm upset!" Now she really was crying, but the release felt wonderful. She'd been saving up for this a long time. "You and the governor never cared about me in the first place! You just wanted me out of the way!"

"Shannon, now that's not true, and you know it!"

"Then why is it you're the only one who ever calls me?"

"Shannon, I told you, the governor is busy, so I call on his behalf."

"Then why is it every time you call it's always about the same thing: 'Are you all right, Shannon? Are you getting over it, Shannon? You haven't told anybody, have you, Shannon?'"

Now he was really getting flustered. Even through the flood of her emotions, Shannon could tell she'd hit the right nerve.

"Shannon, now . . . you know that isn't true! We're thinking of you and your future. That's what the scholarship was all about."

"You're thinking of you and the governor and the election—that's what you're thinking about! I don't think you even cared about Hillary! I know the governor never did!"

Oh-oh. Devin switched to stern parent mode. "Now hold on, young lady! That was uncalled for!"

She wasn't intimidated by this guy anymore. He wasn't her mother or her father, and besides that, he was far away, a little voice on the phone that she realized she hated. "Oh, is that so? Well, Hillary used to tell me about it—she used to cry about it, how she never even saw him, how he didn't care about her, he was always gone, always doing his political thing. But now that she's dead she's important to him! Now that she's dead he cares about her precious reputation!"

"Hillary . . ." he bumbled. "Shannon . . . it's late, and you're tired, and things are going to look a lot different in the morning. Why don't you sleep on it, okay? We can talk again tomorrow. Give me a call, okay?"

"I don't want to call you. I don't want to talk to you . . . not ever again. I'm sick of talking to you."

"Now, Shannon, you call me tomorrow, after you've had some time to think about things. We have a lot invested in you, and we don't want to see you throw it all away."

That was enough. That one little attempt at another guilt trip was just enough to spur Shannon on to new heights of courage. She slammed the phone in his face.

Then she wept, half from sorrow and pain and half from a

new freedom and release. Before this moment she'd not realized how bound she was, how heavily weighted down.

Martin Devin did not sleep much that night. He lay in bed, staring at the ceiling, staring at the wall, turning this way and that, and having a long, furious conference with himself: agenda, second agenda, course of action, alternatives, information selection, presentation, first impression, second impression, arguments, counterarguments. He rehearsed conversations with the governor, babbling to himself under the sheets. He came to dead ends, pounded the mattress with his fist, and started over.

What could he say? What could he not say? How much did the governor really need to know? How much should he tell the governor in any case? Which information would be to his own advantage and which would not? What would the consequences be?

Well, he would have to say something. The last thing he needed was for the governor to find all this out from someone else.

One thought came across his mental desk more than once that night: *Barrett has the tape. I know he has the tape.*

And that thought was always connected with another: *Your goose is cooked. Checkmate. You've had it. Cash in your chips—you're out of the game.*

Oh no, was his reply. *Not me. I'm never out. Somebody else is going to fall, but it isn't going to be me. I'll find a way. Yes sir, I'll find a way.*

And he stayed awake most of the night trying to do just that.

On a TV screen: Rosalind Kline, sexy, sultry actress from the TV sitcom "Who's Got Problems?," teases and cavorts with a handsome, hairy-chested man in a large, ornate bedroom. He embraces her. She teasingly begins to finger the top button of her blouse, and then, with a little laugh and a flip of her blonde tresses, she says in her breathy voice, "Oh, I can't take this off. I'll catch cold!"

"Cut!" says the director off-camera.

Another angle: We see the camera crew, the sound technicians, the lights of a TV soundstage. Rosalind and the male actor break character. She gives him a pat on the shoulder as he walks off the set and is handed a can of soft drink. Rosalind turns and walks toward us, away from the bedroom set. Her name appears across the bottom of the screen: "Rosalind Kline, star of 'Who's Got Problems?'"

She looks directly at the camera and says in all seriousness, "There was a time when talented women like me were regarded as objects and playthings, but thanks to visionary people like Hiram Slater that was then and this is now. Women enjoy a new dignity and equality, and with important changes occurring every day in the workplace women are finding opportunities for personal growth and advancement not open to them only a few years ago. But much remains to be done, and that's why I'm asking you to reelect Governor Hiram Slater. This is one man who cares about women."

Cut to bold, Mount Rushmore-ish shot of Hiram Slater's stern countenance and the slogan, "The New Dawn Lives On. Hiram Slater for Governor."

Small letters across the bottom: "Paid for by the Committee to Reelect Governor Slater, Wilma Benthoff, Chairperson."

Governor Hiram Slater backed away from the television set and clapped his hands in glee. "Beautiful! Absolutely beautiful!" Then he quipped, "And the ad wasn't bad either!"

He was in his office, his desk cluttered with some serious work to be done, but . . . well, he knew the ad would be running in between some of the soap operas, and he just had to see it—not just on video, but on the air, for real, the same way the public would be seeing it. The experience was downright thrilling. Rowen and Hartly, his PR men, were doing an exquisite job.

"Mr. Governor?" came Miss Rhodes' voice on the intercom. "Mr. Devin is here to see you."

Slater was delighted. Now he'd have someone to share his delight with. "Great. Send him in."

Devin came through the door looking tired and worn. His eyes were puffy and his expression somber.

"Well, Martin, things are rolling! The celebrity ads are starting to air, and they look sensational!" Then the governor noticed Devin's countenance. "And you look like you could use some good news."

Devin smiled weakly. "I could, sir."

Slater went to his desk and produced a report. "Well, have you seen this? I just got an endorsement from the United Feminist Front. They're backing me 100 percent, and that's quite a statement!"

"Yes, sir. That's marvelous." Devin smiled again, but he did not dance for joy. "Mr. Governor, I'm afraid I may have to rain on your parade. You'll recall the assignment you gave me the last time we talked. Well, I have a report for you."

Slater sobered up, sat at his desk, and gestured toward a chair for Devin.

Devin sat and tried to recall the outline he'd written in his head all through the night. "First of all, I had dinner with Tina Lewis last night. She's been able to confirm that John Barrett, the anchorman, and Leslie Albright, a reporter, are working on something having to do with your daughter Hillary. They're digging it up again."

The governor tried to remain calm, but he was visibly upset and his voice strained. "Did she say why? What are they after?"

Devin shook his head and threw up his hands. "She doesn't know."

"She doesn't know? Are you serious?"

"They're working on something, but they haven't presented it to their bosses yet, and until and unless the story is pitched to the producers and editors, whoever's in charge, there really isn't anything Tina can do about it. It's policy that—"

Slater held up his hand to stop Devin in midsentence.

"No, no, Martin, that's where you're wrong, or she's wrong, or both of you are wrong. We are going to do something about it. You are definitely going to do something about it; you can consider that part of your job."

Devin tried to maintain the appearance of strength and confidence, though he certainly felt neither strong nor confident. "Sir, unfortunately for us, it's a free country, and . . .

realistically, we can't stop them from asking questions. They're not doing anything illegal that anyone knows of, and they're not violating any policy at Channel 6."

The governor softened a little, although he didn't like it. Devin was right. "Well . . . what else?"

"I have one small comfort: Tina says it doesn't matter what they're working on because whatever it is, it won't get past her. She has enough influence to frustrate—hopefully even block—the story, and she's agreed to do that."

"She can block it?"

"Yes, sir." Then Devin tried to rebuild his worth in Slater's eyes by adding, "She does things for me. We have a certain . . . working relationship going, if you know what I mean."

"Well . . ." Slater leaned back in his chair and considered that possibility. "Your little liaison may buy us some time, but it won't save us. This does not look good, Martin." He brought his weight forward again. "What about our old nemesis—Mr. Ed Lake? Is he the one who leaked to the press?"

This was a delicate subject for Devin, but he had to say something. "I have strong suspicions about him, but I haven't found him yet. He's left town indefinitely, and that says a lot right there."

"Yes, it does. Well . . . if it is him, I'd sure like to know how he found out and what he told them."

"I would too, sir. Right now I have no idea." Almost no idea, would have been more truthful.

"Well, find out. Twist his arm a little."

"Oh, I will. You can count on that. But there's more. Tina said Barrett and Albright checked out the videotape the station had on Hillary's death and funeral, and also your presentation of the scholarship to Shannon DuPliese."

Slater saw it coming. "Oh no . . ."

Devin nodded. "I called Shannon last night after dinner with Tina, and . . ." He broke the news gently. "She told me she'd gotten a call from Leslie Albright at Channel 6."

At that, the governor groaned, sank into his chair, and rested his brow on his fingertips.

Devin kept going, trying to keep himself and Slater afloat. "She said she didn't tell Albright anything."

The governor blurted, "And you actually trust her?"

Devin hadn't rehearsed any answer to that question last night. "Uh . . . well, that's difficult to answer . . . Haven't we been trusting her all along?"

Slater pondered that, then nodded with realization. "Martin, that was our biggest mistake."

"But what else could we do? She was . . . she was there, with Hillary. She saw the whole thing. Her voice is—was—on that 911 recording . . ."

Slater continued, his voice rising. "These reporters have been talking to Dr. Matthews, they've been talking to Shannon, and who knows who else they've talked to or will be talking to . . . But, Martin, Shannon is the one person who can testify to anything of real consequence, and I do believe that sooner or later she is going to talk! The press is going to find out. We'd be fools to think otherwise." He shook his head and muttered, "The old prophet was right about that."

He got up and paced about the room, looking out the window, glaring at the floor, glaring at Devin. "So maybe it started with Lake, but does that really matter now? Not really. The press is going after it, and sooner or later they will find the leaks, and one leak will lead to another until finally the story will explode all over the media, and there will go the campaign. Bob Wilson will love this!"

Devin had come to that conclusion himself last night. "You're absolutely right, sir. It will come out, one way or another. But I've been thinking about that."

Slater sounded a little sarcastic when he said, "Oh, I'm very glad."

Devin rose and approached the governor, lowering his voice. "Maybe you can't keep it from coming out, but perhaps you can control how it comes out. We have some connections with the media, and we have Rowen and Hartly, our PR boys. Perhaps we could get the jump on this story and release it *our* way. If we go public first, Barrett and Albright lose their momentum. They won't be able to strike the first blow, and their story will lose its novelty. We'll steal it from them."

Devin had struck the right chord. The governor calmed immediately. His brow furrowed as he processed the idea.

"It could work."

"I have great confidence that it will work, sir."

"Except for the timing. We don't control that yet."

"Sir?"

Governor Slater looked directly at Devin with cold and calculating eyes. "If we're going to build momentum, or even shape the information the way we want it, we have to control *when* the information gets out. If the media get their hands on it first, before we have a chance to shape it . . ." The governor took a quick mental inventory and then concluded, "I think all the other potential leaks are slow enough. Matthews values his job and hasn't revealed anything up to this point, and chances are he never will, not willingly or directly. The autopsy report can't be seen without a court order, which the press isn't about to get. What about the Adam Bryant School?"

Devin shook his head. "I talked to Erica Tyler, the principal. The school doesn't want any trouble or any connection with any trouble. We're safe there."

"Good. Good."

The governor had a thought, but then dismissed it. "Hm. There was that recording of Shannon's 911 call, but that's destroyed."

"Yes, sir. Destroyed long ago." It wasn't hard for Devin to lie when necessary.

"And the master recording at the dispatch center is confidential. Ehh, I suppose we took a risk having that copy made."

"A necessary risk, sir. We had to know who made that call."

"Which brings us back to Shannon. She's the only high-risk factor. The media have already contacted her, and we can't count on her silence. Martin, have you done a lot of thinking about this?"

"All last night, sir."

"So what's your plan for dealing with Shannon?"

Oh-oh. "Uh . . . I haven't thought of one yet, sir."

The governor's tone was that classic command tone that was not to be ignored, that allowed no hesitation. "Think of one."

The next afternoon Leslie was busy at her computer, trying to clarify that the hit-and-run driver who fled from police in a harrowing car chase crashed through the front window of the Parkland Credit Union after he hit the pedestrian standing outside, but that this pedestrian was not in the van the driver hit in the first place before the chase and the ensuing crash, that it was the lady with all the groceries who was first seen on the sidewalk after the initial crash and who identified the driver of the hit-and-run vehicle just before the chase ensued, and that the crash through the window was an accident in addition to the first one, and by now . . .

She was glad when the phone rang. She'd straighten out her notes later. "Hello, this is Leslie."

"Hello. Leslie Albright?"

"Yes."

"This is Dr. Mark Denning. You spoke to my wife a few days ago."

Leslie scrambled, shoving her other notes aside and flipping to a fresh sheet in her notepad as she spoke amiably. "Oh yes, Dr. Denning, thank you so much for calling. I enjoyed my visit with Barbara."

"Yes, she did too."

"So how did things go in Sacramento?"

"Well, just great. I have a job, so we'll be moving."

"Terrific."

"Anyway . . . Now, I take it you know the Brewers?"

"Yes. Myself and John Barrett have been working with them trying to come to a conclusion about the death of their daughter."

"Well, let me tell you what I can do . . ."

John was busily editing the script for the Five O'clock and having trouble with a story about a hit-and-run driver in a car chase with the cops after hitting a lady with some groceries . . . it wasn't making a lot of sense just yet . . . when someone came alongside his desk. Leslie. She was looking rather pleasant, maybe even victorious, holding some notes in her hand.

She spoke softly. "John, I'm going to start praying more. I just got a call from Dr. Mark Denning."

John leaned back in his chair and looked up at her, his eyes wide with expectation. "Do tell."

"He just got back from Sacramento. He managed to get a job down there, so he was in a pretty good mood." She looked at her notes. "He has a copy of Annie's autopsy report in his own files, and he's prepared to release it."

"Praise God!" John exclaimed quietly. He noticed he was beginning to revert back to his Pentecostal roots during moments of joy, but he didn't mind. "But . . . does it . . . ?"

Leslie smiled and nodded. "Oh yeah. It confirms the cause of death to be septic abortion." She held up her finger. "But hold on, there are a few details to be worked out. The rules I got from his wife are the same: He'll release it only to the Brewers, and he'd prefer some kind of legal document that would authorize him to do so. I asked him if he'd accept a Request for Medical Records like the one we used at the Women's Medical Center, and he said that would be perfect." She chuckled. "He says he doesn't really need one, but if a question ever comes up he wants to cover his rear as best he can."

"Well, let's call Aaron Hart."

"I did. He said I'm not his client . . . Deanne Brewer is. She'll have to ask him to draft the letter."

"So, will she?"

Leslie was happy to report, "Deanne's ready. She was just waiting to hear what the next move would be."

"What about Max?"

"Well . . . he's simmered down a little. She says he hasn't really abandoned us, that he still respects the memory of your father. He's just trying to sort it out."

"That autopsy report would make a nice peace offering, wouldn't it?"

"I think it would. It'll mean something finally went right for the Brewers after all this time. I think Max is afraid it won't, and that's why he won't stick his neck out again. But he says if Deanne wants to get her hopes up, he won't stop her."

"So when will it happen?"

"Aaron Hart will have the Request Letter ready by tomorrow, and I've made the appointment for Deanne and me to go see Denning tomorrow night."

John gave a low whistle. "I think this thing is going down, as they say. It's happening fast."

"Well, the faster the better . . . before something else goes wrong."

"But you know what? Once we get that report, proof of how Annie died . . . I think we'll be that much closer to breaking through to Shannon."

"And if we asked Deanne to call her . . ."

That thought flowed through John's mind like warm, soothing oil. "Deanne?" He looked up at Leslie with a profound new respect. "Of course. They've had basically the same experience—they're feeling the same pain."

"Of all the people who could talk to Shannon, Deanne's the one who could do the most good."

John's heart was stirring. "We could be getting close to linking the two deaths at the same clinic."

"Maybe," Leslie cautioned.

"We'll see. But now . . . one more question."

"What?"

John pointed at the computer screen. "The lady carrying the groceries—was she standing outside the Credit Union when the van came through, or was it the other pedestrian?"

"Oh, come on! You can't make sense of that?"

"Hey, it has your name on it. Explain it to me."

They got it straightened out.

twenty-five

The driver of the big city bus hit the brakes and lurched to a stop halfway into the crosswalk, almost spilling his passengers from their seats. Now they were griping at him, and the pedestrian he almost ran over was making an obscene gesture as he bounded onto the curb.

"Watch where you're going!" the driver yelled through the windshield.

"Watch where you're going, idiot!" yelled the pedestrian as the bus continued down the street. "Stupid jerk, trying to kill people out here . . . Stupid bus!"

On the side of the bus, a bold poster of John Barrett and Ali Downs reminded him that they were doing a full hour of news starting at 5.

The man cursed. "Yeah, that figures!"

It was night—the best time to meet with people you don't want to be seen meeting with, and Martin Devin had an appointment.

He ducked into Clancy's, a boisterous night spot with a lounge, dance floor, and pool hall, located a few blocks up from the waterfront in a district you wouldn't want to be seen visiting, which was okay—none of your friends would ever go near the place to find you there.

The heavy brass door swung open with a substantial tug, and the warm, beer-scented air washed over his face as he stepped inside. The street outside was noisy; in here it was noisier. The jukebox demanded you listen to fifties oldie-goldies whether you wanted to or not. The neon beer logos hanging on the walls persuaded you to drink. The menu on the wall persuaded you to eat the greasy food. The blue haze in the air persuaded you to smoke. The girls draping their frames here and there over furniture, bar stools, and booths persuaded you they were fun to get to know.

Well, they would never know Martin Devin, at least not as Martin Devin, not tonight. He wore an old jacket, a ragged pair of work jeans, a baseball cap with a beer logo on the front, and a pair of dark glasses, trying to look the part of a blue-collar, beer-drinking, good old boy. He even walked tall and tough, using the same gait that used to intimidate the underclassmen in high school. Despite his appearance, though, he still tried not to look anyone in the eye. This was a world he wanted nothing to do with, at least not directly. The kinds of things that happened in this world could be distasteful to someone of his stature. They were things he never wanted to touch and did not want touching him and certainly did not want to be associated with.

But sometimes . . . like now . . . such things were necessary, even unavoidable.

The same was true for Willy, the man who could provide such . . . things. He was the kind of man it was best to avoid; *distasteful* described him well. Devin had never met him face to face. He'd heard of Willy through a mutual friend, a politically active fellow of substantial means and influence who could do favors for those in power—in exchange for favors, of course. All contact Devin ever had with Willy had been by telephone up to this point, and all paychecks to Willy were mailed to a Post Office box with no questions asked. The jobs got done; that was all Devin cared to know.

But now Devin considered the situation to be somewhat desperate, calling for a less casual approach. He had to meet this Willy face to face. He had to be sure they really understood each other. Maybe this would be the only meeting of this kind. Perhaps the business would be finished quickly and their relationship could immediately dissolve. Devin hoped so.

He turned and walked down the aisle between the bar and booths, then wound his way through the tables in the lounge toward a dark corner in the back. On a small stage across the room, under multicolored spotlights, a trio of musicians maintained a flow of not-quite-right pop tunes while couples meandered around the hardwood dance floor. This was a good place to meet—dark, noisy, distracting.

He saw a hand wave to him from the corner booth, just wiggling above the surface of a table, not in the air. The face above the hand wasn't much of a surprise. It looked old, held a grim expression, and, as Devin could see as he drew nearer, had been in more than a few fights over the years.

"Are you Willy?" Devin asked.

The thin lips pulled back into a smile that revealed some teeth missing and one tooth filled with silver. "Have a seat, Mr. Jones or Smith or whoever you want to be."

Devin didn't think that was funny and let his expression say so as he slid into the booth.

"Will you have a drink?" Willy asked.

"I won't be staying long."

"Long enough for a beer maybe?"

Devin didn't want to antagonize the man. "Okay."

A miniskirted waitress took the order and hurried away.

"So," Willy began, "what brings you into my neck of the woods?"

Devin took another look around to make sure they would be speaking in private. "Things are getting out of control. John Barrett has the tape, and he's going after a news story."

Willy smiled a so-what smile and nodded lazily. "Well, now we finally know where it is. I knew that tape would turn up sooner or later."

Devin was not about to make a scene, but he did touch Willy's arm quite firmly for emphasis. "Listen, you—if your guys would've done their job correctly, we wouldn't be in this mess. I hired you to get that tape back, not kill somebody, and now I hope you've figured out that neither of us can afford for anyone to find out what happened."

Willy looked him in the eye for a moment and saw the steel in Devin's gaze. He finally nodded in agreement.

"What makes you so sure Barrett has the tape?"

"He's—" The waitress came with Devin's beer. When she left, he continued, "He's the son of the man you killed, and now he's tracking down Shannon DuPliese. What more do you want?"

Willy nodded slowly. "That's enough."

Devin was seething. "The way your boys got such perfect results at the kickoff rally, I was sure they could handle this situation without turning it into a major scandal! A simple mugging would have been enough. We could have survived that, we could have stayed clean—"

"We didn't plan to kill him."

"Well, that doesn't make much difference now, does it?"

"The cops aren't on our trail, are they?"

Devin had no immediate answer.

"Looks like Ted and Howie covered their tracks pretty well if we haven't heard anything by now."

"Suppose Barrett takes that tape to the police. You don't think that will stir things up?"

Willy nodded. "That will stir things up."

Devin locked eyes with him. "So let's talk completion. I want the job completed to my satisfaction."

"You want John Barrett roughed up?"

"Don't be ridiculous! He's a public figure, right out in the open!" Devin drew closer so he could talk more quietly. "I'm talking about Ed Lake, for one. He had that tape in the first place, and he knows what's on it. We have to keep him quiet about this."

"Well, he's a weak little man. When Ted and Howie got him down on the ground, he blabbed everything, told 'em exactly who he gave the tape to, where to find the guy. He didn't have a lot of fortitude, you know? And I hear he's skipped town. He's scared. But if you want us to, we can scare him again."

Devin thought for a moment. "We absolutely cannot afford for anyone to find out what happened. Keep Lake quiet. Do what you have to."

"All right. We'll do that. And you can send the check to the same mailbox—"

"You're not through yet."

Willy wheezed a beer-stenched chuckle. "Oh, yeah, the girl, the girl. Yeah, I suppose you're concerned about her. I would be. Barrett has the tape, but what does it prove? That Hillary Slater had an abortion—maybe. Big deal. Who doesn't these days? But now Barrett's father is killed for a tape with Shannon's voice on it—a tough break, I admit it—and Shannon knows how certain people would benefit from that . . . which could make old man Barrett's death look like more than an accident, which should get the cops interested."

Devin knew this thug was tormenting him. He grabbed for authority, something impressive. "The governor wants this whole mess cleaned up neatly and quietly. We're prepared to pay you—"

Another wheezy chuckle. "Hey, don't give me this governor business! I never got any call from the governor; I only got a call from you." Willy's eyes took on a tormenting twinkle. "And I'd be willing to wager the governor doesn't know a thing about this. You got yourself into this mess, right up to your little beady eyeballs—"

Devin placed his hand around Willy's throat. He didn't squeeze. He just put it there to make a point. "I didn't get myself into this. You and your thugs got us both into it through sheer incompetence. Agreed?"

Willy gave in quietly. "Hey, I don't deny it. Such are the hazards of the business."

Devin removed his hand. "And you are going to do whatever is necessary to get us both out. Neither one of us wants to hang, but if I hang, I'll see to it that you hang with me. I'm sure you understand."

Willy nodded. "I'd do the same for you."

Devin relaxed just a little. "Then we do understand each other. That's good."

"So okay, then . . . No more mistakes. Let's get to the girl. She's your biggest problem. Aren't you the one who handled the scholarship money?"

"That's right."

"And you were telling me the other day how you were trying to ride herd on her to keep her quiet."

Devin nodded.

Willy allowed himself a little chuckle, but not too much of one. "Well, considering all that, if she ever does talk, she'll probably talk about you first."

"Correct. So obviously I need something quick and decisive, if your boys can do it."

"Ted's available."

"Ted! He was supposed to intimidate the old man and ended up killing him!"

Willy shrugged and gave a little smile. "Well, it's what you're going to want in this case, and it's what he does best. And he's better with women."

"Well, can he keep it from looking like a crime?"

Willy snorted and waved away that comment. "Ehhh, college coeds get raped and killed all the time. It'll make the news for a while, then get blamed on some serial rapist or something, and then the whole thing will fade, especially since Ted will be back here, far away."

Devin was hearing too much. He held up his hand. "I don't want to know how you do it. I just want it done."

Willy was pleased enough with that. "I'll be in touch."

Devin finished his beer quickly and got out of there.

The front door to the big house at 19202 N.E. Barlow opened, and a handsome, dark-haired man looked out at Leslie and Deanne. He was expecting them. "Well . . . Hello . . . Come on in."

Leslie made the introductions as they stepped inside. "Dr. Denning, this is Deanne Brewer."

Deanne shook his hand, feeling nervous, trying to appear calm and sociable even as hope and despair battled within her. "I'm pleased to meet you."

He returned the greeting. "I'm pleased to meet you."

She just had to ask, even before Barbara Denning took her coat. "Doctor, can you help us? If you can't, then I won't take any more of your time."

He nodded as he understood her feelings. "I think I can. Why don't you come in and sit down?"

They settled into the soft couch in the Dennings' living room while the doctor and his wife sat in another couch opposite them. They talked about how nice the house was, and how distinctive the china cabinet and dinette looked, and how long Barbara Denning had been collecting Hummel figurines, and then they discussed the TV news business and how reporting worked, which finally brought them around to the subject for the evening.

"I understand one story got away from you," said Denning.

Both Leslie and Deanne made an unpleasant face at the recollection.

"At Deanne's expense, most certainly," said Leslie.

"Did you see it?" asked Deanne.

"Barbara told me about it."

Leslie said, "It was a terrible setback. It almost came between us."

"Max is still upset. He doesn't want to trust anybody," said Deanne.

Denning leaned forward, concern filling his eyes. "Then . . . if I may ask, what's to keep the information I have from being misused as well?"

They were all looking at Leslie, even Deanne, needing an answer to a valid question. Leslie had determined she would be forthright. "Um . . . to be perfectly honest . . . present circumstances in the newsroom being what they are, I don't think this information has much chance of a fair treatment or of even being noticed at all." She quickly added, "And Deanne and I have talked about the newsworthiness of this and whether or not that mattered, and we've agreed that it really doesn't. I mean . . . at one time I thought it would be a news story. Then after it became one, I was sorry it did. Maybe if the picture becomes clear enough and the climate in the media is right, we could do something on it, but we're not concerned with that right now. My real concern is with Deanne and Max. We started something with them, and I want to finish it." She looked at Deanne, yielding the floor.

Deanne spoke her part. "Dr. Denning, my husband and I have our own life to live and our own children to raise and our own affairs to manage, and that's always going to be the same whether it's ever seen on television or not. We've lost our daughter, and we want to know why. Even if nobody else ever hears what happened to her, at least we'll know. That's what we want, at the very least."

Dr. Denning seemed pleased with that, though still

troubled. "It's hard to get people to view things through clear, untainted glasses, don't you agree?"

Leslie nodded. "Certainly. We're all up against that. Even an unbiased news story won't please a biased viewer, and sometimes you can't win no matter what you do."

Denning laughed. "Well, the medical profession is no exception, let me tell you. We're supposed to be the empirical, objective professionals, but we have our biases too. There are some things we want to know and some we don't. There are findings our peers will accept and findings our peers will not find acceptable. Part of surviving in the medical profession is to learn how to handle certain information. There are rules."

Leslie ventured, "Such as . . ."

"Botched abortions, you don't talk about. Your peers moonlighting at abortion clinics, you don't talk about. Nonphysicians performing abortions in place of the physician who's late, you don't talk about. Prescriptions being written by nonphysicians on forms signed in advance by the physician who isn't even there, you don't talk about. Unsanitary conditions, rushed procedures, little fudges here and there for the sake of saving time and making money, you don't talk about." Denning was showing some frustration now. "Because if you do talk about it, that makes you anti-abortion. You're branded. You're not politically correct. You're not one of the recognized professionals anymore." He looked at Leslie with a glint in his eye. "And you know, even as I sit here, talking to a news reporter—a news reporter!—I feel perfectly safe. I know I can tell you all kinds of hair raisers, story after story, but you won't talk about it either, and even if you tried to . . . well, we've already seen what happens."

Leslie said nothing for a moment, having no reply. Finally she offered, very quietly, "At the present time I can't disagree."

"So," Denning said with a sigh, "we all climb aboard and let the profession carry us where it will, and we obey the rules, don't we, because we don't want to be kicked off."

"As you were?"

Denning nodded. "Mm-hm. Do you know how many

abortion-related cases come through Westland Memorial Hospital each month?"

"How many?"

Denning shrugged. "I don't know. No one does. Ask the Records Department and you get a blank stare. Dig through the files and you get vague entries on the charts. There's an entrenched mentality in that place, and you fall in line or you don't last long." He paused for an emotional breather and then told Deanne, "As far as my personal knowledge is concerned, as far as what I saw in pathology, your daughter Annie was only one among many over the last few years."

Deanne nodded grimly. She was not surprised.

"But who ever hears about it?" Denning reiterated.

"We did," Deanne said gratefully, "and we owe you a debt of thanks."

Denning smiled resignedly. "Well, I think your husband and his friend, that older fellow . . ."

"John Barrett, Sr.," said Leslie. "He was the father of John Barrett, the news anchor at Channel 6."

Denning found that strangely amusing. "I wonder how that old man and his son get along?"

"They . . . didn't . . . get along too well, obviously."

Denning caught Leslie's emphasized past tense. "Oh? Is the elder Barrett deceased?"

Leslie nodded. "Killed a few weeks ago in a warehouse accident."

Denning slowed his pace a little to show respect. "I'm sorry to hear that." He reflected on his experience with John Barrett, Sr. and smiled. "That man didn't blend in much, not around that hospital. It was startling—well, refreshing, really—to encounter someone so opposite in his thinking from the people I worked with day in and day out. I think that might be why I took the risk I did. As I was going to say, Mr. Brewer and Mr. Barrett caught me at a good time. I was just frustrated enough with being pulled around by the prevailing winds at that hospital that I was glad for the opportunity to do something, just one thing, for conscience' sake. I never lied on an autopsy report; what I found, I recorded. But I knew the rules—plus the written policy about anything abortion-related being inaccessible to parents—so I went along with that. And if someone chanced to pirate some information from a patient chart while my back was turned, well . . ."

"I understand it still got you fired," said Leslie.

"I believe so. There's no record of that, and no one will admit it, but . . ." He looked at Deanne. "Please don't blame your husband. I think he was right to cause the fuss he did and make the demands he did, but . . ."

"He got you in trouble," said Deanne.

Denning nodded. "It all got traced back to me in short order, and that was that. I didn't think I was snitching on my peers, but they saw it differently."

"And what about Dr. Lawrence, the ob-gyn on Annie's case?" asked Leslie. "I suppose he had a voice in your demise."

"He did. And you'll be interested to know that Dr. Lawrence and Dr. Huronac are good friends."

Deanne asked, "Who's Dr. Huronac?"

Denning chuckled at himself. "Well, see how little anyone knows? Dr. Michael Huronac does most of the abortions at the Women's Medical Center. It's basically all he does, six days a week. You see the connections here? Birds of a feather look out for each other, and the odd birds have to watch out."

"So . . . you did get another job okay?" Leslie asked.

"At a Catholic hospital. I won't say it's heaven on earth, but at least abortion isn't an issue we have to grapple with."

Leslie had a thought and muttered to herself. "Catholic. A Catholic school . . ."

"Hm?"

Deanne took a notepad from her handbag. "Could I have that doctor's name again?"

Denning spelled it out for her. "H-u-r-o-n-a-c. Michael. It's none of my business, but might you be considering some litigation?"

"We really don't know yet."

"Well . . . I might be able to help you out if it ever comes to that."

That really got Deanne's attention, and Leslie's.

"Really?"

"Did you happen to bring a legal request of some kind?"

Deanne hurriedly dug through her handbag and produced an envelope from Hart, McLoughlin, Peters, and Sanborn. "Here . . . I'm the personal representative of my daughter's estate, and as such I have legal power to request her medical records . . ."

Denning rose from the couch and took it from her. He opened the envelope, scanned the letter inside, and said, "Great. This protects my rear. I didn't leak it to you, you asked for it legally. I'll be right back."

He left the room for a short moment while Barbara, Leslie, and Deanne refilled their coffee cups. When he returned, he held out a thick, white envelope.

Deanne stood and reached out to receive it. Leslie stood too. Such a moment you could not take casually. This was a treasure, the end of a quest.

As Deanne opened the envelope to look at the contents, Denning briefly explained, "It's all there—all the findings. I can explain any of it that you don't understand, but the bottom line you already know. The abortion was hurried and sloppy, there were parts of the fetus and placenta still left inside and festering, the uterus was perforated, and the infection had spread generally throughout Annie's system. So the primary cause of death was generalized septicemia, which is bacterial infection of the bloodstream, and the secondary cause was septic abortion, something for which the abortionist is responsible, in my opinion."

Deanne asked, "And . . . are you saying you'd be willing to testify to this in court?"

Denning did not answer lightly. "Yes, I would. My employment situation is not quite as shaky now, but even if it was . . . it felt so good to be honest that one time that I'm ready to try it again."

Deanne wanted to hug him, but restrained herself. "That . . . that would just be so wonderful!"

"But do you have any way to prove which clinic is responsible? I'm willing to bet it was the Women's Medical Center and Dr. Huronac, but I have no way of knowing that for sure."

"We'll work on it," said Leslie.

"And . . . I suppose you'd like something on-camera?"

Leslie was surprised, not really expecting the offer. "Well, like I said, that's secondary to just getting the truth for the Brewers."

Denning just gave a what-the-heck shrug. "If you can use it . . . sometime, who knows when, fine. But we'll have to do it soon. Barbara and I will be moving."

"Well, let's set a time then."

"Good enough."

Deanne just kept gazing at that autopsy report, in their hands at long last, the first solid evidence to prove what happened to Annie Delores Brewer.

Max Brewer, a scowl on his face, his wife Deanne by his side, received the thick white envelope from John Barrett, his son Carl, and Leslie Albright as they all stood in the Brewers' living room. It was like a little ceremony, the presentation of a peace offering. Hopefully it would result in John and Leslie being able to stick around for a while instead of being thrown out.

Max opened the envelope, pulled out the autopsy report, and took the time to flip through every page, the scowl never leaving his face until . . . as he looked upon the last two pages, realizing it was all there, and reading once again what it contained, the scowl melted into tears and he started sniffing, holding Deanne close.

John had said it before, but now, seeing Max soften so, he tried saying it again. "Max, we never intended for the story to get twisted around like it did. We're on your side, and we sincerely apologize for the grief we may have caused you." Max said nothing, but their eyes were on each other, and Max was listening. "This whole thing has been a moral struggle for me, and I know I'm still not finished, but for whatever it's worth, it was no fun having to anchor that story the way it came out. I hope I never find myself in that kind of predicament again. I'm sorry, Max."

Max looked at Deanne and then at the autopsy report and then muttered, "Aw, I guess there ain't that much harm been done." Then he glared at John with that look John had come to recognize—eyes of fire, heart of gold. "We'll see. You mess with me again, I might get mad. But we'll see."

John smiled and offered his hand. Max took it, and they were friends again.

"There's more," said John as Carl set up a cassette player on the dining room table.

Midwestern University. Ted Canan stood on the steps overlooking the Quad Plaza at the center of the campus and took it all in. Yeah, Willy said it would be a big place, and he was right. Lots of fancy red brick buildings, close-mowed lawns, brick sidewalks, ivy, shade trees, noontime carillon bells, sweet-looking chicks swivel-hipping their way across campus. Mmmmmm-hm!

I should have gone to college, he thought to himself. *Think of how things would have turned out. I could've been a rocket scientist or something. Oh well. How many of these kids have control like me? I got control. I call the shots. I make the moves I want to make. And I get paid to do it!*

He looked himself over, wondering if he would blend in very well. Not really. He was big, which was fine, but he was a little older than all these spring chickens, and the tattoos on his arms made him look more like a street thug than a rocket scientist-to-be. What about the black, greasy hair? Well, he was seeing all kinds of hair walk by, so that was no problem. But he'd get some better duds right away, something clean and maybe natural-looking. He didn't want anyone to think he'd hurt them.

He pulled out a map of the campus Willy had gotten from some big wheel in the state government and checked again for the location of Clark Hall, one of the girls' dorms. Yeah, there it was. He'd go check it out. He was hoping there'd be some trees around that place somewhere, some dark areas, some bushes or something. That would make his job easier.

"And did you say she's bleeding?"

"Yes, and it won't stop!"

"Where is the blood coming from?"

Max and Deanne sat at their dining room table, listening intently to the brief tape recording John, Carl, and Leslie had become thoroughly familiar with.

"Where is the blood coming from?" asked the dispatcher. "Where is the wound?"

"She had an abortion," came the voice of Shannon DuPliese.

Max mouthed a cussword, not out of anger, but out of horror, resting on his elbow, his head only inches from the cassette player's speaker.

"District Twelve, Rescue 231, Medic 231, vaginal bleed, the governor's residence, 1527 Roanoke . . ."

John, Carl, and Leslie sat with the Brewers at the table, not saying a word, just letting the tape speak for itself.

The dispatcher's voice: "Hello? Are you there?"

A man's voice, desperate, urgent: "Who is this? I need the phone—"

"Sir, this is District Twelve Fire Emergency. We have dispatched Medic One and an aid unit to the governor's residence. Who are you, sir?"

"I'm Governor Slater! It's my daughter!"

"Is she conscious, sir?"

"No, no, I don't believe so."

"Is she breathing normally?"

The governor called off the phone, "Is she breathing? Ashley! Is she breathing?" A woman screamed something in the background. The governor came back on the phone. "She's breathing, but we don't think she's conscious."

"Does it sound like she's breathing normally?"

"No. No, she's gasping . . . it's very labored breathing."

"Would you like to do CPR? I can help you."

"Yes! I just need to—"

The woman shouted something. There were thumping sounds, doors opening, footsteps, voices.

"Oh, they're here! Thank God!"

The tape ran a few more seconds as the aid crew arrived and then went silent. John hit the Stop button.

Max remained frozen by the speaker for a moment as if hypnotized by what he'd heard. Deanne had grabbed his hand at some point during the tape, and now her hand was locked there. It took both of them several seconds to relax, to turn from stone to flesh again and ease back from the speakers. Max even took some extra breaths to make up for those he'd lost during the playing of the tape.

"O God Almighty!" said Max.

"O Jesus," Deanne prayed, "what's become of us?"

Max asked Leslie, "What was it Denning said? That there were others besides Annie?"

Leslie nodded. "I guess Hillary Slater would fall into that category."

John added, "And I think Dad knew that both deaths occurred in the same clinic, the Women's Medical Center. That's what he was setting out to prove."

"Well, he even knew about Hillary Slater's death before he got this tape," said Carl. "He went down and bought a copy of her death certificate just a few days after she died, and he wrote to the governor about it too, right about that same time. He was onto something, and the governor knew it."

"And now he's dead," said Max. "Is that what I told you? Huh?"

"Well, there's still a lot we just plain don't know," said John. "We have hunches, sure, but we don't have any solid connection between Dad, the tape, and whoever killed him."

"We'll find 'em . . . or they'll find us, either way." Max's words had a sobering effect on them all.

Leslie offered, "Well, we may be in the dark about what happened to Dad Barrett, but as far as what happened to Annie and to Hillary Slater, I think we're close. It all hinges on two key witnesses who can link the two girls' deaths at the same clinic. One is that girl who calls herself 'Mary,' the one we talked to at the Human Life Services Center, and the other . . ." She gestured toward the cassette player. ". . . is Shannon DuPliese. And, Deanne, you're the one who will have to talk to them. You've been through it. You can relate to these girls."

"And you're not the press," said John. "You're a mother, just a plain and simple, totally real person with a real concern."

"Well . . ." Deanne felt complimented but didn't know what to say.

John explained, "We've got to handle this thing on a real level—person-to-person and not person-to-media machine. If a news story comes of it later, fine, but . . . I've lost my father, and you've lost your daughter, and maybe a lot of other folks have lost someone because of . . . whatever this is . . . and I'd just as soon approach it on that level alone."

Carl spoke up. "Dad, would it be accurate to say we're doing this because it's the right thing to do?"

John smiled at his son. "Yeah, and that should be reason enough. Whether this ever gets two minutes on the 5 o'clock news is secondary and maybe doesn't even matter. It's still something we have to do."

Max nodded. "Yeah, I do feel better about that."

Deanne asked, "So what should I do?"

Leslie answered, "Call Shannon DuPliese. It's too late now, she's two hours later than we are here, but maybe tomorrow night . . ."

"But what do I say to her?"

"Just tell her the Truth," said John, "and then ask her if she'll be truthful with you."

twenty-six

AS the public watched:

Video: The majestic mountains and tall timber. A bald eagle soars above the peaks. Some elk graze lazily in a green meadow among colorful wildflowers as a breeze rustles the grass. A whale breaks the surface of the sea, spouting and slapping his tail on the surface with a violent, white-watered splash.

Voice over drum and flute music: "The Native Americans say the Earth is our Mother. Perhaps they are right. As human creatures, we share the Earth with all of nature, from the trees to the birds, from herds of deer to schools of spouting whales. For all of us, the Earth is home." On a high mountain ridge, walking along a trail with jagged, snowcapped peaks in the background, a durable, handsome young man approaches the camera, walking stick in his hand, coat over his shoulder. At the bottom of the screen appear the words, "Eddie Kingland, star of the TV show 'Love Thy Neighbor.'" Eddie looks sincerely into the camera and continues, the mountain breeze making his hair wave and play about his backlit head. "I've devoted much of my time to the protection of our precious natural resources because, as we should realize, we and the Earth will all live, or all die, together, and our children's fate, their world, is in our hands to form now. That's why I'm happy to give my support to the man who has served your state—and the Earth—with care, respect, and vision. Hiram Slater loves the Earth he came from and knows how much he owes her. If you love the Earth, you owe Hiram Slater your vote."

Cut to an eagle flying against a burning, sunset sky. As it floats on the wind, the words appear below it: "Hiram Slater: the New Dawn Lives On.

"Paid for by the Committee to Reelect Governor Slater, Wilma Benthoff, Chairperson."

The NewsSix logo appears on the screen, along with the words in gentle, flowing script, "A Window on Life," as a piano plays softly, soothingly.

John Barrett appears in a living room setting, dressed casually, sitting in a comfortable chair, his weight forward, talking to someone off-camera. "I often feel a special closeness to the people we report on because when a story breaks real people are involved, and when our cameras enter their world it's like opening a window through which we can share their experience—their joy or pain or hope . . . well, just anything and everything that makes us human. No other medium can bring us that close." He reflects a moment, then smiles at a moving thought. "You know, I see life through the eyes of new people every evening, and . . . it sure can expand your way of looking at things."

The screen goes to soft white as the words appear in gentle, flowing script—"NewsSix. We'll Be There."

The little portable television in Dad's shop sat cold, silent, and dead, its eye blank and staring into the room with nothing to say, no message to bring, and no one watching.

But the room was filled with warmth and joy anyway as John and Carl began to cover the little rowboat's ribbing with marine plywood. They talked as they worked, sometimes on big issues, sometimes on the foolish things, often laughing, sometimes even arguing, but they talked and worked together the whole morning.

Later that evening John sat at his computer in the bustling NewsSix newsroom, trying to get the script ready for the Seven O'clock. Even though some of the stories seemed wordy and too long, he decided they would just have to do—he couldn't concentrate enough to bother with them any longer. He was thinking about the Brewers and wondering how things were going.

Carl was working on the rowboat at the time, and as long as he had to line up the seams and seal them just so, his mind was on that task. But as soon as the plywood was in place and he'd set the bar clamp to hold it, his mind went to the Brewers. *Come on, Deanne, make us all proud of you!*

It was just after dinnertime at the Brewers'. Deanne and the kids had all hustled to get the dinner dishes washed and put away, and now the house was settling down to a relative quiet. Deanne took her place in Max's easy chair, the telephone on the stand right beside her. Leslie had already given Deanne the phone number, along with Leslie's calling card number for charging the call, and Deanne had them scribbled at the top of a sheet of notes she'd made.

"Still don't know what I'm going to say," she said with a bewildered shake of her head.

"Don't worry, babe," said Max. "You're Annie's mom. You just remember that, and the words'll come."

"I know John and Carl and Mrs. Barrett are all praying for you," said Leslie. Then she added, "And so am I."

"O Jesus," Deanne prayed, looking toward Heaven, "I'm praying too. Help me do it right."

She picked up the receiver and started dialing the number. "Now watch her not be there . . ." A recording asked her to enter the calling card number, and she did, consulting the number at the top of her notes.

A short pause.

"It's ringing," she reported.

Click. "Hello?"

Okay, Deanne told herself. *It's all yours now.* "Hi, is this Shannon?"

"No, this is her roommate Olivia."

"Oh, is Shannon there please?"

"Just a minute." Then away from the phone, "Shannon, it's for you."

Deanne looked at Max and Leslie, and they just looked back at her, their faces full of support.

"Hello?" came another voice.

"Hello . . . Shannon?"

"This is she."

"Shannon . . . my name is Deanne Brewer. I'm a mother, I've got four kids . . . Well, I had four kids, now it's just three . . ." Deanne hesitated, much as a novice skydiver would do at the door of the airplane before jumping. "Shannon . . . I know you don't know me, but . . ." There was nothing left to say but the Truth. Deanne looked toward Heaven even as she spoke the words. "Shannon, I used to have four kids, but my oldest, Annie, who was seventeen, died from an abortion she got at the Women's Medical Center, that abortion place down on Kingsley Avenue. And I . . ." Deanne's hands were shaking, and her voice was beginning to quiver. "Well, Annie died in May. May 24th. And I don't mean to . . . Are you still there?"

There was silence. Deanne looked at Leslie and Max, worry in her eyes.

"Shannon?"

Shannon's voice sounded weak. "*Where* did she die?"

"The Women's Medical Center, that clinic on Kingsley Avenue."

That seemed to hit home. Shannon said nothing for a moment, fidgeting with the receiver. Then she said, "O God . . ."

"Shannon? Honey, are you still with me?"

"Pardon me, what was your name again?"

"Deanne Brewer. My husband's name is Max, and our daughter's name was Annie."

"Mrs. Brewer . . . what did they do to her?"

"Well . . ."

"Did she bleed to death?"

"No. They . . . well, they hurried too much, I guess. They left parts of the baby inside and perforated her uterus, and she got an infection and died."

Shannon's voice was quivering and weak. She could have been crying. "How did you know to call me?"

Deanne struggled for just a moment and then remembered John's words: "Just tell the Truth." She decided to do just that. "Shannon, my husband Max and I have been trying to find out what happened to Annie and who was responsible, and some good people from the TV station, from Channel 6, have been helping us. We just got a genuine copy of Annie's autopsy report last night, and that's the first real proof we've had. The clinic won't tell us a thing—they're hiding it."

"Channel 6?"

"Yes, that's right. They know there's something going on at that clinic, and they've been helping us."

"I got a call from a Leslie Albright just a few nights ago."

Deanne could see Leslie getting anxious about all this truthfulness, but Deanne was going to go with it do or die. "Mm-hm. Well, Leslie's here right now—she's sitting right next to me."

"But . . . she said she was trying to do a follow-up story on me as the first recipient of the Hillary Slater scholarship."

Deanne had no answer for that. "Well, would you like to talk to her?"

Shannon hesitated.

"Maybe you can ask her about that and she can explain it to you."

"Okay."

Deanne held the phone out to Leslie.

Leslie sank just a little, feeling she'd been cornered and caught. Well, time to come clean and die all, die merrily. She took the phone. "Hello, Shannon. This is Leslie."

"Hi. Are you the one who called me?"

"Yes. It was Tuesday night, I think. We were talking about your being the first one to get the Hillary Slater scholarship and . . . well, I guess I—"

"Do you still want that story?"

Leslie perked up at that. "Um . . . well, Shannon, I have to tell you . . . I wasn't really after that in the first place, I just—"

"I'll talk to you. And I want to talk to the other lady too."

"Mrs. Brewer?"

"Yes. I've had time to think, and I know I have to talk to somebody. I can't carry this . . ." Emotion overtook her. "Excuse me."

"Shannon . . ." Leslie could hear her crying, so she spoke gently. "I'm going to let you talk to Mrs. Brewer again, okay? She knows how you feel more than anybody else does."

Leslie handed the phone back, whispering, "She's crying."

Deanne felt she was reaching out to a daughter. "Shannon, I'm here." Deanne listened to the girl weep and began to shed tears herself. "You go ahead and cry, honey. I've got my arms around you, hear? I've got my arms around you."

They met and embraced for real under a spreading oak tree in the center of Balen Commons, the centerpiece of the Midwestern University campus, a pleasantly meandering mall of groomed lawns, hundred-year-old trees, brick walkways, and gently rolling terrain. On all sides were the original brick buildings from the nineteenth century. Nearby a fountain with sporting bronze porpoises trickled and sprayed, and here and there bronze, marble, and granite sculptures jutted out of the evenly mowed grass like oversized toys. It was Saturday afternoon, a warm and pleasant day for October.

"This is my husband Max."

Max offered his big hand, and Shannon took it warmly.

"I'm gonna take myself a tour of this place for a while," he said, "and let you ladies talk. When you want to meet?"

They consulted their watches and agreed on a time about an hour later. Max walked away, just taking in the campus and looking for something interesting to do.

Shannon and Deanne found a bench in a pleasant little hideaway bordered by shrubbery alive with tiny, chattering birds. They talked for a while about themselves and their different backgrounds—Deanne, raised in the inner city by staunch Baptist parents, never well-to-do nor career-oriented, but happy to be the wife of a welder and a mother of four; Shannon, raised in a wealthy home by social-activist, Presbyterian parents, with the children of VIPs for friends, including the governor's daughter, and now aspiring to study law and economics.

And then they talked about Annie, not much younger than Shannon herself at the time of her death, a young lady with a bright future and the mind and will to tackle it. Understanding and appreciating her life was easy. Trying to derive some sense or meaning from her death and all the factors that caused it was another matter.

Then Shannon said abruptly, "Please don't hate me."

Deanne was shocked at that. "Shannon, why would I hate you?"

Shannon looked across the campus as she gathered her thoughts and controlled her emotions. She was determined that they would serve and not rule her today. "It's my understanding that, had I spoken up, had I said something, had that clinic been investigated, Annie could very well be alive today. Ever since Hillary was killed, I was always afraid that it might happen to someone else, and when you called . . . well, I knew it had happened. That's what I'm having to live with now."

She returned her gaze to Deanne, her face tense with emotion, her eyes watery. "Mrs. Brewer, I've been under tremendous pressure not to say anything, I want you to understand that. And not being perfect, and having morals that are somewhat undefined at this point in my life . . . I did choose the easy route, or what I thought was the easy route. It's been that way ever since April, when Hillary died. But I can't go on with it. It just can't continue. I've thought a lot about it, and I arrived at two possible choices. I could stay quiet about it and die inside—just cease living as a true human being. Or I could speak up and probably ruin my educational future. But . . . since either course will be a kind of death anyway, I figured that last death I could live with." She smiled at the paradox of the words.

Then she looked away again. Just looking across the lawn and the leaves turning gold made it easier to think, speak, and hold her emotions in check. "I'm sorry if I don't look you in the eye very much. I'm feeling a lot of shame right now."

Deanne reached over and touched her hand. "Honey, don't carry any shame for me, or for Annie. I forgive you, and I know she would. And God will, if you just ask Him."

Shannon closed her eyes and drew a deep, shuddering breath as her jaw trembled. For several moments she fought back her emotions, her hands frequently going to her face to cover it or to dab away tears. "I do appreciate that. I need to dig my way out of this pit somehow, and I do appreciate your understanding."

Then with trembling hands she reached into her carrying bag and produced a spiral notebook. "We really need to get into this while I still have the strength." She opened the notebook in her lap and paged through it until she found the first of many pages of notes. "Do you want to record this?"

Deanne shook her head. "Honey, this isn't an interview. We're just talking, that's all. If you decide you ever want to talk to Leslie and John and do it for a camera or a tape recorder, that's entirely up to you. Right now it's just you and me."

She nodded. "Well, I could use a dry run anyway." Then, starting at the top of the first page, she pressed forward, purposefully forcing herself over rough and difficult emotional terrain. Deanne didn't know what else to do but slide close to her and touch her whenever she needed it, which was most of the time.

"Hillary Slater and I were best friends from the time we were little. We went to Bowers Elementary together, and then we both started fourth grade at the Adam Bryant School. I think it was because our fathers were both involved in politics and it was that kind of school, a school for the children of the elite, the influential. Hey, we were privileged kids; we had the best.

"So Hillary and I grew up together, and we got to know each other's family, and I always knew that Hillary's dad was a driven man. If something didn't bring him success or power or influence in political circles, he didn't show much interest in it. And that's how it was with his children. He drove them too. He was very demanding, and he expected them to play the political game with him. I can remember the whole family putting on the smiles and standing together for pictures and publicity during his last campaign, everything rosy and the wife happy and the kids doing fine.

"But it was all public image. Hiram Slater can be cruel, and I saw him slap Hillary a few times to keep her in line, to keep her going along with his program. She was the governor's daughter, and she had to perform and look good to make him look good, and for the most part she did that—she maintained the image.

"Until she got pregnant. I know who the boy was, but

that's immaterial. He's in college now, and I suppose he's dating other girls, and all I can hope is that he's learned a lesson, but who knows?

"But I remember Hillary was really scared and kept talking about how her father would just kill her, and she didn't want anybody to know about it, she just wanted to get it taken care of and go on with her life. Knowing her father and how publicly oriented he was, and how public everything was with their family, I didn't blame her.

"I remember on April 16th—a Tuesday—I was called down to Mrs. Ames' office—she's a counselor at the school. Hillary was there in the room, and she and I and Mrs. Ames had a private meeting, and that's when I learned that Hillary was pregnant. She'd had a pregnancy test done by the school nurse, Mrs. Hunt, and the test had come up positive. So now Mrs. Ames had made an appointment for Hillary to get an abortion, and Hillary chose me to be the one who would drive her to the clinic and then take her home afterward. We had a lot of trust between us. We'd shared a lot of secrets, and now we were sharing this one.

"Mrs. Ames picked the Women's Medical Center because it was across town, in the south end, where the lower-income girls usually went. She figured that would be the best place because no one would know Hillary there, and we could get in and out of the area without being seen or noticed. They would even accept a phony name as long as you used the same one in all your dealings with them. So we picked out a false name, Susan Quinto. We got the idea from 'Suzy Q.' It was dumb, but that's what we picked. So on Friday we both went to school like always, but then got excused from classes at lunchtime—Mrs. Hunt wrote both of us medical excuses—and we drove over to the clinic.

"And that place was busy—it was just crammed. A whole van full of girls got there right before we did, and . . . everybody was quite stressed, there was a lot of tension. The clinic people were stressed and yelling at us, and . . ." Shannon drew a few deep breaths. "And the doctors were stressed as well. We could hear them yelling in the back, and we could hear some of the girls screaming . . ."

Shannon couldn't hold back her tears at this point. She wept, pulling out a tissue to wipe her eyes and nose. And she was angry with herself for crying.

Deanne put her hand on Shannon's shoulder and spoke earnestly. "No, now don't you mind it. If you don't cry you'll break. You go ahead."

Shannon continued even though her voice was shaking and she spoke an octave higher. "And Hillary was so frightened . . . She just wanted to run, to get out of that place . . . She said . . . I remember her saying, 'This is Hell—why do I have to go through this?' . . . And I kept telling her to just be brave, just go through with it, and then everything will be all right, it'll all be over . . ." She blew her nose, tried to gather herself, and then pressed on. "And then her turn came, and the lady—I don't know if she was a nurse or just a counselor or what—came and got her and took her through the big door, and the door closed, and . . . and I didn't know what they were going to do to her. I didn't know they were going to kill her . . ."

"No, honey, of course you didn't."

Shannon pulled herself together somewhat, at least enough to continue in a normal octave, though still shakily.

"And it didn't take long at all. I think it was maybe a half hour later, the lady—the same lady—came into the waiting room and told me to drive around to the back door to pick up Hillary—she was ready to leave. So I got the car and drove around to the back door, and they brought her out . . . the counselor lady and then some other assistant, one on each side of her to help her walk . . . and they said she should lie down in the backseat, so she did, and she had some birth control pills they gave her, and some instructions to follow . . ." She dug through her bag. "I've got those somewhere . . ." She leafed through a folder and pulled out a green sheet of paper, somewhat wrinkled, with text photocopied on both sides. Deanne received it from her and looked it over. At the top was the name and address of the clinic and then the title, "Post-Operative Instructions."

"The lady gave me that copy so I could help Hillary remember what to do. Hillary was so . . . she was just . . . I can't describe it. She just lay there in pain, just real sick . . . and it was like . . . like she was already gone, like she'd already died. She just wasn't the same, and she just kept saying, 'Take me home, just get me home.' And the lady told us to watch the bleeding, that it would stop after a while, but we had to keep a fresh pad on it. She said to get Hillary home and get her to bed and everything would be okay, so I started driving her home, but the bleeding just got worse, and we had to stop and change her pads and . . ." Shannon buried her face in her hands. She spoke through them, her voice muffled. "And the blood was everywhere . . ."

Max had taken a casual walk around the campus and now was returning to Balen Commons. He reached the top of the knoll where the big oak tree stood and from there could see Deanne and Shannon sitting together some distance away. It was obvious they were in the middle of something very intense. Deanne had her arm around Shannon, and Shannon appeared to be crying. It looked like he'd be taking another lap around the campus, which was okay with him. This was why they flew out here, to find out—Hold on.

Max moved quickly behind the oak tree and tried to look casual as he carefully peered around it.

Who was that sitting over there, that guy with the newspaper? He was close, not more than forty feet away, sitting on the edge of one of the big bronze sculptures, just flipping through the newspaper and trying to look casual. He was dressed in jeans and a long-sleeved shirt, nothing remarkable, but his face was easy enough to see.

And Max remembered that face very well. He'd had a close look at it moments before he planted his ham-sized fist right into it and knocked the guy down.

That guy was at the rally! Yeah! He was one of those guys who started the big fight at the governor's rally!

And he was watching Deanne and Shannon!

Max didn't notice, but his hand had turned into a dangerous, tight fist as he stood there behind the tree.

Shannon sat up straight, wiping her eyes and nose, and pressed on as steadily as she could. "I got her home, and the rest of the family was away. We knew they would be. The governor had some kind of speaking engagement, and Mrs. Slater and Hayley and Hyatt went with him, and they weren't supposed to be back until that evening. We thought we could just get the abortion done and Hillary would be okay and no one would know the difference. That was the plan, but it didn't work.

"I remember how weak she was . . . just dragging. I could hardly get her up the stairs to her room. And by then I was getting scared, and I said maybe we should call somebody, but Hillary kept begging me not to, not to let anybody know, not to call anybody. She said she'd be okay, and so we just kept soaking up the blood and changing the pads and . . . and it just wouldn't stop!

"Finally I called the clinic, but the line was busy, and I called again, and the line was still busy . . . and Hillary just kept bleeding and getting worse and worse. She started sweating and gasping for air, and I called again, and somebody finally answered, and I told them the bleeding just wouldn't stop, and . . . and that woman didn't know what to tell me! She asked, 'Well, are you following the instructions on the green sheet?' and I said sure, but there was nothing on the instructions about this much bleeding, and then she said, 'Well, if it doesn't stop by tomorrow morning, give us a call,' and she acted like she didn't want to talk, like she didn't have time, and . . . I think she was just putting me off, she didn't want to talk to me, she was too busy. And she just hung up.

"And then I looked at Hillary, and she was starting to turn blue, and she wouldn't respond to me anymore. She was fading. So I couldn't wait any longer. I called 911 and got help, and . . . and then the governor came home. I saw the headlights in the driveway and heard the garage door opening, and . . ."

Shannon paused, looking out across the commons. "I . . . I think this is where I went wrong, where all this other trouble started, because I panicked and ran out the back door. I just dropped the phone and got out of there. I thought Hillary would be okay because I called 911 and they were going to send somebody . . . but I was scared. I didn't want to be there when the governor came in and saw Hillary and all the blood and found out . . . I didn't know what he'd do.

"So I ran to my car . . . We'd shuffled cars around. I'd driven over to Hillary's and then we both rode in her car to school and then back to her house from the clinic. We were trying to keep everything secret, you know? So my car was parked a few blocks away, and I ran and got in my car and drove home, and my folks weren't home yet, which was a good thing because I know they would have seen something was wrong. But by the time they got home the word was getting around, and they'd already heard that Hillary had been taken to the hospital, and then they told me and . . . from then on I didn't have to hide how upset I was, I could just flow with it because everybody was upset.

"So . . . when Hillary died I just came apart, and my mom and dad felt real sorry for me, and they were great, but . . . I never told them what really happened. I never said a word, even after the governor told my dad that story about Hillary taking her pills by mistake . . . even after it came out on the news.

"And you know, for a while I wasn't really sure. I thought maybe that really was what caused it. Maybe Hillary was taking those pills and then had the abortion and then had the bleeding because of the pills, but . . . I know she wasn't having her period. I mean, she was pregnant!—so why would she be taking pills for menstrual cramps? And why would she get into her father's pills in the first place? She had her own bottle of pills in her room and she knew what they looked like. She wasn't stupid.

"But then the governor came to see me. He came over to the house to have a private little talk with me, to give me some comfort, you know, and my folks were really glad he was being so thoughtful. But you know what? He came to make sure I wasn't going to say anything. I don't know how he figured out I knew anything about it. I didn't ask, and . . . you know, neither one of us said anything directly about it. He just said things like, 'We both loved Hillary very much, and we wouldn't want anyone to know things about her that are private and her own business.' And then he told me, 'I believe in privacy, so I'm not going to ask any personal questions, not about you, and not about Hillary.' And then he said, 'But I'd like you to do me a favor, a very big favor, and that is, please respect Hillary's privacy and reputation, and keep this as something only you and Hillary shared.' "

Shannon laughed a small, derisive laugh. "Something only I and Hillary shared. He made it sound so honorable, so virtuous, like I was doing my best friend a favor as only a best friend can do.

"And you know, it took me a while to figure out what he was really doing. I wasn't going to tell anyone anyway, but then he came and gave me his big 'privacy' pitch, and then, just a few days after that, his number two man, Martin Devin, called me and told me I'd been chosen to receive the first scholarship and that I could go to Midwestern if I wanted, all expenses paid, and . . ." She shook her head incredulously. "And I still didn't get it. I accepted the scholarship and enrolled at the university, and I had this big idea in my head that I was going in Hillary's memory, and I thought that was so great, but . . . I always had an inkling that the governor had his own agenda in mind, and now I'm convinced of it."

She got a sudden thought that wasn't in her notes. "And you know what else convinces me? He took Hayley and Hyatt out of the Adam Bryant School right after all this, and it was close to the end of the school year! Nobody really knew why, but it all makes sense to me now. The school sent Hillary to that clinic to have an abortion behind her father's back, and he couldn't stand that. Hayley and Hyatt are going to a Catholic school now—surprise, surprise! Governor Slater talks all about privacy, privacy, privacy, but when it happens to his own kids, watch out!

"Anyway, I get a call from this Martin Devin character almost every week, and he's getting to be a real pest. He just keeps calling to make sure I'm okay and make sure I know they're still watching me, still making sure I keep quiet. Well, last time I told him the press wanted to talk to me and I just might talk to them, and I told him he could have the money back, that I was sick of the whole thing." Shannon heaved a deep sigh. "Oh, and did that ever feel good! He got real upset, but I felt great. Now I know what I'm going to do, and . . . Well, a lot of people aren't going to like it, I know, but I have to do it anyway. I can't carry this anymore."

Deanne put her arm around Shannon and pulled her close.

Shannon returned the embrace, and they remained that way for a moment, just savoring the closeness and kinship that had formed between them in such a short time. Their stories, their pains, and their fears were so very much the same, and now each woman had found in the other a beautiful answer to her need.

Max didn't want to leave the Commons in case the guy from the rally decided to slip away or, worse yet, attack Deanne and Shannon. He kept an eye on the character with the newspaper, but then managed to catch the attention of a passing student.

"Hey kid!" he almost whispered, beckoning to the young man.

The young man stopped, a little curious, a little suspicious. "Yeah?"

"You got police around here?"

The young man smelled trouble. He was interested.

"Campus police?"

"Yeah, *any* police!"

"Sure."

"Call 'em. Get me one . . . right now!"

twenty-seven

Night fell over the Midwestern University campus, and with the loss of the sun the temperature dropped to that crawling, autumn kind of cold that settles into the pockets and valleys like clouds of dry ice and turns the edges of the leaves and grass frosty-white by morning. The between-class bustle and rush of the daytime was now an intermittent trickle of students, most wearing warm coats, crossing the campus to attend libraries, late classes, cultural events, and political meetings. Now the amber floodlights came on to illumine the main walkways and malls, and the shadows beneath the trees and behind the thick shrubbery became ink-black.

Ted Canan was ready—ready and altogether patient, like a skilled and ruthless hunter. He would only have one chance, one opportunity, and he was willing to wait for the right one. When it came, he would be quick, the results would be final, and he would be out of there, ready to fly back west and collect his payment.

He'd gotten to know the landscaping around the campus, especially the pockets of blackness and covering that lay along the several routes to Clark Hall, one of the girls' dormitories—*the* dormitory he was most interested in. He'd kept track of Shannon DuPliese all through the day, even during the hours she'd visited with that black lady, whoever she was. He hadn't been on campus long enough to find a reliable pattern in the girl's routine, but tonight showed some promise because he knew where she was now, where she would be, and when. After having dinner with those black folks at the North Campus Diner, she'd gone to the Research Library. The Library closed at 11:00, and that hour was fast approaching. Unless she took a long, circuitous route around the perimeter of the campus, she would have to choose between two possible routes back to Clark Hall, both of which presented very short but very good windows of opportunity.

The most favorable route included a narrow stretch of

concrete walkway that ran behind the stadium bleachers, flanked by a sheer concrete wall on one side and a thick, wooded area on the other. At a key spot there was a small trail leading from the walkway into the woods with one row of bushes forming a perfect blind where he could wait. He'd plotted out several quick escape routes from that area—one down a service alley behind the BioMed Library and out to the avenue bordering the campus' west side, the other south through a botanical garden that was perfectly designed to hide a fleeing killer like him and bordered on the main street leading to the Medical Center. Either way, if things went well he would be long gone before this girl was even missed.

The other route she might follow would be a little riskier because the vegetation wasn't quite as thick and an escape route was further away, across open space. If she chose that route, he might not make his move tonight.

In any event he'd picked out a vantage point from which he could see which route she chose and then outrace her to the place of ambush. And that was where he now crouched, silent, dressed in black, patient.

Shannon DuPliese tried to study but couldn't keep her mind on it. She looked up at the clock on the wall. 10:55 P.M. The Research Library would be closing soon, and she was getting very nervous. She put her book away. She might as well quit for the night.

11:05 P.M. As Ted Canan watched from his vantage point, two young men walked along the main thoroughfare from the Research Library, talking quietly, their heads and shoulders illumined by the amber floodlights. Then two women. Then a man and woman holding hands and laughing. He remained still. She would come soon.

Two faculty members came by, one of them earnestly trying to make a point and the other not going along with it until they rounded a corner and their voices faded.

Then one lone man, walking briskly in the cold.

Then, some distance behind him, alone, came Shannon

DuPliese. He recognized her long, brown coat and the thick stocking cap she wore on the crown of her head, now pulled down around her face against the cold. She was carrying her large canvas carrier over her shoulder in typical fashion, and she seemed to be in a hurry.

Okay, baby, which will it be? He watched as she approached the Graphic Arts building, for at that point she would turn right and follow the path that went behind the stadium bleachers or would turn left and walk up the steeper route through the trees and along the parking lot.

She reached the Graphic Arts building. She stopped. What was she doing? She set her bag on the pavement and looked through it. Had she forgotten something? *Too late now, baby, the library's closed.*

She looked back his direction. He didn't flinch. He knew she couldn't see him up in these bushes.

Then she seemed to make up her mind. She picked up her bag . . . and turned right.

C'mon, c'mon, do it, make me happy. Yeah! She was going to take the better route for sure.

She was heading that way, not turning back.

He bolted from his hiding place, bounded up the hill, over a short bridge, and down the winding path toward the stadium. Then, at a predetermined entry point, he bounded like a black gazelle into the woods and wove his way through the trees and bushes to the ambush point, making it there well ahead of her.

He crouched behind the bush blind, his heart racing, his adrenaline pumping. He was already seeing it happen in his mind's eye; he could already feel his hand around her throat.

Looking up the walkway, he could just see the boundary of the last floodlight's amber circle. Between that circle and himself was just the right kind of darkness, and so far there were no other human beings passing by.

He heard her footsteps before he saw her. His body tensed, and he fell especially silent.

The footsteps continued, clicking evenly and quickly along

the concrete, growing louder and more definite as they approached.

Then he saw her pass through the last reach of the amber light and into the darkness, into his snare.

She was walking down the center of the walkway, her head down, the cap pulled down against the cold, her arms close to her chest, her bag over her shoulder. She was walking blind. He'd be on her before she knew a thing.

She came closer. He prepared for his leap.

She came alongside his hiding place.

He leaped from behind the blind, silent as a spirit, a blurred shadow, a sinewy demon of death. His arms closed about her shoulders, his hand clamped over her mouth, and she made no sound. She struggled, bending, twisting, but he had her in a steel grip and now he was going to finish it quickly. He began pulling her toward the woods.

Uuuhhh! He felt like his groin would come out his throat. The blow kinked his spine, and the pain numbed his brain except for one thought: *hang onto her, hang on.* He managed to keep his grip on her as he tried to recover from the pain that coursed up his body.

Wump! An elbow rammed his ribs so hard he felt he would never breathe again.

Somehow one of her arms got free, and her palm slammed into his face. He stumbled backward. How did her foot get behind him? He tripped over it and slammed flat on the pavement.

Footsteps! Running footsteps! They were closing on him! The game was over. The hunter had become the hunted.

He got to his feet, his legs wobbly, his back bent, his guts threatening to pour out of his quivering body.

"Freeze!" came the shout from further up the walkway. "Police!"

He pushed with his legs, one at a time—it didn't feel like running—and made for the woods. Out of the corner of his eye he could see a cop dressed up like Shannon DuPliese aiming a .38 at him.

He got to the edge of the woods, took two painful steps

into the bushes, and ran into a huge, muscular wall with powerful arms and raging eyes.

"Where you goin', man?" the wall asked before shoving him back onto the concrete where he went tumbling again.

He got back on his feet in an instant, ready to run, but the big black man already had him by the collar and belt and slammed him up against the concrete wall. He bounced off and fell backward into the arms of two? three? a dozen? police officers who swarmed, tackled, pinned, and cuffed him.

It was over. Boy, was it over!

"You have the right to remain silent . . ." said one officer.

Ted Canan looked up from the concrete to see a cop remove a wig and stocking cap, another cop holstering his gun, two campus police standing ready with night sticks, and the lone, uniformed orator reading him his rights.

As for that wall that met him in the woods . . . it was a huge black man, standing over him with muscular arms crossed over his chest, smiling knowingly, just glaring at him like a lion eyeing his kill.

"We got you, punk, and now you better sing!"

The phone rang in Shannon's dorm room. She got up from her desk where she'd been waiting and picked up the phone.

"Shannon?" came the voice of a police officer.

"Yes."

"We got him."

The dispatcher's voice: "Hello? Are you there?"

A man's voice, desperate, urgent: "Who is this? I need the phone—"

"Sir, this is District Twelve Fire Emergency. We have dispatched Medic One and an aid unit to the governor's residence. Who are you, sir?"

'I'm Governor Slater! It's my daughter!"

"Is she conscious, sir?"

"No, no, I don't believe so."

"Is she breathing normally?"

The governor calls off the phone, "Is she breathing? Ashley! Is she breathing?" A woman screams something in the background. The governor comes back on the phone.

"She's breathing, but we don't think she's conscious."

"Does it sound like she's breathing normally?"

"No. No, she's gasping . . . it's very labored breathing."

"Would you like to do CPR? I can help you."

"Yes! I just need to—"

The woman shouts something. There are thumping sounds, doors opening, footsteps, voices. "Oh, they're here! Thank God!"

"The aid crew is there, sir?"

"Yes!"

"Very good, sir, they'll take it from here, all right?"

"Yes, thank you."

"Good-bye."

Click.

The tape went silent. John hit the Stop button.

Monday night, a little after 8 P.M.

Detective Bob Henderson sat there on the edge of John's easy chair and just stared blank-faced at the cassette player for a significant length of time. Finally, in as cool and efficient a tone of voice as he could muster, he asked John, "Is that one tape your only copy?"

"I've made some others, and they're in safe keeping," John answered.

Henderson went back to staring at the cassette player again, thinking, rubbing his chin, his mouth. "Okay . . . so it's just like Shannon DuPliese says—Hillary Slater died from an abortion."

Leslie answered directly, "That's right." No ifs, ands, or buts.

Deanne reminded the detective, "She was there, Mr. Henderson. She saw it, and she's ready to testify to it."

"I know," said Henderson, "she told me on the phone. She even knows the false name Hillary used in case we need to subpoena the clinic records."

"And that's why that Canan punk tried to kill her," Max added. "She knew too much, and they were afraid she'd talk!"

Henderson held up his hand. "Now, now, let's not go too fast. Let's get all the facts in hand before we jump to conclusions."

Max was quite ready for conclusions. "What more facts you need? John Barrett, Sr. had that tape, and he got killed. Shannon DuPliese is the one talking on the tape, and somebody just tried to waste her on Saturday! You oughta be askin' yourself who and why."

"I'm asking myself, *qui bono?,*" said Henderson.

"What's that?" asked Max.

"Who benefits?" Henderson stared at the floor and rubbed his face some more. "And listen, I really do not like the answer to that question. I've got to be really careful!" He pointed his finger right at John and then Leslie. "And you people in the media have to be careful too! Do you have any idea how explosive this is?"

John shrugged. "That's why we called you. We thought we finally had something you could run with."

Henderson only shook his head and whispered a mournful oath, followed by a quick "Excuse me." He reviewed some facts in his head. "Well . . . Shannon is convinced the governor and his chief of staff were trying to hush her up—permanently. She says Devin was hounding her, trying to keep her quiet, and she told him she just might talk, and then—a few days later—here's Canan jumping her—well, the decoy of her."

"So okay!" said Max. "There you are."

"Yeah, here I am—in a very sticky situation where I'd better be right, and I mean absolutely, totally right, before I make a move on this thing." Henderson took a deep breath and switched from a dumbfounded to a methodical mode. "Well, we've got something started. I've been in touch with the police back at Midwestern University, and we've got a firm ID on Ted Canan. I know the guy. He's from right around here, and he's got a record as long as three of our arms. I've run him in a few times myself. So I think it's fair to ask what a two-bit hood was doing clear over in the Midwest, attacking the only girl on that campus who just happened to be best friends with the governor's dead daughter." He looked at Leslie. "Now was it you that had that video . . . ?"

Leslie nodded. "Right . . . the video of the governor's rally. Ted Canan is in it, and I think one other character who started that fight."

"Yeah, I need to see that before Canan gets extradited back here. I want to know if he's got any immediate friends I can pressure."

"I'll have it for you tomorrow."

Henderson looked over the scribbled notes in his hand, notes from the conversations he'd had with Shannon, with the Brewers, with John and Leslie, and now from the playing of the 911 tape. "A lot of pieces here . . . but a lot of the puzzle." He flipped a page over. "Looks like Governor Slater either lied or somebody lied to him. I'd like to get to the bottom of that, find out who and why—" He cut off any objection from Max by looking at him and adding, "—for sure. And then . . ." He looked at John. "You know, that whole pipe rack theory of yours makes a lot more sense now, doesn't it? With no clear fingerprints on the forklift, we've needed another trail of some kind. Well, now we've just about got ourselves a smoking gun here, a motive and a possible connection to the party who pulled the trigger. It's getting credible . . . very credible. But I still have one big question: just how the heck did your father get that 911 tape?"

John answered, "We've looked in the governor's direction. I have a friend who's trying to find out if the governor's made any recent enemies, someone on the inside who'd know about all this."

Henderson tightened his lips at a difficult thought. "You're talking about somebody way inside."

"Maybe so. But the guys at the warehouse say Dad did have a visitor that day I dropped by to see him and saw him with Chuck's walkman."

"I'll drop by and get the description from them. We've got to find the guy, whoever he is."

"He may have just been a courier for someone else, we don't know."

"No, we sure don't." Henderson flipped to a page with some room on it. "John, if you don't mind my asking, why do you think your father got that tape? I mean, the guy was a plumbing wholesaler! Why give a tape like that to a plumbing wholesaler?"

"Well . . . remember what I said about his religious leanings?"

Henderson gave a big nod. "Ah, yeah, the pro-lifer making pro-choice enemies. So he did have his hands in the political realm."

"And he was making the governor nervous, I know that. He wrote to the governor about his daughter and apparently knew all about the abortion before he even got this tape."

Henderson looked up from his notes. "How'd he know?"

John shrugged. "He was a prophet."

Henderson's face got a little lopsided. "You want me to write that down?"

John smiled. "That's the predominant theory at this time, yes."

Henderson wrote it down. "This case is full of surprises, I want to tell you . . ." Then he looked at all of them. "So all right, I'm going to make a nearly impossible request of all of you. Try to control yourselves. Don't blab this around. It's just too big, too dangerous, and if something gets blown before we're ready, we could lose it all, you understand? And that goes for you people in the media!"

Leslie retorted, "And you too, Henderson! Let me remind you that there are beat reporters around the police precinct all the time who would just about kill for a scoop like this. But you know and I know that we're dealing with people who specialize in lying and phony images, and if they suspect we're onto them . . ."

Henderson laughed. "Suspect? They know! Their hired thug just got arrested, for crying out loud!"

Leslie backed off. "Yeah, good point. So . . . how about we all move fast and move quiet?"

"And keep our cool! We don't know anything for sure yet. Keep telling yourself that—and don't jump to conclusions. Let's get the whole picture first."

"Fair enough," said John.

"Agreed," said Leslie.

"I'd say you better hurry," said Max.

"Okay, I'm outa here," said Henderson, rising. "I'll be in touch. Leslie, give me a call and we'll see that tape. And, John, if Shannon has anything more to say, let me know."

John rose to shake Henderson's hand. "I've contacted a friend at a TV station over there. He's going to interview Shannon on-camera and send me the raw tape. We'll be in constant contact getting ready for that."

"Good enough."

"Oh, and Leslie . . ." John beckoned to her.

"Yeah?"

"You've got a copy of the 'Post-Operative Instructions' from the clinic?"

Leslie dug into her carry bag. "Oh, yeah, right." She handed a photocopy to Henderson. "Here . . . I got the original from Shannon, and she got it direct from the Women's Medical Center. You can see the Center's name and address right at the top."

Henderson was intrigued.

John continued, "And, Leslie, make sure you get one of those to Mrs. Westfall at the Human Life Services Center. Tell her about Shannon. Maybe Mary will come forward now that she has a corroborating witness."

"Maybe Mary has her own copy," Leslie mused.

Carl gave a clap of his hands. "Man, wouldn't that be something? That would cinch both abortions happening at the same clinic for sure!"

"I'll call her tomorrow," said Leslie.

"And I suppose Aaron Hart, the lawyer, needs to find out what's going on," John considered.

They were all busily chattering when Henderson closed the door to John's apartment behind him and walked slowly down the stairs to his car, deep in thought, heavily perplexed, still dumbfounded. This was turning out to be some kind of day, almost more than he could take all at once.

He got to his unmarked squad car and leaned against it for just a moment.

"*Qui bono?*" he asked himself, looking out over the city. It just seemed that all the arrows pointed in the same direction. Hoo boy. A bigger can of worms he'd never find.

He got into the car, his mind still processing a substantial load of data, sorting it, filing it in little slots and folders in his head, arranging it all into some rather unthinkable revelations.

"Who benefits?" he asked again and then let his head rest with a bump on the steering wheel at the obvious answer.

The meeting behind the tall oak doors of the Executive Conference Room convened early on Tuesday morning, with all those invited arriving promptly despite the short notice.

Hiram Slater stood at the head of the long conference table. At his right sat his special assistant and the meeting's organizer, Martin Devin. At his left sat Wilma Benthoff, the governor's campaign manager, and to his left sat Mason Hartly and Eugene Rowen, the governor's innovative publicity team.

The others sitting at the table were their special guests, handpicked by Slater and Devin, persons crucial to the carefully laid plan they were about to present.

The first was Tina Lewis, close business acquaintance of Martin Devin and executive news producer for Channel 6.

To her right, Gretchen Rafferty, red-haired, grim-faced feminist, political activist, and director of the League for Abortion Rights.

Next to her, Candice Delano, a well-weathered, white-haired pillar of radical feminism and president of the United Feminist Front, a woman who hated men and was never timorous in saying so.

Across the table from them was an attractive and articulate black woman named Fanny Wolfe, president and spokeswoman for the Federation for Controlled Parenthood.

Next to her, with weathered face and thinning gray hair combed straight back, was Murphy Bolen, news editor for the city's biggest newspaper, *The News Journal*.

They had just heard the truth about Hillary Slater's death from Hiram Slater himself, followed by a quick report from Tina Lewis about the news story now brewing somewhere behind the scenes at Channel 6.

Gretchen Rafferty turned red and set her jaw more firmly than ever. Candice Delano let out an unabashed string of obscenities. Fanny Wolfe started jotting questions of strategy on her yellow legal pad. And Murphy Bolen raised his eyebrows, leaned his chin on his knuckles, and whistled one long, mournful note.

Gretchen Rafferty was the first to speak. "Well, whose business is it anyway? Nobody needs to know."

Candice Delano added quite loudly, "Whatever happened to privacy? Isn't that what we've been marching for all these years?"

Tina waved her hand for a chance to respond and then answered curtly—the pressure was going to be on her and she knew it, "It's going to come out. That's a given we all have to accept."

Candice Delano was not about to accept it. "From your own people? You're telling us that you have no control over these muckrakers?"

"I can do what I can, but—"

"Then stop them, fire them, do something! We don't need this kind of—"

Tina became angrily defensive. "I'm in no position to fire anyone, and I can't stop them from snooping—it's a free country—"

"Snooping? You can't stop them from snooping?"

"Now hold on," said Murphy Bolen, coming to Tina's rescue. "The fact of the matter is, for some people this news is gonna be hot. It's gonna be just the thing they're looking for to cook the governor's goose. So you can take up our time blaming whoever you want, but Tina's right—it's going to come out. If her people don't spread it, somebody else will."

"Anti-choice bigots . . ." Candice muttered.

"Of course," Gretchen Rafferty agreed.

Martin Devin grabbed for control. "This is the reason we've called you all together. Now the way we see it, we can't keep the news from getting out. But look around the room, folks. We do have the power to control how it comes out, how it sounds, how it looks. We can take control of it and put it out our way first. What are a few little people down at Channel 6 compared to our combined efforts, especially if we scoop them on this?"

Fanny Wolfe was ready to jot down ideas. "So what are you proposing?"

Devin had an outline already printed and passed it out to all those present. "This is an initial battle plan, wide open for discussion, improvement, comment, whatever. But remember, we have to move on this today if we're going to get the jump on the enemy. If the story breaks before we have a chance to break it first, we'll lose the high ground. But if we can move first and build some momentum in molding public opinion, our enemies will look pretty feeble trying to catch up from behind."

They all perused the notes Devin had passed out. No one jumped for joy or remarked how clever the plan was, but no one had any better ideas.

Hiram Slater guided them through the outline himself. "You'll notice we've called for some pretty harsh measures, maybe even some sacrifices on the altar of the cause, and that's one reason I had to have you all here to see this. If I hadn't called you in and shown you this and made it clear to you, I'm sure some of you would have thought I'd betrayed you, that I'd become a turncoat."

"I dare say," Gretchen Rafferty replied.

Fanny Wolfe nodded to herself. The plan seemed to make sense to her.

Murphy Bolen just smiled as headlines paraded through his head.

Slater referred to his copy. "Now to quickly outline the plan, Phase One will be a press release from myself, possibly a press conference or a speech in which I'll release the information that Hillary died from an abortion—"

Candice Delano slammed the table and let out a cry of indignity. "No! That will never work, Governor! You'll be walking right into the enemy's cannons!"

"Now, Candice," cautioned Fanny Wolfe, "hear him out. There are times to be forceful and direct, and there are times to be subtle."

Gretchen agreed. "Go ahead, Governor."

Slater continued, "Fanny used the right word: *subtle.* I'm sure we're all aware that how we say things can have a great effect on the public's reaction. What I'm proposing is that I go ahead and release the information about Hillary's death, but deliver it from the position that I never knew about it until recently—and that even upon knowing it, I have no regrets that I didn't know because Ashley and I respected Hillary's privacy—and even though an unfortunate accident occurred, the higher ideal of personal privacy remained intact. Listen, if we truly believe in total reproductive privacy, then the rules have to apply to everybody, including me and my own children, and that's what I intend to say."

Now Candice mellowed a little, chewing on this new morsel. She liked the taste of it.

"So . . ." Slater continued, "we'll work out the details on that later. But then will come Phase Two, which is to answer the questions that are going to arise about the safety of legal abortions in this state. This is where some sacrifice might be necessary, and that's why you people are here. I need your input on this.

"My PR men here . . ." The governor looked toward Rowen and Hartly. ". . . have a nice little slogan I've adopted: *Image Is Everything.* Based on that idea, we must deal with the cause of Hillary's death publicly to assuage any fears that might arise in the public mind. So publicly I'm going to launch an investigation into abortion malpractice, not because I have anything against abortion, but because—and our PR program will emphasize this—Governor Hiram Slater cares about women."

Now Candice got agitated again, but this time Gretchen and Fanny joined her.

Candice spoke first. "Sir, you can't investigate the clinics! That would mean government interference, and that would mean war! Our friends would never stand for it!"

Gretchen added, right on top of Candice, "They absolutely will not stand for it; *I* won't stand for it! It would be tantamount to harassment!"

Fanny tried to sound reasonable. "You would be opening a dangerous crack in the wall of privacy, sir, and who knows how large a flood of invasion and regulation would break through after that?"

Candice quoted an old marching chant, "Not the church, not the state, women must decide their fate!"

Devin tapped the table with his pen to call for order. "Ladies . . . gentlemen . . . please hear us out. We are dealing with cold, vicious reality here. The anti-abortion forces are going to be crying for just such an investigation. They will most certainly cash in on this politically, and we have to find a way to defuse it, all right?"

Governor Slater was visibly feeling the stress of all this. "If I must defend my own sincerity . . . Let me inform you that we did our best to conceal all of this when it first happened because I knew it would be politically devastating. If I'd taken any action at the time, you people would have branded me as anti-choice, and you know it; if I did nothing, then the opposition would have branded me a heartless politician who doesn't care about what happens to his own children. I didn't want to find myself in such a position, and I definitely didn't want your interests jeopardized. But now we—and I mean all of us—are in this position, and we have to do whatever is necessary to dig ourselves out."

They quieted themselves and were ready to listen again.

"Now let me just say, I don't know which clinic is responsible for my daughter's death, I don't want to know, and I have no intention of finding out."

"Well, we won't tell you either," Candice blurted.

"May I finish?" the governor said in rebuke and then continued, "When I say that I'll publicly launch an investigation, I mean I'll be doing something for the public to see. I'll appoint some people, or I'll have Martin handle that . . ." Devin nodded. "He can make some calls, ask some questions, interview each of you, perhaps even get you to serve on a committee. Together you can compose some effective soundbites on the safety of the industry, get some pictures of your activities on-camera for television, go through the motions, all right? We'll do something for the public to see and hear, and we'll structure the information so as to calm the public mind, just put the whole thing to rest. And then . . ." The governor looked at Tina Lewis. "With help from our friends in the media, the story can just fade away—am I right?"

Tina commented, "Well, it's going to be a big story initially. There isn't much we can do to change that. But with that as a given, there are two factors that come into play here, as I see it. Number One, the subject matter is something the media in general are not going to want for very long. It's like a hot potato; no matter how you report it, you're going to have somebody screaming at you, and that gets tiring real fast. So far as my own associates are concerned, I don't think the story will be carried for long. Second, in our medium, old news is virtually no news. We have to get people to tune in, which means we can't tell them old things they already know. They want new stuff that's hot, fresh, immediate. Well, this story has oldness built into it; it happened months ago. I think that if we drop the story onto them quickly, with all the loose ends tied up right from the start, sure, it'll hit big and play big on a newscast, but it'll hit complete, which means we can drop it just as quickly with no need for follow-up and let it die from neglect. After the initial shock, the public will eventually lose interest and want to hear about something else. It happens all the time." She looked at Murphy Bolen, petitioning his view.

Murphy nodded resignedly. "Ehhh . . . yeah, it would get buried pretty quickly. A story as unsavory as this one won't be followed for very long. I know a lot of reporters who won't want their names on it. Whoever does write it is going to be walking a thin line back at the office, if you know what I mean. And once it's over with, once it's buried, I can't imagine any reporter's gonna stick his professional neck out to dig it up again." Then he added, "But, Governor, just be sure that whatever you say you're gonna do, at least do something that comes close. If we're gonna report something we have to be honest."

"I understand," the governor responded. Then he looked sternly at Gretchen, Candice, and Fanny. "But before we go on, let me say this for the record: Don't you people forget that I'm not just covering for myself and my policies—I'm also covering for you. I didn't ask for any of this to happen, and I sure didn't ask to have my daughter killed, and if there's any blame to be found for our present circumstances it is not with this administration but with the industry that got sloppy enough to let it happen. So all three of you need to carefully appraise your demand that I not launch a real investigation into this because as far as I'm concerned, if I don't do anything about this, then you and your friends in all those clinics had *better* do something! I've stood by you, I've pushed legislation that benefits you, I've protected your sacred privacy and stayed out of your way. But if you're going to start killing people, it's going to be bad for both of us—you follow me?"

They paid attention to him and heard what he said, but their response was a chilling, stony silence. Gretchen's jaw was quite prominent, Candice only scowled at him, and Fanny wouldn't raise her eyes, but went back to doodling on her notes.

"Now . . ." the governor continued, "as for Phase Three, considering that no amount of subtlety or craft will satisfy the anti-abortion camp, and anticipating that they'll try to make a big deal out of Hillary's death, we're going to be working on shifting the public's attention away from the fact of the death itself and toward this administration's concern for women and their right to privacy—safe, sane, legal privacy. It's going to be an image war, to put it quite simply." The governor looked at Rowen and Hartly. This was their cue.

Eugene Rowen, horn-rimmed glasses in place and tie still crooked, stood to speak. "We've contact the agents of several celebrities who have already contracted with us for the campaign ads, and we're now working on what you might call counter-information ads—special ads that will underline in the public mind the real motivation behind Governor Slater's action, or inaction as it were—that Governor Hiram Slater cares about women."

Mason Hartly spoke up without standing. "The whole point is, the opposition might try to stir up gossip and innuendo about what the governor should or shouldn't have done about Hillary's death, but we'll just hit that head-on with a firm presentation of his motivations and reasons for doing—or not doing—what he . . . uh . . . did or didn't do. Am I making sense?"

"So far," said Fanny.

"How are you going to protect choice?" Candice asked.

Rowen fumbled through the papers in front of him just a moment, then answered, "Well, look at it this way. The opposition says something like, 'Hiram Slater doesn't care if his own daughter dies in an abortion clinic,' and so we just come right back and say, 'Hiram Slater believes in the sanctity of privacy, even to his own hurt, so deep are his convictions.'"

Gretchen was impressed. "Wow . . ."

Fanny nodded, smiling. "Very smooth."

Candice kept scowling but nodded her approval.

Rowen continued, "And . . . um . . . the opposition might say something like, 'If the governor's own daughter can die in an abortion clinic, then is anyone safe?' and we can turn right around and say, 'Governor Slater understands in the deepest, personal sense the need for safe, legal abortions and stands with all women in the fight to fulfill this need.'"

Now even Candice smiled. "Mm-hmm."

Hartly added, excitement in his voice, "And get this—we've just talked with Anita Diamond's agent—uh, she's the black pop singer, right?—and she has agreed . . ." He took a moment to look them all in the eye, to bait them a little. ". . . to do an ad for us in which she admits to having an abortion and how it did wonders for her career and how people like Hiram Slater are the answer for up-and-coming down-and-outers like her, or something to that effect."

Springtime, sunshine, and heavenly sparkles floated into the room, at least where the three women activists were sitting. They liked what they were hearing.

Rowen concluded, "We'll work this new material in so that it meshes perfectly with the ad campaign already under way. That way the public will immediately identify with the graphics and the style and fall into line, just flowing with it, not being jarred by any abrupt change in direction."

Hartly concluded, "And this work is under way right now, as we speak, ready for airing within two or three days."

Devin took back the floor. "So this is the basic plan, and we'll have more details for you as soon as they develop. Any questions?"

Fanny asked, "What about Loren Harris, the general manager at Channel 6? Can he be persuaded to intervene on this—at least stall it a while?"

Devin nodded, pleased with the question. "We are looking into speaking with him—not only regarding stalling the story that seems to be brewing there among some of the news staff, but also regarding the advertising we'll be buying from the station. We've been worth a lot of money to them in the past and hope to be worth even more in the near future, as we've already discussed." His eyes took on an additional devilish glint. "He knows we're very close to several of his regular advertising clients—and that our influence could send those advertising dollars elsewhere. Considering all that, I think Loren Harris might be persuaded to see things as we see them."

The governor added, "Loren and I are friends, and I'm very careful about not abusing our friendship to slant the news coverage, but . . . I think he'd be open to changing some timing here and there, perhaps changing some emphasis. We can deal with him. I'm confident something can be worked out."

"Any more questions?" Devin asked.

Not really—at least no question anyone felt like speaking. And besides, this was a quickly called meeting—they all had other places they needed to be. The meeting broke up, and they all headed down the hall toward the exits.

Devin made sure Tina Lewis would have to pass close by him to get out the conference room door. "Thanks for coming."

"Thanks for having me."

He checked her over, enjoying the view. "We'll need to stay in close contact during this whole process, I imagine."

She knew he was eyeing her, but catered to his interest. The hungrier he was, the more useful he would be. "We'll do that."

He leaned close and spoke very softly. "Any further word on the death of John Barrett's father? Are the cops looking into it?"

'I haven't heard a thing, Martin." Then she gave him a curious look. "Just why are you so interested?"

Devin chuckled. "Well . . . I guess because I have strong feelings about John Barrett and his kooky father."

She accepted that. "I'll look into it."

"If you get the chance. Gotta go." He ducked out and hurried toward his office, feeling much the conqueror.

Fanny Wolfe and Candice Delano conversed quietly as they walked along.

Candice asked, "So what do you think?"

Fanny answered, "I think our people will get behind the governor on this. It's really the best course of action, and this kind of thing has worked in the past. What about your people?"

"They'll back him, provided he doesn't say much. The more he talks about this, the more trouble I'm going to have cooperating."

Murphy Bolen just happened to overtake them, being a faster walker.

"What do you think of the plan?" Fanny asked him.

Murphy just smiled and quipped, "He's dead" as he stopped at the drinking fountain.

Martin Devin, some distance behind them, heard the comment but pretended to ignore it. He didn't need to hear that kind of talk or entertain those kinds of thoughts at a time like this. Winners kept their eye on the finish line, not on the obstacles. He would make it.

It would be extremely comforting to get a progress report from Willy on the whole Shannon DuPliese thing. But still, he would make it. He stepped into his office, feeling good about the meeting.

Until he saw a man sitting there waiting for him.

"Uh . . . yes, can I help you?"

The man stood, smiling pleasantly. "Hi there. The secretary let me in—she said you'd be out of your meeting real soon." He reached into his suit coat pocket and produced a badge. "Detective Bob Henderson, homicide."

twenty-eight

SURELY there could be no greater feeling of insecurity than trying to look innocent in front of a cop, especially a cop from homicide. Devin could feel an abrupt and intense reaction in his body—a painful twist in his stomach, a pronounced speeding of his heart rate, a trembling in his extremities. He tried to control it, drawing on all the acting ability he could muster.

Watch your voice now, Martin. Low, even tone. "Yes, Detective, how may I help you?"

Henderson stood there a moment, observing. He seemed to be reading Devin like a book. "Feeling all right?"

Devin sat behind his desk. It would be a good place to sit, to hide as much of his body as possible and regain control of the situation. "Well, actually, no. I think I'm battling a touch of the flu this morning, so. . . ."

"Oh, I won't take long. I'm just out gathering some information on a case, and I figured you'd be able to help me."

"I'll try."

Henderson got out his notepad and flipped through the pages to a particular spot. "Well, of course you would be familiar with Shannon DuPliese, the young lady who received the first Hillary Slater Scholarship?"

Control, Martin, control! "Why, yes, of course. She's attending Midwestern University now, and I understand she's doing quite well."

"Have you heard from her lately?"

"No, not lately." Then Devin even managed to show some concern. "Uh . . . is she all right?"

Henderson smiled. "Oh, she's fine. A little shaken up, but she's fine." Henderson waited for just one beat and then hit Devin with the news. "But some thug tried to jump her this weekend, and we're looking into it."

This was terrible news. Devin didn't have to act stunned, but he did try to appear stunned for the right reason. "I'm . . . I'm shocked."

Henderson just stood there observing. "Well, that's understandable. I gather you were pretty close to Shannon, working with her on the scholarship thing, helping her enroll at Midwestern University, taking care of all the details."

This guy had been doing his homework. "Well . . . yes. We . . . I've, uh . . . I've been very happy, very encouraged to be a part of it. It's been good for the governor too to see a bright young lady like Shannon have the opportunity to excel in the place of the daughter he lost. It's been very helpful."

Henderson consulted his notes. "Did you call Shannon the night of Tuesday, October 1st?"

Devin's mind raced. *What was that? When was that? Why was that? Did I? Didn't I? Can I deny it, or should I admit it? What harm will I do myself?*

"Uh . . . I'm not sure of the date, but I did call her last week, and it was in the evening, yes."

Henderson nodded and checked something off in his notes. "Can you tell me what the conversation was about?"

Devin found a shield to hide behind. "Well, no, not really, not without Shannon's permission. We talked regarding the scholarship, her studies, that sort of thing. Under the agreements we have, such matters are kept in confidence."

"Sure. That's fine. But tell me, did you threaten her?"

Devin actually did feel indignant. "Excuse me?"

"Did you pressure her or threaten her regarding anything?"

"Regarding what, if I may ask? And just what do you mean by 'threaten'?"

Henderson smiled. "Hey, it's okay. These are routine questions. Nobody's accusing you of anything."

"Well, I should hope not! Shannon and I have had a good relationship. The governor's family and her family have been friends for many years. I . . . I really find such questions offensive."

"Certainly. Just have to cover all the bases, that's all." Henderson scribbled a little more. "Let me tell you what's going on—maybe that'll help. You see, Saturday night the police out at Midwestern caught a punk named Ted Canan, and from what they've been able to gather so far, he'd been following Shannon for a few days, just waiting for a chance to attack her. They caught him first, fortunately. But here's the question I have to deal with: Ted Canan's a local hood, from around here, and Shannon DuPliese is from around here too. Now apart from assaulting Shannon, we can't think of any reason why Ted Canan would be halfway across the country singling out a girl who was from the same town as himself, a girl I'm sure he'd never met before. You see the problem here?"

A question popped into Devin's mind: What did Murphy Bolen say out in the hall? "He's dead"? Who was he talking about?

Henderson was waiting for an answer, so Devin gave him one as best he could. "I . . . uh . . . I think I do. This is all so sudden, so bizarre."

"Yeah, it sure is. So let me just ask you, you know, for the record, just so I can say I asked, Would you have any idea why someone would come after Shannon?"

"Well, I . . . I don't . . . no, I just don't know why anyone would want to kill her." A new idea came to mind. "Except, maybe . . . that wasn't his real intention. Perhaps he intended to . . . uh . . . take moral advantage of her. Maybe he saw her here . . . saw her on television when she received the scholarship and decided to follow her. Maybe he gets a kick out of degrading important people, people recognized for achievement . . . people like Shannon . . ."

Henderson seemed to be writing down Devin's ideas, then looked up. "Nobody said Ted Canan intended to *kill* her, Mr. Devin. But maybe you're right. Maybe he just wanted to take moral advantage."

"Well . . ."

"But that is difficult to swallow, isn't it? That he'd go halfway across the country to do something like that? And there's another thing—the plane fare was over eight hundred bucks, and Ted Canan's never had that kind of money—except when somebody else hires him."

"Well . . . what did this Ted have to say about all this?"

"Oh, he isn't talking. He's pleading the Fifth."

"Hmm." Good news? Not really. "And what does Shannon think?"

"Oh, we're still talking to her. We don't have the whole picture yet. Oh, and I never got an answer to that question that offended you. You want to answer, just for the record? Did you threaten Shannon when you called her?"

The question was still offensive—too close to the target, actually. "Absolutely not. I categorically deny threatening her!"

"All right then, did you strongly urge her to remain quiet about certain matters pertaining to the governor's daughter Hillary?"

Henderson was trying to nail him to the wall, and Devin knew it. Well, there was no sense in denying it. "Listen . . . Shannon and I have talked about this matter of Hillary before. The governor is a public figure who needs his privacy, and I felt a need to remind Shannon of that. She was close to Hillary, and so . . . Well, there could always be a temptation for her to talk to the press, and . . . the governor simply didn't want that to become a pattern."

"Okay. Got it." Henderson scribbled it down and then said, "Well, that'll do it for now. Thanks a lot for your time. I'll call if I have any more questions."

"Good day, Detective."

Henderson pocketed his notepad and went out quietly, just quietly and calmly enough to make Devin wonder what he was thinking.

Willy! Where was he? What had happened?

Devin gave Henderson enough time to leave and then hurried out of the building and walked three blocks to a hotel. Toward the back of the lobby, just outside the elevators, he hunched over a pay phone, carefully concealing his face as he placed a call to a number he kept only in his head. The phone at the other end rang several times, and finally a sleepy voice answered. "Yeah?"

Devin tried to sound tough and unidentifiable. "Let me talk to Willy."

"Not today, man—he's gone."

No! That wasn't what Devin wanted to hear at all.

"What do you mean *gone?*"

"Oh, he's left town. Probably some heat on somewhere—you know how that is."

"Well, did he say where he was going?"

"Are you kidding? He never does. And I don't know anything, all right?"

Click.

Easy Martin, easy. Just think. Work it out. There's an answer somewhere.

But he was shaking all over.

He hurried back to the office, passing by a small lunch counter where Detective Bob Henderson stood concealed behind a rack of magazines, munching a hot dog, watching him go by.

"Dr. Harlan Matthews?"

The doctor looked up from his desk as the thought *Now what?* went through his mind. The pressure around Bayview Hospital had been bad enough ever since that woman reporter came to see him. He didn't need any more trouble of that kind.

Well . . . it wasn't Leslie Albright. But it did look like more trouble of that kind, and maybe worse. He immediately recognized the well-known face of John Barrett, NewsSix anchorman, and the man standing beside Barrett was showing a police badge.

"I'm Detective Bob Henderson, homicide, and this is John Barrett, with Channel 6 News, though he's here unofficially at the moment."

"And what in the world can I do for you?" Matthews was getting fed up and couldn't keep from showing it. "I recall talking to another reporter from Channel 6, here as unofficially as you, Mr. Barrett."

John replied, "We haven't released any information or done any story pertaining to you, and we won't do so without your knowledge."

"That doesn't mean it won't happen."

Henderson said, "Well, this won't take long, and quite truthfully you don't have to say anything if you don't want—the law's clear on that. But we were wondering if you'd be willing to open the file on Hillary Slater and confirm for us the real cause of death. We need the information for a possible murder investigation."

Matthews gave a slow shrug. "I'll need a court order, gentlemen."

Henderson expected as much. "Mm . . . Okay. Can't hurt to ask. We'll get the court order."

John ventured, "Dr. Matthews, through some investigation of our own we've found other evidence to indicate Hillary Slater died from abortion malpractice. We just need you to verify that's the case."

Matthews leaned forward, his chin resting on his hands, and considered John's question for a moment. "*Other* evidence?"

"Yes, sir. Very strong evidence, possibly enough to break the story with or without your involvement."

He smiled at that. "Without, most likely."

"Except for . . ."

"Yes?"

John thought for a moment, formulating his argument. "If and when we break the story, the governor's going to deny knowing the cause of death at the time, which means he'll have to argue that he was given erroneous information, which means . . . Well, doesn't it make sense, sir, that the finger of blame is going to have to point somewhere? And do you imagine that your superiors are going to point it at themselves? If you filed a correct and truthful report and were honest about the real cause of Hillary's death, it may be in your best interests to establish that before someone else makes you out to be incompetent."

That actually made Matthews laugh, nodding approvingly. "One would think you worked here."

Henderson stole a glance at John, visibly impressed.

Matthews asked, "Can you guys get a court order and make me produce the report?"

Henderson smiled. "Yeah. We could do that. It would provide you with personal protection if you feel you need it."

Matthews went back to the work on his desk, his way of dismissing them. "Bring me a court order and I'll see what I can do."

As John and Henderson went down the hall, Henderson whispered, "What he's really going to get is a search warrant. I just didn't want to scare him."

"John!" Leslie saw him come into the newsroom and ran to meet him in front of the assignment desk, her face full of urgency.

He shook his head. "Matthews won't release a thing without a court order—"

"Slater's going public!"

The sudden change of gears was jarring. "What?"

Leslie started back into the newsroom, and John had to follow her to hear what she was saying. "Tina got the tip this morning and sent Marian Gibbons after the story. He's going public with Hillary's abortion."

Now that was intriguing! "Oh, is he now!"

They hurried over to a bank of monitors in the corner of the newsroom. One monitor showed what was on the air at that moment—a soap opera being carried on the network; one showed the newsroom—the screen was black at the moment; and one showed any live feeds from out in the field. On this monitor they could see a blue podium in front of a large convention hall. A large lady in a blue dress was introducing people, going through preliminaries.

"It's a fund-raiser put on by the Women's Citizen League," Leslie explained. "They're backing Slater, and he's scheduled to speak."

John noticed some familiar faces sitting at the head table on either side of the podium. "Gretchen Rafferty . . . Fanny Wolfe!"

"I think Candice Delano's there too, down at the other end."

John looked at Leslie. "Then they're all in this together."

"You know they are. They're jumping our story."

"And Tina got the tip, of course!"

"If you want to call it a tip. She could have been one of the organizers. She sent Marian Gibbons to cover it, and that says plenty. She's having it fed directly here so she can see the speech herself. She and Rush are up in the control room right now." Leslie's eyes were glued to the screen as she whispered, "What are we going to do?"

"Listen . . . very carefully."

Wilma Benthoff, the governor's campaign manager, her blonde hair billowing and her black, sequined dress sparkling, made the introduction. "Ladies . . . and you men out there too . . . please welcome to the podium the Architect of the New Dawn, Governor Hiram Slater!"

Thunderous applause. The camera followed Slater as he rose from the table and walked to the podium, the written speech in his hand.

John ran to his desk for his notepad and got back in time to hear Slater begin his speech.

"Fellow citizens," the governor began, "and I do emphasize the word *citizens*, in these days, more than ever, the meaning of that word as it applies to everyone—all races, creeds, genders, and lifestyles—is crucial and a part of what this campaign is all about . . ." He went on, reiterating his platform and ideals and getting plenty of applause.

Leslie took a turn listening and jotting notes, while John went to his desk to start editing for the Five O'clock. Then John stood and listened while she went to her desk to polish up her day's work. It looked better than just standing there gawking at the screen.

Snap! Snap! Snap! John was snapping his fingers, signaling her. She bounded from her desk, catching her wastebasket with her toe and flinging it into the aisle where it promptly drew attention from the other staff.

"Man, what's up?" someone said.

Leslie and John listened raptly as Governor Slater continued his speech and other newsroom staff began to gather out of curiosity.

". . . a woman's inalienable, inviolable right to choose . . ." the governor said loftily. "I have not compromised on that ideal, and I always knew, even as we have all learned time and again together, that such freedom comes with a price, and that eternal vigilance is only one of its costs. As an army marches to victory, every soldier in the ranks knows he or she may not come back from the battle, that he—or she—may be called upon to make the ultimate sacrifice in order that those who come after can walk on ground that was gained through that sacrifice. And so it is not with shame but with pride—and with hope that your hearts may be encouraged—that I share with you, just for a moment, how the battle for abortion rights has affected my own home, my own family."

At this moment the camera captured some reaction shots of Slater's family—his wife Ashley, his daughter Hayley, and his son Hyatt, all present to publicly support him.

Slater continued, "My daughter Hillary was a young woman after my own heart, and I want her to be remembered for the fierce fighter she was. She was a soldier for justice, striving right alongside with her daddy for the ideals my family and I—and you—all share. And so . . . it did not come to me as any great surprise or shock to receive the news that Hillary had given her life on the battlefield of women's rights. It did not shame me to learn just recently that the original medical assessments in Hillary's case were incomplete, that some fine details had been overlooked, and that, contrary to the original conclusions of the skilled medical team who tried to save her life on that fateful night in April, she did not die from mislabeled drugs or from a foolish mistake or from any overdose. Rather, knowing the risks but standing firm nevertheless on her right to choose for herself whether to embrace those risks, she willingly and gladly received an abortion. She chose to control her own body, her own life, and to carry on with her future."

Leslie just about fell over and did manage to compare Slater's words with stuff one might encounter in a barnyard. John just shook his head and kept listening, his spirit churning within him to such a degree that his hands began to shake.

Slater continued, "Now, exactly how she died is unimportant. No medical procedure is totally without risks, we all know that, and there is no point in dwelling on the odds of such a thing happening or trying to fathom the unfathomable luck of the draw or hunt down who is to blame, if anyone. What if we did? Friends, it would be tantamount to marching backward, and I know Hillary would not want that. I also know that the enemies of choice would want that.

"Did we know she was pregnant? No, we did not. Did we know she had chosen to have an abortion? No, we did not. Did we want to know these things, before or afterward or ever?" Then, with great emphasis, he said with special intensity, "No, we did not!" He paused. The crowd let it sink in a moment, adjusted to this new revelation, and then, in a slow crescendo of approval and encouragement, rose to their feet and applauded. The governor had become all the more their champion.

In the newsroom Erica Johnson, the managing editor, indulged in some short applause herself, as did Valerie Hunter, special assignment reporter, and Barry Gauge, the commentator. Leslie didn't applaud, and it caught her interest that only a month ago she probably would have.

Governor Slater looked at the people sitting on either side of him, and the camera got close-ups of his supporters, including Fanny Wolfe, Gretchen Rafferty, and Candice Delano as he continued. "As a family, we have stood for the sanctity of privacy for all our children, and though trust and communication are foundational to our home, we still understand there are lines of privacy that cannot be crossed. I believe Hillary did what was right for her at that time, at that place in her life, and I will stand by her proudly, even in her death. I want you to do the same." More applause, from the audience and from the newsroom.

Leslie could feel some eyes staring at the back of her neck, but her arms remained firmly crossed, her hands silent.

"Are abortions safe in this state? Of course they are, as my good friends here on the platform with me can and will guarantee. But we would be blind and shortsighted if we didn't expect our enemies to dig and pry and demand to know more than they are entitled to know. Demagoguery is unavoidable in a situation like this, especially with the election coming up. So before my worthy opponent Bob Wilson begins to whine about this, let me say from the very outset that I intend to appoint a special committee to evaluate the safety, sanitary, and procedural standards of clinics licensed in this state. The committee will include Ms. Fanny Wolfe, president of the Federation for Controlled Parenthood and well-known to you all . . . and also Gretchen Rafferty, director of the League for Abortion Rights."

Leslie and John exchanged a glance. They both understood that foxes were being appointed to guard the chickens.

"I will also appoint distinguished members of the medical community to assist them, people who are intimately acquainted with the needs of women and equal to the delicacy of their task. I know their work will be to the advantage, and not the detriment, of women and women's rights, and as a result none of us will ever need to worry over the safety of loved ones who may have to make this difficult choice in the privacy of their own hearts.

"Your governor cares about women and their sacred right, and it is his desire to protect it, strengthen it, and establish it without fear or misgivings, so help me God!"

Another standing ovation, the crowd cheering, waving their hands, some even jumping up and down with ecstasy. Some whoops also rose from the newsroom.

John watched it all, and then, as if Carl were standing beside him, he heard the question Carl had first asked that rock group at the concert he attended and then left: "Where are we going? Where are you taking us?" He looked around the newsroom, then back at the monitor as the governor began his closing remarks, and once again he could hear that low rumble, could sense the same impending darkness he'd encountered in the shopping mall.

Leslie couldn't hold it in any longer. "Mommy, the emperor is naked!"

That brought some mutterings from the others. She could feel the chill in the air.

"Hey," said Valerie Hunter, "whose side are you on anyway?"

Leslie glared at her and pointed at the monitor. "That is the biggest pile of tripe I have ever heard! The guy's crazy!"

Two reporters looked at her and moaned as if she'd just told a stupid joke.

Ali Downs, John's co-anchor, looked at John and Leslie as if they'd caught a fatal disease. "What's gotten into you two?"

Valerie reprimanded her. "Leslie, you're being unprofessional!"

"Yeah, pretty emotional," said Barry Gauge as he turned back to his computer console.

Leslie turned to John and saw tears in his eyes. "He's crazy!" she told him, hoping he'd agree.

"And doomed," said John.

The governor was just finishing his remarks. Now he was returning to his seat.

John's eyes were glued to the screen. He knew what he was seeing now was not really on the monitor, but he knew he'd better watch carefully.

He could have been staring at the glass door of a large washing machine. Inside, like so much laundry, the hundreds of people attending that rally were swirling, tumbling, screaming, and receding as if going down a huge, black drain.

And there was the governor, tumbling past the window, headed for certain destruction, but beckoning to them, shouting to them to follow. Sometimes people would come against the glass and bang on it, trying to get out, but then their faces would vanish in the crowd to be seen no more.

"Where are we going?" John asked quietly. "Where are you taking us?"

"Forward, John!" said Ali Downs, turning away. "He's taking us forward, and you'd better wake up and come along!"

But Leslie understood what John was going through. "What do you see, John?"

The monitor had gone blank. The feed of the governor's speech was completed, and now Marian Gibbons was most likely doing her opening and closing stand-ups for the camera, trying various summaries of the governor's comments in several different takes. Upon her return to the station she would select the one to include in her final package.

John stared at the blank screen. "He's caught in there. He's ensnared in his own illusion." Then he backed away, pointing at the blank screen. "You look at that thing long enough, it starts sucking you in, you know that?"

She put her hand on his shoulder. "What do we do now, John? What about our story?"

He turned away from the screen all the more determined. "You're going to get the Brewers on-camera tonight, right?"

"They're ready. After this whole business with Shannon they've got the fire back in their eyes."

"Okay. I'm still expecting that tape of Shannon's interview from Tom Carey. He said he Fed Ex'd it yesterday, so it should be in today. Carl and I will take a look at it tonight." Another thought. "Oh, have you called Mrs. Westfall?"

"Yeah, this morning. I told her all about Shannon, and I asked her if Mary might have a copy of the 'Post-Operative Instructions' as well. She's going to contact Mary and try to persuade her to meet with us. She can't guarantee Mary will go on-camera though."

"We've got to get this story together, Leslie, and we've got to do it fast. Hiram Slater's already come off the starting line!"

Clancy's, the boisterous night spot, lounge, and pool hall, was enjoying its afternoon, right-after-work crowd. Though the place was noisy, it wasn't as crowded and definitely not as dark as the other night.

So much the worse for Martin Devin, who wanted very much not to be seen or recognized, but who felt he would have to take the risk as he stepped up to the bar.

"Yeah, what'll you have?" asked the bartender.

Devin, dressed in his blue-collar worker disguise and wearing the same dark glasses, asked in a low voice, "Have you seen Willy around?"

The bartender immediately eyed Devin suspiciously. "Who's asking?"

"A friend."

The bartender only sneered at Devin, drying some shot glasses with a white towel. "I don't think we've been introduced, mister."

Devin was past being cool or professional. "Hey, cut the crap, will you? I've got to talk to him!"

"He's gone."

"Gone? Gone where?"

The bartender shrugged. "Like I said, buddy, we haven't been introduced, and I value Willy's patronage, you follow?"

"But . . . but what about . . ." Devin lowered his voice. ". . . what about Ted Canan? I heard he was in a jam."

Now the bartender's eyes filled with malice. "You know what? You ask too many questions."

Devin tried to grab him. "Now listen, you—" But the bartender backed away, and at the same moment four big, able-bodied friends of the establishment turned to give Devin their full, icy attention, burly arms ready.

Devin backed off. "Hey . . . I don't want any trouble—"

"Then get outa here!" said the bartender.

Martin Devin, chief of staff and special assistant to the governor, got out of there like a dog shooed out of the house.

Video: John Barrett and Ali Downs in a quick-cutting montage of different shots, a video scrapbook. Both of them looking out over the city as the sun sparkles on the skyscrapers; John interviewing a fire captain as fire fighters douse a burning warehouse in the background; Ali showing a class of first graders some flash cards about AIDS; John and Ali working together on a newscast script, laughing at a joke, talking to a camera.

Audio: A low, mellow voice borrowed from a wine commercial that uses only periods, no commas: "For the third year in a row NewsSix is number one. NewsSix. Ali Downs. John Barrett. Your premiere news gathering team. Again."

"Nice ad," said John.

"They're all nice," said Carl. Then he laughed. "If all those people out there only knew!"

They were in John's apartment, the television playing while John tinkered with a Beta cassette deck an engineer had let him borrow from the station.

John knew Carl was testing him and joined the game as he prepared the equipment. "Hey, come on. I've been coming across pretty good on the tube, you have to admit. I don't even wiggle my thumbs anymore, did you notice?"

"Oh, I've noticed, Dad, I really have. It's made a world of difference!"

"Well, there you go." John's eyes twinkled as he measured a quarter inch between his thumb and forefinger. "Now I'm that far from perfect!"

Carl laughed, lounging on the couch. "Aw, get outa town!"

"No, just ask my public out there!"

"Well, sure, they get to watch you, but I have to have you for my old man." He held up his root beer in a toast. "*Viva la difference!*"

John shook his head. "Well, we press on toward the mark. We press on."

"So press the Play button. Let's roll this thing!"

"Right on."

Blip. John hit the Play button, and the cassette from Midwestern University began to roll. Tom Carey, a reporter for a Midwest station and a longtime associate of John's, had sent it Federal Express, and it had arrived on John's desk that afternoon. John didn't open the package at the station, but hid it in his briefcase, did the Five O'clock, did the Seven O'clock, and then got safely home first.

Shannon DuPliese appeared on the screen in a typical talking-head interview format, looking off-camera, a bit of halogen lighting on her face, a small, black, clip-on microphone attached to her blouse.

"Okay," came Tom Carey's voice off-camera, "this is the interview with Shannon DuPliese, 2:41 P.M., October 9, 1991. This is for you, John, old buddy."

Shannon looked at the camera and smiled good-naturedly, though she seemed nervous.

Then Tom had another thought, "Oh, and John . . ." He stuck his head between Shannon and the camera, and though his face was a little blurred, his big glasses and wild head of black hair were unmistakable. "Hi, it's me. Listen, we can do this both ways if you want. Shannon says she'd just as soon have her face shown, she's got nothing to hide, but we'll go back and do some key soundbites with her in silhouette in case you decide to go that way." He vanished from the screen with a Muppet-like jerk and began the interview.

"So, Shannon," came his voice, "why don't you start by telling us who you are?"

She looked off-camera at Tom and introduced herself. "My name is Shannon DuPliese, I'm nineteen, and right now I'm going to Midwestern University . . ."

Wow, thought John, *this is gonna be heavy. The real scoop, straight from the person who was there. What a story—if it ever becomes one.*

The phone rang. "Oh-oh," John said, hitting the Pause button. "Come on, Leslie, don't tell me you couldn't get together with the Brewers . . ."

John strode over to the kitchen counter and grabbed the phone. "John Barrett."

"John, this is Charley Manning."

Well! Charley Manning, John's friend with close ties to the governor's office!

"Hey, Charley, what do you know?"

"John, I've come up with a pretty good hunch. See what you think of it. Right before the governor's campaign started, he had two special assistants. Martin Devin was one, and the other one was an older guy named Ed Lake. Lake was there first and served as chief of staff during the governor's first term until Devin came on the scene as special assistant and the chain of command got muddled. After that, those two men couldn't agree on who was special assistant and who was chief of staff, and what those titles meant anyway, and then this Devin character started muscling his way directly to the governor instead of going through Lake. Some of the governor's staff told me they had a real feud going for a while.

"Well anyway, things finally came to a head, and Lake was forced out. And check this timing—he left the job the Monday after the governor's kickoff rally."

John immediately saw the connection. "Monday after the rally . . . That's when Dad got that tape."

"From what some of the staffers told me, Lake and Devin were always trying power plays on each other. It sounds to me like Lake gave the tape to your dad just to knife Martin Devin."

"So where's Lake now?"

"Gone. He's left town—to begin his retirement, I understand. He might be with a sister in Alaska or at a winter home he owns in Florida, either one. Or he could be somewhere else we don't know about."

"Thanks, Charley."

"Well, it isn't much, I know."

"It'll help. We'll follow it up."

twenty-nine

video: A black-and-white still from an old TV show showing a handsome doctor and a mischievous, ponytailed nurse.

Voice over the picture: "I'm not a doctor, but I've played one on TV . . ."

Video: The black-and-white TV still lap dissolves to another still, this one showing an older doctor surrounded by bright-eyed, somewhat ragged children.

Voice over the picture: ". . . and the role of Dr. Harrigan in the classic film *Angels in White* was one of my most memorable."

Cut to the present, color video, as Theodore Packard, silver-haired, distinguished actor of stage and screen, dressed in a smartly tailored suit, replaces a thick book on one of many full bookshelves that cover the whole wall behind him. He looks with eyes of wisdom at the camera.

"Having identified as an actor with the high drama of medicine, I am daily reminded that . . ." As he speaks, he crosses to his desk and sits on the corner of it. Behind him a microscope can be seen on a table, and on another wall full-color anatomy charts. ". . . not too many years ago, women, free citizens of this country, were still forced by society's bonds and ignorance to resort to unspeakable, desperate measures in attempting to undo a crisis, unwanted pregnancy." He turns his head to one side just as another camera picks him up looking straight into the lens, a closer shot.

"Now, thanks to visionaries like Governor Hiram Slater, those days are finally coming to a permanent end, and I'm happy to relate that your governor is still at work to insure that all abortions in this state will be not only legal but available and, most of all, safe. Hiram Slater cares about women. He will fight for them and for their privacy . . ." His voice takes on an especially gentle, compassionate tone. ". . . and has done so, even to the point of personal sacrifice." He rises from the desk and walks toward a third camera, his marvelous study full of books spread out behind him. "I hope you'll share Hiram Slater's dream and place your vote where your heart is this November."

Fade to a heavenly, ethereal, slow-motion shot of a young mother dressed in flowing white, lifting a tiny pink baby and cuddling it close. A soft, soothing female voice: "That we may choose if . . . and when . . . without fear."

Freeze frame. Lacy, gentle script appears over the mother and child: "Hiram Slater cares about women."

Small title across bottom of screen: "Paid for by the Committee to Reelect Governor Slater, Wilma Benthoff, Chairperson."

Wednesday morning, 10 o'clock, Bayview Memorial Hospital. Dr. Harlan Matthews, pathologist, expected to hear the knock on his open office door. Looking up, he saw his visitors from yesterday. The detective was holding a folded sheet of paper.

"Good morning, Doctor," said Henderson. "I brought you something."

Matthews rose from his desk, received the sheet of paper from Henderson's hand, and took the time to read it thoroughly.

He laughed. "A search warrant! Ah, that's even better!"

Then he closed his office door, but not before John dragged a large carrying case in from the hall.

Matthews looked at Henderson who shrugged and replied, "Hey, I owe him a lot. We've got a buddy system going here."

Matthews placed the search warrant reverently upon his desk and answered, "Let's have a little meeting first. Have a seat, gentlemen."

Dr. Matthews already had two chairs ready and waiting for them. They sat, and then Matthews took his place behind his desk, slid open the center drawer, and immediately produced two manila folders. One he kept for himself, the other he handed to Henderson.

"To encapsulate the findings of the report . . . give you the bottom line, in other words . . ." He watched as they opened their folder and perused their copy. ". . . the patient died from hypovolemic shock, which is a severe drop in the volume of blood to the vital organs—the brain, kidneys, liver, even the heart itself—resulting in death. The hypovolemic shock was due to exsanguination, severe loss of blood, which was due to . . ." Matthews flipped through his copy of the report. "Here it is, written out briefly, the bottom of the last page, just that one paragraph, you see there?"

They found it.

"Of course, I'm sure you realize that the death certificate said nothing about this, but found the third cause to be hypoprothrombinemia, due to an accidental overdose of Warfarin."

"That's the story we all got," said John.

"Well, here are my findings. 'Obstetrical hemorrhage,' bleeding due to retained products of conception and endometrial lacerations. In other words, whoever did the abortion was in a big hurry, didn't finish the job, and botched it besides."

Matthews set down his copy and leaned back in his chair, ready to explain a little. "When a normal birth occurs, or even an induced abortion done properly, the uterus naturally clamps down and stops its own bleeding. But in this patient's case, most of the placenta was left inside, and the wall of the uterus was lacerated, and that natural stoppage didn't happen. The patient bled out in a matter of hours."

Henderson muttered a low curse, staring at the report.

John wondered, "But . . . surely someone at the abortion clinic would have noticed the bleeding."

Matthews was unhappy about this whole case, that was obvious. "*Should* have noticed the bleeding but didn't. There's always bleeding after an abortion. That's normal. What someone didn't see or didn't report or didn't think to do anything about was heavy, continuous bleeding. And I can imagine it not being seen, given the sinking standards of this business. You have to realize, abortion clinics aren't like your typical family practice. They're under tremendous pressure from two sources: money and fear.

"On the one hand, abortions are lucrative; you can bring in

a lot of money in a short time with minimum effort. The more abortions you do, the more money you make, so the natural inclination is to do them as quickly as possible and cut corners if you can. You get the procedure down to just a few minutes, you get an assembly line going, and you don't hire RNs to help in the back rooms because they get too picky about procedure, sterilizing the equipment, sanitation. All that stuff takes time, and you can have some thirty girls waiting in line. So instead you hire health-care workers—often marginally trained—to do all the assisting, attending, and observing, most of whom are there because they're cause-oriented. They're dedicated to the cause of abortion at any cost and aren't about to jeopardize that cause by making waves or finding fault.

"On the other hand, you've got the intense political pressure over this whole issue, which makes you circle the wagons all the tighter to protect yourself from intrusion, discovery, regulation, standardization. If you slip up, the last thing you want is for anyone to know about it, least of all your peers. There's also an unwritten code out there: you don't snitch—you don't make trouble. Couple that with the women who get the abortions. Most of them are there secretly. They come in secretly, they go out secretly, they even use false names a lot of the time, and if something goes wrong, they're not likely to say anything to anyone about it because they don't want to be discovered—the young girls especially, and sometimes . . ." Matthews picked up the autopsy report and slapped it down on his desk for effect ". . . sometimes this is the result. And the whole thing was secret, from start to finish. It took a search warrant for anyone to even know about it."

Henderson asked, "Did Governor Slater know about it?"

Matthews knew that was a ticklish question and balked just a little before answering. "He knew his daughter died from an abortion, yes. I'm the one who told him."

"Uh . . . when was that?" John asked.

"The day after . . . that would be Saturday. Hillary died Friday evening, we did the autopsy the next day, and then . . ." Matthews fidgeted a little, looking around the room in frustration. "And then the governor came for a conference with Dr. Leland Gray, his personal physician who handled the case, and I was in on that meeting to share my findings."

Henderson held up his hand. "Now hold on, Doctor, let me be sure I'm following this. You say you and Dr. Gray sat down with the governor and told him exactly what happened to Hillary?"

"Yes, sir, we did."

"And you told the governor she died from a botched abortion?"

"I used the same words with him as I just now used with you in describing the cause of her death."

"So . . . where did this wrong drug story come from?"

Matthews sighed and stared at the report. "Gentlemen, I did my job as best I could. I performed the autopsy and submitted my findings to the attending physician, Dr. Gray. After that, I was out of the loop. Dr. Gray filled out the death certificate, changing the last entry as to cause of death from obstetrical hemorrhage to Warfarin overdose. And as you know, that's the story that was released to the press, with the governor's full knowledge and approval. Obviously much of my report was . . . circumvented, ignored."

"They circled the wagons," said John.

Matthews nodded. "You're getting the picture."

"And . . . all the time you knew this and didn't say anything? You didn't take any action?"

"Try it yourself sometime. Just see what happens. Dr. Gray is not one to be tangled with if you value your job."

Henderson quipped at John, "Looks like you're about to stir the waters up a little."

John looked at the camera case on the floor. "Well . . . what do you think, Dr. Matthews? You're talking about it now."

Matthews shrugged. "The governor's already made it public, so it's going to come out anyway, and most importantly . . ." He pointed to the search warrant. ". . . you made me."

John reached tentatively for the camera case. "Well, since you've already made the information somewhat public . . . and the governor has too . . ."

"And somebody out there is going to wonder why he thought it was a Warfarin overdose all this time and only recently found out it was obstetrical hemorrhage . . ."

"Yeah, right."

Matthews hesitated, then went on, "And since the fingers are going to be pointing and will have to land on somebody . . ."

"You, do you think?"

Matthews thought a moment, then said, "Set it up."

John grinned and opened the case. "It could take a while. I don't have a cameraman, so I'll have to do it all myself."

Matthews got up. "Let me help. I can handle that tripod."

"Where's an outlet for these lights?" asked Henderson.

TV lights illumined the wall of the reception area in the Human Life Services Center. Seated in shadow, a silhouette in front of their hot, white glow, "Mary" was talking honestly and directly with Leslie Albright, reporter for NewsSix, as a television camera perched on a tripod beside Leslie captured it all.

"Mary's" real name was Cindy Danforth. She was eighteen, black, and insecure, but had some new friends. She'd recently spoken with Shannon DuPliese by telephone. They'd shared their fears, wounds, and sorrows, and the healing process had begun for them both. The greatest balm for Cindy was just finding someone else who could identify with her experience, especially her experience at the Women's Medical Center.

But Shannon was not the only supporting influence that had brought Cindy to this point. Rachel Franklin, the waitress who first told John and Carl about Annie, was right there in the room at this moment, behind Cindy 100 percent. Mrs. Westfall had introduced Rachel and Cindy to each other only yesterday, and now they were like sisters. Again, they had an experience, a particular place, in common.

Deanne Brewer was also there, a loving mother who actually understood and accepted everyone as they were and where they were. Also, the fact that she was Annie's mother evoked a deep and warm respect from the girls. They'd welcomed Deanne into their lives.

So now, even though the camera would see only her silhouette, the protective screen from the last visit was gone, and Cindy faced Leslie Albright directly to tell her story. The interview lasted almost an hour.

Leslie asked a closing question, still using Cindy's code name. "Mary, why have you come forward to tell us your story? What do you hope to accomplish?"

Cindy spoke in a timid voice, but had a firm grip on the answer. "Well, you know, I don't want to hurt anybody, and I'm not out for revenge, but . . . after what happened to Annie, I just have to do what I can to keep it from happening to somebody else. Hillary Slater died, and nobody said anything; so then Annie died, and now if I don't say anything about Annie, somebody else might die. Somebody has to say something, and somebody has to do something, that's all."

"Is there anything else you'd like to say, anything that I haven't asked you about?"

Cindy thought for just a moment. "Just . . . I just want to tell all the girls out there, be careful. Abortion isn't worth going through."

"Thank you. You're a courageous young woman."

Cindy smiled shyly. "Thanks . . ."

Leslie looked around at the others—at Mrs. Westfall, Rachel, and Deanne Brewer. They were all quite pleased and proud of Cindy. They began to applaud.

"Guess that'll do it," said Leslie, standing up to turn off the camera. "Great job. Really great job."

"When's this gonna be on TV?" Cindy asked.

Leslie answered honestly. "I really don't know, Cindy. It might get on TV, and maybe it never will. What matters is that it's on record. You've told your story, and someday it will hopefully make a difference."

Rachel was matter-of-fact. "It might not be news."

Leslie encouraged them, "But it's still the Truth, and someday . . . someday people are going to know."

"That's why we're doing any of this," said Mrs. Westfall. "That's why Shannon talked on-camera back east—and why Mr. and Mrs. Brewer did an interview. Someday the story's going to be heard, but first *we* have to tell it."

Leslie reached through her carry bag. "That reminds me . . . I got a copy of Shannon's interview today, and she said to be sure you got a copy." She pulled out a VHS cassette and gave it to Cindy.

Cindy received it but looked troubled. "Um . . . we don't have a VCR."

Mrs. Westfall offered, "You can use ours."

Rachel asked, "I'd like to see that myself."

"Well, you can all watch it," said Leslie. "Shannon wants you to see it. And by the way, she'll be coming back in a few days. She's withdrawing from Midwestern. She wants to go to school here like she originally planned. So you'll all have a chance to meet each other."

Mrs. Westfall asked, "Do you think there's any possibility of legal action? There just seems to be so much information coming out now."

Deanne shrugged. "We just aren't sure yet. We're thinking of getting everyone together to talk to Aaron Hart, the lawyer. If getting on TV doesn't work, maybe going to court will."

"Oh!" Leslie was reminded of something else. "Cindy, I was supposed to ask you about those post-operative instructions the clinic gives out . . ."

Cindy remembered it too. "Oh yeah. Just a minute."

She went back into Mrs. Westfall's office, rummaged through her schoolbooks, and came back with a wrinkled, slightly torn, original green copy of the "Post-Operative Instructions" from the Women's Medical Center. "I always kept it in case something went wrong later on. I didn't know what was gonna happen."

Leslie reached into her carrying bag and took out the copy she'd gotten from Shannon DuPliese. The two were identical, with the clinic's name, address, and telephone number clearly printed on the top.

"Bingo."

It could be a music video. Amid stage smoke, pulsating, hot-colored lights, and bare-chested, male dancers slick with sweat, Anita Diamond, rock music legend and poser for porn, high-kicks, jerks, and swivels her way through a bombastic song-and-dance routine, wailing something about not touching her body unless she asks you to, and if you make her happy, you'll see what she can do . . . to you . . . yeahhhh!

The speaking voice of Anita Diamond rises as the music soundtrack falls. "This is Anita Diamond, coming to you free and easy. I know what I want out of life, and so do you . . ."

Lap dissolve. Now Anita walks down the long aisle of an empty concert hall, dressed in her trademark black leather, a cocky tilt to her head as if one earring weighs several pounds. "I'm free to sing and make you happy because I was free to choose. Sure, I had an abortion. I wasn't afraid of it then, and I don't regret it now. Someday I'll have a family, but right now I'm making music and making love with you, and that's me, you know?"

She spins in a hot dance step, then prances up the aisle, the huge stage behind her, the camera dollying back in pace with her. "That's what I like about Hiram Slater, your governor. He wants people like me to be free to be all we can be, and he's one governor who won't slow you down! So keep Hiram working for you, and we'll all take life in our own hands, call our own shots, and do it!"

Lap dissolve back to the thunderous, hot, song-and-dance number on the smoke-filled, brightly lit stage. Anita Diamond spins, leaps, and ends the song with one long, soulful wail as . . .

Freeze frame.

Title above Anita's grimacing face: "Hiram Slater cares about women."

Small title across bottom of screen: "Paid for by the

Committee to Reelect Governor Slater, Wilma Benthoff, Chairperson."

Ben Oliver dropped the pile of notes, news copy, and several videotapes onto his desk with a definite *whap,* and then backed away just a little to stare at it, at a loss for words—for just a moment. Then the words came, few of them repeatable, ending with, "What the *&%@@# is going on here?"

It was Monday, October 14th, just a little after 1 in the afternoon. People were returning from lunch, but Ben had remained in his office going through all this stuff, and now he was agitated, to put it mildly.

John stood in the doorway of Ben's office, waiting to hear Ben's reaction to the materials he and Leslie had gathered, including the interviews with Shannon DuPliese, Cindy "Mary" Danforth, pathologist Dr. Harlan Matthews, pathologist Dr. Mark Denning, Marilyn Westfall, and last but not least Max and Deanne Brewer. From where John stood, Ben's reaction seemed pretty strong. He was pacing back and forth like a steel ball in a pinball machine, sort of bouncing from his desk to the opposite wall, then to the bookshelf by the door, and then back to the desk.

"Looks like you've seen it all," John prompted.

"Just finished watching the Brewer interview," Ben replied and then took the Lord's name in vain.

"He has been helpful in putting this together, yes," said John.

"Sorry. I know you're religious."

"Okay."

Ben pulled a pen from his shirt pocket and stuck it in his mouth, a mannerism that showed he was nervous and missed the pipe he had given up some time ago. He even fumbled absentmindedly in his pocket for matches until he caught himself. "When was that big speech by the governor? Last week . . . uh . . ."

"Last Wednesday, to be exact," John assisted.

"Yeah, last Wednesday . . . Just last Wednesday the governor makes his big confession, says he didn't know about the abortion and he's proud of it, didn't want to know, still doesn't want to know . . ." Ben swore again. "Do you know how much his committee's paid for ads on this station? It's frightening! He is working hard to smooth this thing over, and we are doing the best we can to oblige him, are you aware of that?"

"Yes, sir."

"We broadcast those . . . what the *&%#$ are they? . . . 'Hiram Slater cares about women' ads . . . every few minutes, every commercial break, it seems. He cares about women, he cares about women, he cares about women! I'm ready to kick the tube in, and it's my own station! That goofball's using us, that's what! We have become, in one high-priced week, the city's premiere purveyors of political horse crap!"

Ben flopped into his chair and glared at the videotapes in front of him. "And it's all your fault, isn't it? Huh?" He had just a hint of a smile at the corners of his mouth. "Slater's running, isn't he? He's trying to beat you to the punch and say it all first!"

"I believe that's exactly what he's doing."

Ben looked past John into the newsroom. "And I don't hear anybody complaining. Nobody's asking questions. Nobody's wondering, 'What's the matter with those doctors—are they stupid?' Worse yet, I don't hear anybody saying, 'Well, what's he telling us this for? Who asked him?'" Ben chuckled and shook his head. "No, he's running—with his pants down—and he's gonna trip if he isn't careful."

John asked, "I take it you're buying the story?"

Ben's smile weakened in slow, steady increments until it had vanished from his face. He looked out the glass again into the newsroom. "John, I'd love for life to be simple. I'd love to go out there and tell everybody, 'It happened, so let's report it,' but you can bet your little heinie the rules are gonna change while the words are still in my mouth."

John expected this. "Well . . . it's going to come out somehow. I just figured you'd like to see it."

Ben built up to another burst of anger and then exploded with a curse. "This is maddening! This is a hot, hot scoop—

it's almost scandalous, and . . . and I know nobody's gonna want it!"

"It's the Truth."

"But is it news?"

"Ben, you know it is!"

Ben was not frustrated and angry with John, but he couldn't help raising his voice anyway and making John the brunt of it. "Does our Accounting Department know it? Does Loren Harris know it? He and the governor are friends, remember? What about Tina Lewis and all those people on the news staff applauding the governor when he gave his speech, huh? Do they know it?"

John leaned over Ben's desk. "Ben, a young, poor, black girl is dead because—"

Ben bolted from his chair in a burst of anger. "I am not stupid, mister! I've got eyes, I've got ears, and I hope I still have brains!" He pointed over John's shoulder. "Close that door, I don't need all those big ears out there listening in on us . . ."

John closed the door.

"John, you and I are sitting in the middle of a big threshing machine that . . . that gobbles up Truth and then packages and sells it and is very concerned about the quality and salability of its product." He calmed a little, his anger displaced with a depressing regret. "We're talking . . . NewsSix . . . Channel 6 . . . the Business, the Entity, the outfit we all work for, with bosses and paychecks and policies, and . . ." Ben threw up his hands. "And why am I telling you all this? You've already been through it once with the Brewers—I'm sure you remember that."

"That's why I think you owe me, Ben, if I may be so bold. And not just me. You owe the Brewers. Those people trusted us once, and we let them down. We owe it to them. We owe the people out there the Truth."

Ben faced the wall just to get away from John's gaze so he could sort out the situation. It didn't take long. He turned, looked once more at the pile on his desk, and said quietly, "I'll see what I can do."

John nodded. He understood Ben's limitations. "That's good enough for me, Ben."

Ben held up his finger. "On one condition . . ."

"What?"

Ben sighed as he fell back on the old axiom of news reporting. "We still need to get the governor's side of all this."

John expected to hear that, but he didn't especially like it. "As if we haven't already heard his side."

"Mm . . . There are a few specifics he'll have to address, such as the suggestion that he's indirectly responsible for a young girl's death—maybe several deaths, if Denning's right—that he's put politics ahead of his own kid—that maybe he doesn't care about women as much as his slick ads say he does—that he's a clever but bald-faced liar. John, there are all kinds of nasty inferences to be drawn from this story. The governor should have his chance to reply to any and all of them . . . if we're going to play fair."

John acquiesced. "If we're going to play it fair, by the book, I suppose you're right."

"But *I'll* call him. Cuss me out if you want, but I'm gonna have some control of this thing. I want to hear from the man myself before I stick my neck out, and definitely before I let you bring the station heads down on us."

John took a moment to accept that and then closed the conversation. "Then I'll get to work on the Five O'clock. Thanks for your time and involvement, Ben."

"You're welcome. Just don't let it happen too often."

At that moment Leslie Albright and Detective Bob Henderson were sitting in the station's Client Viewing Room, a small conference room where clients who bought advertising could view their commercials, approve or disapprove, haggle, and swing deals. Leslie managed to find a time when the room would be free and chose to use it instead of the glass cubicles down in the Editing Department where the editing staff—and anyone else who wanted to—would see what they were watching.

They were seated on comfortable, padded chairs, their eyes

directed to the large television monitor built into the dark cabinetwork against the wall. As Leslie operated the tape player, fast forwarding, pausing, rewinding, and searching through the footage of the governor's kickoff rally, Henderson kept eyeing the crowd, looking for a familiar face.

"I want to tell you, this was an awful experience!" she said as they viewed Leslie herself standing before the camera trying to do her stand-up and looking extremely nervous, her hair tousled, holding her ground as a sea of enraged humanity boiled and bubbled behind her and one lone man stood above the crowd, shouting words no one could hear.

Then the Leslie on the screen started talking. "John, this is where it all begins for Governor Hiram Slater. Even though the polls show Bob Wilson gaining support, the governor has proven he has supporters too, as you can see by the vast crowd behind me."

Henderson laughed. "Supporters! They're about to riot!"

Leslie fast forwarded a little. "I think the fight started right after I did my outcue for John. Let's see . . . right about here . . ."

The Leslie on the tape almost shouted her cue line over the hubbub of the crowd. "So, John and Ali, this campaign could be an exciting roller coaster ride for both candidates, and the whole thing—" Someone screamed. "The whole thing begins in just a few minutes!"

"Okay," said Leslie. "There! You see them?"

Henderson jumped from his chair and got close to the screen as the two new bodies appeared in the crowd, swinging at people and starting the fighting. "Yeah. There's Canan right there." He pointed to Ted Canan, recognizable by his greasy black hair and tattooed arms. "And now . . . who's this other guy? Roll it forward."

Leslie inched the tape player as the crowd and the two thugs moved in jerky stop-motion. It looked like an instant replay of a free-for-all.

Then the two thugs moved behind the big, on-screen Leslie for a moment.

"Aw, come on . . ." said Henderson.

Leslie moved the tape forward a little more quickly. "I think they do come out on the other side."

They did eventually, helped on their way by a gigantic black man.

"Well!" said Henderson. "Max in action!"

More jerky stop-motion. Ted Canan grabbed a woman by her hair and flung her sideways. Right behind him his associate jerked backward, Max Brewer's hand grabbing his shoulder and turning him around for a haymaker to the jaw.

"Hold it!" said Henderson.

Leslie stopped the tape. Thug number two was in full view now, his face held high and visible thanks to Max's grip on him.

Henderson snapped his fingers. "Hmph! Okay . . . I know who that is. Howie Metzger. I had a hunch it would be him. Ted and Howie are like salt and pepper shakers. You hardly see one without the other. I'm going to put out a bulletin on him right away."

Leslie ran the tape a little further, and Howie's face was visible for only another second before Max decked him.

Henderson laughed. "I'll tell them to look for a hood with a broken jaw."

Leslie stopped the tape player. "And what do you think you'll find anyway?"

Henderson gave a slight shrug. "Oh, more info on Howie's buddy Ted, and who knows? Maybe I'll find John Barrett's killer."

thirty

Ben Oliver had the door closed to his office when he placed the call to the governor. Of course, his call did not go directly through. He had to talk to a switchboard operator and then the receptionist/secretary in the Executive Offices who gave him a bit of a runaround before he told her the nature of his business. She then connected him with Miss Rhodes, the governor's personal secretary.

"This is Ben Oliver, news director at Channel 6. We're preparing to do a story on the governor, and I need to present the story to him for his comment."

Miss Rhodes was polite, but Ben knew she would be unbending. "Any inquiries from the press are handled either by his campaign manager, Wilma Benthoff, or by his chief of staff, Martin Devin. I believe Mr. Devin is in. Shall I ring his office?"

"Sure, go ahead."

Another secretary answered. "Mr. Devin's office."

"Hi, this is Ben Oliver, news director at Channel 6. We're preparing to do a story on the governor, and I need to present the story to him for his comment."

"One moment."

Devin's voice came on the line. "Martin Devin."

Ben said the whole thing again. "Hi, this is Ben Oliver, news director at Channel 6. We're preparing to do a story on the governor, and I need to present the story to him for his comment."

"Channel 6?" Devin didn't sound too happy.

"That's right. NewsSix. We're putting a story together on the governor and—"

"What kind of story?"

Ben noted Devin's sharp tone. Yeah, Barrett and Albright had exposed some nerves over there, all right. "Well . . . you be the judge, but some of it gets kind of personal, and perhaps the governor would like to hear it for himself."

Devin paused, apparently thinking it over. "Just a minute."

He put Ben on hold for several minutes. Ben used the time to rehearse what he would ask. Whomever he talked to, he expected the experience to be somewhat unpleasant.

Devin came back on the line. "Mr. Oliver, the governor will talk to you. Please hold."

Well, what do you know! Ben got his pen ready, not to chew on, but to scribble notes.

"Yes, this is Governor Slater." He didn't sound too happy either.

"Governor Slater, this is Ben Oliver, news director at Channel 6. We're working on a possible news story regarding the true cause of your daughter Hillary's death and your knowledge of that true cause, and . . . Well, considering the delicate nature of the story, we'd like to discuss it with you and give you an opportunity to comment."

The governor's tone was sharp. "Mr. Oliver, I've said all I'm going to say about that. I know you covered my address to the Women's Citizen League, and in that address I shared as much personal information as I thought necessary. If it's all the same to you, I'd prefer you just be content with that."

"Mm-hm. Well, you need to know that we have since uncovered some additional information, and in the interest of fairness I'd really like to discuss it with you before we go any further. Would you be agreeable to that, sir?"

"What information?"

Ben consulted his notes. "Well, first of all, we've been able to establish that you knew about the abortion all along and that the Warfarin story was essentially a cover-up that you had full knowledge of and approved." Ben waited for a reaction. There was none. "Uh . . . would that be accurate?"

The governor seemed remarkably calm—cold but calm. "What else?"

"We've been able to establish that Shannon DuPliese, Hillary's best friend, was a witness and party to the abortion, and that you and your office put financial and psychological pressure on her to remain silent about it."

That got a direct curse from the governor, and then he demanded in an angry tone, "What else?"

"I understand this could be difficult for you, sir." Ben was trying to maintain as nice a manner as he could, but there seemed to be no way to avoid the governor's wrath. He rubbed his brow nervously and continued. What else could he do? "We've also been able to establish which abortion clinic was responsible, and we've discovered that only a month after Hillary's death at least one other girl died in the same clinic."

Now there was a deathly silence. *Hoo boy,* thought Ben, *that had to hurt.* "Uh . . . were you aware of that, sir?"

Then the governor cursed slowly, employing whole phrases. "What kind of a cheap, supermarket tabloid stunt is this? You think for one minute people are going to believe that crap?"

"Uh, well, as I said, this is a rather tedious story, and that's why I'm calling to discuss it with you, to get your comment—you know, get your side of it."

"What does Loren Harris have to say about this?"

"I haven't discussed it with him yet. This is pretty fresh material, it just came across my desk, and I'm trying to get some things nailed down first. I thought I'd get your reaction and perhaps set up an interview so you can respond. Would you be interested, Mr. Governor?"

"Is John Barrett behind this?"

Well . . . why hide it? "Yes, sir, this is a story he's been working on, he and one other reporter."

Now the governor cussed out John Barrett. "I should have known . . . that little pretty-boy TV star and his kooky, bigoted father. It must run in the family!"

Ben scribbled that quote down. "Uh . . . should I consider that a quote? A response?"

Slater exploded. "Lay off the objective reporter routine, Oliver! You don't think I know what you're doing? You don't think I know what Barrett's up to?"

"Perhaps you'd like to discuss this with John Barrett and review the material he's gathered?"

'I'm talking to Loren Harris about this! This has gone far enough!"

"Well, perhaps you'd like to hear some more details—"

Click.

Ben hung up, went over his notes, thought for a moment, and then went out into the newsroom.

He found John sitting at his desk, editing the script for the Five O'clock.

"John."

John looked up and immediately knew there was trouble.

"What's happening?"

Ben bent close and talked quietly. "I just talked to the governor."

John could see the answer in Ben's face but asked anyway. "How'd it go?"

"I'm on my way to the restroom to wash my ear out. But tell me, do you have copies of all that stuff you gave me?"

"Yeah, we copied everything."

"The tapes too?"

"Yeah."

Ben nodded with satisfaction. "Good. Keep 'em in a safe place, will you? There's no telling what'll happen to this story in the next hour or so." He straightened up and looked around the newsroom, his domain. "I'll be in my office. I'm expecting a call from Loren Harris any moment."

Ben went back toward his office, tapping Leslie on the shoulder as he passed her desk. "Better finish up your work quick. You're going to be busy on something else today."

Two floors up, Loren Harris, short in stature but imposing in position, slammed down his telephone, took just a moment to brew up some appropriate and professional demeanor, and then grabbed up the phone again, banging out Ben Oliver's number.

He'd just heard from Governor Hiram Slater.

Slam! Tina Lewis put down her phone, incensed. She needed a moment to regain control. She sat in her chair, trying to do some deep yogic breathing, think of beautiful ocean beaches, anything. But all she could visualize was tearing out John and Leslie's hair by the roots. Finally she decided she should be up-front, direct, honest, and confrontational, and she bounded from her office to have words with Ben Oliver. She'd just heard from chief of staff Martin Devin.

Hal Rosen the weatherman knew the forecast was going to be pleasant—outdoors. But in the newsroom it didn't take weather radar or a satellite to see some dark clouds gathering. They were moving right past the weather desk, in full view. First came Ben Oliver, walking tall and alone like Gary Cooper in *High Noon,* heading back to his office as if he would be facing death.

Oh-oh! Here came Tina Lewis, bursting from her office with her weight so far forward he was afraid she would crash right on top of him instead of making that sharp right turn toward Ben's office.

Whew! She made the turn. At least Ben would catch all that thunder and not Hal!

Tina got to Ben's door and waited, leaning against the doorpost on one foot, the other swinging in little circles and punching holes in the carpet. Ben was on the phone.

Then he came out of his office again, carrying some papers and videotapes. She started whispering something to him with such force that he grimaced and turned his head to protect his ear.

"C'mon," Hal heard him say. "We're meeting Loren Harris up in the viewing room."

And away they went, around the corner and out of sight, Tina still whispering, and Ben trying to hold her off until they got upstairs.

Loren Harris! Now this was going to be weather!

Loren Harris had done many a Channel 6 Editorial, and on-camera his manner had always been studious, reserved, and proper. Now, as he stood before the gathering in the Client Viewing Room, his suit coat buttoned, his tie subdued in color and straight in knot, and his posture exuding dignity, he was trying very hard to maintain that image, to look like the man in control, the wielder of power, now deigning to descend into the sweating, groaning galley of the ship.

John and Leslie had just come up from the newsroom and joined Tina and Ben at the small conference table. They could feel the tightly wound tension in the room the moment they stepped inside. Ben's eyes were locked into that narrow gaze that meant a toe-to-toe tangle, and Tina was into her treed cougar role.

As for Loren Harris, he would not have appreciated being described as shaken and discomfited. It would have been better to say he was approaching a power of conviction and a fervency of delivery they'd never seen before—and should pray they would never see again. He glared at them, one by one, looking for weakness, testing for guilt.

Then he spoke. "Ladies and gentlemen, we have a choice before us, an immediate question of agenda. Do we settle this quickly and professionally, with the best interests of Channel 6 at heart and our emotions and personal views safely in check, or do we take off the gloves and let our feelings totally disrupt the orderly process so that we get nowhere? Decide now which it will be."

He looked at them, and they looked at each other. There were no outbursts, but neither were there any concessions. Each person stood his ground.

Harris made the choice for everyone. "We will settle this matter quickly and professionally and then continue with our normal business. Understood?"

Leslie said, "Understood."

John nodded.

Tina glared holes in the table.

Ben just looked out the window.

Harris proceeded. "Now, John and Leslie, for your information, the rest of us have seen excerpts of the video and have perused your notes, and there is no question that this is going to be a delicate matter not only for the governor but for this station."

"And for women everywhere . . ." Tina muttered, still glaring holes in the table.

"Excuse me?"

'Nothing, sir."

Harris let it slide. "For your information, I've just had a conversation with Governor Hiram Slater, and he was . . ." Harris showed a slight grimace at the memory. ". . . he was furious, he was indignant, he used an abundant amount of profanity, and he made as strong an appeal as he could to me as a friend to take control of this situation." He paused to see if his words had produced any effect, any reactions.

"Are you going to kill the story, sir?" John asked.

Tina hissed, "There's no story to kill! This isn't a story! This is trash!"

Harris cut them both off. "I will finish what I have to say, thank you very much!"

They looked his way.

"The governor has his opinion about all this, naturally. He's convinced that we're about to do a very damaging story about him, something slanderous to himself and his family, and he put my feet to the fire, suggesting in the strongest terms that we were doing this only because this is an election year and he's right in the middle of a campaign. He accused us of pursuing a political hatchet job—a suggestion I find revolting and offensive, and I told him so. Nevertheless, he then went on to bemoan how he once trusted us, how he always thought our station had a favorable position toward him, or at least an unbiased position, and asked how I, being his friend, could tolerate such sleazy, muckraking, gossip-mongering reporters on my news staff, including . . ." He looked at Ben. ". . . my news director."

Ben raised an eyebrow but held his peace.

Tina crossed her arms and smirked at John and Leslie. Had she been a schoolgirl she would have been sticking out her tongue.

John and Leslie just waited to see what direction Harris was going.

Harris continued, "So, ladies and gentlemen, I now find

myself in a substantial bind, caught between the ideals of journalistic freedom and . . . the higher ideals of friendship, decorum, restraint . . ."

"Pragmatism," Ben suggested.

Harris didn't like the contribution but couldn't disagree. "Perhaps."

Ben was ready to push it, and he did. "The governor's your friend, you voted for him—" He shot a glance at Tina. "—like most of the news staff did—and the only bias that ever gets caught around here and condemned is bias against Slater and his kind of politics. Couple that with the bucks he's pouring into this station for all that slick advertising, and you've got yourself a teflon governor we don't want to stick anything to. Excuse my frankness, sir, but that's the way I see it."

Harris didn't receive that well. "I take it you think we should run the story, Ben."

"You're darn right I do. This is a big story. It has everything to do with Slater's credibility as a candidate, the sincerity of his agenda, whether he has any respect for the public's ability to think!"

Tina wasn't about to let this slide by. "Mr. Harris, I think the real bias here is obvious! This . . . this is utter madness! It isn't news!"

Ben shot back, "It's news! Get used to it."

"It's trash! It's . . . it's slanderous and damaging, and what purpose could any of it possibly serve anyone? So the governor's daughter died from one unfortunate accident! He's already revealed that! He's freely admitted it to the world!"

"Freely admitted!" Leslie jumped on that. "Mr. Harris, he only went public with that information because he knew we were about to, and he didn't tell the whole story, not at all!"

"He told enough! It's his life, his privacy. Why drag it all out again? What's the point?"

"I think the point is obvious! If present policies and laws allow this to happen—"

"There is nothing wrong with the present laws! The laws are in place to protect privacy!"

Fortunately, there was a table between them, though Leslie

seemed about to jump over it. "You mean to protect that clinic and Dr. Huronac and any other quacks out there!"

"All right, ladies . . ." Ben cautioned.

"Well, so much for objectivity!" Tina shouted without reserve. "This is a hatchet job!" She turned to Harris. "This is a hatchet job! It's sleaze, pure and simple!"

"Tina!" Ben cautioned more loudly.

She was virtually screaming for help. "Mr. Harris, you've got to do something!"

"QUIET!"

It was Loren Harris who shouted that. No one could believe it. They all fell silent immediately.

Harris began to tap the table with his finger rapid-fire as he spoke slowly and deliberately. "This . . . is what . . . we are up against, people! A story that inflames, divides, tears the scabs off old wounds, that disrupts my News Department—"

"But a story that is true," said John.

"You haven't sold me," Harris retorted.

"What's to sell?" Ben fumed. "You've seen the video. We've got a governor who cares more about politics than the safety of his own family, or anybody else for that matter. There's another girl dead because he tried to bury this, and another girl who's been virtually scared into silence!"

Harris had heard enough. "Ben . . ."

"And you're gonna stick up for this guy? You're gonna bury this just for him? If you bury this, you're just as bad as he is!"

"BEN!"

Ben stopped.

"That will be more than enough!"

John raised his hand. "Sir, there's something we haven't brought up yet, and that's the matter of the Brewers. They were simply trying to find out the true cause of their daughter Annie's death when this station did a story on them that virtually portrayed them as pro-life invaders of privacy trying to weasel their way around the laws. It was a terrible injustice toward them—"

"It was a factual and reliable piece!" Tina objected.

"Oh, right," Leslie said with a leer, "totally objective and unbiased!"

Tina spat right back, "I'm sorry if the story did not favor your position!"

"Oh, that reminds me!" Leslie dug through the notes on the table and produced Dr. Mark Denning's autopsy report. "Here, Executive News Producer!" She slapped it down on the table in front of Tina. "I still remember how you made such a big deal about the Brewers having no *bona fide* autopsy report to prove what killed their daughter. You may consider this *bona fide* autopsy report shoved up your nose!"

That brought a long enough silence from Tina for Harris to interject, "John, your point?"

"As I told Ben, we owe it to the Brewers to finish their story. The first time they came up dry—they didn't find out anything. Now all the facts are assembled. Their daughter died on May 26th after undergoing an abortion at the Women's Medical Center on May 24th. We have a witness, we have documents, we have a pathologist, and . . ." He nodded toward the autopsy report Tina refused to look at. ". . . a complete autopsy report. We can prove it all."

"And this is the second victim of the clinic, Hillary Slater being the first, is that right?"

John gave a deep, emphatic nod.

Tina cut in with, "I strongly object to the use of the word 'victim.'"

"They're both dead, aren't they?" Ben asked.

Harris seemed to be softening. He was obviously thinking about it.

Tina spoke in desperation. "Mr. Harris, please don't let them run this story. It just isn't worth the horrible damage it will do!"

"Tell that to Hillary and Annie!" Leslie was quick to say.

Tina lashed back with, "If you don't stop—!" Her hand actually raised as if it would strike. She stopped herself, settled back in her chair, and covered her eyes with her hand.

"I'll hear what you have to say, Tina," said Harris.

When Tina lowered her hand from her face, her eyes were

watery. She looked at Leslie and John, her eyes burning with anger . . . and pain. It was as if her hardened emotional armor had worn thin from the onslaught and something deeply human was finally showing through. "You . . . you people keep talking like somebody did some horrible thing. Mistakes can happen . . . But women have a right to do what they have to do, and it simply is no one else's business."

Ben asked, "Tina, do you need a break?"

"No, thank you."

"You sure?"

"I said no, thank you!"

John caught her eye. "Tina . . . for whatever this is worth, I want you to know I understand. I really do. I know where your pain is coming from."

She cursed him. "You religious bigots are all alike. What right do you have to judge me?"

Harris intervened. "No one is judging anyone—we are trying to judge the newsworthiness of this story—that is, if we can keep our own feelings separate from the deliberations!"

Tina didn't seem to hear him. She was still looking at John with both hurt and hatred in her eyes. "I didn't do anything wrong!"

John knew he'd heard her say it herself, the outward Tina, the one sitting across from him, and both of them knew what Tina was talking about.

A tear escaped her eye and ran down her face as she said it again, looking directly at John. "I didn't do anything wrong!"

Ben broke in, not realizing her real meaning. "Nobody's saying anybody did anything wrong! I authorized that story, and we ran it. It was all in a day's work, and hey, you win some, you lose some, but you keep trying."

Tina gave Ben a quick, obligatory glance as she recovered quickly and deliberately, getting her armor snugly back in place. Then, upon wiping her eyes and nose with a tissue, she summarized her position. "The story . . . the information . . . is inflammatory and prejudicial. It is long, long after the fact, lacks currency, and is therefore irrelevant. And as executive news producer I consider it far outside the bounds of propriety. For these reasons, and others, I do not consider it news, and I see no way that a story of this nature would be in the best interests of Channel 6."

Harris seemed affected by Tina's words, and perhaps by her emotion. "I would tend to agree with that."

Ben countered, "So we're just going to look the other way and let the governor lie, is that it?"

Tina found fresh rage. "We are not here to judge the governor's character! We are here to report what has happened—"

Ben jumped all over that. "What's happened, Tina? What's happened? So all right! Let's run the story."

Harris offered, "Ben, now wait a minute. Don't you think the governor's met us halfway on this? He's come out in public and revealed some very sensitive information on his daughter. He's essentially opened the bedroom doors of his home for public viewing—pardon me, but isn't that about it? In all honesty, people, isn't that enough? Hasn't the governor opened himself up enough and borne enough pain? It seems to me he's answered every reason you want to run this story. He's revealed how his daughter really died, and he's promised to look into the safety of abortion clinics."

Leslie reiterated, "He's running. I'm convinced of it. He's trying to cover his tracks by getting the jump on us."

"Which in itself is another reason not to run this story," said Tina. "This is still another way in which the story is after the fact. It'll be old before it gets on the air, and . . . really, after everything the governor has already done to make the whole matter public, we're going to sound like we're eating sour grapes, like we're flinging mud at his backside now that he's passed us in doing the right thing." She appealed to Harris. "Really, I think the dignity and credibility of Channel 6 is at stake here."

John insisted, "But we're overlooking the whole matter of the Truth, Mr. Harris. The Truth is at stake here! To be silent is tantamount to maintaining the lie. I agree with Ben—if we help Slater cover his tracks, we'll be just as bad as he is. He covered it all up for political reasons, and won't we be doing the same thing? It wouldn't be right."

Harris leaned toward him. "John, you can moralize about the proper path for this station to take, but you need to remember, it's part of my job to be sure this station survives. And in that light, the governor's public confession may have to be adequate for us."

"Yes," Tina almost whispered, just barely pounding the table with her fist. "Yes, yes!"

"He's confessed nothing!" John argued. "He's taken a shameful and regrettable situation and turned it into a symbol, a rallying point for his political agenda! There's no remorse, no regret, no confession of wrong. He's not being truthful, sir, and if we let this go we won't be truthful either! We have an obligation to the Truth, whether we like it or not, whether it hurts us or not, whether it benefits our own pocketbooks or not." John drew a breath and delivered his next words with extra punch. "We have to do the right thing."

Leslie agreed, repeating the phrase, "Yeah, the right thing."

Harris unbuttoned his suit coat. It was getting a bit stuffy in the room, and he was definitely getting hot under the collar. "Mr. Barrett, freedom of the press means we have just as much freedom to remain silent as we have freedom to speak."

John had the strange sensation he was mimicking his father as he replied, "Sir . . . I don't have that freedom." He could sense he was saying too much, pushing his bounds, but the words seemed to jump out of him. "It's . . . it's hard to explain, sir, but . . . I've been through a lot this past month or so, and . . . if you can accept this, sir, I feel an obligation toward God to be as honest as I can. I'm human, sir, and I'll admit the Truth can be painful at times, and even a little elusive, but . . . as best as I can, I must speak the Truth and address things as they are. I don't feel I have any right to take the Truth and cut it up, rearrange it, select what I want and delete what I want just so it'll align with my politics or my Accounting Department."

"Mr. Barrett . . ." Harris had heard enough, and now he was leaning with his hands on the table, casting the shadow of disfavor over John as only the Boss could do. "In the interests of bringing this meeting to a conclusion, I think it's time you remembered who you really are. You may think you're a celebrity—a household name—a famous face. But you'd better remember, you are only those things because this station, this business entity, made you those things, and not for your benefit, but for ours. *Our* benefit, *our* ratings, *our* advertising dollars, *our* profit margin. Mr. Barrett, regardless of your obligations to God, you need to keep in mind that first and foremost you are an employee of this organization. An *employee.* And I expect all employees to have not their own nor God's but this station's best interests in mind at all times."

He stepped back from John to address them all. "We all have our convictions and our ideals. We all have our feelings about what journalists have a right to print and say. We all like to spout about the First Amendment and freedom of the press. But let me introduce you to the real world. Freedom of the press belongs to him who owns the press, and Mr. Barrett—and the rest of you—that's *me.* I run this press. As long as you work for this press, freedom of the press stops . . ." He pointed at his nose. ". . . right here. It stops with your boss, your paycheck. In the final analysis the Truth doesn't call the shots here. The Truth doesn't matter. I call the shots, and what I want matters. Right now, that's the only truth you need to deal with."

Ben cut in before anyone else could. "Loren, Mr. Harris, sir, perhaps we've heard John and Leslie's positions clearly enough, and the afternoon's getting on. Why don't we let them go back to their work while the three of us finish this?"

Harris looked at John and Leslie with an expression that indicated he was quite tired of their company. "I think that would be an excellent idea."

The doors to the viewing room closed behind John and Leslie as they went out to return to their work—and to wait.

thirty-one

John and Leslie gave at least token service to their work, going through the mechanics of editing their materials for the evening newscasts. Leslie was doing a story on a battle between loggers and environmentalists and a night-long hearing that brought no firm results. It was almost a "same old, same old" story, and the copy was sounding "same old, same old." As for John . . . well, the Five O'clock looked good, the script felt tight and well-paced, there were no big problems with it. In other words, compared to the story now being chewed on, poked at, dissected, pushed, pulled, and ultimately decided upon upstairs, this stuff on their computer screens was not that engaging.

Oh-oh. There was Tina Lewis, walking briskly into the newsroom, not making eye contact with anyone, not even allowing her face to turn his direction. When she went by Leslie's desk she picked up some extra speed and kept her eyes straight forward.

Leslie shot a glance at him, her eyebrows soaring in surprise. Could this be a good sign?

Tina disappeared into her office and closed the door with a loud slam. One would think that was a good indicator that she had not prevailed in her desire to kill the story. And yet . . .

John felt trouble in his spirit. He knew—and he felt it was from the Lord—that the decision was in some ways favorable and in some ways not.

He turned back to his computer, took a deep breath, and prayed for just a moment, silently, not even closing his eyes. It didn't really matter, he told the Lord. Whatever God wanted was fine with him. Whether the story actually ran on the air was secondary. What was truly important was that John remain sensitive to what God was doing and saying, and that the Truth prevail.

"Lord God," he whispered, "I just want to be obedient for once."

There was Ben, just now coming into the newsroom. He stopped briefly at the assignment desk to grab a fresh copy of the Outlook Sheet from George Hayami, the assignment editor. They talked a moment, and then Ben went over to Leslie's desk.

"Leslie . . ."

She looked up. Oh-oh. Now would come the verdict. "Okay. Break it to me gently."

He leaned close, his back toward the room, and particularly toward John's desk. "It isn't all good news, okay? But I want you to listen carefully and do what I tell you."

"Yes, sir."

"First of all, the story's gonna run, probably tomorrow."

She didn't allow herself any joy at that news, knowing the bad news was still coming. "And?"

"And . . ." He looked toward Tina's office and then back at Leslie. "And I want you to take a few days off, starting right now."

That hit Leslie in the stomach. "What . . . I don't understand."

"I'm giving it to you straight. Tina did not want this story to go on the air, but I prevailed, after a fashion, and right now she is one hot-under-the-collar lady. It's gonna be an interesting next few days around here. I think all Hell is gonna break loose, and . . . with all due respect to you, I don't want you in the middle of it, or possibly being a part of it. I think you need to lay low for a while."

Of course, Leslie had to argue with him. "But, Ben, that's . . . that's ridiculous . . ."

He smiled, knowing better. "Oh, is it now? No matter what Tina says or does, you're just going to sit quietly and take it, aren't you? You're going to be a good little girl and let Tina call all the shots and not say a word?"

Leslie could see his point. She tried to justify herself. "Ben, I never wanted any trouble . . ."

"Well, neither do I. The problem is, you're like uranium, and Tina's like plutonium, and when the two of you get together you achieve critical mass. I don't need that in my newsroom, and considering what's coming up, it's unavoidable unless I get one of you out of the picture. So let the story air first, and I'll give you a call when the coast is clear and it's safe to come back."

"But, Ben . . . who's going to do the story?"

"I'm gonna let John do it."

Leslie could sense something coming. "By himself?"

"Yeah. All by himself."

"And then what?"

He hesitated, then answered, "It's too early to say. But go on—pack up your stuff and clear out right now. I don't want to see you around here until this is over, and then I'll call you." He reassured her, "You're not fired, you understand. I just want you far, far away for a while."

She got brave enough to protest, "Ben, that story was both of ours. I worked on it too."

"I haven't forgotten that."

"So . . . whatever happens to John . . ."

He stopped her. "Hey, nothing's happened yet! Just wait and see—elsewhere. That's an order."

John could see Leslie turn off her computer and start clearing her desk. Now Ben was coming his way. John reached and grabbed an available chair, pulling it close to his desk just in time for Ben to sit down.

Ben stole a quick glance back toward Leslie, who looked right back at him with resistance in her eyes even as she continued packing. Then Ben told John, "Leslie's getting clear of the situation for a few days."

John watched Leslie throw some items into her carry bag and then grab her coat. "I think that's a good idea, Ben. I appreciate it."

"So . . . you ready to hear the final word?"

"It looks like the story's going to run."

Ben did not appear to be sharing good news. "Tomorrow, if you can get it together."

"I suppose I can. It'll be tough without Leslie, but I'll give it a shot."

"You'll have to get over to see the governor tomorrow morning. Loren Harris is already setting that up." Ben paused, preparing to be up-front and honest with his anchorman. "He's hoping the governor will be able to talk you out of it—or scare you out of it, I don't know which. But you'll take a cameraman with you and get the governor's comments, if he has any. Then . . . you put the story together and we'll run it on the Five O'clock and the Seven O'clock. You'll have two minutes maximum and will do your own lead-in and voice-over. It'll be all yours, from start to finish. Nobody else's name on it." Ben gave an apologetic shrug. "Part of the deal with Loren."

John understood. He knew. "That's why you sent Leslie home, isn't it? The story's going to be buried."

Ben looked away as he said, "And probably you with it." He looked back at John. "I don't know that for sure, but . . . let's face it, you're not making friends around here. You're violating the unwritten rules—that is, if you still want to go through with it."

"I'm not so sure I *want* to. I just know I *have* to."

"Why, John? You still think you owe something to the Brewers?"

"That's part of it. But at the risk of generalizing, I feel I owe something to everyone. I owe them the Truth."

Ben leaned back in his chair, somewhat forlorn. "Well . . . we'll see how much of it they get. I swung a deal for you, but I'm not that impressed with it."

"Yeah, I know." John began to recount the meeting as if he'd been there. "Tina was against running the story, you were for it, Harris was caught in the middle and concerned for the station and his standing with his peers. You came up with the idea. Hey, as big as the story is, we can't honestly ignore it. But why not let Barrett carry the whole thing on his own shoulders, give him a fair shot at it, then tuck it away in the middle if you want, make a lot of noise on either side. If the story dies, people will forget and we're off the hook; if it turns out to be hot, we can always say we broke the story here first. In any case Barrett and Albright will get it out of their system. All very pragmatic."

Ben laughed. "You *have* been paying attention all these years."

John knew he was right on the money, but he wasn't happy about it. "Kind of like a picture I saw in the mall a while ago. It would be too hard to explain, but . . . it made me consider the fact that the media being what it is, you don't have to withhold information. You don't even have to lie that much. Just pour on enough distraction and people won't know which way to look."

Ben thought that over grimly. "And in that area, the gov's got a big head start on you."

"And I suppose he always will."

"But you still want to go ahead with this?"

John smiled at the peace he felt about it. "I can do it. Like you all agreed in the meeting, I'll have it out of my system. I'll have done what I need to do."

Ben probed, "And . . . what do you think, John? Is this your concept of a sharp, in-control kind of guy, the man the public can trust to bring them the news with sobriety, integrity, and grit . . . all that stuff we talked about?"

"A man like that would tell the Truth, wouldn't he?"

Ben nodded. "That's what I told Loren Harris."

This time they both laughed, if only to relieve the pressure.

Then Ben got serious again. "But, John, I get the feeling you know a lot more than you're telling. This is no one-shot story, is it? It's leading somewhere."

John sorted what he could say from what he could not. 'Well, Ben, to be honest . . ."

"Of course."

John nodded. "It's leading somewhere. It's going to get bigger, a lot bigger, and it'll be interesting to see how big it has to get before it can't be swept under the carpet anymore." He chuckled. "Well, I suppose you could sweep an elephant under the carpet and get away with it—as long as you keep everyone looking the other way."

"An elephant? Now you've got me curious."

"I'm sorry to do that, Ben. But right now I've got a promise going with certain parties that I won't talk about it until they've completed their work on this."

Howie Metzger, small-time hood and thug-for-hire, sat calmly at the little table in the interrogation room, dragging on a loaned cigarette and trying to maintain a cool, unshakable image while Detective Henderson's partner, Clay Oakley, read Howie his rights.

"You have the right to remain silent. Anything you say or sign can be used as evidence against you in a court of law. . . ." Henderson had chosen Room 1027 on the top floor of the County Courthouse, a six by eight foot cubicle just down the hall from the jail, and known for its gloominess, with no windows except for the two-way glass in the door, its walls painted a dingy, graying yellow. He wanted the mood to be just right when they talked to Howie.

Oakley finished. "You have the right to exercise any of these rights at any time before or during questioning or the making of any statement. Now . . . do you understand these rights?"

"Sure," said Howie.

"Keeping these rights in mind, do you wish to talk to us now?"

"Maybe."

Henderson knew Howie was probing. "Howie, I saw you and your old buddy Ted on television, busting heads at the governor's rally last month. You remember that?"

"Yeah, I remember that."

"We're about to extradite Ted back here on a murder rap, and he's put the finger on you. He says you were there, that you killed the old man."

Howie was skeptical. "Oh, did he now?"

Henderson came close to the table. "So . . . hey, we've played this game so many times, you know the rules. You help the prosecutor, and the prosecutor helps you. Ted's given us his side of it. We'd like to hear yours. You want to talk to us?"

Howie laughed and took another drag on the cigarette. "Let's hear his side of it."

Henderson flipped open his notebook and consulted some notes he'd written. "You went together to Barrett Plumbing and Fixtures looking for a tape cassette. You roughed up the proprietor, John Barrett, Sr., trying to get him to tell you where the tape was. Ted says he wouldn't talk, so you, Howie, got really rough with him and finally beat him so hard you killed him."

Howie shook his head. "No way! No way!"

"Are you talking to us, Howie?"

"Yeah, I'm talking to you! And you'd better be listening!"

"So that isn't what happened?"

Howie was insulted. "No, no, no . . . now that's *Ted* talking, man! What do you *expect* he's gonna say?"

"So where'd he go wrong?"

"I didn't kill the old man!"

"So Ted did?"

"Well . . ."

"Well what?"

"Nobody killed anybody. We roughed him up, that's all. We wanted the tape, and he wouldn't tell us where it was, so we just tried to persuade him a little."

"I'd say you persuaded him a lot, so much that he died."

"Hey, he had a heart attack or something. We didn't hit him that hard. We hit another old guy, and *he* didn't die like that."

"What other guy?"

"Oh . . . Ted didn't tell you about that?"

"What other guy?"

Howie smiled. "See? Now you're talking to the right man! I'm not holding out on you—I'm cooperating. You remember that later. The other guy . . . Lake . . . We went after him first 'cause we thought he had the tape. We cornered him right outside his house and . . . man, I don't remember if we hit him first or if he talked first . . . The guy had no guts at all, you know? Soon as we grabbed him, he started squealing, 'I don't have it, I don't have it!' I think Ted slapped him once or twice. Ted's cruel, you know? I don't go for that cruel stuff."

"No, of course not."

"But he told us right away, 'I gave it to John Barrett, the old guy that runs that plumbing warehouse,' and he told us where the warehouse was and everything. He spilled his guts, man, so we let him go. He was a pushover."

Oakley thought that was intriguing. "So, it sounds like you hardly hit him at all."

"No. Guess not."

Henderson renewed his charge. "But you had to hit Barrett a little harder, didn't you?"

"Well hey, man . . ."

"So hard you *killed* him."

Howie shook his head, indignant. "Hey, nobody killed anybody!"

"Lake. You said the other man's name was Lake? Got a first name?"

"Uh . . . Edward, I think. Willy said he used to be some head honcho with the government. I don't know what he did."

"All right. So who dumped the pipe rack over on old man Barrett? Was that your idea?"

"No, no, it was Ted's idea! Hey, I'm not that smart! I don't kill people for a living! Ted does that stuff. He's good at it. He said we had to make it look like an accident."

"So you drove the forklift—"

"*Ted* drove the forklift! Man, will you quit looking at *me*? Ted's the killer. I'm a witness. I'm telling you what really happened."

"And you never found the tape?"

"Didn't stick around to look for it. Once the old man was dead we just dumped the pipe rack and got out of there."

"Who's Willy?"

"Huh?"

"You said *Willy* told you about Lake. Who's Willy?"

Oakley asked, "Willy Ferrini?"

Howie brightened. "Yeah, The Fixer. Ferrini the Fixer."

Henderson chuckled. "The would-be godfather."
Howie thought that was funny. "Yeah. Even tries to mumble like Marlon Brando!"
"So where does *he* come in?"
"We work for him sometimes. He's the guy who hired us to bust heads at the governor's rally, and he's the guy who sent us after Lake and that tape."
"So what was on the tape—did he ever tell you?"
Howie shrugged a little. "Top-secret stuff, like wiretaps, secret conversations, surveillance—that kind of stuff. Sounded big-time."
"So who hired Willy?"
Howie shrugged. "Ask Willy."

Tuesday morning, at about a quarter to 9, John and Mel the cameraman parked their white NewsSix fastback in one of the press stalls behind the capitol building and started across the vast lawns of the Capitol Plaza toward the Executive Offices, a four-story, marble-and-concrete complex that faced the capitol and emulated the classic architecture of the landmarks around it. John thought the building looked rather dismal and box-like, almost as if nice offices and large windows had been installed in a parking garage, with huge pillars added in front for no apparent reason. Oh well, today he wasn't feeling too good about this place anyway.

Across the plaza they went, like two tiny sojourners crossing a sea of green, Mel lugging the camera on his shoulder and the equipment bag at his side, John carrying the tripod and some extra lights, as well as his notebook. They drew a few looks but only briefly. News crews were a common sight around here.

John looked at his watch. The governor was expecting them at 9 sharp. They should be on time.

But the walk seemed very long, not only because they were lugging the equipment, but because neither one of them was looking forward to this interview. All the way over here in the car, Mel kept saying things like, "Well, you've got guts, John, I'll hand you that," and "Yes sir, this one ain't gonna be easy," and "Hope they remember I'm just the cameraman," and "What are you gonna ask him anyway?"

John had an odd feeling walking toward this interview, a strange mixture of anxiety over the interview itself and how it might turn out, and exhilaration from the whole sense of adventure surrounding the story. He looked around, noticing how tiny and insignificant he and Mel looked out here in the middle of the plaza. Like ants. Very lonely ants. Yes, the loneliness was part of the adventure.

It took some struggle to get the equipment through the revolving door and into the lobby. Then they had to pass through security, letting two guards in blue uniforms check their IDs, go through their equipment, X-ray their bags and cases, and watch them walk through the metal detector. Mel kept making the thing beep until he took off his earring—he'd chosen a rather large one today.

Finally, they were *inside,* feeling the awe and intimidation of having breached a fortress. This was where the Big People worked, the Giants, the Rulers and Kings. Here, in these halls of marble, under these high ceilings and brass chandeliers, the Holders of Power made their decisions and turned the tide of history. In the movies lofty background music always played whenever a character found himself in such a setting. John couldn't help thinking of *Mr. Smith Goes to Washington* with James Stewart.

Then the thought "Elijah the prophet confronts King Ahab" struck him, and he felt the size of an ant again.

When the elevator door opened at the fourth floor, it unveiled the hallowed halls of the King: an expansive lobby and reception area, mostly marble, with murals of state history on the walls and a reception desk standing like a bastion in the middle of the red carpet, the skinny lady with glasses on the chain around her neck facing the elevator like a guard on the ramparts, ready to ward off invaders. Over in one corner to the right a uniformed guard sat at a desk, doing nothing in particular.

John introduced himself and Mel. The lady smiled and made a call.

Then, from the far end of a cavernous hall, a woman appeared, walking briskly toward them, her high heels tapping out a tight little rhythm that echoed off the ceiling and floors and sounded like distant gunfire. At first she was so far away they couldn't even make out her face. But as she approached and grew steadily in size, they could discern a sharp-looking, thin woman with stare-you-down eyes and billowing, curly blonde hair.

When she finally reached the reception area, she extended her hand in greeting. "Mr. Barrett, I'm Wilma Benthoff, the governor's campaign manager and head of public relations. Will you come with me please?"

John picked up the tripod and lights, Mel grabbed his camera and carry bag, and they followed her down the vast hallway, walking under huge marble arches and bronze chandeliers with myriads of tiny bulbs glowing gold. Mel had worn a conventional shirt instead of his usual T-shirt, but now he was wishing he owned a tie.

"There is to be no eating, drinking, or smoking anywhere on this floor, and you are not to touch any of the brass railings or fixtures," Ms. Benthoff instructed over her shoulder. "Any umbrellas, canes, tools, or implements must be checked outside the chamber door except those items necessary for the interview."

"Yes, ma'am."

"Yes, ma'am."

"The governor has granted you one half-hour for the interview and reserves the right to terminate the interview at any time. You must address him as Mr. Governor, you must ask your questions only when he has indicated he is ready to receive them, and you must not interrupt him when he speaks. You must frame your questions clearly and succinctly."

"Right."

"Right on."

"Please observe protocol at all times, and follow the directions given you as to where and how you may set up your camera."

"Yes, ma'am."

"Yes, ma'am."

At the end of the hall were two huge, ornately carved oak doors with bronze hinges and handles. Ms. Benthoff put her full weight into swinging one of them open and held it steady while they passed quickly through.

Now they were in the mini-kingdom of Miss Rhodes, the governor's secretary, the comfortable, well-furnished chamber that lay between the outside world and *the* chamber, the governor's office. Had any other mortal ever gotten this close?

Miss Rhodes, a matronly, round-faced woman with hair dyed reddish-brown, rose from her desk to greet them. "I'll let the governor know you're here."

She picked up her telephone, spoke very quietly, and set it down.

The big oak door to the governor's office swung open with a burst of wind, and a tall, strong, handsome man emerged, jabbing out his hand in greeting. "Good morning, gentlemen," he said. "I'm Martin Devin, chief of staff and special assistant to the governor." John and Mel each had a turn having their whole frame shaken by his handshake.

"Won't you come in?" They followed him around the last bastion—Miss Rhodes' desk—and through the big oak door, into the Office of the Governor.

This was a wondrous room, with ornate paneling on the walls, brass hardware on every door, window, cupboard, and cabinet, a central chandelier for general lighting, ornate brass wall sconces for mood lighting, floor and table lamps positioned just so. Two walls were lined with bookshelves full of books and fine collectibles of brass, iron, and pottery. Art hung on the walls, a huge globe stood in the corner, and through the ceiling-high window behind the governor's chair the capitol dome rose against a blue sky, a soul-stirring symbol of honor, duty, and country. John could hear lofty, patriotic music rising in his mind, and now he felt very much like Jimmy Stewart's Mr. Smith.

Mr. Devin stood to one side of the governor's desk, ready

to do his bidding. Ms. Benthoff took a seat on the other side, a writing pad ready for taking notes.

But where was the governor?

"Gentlemen," Mr. Devin said, "Governor Hiram Slater."

"Uh, hello, sir . . ." John heard Mel say. "I'm honored."

Mel was looking toward the governor's desk, but John didn't see anyone there.

No, wait, there was someone. John could just see the top of someone's head poking up from behind the desk.

Governor Slater? Governor Hiram Slater, the Architect of the New Dawn? The towering icon of progress? The Fate of the State? The King atop the highest pinnacle of power?

John saw a little man, no taller than four feet, peering out over the top of the desk, his eyes wide with fear, his little fingers gripping the edge of the desk in a death grip.

"And you must be the anchorman John Barrett," came the governor's voice, somewhat higher-pitched but normal for Governor Slater.

John recovered from his vision in time to see the full-size governor standing behind his desk in a perfectly tailored blue, pin-striped suit, with white shirt and red tie, one hand resting on the glassy smooth desktop, the other extended toward him.

John was amazed and couldn't help appearing so as he took the governor's hand and shook it. "Hello, Mr. Governor," he said, even smiling a little, not in a socially pleasant way but in relief and even amusement.

The governor looked at Mel and also threw some prompting glances at Ms. Benthoff as he said, "Why don't you go ahead and set your things down for a moment? The interview is somewhat contingent at this time. I think we'll just talk first." Ms. Benthoff guided Mel to a nice area some distance from the governor's desk where he could set everything down and then placed a chair there for him to sit in. "Thank you for your patience," she said in a tone that said he'd better be patient.

The governor looked at John again. "Mr. Barrett, with little time afforded us, I think we should come to an understanding in short order. Won't you sit down?"

John watched as the little four-foot Hiram backed away from him, bumped into his chair, and then ducked behind the desk.

Bump! A chair came up behind John's knees, and he just about fell backward into it. Mr. Devin was quick to facilitate the governor's wishes. John sat.

The governor—the "real" governor—sat, eyeing John for a moment. Then, leaning forward, his hands folded on the desk, he said, "First of all, I'd like to know just where you're coming from, Mr. Barrett, and why you're doing this story. Now I might be wrong in assuming this, but I'm sure you and your father have had many conversations about me, hmm?"

John made a conscious effort to look normal and not gawk. But he was distracted by the realization that his eyes were open. He could see. He could *really* see. "Um . . . only one conversation actually. It was after your kickoff rally. I was trying to tell him to leave you alone and stop preaching at you."

The governor's eyebrows went up, and he exchanged a glance with Mr. Devin. "That's very interesting, Mr. Barrett, considering the approach you're taking now."

John continued to build his answer. "I was embarrassed by his behavior. Most everyone knew who he was, and here *I* was, an up-and-coming television news anchor very concerned for my image and reputation, with a religious kook for a father."

The governor said nothing but eyed John warily.

John continued, figuring the governor was giving him the floor. "But his religious zeal aside, as I considered the gist of what he had to say . . . I came to realize he had a valid point. Mr. Governor . . ." John tried to keep a gentle, even tone. He was venturing onto thin ice, and he knew it. "I was running scared. Running from the Truth, running from the man I truly was, hiding behind an image that portrayed me as more than I truly was. I couldn't see that Dad was just trying to warn you—all of us actually—that we're not being honest with ourselves or with others or with God. Mr. Governor, contrary to what your PR people have told you, image is *not* everything. It's an illusion, a trick, a lie that we even start to believe ourselves. And like Dad said, someday the image will collapse—your image, my image—and . . . well, I had to ask myself, when the image collapses, will there be a real man left standing in its place?"

The governor grew restless. "So please tell me what all this has to do with the story you're doing and with the interview."

"The story, and this interview, have to do with Truth. Dad told me once that the Truth can be your best friend or your worst enemy. If you're willing to hear the Truth, it might hurt a little, but you'll come out ahead, you'll benefit. If you're encasing yourself in an illusion and running from the Truth . . . well, sooner or later it'll catch up to you, and then the blow will be a lot more severe. You may not be able to pick up the pieces. That's what Dad was trying to get across, and I've since concluded that he was right."

Governor Hiram Slater sneered just a little. "And now . . . I suppose you have picked up the mantle of your father—hence this vindictive, prying, moralizing story of yours?"

"I've come to know the same God my father knew, and I've tried to know and live according to God's Truth. That's what brought about this story."

"But you do realize what you're up against?"

"A bubble? An illusion?"

Slater slammed the top of his desk in anger.

Devin stepped forward. "Okay, that's enough. The interview's over—"

Slater put out his hand. "No, Martin, not yet. I'm not through with this . . . this self-righteous, hypocritical bigot . . . this . . . this . . ." Not able to think of a greater insult, he skipped ahead. "Barrett, we're going to talk in practical terms here. We're going to be reasonable. We're going to weigh the alternatives and come to an understanding, all right?

"Now, what do I have? Let's just lay it out in the open. I have an ad campaign saturating every household in the state even as we speak, and it's weeks ahead of you. I've already come out publicly with the true cause of Hillary's death, and I've pledged to look into the safety standards of abortion clinics. I have the public mind on my side, *way* on my side. I'm on your 1-yard line, all right?

"Now, what do you have? Some little mud-slinging story about . . . what? That I knew how my daughter died in the first place but covered it up and so another girl died in the same clinic. Well, big deal. You really think anybody out there really cares? And how much time do you have to do the story? Two minutes! Just two minutes! Yes, I've talked to Loren Harris. He's a friend of mine. We look out for each other, which means *you'd* better look out!

"So just imagine how much effect your little two-minute package is going to have against all the other media saturation we've already established, not even including the past advertisements! Hey, the papers are telling *my* side of the story, and so are all the other stations, and tomorrow, Barrett, so will *your* station! It'll be like you were never there, like you never said a word!

"So why do the story? That's what I want you to tell me. Why even attempt something so futile and potentially self-destructive?"

John could see Slater thought he was prevailing in this bout of ideas and wills, and yet . . . there was that little four-footer again, saying the same words but in stark terror, as if begging for his life.

John slowly rose from his chair. The power—the conviction—of his words was too much for him to remain sitting. "Mr. Governor, the image you have built has drawn the eyes of the people, and many of them believe the image and praise it. But the image will topple, and then, Mr. Governor, will a man remain in its place?"

Slater shouted at him, his face reddening in anger.

"Just answer my question, Barrett! Give me one good reason why you're trying to destroy yourself!"

John could see it even as he said it. "All your life you've devoted yourself to the building of an image, and now . . . full of fear, you're tumbling around inside it, getting smaller and smaller . . . You're lost in there, but you're afraid to come out, afraid of the Truth. That's why you're afraid of this story."

Devin rushed forward again. "Mr. Governor, you don't have to put up with this nut!"

John could see the little four-foot man scream back at his special assistant, "Leave me alone! I can handle this!" The little man looked at John, his eyes burning with anger—and fear. "I can handle *you*—anytime, anywhere! You're nothing, you hear me? *Nothing!*" He was like a child screaming in defiance at his parents.

John spoke it even as he came to know it. "You will win the election, Mr. Governor."

That at least stopped the escalation of the governor's anger. He backed off a little, then even forced a smile.

"So you admit that."

"But win . . . and serve . . . as *what?* What will you be? What will the people elect?" John sat back down, pondering out loud. "The Adam Bryant School has survived their involvement in the death of Hillary Slater, but . . . as what? Are they better people now? Have they become more human, more virtuous for having deceived others? The doctor who falsified the death certificate has survived, and his practice remains, but . . . as what? What has he gained that is worth surviving *for?* Not more integrity. Not more dignity. Not more honor.

"And what about the women? Now they have the right to choose, and yet . . . how will they find the sacredness of their own lives if life itself is no longer sacred?" John looked directly at the governor. "But even as all those have survived as less than what they were before . . . *we*—you, the Brewers, all of us—have survived, but none of us are richer. Just consider what we've lost—our character, our integrity, our honor, our sacredness, and now . . . our *children.*"

The governor took a deep breath, straightened his spine, and responded, "But I *will* win the election, Mr. Barrett, no matter what you try to do! You can put *that* on your little videotape and report it!"

"You will win the election," John repeated, "but by a smaller margin than you're projecting now." Then he added firmly, "And you'll be unable to complete your term of office."

The governor looked laughingly at Mr. Devin, who broke into a mocking smile of his own.

Slater asked with a sneer, "What's this—a doomsday message from the junior prophet?"

John continued quietly but firmly, his eyes locked on the governor. "The image will collapse, and the man inside will wither from shame."

Before the governor could dismiss the words, John jumped in with some more. "And here's how you'll know that the Lord has given you this message: Before you go home tonight, you'll spill coffee on yourself."

The governor rolled his eyes, leaning back in his chair incredulously. Mr. Devin broke out in rude, mocking laughter. Slater's voice was cracking up with laughter as he asked, "That's it? No bolts of lightning? No earthquakes?"

John received more. Even he was amazed. "There's more. When you go home tonight, you'll receive a new pair of running shoes. Uh. . . . navy-blue running shoes."

Now Mr. Devin approached the governor's desk, amused and not wanting to miss a thing. "Mr. Governor, we should have sold tickets. This is great."

"There's more," said John, and now even Mel the cameraman was coming closer, all ears. "On Wednesday you'll discover that your chief of staff has been lying to you."

Mr. Devin didn't think that was funny at all. "Are you talking about me, Barrett? I'd be careful if I were you."

John looked Devin squarely in the eye and told him, "You never destroyed that tape cassette of Shannon DuPliese's 911 call. Instead you kept it in your desk, hoping to use it to further your own power. But Ed Lake stole it from your desk drawer, hoping to use it himself, and after you fired him, he gave it to my father . . ." John looked at the governor. ". . . and that's how this whole news story began."

Devin cursed loudly, denying the charge, then grabbed John by the arm. "That's it, buddy, you're out of here!"

"Hold it, Martin!" ordered the governor.

Devin stopped and put on a sudden grin. "Mr. Governor,

this guy's a loony! He isn't making a bit of sense! I'd just as soon be rid of him."

Hiram Slater's countenance was filled with rage and loathing. He glared at the prophet and said, "What else?"

Devin's big hand was locked around John's arm, ready to snatch him out of his chair, but John spoke anyway. "On Wednesday you'll also learn that your other daughter, Hayley, is pregnant." John saw the little four-footer leap onto the desk, jumping and screaming like a wild dwarf, his eyes wild with fear, "Out! Out! Get away from me!"

Hiram Slater was on his feet, yelling, "Of all the indecency! Of all the arrogance!"

Devin's grip tightened on John's arm. Devin was just waiting for a word from the governor.

"First your father," the governor said seethingly, his face red with fury, his body trembling, "and now *you!*" He looked at Devin. "Get this kook out of here!"

John was lifted out of the chair. Devin's huge hand was crushing his arm as the chief of staff dragged him toward the door.

Devin pushed the door open and practically carried John around Miss Rhodes' desk, finally releasing him just inside the huge, carved oak doors.

John straightened his clothing and looked back, wondering what had become of Mel.

The door to the governor's office burst open once again, and out came Mel like a man escaping a burning building. "And you can be sure Loren Harris will hear about this!" came the governor's final words over Mel's shoulder. Mel dragged all the equipment through the door as quickly as he could, hoping Mr. Devin would see he didn't need any assistance. John dashed over to help him, and Mel could only puff, "Boy, you sure got us in deep soup this time!"

Devin swung the big door open and held it there. "Good day, gentlemen."

John let his eyes meet Devin's just one more time before they went into the hall and began to work their way back out of the King's lofty chambers.

thirty-two

In front of a bank of monitors with still pictures pasted over their screens, Ali Downs was ready for the camera, looking stunning as usual. Walt Bruechner, the late-night news anchor with the big teeth and thinning hair, looked pretty good, all made-up and suited up and ready to sell the news. Marvin the photographer was back again, chubby, bearded, and fretting, all his strobes, umbrella reflectors, and floodlights in place, and just like before, he was peering through the viewfinder of his big camera on a tripod and trying to elicit the right response from his subjects.

"All right, all right, gimme news, gimme action, gimme that old intensity," he chattered.

Ali and Walt had some dummy scripts and looked at them. "Ali," Marvin said, waving his hand at them, "you're checking a story with Walt, checking for accuracy, okay?"

Ali held her script so Walt could see it. "John—I mean, Walt—what do you think of this? I don't trust the source. And look at that spelling!" *Flash.*

"Hmmm," said Walt, "just how do you spell supercalifragilisticexpialidocious?" Then he cracked up. He loved his jokes. *Flash.*

"Hey, come on, come on, let's get serious!" said Marvin.

Walt read from the script, "The annual Ostrich Egg Toss was held in Veteran's Park yesterday, and as always there was no winner . . ."

"Yeah, that's good, that's good." Marvin kept peering down through the viewfinder. All they could see was the top of his head. "Now look at me. Make me trust you."

"I wouldn't lie to you," said Ali in mock seriousness. *Flash.*

They smiled. *Flash.*

They looked at the script again. *Flash.*

They posed with a TV camera. *Flash.*

Walt in shirt sleeves. *Flash.*

Ali close-up, jotting notes. *Flash. Flash.*

"Wet your lips and smile." *Flash.* "Lean forward, Walt. Ali, move in." *Flash.* "Okay, turn this way a little. Closer together." *Flash. Flash. Flash.*

Then the video shoot. Mounted cameras, hand-held cameras, high angles, floor angles, close-ups, traveling shots. News in the making. Faces full of business, like the world's going to end if we don't get this story out, working, editing, rushing about, hand-held shots racing through the newsroom, quick conversations, zoom-in shots of Walt, then a blurry pan, then Ali brought into focus and zoomed in some more. Intensity, intensity. Walt with sleeves rolled up, banging away at the computer, not just taking but *tearing* news copy from the printer, nodding in agreement with no one in particular. Ali busy at work, then consulting with a reporter (over-the-shoulder shot), then a wry, you're-not-fooling-me smile at someone off-camera.

From his office door Ben Oliver caught glimpses of the process, the same old process, but made no comment. Toward the end, while Walt and Ali strode through the newsroom toward nothing in particular while a camera dollied alongside them to catch their determined expressions and purposeful gait, he finally allowed himself one bitter expletive and went inside his office, closing the door behind him.

Something was up. The whole news staff knew it. News—whether it was from reliable sources or not—rippled across the newsroom from cubicle to cubicle, through the computer system and over the phones.

"Leslie Albright's been canned," came one report.

"John is definitely history," came another.

"Be careful," came a warning. "Loren Harris is on the warpath, and you might be next."

"Walt Bruechner? Give me a break!"

Tina Lewis didn't seem to want to talk about it, but she did let the little drops of poison slip through to the right people from time to time. From these bits and pieces the story began to develop.

"They tried to push through an anti-abortion story."

"They still are, and Loren Harris is taking the coward's way out."

"So what's Ben Oliver doing about it?"

"The governor's putting on the heat. We could get burned on this one."

"Somebody had an abortion? Who?" "Who cares?"

Then Tina had a meeting with Rush Torrance, the Five O'clock producer, and some of the overheard conversation regarded a story John Barrett would be doing alone that evening, something about the governor's daughter and how she died, and how the governor did nothing about it when he should have, and how another girl died in the same clinic due to the governor's negligence or indifference.

Now the polarizing started.

"I gotta hear more about this." "You don't need to. It's nobody's business, and especially not ours."

"You call this news? It's gossip, it's sensationalism."

"Eh, pure politics, that's what it is."

"Man, digging up something this cheap, Barrett and Albright *deserve* to be canned!" "But what if it's true?" "So what if it is? That doesn't make it news."

"The public doesn't need to know any of this stuff."

"It's a political smear tactic, can't you see that? I wouldn't touch it with a ten-foot cattle prod!" "It happened, didn't it?" "We don't know that." "Do we even want to know?"

"Don't you have work to do?"

"The governor's kid died from an abortion? Oh man. Quick, where do I hide?"

"Are you sure Barrett's doing the story? I don't want *my* name on it!"

Video: Replayed excerpts from the governor's address to the Women's Citizen League's fund-raising luncheon.

As stirring music rises in the background, Hiram Slater once again delivers those stirring words: ". . . a woman's inalienable, inviolable right to choose. I have not compromised on that ideal . . ." Lap dissolve to another angle: ". . . As an army marches to victory, every soldier in the ranks knows he or she may not come back from the battle, that he—or she—may be called upon to make the ultimate sacrifice in order that those who come after can walk on ground that was gained through that sacrifice . . ."

Dissolve to a shot of Slater sitting with Hillary, his arm around her. The camera slowly zooms in on their smiling faces.

"As a family, we have stood for the sanctity of privacy for all our children . . . I believe Hillary did what was right for her, at that time, at that place in her life, and I will stand by her proudly, even in her death. I want you to do the same."

Back to Governor Hiram Slater, his words and the music reaching a crescendo. "Your governor cares about women and their sacred right, and it is his desire to protect it, strengthen it, and establish it without fear or misgivings, so help me God!"

Applause, applause, applause.

Freeze frame. The picture of Slater fades to a soft-hued portrait on parchment as the solemn words appear: "Governor Hiram Slater. His Pain . . . Your Gain."

Small title across bottom of screen: "Paid for by the Committee to Reelect Governor Slater, Wilma Benthoff, Chairperson."

John and Mel arrived back at the station a little before 10 o'clock and immediately felt a certain uneasiness in the newsroom, as if they'd just returned from covering a nuclear disaster and might be contaminated.

"How'd it go?" George Hayami asked from behind the assignment desk when they reported in.

Mel just cussed a blue streak and then reported, "You should've seen it. The gov about scratched John's eyes out."

George flashed a questioning glance at John.

John just shrugged as he made himself a cup of coffee. "I would say he was unavailable for comment."

"So did you get anything on-camera?"

Mel shook his head. "We didn't even get that far before he threw us out of there."

By now Erica Johnson was standing there, having a professional as well as personal interest. As managing editor she was responsible for story assignments and content and needed a report on how it went and what would be available for the evening newscasts. As a person, well, she—and almost the whole newsroom—was just plain curious.

"So what've we got for tonight?" she asked.

Mel took that as a cue to detach himself. "I'm getting another assignment. Excuse me."

John answered, "Well, it'll be what we discussed with Ben, a two-minute package. I'll voice the whole thing and work in soundbites."

"But no reacts from the governor, I take it?"

What else could John say? "I guess I'll just have to say he was unavailable for comment."

"So now you don't have reacts from the governor and you don't have anything from the Women's Medical Center either."

"Hey, I called them this morning, and their reaction was pretty much the same as the governor's. They couldn't throw me out, but they did hang up."

"The governor threw you out?"

"Yeah, I'm afraid so."

"What happened?"

"Well . . . before we could do the interview he wanted to talk to me about my motivations for doing the story, and so we talked about my motivations, and then we grappled over which would prevail—my obsession with Truth or his obsession with image and power, and . . . well, the upshot of it was that he had no interest in participating in the kind of moralizing, muckraking story I was pursuing. It was his office, so he asserted his sovereignty and threw me out."

"Hoo boy . . ."

"I suppose Loren Harris has heard about it?"

Erica shook her head. "Loren Harris isn't here today. He's gone far away, and he can't be contacted."

Well, that was interesting.

Erica continued, "Which means the last avenue of appeal is closed until this is over." She sighed in resignation. "So go ahead. Put it together. I've got you slotted for the Five O'clock and the Seven O'clock." She walked away with nothing more to say, and John went to his desk to begin.

The main body of the story would be prerecorded ahead of time, with narrative and video; on the live newscast he would introduce the story with a short lead-in, then the cassette would roll, and then he would come back to do a short closing tag. According to Ben, everything—the lead-in, the prerecorded package, and the tag—had to fit within two minutes.

He clicked on the computer console and stared at the blank screen. Two minutes. Two minutes. How could he say it all in two minutes?

He tapped out a short list of the main points:

—Hillary Slater dead from abortion. —already stated by gov.

—Women's Medical Center responsible. —they refused to comment.

—gov covers it up. —do we say for political reasons?

—gov buys silence from Shannon DuPliese (?)

—second girl dies in same clinic. Annie Brewer.

—no comment as yet from Governor Slater.

He felt a doubt. The question arose in his mind: *So what?*

Maybe the governor was right. Who really cares? Maybe Tina was right. We've already covered this—why drag it all out again?

In light of everything else already said, written, and broadcast about this whole case . . . maybe this was a non-story. Maybe the thunder was really gone.

He took a deep breath and kept going.

Tap tap tataptap . . . He put down ideas for soundbites.

—true cause of Hillary's death: Dr. Harlan Matthews, pathologist, Bayview Memorial Hospital.

—gov knew true cause: Matthews again.

—cover-up, pressuring Shannon DuPliese to silence: Shannon DuPliese.

—Women's Medical Center responsible: Shannon DuPliese, with "Post-Operative Instructions."

—Annie Brewer also died from botched abortion: Dr. Mark Denning, pathologist, formerly at Westland Memorial Hospital.

—Annie died in same clinic: Cindy Danforth, eyewitness account, plus "Post-Operative Instructions."

He tapped in the Print command, and the printer just a few desks away began to zip off a hard copy of his notes. The printing was finished by the time he got there, and he tore off the single sheet of paper, looking it over again.

Two minutes. This was going to be one tight, rushed story.

He pulled a box from under his desk and gathered up all the raw videotape they'd shot, all the interviews, establishing shots, reacts, etc. Now that he had some idea of what form the story would take, he had to review the tapes and pick out the soundbites. And he had to do it *fast.*

"I'm sorry about John Barrett, Sr. I really am. I had no idea . . ."

Ed Lake poured coffee for his visitors, Detectives Henderson and Oakley, as they all sat in Lake's dining room. He'd been gone for a while, hoping to remain untainted, but no sooner had he returned than they were knocking at his door. He figured it was time to face the music while he still had some chance of calling the tune.

"But you feared for your *own* safety," Henderson countered.

"I won't discuss that without an attorney present. But you do understand, don't you, that I'm telling you about the tape because I want you to know who's really responsible for John Barrett's murder?"

"And that is—?"

Lake sipped from his coffee, buying some time to think. "I guess I can't speak from personal knowledge, but consider the flow of events. First the governor has Martin Devin go down to the Fire and Emergency Dispatcher to secure a copy of the recorded emergency call. Why? Well, I take it you've heard the tape. I listened to it, of course, and having done so, it's easy to conclude that Slater wanted to know who made the call so he could cover his rear, if possible, which is consistent with the fact that the governor immediately became very fatherly toward this Shannon DuPliese. Anybody need a refill?"

Oakley put his cup forward, and Lake refilled it.

Lake continued, "I picked all this up just keeping my eyes and ears open. They tried to keep me out of the loop, but I had my ways of worming my way in. Anyway, when it came down to that tape and what to do with it . . ." Lake had to laugh. "Governor Slater handed it to Devin and told him to destroy it. Talk about putting the fox in charge of the chickens! I saw Devin put the tape in his desk drawer—that was back before he had that nice inner office he has now—and I knew we'd never see it again. But I also knew he had no intention of destroying it.

"Well, Devin and I weren't getting along too well—you may have heard about that. So I decided a little insurance wouldn't hurt. I happened by his desk one day when he wasn't there, slid the drawer open, found the tape, and slipped it into my pocket. Either he never missed it or he was afraid to ask anyone about it. He was supposed to destroy it, remember, and he couldn't let anyone know he'd failed to do his job.

"Then came the big blowup between me and Devin, and this time he had the upper hand. The governor had appointed him as chief of staff, and he made it his first task to fire me. So out I went, but I had that tape with me, and I intended to use it somehow."

Henderson asked, "But why give it to John Barrett, Sr.?"

Lake smiled. "Poetic justice, I suppose. Barrett was a thorn in the governor's side. Slater couldn't stand the guy. Everywhere he went, there was that old prophet, shouting and denouncing him and taking him to task, and I knew, I just knew, that giving John Barrett, Sr. the governor's most guarded secret would be the perfect stab. You know, besides being a right-wing fundamentalist kook, Barrett was also an active pro-lifer, and the fact that his son happens to be the number one news anchor in the city did not escape my notice either.

"I hired a young man to be a courier for me. He'd served papers before for some attorney friends of mine, so I knew he was trustworthy. I believe he even disguised himself as a salesman or something, but he delivered the tape, along with a copy of Hillary Slater's death certificate, to John Barrett, Sr. at Barrett's plumbing supply warehouse on . . . I believe it was Monday, the 9th of September.

"I was accosted by hired thugs the very next day, just outside my home here, and they demanded the tape and threatened me with bodily harm if I didn't produce it." Lake shook his head and laughed at himself. "You never know how you'll react in such a situation. I did remember a crime prevention show I watched once where they said, 'If someone tries to hold you up, don't resist, just let him have your wallet. Your wallet isn't worth your life.' I guess I adapted that idea and quickly gave them the information they needed, figuring it wasn't worth my life. I told them where they could find the tape, and they left me alone after only a few blows to the face.

"Anyway, gentlemen, I find no difficulty in deducing who sent the thugs. They came for the tape. Now who do you suppose would want it? Only Martin Devin." Then he looked down at the table forlornly. "But I am truly sorry about John Barrett, Sr. If he'd taken the course of action I chose and simply given them what they wanted . . ."

Henderson and Oakley had heard enough for now. They'd jotted it all down. They rose from the table.

"Thanks for the coffee," said Henderson. "And, uh, you'll be sticking around town, won't you?"

"I'll be here."

Up in the editing room, a tight, busy place that resembled a miniature Mission Control at Cape Canaveral, the editors were working intensely at their consoles and television monitors, putting together the stories for the evening newscasts, electronically selecting, cutting, pasting, and forming a quick, instant, encapsulated TV reality to be played during the forty-eight minutes of air time for the Five O'clock and twenty-two minutes for the Seven O'clock. It was a marvel to watch, as images and soundbites were selected from the raw video and joined with the spoken copy to form an audiovisual package.

One editor was assembling a cops-and-speeder story, following the script given him by the reporter who'd covered it. The reporter had already recorded his narration in several different takes, and the editor had assembled the good takes into a smooth stream of narrative, recording it all on one track of the cassette that would be used that evening. Now he was adding the images to be matched to the narrative. The reporter had written into the script the exact images he'd selected from the raw tape to insert behind his words, along with the electronic time code imprinted on the tape by the camera's recorder that would tell the editor exactly where on the tape to find the required footage.

"The red pickup led police on a high-speed chase up I-5 for three miles . . ." came the reporter's recorded voice-over, and the editor found video footage of the freeway taken from the moving news car and placed that behind the spoken phrase. ". . . until crashing through the guardrail, rolling several times, and coming to rest upside-down in the Zip's Market parking lot . . ." In went shots of the broken guardrail, the big sign over the grocery store identifying it as Zip's, and then the mangled remains of the pickup, several cops, some startled and shaken bystanders. As the story came together, pictures smoothly accompanied the spoken words of the reporter, and the TV viewer would have information both to hear and see, running at the same time.

The editors were good at it and worked fast, pressing buttons and whirling knobs, watching people and events scurry across the monitors in comical, rapid motion, forward, backward, still, then forward slowly, then backward slowly, then frozen, marked, recorded, and then rushed forward and backward again as the editors picked out the right images to go with the spoken copy.

When John came into the editing room with his pile of notes and raw video, he was hoping and praying there would be someone there willing to help him. He'd selected the soundbites from the tapes and scripted the story out in the computer, but the story was still too ponderous. The whole adventure, the experience, the turmoil, the issues, the fibers, threads, and ideas just weren't falling easily into a two-minute package, and he was running out of time.

And now no one would look at him. Sure, they were busy at their work and watching the images fluttering and scurrying across their monitors, and yet . . . he'd come into this room many times before and always got a greeting from somebody, but not this time.

Where was Bill? They'd worked together before and gotten along great. Maybe Bill would be willing . . .

"Hi, John."

"Oh, hi, Bill."

Great. Bill didn't seem any different—still the young, witty, bespectacled technician John was used to. Bill was already eyeing the pile of material John was holding.

"Bill, I've got a problem here . . ."

"Yeah, looks like it. And you've got to have it ready for the Five O'clock?"

"Afraid so."

"Well, come on. I think Booth Two is open."

John followed Bill down the narrow aisle toward one of three enclosed editing booths, normally used for assembling special projects, teasers, promos, and commercial spots. They squeezed their way into the small booth, and Bill closed the glass door.

Bill sat down at the editing console and began to sort through John's script and videos.

John explained, "I've picked out the soundbites and scripted the thing, and I've cut and I've cut, but I still can't get it into two minutes."

Bill scanned the script. "Well, what are the essential points?"

"I had about a hundred, but I've cut it down to three: The governor knew at the time how his daughter died, he purposely covered it up, and now another girl has died in the same clinic."

Bill cracked up as if he'd just gotten the punch line of a joke. "Ohhhh . . . yes, yes . . . *Now* I understand what's going on around here."

John figured he'd better give Bill a way out. "And of course it's up to you whether you want to be involved in this . . ."

Bill was matter-of-fact. "Well, it's news, isn't it?" He set the script on the console ledge and took out his pen. "So let's just do the best job we can."

Rachel Franklin was working the day shift at Hudson's Restaurant and having a pretty good afternoon with nothing to be too anxious about—until Carl Barrett came in the door looking for her. She hardly recognized him with his hair cut and his jewelry gone, but there was no mistaking those intense, probing eyes.

She busied herself arranging water glasses and silverware as she greeted him. "Hi. How are you?"

"Better."

"How's your father?" This question carried a tone of distaste.

"About to go on the tube and talk about Annie Brewer."

That got her attention. "When?"

"Tonight—hopefully on the Five and Seven O'clock newscasts. He's going to try to cover the whole thing we've been working on—the governor's daughter, the clinic, Annie. The general manager said he could have two minutes."

Her face fell a little when she heard that.

Carl understood immediately. "Yeah, two minutes—big deal. How do you say it all in two minutes?"

She sighed in a kind of defeat. "I guess I just don't know who to blame. I get so mad about it all, and I think I'm entitled to be, but . . . I can't blame you—or your father. I just don't know . . ."

Carl looked around. He knew he shouldn't keep her from her work. "Well anyway, I just wanted you to know that he's trying. I don't know how well he'll succeed, but . . . he is trying to let people know."

She allowed herself a smile. "Well, tell him I appreciate it."

He touched her shoulder and turned to go.

John felt he was living out a whole new meaning to the phrase, "In the few seconds we have left . . ." Soon he would have to get going on the rest of the script for the Five O'clock, but the script for his own two-minute story was becoming a lingering, insurmountable nightmare of a task.

He read aloud through the cut and slashed script one more time, even trying to read quickly, one eye on the script and one eye on the digital clock on the editing machine.

"After the death of Hillary Slater, the Women's Medical Center continued business as usual. There was no inquiry, no investigation of—"

"Time," said Bill.

John sank in his chair.

"We've got to cut more," Bill said.

John lamented, "We've already cut half the heart and soul out of this thing."

Bill whistled. "Sounds artistic!"

"Just human."

"Well . . . okay, what about the governor's opening soundbite?"

"Okay, we'll start there."

Bill rolled a cassette back to a brief excerpt from the governor's speech to the Women's Citizen League. There was the governor, frozen in time on the monitor. Bill hit the Play button, and the governor came to life, speaking as Bill and John followed along, reading the script.

". . . knowing the risks, but standing firm nevertheless on her right to choose for herself whether to embrace those risks, she willingly and gladly chose to terminate her pregnancy. She *chose* to control her own body, her own life, and carry on with her future."

"Let's cut all that first part," said John, marking the script, "up to . . . 'she willingly and gladly chose . . .'"

Bill rewound the tape as the governor's voice rose to a garbled squeal, his head bobbed and jerked, and his mouth chattered. Bill hit the Play button.

". . . embrace those risks, she willingly—"

"That's it," said John.

"Okay, we'll trim it down . . ." Bill rewound the tape to the cut point and noted the time code on the LED counter.

"That'll save you seven seconds. What about the Brewers?"

John was emphatic. "No. The Brewers have to stay—absolutely. We'll just have to cut something else."

"Okay," Bill said with a sigh. He scanned the script.

"What about Shannon DuPliese? She had a lot to say."

"Let's take a look at it."

Bill ejected the governor cassette and dropped in the interview with Shannon DuPliese. It was already cued to the soundbite they'd hoped to use.

Play. Shannon sitting comfortably, well-lit, speaking to the interviewer off-camera: "The bleeding just wouldn't stop, and Hillary kept saying, 'Don't tell anyone, I don't want my father to find out.'" Pause.

Bill consulted the script. "And then you say, 'Shannon finally called 911 and help arrived . . .'"

John nodded, grabbing the pen. "Yeah, we can cut that out. People know how Hillary died . . . I guess."

Bill regretted the cut too. "Yeah, it's too bad. This is powerful stuff." He fast forwarded the tape. "So now we've got that other part . . ."

Stop. Play.

Bill and John followed along in the script as Shannon spoke on the tape. "Well, first it was the governor. He came over to visit me after Hillary died, and kept saying things like, 'Well, we want to protect Hillary's memory, don't we?' and 'Nobody needs to know what happened, and I'm not going to ask, and don't think you need to ever tell anyone,' and I didn't get it at first. I thought, well, of course, I won't tell anyone, it's a private matter . . ." John shook his head. The paragraph on the script looked long, and Shannon was sure taking a long time to speak it.

"Okay, there's got to be something we can cut here."

"Let's just find a piece of it."

John looked up and down the long paragraph while the Shannon on the tape kept talking. ". . . But after I started school, Martin Devin started calling me on a regular basis, and I realized that . . . hey, these people didn't trust me. They were going to keep an eye on me and make sure I kept my part of the bargain—and I didn't even know there *was* a bargain."

"We can cut that last part about not knowing there was a bargain," John thought out loud.

"No, come on, give me more than that."

"All right, all right. Uh . . . cut . . . how about from 'and I'm not going to ask' up through . . . 'private matter'?"

Bill balked a little. "Cut something from the middle? Do you have a reaction shot anywhere to cover the cut?"

John could feel the tension twisting his stomach. "Oh . . . man, I don't know. A friend of mine did this interview and I'm not sure—"

"We could dissolve it. It'll look kind of tacky, but . . ."

"No, just . . . just cut it from that point. Cut the whole thing . . ." John had a second thought. "But then we'll lose the part about Martin Devin."

"Well, let's try the cut in the middle and also take off the part about the bargain."

"Okay."

Cue to the cut. Check the time codes. Cue to the other cut. Check the time codes. Add it up.

"2:59."

"Nuts!"

"You're sure you don't want to cut the Brewers?"

John didn't answer so quickly this time. "Well . . . can we shorten them a bit without cutting them out?"

Bill slapped in the Brewers interview and cued it up.

There was Deanne, sitting on the couch with Max.

Deanne: "When Annie died, the doctor told us it was from toxic shock syndrome, but . . ." She fumbled, dealing with emotion. "We . . . we just weren't sure about that, and . . . we didn't know where to turn. . . ."

John grew impatient. "Come on, Deanne, just *say* it!"

Bill observed, "If you want this one, you'll have to cut the tears and just keep the statement. She takes too long when she's crying."

John decided, "Cut the tears, trim back to the statement."

"Righty-oh."

Cut. Play. Time.

"2:45."

"Oh, come on!"

Bill was getting short-tempered. "John, you can't have everything—you have to accept that!"

"Okay, okay."

He scanned the script, desperately looking for anything else dispensable.

Bill suggested, "How about this line: 'Max and Deanne Brewer had their suspicions but were unable to learn anything because of the reproductive privacy laws'?"

"You mean shorten it?"

"I mean cut it."

John winced. "But it's an important point! The privacy laws . . . I've got to point out—"

"Hey, wait a minute. Doesn't Max sort of capture that in his soundbite?"

He cued the tape to Max's soundbite as John consulted the script.

Play.

Max, sitting on the couch next to Deanne: "'s long as your daughter's alive you got no right to know what she's doin', or what somebody's doin' to *her.* Only reason we could find out what happened to Annie was 'cause she was *dead,* and I think that's a little late."

Bill looked to John for a verdict.

John thought it over quickly and then nodded.

"Okay," said Bill, "we scratch the whole paragraph about the privacy laws."

Cut. Play. Time.

"2:38."

John flopped back in his chair. "Well, we're getting closer."

thirty-three

GOVERNOR Hiram Slater was ready to call it a day and hopefully forget that this day had ever occurred. The business and the normal routine had been substantially disrupted by that unfortunate encounter with Mad Prophet Junior, leaving the governor shaken, disgruntled, and distracted. Not being able to reach Loren Harris and rake him over the coals left Slater even more shaken and disgruntled. And as for Martin Devin, he was no help at all, disappearing after ousting the prophet and seeming to be busy everywhere except in the governor's presence.

So now some dirty-laundry story was probably going to run on Channel 6 that night, and all Slater could hope was that Rowen and Hartly would be able to wash it out with a counter-campaign of their own. Wilma Benthoff was already looking into that.

Well, he had to get home. He had to address the Fellowship of Business that night, and he really wanted a nap and a shower first. He knew he'd feel better after that.

He had Miss Rhodes call his chauffeur, grabbed his overcoat, and headed down the long, ornate hallway, saying quick good nights to Miss Rhodes and the female sentry on duty at the main reception desk.

Bryan, a part-time law student, serving as his chauffeur, met him in the main lobby as he emerged from the elevator. "Good evening, sir."

"Good evening, Bryan. Let's get me home. I'm tired."

"Very good, sir."

And then, just as Bryan did every day, he offered the governor his usual cup of coffee in a styrofoam cup with a plastic lid.

The governor stopped dead in his tracks. He stared at the cup of coffee, and then he chuckled, shaking his head.

"Ooohhh, boy . . ."

"Sir?"

"Bryan, now this is going to sound odd . . ."

Bryan chuckled too. *Something* was funny.

The governor looked across the room at a drinking fountain. "Bryan, why don't you go over there to that drinking fountain and . . ." He made a slow, deliberate pouring motion with his hand. ". . . pour that coffee down the drain, down that drinking fountain."

Bryan was bewildered. "Down the drinking fountain, sir?"

The governor laughed and even backed away from the coffee cup. "It's, uh . . . well, I've got a little bet going."

Bryan shrugged. "Okay. Yes, sir."

He walked briskly toward the drinking fountain to carry out his orders. Governor Slater stood still, looking all around for any coffee that might float by in the hands of angels or gremlins, and then watched as Bryan slowly and carefully emptied the coffee cup and tossed it into a waste receptacle.

Bryan returned, and the governor released a mock sigh of relief. "Good enough." He started walking, not looking. "Well, let's get going—" *Oof!* Too late, the governor abruptly encountered a wall of gray wool and felt hot drops of liquid striking his face.

"Oh, man! Sorry, Governor!"

Slater backed away from Ron Brennon, the Senate Majority Leader who was wearing a gray wool overcoat and carrying a cup of coffee. The cup had no lid, unfortunately.

Bryan was all over the governor with a handkerchief. Slater beat him off. "Okay, okay, leave me alone!"

Brennon thought it was kind of funny and ventured a little laugh.

Slater didn't think it was funny at all. "Why don't you watch where you're going?"

Brennon shook his head innocently. "Hey, I wasn't going at all, Governor! I was just standing here. *You* walked into *me*. Sorry . . ."

The governor looked at Brennon, then at Bryan, then at the coffee soaking into his overcoat, and tried to calm himself. "Well," he struggled to say, "it's no big deal."

That's what he absolutely had to believe.

4:45 P.M.

Mardell the floor director, her long, black hair tied back with a bow and her headset in place, was at her post behind Cameras One, Two, and Three on the news set, as were the camera operators. The lights were coming on, and the robotic camera on the boom was being checked for its nightly dive out of the rafters.

John stood in the makeup room before the huge, illuminated mirror, putting on his best face and having strange, fatalistic thoughts about the future. *This must be what it feels like to go to your execution,* he thought. Quite honestly, he didn't feel all that excited about being a martyr. Not for what could turn out to be a non-story. But it was all in the Lord's hands now. Whatever would come, would come.

He and Bill had finally finished the package early in the afternoon, and now the cassette was ready and waiting up in the control room. The final script was a mere fraction of the story John started out with, which was a mere fraction of the whole incredible adventure he and the others had been through over the past month or so. It would have taken an hour-long television special to capture even half of it, and all he had for tonight, and maybe forever, was two minutes.

But he had some good feelings as well, especially gratitude. He had to be thankful to God that he'd even gotten this far with the story. It was like getting a second chance, a chance to make things right. And for all the pain he now felt, he also enjoyed a deeper feeling of peace. He just hoped Max and Deanne were watching, not to mention Rachel, Cindy, Shannon, and Mrs. Westfall. And Carl. And Mom.

Carl came in from Grandpa's shop in time to wash up and get not only the television but also the VCR turned on and a blank tape ready to roll. A thing like this was only going to happen once, and he didn't want to miss it.

"Grandma, it's almost 5!"

"Ohh," came a cry from the kitchen. "Lord Jesus, help my Johnny!"

At the Human Life Services Center, Marilyn Westfall set a small portable television on the corner of her desk. She usually went home at 5 o'clock, but if she did this time, she might miss the story while she was out on the road driving, so she'd stick around the Center a little longer, along with her volunteers.

4:50 P.M.

John slipped into his suit jacket and walked around the plywood backdrop and onto the news set just as he had done so many times before. Ali Downs was already there, putting in her earpiece and concealing the cord behind her back and under her jacket. Bing Dingham the sports announcer was ready at his post and fidgeting a little. Hal Rosen was in his place on the right end of the news desk, his hands folded in front of him, ready for a friendly chat.

In the control room Susan the director sat at the console in front of the wall of monitors, paging through the script with Rush Torrance and Tina Lewis as the syndicated controversial talk show babbled quietly from the On Air monitor.

"So we open with 130, job cutbacks at Benson Dynamics . . ." said Susan.

"And 140's out," said Rush.

"140, Car Wash . . ." She chuckled. "Too bad. I liked that one. But okay, where's Wendell?" She glanced up at one of the black-and-white monitors near the ceiling and saw Wendell Southcott standing in front of the main office of Benson Dynamics, waiting to do his live feed, the camera capturing the company logo on the building over his shoulder.

"Okay, he's ready." Susan turned to the console and started setting up the cameras on the set below. "Okay, coming up on the teaser, Camera Two, four-shot, Camera One on Bing, Camera Three on Hal. Stand by."

Rachel Franklin got off work at 4 and made it home in time to flip on the television. John Barrett was going to do a story on the whole Annie Brewer thing? Well, that remained to be seen.

Shannon DuPliese, now back home, sat on the couch with her mother, just waiting for the news to come on. Her father stood behind them, his hand on his wife's shoulder. Ever since Shannon decided to withdraw from Midwestern and return the scholarship, she and her parents had been talking—really working it through. Of course they had to deal with pain, bewilderment, and disappointment, but there were no longer any secrets.

So far two things were certain in the DuPliese home: Shannon had done the right thing in coming home and opening up about everything, and as for Hiram Slater . . . well, he would have some explaining to do to a family that had once trusted him.

4:56 P.M.

Time for the before-show teaser, right on the tail-end of the syndicated controversial talk show.

Rush counted down, "Four . . . three . . . two . . . one . . ."

"Up . . ." said Susan, "and . . . cue. Stand by cassette." The On Air monitor in front of Susan showed Hal, John, Ali, and Bing sitting happily at the news desk, all looking at Camera Two as busy theme music played in the background.

John read the script mirrored over the lens of Camera Two. "Good evening, coming up on NewsSix at Five O'clock . . ."

"Roll cassette," said Susan.

Video: The main office building of Benson Dynamics. Workers leaving one of Benson's factories. Big airplanes under construction in a hangar.

John's voice over the video: "A big cutback in orders could mean a big cutback in jobs at Benson Dynamics."

Wipe to video: Cops coming out of a small house in a low-rent district. Yellow plastic tape stretched around the house. Flashing red and blue lights. Bags and bags of white powder.

Ali Downs's voice over the video: "Police who thought they were breaking up a local crack house found more than they bargained for . . ."

Wipe to video: Some shots of a red pickup truck, upside-down and mangled.

John's voice over the video: "And a high-speed chase ends in a spectacular and fatal crash."

Camera Two, all four.

John intro'd Hal Rosen. "And a cooler but cleaner Tuesday?"

Camera Three, head-on to Hal.

Hal looked chatty enough as he said, "Nice air, clear skies, lower temperatures, beautiful colors, and maybe a touch of rain. Not bad for fall. I'll tell you all about it."

Camera Two, showing all four.

Ali intro'd Bing Dingham. "And fall is bringing out the colors on the football field as well . . ."

Camera One, head-on to Bing.

Bing was excited and bubbly. "The Tigers bring home a big win against the Cutters, and second-string quarterback Jeff Bailey played a first-string game. We'll have highlights."

Back to Camera Two on all four of them.

John faced Camera Two and closed the teaser. "All that and more coming up on NewsSix at Five, your Premiere News Source."

Commercial. They were off the air.

Hal and Bing took out their earpieces and left the news desk until it was their time to be on again.

John paged through his script, making little marks here and there to remind him, warn him, cue him. Strange how quiet it was on the news set tonight. Normally things were a little more chatty between the techs and the talent.

John found the Slater Cover-up Story, still safe and sound in section five, Number 540. Any minute he expected to hear Rush in his earpiece saying the story was bumped, but so far so good.

Marilyn Westfall was ready, as were two volunteers from the center, a young mother and a grandmother, seated next to her.

But a special guest joining them for the occasion was Cindy Danforth, who'd found a comfortable perch on the arm of one of the chairs.

"Two minutes?" asked the grandmother.

"That's all," said Mrs. Westfall.
"Don't blink, anybody," said Cindy.

Max, Deanne, and all three kids were seated in front of the television again, and this time all of them were nervous about it, remembering the ill feelings that had resulted from the last time Deanne had been on TV.

"Are you gonna be on this time, Mommy?" asked young George.

"I don't know, honey. We'll just have to see."

"I'm not gettin' my hopes up," Max said quietly.

4:58 P.M.

Susan the director set things up for the Five O'clock. "Camera Two, two-shot of John and Ali. Camera Three, head-on to John—we'll pan for a Benson box . . . I thought I saw one in there. I don't know that for sure. Graphics, do you have a Benson box? Cassette One is 130, Benson Cutbacks . . . Camera One, you'll be shooting the two-shot for the DVE box to John and Ali's left. Uh . . . no, we're yanking the Car Wash. Yank 140. 140 is out."

John and Ali pulled the car wash story from their scripts. John would be opening with the first story on the Benson Dynamics cutbacks, and they would be talking to Wendell Southcott as he appeared in the false frame at the left end of the news desk.

As Rush and Susan chattered away, working against the clock, Tina Lewis stood silently against the back wall of the control room, watching with an intense, brooding interest, a script in her hand.

"Okay," said Rush, "ten seconds."

"Here we go, everybody," said Susan.

"Here we go," John told the Lord, his eyes closed for a one-second prayer.

"Five . . . four . . ."

"Roll cassette."

On the Preview Monitor, the Opening Cassette showed the

numerals counting down as Rush counted out loud, "Three . . . two . . . one . . ."

On the air.

Music. Big music that sounded like news, rushing along, charging along, sounding the call, *News is happening, happening, happening.*

Video. Moving, aerial shot of the city, the Adams Tower, downtown. Traffic rushing back and forth, ferries pulling out from the dock.

Deep, sandy, booming voice: "This is Channel 6, The City's Premiere News and Information Station, your number one source for up-to-the-minute news . . ." Pictures, *fast* pictures: a cameraman runs toward a fast-breaking story, zooming in, focusing; a female reporter stands in front of more news, hair blowing, microphone ready; a male reporter scrambles from a NewsSix car, his eyes locked on an off-screen event; Chopper Six lands with a bump; technicians bang switches in the control room . . .

New video. The city skyline from high above, the picture rocking, dipping a bit with the helicopter as it banks over the skyscrapers, catching the glint of the evening sun off the vast panes of glass . . .

Voice still going: "And now, from the NewsSix newsroom, this is NewsSix at Five, with John Barrett . . ." As the camera flies through the air, circling over the freeway where the traffic flows like blood through an artery, a box appears at the upper left. John Barrett flashes a knowing smile at the camera.

". . . Ali Downs . . ." Box at lower right. She has a new hairdo, a new look, and delivers a shining smile.

The boxes disappear as the camera drops toward an imposing tower of glass adorned with a big red 6.

"Bing Dingham with sports . . ." A box containing Dingham's face leaps out from the tower and slams into the upper-right position. Bing Dingham looks at the camera and cracks up as always.

"And Hal Rosen, weather . . ." His box flies out of the tower and comes to rest at the lower left as he looks at the camera and winks.

The boxes disappear. Here comes that tower, closer, closer, we're coming in for a landing, the BIG RED 6 filling the screen, closer, faster, *closer, faster* . . .

"The NewsSix News Team. NewsSix at Five!" *Crash!* We're inside the building, sailing past rafters, cables, floodlights, and then, like a roller coaster going over the top, we nose over, dropping down past rigging, wires, lights, monitors, into the open expanse of the NewsSix set, heading for the floor and the news desk where John Barrett and Ali Downs are ready and waiting to inform us, accepting with ease that we have fallen from the sky and through their ceiling to get there.

Two-shot: John and Ali at the desk, looking into Camera Two, the false video monitors behind them.

"Good evening," said Ali, "and welcome to NewsSix at Five."

Camera Three, head-on to John. The camera pans to the right as a graphics box appears over John's left shoulder. The graphics box shows the Benson Dynamics logo over a silhouetted airplane and the large word beneath the box: "CUTBACKS."

John read the copy to lead into Wendell Southcott's report. "Big news today from Benson Dynamics, one of the city's biggest employers. Due to canceled airline orders and government contracts, the company will be cutting back its work force."

The red light atop Camera One lit up, and John looked in that direction, continuing, "Wendell Southcott has been tracking that story . . ." Mardell held out her hand, indicating where the DVE box would appear. John and Ali looked at the wall as if looking at Wendell. ". . . and now has this live report. Wendell?" Camera One captured John and Ali looking at the box with Wendell Southcott looking back at them, microphone in hand, the Benson Dynamics building behind him.

"Stand by Cassette One."

Wendell went to full-screen as he began his report. "Well, John, U.S. and foreign airlines have cut back delivery on

2100s and 2200s, and Benson has also been hit hard by defense cuts."

"Roll Cassette One."

A missile appears on the screen, blasting into the air. Title at bottom of screen: "Benson. Cutbacks."

Wendell Southcott's voice over the video: "Benson took a big hit with the cancellation of the WeeWinder missile . . ."

Carl and Mom sat on the couch, watching anxiously as the newscast hurried along and the VCR rolled, recording the event. They sat through the Benson story, then a related story on the local economic impact of the Benson cutbacks, then a story about a police raid of a crack house, and then a story about a high-speed chase and a wrecked pickup truck.

A commercial brought a chance for Mom to break eye contact with the television screen and say, "Did John say when he would be doing the story?"

Carl didn't like the answer. "Well . . . he said they were going to bury it, and that meant they'd probably put it somewhere in the middle with other stories on either side, and definitely not right before or after a commercial."

"I don't understand."

"People might remember it if it's the first thing they see after a commercial—if it's the top story in that section. But you can't have it right before a commercial either because then people can think about it during the commercial."

Mom was shocked. "They actually *plan* it that way?"

Carl laughed but just a little. "Who knows? That's just Dad's theory."

"Well, we'll see if he's right."

"The point is, he's doing it."

Mom gave a solemn nod and a proud smile.

"I only wish Grandpa could see this," Carl sighed.

Mom patted Carl's hand. "Dad saw this moment a long time ago. He knew this day would come."

The newscast continued on through another section and another commercial break. Then more news: a house fire, a yacht sinking in the bay, an environmental fracas over a new garbage incinerator.

Then came a quick update on the gubernatorial campaign, reported by Todd Baker. Challenger Bob Wilson was still coming on strong, at least in his rhetoric—"Slater says he cares about women, but I don't see the *family* anywhere in all that talk!"—but the polls showed Hiram Slater well ahead, so the governor remained confident of victory: "Four years ago I received a mandate from the people, and I believe the people still believe in the causes for which they first elected me. I have no question that we will prevail." It wasn't anything new or startling. Same old, same old.

Moving right along: "The cross-Bay bridge, a real possibility? A planning committee released its findings today." Jim Eng had the story. Jim Eng did the story. John asked a scripted question: "Well, Jim, how many members of the committee really view the Meyer's Point route as feasible?"

"John, as a group the committee members would not commit themselves, but one member who asked not to be named felt the route would be approved . . ."

Commercial break.

Next section. The opening of the city's new art museum. Consumer specialist Dave Nicholson's investigation into a mail-order meat packing scam.

Then Bing Dingham with sports. The Tigers and Cutters game. Some tennis. Another HIV-positive superstar admitting to having sex with hundreds of women and insisting the Administration isn't doing enough.

Hal Rosen with current weather and the national weather situation, the five-day forecast coming up later in the program.

Then the teaser.

Camera Two, two-shot of John and Ali, zooming back a bit. Their names appear under them: "JOHN BARRETT. ALI DOWNS." Between the names, the NewsSix logo. Behind the anchors, the backdrop with the false monitor screens.

Ali took the first tease: "Hate crimes in this area are on the rise, and a white supremacist group vows to make Waterton a national haven for whites only."

"Roll Cassette 530."

Video: A burning cross in the front yard of a nice house; white men with close-cropped haircuts marching with banners and giving Nazi salutes.

Title at bottom of screen: "AHEAD." John's voice over the video: "A local African-American family is threatened by still another cross burning but vow to stay, even as the American Aryans open a local chapter only blocks from their home."

Video: A wild rhinoceros rams a safari jeep as the passengers scurry in all directions, screaming, hollering.

Ali's voice over the video: "And a frightening incident at the Wildwood Animal Safari as a rhinoceros goes on a rampage, all captured on home video."

A banner graphic wipes onto the screen. "Business. The Dow Jones Averages, up 5.59." Then six local stocks and how they did.

Commercial break.

John flipped the pages of his script in Section Five. There were only three stories slotted for this section: the hate crimes/white supremacist story, the home video of the rampaging rhino, and . . . the Slater Story, sandwiched between the other two.

"Three . . . two . . . one . . ."

Ali began Section Five. "Another cross burning, this time on the front lawn of an African-American family in the Waterton district . . ."

John watched the monitor in the news desk as the video played and special assignment reporter Valerie Hunter did the reporting. It was impressive stuff, even scary. The frightened family, the charred cross still on their front lawn, the mother and father voicing their fears and concerns, followed by the grandiose and hateful boasts of the white supremacists.

A powerful story. A disturbing story. And it would be followed by . . . what? John's non-story? His after-the-fact indulgence in finger-pointing? For just a moment he even considered calling Rush and canceling the story, but of course by now that was impossible. The newscast was rolling; the scripts, teleprompters, and cassettes were all in place. The story was going to air, and he was going to read it.

Mom and Carl knew the time was passing. The newscast had already been going for forty minutes. The Slater story had to be coming up soon.

Mrs. Westfall, Cindy Danforth, and the two volunteers were beginning to wonder if the story would air at all. They felt they'd been sitting an awfully long time.

Rachel was only inches from turning the television off and going on with her life. She figured she'd give the show just a few more minutes and that would be it.

Shannon and her parents were discussing whether they'd been told the wrong date, and Shannon was beginning to have serious doubts whether she'd heard Carl correctly.

Max and the kids were getting restless and hungry, and Max was muttering phrases along the lines of, "All this waiting for two lousy minutes . . ."

Deanne began setting the table and heating up the leftovers. If something came on, she would hear it and be able to run over to watch.

John had the script ready in front of him, the anchor lead-in highlighted. Ali would be doing a closing tag on the hate crimes/white supremacists story facing Camera Two, and then, on her outcue, ". . . there are no suspects, but the investigation continues," John would begin.

John could see Camera Three positioning for his anchor lead-in. He got ready.

In the control room Tina eyed his face as it appeared in the Preview Monitor. She could read the tension in John Barrett's eyes.

"You just had to push it, didn't you?" she muttered. "You just *had* to push it!"

Rush and Susan were too busy directing the newscast to hear her.

Ali closed the hate crimes story, looking into Camera Two. "The American Aryans deny any involvement in the cross burning, and so far there are no suspects, but the investigation continues."

The red light on Camera Three lit up. John remained in professional mode, facing the camera and reading from the script mirrored in front of its lens. He let his mind run automatically as he detached himself from the story. This was nothing special, he told himself, nothing different, it wasn't his story. It was news. It was his job. He had no intention other than to do it right, to do the best job he could do.

Camera Three, head-on. No pan, no box, just John.

"Stand-by Cassette 540."

"A week after Governor Slater went public with the abortion death of his daughter Hillary . . ."

The Brewer kids all squealed, "Mom! Mom!" and Deanne came running.

". . . new questions are being raised: Did the governor know from the beginning how his daughter died, and if so, was he involved in a cover-up that may have cost at least one more life?"

"Roll cassette," said Susan.

The package began.

Video: The governor, addressing the Women's Citizen League. An excerpt from his great announcement a week ago. Title at bottom of screen: "October 9th."

Governor: ". . . she willingly and gladly chose to terminate her pregnancy . . ."

Governor's voice drops as John's voice-over begins.

"Governor Slater claimed he had just learned Hillary did not die from mislabeled drugs but from abortion malpractice."

Video: Dr. Harlan Matthews sitting in his office, talking to the off-camera interviewer, his voice muffled under John's voice-over.

"Pathologist Dr. Harlan Matthews confirms the cause of

Hillary's death, but insists the governor knew the cause of death the day after it happened."

Title at bottom of screen: "Dr. Harlan Matthews, Pathologist, Bayview Memorial Hospital."

Matthews's voice comes up to volume: ". . . it was an abortion, performed quite hurriedly and clumsily."

John's voice off-camera: "And was the governor made aware of this?"

"He knew his daughter died from an abortion, yes. I'm the one who told him."

Video: The exterior of the Women's Medical Center.

John's voice-over: "Hillary received an abortion at the Women's Medical Center on the 19th of April."

Video: Shannon DuPliese talking to an off-camera interviewer.

"Shannon DuPliese, a close friend, drove Hillary to the clinic and then home to the governor's residence, where Hillary died a few hours later."

Video: Old clip of Shannon receiving the scholarship from Governor Slater.

"When Shannon was awarded the Hillary Slater Memorial Scholarship, she soon realized the scholarship came with a price—her silence."

Video: Back to Shannon being interviewed.

Title: "Shannon DuPliese, friend of Hillary Slater."

Shannon: "Well, first it was the governor. He came over to visit me after Hillary died, and kept saying things like, 'Well, we want to protect Hillary's memory, don't we?'" A shot of her hands wringing nervously in her lap, something Bill found near the end of the tape and used to cover the cut. Shannon continues, "But after I started school"—viewers see her face again—"Martin Devin started calling me on a regular basis, and I realized that . . . hey, these people didn't trust me. They were going to keep an eye on me and make sure I kept my part of the bargain—"

Video: Exterior shot of the Women's Medical Center.

John's voice-over: "After the death of Hillary Slater, the

Women's Medical Center continued business as usual. There was no investigation of malpractice."

Video: A shot of Annie Brewer's senior picture. The camera zooms in slowly to heighten the intensity.

"A month later Annie Brewer, a high-school senior, also died from an abortion she received at the Women's Medical Center."

Video: Cindy Danforth in silhouette. Title on bottom of screen: "Mary, witnessed abortion."

Cindy: "Annie was right across the hall from me, and I could hear her screaming, and after we got out of there, I knew something wasn't right. She was hurting."

Video: Max and Deanne, sitting on their couch. Title: "Max and Deanne Brewer, Annie's parents."

Max: "'s long as your daughter's alive you got no right to know what she's doin', or what somebody's doin' to *her*. Only reason we could find out what happened to Annie was 'cause she was *dead*, and I think that's a little late."

John's voice-over: "Max and Deanne Brewer had to take legal action to obtain Annie's autopsy report."

Video: Dr. Mark Denning. Title: "Dr. Mark Denning. Performed the autopsy."

Denning: "The primary cause of death was generalized septicemia, due to septic abortion, something for which the abortionist is responsible, in my opinion."

The package was over.

Camera Three, head-on to John.

John spoke his closing tag. "The Women's Medical Center refused to comment, and Governor Slater was unavailable for comment. Ali?"

Ali spoke to Camera Two. "Well, a drive through the Wildwood Animal Safari turned into a real nightmare . . ."

"Roll Cassette 550."

Video: The rhinoceros stampling and lumbering about in the tall grass, charging a land rover, making it jolt and rock as tourists run for cover, screaming, the camera shaking and jerking. Exciting stuff.

Ali's voice-over: ". . . when one of the wild animal park's rhinos went on a rampage . . ."

Carl leaped from the couch and let out a whoop, then a loud "YES!," then danced a little, then shouted, "He did it! He really did it!"

Mom just sat on the couch, quietly clapping her hands, tears in her eyes, praying, "O Lord, my dear Lord, Johnny's come home. He's come home!"

Carl pointed at the television, oblivious to the rhinoceros video and then the car commercial. He had only one thought on his mind. "That was my dad! That was the *man!*"

Mrs. Westfall and the two volunteers all gave Cindy a big hug.

"You did great, honey."

"God bless you—you're very brave."

"Good job, good job."

Rachel finally relaxed. Two minutes. Well . . . okay. He did okay.

Shannon and her folks got up and went to eat dinner. They knew better than to expect any more than what they had just seen, but they were satisfied. They had to give John Barrett credit for saying as much as he did.

Deanne looked at Max, trying to fathom his brooding expression even as the kids got up and babbled in excitement.

"I saw both of you!" said George.

"*I* wanna be on TV!" said Victoria.

"Well, sugar, aren't you going to say something?" Deanne asked.

Max drew one long, slow breath and looked at his wife. "Well . . . it wasn't much." Then he broke into a smile. "But it wasn't bad!"

They embraced.

The rhinoceros story ended, and NewsSix went to a commercial.

Susan the director swiveled around in her chair and let out

a quiet cussword of amazement. "How come I never heard about this before?"

Tina stood against the back wall, staring at John Barrett's face on the Camera Three monitor. "Heard about what?"

"This thing about Slater's daughter!"

Tina seemed to ignore the question and addressed Rush. "That story took too long. We hardly had room for the rhinoceros video."

Rush glanced at his script. "Yeah, well, you might want to drop it from the Seven O'clock."

"Oh no, you don't—drop the rhinoceros!" said Susan.

"You just do your job!" Tina snapped. *"I'll* decide what gets dropped!"

Susan closed right up, knowing better than to say another word. She took a deep breath, swiveled back to the console, and went back to doing her job. "All right, Camera Two, head-on to Ali. And, Camera One, you'll be doing Barry's commentary . . ."

John could feel the chill coming from Ali's side of the news desk, but he stayed professional, getting ready for the next section. He'd delivered the story, but the adventure wasn't over yet. There was still the rest of this newscast, and there was still the Seven O'clock.

thirty-four

GOVERNOR Hiram Slater said good evening to Bryan the chauffeur and went in the back door of the mansion, carrying his coffee-stained overcoat over his arm.

He found Alice the maid busy in the kitchen, putting dinner together. She was a very sweet older gal, a widow. She and her late husband had been friends of the family for years.

"Hi, Governor."

He didn't look her way when he said, "Hi, Alice."

She noticed his sullen mood. "Oh, tough day?"

He stopped and softened enough to chuckle at his own misfortune, unfolding the overcoat for her to see. "Spilled coffee on my coat . . ."

She immediately took it from him. "Well, don't you worry. You just let Alice take care of it."

"Where's Ashley?"

"Oh, out shopping for plants and bulbs, I think. She should be home any minute."

The governor almost felt stupid asking the question, but he had to ask. "Uh . . . where'd she go—Warren's Nursery?"

"Oh, right. That's what she said. They're having a sale right now."

"So she . . . well, she wasn't going anywhere else—to buy clothes or shoes or anything?"

Alice laughed. "Oh dear, I wouldn't know, Governor."

"Mm. Any mail?"

She pointed to the kitchen table where all the mail was routinely placed for his perusal. He could see there were no packages of any kind.

"Have any packages come today—anything from UPS?"

"No. The mail on the table is all there is."

He felt better. "All right . . . Good enough . . . Well, I'm going to take a shower and close my eyes until dinner."

"I'll call you when it's ready."

He hurried through the big house and up the stairs to the

bedroom, feeling his nerves starting to ease. Ahhh. His own home, his safe haven, his castle the public—and the prophets—could not enter. What a feeling.

He took off his suit jacket and tossed it lazily onto the bed, then started removing his tie as he went into the master bathroom, humming a little tune. A good hot shower, yes sir, that was what he needed.

Oh no. What was that by his vanity sink?

He stood staring at it, afraid to approach it, unwilling to believe it really was . . . a shoe box. Only when he finally decided it had to be a gag, an elaborate hoax, did he approach the shoe box and remove the lid.

Sure. Of course he found navy-blue running shoes inside.

He slipped off his dress shoes and tried on the running shoes. Great fit.

"Hello," came Ashley's voice in the bedroom. "Did you find something?" She had that teasing tone she always had whenever she surprised him with something.

He was not pleased as he strode out of the bathroom, the shoes still on his feet. "What's the meaning of this?"

She was pleased. "Oh, looks like they fit!"

"Yes, they do!" Slater replied angrily. "Perfectly! So where did they come from?"

She was taken aback by his angry tone. "Well . . . Hiram, they didn't cost a thing!"

He was yelling now. "Where did they come from?"

And now she was starting to yell back. "From Wade Sheldon!"

"Wade Sheldon!" The governor was shocked and perplexed. Wade Sheldon and he had worked out together at the health club for a few years now. "Where'd *he* get them?"

Ashley was indignant and defensive. "I thought you'd be pleased."

"Just answer the question!"

"He got them from a mail-order catalog. They didn't fit him, so he thought he'd give them to you. I got them this morning when I went to see Marcy."

Marcy. Wade's wife. This wasn't making sense. Did the

Sheldons know John Barrett? Did Ashley get the shoes from Marcy before John Barrett gave his little prophecy or afterward? How did John Barrett know Ashley would be visiting Marcy? How did he even know Wade had ordered the shoes?

"What time did you go visit Marcy?"

"About 10. Why?"

Slater sat on the bed. He kicked the shoes off as if they were his enemies. "I'm just . . . I'm just trying to figure this out, that's all. There's an explanation! There has to be!"

Ashley had had her fill of abuse for now. "It might be because Wade is your friend, or is friendship that foreign a concept to you?"

"It's not that simple!"

"So what do you think the shoes are, a *bribe?*"

"Not a bribe . . . Maybe a trick . . ."

"Hiram Slater . . ." She told him where he could go and fled from the room.

6:50 P.M.

John rechecked his makeup in the makeup room, standing all by himself in front of the huge illuminated mirror and taking some deep breaths just to steady himself. It was getting tough to maintain his professional edge when such conflicting feelings raged inside him.

One part of him—the professional, go-with-the-flow part—was lashing out at him, chastising him, screaming at him that he was doing a monumental disservice to his profession, to the people he worked for, to the whole industry that had made him a household name.

At the same time, one steady, unshakable voice from somewhere else inside him—probably his heart, but right now his feelings were too scrambled for him to tell—kept him standing firm on this chosen path, with no other assurance than the knowledge that he was doing the right thing.

The overall effect of this inward battle was a twisting, wrenching, nauseating conflict that closely resembled a coronary, and he couldn't wait for the whole miserable experience to be over.

He was glad Leslie wasn't here right now. She'd be getting herself in trouble for sure, and he could just imagine how much harder it would be with her stirring things up.

He was wondering why Ben Oliver was nowhere to be seen. Had he gone home? Had he ducked out the way Loren Harris had? Aw, Ben, you helped get me into this—the least you could have done was walk me to the gallows and say good-bye.

Why do I even stick around? He wondered. *If I'm as good as dead as a news anchor, why don't I just walk off the job right now instead of prolonging the pain?*

Oh, but there came that voice again: *Press on, press on, you're doing the right thing. Finish it.*

Oh, I'm going to finish it, all right. I'm probably going to finish everything, *including myself.*

"It's hard, son," came a voice from his memory, "to have God show you things and tell you things and then not know what to do with what you've been given." Oh great. Just what I need. Another emotion. John leaned on the counter in front of the mirror as his face turned hot and his eyes flooded with tears.

More of Dad's lamentation came to his memory. "'Eat the scroll, John.' That's what the Lord said. 'In your mouth it will taste sweet, but it will make your stomach bitter.' And He was right. Up front, when you hear things and see things and God entrusts you with knowing things, you think of how privileged you are, how wonderful it is to see Truth parading right in front of you. And then . . . when you try to speak it and nobody listens . . . and you see people heading for a cliff and you just can't turn them back . . . and when you find out things you would have been happier not knowing . . ."

John wanted to break right down and cry, but there wasn't time. The clock on the wall said 6:54. He had to get to the news set and do the 6:56 teaser and then the Seven O'clock, and he had to be on top of it and look good and be the professional the viewers out there had learned to trust, and he couldn't go on-camera with tears in his eyes and his voice quaking just because he understood for the first time how

Dad must have felt standing up on that planter before that hostile crowd . . .

He broke down anyway, pulling a tissue from the dispenser to sop up his tears. He could only cry in the few seconds he had left. Watching the clock, he made sure his emotions stayed within the schedule, and he pulled a drawer open looking for some eyedrops. Yes, there they were. Hopefully they would get the red out of his eyes before he went on-camera.

6:56 P.M.

"Good evening. Coming up next on NewsSix at Seven, a big cutback in orders could mean a big cutback in jobs at Benson Dynamics . . ."

And then Ali said her lines, and then John gave a quick preview of the crack house bust story, and then Hal Rosen gave a hint of what the weather would be but you'd have to watch the show to find out the rest. The whole teaser went just fine, and they were off the air for a few minutes.

Then he and Ali checked their scripts and listened for any late changes coming from the control room.

John could feel his emotions right at the brink of his eyes, but he kept them down. He kept his mind on the script, on Mardell's directions, on the whole newscast.

Tina Lewis and Pete Woodman, the Seven O'clock show producer, quickly paged through the script for the half-hour newscast. Susan was at her post again, ready to direct.

"I hear you had trouble with the car wash story last time," said Pete.

"Mm, too long, I think," Tina answered. "But hey, we bumped it from the Five O'clock, let's see if we can run it this time."

Pete found it. "Okay . . . 140. Yeah, it's going to be tight."

"So let's bump something else. We'll see how it goes." Susan could hear something coming but busied herself with her job, wanting very much to keep it. "Camera Two, two-shot of John and Ali. Camera One, head-on to Ali to start. Um . . . is the Barry Gauge commentary in or out?"

"It's in, Section Four," said Pete.

"Good enough."

"Ten seconds."

Susan got the show rolling. "Here we go, everybody."

Pete counted down, "Three . . . two . . . one . . ."

The Seven O'clock went like clockwork as John and Ali anchored story after story, taking turns back and forth.

The first section got long.

"We'll bump the high-speed chase with the pickup truck, 180," said Pete.

Tina jumped on that. "No, move it to Section Two."

Pete objected. "We don't have room in Section Two."

"So move . . . uh . . . move 280, the garbage incinerator, up to Section Three."

Pete was getting edgy. "Tina, something's gotta go, come on!"

"We'll see."

Pete just shook his head. "We'll see all right."

John and Ali got the word through their earpieces. They would do 160, the big crack house bust, and then cut for the commercial. 180, the high-speed chase, would start Section Two. 280, the garbage incinerator, would start Section Three.

They marked their scripts. Ali finished the crack house story. They did a quick tease of stories coming up and went to the commercial.

"Okay," said Susan through their earpieces, "remember, we'll start Section Two with 180, the high-speed chase. Camera Three, head-on to John. Stand by."

Section Two went smoothly, and the change worked well, even saving them a few seconds. They filled the time with cute anchor chatter.

Commercial break.

Pete shook his head. "Okay, Tina, Section Three coming up, and there's too much there."

Tina already had the problem solved. "Push 370, the campaign, forward to Section Four."

Pete could count. There were too many stories in Section Four and not enough time. "And what do we bump?"

Susan muttered to herself but loud enough to be heard, "I bet it won't be the rhinoceros."

Tina heard the wisecrack but remained steady and determined. "Bump 430, the Slater story. We'll do the campaign, then Barry's commentary, and finish out with the rhinoceros."

Pete balked for just a moment. "You're . . . uh . . . you're sure?"

Tina showed such incredible patience. "Oh, excuse me, was I unclear?"

He caught her gaze and gave in. "Okay. You're the boss."

He found 430, the Slater Story, and pulled it out, dropping it page by page onto the floor. "430 is out."

John got the word through his earpiece. "Heads up. We're pushing 370, the campaign story, ahead into Section Four, and we're bumping 430, the Slater Story. Slater is out."

John felt more conflict deep inside—anger at being double-crossed mixed with the naughty joy of escaping a responsibility—crushing disappointment mixed with a relief John felt uncomfortable about feeling.

He could see Ali flipping through her script and tossing the pages onto the floor. He found the pages in his own script, pulled them out, but kept them to one side. He was definitely *not* going to toss them onto the floor.

"Stand by," said Marshall, ready to count down.

As John looked her way, he could see—or did he imagine?—a vast crowd materializing behind those three cameras. He could hear their voices rising as if a sound engineer were slowly bringing up the volume.

Almost immediately he recognized them. They were the crowd at the governor's kickoff rally, and now he was standing above them, up on the planter, in Dad's shoes, wearing Dad's overcoat. They were jeering him, chanting, shaking their fists, waving signs.

He blinked the vision away.

Mardell counted down, "Three . . . two . . . one."

She pointed at them, and they started Section Three.

The newscast galloped through Section Three, and Section Four proceeded as a foregone conclusion. First came the latest update from the gubernatorial campaign, with both candidates making their splashes and Slater looking a lot better on television than Wilson. Then came a prerecorded Barry Gauge commentary, but John didn't hear a word of it.

Then came the home video of the rampaging rhino, with plenty of time to include some of the really great shots—the rhino charging, hooking its tusk under the land rover and just about turning it over while a man with a rifle struggled to get a safe aim. In the interest of good taste, the video was cut short before the rifle was fired.

Music. Busy music. It was time to go.

Camera Two, two-shot of John and Ali.

John started the closing. "And that's it for NewsSix at Seven. Thank you for joining us."

Ali took her turn. "Stay tuned now for the premiere of a new Channel 6 TV magazine, 'Here and there,' coming up next."

"Good night."

More music as Camera Two zoomed out to include more of the news set.

Commercial.

Mardell waved. The show was over, the cameras were off. "Okay, everybody, good show."

"Good show, John," said Ali, gathering up her script. It was the first time she'd said anything to him all night.

"Thanks." John reached for the pulled pages—430, the Slater Story. "But I still have one more story to do."

"Huh?" Ali watched him, perplexed.

John held the script in front of him, faced Camera Three even as the cameraman backed it away to park it, and began to read. "A week after Governor Slater went public with the abortion death of his daughter Hillary, new questions are being raised . . ."

Ali rolled her eyes. "John . . . come on, let it go."

". . . Did the governor know from the beginning how his daughter died . . ."

"John!"

". . . and if so, was he involved in a cover-up story that may have cost at least one more life?"

Ali gave up and walked out, shaking her head in disbelief.

John could see the rally mob again, still moving by like a churning river, bothered by his words, waving their signs, telling him to shut up. He kept reading. "Governor Slater claimed he had just learned Hillary did not die from mislabeled drugs but from abortion malpractice . . ."

Mardell felt terribly awkward standing there behind the dead cameras while John kept reading the story. Was she supposed to stand there and listen or what?

John looked at Camera Two now. It was closer, even though it was one big dead machine. "Pathologist Dr. Harlan Matthews confirms the cause of Hillary's death, but insists the governor knew the cause of death the day after it happened."

Mardell exchanged a look with the camera operators, and their expressions all agreed—this guy was finally losing it.

"Let's get out of here," said a cameraman.

"Yeah, don't give him an audience and maybe he'll stop," said another.

Mardell and the camera operators left quietly.

John had no audience but the dead cameras and the vast crowd he saw in his mind. He kept going. "Hillary received an abortion at the Women's Medical Center on the 19th of April. Shannon DuPliese, a close friend, drove Hillary to the clinic and then home to the governor's residence, where Hillary died a few hours later."

Carl turned off the television feeling a little disappointed. "He said he was going to do the story on the Seven O'clock too. I wonder what happened?"

Mom reached out and took his hand. "Carl . . . he's doing the story. Right now."

Carl was puzzled, but he trusted her. "What do you mean?"

She pulled him down, and he sat next to her. "He's speaking the Truth right now. I don't know who's listening, but he's doing what he has to do, I know."

Up in the control room the monitors were cold, black, and silent. There was no sound. Susan was picking up the pages she'd tossed on the floor, still musing about what had happened. Tina was brutally tearing hers in half and throwing them in the waste can.

Pete was standing by the window that overlooked the news set. "What's John doing down there?"

John kept reading as the lights on the set shut down and the room went semi-dark. "When Shannon was awarded the Hillary Slater Memorial Scholarship, she soon realized the scholarship came with a price—her silence. After the death of Hillary Slater, the Women's Medical Center continued business as usual. There was no investigation of malpractice."

Now Susan and Tina had joined Pete at the window.

Pete chuckled incredulously. 'He's doing 430, the Slater Story."

Susan was awestruck. "He's doing it anyway!"

Tina murmured, "Like father, like son" and turned away.

John slowed down as he read the final lines of his narration. The clock wasn't running now, and he would never get the chance to read the lines again. "A month later Annie Brewer, a high-school senior, died from an abortion she received at the Women's Medical Center." And then there was silence. No commercial break with its bright lights, loud music, new cars or cold, inviting bottles of beer. No angry throng seething and ranting around him.

Just silence. John could almost sense his words still echoing somewhere in the room.

He'd said it. He'd done the story. He laid the script down gently, respectfully, and then sat there for a moment, leaning on his elbows, his knuckles against his chin, just decompressing, allowing himself to feel.

It was so quiet. Had it ever been this quiet in his life before?

"Barrett, you are one weird fellow, you know that?"

Ben Oliver was standing at the other end of the news desk. How long had he been standing there?"

"Hi, Ben."

Ben rested his elbows near the spot where Bing Dingham usually did his sports reporting. He just stood there and studied John for a moment. "So Tina bumped the story."

"It got on the Five O'clock, but she bumped it from the Seven."

"You lost out to the rhinoceros."

"Afraid so."

Ben laughed derisively and threw in a well-woven curse as well. "Yeah, I know . . . I should've been here. But I won't lie to you, John . . . I just plain didn't want to be. It would've meant trouble, the kind I don't like and don't need any more of." He sniffed in disgust. "I couldn't have made much difference anyway. You push your weight around too much, you get accused of bending the news, you know?"

"I can appreciate that."

Then there was silence, the ominous kind. John finally broke it by asking, "So, Ben, will I be working here tomorrow?"

Ben's gaze fell to the top of the desk for a moment and then returned to meet John's. "Well . . . Loren Harris went over your contract. The contract says we can't fire you, but it does allow us to reassign you."

John was expecting this. "Uh . . . to what? Feature reporting?"

"Yeah . . . reporting fluff. Soft features. Barbershop quartets and oyster eating contests and slug races, things like that. Of course, it'll mean fewer hours. You'll only be working part-time."

John leaned back in his chair and laughed quietly. He'd heard this kind of offer being made before, usually to reporters who didn't show up the next day.

Ben had to laugh too. He knew he wasn't fooling anyone. "You know how it works, John. Loren's forcing you to quit. That way we kill our scapegoat and we don't have to give him any severance pay. Such a deal!"

"Can I have a day or two to think about it?"

"Oh gosh, yes."

Another moment of pensive silence. John gathered up his script. "Ben . . ."

"Yeah."

"Do you . . . do you understand what I did here today? Do you know why I did it?"

Ben looked at John with eyes that hadn't missed a thing.

"For the same reason you're getting . . . reassigned. You're not being a good citizen in La-La Land; you don't believe all this stuff anymore." He looked at the plywood backdrop with the city skyline, the false monitors, the textured blues and greens. "I think . . . I think Loren's afraid that one of these days you're finally gonna lose it and start hollering, 'We've been lying to you! The city you see behind me isn't real—it's just *painted* there, you hear me?' "

"'Mommy, the emperor's naked . . .'"

Ben put a finger to his lips. "Shhh! You want to get us *both* fired?"

John had to laugh. Ben did understand.

Ben came closer and sat in Ali's chair. "But let me tell you something, John, just for the record. I was watching your performance just now, when nobody else was. You did all right. As a matter of fact, I think it was the best you ever did." Ben's eyes twinkled. "You went over by at least thirty seconds, but you did all right."

"I believed it. It was true."

Ben nodded. Then he added in all sincerity, "John . . . you did the right thing."

Willy Ferrini had just gotten back in town and was enjoying another one of those Hiram Slater commercials on the wide-screen television at Clancy's when Henderson took him aside for a chat—*way* aside actually, all the way down to headquarters.

Willy was not a noble person, of course. He had no one's interests but his own in mind. "Hey, you don't wanna talk to me. Talk to the man on top—Martin Devin. He's the one who hired me to . . . uh . . ."

"To what?" Henderson asked, circling impatiently around the same interrogation room where he'd grilled Howie Metzger.

"To get the tape from Ed Lake and then from that old Barrett character."

"Did he tell you to kill Barrett?"

Willy shook his head and waved aside that notion. "Hey, he just said to do whatever it took. He wanted that tape back. He said not to come back without it, and that's what I told Ted and Howie."

"You mean, of course, *the* Martin Devin, the governor's chief of staff?"

Willy liked the important sound of that. He smiled and nodded.

Henderson instructed, "Say yes for the tape."

Willy remembered his confession was being taped. "Oh yeah . . . Yes."

The phone in John's apartment rang two times, and then the answering machine clicked on, playing a message John had recorded as soon as he got home. "Hi, this is John. I hope you won't mind if I don't answer the phone right now. I'm all right, but I . . . well, I need to be alone for a while. Maybe we can touch base again tomorrow, okay? Go ahead and leave a message after the beep."

"Hi," came a familiar and concerned voice. "This is Leslie. I saw the Five and Seven O'clock, and I can just guess what happened. Listen, hang in there, John, and remember, we're all behind you. As soon as you're ready, I want to talk about it, so give me a ring."

John sat in a chair at the dining table, looking out at the city coming alive with lights as the darkness of night deepened. The newscast was over now. He'd told Mom and Carl how he needed this night to himself, and they understood. Now he could feel all he wanted until the feelings made sense. He could even cry.

Another call came in. "Hey, John, this is Susan—you know, the show director. Hey, guy, I've never done this before—you know, just stuck my neck out like this, but . . . I just want to say I'm sorry you got bumped. That story on Slater—I don't think it's going to go away. I think you've really uncovered something, and you should feel good about it, and uh . . . that's . . . well, I guess that's all I need to say. I hope to see you around. Good-bye."

John appreciated Susan's call. Someday those encouraging words would work their way through his sorrow and do him some good. Someday.

But tonight as John sat there quietly, motionless, looking out over the city, all he could do was weep over it.

Just like Dad.

Another call. "Hi, John. This is Aaron Hart. Listen, we were all watching tonight, and you did great. I won't bother you about this until you're ready, but you'll be interested to know that the Brewers are going to go after the clinic, and they'll be getting help from . . . uh . . . Rachel Franklin, Shannon DuPliese, and Cindy Danforth. Dr. Huronac and that Claire from the clinic too. Anyway, as soon as you get the chance we need to pool all the information and see what we have—but not until you're ready, okay? You just take it easy, be encouraged, and . . . we'll hear from you in your own good time. Bye."

John reached over and turned off the phone's ringer and the answering machine's volume. Then he sat there in the silence, alone with himself.

Despair. That's what he was battling right now.

Aaron . . . what good will you do, really? If you shut down one clinic, another will pop up somewhere else; tear one clinic down, they'll just build another one. The problem isn't that clinic; it's in the hearts of all those lost and crying souls out there. The answer's got to come to them, to each heart, to each and every pain and resentment, to every wound that ever needed healing, to every soiled conscience that ever needed cleansing. It would take a miracle!

And tonight . . . what good did I do, really? What difference did I make? Was anybody out there even listening?

John's Bible lay on the table. He'd turned to 1 Kings 19, where Elijah the prophet was hiding for his life in a cave and cried out to the Lord, "I have been very zealous for the LORD God Almighty. The Israelites have rejected your covenant, broken down your altars, and put your prophets to death with the sword. I am the only one left, and now they are trying to kill me too." He read the passage several times as he sat there alone in the dim lamplight of his dining room. Elijah's words captured just how he felt.

"Well, Lord, now it's over, so maybe You'll tell me just what it was all about." John heard no answer. He saw no vision.

He pointed toward the city and began to weep again. "Lord God, what about their cries? Why do You let me hear them? What can *I* do about it?"

John sat up straight in the chair, watching the city, hoping for a thought, an insight, an answer from God, anything that would bring sense to his misery.

But God remained silent.

"Lord . . . what's to become of us?"

That was his last question. He listened only a moment longer and then, drained of tears, despondent in spirit, he settled back in his chair with nothing more to say or think or do or hope, his eyes closed to the whole helpless world. And there he stayed, he didn't know for how long.

John opened his eyes, for no reason he was aware of except that something had prodded him, much as a sound, a light, a bump, or a squeak might wake a person without his knowing exactly what had done it.

The first thing he noticed was the pattern of the vinyl flooring on the dining room floor. There was nothing unusual about it, except that he was seeing it so clearly where before the light had been too dim.

Light? Yes. Light that wasn't there before.

Fascinated, he sat there and watched as the light grew, fanning out gently, displacing the shadows, steadily building and widening until it filled a long rectangle across the dining room floor.

It was coming from his bedroom, shining through the open doorway. Had the light come on in there?

Couldn't be. This light was not from some fixture or lamp. It was more like the glimmer from diamonds or the glint from polished silver, and yet it was soft, warm, comforting, with a hint of gold that seemed to move within it like myriads of tiny flames.

John moved for the first time and only then became aware of his muscles and the weight and size of his body. He rose from the chair and stood on his feet. Yes, his feet, his physical feet on the physical floor in his real, physical apartment. He was really here, the light was really here, and this was no dream.

A vision, maybe? Well, maybe.

The light had fully arrived, no longer growing in intensity but remaining steady now, shining out of his bedroom and lighting up much of the apartment. John moved step by step toward the bedroom door, knowing he would find *something* but having no idea what it might be. An angel perhaps? Things like that happened in the Bible, and he'd heard stories about such encounters from some of the saints in church years ago.

God? He stopped for a moment. If this was going to be a burning bush, he sure didn't feel like a Moses.

But there was no fear. Only awe—and extreme curiosity. He took another step and then another.

Now he could see his bed, the bedspread brightly illumined.

Then the pillows neatly arranged at the headboard.

And there it was.

A lamb.

Warmth and joy flooded him, flowing like warm oil from his head and on down to his feet. He relaxed and even smiled, leaning against the doorpost, looking at that little creature now looking back at him with gentle, golden eyes, the lashes blinking every once in a while, the legs tucked neatly under its perfect, unblemished body.

The lamb! They'd met before, when John was ten. And as John stood there in awe, drinking in the vision, he remembered the details he'd seen back then—the white wool, so perfect it glowed; the attentive, flitting ears; the kind, gentle eyes; and the remarkably peaceful demeanor. The lamb looked exactly the same, in every detail.

"Hello," he ventured to say, but very softly, afraid he might startle his guest.

The lamb raised its head attentively and returned the greeting with its eyes.

"It's . . . uh . . . it's been a while. I'm very happy to see you again."

He dared to enter the room approaching the lamb so very furtively, his hand outstretched.

The lamb rose to its feet, the little black hooves glistening, the bed sinking only slightly under its weight, and took a few steps toward him.

John chuckled as he stroked the lamb's nose. This little guy wasn't afraid of anything.

Then it entered John's mind to find a treat of some kind, some token of friendship—or loyalty. "Uh . . . carrots. Would you like a carrot?"

The lamb didn't respond one way or the other. John backed away, speaking gently. "Let me . . . let me bring you something, okay? I have to, you know, be a good host, right?"

He hurried into the kitchen and threw on the light.

Then he scrambled through the refrigerator for a carrot.

"Okay!" he said, closing the refrigerator. "Here you go!"

Oh. He stopped and fell silent.

The lamb was standing at the sliding glass door, looking out at the city, its body motionless with attention.

Suddenly the carrot was unimportant. John set it on the counter and quietly joined the lamb, kneeling beside it, looking out through the glass.

They remained there for quite some time, just listening. The lamb looked up at him, the eyes troubled.

He nodded. "Yeah, I hear them too." He looked toward the city once more as the lamb followed his gaze. "I hear them too."

That night John slept peacefully for the first time in over a month, the lamb curled serenely on the bed near his feet, keeping watch.

thirty-five

The very next day John Barrett was not seen in the newsroom, and few were surprised. In his place, Walt Bruechner hurried about, getting acquainted with the daytime staff, getting accustomed to the daytime routine.

Out in the station's lobby, a maintenance man carefully removed the fasteners from the brightly lit, full-color, three-foot-high photograph of John Barrett, news anchor, and took it down from the wall, removing it from the company of the other great names and faces.

Above the avenues, streets, and freeways here and there around the city, workmen began to peel the face of John Barrett from the billboards, removing him in long, jagged strips that fell into the bed of a truck parked below.

At the city garage, the Barrett and Downs posters were removed from the sides of the buses to make room for new posters that were due to arrive any day, new posters with the face of Ali Downs plus the new face of Walt Bruechner. The old posters were rolled up tightly and deposited in the trash bin.

Throughout that day's programming on Channel 6, bold new promo spots began to air. Impressive video images of the hot new NewsSix team—Bruechner and Downs—flashed across the screen, exuding integrity and incisiveness.

By the day's end John Barrett, bold, incisive, trustworthy, accurate, and up-to-the-minute anchorman, would silently slip out of existence in the popular culture and within weeks would vanish completely from the public mind.

John Barrett, high, lofty, untouchable, and altogether perfect, was still gazing down with honest eyes from the rafters of Dad Barrett's shop as Carl positioned a ladder just beneath him, climbed up the rungs, and removed the portrait from its place. The stern look of honesty never changed as the portrait made the trip down the ladder in Carl's hands, and the eyes showed no response as Carl broke the wooden frame with a hatchet and neatly folded the canvas into quarters. When the folded canvas and its wooden frame were ceremoniously placed in the garbage, the face wasn't even seeing the light of day, but was folded upon itself in darkness, never to be seen again.

Carl placed the lid back on the garbage can, fastened it down with an elastic strap, and then let out a whoop the whole neighborhood must have heard, his face toward Heaven, his arms stretching upward.

Mom Barrett stuck her head out the back door. "Carl! What's wrong—"

When she saw him standing by the garbage can and noticed the joy on his face, she pieced it all together and went back inside, indulging in a quiet little whoop of her own.

Governor Hiram Slater wasted no time. The moment he arrived at his office he told Miss Rhodes, "Get Martin Devin in here right now, right away, pronto, no excuses!"

She gasped at his manner but carried out his order immediately, grabbing up her telephone to make the call.

Slater went into his office and immediately removed his suit jacket, throwing it on the deep, leather-covered sofa. He would talk to Martin Devin this morning, and he would get the straight scoop from him on *everything* or Devin was going to walk that very day, that very hour!

First the spilled coffee, and then the blue running shoes, and now . . . well, everything the prophet had said about Devin yesterday did make sense. The 911 tape! Of course. It would have been the easiest, most direct way for Barrett and Albright to find out about Shannon DuPliese.

That tape could have triggered everything. That tape that Martin Devin was supposed to destroy!

Well, did he? *Did he?*

The governor hit his intercom button. "Miss Rhodes! Have you talked to Devin?"

"Sir . . ." She sounded hesitant. "Mr. Devin says he's with some visitors right now and can't get away." The governor wouldn't accept that, and then thought that maybe he should, and then decided he wouldn't. He called Devin's office himself. Devin's secretary answered.

"This is the governor! I want to talk to—"

Miss Rhodes' voice squawked out of the intercom. "Mr. Governor, Mr. Devin is here now."

The governor hung up on Devin's secretary as the office door opened and Martin Devin came in with two gentlemen.

That perturbed the governor even more. "Devin, we need to have a conference immediately." He looked at the two men. "Gentlemen, if you'll excuse us?"

"Uh, Mr. Governor," said Devin, "these men are from the Police Department. I'd like you to meet Detective Robert Henderson and his partner, Detective Clay Oakley."

No one made a move to shake hands. The two detectives only nodded at the governor, and he replied, "Gentlemen . . ."

Devin explained, "Mr. Governor, I'm sure you'll want to know that these two gentlemen are here to take me into custody."

That didn't register. It was just too outrageous.

"Custody? What do you mean, *custody?*"

"They're . . . uh . . . they're placing me under arrest."

For one of the few times in his life Hiram Slater was at a loss for words. He just stood there, his mouth hanging open and trembling, his eyes darting from face to face, looking for some safe place to land.

Devin figured he'd better sew up some loose ends before he left. "Wilma Benthoff has the new poll results, and she'll be bringing them by this afternoon. You're doing well—still way ahead of Wilson. Rowen and Hartly are preparing a new package of TV and radio promos. Uh . . . I've told them to be available in case you need to do any image repair. They should be getting in touch with you today or tomorrow."

But of course that wasn't what the governor wanted to talk about. "Martin! They're arresting you on . . . on what charges?"

Devin thought for a moment, then answered directly, "Oh . . . accessory to murder, conspiracy to commit murder . . . it all has to do with murder."

"What? What are you talking about—"

Devin held up his hand. "Mr. Governor, I can't discuss it . . . I'm sure you understand." Then, "But maybe I can tell you this much . . . Remember Mad Prophet Junior from yesterday? He was right." He allowed himself a self-mocking laugh. "See what happens when you lie?" Devin looked at the cops again. "Okay, gentlemen, let's go."

The governor was flabbergasted and could only stand there while Oakley took some handcuffs out of his pocket.

Henderson tried to be gracious and told Oakley, "We'll wait until we get outside."

Oakley shrugged and put the cuffs away.

Then Henderson said to the governor, "Nice to meet you, sir. Oh . . . if I may give you some advice . . . you should seek legal counsel, sir, right away."

With a nod from Henderson, all three left the room and went by Miss Rhodes' desk and on down the long, ornate hallway to the elevators.

The governor went as far as the big oak doors to watch them depart, his face pale with horror. This couldn't be happening.

What *was* happening? He looked at Miss Rhodes, but she didn't have any answers and only gave him her most blank, most perplexed expression. "Should I . . . call an attorney or something?" she inquired.

"Call Rowen and Hartly . . . and Wilma Benthoff . . . oh, and Clyde Johnson, my attorney." He saw the elevator door open. Devin and the two cops got on the elevator, and someone got off, stepping into the reception area.

Oh no. It was Ashley . . . Mrs. Hiram Slater. She was not expected.

But then, *nothing* that had happened so far had been expected, although he was beginning to think it *should* have been.

By the time Ashley Slater got to her husband's office, he was standing by the big window, looking out toward the capitol dome.

"Hiram, I'm sorry to come in unannounced, but . . . I'm afraid we have to talk."

He turned slowly from the window, defeat and surrender just beginning to darken his expression. Abruptly he stated the fact before she did. "Hayley is pregnant."

Now it was Mrs. Slater's turn to be shocked. "How . . . how did you know?"

Slater looked down at the deep, royal-blue carpet as he recalled the prophet's words from yesterday. "It's Wednesday."

Leslie got her call from Ben Oliver that morning. The big battle was over, he said, and the dust was settling. If she could come back without kicking it all up again, she was welcome.

Well . . . she would try to be a good girl, but she knew it wouldn't be easy. At 9 o'clock she was back in the newsroom, ready for that day's assignment, ready to participate in the story planning session around Erica Johnson's desk. Tina was at that meeting, but their eyes never met, and they didn't say a word to each other. It was clear they'd both had a talking-to from Ben.

The day's outlook seemed routine enough. There'd been a fire on the waterfront that needed a quick follow-up; Benson Dynamics was still wallowing in red ink and passing out pink slips; the mayor was appointing a special investigator to find out whom to blame for the new sidewalk buckling down at the public market. Leslie got assigned the buckling sidewalk story, something relatively tame, easy, and nonhazardous.

When the meeting ended, she went to her desk to gather her gear and wait for her cameraman. John was on her mind. She hadn't seen him or talked to him since the day before yesterday, and she was dying to know how he was doing, what he was doing, what he would be doing. Too much remained unresolved, and it was driving her crazy.

Someone stopped at her desk. She looked up.

It was Tina Lewis. "Hi."

Now you be a good girl, Leslie! "Uh . . . hi, Tina. How are you?"

The moment Leslie asked that question, Tina's eyes fell, and Leslie could see the old fight was gone. The fire in her eyes was all but extinguished. Tina seemed crestfallen. Something terrible must have happened since the morning meeting.

"Tina? Are you feeling all right?"

Tina raised her head again, drew a controlled breath, and said softly, "I'm . . . Well, I hope I'm just a little bit smarter now, smart enough to tell you . . . I'm sorry." She struggled, trying to qualify the statement. "I'm not . . . well, I'm not abandoning my position on things. But I'm just trying to see things more accurately, get a fuller picture." She got frustrated trying to explain herself. "I still have to think it through, but . . . let me say this much. You and John were right—*in certain areas.* In certain areas you were right on the money, you were following your instincts well, and I can see that now."

"Well . . . thank you."

"Anyway . . . it's good to have you back." And with that, Tina turned and hurried away.

Leslie leaned back in her chair, a smile widening on her face and her eyes widening with surprise. "Well . . . what do you know about that?"

What on earth had gotten into Tina? What was happening around here?

Whoa! What was this? Ben Oliver and Erica Johnson came scurrying into the room and over to Erica's desk where Erica started scanning the day's story assignments and having a muttered meeting with Ben. Then they both looked her way.

"Leslie?" said Erica, beckoning with her finger.

Oh-oh. This might be the answer right here. Leslie got over there, trying to play along with the low-key, semi-secretive mood.

Erica looked at Ben, and Ben took the floor. "We're putting you on another story." He touched Leslie's arm. "Hang on to yourself. I don't want the whole newsroom coming unglued, at least not all at once." Then he broke the news. "Martin Devin's just been arrested—charged with murder."

Leslie tried to hang on to herself, but she could feel her heart racing, and when she spoke, her voice wanted to squeal. "Does . . . does John know?"

Ben was still stunned himself. "If you want to know what

I think, I think he *always* knew. He's the one who called just now."

Leslie made an easy connection. "You mean . . . you mean the murder is . . . is—"

"The victim is John's father." Ben sniffed a tight little laugh at himself. "I *knew* that story you two were working on was leading somewhere. Now we've got something that's going to explode all over the state for months."

Leslie grabbed for the nearest phone. Ben shot out his hand and stopped her.

"Ben! I gotta talk to John!"

He forced her to look him in the eye. "Leslie, you get yourself a cameraman, you get down to the precinct and get the details, then you get in touch with the governor's office to see what they have to say, and then you get in touch with anybody and everybody who might know something about this—and I'm sure you do know some key people, don't you? People close to the victim, people close to the governor's family, people who might have something to say about the possible motive for the murder? Hm?"

Leslie nodded furiously. "Yes! Yes, sir, Ben—yes!" She was like a racehorse being held back at the starting gate.

Ben kept a steady hand on her arm and kept looking her in the eye, demanding her attention. "The story's yours, Albright. You earned it. Now don't mess it up." He let her go, and she went straight to her desk, straight to her phone.

The phone rang just as she got there.

"Hey, Leslie, this is Detective Henderson. I'm down at the precinct, and I've got a story for you—"

"Yes!" she shouted, unable to keep her voice down. "You've arrested Martin Devin!"

That caught the ears of several reporters at their desks. Ben moaned, "Oh boy, here we go!"

Henderson was amazed. "Boy, news travels fast . . ."

"I'll be right there!" said Leslie.

"Okay. I've got a bunch of info for you, so bring a camera."

"Thanks. See you in a bit."

She called John's apartment, but John didn't answer. She left a frantic message on his answering machine.

She called Mom Barrett.

"Hello?"

"Mom Barrett, this is Leslie!"

Mom was excited. "Oh, Leslie! Have you heard?"

"About Martin Devin?"

"Yes! John told me. I'm still in shock!"

"It's incredible! It's absolutely incredible! I've just got to talk to John!"

Mom toned down just a little. "Oh . . . well, he isn't here."

"Do you know where he is?"

"Well . . . yes, but—"

"Where? I've got to talk to him! How did he find out? What does he know?"

"Well, Detective Henderson called him this morning, and then John called Mr. Oliver at the station. But listen, Leslie, I'll tell him you called, and I know he'll want to get back to you."

"Well, where is he?"

"Oh . . ." Mom fretted a bit. "I should have known this was going to be a problem. I promised him I wouldn't tell."

"What?"

"He and Carl went somewhere together, that's all I can say. But they should be back later today."

Leslie stopped short when she heard that. She began to understand. "Oh . . . Oh, okay. Well . . . um . . . tell him I'm . . ." She felt fully charged with energy. "Tell him I'm back doing the news, will you? Tell him Ben gave *me* the story!"

"Oh, honey, that's wonderful!"

"And tell him not to worry!"

Mom laughed. "I'll tell him."

Dad's old pickup came to a stop in the gravel only a few yards from the edge of a great body of water. The doors squeaked open, and two wayfaring seamen dressed in boots and warm coats got out, ready to challenge the briny deep.

Actually it was just a small lake in the middle of a park, but the spirit of a magnificent voyage was still in the air.

John, a warm stocking cap on his head, reached into the truck bed and threw back the canvas cover. "Okay, girl, here comes your maiden voyage."

Carl helped pull the cover off the little rowboat. "We still need to name it something. Something like *Invincible* or . . ."

"*Impenetrable* . . ."

"Yeah, right. *Impermeable. Unsinkable.*"

"Well . . . we'll find out about that, won't we?"

Carl jumped into the truck bed to take the bow, while John took hold of the stern, and without much trouble at all the little craft was half in the water, ready to shove off.

John had to stand there for just a moment, admiring the boat in its natural setting, the small lake waves lapping at its sides. So far no water was leaking in.

He put an arm around Carl's shoulders. "You did a good job, son."

Carl returned the arm around. "So did you."

They loaded the oars and a duffel bag containing their lunch and then flipped a coin to see who would row first. Carl won.

The little boat sliced through the water like a champ, propelled along by Carl's strong, even strokes. Out across the lake they went, father and son, laughing it up, talking it up. From far away you could hear their conversation carrying across the still water.

"So . . ." came Carl's voice, "it's Grandpa's sister Alice who married Robert . . . and then his brother Roger who married Doris . . ."

"No," came John's correction. "Roger married Marie."

"Oh yeah, yeah . . . Marie."

"And they had four kids—Linda, Debbie, Bobby, and Jason."

"And Debbie's the one who's married."

"*Linda's* the one who's married—to Burt."

"Burt. Did I meet him?"

"He's the guy with the crew cut."

"No, I didn't meet him."

As the time passed lazily by, they rowed up to one end of

the lake and then headed back again, then took a side trip to circle a little island populated with ducks.

"So what'll you do now?" Carl asked.

"Oh, be a columnist maybe," came John's answer. "I know some people at the *Journal* who've wanted me before."

Their approach alarmed some ducks that skittered across the water and took to the sky.

"Sorry," Carl called to the ducks.

"They look great, don't they?"

"Hey, you want to row for a while?"

"Sure."

They carefully traded places. John took the middle seat and the oars, while Carl sat in the stern.

John started pulling at the oars. "Ah! Feels great!"

"You know it."

"So what'll *you* do now?"

"Oh, maybe I'll go back to school. That whole idea feels better to me now."

"Well, you're good at what you do, Carl. Real good. I think you'll succeed."

"I think so too."

John pulled briskly at the oars, and they started up the lake again with no real destination in mind. They just wanted to row and ride and talk. They talked about love and John's marriage that didn't work and whether John might get married again—he might—and whether Carl had thought about where he'd live and if he thought he'd like to get married and about Grandpa and Grandma and all the family that was so hard to keep straight and about God and what He was all about.

John finally set the oars down. "Oh, that reminds me." He chuckled. "Well, it doesn't really remind me—I've been thinking about it all along, but . . . now would be a good time for a little ceremony."

Carl laughed, expecting something corny. "Oh brother, what now?"

John had brought the duffel bag along, supposedly with only their lunch inside. Well, the lunch was in there all right, but there was also a very familiar old overcoat. He pulled it out of the bag and shook it out. "Dad gave this to me, and now, for some vague religious reason I haven't clarified yet, I think I should pass it on to you."

Carl smiled and shook his head. "Naw, that's from your father. Grandpa gave that to *you.*"

John held it toward him. "Come on, try it on."

"Aw . . ."

"Go on, take it. Humor your religious old man."

Carl shrugged and laughed and slipped the overcoat on over his other coat. "Don't know if it'll fit me."

John sat there and watched, just to see if it would.

Carl pulled it closed and fastened some of the buttons, then looked up to get John's reaction. "What do you think?"

John looked at the coat on his son and thought it looked a little big or maybe a little out of style for one such as Carl, and he was about to say so. But at that moment John noticed Carl was looking toward the shore, his face full of perplexity and wonder.

"Hey, Dad . . ."

"Yeah?"

"Look at that."

John looked where Carl was pointing.

Far across the water, on the distant shore, the green trees of the park and the skyline of the city rising behind it, a lamb stood very still, its wool shining in the sun, its head held high, watching them.

"Is that a . . . well, it looks like a lamb!" said Carl.

John looked from the lamb to his son and back again.

"You see it, Carl? You see the lamb too?"

Carl looked at his father, puzzled by the question.

"Well . . . sure."

John looked a second time at his son and at the fit of Dad's old overcoat. Now he changed his mind.

He reached out and gave Carl a loving tap on the side of the knee, then fingered the hem of the old overcoat.

"Don't worry about the coat, son. You'll grow into it."

If you enjoyed reading *Prophet*, you'll want to get these other Frank Peretti titles:

This Present Darkness

Ashton is just a typical small town. But when reporter Marshall Hogan and pastor Hank Busche begin to compare notes, they suddenly find themselves fighting a hideous plot to subjugate the townspeople—and eventually the entire human race.

A fast-moving, riveting thriller, *This Present Darkness* offers a fascinating glimpse into the unseen world of spiritual warfare—and the power of prayer.

This Present Darkness
AUDIO CASSETTE

You've never experienced this riveting best-seller in such a powerful way! *This Present Darkness* is available on audio cassette—and read by author Frank Peretti, who, besides his phenomenal success as a writer, is also a master storyteller. These two 90-minute tapes are packed with special music, stirring effects, and all the drama and excitement of the full-length novel.

Piercing the Darkness

The veil between the natural and supernatural is opened again with *Piercing the Darkness*. In the tiny farming community of Bacon's Corner, the hosts of heaven and Satan's hordes come face-to-face in a titanic spiritual struggle centering on Sally Beth Roe, a young drifter with a dark past.

Across a vast panorama of heart-stopping action—including Sally's attempts to escape the relentless pursuit of a mysterious group—*Piercing the Darkness* illustrates the reality of spiritual warfare and the ability of God's truth to burst through the darkness.

Piercing the Darkness
AUDIO CASSETTE

Read by the author himself, this audio abridgment of *Piercing the Darkness* is fortified with dramatic sound effects and music that bring to life all the intrigue and spiritual impact of the beloved novel on two 90-minute cassettes. Great for listening to in the car, while working around the house, or to enjoy as a family.

Tilly

Kathy and Dan Ross are just like any other young couple . . . except for the secrets that lie buried in their souls. When Kathy is captivated by the simple name "Tilly" on a small grave marker, both her life and Dan's are changed forever.

Tilly is the deeply moving story of a woman's struggle to reconcile herself with a long-ago abortion, and a couple's efforts to ultimately move forward with their lives. This powerful tale of forgiveness will shake the most stoic soul.

The Cooper Kids Adventure Series

A four-volume set of Frank E. Peretti's "Indiana Jones-style" adventure series. Build sound values in kids ages 9–14 while keeping them glued to their seats. Nearly 2,000,000 copies sold!

BOOK 1:
The Door in the Dragon's Throat

Jay and Lila Cooper have been on adventures with their archaeologist father before, but nothing like this! As they make their way through the dark and mysterious cavern called The Dragon's Throat, they can't help thinking about the other exploration parties that tried to open the Door leading into it. All fled in panic or died terrible deaths!

What really lies behind the Door? Incredible riches from a lost kingdom? Some ancient evil? Will they be able to overcome whatever force lurks behind the Door in the Dragon's Throat? Join them as they solve this dreaded desert mystery, which ends with a gigantic clash between the forces of good and evil.

BOOK 2:
Escape from the Island of Aquarius

When Jay and Lila travel with their adventurous father to an exotic South Seas island to find a missing missionary, they discover some very strange things going on. It appears that the arrogant leader of the island colony is the man they've been sent to find. But if that's true, then why is he acting so strange? As the Coopers attempt to solve the mystery, they find they also must find a way to overcome the evil that holds the colonists in a death grip—before the entire island breaks apart.

BOOK 3:
The Tombs of Anak

When Jay and Lila Cooper enter the cave-tombs of Anak with their father, they hope to find a coworker who has unaccountably disappeared. Instead, they stumble onto a frightening religion and new mysteries that soon put them all into incredible danger.

Who or what is Ha-Raphah? How does he hold the local villagers in overwhelming fear?

The Coopers desperately search for answers and begin to unravel the mystery, but more peril lies ahead. Will they understand the truth in time to avoid disaster, or will they be swept away in a last desperate attempt by Ha-Raphah to preserve his evil powers?

BOOK 4:
Trapped at the Bottom of the Sea

When Lila insisted on leaving her father's teaching expedition to go back to the States, she never suspected that her flight would be hijacked! Now she is a prisoner, trapped at the bottom of the sea in a locked, top-secret weapons pod with no way of escape. Meanwhile, her dad, Dr. Jake Cooper, her brother Jay, and darling adventure-journalist Meaghan Flaherty are trying to pick up Lila's trail.

Pursued by angry terrorists, they island-hop in a remote corner of the Pacific, hoping against hope to find the plane. But will they reach Lila before her air runs out? Or before the pod is found by another hostile group searching for it?